Shadowrise

Volume Three

TAD WILLIAMS

Shadowrise

Volume Three of Shadowmarch

DAW BOOKS, INC.

DONALD A. WOLLHEIM, FOUNDER

375 Hudson Street, New York, NY 10014

ELIZABETH R. WOLLHEIM
SHEILA E. GILBERT
PUBLISHERS

http://www.dawbooks.com

First printing, November 2010
1 2 3 4 5 6 7 8 9

DAW TRADEMARK REGISTERED
U.S. PAT. AND TM. OFF. AND FOREIGN COUNTRIES
—MARCA REGISTRADA
HECHO EN U.S.A.

PRINTED IN THE U.S.A.

Like the first two volumes, *Shadowrise* is dedicated to our children Connor Williams and Devon Beale, who continue to oppress me with a mighty, mighty love. They are the two coolest kids in the world.

Causeway to Mainland Southmarch

W N

Brenn's Bay

S E

Basilisk Gate

Trigonate Temple

Market Square

Outwall

Harbor

West Lagoon

(Skimmer's Lagoon)

North Lagoon

Tower
of Spring

Tower of Winter

Funderling Town Gate

New Walls

Observatory

Inner Keep

Tower of Summer

Tower of Autumn

East Lagoon

Southmarch
The Outer Keep

Brenn's Bay

TW 2004

Acknowledgements

Thanks as always to my editors Betsy Wollheim and Sheila Gilbert and everyone else at DAW Books, to my wonderful wife Deborah Beale and to our wonderful assistant Dena Chavez and my crafty agent Matt Bialer. Also many thanks to Lisa Tveit, who has been a hero managing our Web site, www.tadwilliams.com. Please come and join us there. It's fun and the side effects are largely harmless.

Nobody since Dorothy first landed in Oz has been surrounded with as many magical people as I am every day, and I am profoundly grateful for that.

MARCH KINGDOMS

Irisian Ocean

Southmarch

Blueshore

Landers Port

Oscastle

Kertewall

Marrinswalk

Silverside

Whitewood

Elusine River

Great Kertish Road

Weeping Moors

N

W   E

S

Esterian River

Upper SYAN

The Heartwood

TW 2006

Contents

PART THREE, PALL

Synopsis of *Shadowmarch*

❧

Southmarch Castle, the last human city in the north, has stood for two hundred years as a bulwark against the immortal Qar—the fairy folk who have twice fought wars against humanity. This is a bad time for Southmarch, a country whose king, OLIN EDDON, is being held for ransom in another kingdom, leaving only his three children, KENDRICK, the oldest, and the twins BARRICK and BRIONY, to watch over his land and people. Making this uncertain time worse, the Shadowline—the boundary between human lands and the foggy, eternally twilit domain of the Qar—has begun to move closer to Southmarch.

Then Kendrick is murdered in his own castle. SHASO DAN-HEZA, Briony and Barrick's mentor, is imprisoned for the crime and it seems his guilt is undeniable. Briony does not feel entirely convinced but she is distracted by many other concerns, not least the problems of trying to rule alongside Barrick, her sickly, angry twin.

In fact, matters are growing more confused and more dangerous in Southmarch every day. CHERT and OPAL, two Funderlings, a dwarfish folk who live beneath Southmarch, see a child abandoned by mysterious riders from the far side of the Shadowline. The boy is one of the Big Folk—an ordinary sized human—but they give him the Funderling name FLINT and take him home to their town under the castle. Meanwhile, CHAVEN, the royal physician, finds his own attention absorbed by a mysterious mirror, and the even more mysterious entity that seems to live inside it.

Princess Briony places much of the blame for her older brother's death on FERRAS VANSEN, the captain of the royal guard, who she thinks should have done more to protect him. Vansen has an affection for Briony Eddon that goes beyond the bounds of both propriety and good sense. He can only accept mutely when, in part as punishment, she sends him out to the site of a reported attack across the Shadowline by the Qar.

YNNIR, the blind king of those same Qar, has initiated a complicated strategy concerning the castle and its ruling family; dumping the boy Flint near Southmarch was only the first part. That act is already having repercussions: at Kendrick's funeral the Eddon children's great aunt, DUCHESS MEROLANNA, sees the boy Flint and almost faints. She is positive she has seen her own illegitimate child, whose birth was kept secret but who disappeared more than fifty years earlier.

Ynnir is not the only one of the Qar with complicated plans. LADY YASAMMEZ, one of the most powerful of the fairies, has gathered an army and is marching across the Shadowline to attack the mortal lands.

Meanwhile, Barrick and Briony find themselves in an ever stranger situation. Their chief counselor, AVIN BRONE, tells them that the TOLLYS, the most powerful rival family in the March Kingdoms, have been entertaining agents of SULEPIS, the AUTARCH OF XIS, the malevolent southern god-king whose goal seems to be to conquer the whole of the northern continent as he as already enslaved the south. (We have already seen him and his apparent madness in his treatment of QINNITAN, an innocent temple novice whom he has declared his newest wife and moved into the harem called the Seclusion. Strangely, though, the only attention she receives there is a kind of religious instruction and a series of disturbing potions the priests force her to drink.)

Back in the northern continent, things get worse. Ferras Vansen and his troop find themselves lured onto the wrong side of the Shadowline. Several of the soldiers are killed by various creatures, and before they find their way back to the lands of men, Vansen sees the army that Yasammez has mustered heading for the March Kingdoms.

MATT TINWRIGHT, a Southmarch poet down on his luck, is asked to write a letter to the Eddon family on behalf of an apparently simple-minded potboy named GIL. A chore Tinwright thinks of as easy money instead gets him arrested and brought in front of Avin Brone, accused of treason. Princess Briony takes pity on Tinwright and frees him, even allowing him to stay in the household as a poet. Of all the troubled folk in Southmarch Castle, Tinwright alone seems to have found some luck.

The Qar destroy Candlerstown and Princess Briony decides South-march must send an army to halt the fairies' advance. To her surprise, her brother Barrick is the first to volunteer to ride out against the Qar. He has confessed to his sister that their father Olin suffers from a kind of madness that caused him to cripple Barrick some years ago, and Barrick believes he has the madness as well, so he feels he might as well risk his life defending the kingdom. Briony cannot talk him out of this, so she tasks Ferras Vansen, who has finally made his way back from beyond the Shadowline, to protect her brother at any cost.

Beneath the castle in Funderling Town the strange boy known as Flint has disappeared. With the help of one of the tiny ROOFTOPPERS, Chert tracks him down in the mysterious, sacred place beneath even their subterranean city, the holy depths known as the Mysteries. There Flint has somehow made his way to an island in an underground lake where stands the strange stone figure known as the Shining Man, sacred to the Funderling people. Chert brings the boy home. Later, with the potboy Gil, Chert will take a magical artifact the boy has brought back from the Mysteries and give it to Yasammez, the dark lady who leads the Qar forces camped outside the castle walls.

It is mid-winter and the army has gone out to fight the Qar. Briony is taunted in public by HENDON TOLLY with her family's failings and she loses her head so badly that she challenges him to a duel. When he refuses to fight her she is humiliated in front of the court, many of whom already feel she is too young and unstable (and too female) to rule South-march. Later, when she goes to keep an appointment with her pregnant stepmother ANISSA, she is surprised by the sudden appearance of Chaven the physician, who has been missing from the castle for some time.

Back on the southern continent, Qinnitan, the reluctant bride of the Autarch, escapes the royal palace of Xis and manages to talk her way onto a ship bound for the northern continent.

Meanwhile, the Qar prove too powerful and too tricky for the South-march armies: Prince Barrick and the rest are badly defeated. Barrick himself is almost killed by a giant, but Yasammez spares his life. After a short while alone with him she sends him away and he rides toward the Shadowline in a kind of trance. Ferras Vansen sees him, and when he cannot stop or hinder the confused prince, Vansen goes with Barrick to protect him, as Princess Briony had begged him to do.

Meanwhile, Briony's meeting with her stepmother turns horrifying when Anissa's maid proves to be Kendrick's murderer and again uses a magical stone to turn herself into a demonic creature bent on murdering Briony as well. Only Briony's courage saves her; the creature is killed. In the shock of the moment, Anissa goes into labor.

Leaving Chaven behind to take care of her stepmother, Briony sets out to free Shaso, her mentor, who has now been proved innocent of Kendrick's death. When she frees him, though, they find themselves outmaneuvered by Hendon Tolly, who has been manipulating events all this time. He intends to make it look as though Shaso has murdered Briony so Hendon can take the throne. Instead, Briony and Shaso fight their way free and escape Southmarch with the help of some loyal SKIMMERS, a water-loving people who also share the castle. But Briony has been forced to leave her home in the hands of her worst enemies, her brother is gone without trace, and Yasammez and the murderous Qar are now surrounding the castle.

Synopsis of *Shadowplay*

❧

BRIONY EDDON and her twin brother BARRICK, the last heirs of the Southmarch royal family, have been separated. Their castle and country are under the control of HENDON TOLLY, a murderous and particularly nasty relative. The vengeful fairies known as the QAR have surrounded Southmarch Castle.

After escaping Hendon, Briony and her mentor, SHASO, take refuge in a nearby city with one of Shaso's countrymen, but that refuge is soon attacked and burned. Only Briony escapes, but now she is friendless and alone. Starving and ill, she hides in the forest.

Barrick, compelled by something he doesn't understand, heads north through the fairy lands behind the Shadowline in company with the soldier FERRAS VANSEN. They soon gain a third companion, GYIR THE STORM LANTERN, one of the Qar general YASAMMEZ's most trusted servants, who has a mission from her to bring a mirror—the very object the boy FLINT took down into the depths beneath the castle and to the feet of the Shining Man—to YNNIR, the king of the Qar. But Barrick and the others are captured by a monster named JIKUYIN, a demigod who has reopened the mines at Greatdeeps in an attempt to find a way to gain the power of the sleeping gods.

Briony Eddon meets a demigoddess, LISIYA, a forest deity now fallen on hard times, who leads Briony to MAKEWELL'S MEN, a troop of theatrical players on their way south to the powerful nation of Syan. Briony joins them, telling them nothing of her real name and situation.

Back in Qul-na-Qar, the home of the fairies, their QUEEN SAQRI is dying, and King Ynnir is helpless to do anything more for her. His only hope, it seems, are the machinations taking place around the magical mirror currently in the hands of Gyir the Storm Lantern. That mirror, and the agreement about it called the Pact of the Glass, is the only thing keeping vengeful Yasammez and her fairy army from destroying South-march.

At the same time QINNITAN, the escaped bride of SULEPIS, the AUTARCH OF XIS, has made a life for herself in the city of Hierosol, the southernmost port on the northern continent. What she doesn't know is that the Autarch has sent DAIKONAS VO, a mercenary killer, to bring her back, compelling Vo with painful magic. The nature of the powerful Autarch's interest in Qinnitan is still a mystery.

Southmarch Castle remains under the strange non-siege of the Qar. Inside the castle, the poet MATT TINWRIGHT has become enamored of ELAN M'CORY, Hendon Tolly's mistreated lover. Recognizing that Tinwright cares for her, she asks him to help her kill herself. Unwilling to do this, he tricks her by giving her just enough poison to make her senseless, then smuggles her out of the royal residence so that he can hide her from Hendon.

Tolly maintains his hold on power largely because he has named him-self the protector of the newborn ALESSANDROS, heir to the missing KING OLIN. Hendon Tolly appears largely uninterested in the besieging Qar or anything else.

Meanwhile, Olin is being held in the southern city of Hierosol, where he catches a glimpse of Qinnitan (working as a maid in the palace) and sees something strangely familiar in her. He does not have long to think about it before the Autarch's huge navy sweeps up from the south and besieges Hierosol. Olin's captor sells him to the Autarch to secure his own safety, although why the god-king of Xis should be interested in the monarch of a small northern country is not clear.

In Greatdeeps, Barrick Eddon and the other prisoners of the demigod Jikuyin are slated for sacrifice in a ritual meant to open the way to the land of the sleeping gods, but the fairy Gyir sacrifices his own life, defeat-ing the demigod's forces with their own explosives. Gyir dies and Vansen falls through a magical doorway into nothingness. Barrick is left alone to fight his way out of the mines and escape, carrying the mirror that Gyir was meant to take to the fairy-king Ynnir. With his companions gone and only the raven SKURN for company, Barrick begins his lonely jour-ney across the shadowlands toward the fairy city of Qul-na-Qar. His only other companion comes to him solely in dreams—the girl Qinnitan, whom he has never met, but whose thoughts can, for some reason, touch his.

Meanwhile Briony and the theatrical troop have reached the great city of Tessis, capitol of Syan. She and the other players meet DAWET there, the onetime servant of Ludis Drakava, King Olin's captor, but they are all surprised and arrested by Syannese soldiers, although Dawet escapes. The players and Briony are accused of spying. To save her companions, Briony declares her true identity—the princess of Southmarch.

Ferras Vansen, who had fallen into seemingly endless darkness, undergoes a strange, dreamlike journey through the land of the dead at the side of his deceased father. He escapes at last only to find himself no longer behind the Shadowline, but in Funderling Town underneath Southmarch Castle. CHAVEN the physician, who is hiding from Hendon Tolly, is also with the Funderlings now.

Far to the south, in Hierosol, Qinnitan is captured by Daikonas Vo, who takes her to the Autarch Sulepis, but the Autarch has already left Hierosol on a ship bound for the obscure northern kingdom of Southmarch. Vo commandeers another ship and sets out after his cruel master.

The Autarch is not alone on his flagship. Besides his faithful minister PINIMMON VASH, he also has a prisoner—the northern king, OLIN EDDON. And Olin's ultimate fate, Sulepis informs him, will be to die so that the Autarch can gain the power of the sleeping gods.

Prelude

❦

"TELL ME THE REST OF THE STORY, BIRD."

The raven cocked his head. "Story?"

"About the god Kupilas—about Crooked, as you call him. Tell the tale, bird. It's pissing down rain and I'm cold and I'm hungry and I'm lost in the worst place in the world."

"Us is wet and hungry, too," Skurn reminded him. "Us has et scarce but a mashed cocoon or two lately."

That idea didn't make Barrick feel any better. "Just . . . tell me some more of the tale. Please."

The raven smoothed his blotched feathers, mollified. "S'pose us could. What did us tell last?"

"About how he met his great-grandmother. And she was going to teach him . . ."

"Oh, aye. Us recalls it. *'I will teach you how to travel in the lands of Emptiness,'* his great-grandmother did tell Crooked, *'which stand beside everything and are in every place, as close as a thought, as invisible as a prayer.'* Be that what us were telling?"

"That's it."

"Could p'raps find you somewhat to eat, first?" Skurn was in a good mood again. "This part of the wood be full of Whistling Moths . . ." He saw the look on Barrick's face. "Well, then, Sir Too-Good-For-Everything—but don't blame Skurn when you comes over all rumbly-stummicked in the night . . ."

* * *

"Crooked did spend long days at the side of Emptiness, his great-grandmother, learning the secrets of her land and its roads and growing wiser even than he had been. He learned many tricks traveling in his great-grandmother's land, and saw many things when no one thought he watched 'em. And though his body was crippled and he had one leg shorter than the other, walking rickety-raw, rickety-raw like a wagon with a broken wheel, Crooked could travel faster than anyone—even his cousin Tricker, who men do call Zosim.

"Tricker was swiftest of all the clan of the Three Brothers, sly master of roads and poetry and madmen. In truth, clever Tricker had figured out some of Grandmother Emptiness' secrets all on his ownsome, but he also called her 'Old Wind in a Well' when he didn't know she were listening. After that she made sure Tricker never learned anything more about her lands and their weirdling ways.

"But Crooked she kept close to her heart and taught him well. The more Crooked learned, the more words and powers he gained, the more he felt it unfair that his father should have been killed and his mother stolen and his uncle and all his kin banished into the sky while the ones who had done it to them, especially the three biggest brothers—Perin, Kernios, and Erivor, as your folk call 'em— should live and laugh on the earth, happy and singing. Crooked brooded on this a long while until at last he thought of a scheme—the deepest, craftiest scheme that ever was.

"Now all of the three brothers were surrounded by guards and wards of frightsome power, so it were not enough simply to come upon them suddenly, looking to do harm. Water Man Erivor had sea wolves swimming all around his throne, and poison jellies, as well as his water soldiers who guarded him all the green day and green night. Sky Man Perin lived in a palace on the highest mountain of the world, surrounded by rest of his kin, and he carried the great hammer Crackbolt that Crooked himself had made for him, which could break the world itself if it hammered on it long enough. And Stone Man (called Kernios by your folk) had not so many servitors, but lived in his castle deep in the earth among the dead, and was warded round with tricks and words that could burn the eyes from your head or turn your bones to cracksome ice.

"But one weakness all the brothers had, which is the weakness any man has, and that were their wives. For even the Firstborn, it is said, are no better than any others in the eyes of their own women.

"Long had clever Crooked grown his friendships with the wives of two of the brothers: Night, who was Sky Man's queen, and Moon, who had been cast out by

Stone Man and then taken to wife by Water Man, his brother. Both of these queens begrudged their husbands' freedoms and wished that they too could go out and all about in the world, loving who they pleased and doing what they chose. So to these two Crooked gave a potion to put in their husbands' wine cups, telling them, 'This will make them sleep the night long and not wake once. While they slumber you can do as you please.'

"Night and Moon were pleased by Crooked's gift, and promised they would do it that very night.

"The third brother, cold, hard Stone Man, had found Crooked's own mother, Flower—I think your kind calls her Zoria—when was wandering alone and heart-sick after the war's end, and had taken her home to be his wife, casting out his own wife Moon to find her luck in the world. Stone Man then gave Crooked's mother a new name, Bright Dawn, but although he clothed her in heavy gold and jewels and other gifts of the black earth, she never smiled and never spoke, but sat like one of those dead folk Stone Man ruled from his dark throne. So Crooked went to his mother by darkness and told her of his plan. No need did he have to lie to her, either, who had seen her husband killed, her son tortured, and her family banished. When he gave her the potion she still did not speak or even smile, but she kissed Crooked on his head with her cold lips before she turned away and walked back into the endless corridors of Stone Man's house. He would see her only once more again.

"His scheme in place, Crooked went firstly to the house of Water Man, deep beneath the ocean. He traveled through the lands of his great-grandmother, Emptiness, as she had taught him, so that no one in Water Man's house saw him coming. Crooked slipped past the unsleeping sea-wolves like a cold current, and although they guessed he was nearby they could not reach him to tear him to pieces with their sharp teeth. Neither could the poison jellies sting him— Crooked passed through them as though they were nothing but floating lily pads.

"When at last he found Water Man asleep in his chamber, drunken and sense-less with the potion that Moon had given him, Crooked paused, a strange mood come upon him. Water Man had not joined in the torture of Crooked like the other two brothers, and Crooked did not feel the same hatred for him that he felt for Sky Man and Stone Man. Still, Water Man had made war on Crooked's family and helped to make Crooked's mother a widow, and then joined his brothers in banish-ing the rest of Crooked's clan into the sky. Also, while he lived on the earth the line of the Moisture clan, Crooked's enemies, would survive. Showing a kind of mercy, Crooked did not wake Water Man up to learn his fate, but instead opened

a door into a part of the lands of Emptiness where no one had ever gone, a secret place even his great-grandmother had forgotten, and pushed Water Man through as he slept. Then, when Erivor the Water Man was gone from the world, Crooked closed the door again.

"He passed out of the undersea house again through his secret paths, wondering whether to go next to confront Sky Man or Stone Man. Of the three brothers, Sky Man was the strongest and cruelest, and had made himself lord of all the gods. He ruled them from his palace atop the mountain called Xandos—the Staff—and the godly court protected him more completely than any walls. His sons Huntsman, Horseman, and Shieldbearer were almost as powerful as their father, and his daughters Wisdom and Forest could also best almost any warrior, let alone a cripple like Crooked. It would make sense to wait until last to attack Sky Man in his great fortress.

"But the truth was that cold, silent Stone Man, not his raging brother, was the one that frightened Crooked most.

"So he traveled to the Staff on the paths of Emptiness, and all the clan of Moisture felt his passing but could not see or hear or smell him. Only Huntsman of the sharp eyes and Forest of the fleet foot could even guess where he was. Cruel, pretty Forest ran after Crooked but just missed catching him, pulling off a piece of his tunic. Huntsman fired a magical arrow that actually flew into the lost paths where Crooked walked and nicked his ear, so that blood dripped on his shoulder and his hand of ivory. But they could not stop him and soon he was deep in Sky Man's palace, where the lord of the house slept his drugged slumber. Crooked bolted the door behind him.

"'Wake up!' he cried to sleeping Sky Man. He wanted his enemy to know what was happening and who had done it to him. 'Wake up, Loud Voice—I bring your ending!'

"Sky Man was very strong, even after drinking the potion Crooked had created. He sprang from his bed and took down his great hammer Crackbolt, big as a hay-wain, and swung it at Crooked. He missed and broke his own gigantic bed into splinters.

"'That is nothing to worry about,' Crooked told him. 'You will not need that bed again. You will sleep in another, soon—a cold bed in a cold place.'

"Sky Man roared that Crooked was a traitor, then he threw his hammer as hard as his mighty arm could manage. If any other god or man but Crooked had been its target Crackbolt would have smashed him into bits and scorched those bits to charcoal. But the hammer stopped in mid-flight.

"'Did you think I would make a weapon for you that you could use against *me?' Crooked asked him. 'You call me traitor, but you attacked my father—your own brother—and threw him down by treachery. Now you will get what you deserve.'*

"Then Crooked turned Sky Man's hammer against him, and the clamor of the blows were like the rumbling-tumble-roar of the lightning. Sky Man Perin cried out to his family and servants to save him. All who lived atop the Staff came running to his aid. But Crooked opened a doorway into the lands of Emptiness and before Sky Man could say another word, he struck him again with the great hammer and knocked him backward into that doorway. The lands of Emptiness pulled at Sky Man like a sucking wind, but Sky Man held on to the floor with all the strength that was in his mighty hands. He would not let go, but neither could he pull himself back from the empty lands where Crooked's great-grandmother reigned. Crooked smiled at that and stepped back. He opened the door of Sky Man's chamber and hid behind it. All of the other gods of the mountain, Wisdom and Shieldbearer and Clouds and Caretaker, rushed in. Seeing their lord in such danger they ran to help him, grabbing his arms and trying to pull him back, but the magic of Grandmother Emptiness was strong and they could not overcome it. While they struggled, Crooked came out from behind the door and walked up behind scrawny Old Age, who was at the back of the crowd. Old Age could not even reach Sky Man, but he was pulling on Wisdom, who was pulling on Huntsman, who was holding onto Sky Man's hand.

"'I remember how you spit on my father's corpse,' Crooked said to Old Age, then lifted up his hand of bronze and his hand of ivory and shoved the ancient one in the back. Old Age stumbled forward and fell against Wisdom, who fell against Huntsman, and soon all those who had come from all over the palace to save their lord fell into the the land of Emptiness together. That broke Sky Man's grip and they all tumbled into the cold darkness forever, every last one.

"Crooked laughed to see them fall, laughed as they shouted and cursed, laughed hardest when they were gone. He had brooded long on the evil they had done him and he felt no pity.

"One of Sky Man's kin, though, had not come into the chamber to help his lord. That was Tricker, who never did anything he could let others do. When he saw what had happened, how Sky Man, the strongest of all the gods had been bested and banished, Tricker was afraid. He ran down from the palace of the gods to warn his father, Stone Man.

"So it was that when Crooked at last came down from the great mountain Xandos and ran toward the house of Stone Man, swift Tricker had run before him. Crooked had no surprise to help him, so when he reached the great gates of Stone

Man's house he found them locked and barred and guarded by many soldiers. This didn't stop Crooked. He stole around them on the roads only he and his great-grandmother knew, until he found himself outside the chamber of Stone Man himself. Tricker had warned his father and was just sneaking away, but Crooked caught him and they fought. Crooked grabbed him around the throat and wouldn't let go. Tricker changed himself into a bull, a snake, a falcon, and even a living flame, but still Crooked wouldn't let go. At last Tricker gave up and resumed his natural shape, a-begging for his life.

" 'I tried to save your mother,' Tricker whined. 'I tried to help her escape. And I have always been your friend! When all the others were against you, I spoke for you. When they cast you out, did I not take you in and give you wine?'

"Crooked laughed. 'You wanted my mother for yourself and would have had her if she had not escaped. You did not speak for me, you took no side—that is always your way, so that you can ally yourself with whoever wins. And you took me in and gave me wine to make me drunk, so that you would learn from me how to make the magical things I gave to Sky Man and the others, but my ivory hand protected me by breaking the cup, and so you failed.' He lifted Tricker up by the neck and carried him into Stone Man's chamber. Crooked was still afraid of the lord of the dark earth, but he knew that one way or another the end was coming.

"Stone Man Kernios trusted no one, so he had not drunk the potion Crooked's mother had prepared for him. He stood ready now in his frightsome gray armor, his awful spear Earthstar in his hand. He was in the greatness of his strength and in his own palace. But he had one other weapon, too, and when Crooked entered by the roads of Emptiness, appearing from the air in front of him, Stone Man showed that weapon to him.

" 'Here is your mother,' said Stone Man, 'who I brought into my house but who repaid me with treachery.' Stone Man had her grasped tight in his arm and held the point of his spear against her throat. 'If you do not surrender to me, binding yourself with the same spells of Emptiness that have allowed you to murder my brothers, she will die before your eyes.'

"Crooked did not move. 'Your brothers have been shown more mercy than they showed my kin. They are not dead, but only sleeping in cold, empty lands, as you soon will, too.'

"Stone Man laughed. They say it were like a wind from a tomb. 'How is that better than death? Sleeping forever in emptiness? Well, you shall have no such gift, as you deem it. You will destroy yourself or your mother will bleed out her life, then I will kill you anyway.'

"Crooked lifted up Tricker, still choking in the grip of his bronze hand. 'And what about your son?'

"Stone Man's voice was the unkind rumble of the earth shaking. 'I have had many sons. If I survive I can make many more. If I do not, I care not what survives me. Do what you will.'

"Crooked threw Tricker aside. For a long time he and Stone Man looked at each other like wolves over a kill, neither willing to take the first step. Then Crooked's mother raised her trembling hands to the sharp point of the spear and slashed her own throat with it, falling to the floor of Stone Man's chamber in a great wash of blood.

"Stone Man did not wait. Even as Crooked stared at his mother gasping out her life on the floor, the lord of the black earth flung his great spear, still wet with his mother's lifeblood, at Crooked's heart. Crooked tried to make Earthstar obey him but Stone Man had laid his own words of power upon it and Crooked could not bend it to his mastery. Crooked only had time to step sideways into the empty lands. The spear flew past him and struck the wall so hard half the palace fell down and all the lands around shook and quivered.

"When Crooked stepped back out the roads of Emptiness, Stone Man was on him. They wrestled then for a long time as the palace itself fell around them, their strength so great and their contending so mighty that the very stones of the earth were all broken and crushed, so that what had once been a rocky fastness of peaks above Stone Man's house fell down into dust, and the land sunk, and the ocean rushed in all around them, so at last they were fighting on an island of stone amid the waters.

"At last the two of them caught at each other's throats. Stone Man was the stronger, and Crooked could only step into the ways of darkness, but Stone Man held on and was carried with him. As they fell through emptiness, Stone Man bent Crooked's back until it was nearly breaking. Crooked could not draw another breath, and neither could he think as Stone Man crushed out his life.

"'Now look into my eyes,' Stone Man said. 'You will see a darkness greater than anything Emptiness can make or even imagine.'

"Crooked was almost caught, for if he had looked once into the eyes of the Lord of the Black Depths he would have been pulled down into death, but instead he turned his head away and sank his teeth into Stone Man's hand. Stone Man was so pained that his grip loosened and Crooked was able to shake him off, then Stone Man fell away and away into the cloudy, cold dark.

"Crooked wandered a while in the most distant lands of Emptiness, dizzy and *confused, but at last found his way back to Stone Man's house where his mother's body lay. He kneeled over her but found he could not weep. Instead he touched his hand to the place she had kissed him, then bent and kissed her cold cheek.*

" 'I have destroyed your destroyers,' he told her silent form.

"Without warning, a terrible pain went through him as Stone Man's great spear pierced his chest. Crooked staggered to his feet. Tricker stepped from the shadows where he had hidden. The mischief-maker laughed and capered.

" 'And now I have destroyed you,' Tricker Zosim cried. 'All the great ones except for me are all dead, and I alone am left to rule all the world and the seven times seven mountains and seven times seven seas!'

"Crooked grasped with his hand of bronze and his hand of ivory at the spear Earthstar that had stabbed him. The great weapon burst into flames and burned away to a cinder. 'I am not destroyed,' he said, although he was sorely wounded. 'Not yet . . . not yet . . .' "

It was only when the pause had gone on so long that Barrick found himself nodding toward sleep that he finally looked up. "Bird? Skurn? What happened next?" His eyes widened. "Where are you?"

A few moments later a mostly black shape flapped down out of the perpetual gray sky with a horrid something wriggling in its black beak.

"Urm," it said, while most of the legs were still hanging out, kicking in hopeless protest. "Lovely. Us'll finish the tale later. Spotted a whole nest of 'these, us has. Taste just like dead mouse 'fore it bloats too far and bursts. Shall us fetch you one or two?"

"Oh, gods," groaned Barrick as he turned away in disgust. "Wherever you are, alive or dead or sleeping, please give me strength."

The raven sniffed at his foolishness. "Praying for strength be not enough. For us to stay strong, us has to eat."

PART ONE

VEIL

1
The Sham Crown

"As far as I can discover, there is no place upon the two continents or the islands of the sea that is without legends of the fairy folk. But whether they once lived in all these places or their memory was brought to the places by men when they came, no one can say."

—from "A Treatise on the Fairy Peoples of Eion and Xand"

THE TEMPLE BELL WAS RINGING for midday prayers. Briony felt a clutch of shame—she was already an hour later than she had promised, in large part because of Lord Jino and his shrewd, seemingly endless questions.

"Please, my lord," she told him as she rose to her feet. "I apologize, but I truly must go to see my friends." So hard after months of rough living to get the knack of ladylike movement and speech once more—it felt at least as false as any part she'd played for the theater troupe. "I crave your pardon."

"By friends, you mean the players?" Erasmias Jino cocked a stylishly plucked eyebrow. The Syannese lord looked like a fop, but that was only the Syannese style: Jino was renowned for his shrewdness and had also killed three men in duels decreed by the Court of Honor. "Surely, your Highness, you are not still pretending that such as you could truly be friends with . . . such as those. They enabled you to travel in secrecy—a clever stratagem when traveling through unsafe country on dangerous roads—but the time for that imposture is over."

"Nevertheless, I must go to see them. It is my duty." She had to admit that much of what he said was true. She hadn't treated the players as true friends, but had kept all that was most important about herself a secret. They had opened their lives to her but Briony Eddon had not reciprocated, nor even come close: they had been honest, she had been the opposite.

Well, most of them had been honest. "I understand you have released all except Finn Teodoros. He claimed to bear messages for your king from Lord Brone. I am Avin Brone's true monarch and he would not have them kept from me, I know. I would like to hear those messages."

Jino smiled and brushed his fingers through his beard. "Perhaps you will, but that is for my master King Enander to decide, Princess Briony. He will see you later today." The juxtaposition of titles was no accident: Jino was reminding her that she stood below the Syannese king in precedence, and would have even in her own country—but she was not, most definitely not, in her own country.

Lord Jino rose with a smooth grace most women would have envied. "Come. I will take you to the players now."

Father gone, Kendrick gone, Barrick . . . She fought to keep the tears that suddenly trembled on her lower lid from running over. *Shaso, and now Dawet. All gone, most of them dead—maybe all of them . . .* She tried to steady herself before the Syannese official noticed. *And now I must say goodbye to Makewell's Men as well.* It was a strange feeling, this loneliness. Always before she had felt it as something temporary, as something that must be endured until her situation improved. For the first time she was beginning to sense that it might not be temporary at all, that she might have to learn live this way, tall and straight as a statue, hard as stone, but hollow inside. *All, all hollow . . .*

Jino led her across the residence and then through one of Broadhall Palace's great gardens and into a quiet hallway built along the inside of the palace's great wall. Such a vast dwelling—the palace alone as large as all of Southmarch, castle and city. And she knew not a soul here, had no one to trust . . .

Allies. I need allies in this strange land.

The Southmarch players were sitting on a bench in a windowless chamber under the eyes of several guards. Most of them already looked frightened; the sight of Briony, confirmed now as their ruler and dressed in expensive clothes Jino had provided for her, did not make them any less so. Estir Makewell, whose last words to Briony had been angry and unpleasant, even blanched and hunched her shoulders as though she expected to be struck. Of all the players on the bench, only young Feival did not look cowed. He eyed her up and down.

"Look at what they've got you up in!" he said approvingly. "But stand up straight, girl, and wear it as though you mean it!" .

Briony smiled in spite of herself. "I've lost the knack, I guess."

The reprobate Nevin Hewney was eyeing her as well, frowning in wonderment. "By the gods, they told the truth. To think—had I but tried a little harder, I could have knobbed a princess!"

Estir Makewell gasped. Her brother Pedder fell off the bench and two guards lowered their halberds in case this might be the start of some general uprising. "Blessed Zoria save us!" Estir cried hoarsely, staring at the fierce blades. "Hewney, you fool, you will have us all on the headsman's block!"

Briony could not help being a little amused, but did not feel she could afford to show too much familiarity in front of the guards and Jino. "Be assured that should I take offense," she said, "it is only Hewney who would pay the price for his ungovernable tongue." She fixed the playwright with a stern gaze. "And were I to read out the bill of particulars against him I might start with the time he referred to myself and my brother as 'twin whelps sired by Stupidity on the bitch Privilege.' Or perhaps the time he referred to my imprisoned father as 'Ludis Drakava's royal bum-toy.' I think either of those would suffice to put the headsman to work."

Nevin Hewney groaned, a touch too loud to be convincingly repentant—the man was either almost fearless or stupefied by years of drink. "Do you see?" he demanded of his comrades. "That is what comes of youth and sobriety. Her memory is horrifyingly sharp. What a curse— never to forget even the slightest bit of foolishness. Your Highness, you have my pity!"

"Oh, shut up, Hewney," said Briony. "I'm not going to hold you responsible for things you said when you didn't know who I was, but you're not half as charming or clever as you think you are."

"Thank you, Highness." The playwright and actor sketched a bow. "For, since I think quite highly of myself, that still leaves me with a formidable weight of charm."

Briony could only shake her head. She turned to Dowan, the soft-spoken giant for whom she had a particular fondness. "In truth, I've just come to say goodbye. I'll do my best to get them to let Finn go quickly."

"Is it really true, then?" he asked. "Are you really . . . who they say you are, Mistress? Highness?"

"I'm afraid so," she told him. "I did not wish to lie to you, but I feared for my life. I'll never forget the kindness with which you treated me." She turned to the others and even found a smile for Estir. "All of you. Yes, even Master Nevin, although in his case it was interspersed with lechery and his unending love for the music of his own voice."

"Hah!" Pedder Makewell was sitting up again, feeling better. "She has scored another hit on you, Hewney."

"I care not," said the playwright airily. "For the mistress of all Southmarch has proclaimed I am half of the most charming man in the world."

"But I am *not* the mistress of all Southmarch." Briony looked over to Erasmias Jino, who had been watching the entire performance with a polite smile on his face, like a theatergoer who had seen better work only the night before. "And that is why you must not go back there—not yet." She turned to the Syannese nobleman. "News of my presence here will reach Southmarch, will it not?"

He shrugged. "We will not keep it secret—we are not at war with your country, princess. In fact, we are told that Tolly only protects the throne against the return of your father . . . or, presumably, you."

"That's a lie! He tried to kill me."

Jino spread his hands. "I'm certain you are right, Princess Briony. But it is . . . *complicated* . . ."

"Do you see?" she said, turning back to the players. "So you must stay here in Tessis, at least until I know more of what I will do. Play your plays. I'm afraid you'll have to find another actress to play Zoria." She smiled again. "It should not be hard to find a better one, I'm sure."

"In truth I thought you were coming along quite well," Feival told her. "Not enough to make them forget me, thanks to Zosim and all the other gods, but nicely."

"He speaks true," said Dowan Birch. "You could still make a grand player someday, if you but worked at it a little." He looked around, reddening, as the others laughed.

Briony, though, wasn't laughing. She had felt a sharp pang at his words, at the glimpse into an impossible other life where things were different, where she could have lived as she chose. "Thank you, Dowan." She stood up. "Don't fear—we'll soon find you all a place to stay." And in the meantime, Briony could keep the players close by and consider the idea that had come to her. "Farewell, then, until our next meeting."

As the players were conducted out by a pair of guards, Hewney broke away from them and came back to Briony. "In truth," he whispered, "I like you better in this role, child. You play the part of a queen most convincingly. Keep it up and I foresee good reviews for you in future." He gave her a quick kiss scented with wine—and where had he gotten any wine, she wondered, while in King Enander's custody?—before following the others out.

"Well, by the sweet Orphan," Lord Jino said, "that was all most . . . interesting. Sometime you must tell me what it is like to travel with such people. But now, you are called to a more elevated performance—a command performance, as such are called."

It took her a moment. "The king?"

"Yes, Highness. His august Majesty, the King of all Syan, wishes to meet you."

Briony would have been one of the first to admit that the throne room back in Southmarch might be dignified, even impressive, but it was not awesome. The ceiling was full of fine old carvings but they were hard to see in the dark chamber except on festival days when all the candles were set blazing. The ceiling itself was high, but only in comparison to most of the rest of the rooms—there were higher ceilings within many of the great houses of the March Kingdoms. And the colored windows that in her childhood had formed her strongest idea of heaven were not even as nice as those in the great Trigonate temple in the outer keep beyond the Raven's Gate. Still, Briony had always thought that there could not be much difference between her home and the other royal palaces of Eion. Her father was a king, after all, and his father and grandfather had been kings before him—a line that went back generations. Surely the monarchs of Syan and Brenland and Perikal did not live much more grandly, she had thought. But since she had come to famous Broadhall Palace, Briony had quickly lost her illusions.

From the first hour of her capture, as the coach surrounded by a troop of soldiers had passed through the portcullis and gate and onto the palace grounds, she had begun to feel foolish. How could she have thought her family something other than rustic—the same sort of faded, countrified nobles that she and Barrick had found so amusing back home? And now she stood beside Jino in the throne room itself, the voluminous chamber that for centuries had been the heart of the entire continent, and which still was the capital of one of the most powerful nations in the world, and her own witless pretension was a bone in her throat.

The Broadhall throne room was vast, to begin with, the ceiling twice as lofty as that of Southmarch's greatest temple, and carved and painted in such wonderful, startling detail that it looked as though an entire population of Funderlings had worked on it for a century. (That was exactly what had happened, she found out later, although here in Syan they called their small people *Kallikans*.) Each brilliant window stained with sun-bright colors looked as big as the Basilisk Gate back home, and there were dozens of them, so that the huge room seemed to be crowned with rainbows. The floor was a swirling pattern of black and white marble squares, an intricate circular mosaic called Perin's Eye—famous throughout the world, Erasmias Jino informed her as he led her across it. She followed him past the huge but empty throne and the company of armored knights in blue, red, and gold who stood solemnly against the throne room's great walls, still and silent as statues.

"You must permit me to show you the gardens at some point," the marquis told her. "The throne room is very fine, of course, but the royal gardens are *truly* extraordinary."

I take your point, fellow—this is what a true kingdom looks like. She kept her face cheerfully empty, but Jino's high-handedness griped her. *You do not think much of Southmarch or our small problems and you want to remind me what real grandeur and real power look like. Yes, I take your point. You think my family's crown is no more impressive than the sham crown of wood and gold paint that I wore on the stage.*

But the heart of a kingdom is not small just because the kingdom is, she thought.

Jino led her through a door at the back of the throne room, this one surrounded by a group of guards in different, although complementary, shades of blue and red from those lined along the walls of the throne room. "The King's Cabinet," said Jino, opening the door and gesturing for her to go in. A herald in a brilliant sky-blue tabard embroidered with Syan's famous sword and flowering almond branch, asked her name and title, then stamped his gold-topped stick on the floor.

"Briony te Meriel te Krisanthe M'Connord Eddon, Princess Regent of the March Kingdoms," he announced, as casually as if she were the fourth or fifth princess who'd come through the door that day. For all Briony knew, she might have been: two or three dozen guards, servants, and beautifully dressed courtiers filled the richly appointed room, and though many of them watched her entrance, few showed any signs of overwhelming interest.

"Ah, of course, Olin's child!" said the bearded man on the high-backed couch, waving her forward. He was dressed in serious, dark clothes and his voice was deep and strong. "I see his face in yours. This is an unexpected pleasure."

"Thank you, your Majesty." Briony made her curtsies. Enander Karallios was the most powerful ruler in Eion and looked the part. He had gone a little to fat in recent years, but he was a big man and managed to carry it well. His hair was dark, almost black, with only a little gray, and his face, though rounded by age and weight, was still strong and impressive, brow high, eyes wide-set, his nose strong and sharp, so that it was still quite possible to see why as a younger man he had been considered a very dashing and handsome prince indeed. "Come, child, sit down. We are pleased to see you. Your father is dear to us."

"Dear to all of Eion," said the woman in the beautiful pearled gown beside him. This must be Ananka te Voa, Briony realized, a powerful noblewoman in her own right, but also, and far more important, a mistress to kings. Briony was a little shocked to see her sitting at Enander's side so openly. The king's second wife had died some years ago, but the gossip Briony had heard among Makewell's Men suggested that he had only taken up with this woman recently, after Ananka had left her old lover, Hesper, the king of Jael and Jellon.

Hesper the bloody-handed traitor . . . !

Briony, who had been in mid-curtsy, almost lost her balance as she thought of him. There were few men in the world Briony would have seen tortured, but Hesper was one of them. She couldn't help wondering whether Ananka had been at his side when Hesper had decided to imprison Briony's father Olin and then sell him to Ludis Drakava. Looking at the woman's sharp, hard eyes, it was easy enough to believe.

"You are both very kind," Briony said, doing her best to keep her voice even. "My father has always spoken of you with the highest regard and love, King Enander."

"And how is he? Have you had word from him?" Enander was toying with something in his lap and it distracted her. After a moment she saw the bright little eyes peering out from beneath his heavy velvet sleeve. It was a small animal, a tiny dog or a ferret.

"Some letters, yes, but not since I left Southmarch." She couldn't help wondering what the two of them were thinking. They acted as though this was any other audience—did they not know her situation? "Your Majesty is doubtless aware that I left my home . . . well, let us say I did not go by choice. One of my subjects . . . no, one of my father's subjects, Hendon Tolly, has traitorously seized the throne of the March Kingdoms. I suspect he murdered my older brother, as well as his own." In truth, Kendrick's death was the one crime she could not with certainty lay against Hendon Tolly, but he had admitted his role in his own brother Gailon's death.

"Lord Tolly says differently, as you probably know," said Enander, looking troubled. "We cannot take sides—not without knowing more. I'm sure you understand. Lord Tolly claims you ran away, that all he does is protect Olin's remaining heir, the infant Alessandros. That is the boy's name, is it not?" he asked Ananka.

"Yes, Alessandros." She turned back to Briony. "You poor child." Ananka was handsome, but she used too much powder—it accentuated the lines of her thin face rather than hid them. Still, she was the kind of woman who had always made Briony feel like a clumsy, stupid little girl. "How you must have suffered. And we have heard such stories! Is it true Southmarch was attacked by the fairies?"

King Enander gave her an irritated look, perhaps because he did not want to be reminded of Syan's old debt to Anglin's line in the fairy wars of the past.

"Yes, it was, my lady," Briony said. "And as far as I know, still under siege . . ."

"But we hear that you hid yourself among a company of peasants and escaped—walking all the way from Southmarch! How clever! How brave!"

"In truth, it was a company of players . . . ma'am." Briony had learned how to swallow an angry reply, but it did not taste good. "And I was not escaping the siege, but my own treacherous . . ."

"Yes, we have heard—quite a story!" Enander cut her off before she could say more. It was not an accident. "But we have had only the barest bones—of course, you must flesh them out for us soon. Ah-ah," he said, lifting his hand when she might have spoken again. "But no more talk now, my dear—you must be exhausted after your ordeal. Time enough for everything when you are feeling stronger. We will see you tonight at supper."

She thanked him and made another curtsy. *So,* she wondered, *am I a guest? Or a prisoner?* It wasn't entirely clear.

As Lord Jino led her out of the King's Cabinet, Briony fought against anger and unhappiness. Enander had received her kindly and courteously, and so far the Syannese had treated her as well as she could have hoped. Had she expected that the king would stand up, declare undying loyalty to the blood of Anglin's line, and immediately equip her with an army to go back and overthrow the Tollys? Of course not. But she also had the distinct feeling from the king's mien that such a thing wasn't only to be delayed, it was never going to happen at all.

Briony was so immersed in her thoughts that she nearly walked into a tall man coming across the throne room, headed toward the chamber she had just left. As she started back he reached out a strong hand to keep her upright.

"Apologies, Mistress," he said. "Are you well?"

"Your Royal Highness," said Jino. "You are back before we looked for you."

Briony straightened her clothes to cover her confusion. Royal Highness? Then this young man must be Eneas, the prince. She felt her breath getting a little short as she looked up. Was this truly the boy she had thought about so much during that year of her childhood? He was certainly as handsome as the prince she had imagined, tall and slender but wide-shouldered, with a tangled mass of black hair like a horse's mane after a long, fast ride.

"There is much to tell," the prince said. "I rode fast." He looked at Briony, puzzled. "And who is this?"

"Highness, allow me to present Briony te Meriel te Krisanthe . . ." Jino began.

"Briony Eddon?" The prince interrupted him. "Are you truly Briony Eddon? Olin's daughter? But what are you doing here?" Suddenly remembering his manners, he grabbed her hand and lifted it to his lips, but his eyes never left her face.

"I will explain all later, Highness," Jino said. "But your father will want to hear your news about the southern armies. Did everything go well?"

"No," Eneas said. "No, it did not." He turned back to Briony. "Are you dining with us tonight? Say yes."

"Y—yes, of course."

"Good. We will speak more then. It is astounding to see you here. I was just thinking about your father—I admire him greatly, you know. Is he well?" He did not wait for an answer. "Jino is right, I should go. But I look forward to our conversation later." He took her hand, kissed it again, a mere brush of his dry, wind-chapped lips, but looked at her as though he meant to memorize her every feature. "I told them you would grow up a beauty," he said. "I am proved right."

Briony watched Eneas go, staring after him for several moments before she realized her mouth must be hanging open like that of some Dalesman sheepherder getting his first view of a real city. "What did he mean by that?" she said, half to herself. "He couldn't have even known I existed!"

Jino was frowning a little, but he did his best to turn it into a smile. "Oh, but the prince would never lie, Highness, and certainly he would not stoop to flattery." He gave a rueful laugh. "He means well, and he is of course a splendid young man, but in truth his courtly manners leave a bit to be desired." He straightened and extended his arm. "Let me show you back to your rooms now, Princess. We all look forward to the honor of your company again at supper, but you really should rest after your terrifying journey."

Briony's own courtly manners might be a touch rustic by Syannese standards but she understood what Erasmias Jino was saying well enough: *Please, child, get out from under my feet so I can see to more important business— the business of a true kingdom, not a backwater like yours.*

It was another reminder that Briony was at best a distraction for these Syannese, and more likely an annoying problem. Either way, she had no power here, or any friends she could count on. She let herself be led back across the gleaming, echoing throne room, through groups of staring courtiers and more discreet but just as interested servants, already thinking about how that balance might be changed for the better.

2
A Road Beneath the Sea

"According to Rhantys and other scholars from the years before the Great Death, the fairies themselves claim they were not created by the gods, but that rather they 'summoned' the gods."

—from "A Treatise on the Fairy Peoples of Eion and Xand"

FLINT PICKED UP THE BROKEN, bone-white disk in his fingers and waved it at Chert. "What is this?" he demanded, but his adoptive father was several paces ahead and couldn't see what the boy had found.

"Are we walking all the way to Silverside, old man?" Opal asked as she came up from behind them, then she saw what Flint was holding. "What do you have there, boy?" She took it from him and carefully rubbed off the dust, then held the pale half-circle up to the light of her coral lamp. "Why, look, Chert, it's part of a sea imperial. What's it doing down here instead of on a beach? Did someone drop it, do you think?"

"Must have." Chert carefully examined the rock above their heads but it looked reassuringly solid and dry. "Nothing dripping here. Besides, the sea doesn't just dribble if it finds a way in. All that water, all that weight, it'd fill the place in a heartbeat." He could not help remembering the terrible stories his father had told him about the tragedy on Quarrymen's Bank, named after the guild that had been extending their living quarters there.

The first law of Funderling Town was, and always had been, that no serious digging of any kind should ever be undertaken beneath the waterline, since one mistake would be enough to bring the sea flooding into the depths, destroying the district of the Mysteries and the temple of the Metamorphic Brotherhood, as well as everything else in the lower caverns. But on that morning sixty or seventy years earlier the Quarrymen's Guild crew had lost track of how deep they'd dug. It was discovered later that they had also cut too far out toward the edge of the great stony island of Midlan's Mount on which Southmarch stood.

That day, a rumble of dislodged stone had been followed by a shocking spear thrust of chilly seawater that knocked Funderling diggers head over heels. Within moments the tremendous flow of water began widening the crevice; the thin spurt quickly became a barrel-wide gush. The quarrymen labored fruitlessly to close the hole, fighting the overwhelming power of the sea god himself, but the excavated rooms were already beginning to fill. One of the workers defied his foreman and fled to an upper level to let people there know what was happening. Such members of the guilds as were available hurried to the spot and a decision was made by the Highwardens to seal off the entire bank. A dozen Funderlings were pulled out of the flooded level, but almost twice that number had been cut off in other side passages by the rising water and there was no time to search for them. It had been a choice, Chert's father had told him with a kind of sour satisfaction, between twenty-three men doomed by an idiot foreman or the hundreds more below sea level in all the rest of Funderling Town.

It was fortunate, in a terrible way, that the Stone-Cutter's Guild had recently allowed the judicious use of black powder in some particularly difficult diggings: if folk had needed to shift the stone by hand, Chert's father had said, there would have been no saving the lower depths at all. The trapped men must have heard a single loud thump like the very hammer of the Lord of Endless Skies as the black powder brought down the roof of the chamber next to the bank diggings. After that they would have heard nothing but their own terrified voices and the water rising to cover them.

The thought of their dying moments had given Chert nightmares throughout his young life, and even today Funderling children talked in hushed whispers about the haunted, hidden depths of Quarrymen's Bank.

"No—no, there is no hole here," Chert told his family, shaking his head at childhood memories that still made his heart flutter in his chest. He summoned a smile. "And a good thing, since we are well beneath the water and I prefer not to get damp."

"Still, that is a sea imperial the boy's found, without doubt." Opal handed it back to Flint and tousled the boy's hair. Opal knew her shells. She had always enjoyed going up to the surface during the cold season with the other Funderling women to gather mussels in the tidepools along the edge of Brenn's Bay, then bringing them home and boiling them with a hot rock. Chert loved them—they were even sweeter than the many-legged *korabi,* the crevice-crawlers that scuttled over the damp rocks along the Salt Pool—and Opal loved them too, but she hadn't gone out to gather any for a long time. Not since they'd had Flint to care for.

"Imperial . . . ?" the boy said, squinting at the disk.

"That's right—because it looks like a coin, see? But it's a shell, the skeleton of a little sea beast." Chert tugged gently at the boy's elbow. "Come along and I'll tell you something about this place."

"I hope you're going to tell us that we're almost done walking," said Opal. "Who would make such a track so deep and so long? Mad folk is my guess."

Chert laughed. "Yes, we're almost done, my old darling—almost." He reached around and patted the bundle on his back. "And remember, I'm carrying the pack."

Opal scowled. "I hope you're not saying that this sack I'm carrying is light. Because it isn't."

"Of course not." He had told her not to bring half of what she'd put in it, of course, but that was like telling a cat to leave its tail and whiskers behind. How could Opal go anywhere without at least a few pots? And her good spoons, a wedding present from her mother? "Never mind," he said, as much to himself as to his family. "Just walk and I'll tell you about this track—why it's here and who made it.

"Now, back in the days of the second King Kellick, if my grandfather told me the tale rightly, there was a great Funderling named Azurite of the Copper clan, but in those days the more common name for azurite crystals was 'Stormstone,' and that's what everyone called him. Now, as I said, Stormstone Copper was a great man—a rare man—and that was good, because he was born into difficult times."

"How long ago?" Flint asked.

Chert frowned. "Well before my grandfather's day—over a century.

The *first* King Kellick had been good to the Funderlings, honoring them in all his dealings with them, treating them no worse than any other member of his kingdom, and sometimes better, because he valued their craftiness."

"You mean craftsmanship," said Opal, puffing a little.

"I mean craftiness, which means more than just the laying of chisel to stone. It has to do with *knowing*. The first Kellick had been one of the few kings that valued what our folk knew. He was the only king that fought against the fairy folk but didn't treat our people like goblins escaped from behind the Shadowline." Chert shook his head. "But you're getting me distracted, woman. I'm trying to explain about these passages we're in."

"Oh! The cheek of me for interrupting you, Master Blue Quartz! Speak on." But he heard a hint of a smile in her voice. They had been walking a good part of the morning and they were all tired: the distraction was very welcome.

"So after the first Kellick died everyone thought that things would go well under his son, Barin, who seemed much like his father. And so he was, except in one way—he hated fairies and he didn't much like Funderlings, either. During his reign most of the Eight Gates of Funderling Town were sealed, leaving us only one way to go up to the surface and back—the same one we use today. And there were king's guards who stood there at that gate, day after day, searching our people's wagons and troubling them for no reason except to remind them that they were not as important as the Big Folk. It was a great shock to all the Funderlings, especially after the long and happy partnership we'd enjoyed with Barin's father.

"Well, as it turned out, Barin reigned even longer than the first Kellick, almost forty years, and although we were still given work in Southmarch, they were not happy years. Many of our people left and spread out to other cities and countries, especially here in the north where the Qar armies had burned and broken so much.

"When Barin finally died and his son came to the throne—the second Kellick, named after his grandfather—wise old Stormstone Copper met with the other leading Guildsmen and asked them, 'Do you know how the Big Folk kill rabbits? They stop up all their burrow entrances but one, then they put ferrets down the one entrance left and let them run every member of the warren to ground—does and kittens and all.'

"When the other Funderlings asked him why he was taxing them with questions about rabbits when there was a new king being crowned and much to be discussed, Stormstone laughed a scornful laugh. 'Why do you think King Barin stopped up the entrances to all *our* burrows?' he said. 'Because that way, if they ever want to rid themselves of us they have only to send down soldiers with spears and torches, just like they send ferrets down the rabbit holes, and that will be the end of Funderling Town. We were fools to let them do it and we are fools if we do not do something about it as soon as we can.'

"Needless to say, there was a great deal of argument—many of the others in the Guild could not believe that the Big Folk would ever harm them. But Stormstone said, 'This Kellick is not like the first Kellick, just as his father Barin was not, either. Have you not seen the way the Big Folk look at us now, the way they whisper about us? They think us little different from the fairies who are besieging the city. If they grow any more frightened, who knows what the Big Folk may do in their fright and anger?'

" 'But what can we do?' one of the guildsfolk asked. 'Do we beg the new king to change the law and allow us to reopen the other seven gates?'

"Stormstone laughed again. 'What, does the fox ask the hound for permission to run away? No. We will do what we need to do and tell no one.' And so they did what he suggested."

Chert cleared his throat. "See, we are starting to climb up again. That means we will be there soon. I admit it was a roundabout way to go, but a safe one." He put his arm on Flint's shoulder, felt his heart go a little cold when the boy quickly pulled away. "If you like, I will tell you the rest. Do you want to hear the rest?"

At first he thought the boy was ignoring him again, but then he saw a just perceptible nod.

"The Stone-Cutter's Guild did as wise Stormstone told them. They took money from the treasury and over the next dozen years found a few of the Big Folk who liked gold more than questions, and so secretly bought a number of houses in the poorest neighborhoods on the edges of Southmarch. Then they began to dig tunnels down from just beneath these properties and connect them to passages on the outer reaches of Funderling Town, out at the far ends of certain nameless roads which the Big Folk knew nothing about, and that they could not have found if they did, even with a map. At last the roads were ready. A group of our people who had permission from King Kellick the Second to be aboveground after sunset because they were working in a royal granary that was in use during the day brought an extra-large crew to work, mainly by confusing the uplander guards with much coming and going. After nightfall half of them left the granary and made their way by back alleys to the houses the Guild had secretly bought and there broke through the last cubits of earth and stone to the tunnels below. When they were finished they covered the holes in the earth with flagstone floors, each with a stone that could be lifted to reveal a doorway to distant Funderling Town.

"Not all these new passages ended in the outer keep, although that is where many were located. Some even led directly under the water to houses and other places on the mainland." He could have mentioned that he himself had traveled such a road to the Qar camp when he had taken Flint's mirror to the Twilight folk, but didn't for fear of upsetting Opal. "In fact," he went on, "it is said Stormstone even had one tunnel built that came up somewhere in the inner keep—on the grounds of the Throne hall itself!

"By the end of a few months, when our folk were finished with re-building the granary, they had also finished all the entrances to these New Gates, as the Guild elders called them in whispers. And ever since there have always been secret ways in and out of Funderling Town. The fairy folk stayed quiet for a hundred years or more after that, so many of the hidden passages fell into disrepair, but I'm told we have kept the houses and other places aboveground that hide them."

"You had better not be telling us this because you plan to make us walk all the way upground from here," Opal warned him.

"No. We're almost there, my love. The reason I'm telling you all this is that we're in one of those passages right now."

"Almost where?" asked Flint.

"The place we're going—the Metamorphic Brothers' temple."

"But why did we walk so far?" Flint didn't sound like he minded much: he was just curious.

"Because soldiers from upground are waiting at the regular gate and on some of the main roads of Funderling Town itself," Chert explained. "And they're all looking for a fellow called Chert and his wife Opal, as well as a big boy named Flint who stays with them."

"Those are our names," said Flint seriously.

Chert wasn't sure if he was joining in on the joke or not. "Yes, that's what I'm saying. It's us they're looking for, son—and they don't mean us anything good."

Brother Antimony was waiting for them in the middle of the path across the wide expanse of the temple's fungus gardens, his young, broad face creased with unfamiliar worry. Behind him other worried faces peered out of the shadows of the pillared facade of the Temple of the Metamorphic Brothers.

"The brothers aren't happy," Antimony told Chert. "Just to let you know. Grandfather Sulphur's been up all night bellowing that the Days of Inundation are coming soon." He nodded to Opal. "Greetings, Mistress, and the Elders' blessings on you. It's good to see you again."

Chert looked around for Flint, who had wandered off, following a cave cricket's erratic path across the garden. "Is it the boy they're worrying about?"

Antimony shrugged. "I would guess it's the other two Big Folk causing them the most fret, wouldn't you?" He laughed, but not too loud: faces were still peering out at them from the facade. "Not to mention what's happening upground, the war with the fairies and the idea we might be drawn into it. Still, some of us don't mind things being stirred up a little." He nodded vigorously. "It might surprise you, Master Blue Quartz, but the temple is not always the most exciting place to live. Not complaining, mind you, but you have certainly brought us a few welcome distractions over the last season or two."

"Thank you . . . I suppose."

Opal had finally recaptured the boy. Chert beckoned them both toward the temple's front door. His wife's eyes were wide as she looked up at the columned facade. "I'd forgotten how big it is!" Her pace slowed as she neared it, as if she fought a strong wind. In a sense, she did, Chert thought: the centuries of unspoken tradition that insisted the temple was only for the Metamorphic Brothers themselves and a few important outsiders.

Although Chert had been here twice before, he had not yet seen the inside, and as Antimony led them through the portico and into the *pronaos* hall he had to admit he was impressed by the size and craftsmanship of the temple's fixtures. The ceiling of pronaos was almost as far above their heads as the famous carved ceiling of Funderling Town itself, although not half so intricate. The temple's creators had instead taken austerity as their watchword, striving to make every line as clean and simple as possible, as had been the custom during their long-ago era. So the groined vault was decorated not with leaves or flowers or animals, but with broad lines and beautifully rounded edges. It made the hall look like something liquid that had been suddenly frozen, as if the Lord himself had poured the temple from a vast bucket of molten stone that had cooled in an instant.

"It's . . . beautiful," Opal whispered.

Antimony grinned. "Some like it, Mistress. Me, I find it a bit . . . stern. Day in, day out, it's nice to have something to look at that holds your gaze, but I find my eyes sort of slipping and sliding . . ."

"Antimony," someone said sharply, "have you nothing better to do than prattle?" It was the sour-faced Brother Nickel Chert remembered from his first visit, not looking any sweeter than before.

The young monk jumped. "Sorry, Brother. Of course, yes. Better things to do . . ."

"Then go and do them. We will call you if we need you."

Antimony, looking sad now—not so much at having been caught having a pointless conversation, Chert guessed, as at having that conversation curtailed—gave a little bow and lumbered off.

"He's a good lad," Chert said.

"He's a noisy one." Nickel frowned. He nodded briefly toward Opal and ignored Flint completely. "I suppose he told you the sort of uproar the place is in." He led them to a door in one wall of the great hall and through into a side corridor lined with alcoves. The shelves were empty but the smudged dust suggested something had rested in each and been recently moved. "We had more peaceful times before we met you, Chert Blue Quartz."

"The blame is not all mine, surely."

Nickel scowled. "I suppose not. Unpleasant things are happening all over, that is certain. These are the worst days since Highwarden Stormstone."

"Yes, I was just telling my family about him . . ."

"It is a pity that the Big Folk cannot simply leave us alone. We do them no harm," Nickel said angrily. "We wish only to follow our old ways, to serve the Earth Elders."

"Perhaps the Big Folk are part of the Earth Elders' greater plan," Chert said mildly. "Perhaps they are only doing what the Elders wish of them."

Nickel looked at him for a long moment. "You shame me, Chert Blue Quartz." He didn't sound happy about it. A moment later Nickel stopped and pushed open a door. The walls of the room behind it were covered with little baskets filled with glowing coral, so that by comparison to the dark hallway it seemed positively to blaze with light. "Come in and join your friends. They are here, in the library office."

It was certainly a modest room compared to the great main chamber, and that made the two men in it—Big Folk, not Funderlings—seem all the more grotesquely oversized. The physician Chaven smiled but did not get up, perhaps because he was worried about banging his head on the ceiling. Ferras Vansen, who was half a head taller than Chaven, rose into an awkward crouch and took Opal's hand. "Mistress, it is good to see you and your family again. I will never forget the meal you made for me on the night I returned—the single best thing I have ever eaten."

Opal's laugh threatened to become a girlish giggle. "I can't take much credit for that. Cooking for a starving man, well, that's like . . . like . . ."

"Catching a sun-dazzled salamander?" suggested Chert, then wished he hadn't: Opal looked hurt. "You do yourself too little credit, woman. Everyone knows your table is one of the best."

"Yes, she certainly has fed me grandly," said Chaven. "I never thought I could grow to admire a well-cooked mole so much." He smiled at Flint, who was watching the physician with his usual serious stare. "And hello to you too, boy. You're getting tall." Chaven turned back to Chert. "We wait only on the arrival of our last guest . . ."

The door creaked open. A worried-looking acolyte stuck his head in. "Brother Nickel?" the newcomer said. "One of the magisters from the town is here and he wants to use your study in the charterhouse for his council room!"

"My study?" squawked Nickel, then hurried out to defend his territory.

" . . . And that would be him," Chaven finished. "Ah, well. Magister Cinnabar and Brother Nickel will never be friends, I fear."

Chert pulled his old, blunt carving knife out of his pocket and gave it to Flint along with a chunk of soapstone to keep the boy occupied. "Let's see what you make of this," he said. "Take good care and think a little before you cut—that's a nice clean piece."

The door opened again and Cinnabar Quicksilver walked in, Nickel's strident voice echoing behind him. "He thinks he is the abbot already, that one," Cinnabar said, frowning. "Chert Blue Quartz, it is good to see you—and Mistress Opal! Have the brothers treated you well?"

"We just arrived," said Opal.

"You and the boy are welcome to wash away the road dust," Cinnabar said. "But I'm afraid I must steal your husband for a while, Mistress. Although you would be welcome, also. My Vermilion usually sees through problems in a moment that would take the Highwardens an hour."

Nickel appeared now, scowling like a man who has come home to find a stranger sitting in his favorite chair. "Have you started without me? Have you begun to talk without me? Do not forget, the Metamorphic Brotherhood is the host here."

"Nobody has forgotten you, Brother Nickel," said Cinnabar. "After all, we're are going to move this council to your study, remember?"

As the monk gave the magister a look that could have powdered granite, the physician stirred beside him. "Our talk will take much of the afternoon, I fear, and Captain Vansen and I have waited some time already. Is there a chance we could find some refreshment?"

"You may eat with the brothers at the appointed time," said Nickel stiffly. "The evening meal is only a few hours away. We agreed with Master Cinnabar to treat you as our own while you guest with us. Our fare is simple, but healthy."

"Yes," said Chaven with a touch of sadness. "I'm sure it is."

" . . . And so I suddenly found myself here—no longer leagues behind the Shadowline but standing in the center of Funderling Town atop a great mirror." Vansen frowned, his eyes troubled. "No, there was more to the journeying between there and here than that . . . but the rest has slipped away from me . . . like a dream . . ."

"It is a gift to have you with us, Captain," said Chaven, "and a gift to learn that when last you saw him Prince Barrick was alive and well." But the physician looked troubled. Chert had noticed him beginning to frown when Vansen talked of finding himself atop the mirrored floor in the Guildhall council chamber, between twin images of the glowering earth god Kernios.

"Alive—that he certainly was," the soldier said. "Well? I am not so sure . . ."

"Your pardon," Cinnabar said, "but now you must hear my news, for it touches on the young prince. A few of us are still allowed upground into the castle to work on tasks for the Tollys, and one of those, at great risk, brought news of your arrival here to Avin Brone."

"The Lord Constable," said Vansen. "Is he well?"

"He is Lord Constable no longer," said Cinnabar, "but for the rest, you will have to discover for yourself. He sent this for you and my man smuggled it back to me."

Vansen looked over the letter, lips moving soundlessly as he read. "May I read it to you?" he asked. Cinnabar nodded.

" '*Vansen,*

" '*I am pleased to hear that you are safe and even more pleased to hear news of Olin's heir. I do not understand what happened or how you got here—this little man has brought a letter from another little man . . .*' "

"I apologize for the count's manners," Vansen said, coloring.

Cinnabar waved his hand. "We have been called worse. Continue, please."

" '*. . . But I can hardly make sense of it. What is important is that you must not come up from below the ground. T.*'—that would be Hendon Tolly, of course—'*has men watching me at all times, and only the fact that the soldiers still trust me and many have remained as my loyal guards have prevented T. from making an end of me.*

" '*The fairy folk, may the gods curse them, have fallen quiet, but I think only to plan more evil. We can withstand a siege because they have no ships, but they have more weapons than those that one can see. They bring a great weight of fear against everyone who fights them, as you no doubt know . . .*'

"And I do," Vansen said, looking up. "Fear and confusion—their greatest weapons."

He turned back to the letter. " '*There is still no word . . .*' " For a moment he hesitated, as though something stuck in his throat. " '*. . . Still no word about Princess Briony, either, although some claim she was taken as a hostage by Shaso in his escape. It does not bode well that he has been so long gone and we have still heard nothing, though.*' " Vansen took a deep breath before continuing. "*So that is our position. T rules Southmarch in the name of Olin's youngest, the infant Alessandros. The fairies are at our walls and as long as they remain a threat he dares not kill or imprison me. You must stay hidden for now, Vansen, though I hope one day soon to be able to greet you, man to man, to hear the whole of your story and thank you for your many services . . .*' "

He cleared his throat, a little embarrassed. "The rest is unimportant. You have heard all that matters. The Qar have gone silent, but remain. Still, the walls should protect us for a long time, even against fairy spells . . ."

"If the Qar want to get into the castle, they will not bother with the walls," Chert said. "They will come through Funderling Town . . . and through the temple here, where we sit."

Vansen stared as though he had lost his mind. "What do you mean by that?"

"What?" Nickel stood up, trembling. "What are you saying? Why would they care about us or our blessed temple?"

"It has little or nothing to do with the temple," Chert said with a scowl.

"What has it to do with Funderling Town, though?" Cinnabar asked. "Once they are over the castle walls why would they single us out?" He stopped and his eyes went wide. "Oh! By the Elders, you are not speaking of an attack from upground at all . . . !"

"Now you understand me, Magister." Chert turned to Vansen. "There is much you still do not know about us and our city, Captain. But perhaps it is time to tell you . . ."

"You have no right to speak of such things!" Nickel said, almost shrieking. "Not in front of these . . . Big Folk! Not in front of strangers!"

Cinnabar raised his hands. "Calm yourself, Brother. But, Chert, he may be right—this is no ordinary matter and the Guild alone should decide . . ."

Chert banged his fist on the table, startling almost everyone. "Don't any of you understand?" Chert was truly angry now—at the Big Folk's intrigues that had dragged Funderling Town into someone else's wars, at Nickel and the others for their craven unwillingness to see the truth. He was even mad at Opal, he realized, for bringing home Flint, the strange quiet boy who had started all this nonsense in Chert's life. "Don't you see? *Nothing* is ordinary anymore! Nickel, we cannot hide secrets like Stormstone's roads anymore. We cannot pretend that things are as they used to be. I have met the fairies myself—nearly as closely as Captain Vansen. I spoke to their Lady Yasammez, and she'll frighten the spit right out of your mouth. Nothing ordinary about her! My boy there brought the very magic mirror here across the Shadowline in the first place that Vansen said Prince Barrick might be taking back to the great city of the Qar. Is that ordinary? Is *any* of this ordinary?"

He stopped, panting. Everyone at the table was staring at him, most with amazement, Opal with concern, Chaven with a kind of enjoyment.

"I think Captain Vansen is still waiting for an answer to his question," Chaven said. "And so am I. Why do you think Funderling Town is in danger? How could the Qar come here without breaching the walls of Southmarch?"

"Chert Blue Quartz," Brother Nickel said in a hoarse, angry voice, "you have no right. We offered you sanctuary here."

"Then throw me out and I'll take these people somewhere else and tell them. Because the Qar already know, so everyone else needs to know as well. Hush, Opal—don't you start on me. Someone has to take the first step, and it might as well be me." He turned to Chaven. "But don't think I will protect your secrets, either, Doctor. I'll let you tell the story if you prefer, but if not I'll tell them what you told me."

Chaven's look of amusement faltered. "*My* story . . . ?"

"About the mirror. Because that's what got me into this latest trouble, isn't it, with Big Folk guards swarming all over our town? And it was another mirror that brought my boy down here the first time—that same mirror that Captain Vansen's fairy friend carried, the one he gave to Prince Barrick. So if we're going to talk about Stormstone's roads then we're going to talk about mirrors. I'll go first. Everybody listen."

For the second time that day, he began the story. "A century or more ago, during the time of the second Kellick, there was a very wise Funderling named Stormstone . . ."

By the time Chert had finished, Brother Nickel had fallen into a sullen silence and Ferras Vansen was listening with his jaw hanging slack. "Incredible!" said Vansen. "So you're saying we could even use these hidden paths to cross under the water?"

"More likely the cursed fairies will use them to invade Southmarch," Cinnabar told him. "And we Funderlings will have to meet them first."

"Yes, but a road goes two directions," Vansen pointed out. "Perhaps in dire need we could escape the castle that way—is that truly possible?"

"Yes, of course." Chert was tired now and hungry. "I have done it myself. I took the half-fairy called Gil on one of the old, secret roads, right under Brenn's Bay and to the very foot of the dark lady's throne."

"So this whole rock is honeycombed with secret ways—passages I did not know about even when I was captain of the royal guard!" Vansen shook his head. "This castle is even more a-crawl with secrets than I guessed. And this very boy was sent here across the Shadowline with a magical mirror as some kind of spy for the Qar, no doubt—but right under all our noses?"

"He's no spy!" Opal said. "He's just a child."

Vansen stared hard at Flint. "Whatever he is, I still can make no sense of it all. What is happening? It is like a spiderweb, where every strand touches another."

"And all are sticky and dangerous," said Chaven.

Ferras Vansen turned and gave him a sharp look. "Ah, yes. Do not fear I have forgotten you, sir. Chert talked about you and mirrors—now it is your turn. Tell us everything you know. We can no longer afford to keep secrets from each other."

The physician groaned softly and patted his much-shrunken paunch. "My story is a long and distressing one—distressing to me, anyway. I had hoped we could find something to eat before I began, just to strengthen myself."

"I'll confess that I'm hungry too," said Cinnabar, "but I think you will talk better and more to the point, Ulosian, if you know you will not get fed until you finish. It seems there are many stories still to be told before this evening ends—so, Chaven, you first, *then* supper."

Chaven sighed. "I feared you'd say that."

3
Silky Wood

"Another story, related by the Soterian scholar Kyros, is that an old goblin told him 'the gods followed us here' from some original homeland beyond the tracks of the sea."

—from "A Treatise on the Fairy Peoples of Eion and Xand"

"I HAVE A PLAN, BIRD." Barrick Eddon unwound another strand of prickly creeper from his arm, hook by barbed, painful hook. "A very clever plan. *You* find me a path that doesn't take me through every single thornbush in Fairyland . . . and *I* won't flatten your nasty little skull with a rock."

Skurn hopped down to a lower branch, but prudently remained out of Barrick's reach. He fluffed his blotched feathers. "It all do look different from up in sky, don't it?" The raven's tone was sullen. Neither of them had eaten since the middle of the day before. "Us can't always tell."

"Well, fly lower." Barrick stood up and rubbed at the line of small, bleeding holes, then pulled his ragged shirtsleeve back down.

"'Fly lower,' says he," Skurn grumbled. "Like he were the master and Skurn the servant, 'stead of equable partners as us'n be *by agreement*." He flapped his wings. "By agreement!"

Barrick groaned. "Then why does my . . . partner keep leading me through all the pointiest bits of territory? It's taken us a day to go a few hundred paces. At this pace, by the time we bring the . . ." It suddenly occurred to Barrick that perhaps a dark forest, filled with who knew how many or what kind of listening ears, might not the best place to talk about Lady Porcupine's mirror, the object he was sworn to carry all the way to the throne of the Qar. "At this pace, by the time we find them even the immortals will have died."

Skurn seemed to soften a bit. "Can't see the ground from high because trees be too thick, 'special them hartstangle trees. But us daren't fly no lower. Don't you see? Silks be strung in the high branches and some even wave above the treetops, just to catch fine fellows like us."

"Silks?" Barrick began to trudge forward again, using the ancient, corroded spearhead he had found beside the road out of Greatdeeps to clear his way when the undergrowth became too dense. This was not the thickest forest he'd seen since he'd been behind the Shadowline but it was full of stubborn, grasping creepers that made each step hard as wading through mud. Combined with the unchanging twilight of these lands it was enough to make even the boldest heart despair.

"Aye. This be Silky Wood, hereabouts," the raven croaked. "Where them silkins live."

"Silkins? What are those?" They didn't sound particularly threatening, which would be a nice change after dealing with Jack Chain and his monstrous servants. "Are they fairies?"

"If you mean be they High Folk, nay." Skurn fluttered ahead to another branch and waited for Barrick to make his monotonous, slow way after. "They speak not, nor do they go to market."

"Go to *market*?"

"Not like proper fairy folk, no." The bird lifted its head. "Hist," he said sharply. "That sounds like somewhat small and stupid a-dyin'. Suppertime!" The raven sprang from the branch and flapped away through the trees, leaving Barrick alone and bewildered.

He cleared himself a place where the thorny branches seemed thinnest and sat down. His bad arm had been throbbing for hours so he was not entirely unhappy with the chance to rest, but for all the annoyance the bird caused him, Skurn was at least something to talk to in this place of endless shadows and gray skies and forbidding trees hung with black moss. With the bird gone, the silence seemed to close in like a fog.

He put his arms around his knees and squeezed hard to keep from shivering.

★ ★ ★

Barrick supposed that more than half a tennight had passed since Gyir and Vansen had fallen and he had escaped the demigod Jikuyin's twisted underground kingdom. It was always hard to guess at time's passage in the endless Shadowline twilight, but he knew he had slept more than half a dozen times—those long, heavy, but somehow enervating sleeps that were almost all he ever had here. Kerneia had come and gone in the outside world while they had been held underground—Barrick knew that because it had been the monstrous Jikuyin's intention to celebrate the earth lord's day by sacrificing Barrick and the others. Since he knew that he and the others had left Southmarch in Ondekamene to fight the fairy armies, that meant he had not seen his home in over a quarter of a year. What could have happened in so much time? Had the fairies reached it? Was his sister Briony under siege?

For perhaps the first time since that terrible day at Kolkan's Field, Barrick Eddon could plainly see the divide in his own thoughts: he still felt a mysterious, almost slavish loyalty to the terrifying warrior woman who had plucked him from the field and sent him across the Shadowline (although he still could not remember why, or what she had charged him with) but at the same time he knew now that the dark lady was Yasammez the Porcupine, war-scourge of the Qar, single-minded in her hatred of all Sunlanders . . . Barrick's own people. If the Qar were now laying siege to Southmarch, if his sister and the rest of the inhabitants were in danger, or even murdered, it was by that lady's pale and deadly hand.

And now he had inherited a second mission for Yasammez and the Qar. He could not recall the first, which she had given him the day she spared him on the battlefield: it felt as though Yasammez had poured it into him like oil into a jug, then pushed the stopper in so tight that he himself could not take it out. The other mission he had accepted solely on the word of her chief servant Gyir, who had sworn it was for the good of humans as well as fairies, shortly before the faceless fairy had sacrificed his life for Barrick's. So now that he was finally free, instead of doing what any sensible creature would do—which would be to make his way as swiftly as possible to the borders of the Shadowlands and back into the light of the sun—Barrick was instead plunging deeper and deeper into this land of mists and madness.

Mists, he could not help noticing, that appeared to be returning. The world had grown colder since the bird had flown away and curls of the stuff were now rising from the ground. Barrick seemed to be sitting in a field of swaying, ghostly grass; in a few moments the mist would be as high as his head. Barrick didn't like that thought, so he scrambled to his feet.

The fog was thickening along the ground, swirling around the trunks of the gray trees like water—even climbing the trunks themselves. Soon the mist would be everywhere, below and above. Where was that cursed bird? How could he simply fly off and leave a companion this way—what kind of loyalty was that? When was he coming back?

Is he even going to come back?

The thought was a cold fist clutching his heart in midbeat. The old bird had not made a pledge to Gyir as Barrick had. Skurn cared little for the desires of either the Sunlanders or the Qar—little for anything, in fact, except cramming his belly with the disgusting things he liked to eat. Perhaps the raven had suddenly decided he was wasting his time here.

"Skurn!" His voice seemed weak, fluttering out like an arrow from a broken string and disappearing into the eternal, murky evening. "Curse you, you foul bird, where are you?" He heard the anger in his voice and thought better of it. "Come back, Skurn, please! I'll . . . I'll let you sleep under my shirt." He had forbidden this before when the weather had turned cold: the thought of having that stinking old carrion bird and whatever lived in its feathers against his chest had been enough to make his skin crawl and he had told the raven so—told him very sternly.

Now, though, Barrick was beginning to regret his bad temper.

Alone. It was a thought he had not dwelled on, for fear of it overwhelming him. He had spent his entire childhood as half of "the twins," an entity his father and older brother and the servants had spoken of as though they were not two children but one tremendously difficult, two-headed child. And the twins had also been surrounded at nearly all times by servants and courtiers, so much so that they had been desperate to escape and find time alone; much of Barrick Eddon's childhood had been spent trying to find hiding places where he and Briony could escape and be alone. Just now, though, a crowded castle seemed like a beautiful dream.

"Skurn?" It suddenly occurred to him that perhaps shouting his solitude was not the best idea. They had met almost no other creatures in the past days of travel, but that had been largely because Jikuyin and his hungry army of servants had emptied the area of anything bigger than a field mouse for miles in all directions. But he was far from the demigod's diggings now . . .

Barrick shivered again. He knew he should stay in one place, but the mist was rising and he kept thinking he saw signs of movement in the swirling distance, as though some of the pearly white strands moved not by the pressure of the wind but through some choice of their own.

The breeze quickened, chilled. A mournful whisper seemed to pass through the leaves above his head. Barrick clutched the spearhead by its broken haft and began to walk.

The mist limited his vision, but he was able to walk without too much stumbling, although from time to time he had to test with his spear to make sure a dark place in the undergrowth at his feet was not a hole into which he might step and wrench his ankle. But the path before him seemed surprisingly clear, easier to travel by far than the choked and tangled way of the past hours. It only occurred to him after he had traveled a few hundred paces that he was no longer choosing a path, he was *following* one: because the way was clear, he walked where he was led.

And what if someone . . . or something . . . wants me to do just that . . . ?

The question and its implication had only just sunk in when something darted past the edge of his sight. He whirled, but now the space between the trees was empty except for a tendril of mist swirling in the breeze of his own movement; as he turned back something the color of fog flitted across the path in the distance before him, but was gone too quickly for him to make out its shape.

He stopped. Hands trembling, he raised the pitted head of his spear. Things were definitely moving in the mist between the farthest trees, shapes tall as men but pale and maddeningly hard to see. The whisper passed over him again, sounding now less like the wordless voice of the wind and more like the hissing of some incomprehensible, breathy language.

A rustle behind him, the dimmest, softest pad of footfall on leaf—Barrick spun, and for a moment saw a thing that made no sense: the figure was nearly as tall as a man but crooked as a mandrake root, wrapped from head to foot like a royal corpse in threads and tatters white as the mist—perhaps it even *was* the mist, he thought in superstitious horror, taking on some vaguely human shape. In places the mist-wrappings did not quite cover, and what was beneath them bulged and oozed a shiny gray-black. Although it had no visible eyes the apparition seemed to see

Barrick well enough; an instant after he saw it the pale thing vanished back into the mist beside the path. More whispers floated past and echoed above his head. Barrick wheeled toward the front again, fearing to be surrounded, but for the moment the creatures of tangled thread had dropped back into the shrouding fog.

Silkins. That was what the bird had called them, and he had named this poisonous place Silky Wood.

Something thin and clinging as a cobweb brushed his face. He clawed at it but it somehow snarled his arm. Instead of reaching up his other hand to be caught and bound the same way, Barrick ripped at the prisoning strands with the blade of his spear, sawing at them until they parted with a sharp yet silent snap. Another strand floated toward him as though drifting on the wind, but then curled around him with terrifying accuracy. He ripped at it with his spear, felt it snag and grow tense, and looked up to see one of the white-wrapped creatures crouching in the branches above him, dangling silk threads like a puppeteer. With a startled cry of disgust and fear he jabbed at the thing with his spearhead and felt the tip sink into something more solid than mist or even silk thread, but nonetheless not quite like any normal animal or man: it felt as though he had stabbed a bundle of sticks wrapped in wet pudding.

The silkin let out a strange, fluting sigh and scrambled up into the branches where it vanished behind swirls of fog and a pall of silky strands strung between limbs. Barrick risked a look ahead and saw that the path that had seemed so wide and inviting only moments before narrowed now into something scarcely wider than he was, a tunnel of white filaments like the den of a hunting spider. They were trying to force him into this trap, to drive him deeper and deeper until he could not turn back, until his limbs were ensnared and he would be as helpless as a trapped fly.

How had this all happened so fast? Blood pounded in his head. Only moments before he had been sitting, thinking of home—now he was going to die.

Something moved on his left. Barrick swung his spear in a wide arc, desperate to keep the creatures at a distance. He felt a gossamer touch on his neck as another one flung down waving strands from above. Barrick shouted in disgust, flapping his hand in an effort to dislodge the sticky tendrils.

Standing in the middle of the path like this, he knew, would mean his doom. *"Get inside a wall or put your back against something,"* Shaso had always told him. Barrick abruptly plunged off the path and began kicking his way through the undergrowth. He knew he couldn't get clear of the trees entirely, but at least he could pick his own spot to make a stand. Dodging the wisps floating toward him, he fought his way through to a small clearing with a single massive tree with plate-shaped, reddish gold leaves and a broad gray trunk at the center of it; the tree's bark was quirked and knotted as a lizard's hide. Barrick put his back against it. Whatever he was fighting wouldn't get up into those branches easily, since the tree did not seem to touch its neighbors on any side.

Mist eddied around his feet, reaching waist high in places as he peered out into the thickening murk. His crippled arm already burned like fire in the places it had been broken so long ago, but he held his broken spear tightly with both arms, terrified the weapon might be knocked from his grasp.

They were coming toward him out of the murk now, pale, ghostly shapes that seemed little more than mist themselves. These silkins were real enough, though: he had felt it when he pushed the tip of his spear into one. And if they were real enough to stab, they were real enough to kill.

Something tickled his face. Barrick, intent on the shapes moving toward him, unthinkingly reached up to brush it off before he realized what it was and jumped away. Another of the things had crept around behind him to fling its strands of silk, and as he stepped around the wide trunk and confronted it, the not-quite-human shape tipped its silk-wrapped, all-but-featureless knob of a head in almost comic surprise, like a dog startled in some forbidden behavior. Barrick thought he saw a hint of wet darkness that might have been eyes peering between swaths of its elaborate tangle of threads. He jabbed hard at the creature's belly with his spear, shoving in most of the corroded metal of the spearhead. It squelched so deeply into the thing he felt sure he had killed it, but when he yanked the spear back he almost could not pull the broken haft free, and when it did come only a little viscous, dark gray fluid bubbled from the hole in the silk wrappings. Still, the silkin stumbled back in obvious pain before it turned and scuttled away into the mist.

Barrick turned just in time to find another of the things coming toward him across the clearing, tendrils of silk trailing from its fingers. Barrick ducked and the threads stuck to the bark beside his head, and for a moment the creature was trapped by its own weapon. It jerked back its crooked hand, snapping the silk, but even as it did so Barrick shoved his spear into its chest. He did not have a chance to put his strength into the stab, so the spearhead did not pierce very deeply, but he slid his hand up the handle for a better grip and then dragged the spear downward, tearing at the thing's midsection and ripping a great, shallow gout from chest to waist. To his astonishment, this time the wound almost vomited gray ooze, and even as the silkin's silent fellows slunk forward out of the mist, the wounded one slid to the ground and lay twitching like a beheaded snake, wheezing and bubbling.

The things were almost entirely wet inside, like the marrow of cooked bones. Perhaps the wrappings were not clothing, he thought, but more like a shell or hide—something that kept their soft bodies protected. If so, then a spear was almost the worst way to fight them. He needed something with a long, sharp blade—a sword, or even a knife—but he had neither. If any of the half-dozen coming now caught hold of him, they would quickly drag him down. In only moments after that they would be wrapping him just like a captured insect in a spider's web . . .

He thought of Briony, who doubtless believed him dead by now. He thought of the dark-haired girl of his dreams, a vision who might not even be alive herself. How few would miss him! Then he thought of Gyir and of the mirror the brave, faceless fairy had put into his hand, and even of Vansen, who had fallen down into darkness and death in an effort to save him. Would Barrick Eddon let himself be taken, then, like some stupid brute of an animal? Beaten by these . . . mindless things?

"I am a prince of the house of Eddon." His voice was quiet and shaky at first but grew louder. He held his spear up so the things could see it. "The house of Eddon!" Then he set it down by the roots of the tree, digging the spearhead into the bark, and stepped down hard, breaking off most of the haft behind the pitted metal. He picked the spearhead up and held it in his good hand like a dagger. "And if you wretched ghosts think a pack of things like you can bring down the house of Eddon," he cried, his voice rising to a shout, "then *come to me!*"

And come they did, silks waving. If they had moved on him together, attacking from above as well as the front, he would certainly have died: their movements were swift and silent and the mist made it hard to distinguish them. But they did not seem to have the minds of men and came at him instead like hungry beggars, first one and then another grabbing at him and trying to trap him in clinging silk. Barrick managed to use those sticky tendrils to pull one of the attackers toward him, and then ripped out the silkin's middle with what remained of his spear. The hideous thing tumbled to the ground near the corpse of the first one he had killed, bubbling gray from its belly and moaning like a distant wind.

The rest of them rushed toward him then. Barrick did his best to remember the lessons Shaso had taught him so long ago—back when the world had still made sense—but the old Tuani master had never taught them much about knife fighting. Barrick could only do the best he could, struggling to retain his weapon at all costs. He fought as in a dream, with strands of sticky white clinging to his arms and legs and face and obscuring his vision. He grappled with the silkins, holding them with their own threaded, leaf-tangled coverings as he tore at them with his blade. Each time he threw one down another came forward to take its place; after a while he could see nothing except what was just before him, as if all the rest of the world had gone dark. He slashed and slashed and slashed until every bit of his strength was gone, then he fell down at last into utter senselessness, not certain whether he was alive or dead and not caring.

"Nry nnrd nroo noof?" the voice kept asking him—a question for which he did not have an immediate answer.

Barrick opened his eyes to find himself face to face with a nightmare— a thing like a rotting apple-doll. He shrieked, but the sound barely hissed out of his parched throat. The raven flew up and away with much flapping of wings, then settled down a short distance away, dropping the ghastly thing that had dangled from his beak onto the soft ground.

"Why did you move?" Skurn asked Barrick again. "Told you to stay waiting, us did. Said us were coming back."

Barrick rolled over and sat up, staring around in sudden panic, but there was no sign of his attackers anywhere. "Where are they, those silky things? Where did they go?"

The raven shook his head as though dealing with a sadly stupid fledgling. "Exactly, just as us said. This be silkin land, and no place for you to go wandering."

"I *fought* them, you idiot bird!" Barrick staggered to his feet. He ached in every muscle but his crippled arm felt a hundred times worse than that. "I must have killed them all." But even the silkin corpses were gone. Did things just evaporate after they were dead, like dew?

Barrick saw something and bent to pick it up on the end of his broken spear. "Aha!" He jabbed it triumphantly in the direction of the raven, even his good arm trembling with weariness. "What's that then?"

The raven eyed the glob of black goo tangled in broken strands of dirty white. "The dung of somewhat that were sick." Skurn examined the mess with interest. "That be our guess."

"It's from one of those silk-things! I stabbed it—I ripped them open and they bled out this foul stuff."

"Ah. Then we should get on," Skurn said, nodding. "Eat this quick-like. Silkins'll come back with more of their kind soon."

"Ha! Do you see! I *did* kill some!" Barrick paused in sudden confusion. "Hold," he said. "Eat what?"

Skurn nudged at the thing he had dropped on the ground. "Follower, it is. Young one, but cursed heavy to carry."

The dead Follower was about the size of a squirrel, its round little head dominated by a jagged, wide mouth so that it looked like a melon broken under someone's heel. The knobs of bone protruding through its greasy fur, hardened into gray lumps on the adult specimens Barrick had seen the day they found Gyir, were still pink and soft on this young one. It did not add to the thing's beauty. "You want me to . . ." Barrick stared. "You want me to *eat* that . . . ?"

"You'll get no nicer treat today," the raven said crossly. "Trying to do you a favor, us was."

It was all Barrick could do not to be immediately and violently ill.

After he had gathered his strength, he got back onto his feet. In one thing, anyway, the raven was undoubtedly right—it would not be wise to remain too long in this place where he had killed silkins.

"If you're going to eat that horrid thing, eat it," Barrick said. "Don't make me look at it."

"Bring it along, us will, in case you change your mind . . ."

"I'm not going to eat it!" Barrick raised his hand to smack at the black bird but did not have the strength. "Just hurry up and finish it so we can go."

"Too big," said the raven contentedly. "Us has to eat it slow, savory-like. But it's too big for us to carry far, either. Can you . . . ?"

Barrick took a deep, slow breath. Much as it shamed him, he needed this bird. He couldn't forget the loneliness that had surrounded him only an hour before when he thought the raven was gone. "Very well! I'll carry it, if you can find some leaves or something to wrap it in." He shuddered. "But if it starts to stink . . ."

"Then you mought get hungry, us knows. Never fear, us'n'll find a place to stop before then."

When they had covered enough ground that Barrick felt a little safer they settled into a hollow where he would be sheltered from the worst of the wind and mist by a large rock jutting from the side of the dell. Barrick would have given almost anything for a fire, but he had lost his flint and steel in Greatdeeps and he did not know how to make flame any other way.

Kendrick would have been able to do it, he thought bitterly. *Father would, too.*

"At least we seem to be leaving the silkins' territory," he said out loud. "We walked for hours without seeing any."

"Silky Wood goes a long way," the raven said at last. "Us doesn't think we're even halfway to the middle."

"Blood of the gods, you're joking!" Barrick felt despair slide over him like a thundercloud blotting the sun. "Do we have to walk straight through it? Can't we go around it? Is this the only way to go to . . ." he wrestled with the throaty, alien words, "to Qul-na-Qar?"

"We could go round the wood, us guesses," Skurn informed him, "but it would take a long time. We could go sunward of it and then pass through Blind Beggar lands instead. Or withershins, and then we'd be traveling Wormsward. Either way, though, us'll still find trouble on the far side.

"Trouble?"

"Aye. Sunward, in the Beggar lands, us'll have to look out sharp for Old Burning Eye and the Orchard of Metal Bats."

Barrick gulped. He didn't want to know anymore. "Then let's go the other way around."

Skurn nodded gravely. "'Cepting that if we go withershins, us're in a swampy place us heard is called Melt-Your-Bones, and even if we miss the woodsworms we'll have to look smart so we don't get caught by the Suck-down Toothies."

Barrick closed his eyes. He was finding his way back to prayer, he had discovered, although having met the demigod Jikuyin he still had difficulty believing the gods always had his best interests in mind. But with a choice between the murderous silkins, something called Metal Bats, and Suck-down Toothies, it couldn't hurt to pray.

O Gods . . . O Great Ones in Heaven. He tried to think of something to say. *Only a few short days ago I discovered I would have to travel across all this fearful, unknown land of demons and monsters with only two companions, a fairy warrior and the captain of my royal guard. Now I still must make that same journey with only one companion—a dung-eating, insolent bird. If you meant to ease my burdens, great ones, you could have done better.*

It wasn't much of a prayer, Barrick knew, but at least he and the gods were talking again.

"Wake me up if something's going to kill me." As he stretched out on the uneven ground he could hear the wet sounds of Skurn starting on the dead Follower. Barrick's ribs ached; his arm felt like it was full of sharp pieces of broken pottery. "No, on second thought, don't bother waking me. Maybe I'll be lucky and die in my sleep."

4

Without a Heart

"The eminent philosopher Phayallos also maintained that the fairy words meaning 'god' and 'goddess' were very close to their words for 'uncle' and 'aunt' . . ."

—from "A Treatise on the Fairy Peoples of Eion and Xand"

THE CHILD TOOK HER HAND and placed it against his narrow chest, a gesture Qinnitan knew meant, "I'm frightened." She pulled him closer, held him as the movement of the Xixian ship rocked them both. "Don't worry, Pigeon. He won't hurt you. He only brought you to make sure I don't dive over the side and try to swim back to Hierosol."

He gave her a reproachful look: it wasn't just for himself that he was frightened.

"Truly, we'll be well," she said, but they both knew she was lying. Qinnitan lowered her voice to a whisper. "You'll see—we'll find a chance to get away before we catch up with the autarch."

Their cabin door abruptly swung open. The man who had snatched them from the streets of Hierosol stared at them, his eyes and face devoid of expression, as if he were thinking of something else entirely. While disguised as an old woman he had mimed feelings quite convincingly, but now he had thrown that aside as if human nature were only a mask he had been wearing.

"What do you want?" she asked. "Are you afraid we're going to sneak out the locked door? Climb the mast and step off onto a cloud, perhaps?"

He ignored her as he walked past. He yanked hard at the bars on the window, testing them, then turned to survey the tiny cabin.

"What is your name?" Qinnitan demanded.

His lips twitched. "What does it matter?"

"We will be together on this ship until we reach the autarch and you can be paid your blood money. You certainly know my name, and much more—you must have spent weeks following me, watching everything I did. By the Sacred Hive, you even dressed up like an old woman so you could spy on me! The least you could do is tell me who you are."

He didn't respond, and his face remained as expressionless as a dead man's as he turned and left the cabin, every movement as precise and fluid as those of a temple dancer. She might have almost admired it, but she knew it would be like a mouse admiring the murderous grace of a cat.

She felt something damp on her arm. Pigeon was crying.

"Here, here," she said. "Shh, lamb. Don't be afraid. I'll tell you a story. Do you want to hear a story?" She didn't wait for an answer. "Have you heard the true story of Habbili the Crooked? I know you've heard of him—he was the son of the great god Nushash, but when his father was driven into exile, Habbili was treated very badly by Argal and the rest of the demon-gods. For a while it seemed there was no chance he would survive, but in the end he destroyed his enemies and saved his father and even Heaven itself. Do you want to hear about that?"

Pigeon was still sniffling, but she thought she felt him nod.

"Some of it is a little frightening so you have to be brave. Yes? Then I'll tell you." And she told him the tale just as her father had taught it to her.

Long, long ago, when horses could still fly and the great red desert of Xand was covered with grass and flowers and trees, the great god Nushash was riding and met Suya the Dawnflower. Her beauty stole his heart. He went to her father Argal the Thunderer, who was his half brother, and asked to marry her. Argal gave permission, but he had a cruel, dishonorable trick in mind, because he and his brothers were jealous of Nushash.

When Nushash had taken Suya away to meet his family, Argal called his brothers Xergal and Efiyal and told them Nushash had stolen his daughter. The brothers then assembled all their servants and warriors and rode to Moontusk, the house of Xosh, brother of Nushash and Lord of the Moon, where Nushash and his new bride were staying.

The war was long and terrible, and during the years it lasted a son was born to Nushash and Suya. His name was Habbili, and he was a brave, beautiful child, the treasure of his parents, wise and kind beyond his years.

Bright Nushash and his kin were defeated at last by the treachery of his half brothers. Suya Dawnflower escaped the destruction of Moontusk, but was lost in the wilderness for many years until Xergal the Lord of the Deep, Argal's brother, found her and made her his wife.

Xosh the Moonlord was killed in the fighting. Great Nushash was captured, but he was too powerful to destroy, so Argal and the others cut him into many pieces and scattered those pieces over all the lands. But young Habbili, son of Nushash, was tortured by Argal, his own grandfather, and all the rest of that demon clan. They tormented him and lamed him, then at last they cut out his heart and burned it on the fire and left him dead in the ruins of Moontusk.

But a mother serpent came into the ruins looking for a place to lay her egg, and so when she birthed it she hid it in the hole in Habbili's chest. With the poisoned egg in his chest he came to life once more, consumed with anger and vowing revenge.

"How can you do this to me?" the mother snake said. "I have brought you back to life, but my child is in your breast and cannot hatch. If you go away now to attack your enemies you will have returned evil for good."

Habbili thought about this and saw that what she said was true. "Very well," he said. "I will trust you, although my own family has betrayed me more times than I can count. Take back your egg, but go and draw a coal from the fires burning in the rubble and put that in my chest instead." And Habbili reached into his chest, pulled out the serpent's egg, and then fell down dead once more.

The mother snake was honorable. She could have left him then, but instead she went and drew a coal from the fire burning in the ruins of the tower and brought it back, although it burned her mouth badly, which is why ever since all snakes have hissed instead of spoken. She placed it in his chest and he came back to life. He thanked her and went on his way, limping so badly from his many injuries that the mortals who met him named him "Crooked."

For years he wandered and had many adventures and learned many things, but always he thought of the evil done to him by his grandfather and uncles. At last he felt he was ready to resume the sacred feud and to bring his father, Nushash, back to life. But his father's body had been cut in pieces and scattered up and down the lands of the north and the lands of the south so Habbili had to search long and hard to find them. At last he had recovered all but his father's head, which was kept in a crystal casket in the house of Xergal, the god of deep places and the dead, whom northerners call Kernios. Habbili went to Xergal's stronghold and, with the use of charms and spells he had learned, made his way past the guards and into the heart of the house. And as he stole through that dark place, the wife of Xergal came upon him. Crooked did not at first recognize her, but she recognized him—for she was, after all, his mother Suya Dawnflower, whom Xergal had captured and forced into marriage.

"You must run away, my son," she told him. "The Earthlord will be back soon, and when he returns he will be angry and destroy you."

"No," Habbili said. "I have come to steal my father's head, so that I can bring him back to life."

Suya was frightened, but she could not change his mind. "Dark Xergal keeps your father's head in the deepest cellar of his house," she said at last, "in a crystal casket that cannot be broken without the hammer of Argal the Thunderer, his brother. But you cannot steal the hammer without the net of Efiyal, Lord of the Waters, who is brother to both. All three brothers are together on a hunting trip and their treasures are unguarded, so you must go now to steal them, for soon they will return to their houses and then you will never succeed."

So Habbili the Crooked fled from Xergal's house and followed his mother's instructions, diving into the great river and swimming down into its depths to the house of Efiyal. There by his skill he overcame the crocodiles that guarded the river god's throne and stole the net. Next he climbed high to the top of Xandos, the great mountain, to Argal's house on its peak. He threw Efiyal's net over the one hundred deadly warriors there so that they slept at his command, then took the great hammer down from the place where it hung by the door. Then Habbili reclaimed the magic net and climbed down Mount Xandos. He went down into the ground, back to the house where Xergal his uncle, lord of the deep places, kept his throne and all his treasure.

"Please be careful, son," his mother Suya told him. "If Xergal finds you here he will destroy you. He is the god of the dead lands. He will drag you into the shadows and you will stay there forever." But Habbili went down the stairs into the deepest part of the Deathlord's castle and found his father's head in a box of gold and crystal, floating in a pool of quicksilver. When Habbili picked it up his father's eyes opened. But since he had eyes and a mouth but no heart, he did not recognize his own son, and so Nushash's head began to cry, "Help! Xergal, great lord! Someone is trying to steal me!"

At that moment Xergal was returning from his hunting trip. He heard the cry of

Nushash's head and hurried down the tunnel toward the deep vault, his footsteps booming like thunder. Habbili was frightened despite the coal burning hot in his breast—he knew that with his crippled legs he could not outrun the Deathlord—so he set the head of his father down on the floor, took up the Hammer of Argal and the Net of Efiyal, and waited. When Xergal burst into the room, his beard and robes black as a starless, moonless night, his eyes flashing red like rubies, Habbili threw the net over him. For a moment Xergal was slowed by his own brother's sea magic and stopped, amazed. In that moment, Habbili threw the hammer at him and it knocked Xergal the Earthlord to the ground. Habbili picked up the hammer, took the head of his father in its crystal casket, and ran up the stairs with Xergal right behind him, getting closer all the time.

Suya, Habbili's mother, grabbed at the cloak of Xergal as he ran past. "Husband," she cried, "you must come and eat your supper before it is cold."

The Earthlord tried to pull away from her, but she held on. "Woman, let go of me. Someone has stolen what is mine."

Suya clung to him. "But I have turned back the bed. Come and lie with me before the bed is cold."

Still Xergal fought to get away. "Let go of me! Someone has stolen what is mine!"

Suya would not let go. "Come and stay with me. I feel ill, and soon I may die."

Xergal shouted, "You will die now!" and struck her down, but by that time Habbili the Crooked had escaped from of the underground palace and had fled south into the forests around Xandos. There he used the Hammer of Argal to free his father's head from the casket, and then all the pieces of Nushash Whitefire were joined and the Lord of the Sun was alive again.

"Father!" he said. "You live once more!"

"You are a good and faithful son," Nushash told him. "You have saved me. Where is your mother? I wish to see her."

When Habbili told him that Suya the Dawnflower had died so that they could escape from Xergal the Earthlord, great Nushash was full of grief. He went away then to his house in the highest heavens and resumed his old chore of driving the sun chariot across the sky each day. Habbili remained on the earth, where he taught the sons of men the truth about Argal the Thunderer and the rest of that traitorous clan of gods, revealing them all as the enemies of Nushash Whitefire. So the people drove out Argal's supporters and the lands all around Xandos ever after worshipped Nushash, the true king of the sky."

*   *   *

Pigeon squeezed her hand. She looked down and saw the question in his eyes. "Yes," she said, "that is the truth. That is why I told you the story. Habbili the Crooked was dead, with his heart cut out, and yet he returned to defeat his enemies—and they were gods and demons! Yes, he was frightened, but he did not surrender to fear. That is why things turned out right in the end."

Pigeon squeezed her hand.

"You're welcome. So do not fear, little one. We will find a way. The gods will help us. Heaven will preserve us."

She held him for a long time until she noticed that the sound of his breathing had changed. Pigeon had finally fallen asleep.

Against all odds, the crippled boy Habbili survived, she thought to herself. Against all odds. But to save him, his mother had to die.

"Are you a believer, King Olin?" The autarch's golden eyes seemed even brighter than usual.

"A believer?"

"Yes. Do you believe in heaven?"

"I believe in my gods."

"Ah. So you are <i>not</i> a believer—at least in the old sense."

"What does that mean, Xandian? I told you I believe in . . ."

" . . . 'In my gods,' is what you said. I heard." Sulepis turned up his long hands like the two sides of a scale. "Which means you acknowledge that other people have other beliefs . . . other gods. But those who truly believe in their own creed think that other gods cannot exist—that the beliefs of others are superstition or devil-worship." The autarch smiled. For a handsome man, he had a terrible, frightening smile; even after more than a year of serving him Pinimmon Vash had still not grown used to it. "I gather you are not that type."

Olin shrugged, but his words were careful. "I try to understand the world in which I live."

"Which is to say you find it hard to believe in anything so foolish as the idea that every word of the <i>Book of the Trigon</i> is the truth. Ah, no, do not grow angry, Olin! The same is easily said of my people's <i>Revelations of Nushash.</i> Fireside tales for children."

Even Vash, with all his years of practice, could not suppress a small grunt of astonishment. The autarch turned to him, grinning. "Have I offended you, Minister Vash?"

"N-No, Golden One. Nothing you do could ever offend me."

"Hmmm. That sounds like a challenge." Sulepis laughed, the high, careless mirth of a happy child. "But at the moment I am involved in a deep philosophical discussion with King Olin, so perhaps you would be more comfortable doing something else." His smile abruptly disappeared. "In other words—go, Vash."

Vash bowed and immediately backed out of the Golden One's presence. As he passed the Scotarch Prusus lolling in his chair, Vash thought he noticed something other than the usual fear and confusion in that rheumy eye. Had the cripple's interest been pricked by the autarch's careless blasphemy? Was the simpleminded creature actually offended? Vash was coldly amused. Perhaps Sulepis was sending away the wrong man.

Once he had gone into the main cabin, Vash climbed as quickly to the deck above as his old legs would allow, then circled around so that he could stay within earshot of the autarch's voice. One did not reach the paramount minister's exalted age by being ignorant of the substance of important conversations, but since he did not have his usual resources in place here on the royal ship he'd have to do the spying himself, degrading and dangerous as it might be.

Sulepis was still talking when Vash drew near enough to hear.

" . . . No, there is no need for coyness, King Olin," said the autarch. "Wise men know that the ancients spoke secrets in the great religious books that are too powerful for simple folk to hear. Knowledge of that sort is for the elite—for men such as you and I, who have studied the deep arts and know the truth behind the gaudy pageant of history."

Vash leaned forward a little until he could see the back of Olin's head where the northern king stood at the railing below him. The autarch was out of sight, although Vash could tell from Olin's tense stance that he must be near: how well the paramount minister knew the nerve-jumping fear that even an apparently friendly conversation with Sulepis brought.

"You mistake me . . ." Olin began, but the autarch only laughed.

"No, do not argue, my good fellow—a man who has so few breaths left to him in this world should not waste even one. I know much more about you than you do about me, Olin Eddon. I have watched you and your family, you see."

The northerner grew very still beside the rail. Were it not that the green, unsettled waters of the Osteian Sea continued to hump and thrash themselves into white froth beyond Olin's shoulder, Pinimmon Vash would have thought the entire world had suddenly paused like a skipped heartbeat. "You have *watched* us . . . ?"

Sulepis went on as though the other monarch had not spoken. "I know that you, your royal physicians, and other philosophic explorers of your court have made a study of the old teachings, the lost arts . . . and of the days of the gods."

"I do not know what you mean," Olin said stiffly.

"It could be that you did so originally for your own reasons—to learn more of the mystery of your family's tainted blood—but in your years of study you cannot have failed to learn more about the way the world *truly* works than the simpletons who surround you, who call you the monarch anointed by the gods without truly knowing anything about the gods at all." For a moment Sulepis came into view and Vash shrank back, but the autarch only moved closer to Olin, his back turned to Vash's hiding spot. Vash couldn't see any of the guards but he knew they would not like the autarch being so close to the foreign prisoner.

It was a strangely ordinary scene, the two men leaning side-by-side against the rail: had it not been for the autarch's ceremonial costume— the high-peaked headgear known as the Henbane Crown because it resembled the poisonous seed of that plant, the huge golden amulet of the sun on his chest, and of course his golden finger-stalls—Sulepis might have been an ordinary Xandian priest discussing tithes and temple maintenance with some northern counterpart. But to face those golden eyes directly, Vash knew, was to feel quite differently about what sort of creature the autarch was.

The northern king seemed to be surprisingly brave: anyone else feeling the autarch's heat so close, the fever of the Golden One's thoughts, would have shrunk away. People in the Orchard Court whispered that standing near Sulepis was like standing in the unshielded desert sun, that if you stayed too long first your wits, then your very skin and bones would burn away.

Vash shuddered a little. Once he had called such talk nonsense. Now he felt he could believe almost anything about his master, this terrifying god-on-earth.

"Perhaps this is all a bit difficult to grasp." The autarch stretched his long fingers toward the western horizon as if he would pluck the sun setting there like a fig from a branch. "I have perhaps pondered more on these things than you have, Olin, but I know you can grasp them—that you can understand the truth. And when you do . . . well, perhaps then you will feel differently about me and what I plan."

"I doubt that."

The autarch made a comfortable, satisfied noise. "Do you know the story of Melarkh, the hero-king of ancient Jurr? I'm sure you have heard it. His wife was cursed by evil fates and so she could not give him a son. He saved a falcon from a great serpent, and in reward the falcon flew him up to heaven so that he could steal the Seed of Birth from the gods themselves."

Olin looked up, his expression so odd that Vash could not read it. "I have heard something like it told of the great hero Hiliometes."

"Ah, you illustrate my point. Now, most of those who hear that tale believe 'This is a true thing. This is what Melarkh—or Hiliometes, if that is how they hear the tale—this is what the great hero did.'" For a moment the god-king's hand rose again, finger-stalls glittering like fire in the sun's dying rays. "But those, of course, are the very simplest of the simple. Cleverer men—clerics and other wise men, leaders of the common folk, *they* will say, 'Of course Melarkh may not have flown up to heaven on a falcon or brought back the Seed of Birth, but the story speaks of how the secrets of the gods must be discovered by brave men, how mortals can change their fate.' And the wildest minds, the loneliest of philosophers living far from the disapproval of others, might even think, 'Since no falcon large enough to carry a grown man exists, perhaps the tale of Melarkh riding one to heaven is false. And if that tale is false, perhaps others are false too. And if the tales are false, perhaps all the stories they tell are lies. Perhaps the gods themselves do not exist!' And from such blasphemy even the wisest recoil, because they know that such thinking could uproot heaven itself and leave men alone in the void."

The autarch's tone changed now, growing softer and more intimate, so that Vash, cursing his old ears, had to lean down to the point where his back, already sore, began to ache in earnest. He was also terrified that the railing might creak under this greater weight, giving him away.

"But here is what I say to all of them, the stupid and the curious and the brave," the autarch continued, "they are all of them right! And they are all of them wrong as well. Only I understand the truth. Only I of all living things can bend the gods to my will."

Vash took a breath. This was a scope of madness even he had not seen before, and he had witnessed many of the autarch's strangest and most savage ideas.

"I do not . . . I do not understand you." Olin sounded weak and ill now.

"Oh, I think you do. Or at least you grasp the general drift of what I say—because you have thought such things yourself. Admit it, Olin, you are surprised to hear such ideas—ideas more exalted but otherwise not so different from your own—coming from one you think of as so different from yourself. Well, you are right—I *am* different. Because where you have learned these secrets and thought these thoughts in the depths of despair, trying to learn why you and your line are so cursed, I have stepped forward and said, 'These secrets are what I seek, but I will not be the anvil, I will be the hammer. It is *I* who will do the shaping.'" The autarch let out another gleeful laugh. "You see, I know what is beneath your castle, Olin of Southmarch. I know the curse that has bedeviled your family for generations, and I know what caused it. But unlike you, I will shape that power to my own will. Unlike you, I will not let heaven rule me with ancient tales and infantile warnings! The power of the gods will be mine—and then I will *punish heaven itself* for trying to deny me!"

After the autarch returned to his cabin, King Olin remained at the rail, staring silently at the water. Pinimmon Vash, whose knees were throbbing now too, dared not move yet for fear the northern king would notice him. At last, Olin turned and let his guards lead him back toward his small cabin. For a moment Vash could see the foreign king's face clearly, its skin so slack and its hue so ghastly pale that Olin might have already been dead. In fact, the foreigner looked as though he had seen not only his own death, but the end of everything he loved.

Pinimmon Vash, who had never wasted a drop of pity on others, thought of Olin's bloodless face and found himself hoping that the gods would show mercy on the northern king and let him die in his sleep that night.

5

A Droplet of Peace

"During the years of the Great Death, most fairies were driven out of the lands of men, accused of spawning and spreading that terrible plague. But Phayallos and others claim that fairy-villages such as a cave city near Falopetris in Ulos were found empty but for the bodies of dead Qar, who had succumbed to the pox before any man had reached them."

—from "A Treatise on the Fairy Peoples of Eion and Xand"

"NO." THE BARMAID SLAMMED the coin down on the wet, greasy board and walked away.

Matt Tinwright wanted her to take it, but he had to admit to a certain ambivalence. It was the last of his money, a single silver sturgeon borrowed—along with the three he'd already spent in the last fortnight—after a heroic wheedling of old Puzzle, a feat of flattery, exaggeration, and outright sniveling that would be celebrated among the guild of beggars for centuries to come. Not that Tinwright had exaggerated everything he had said to get Puzzle to take his coins out of the odiferous little bag he kept in his boot: he really did need the money, and it really was a matter of life or death.

"Please, Brigid," he said quietly as the barmaid passed him again. There weren't many people in the Quiller's Mint at this time of the day, and those who were would doubtless not know the difference between voices inside their head or outside, but it was not the sort of thing one talked about loudly. "Please. There is no one else who can help me."

"And I don't care." She stopped in front of him, fists on hips, and bent forward so that her face was only a hand's-breadth from his own. Normally he would have been distracted by the amount of bosom this pose displayed, but even his most dominating instincts were at the moment shriveled by fear of his awesome responsibility. "My brothers helped you get her out of her rooms and I helped you get her over to the new place—I even carried the snobby cow while you ran off and piddled your pantaloons."

"A base lie!" he said, then lowered his voice. "I had to go and distract those men. They were priests—clerics from the castle's counting house. They are sober men and would have known right away something was not right." He remembered the terror of that moment, hearing them coming down the passage as he and the serving wench were dragging a dazed, barefoot Elan M'Cory to the room he had rented and prepared for her near Skimmers Lagoon. It had been even more frightening than the time he had thought he was about to be executed by Avin Brone: that time he had not known why he was in trouble, but this time Tinwright had helped a young noblewoman poison herself—although without letting her actually achieve that goal. Now he had to keep the recovering Elan hidden from Hendon Tolly and the others. Almost being caught like that—well, he wouldn't admit it to Brigid, but the state of his clothing *had* been a near thing.

"You know, it's a funny thing, Matty, but I still don't care." Brigid tossed her curly hair. "I'm not interested in your problems anymore. I've got a new man and he's got money. Not just drips and drabs like you and that poor old stick you cadge yours from, but a good living. He's got a house in Oscastle, and a shop, and he has nice clothes and a walking stick with a handle made of real whale ivory . . ."

"And a wife back home?" Tinwright said, none too nicely.

"What of it? She's a sour old cow—he told me so. He'll set me up in a place of my own and I won't have to live in this bloody place anymore and let Conary feel my bubs just to earn my wages."

"But Brigid, I'm in terrible trouble . . . !"

"And who put you there, Matt Tinwright? You did. And who's got to get you out? None other than the same person. Learn that lesson and you'll be halfway to being a man instead of a boy and a fool."

She turned and walked briskly away, but only got a few steps before she turned back. Her face had softened a little. "I don't wish you harm,

Matty. You and I had our laughs, and you're not a bad sort. But you can't build a house on water. You have to find a place to stand."

She left him then. For all his years of chasing the poetic muse, he could not think of a word to say.

"Oh. It's you." Her dark eyes seemed to take up half her face. Elan M'Cory was frighteningly thin—she had not eaten a full meal since she had taken the tanglewife's potion many days ago. "I thought it was that cruel, red-faced woman."

Tinwright sighed. "Brigid is not cruel."

"Do not defend her just because you have had your way with her. I am not a child—I know how the world is wagged. And she *is* cruel. She tried to pour soup down my throat. She nearly drowned me."

"She was trying to get you to eat. You must eat, Elan." He sat down on the end of the bed. It was a cheap, frail thing and it creaked under his weight. "Please, my lady, you will make yourself ill . . ."

"Make myself ill? Who was it that did this to me, I ask you? Who tricked me when I would have ended it all?"

Tinwright hung his head. She had been like this since she had awakened, furious and argumentative or sad and silent, but always miserable. No wonder Brigid refused to come anymore. He couldn't blame himself for not wanting to see the woman he loved take her own life, but he certainly could have wished things might have gone better. "I did," was all he said. It was easier not to argue. As it was, he heard her doleful voice in his head for hours after he left her. He had not been able to write a line in days, and just at a time when he had begun to think he was actually finding his way.

"All I asked of you was the smallest thing—a gift of kindness." She closed her eyes and let herself sink back into the cushion. "You say you love me, say it over and over again, but did you bring me what I wanted? A droplet of soul's peace, that was all I asked. A simple thing."

"It is no simple thing to kill someone," he said. "Even less so when you care for that person as much as I care for you, Lady Elan."

She opened her eyes again, and for a moment he thought she would shout at him, but the wildness went out of her face and her eyes filled with tears. "If your love and concern could have saved me, Matt Tinwright, it would have saved me already. But I am damned. I belong to Kernios and his dark country."

"No, you do not!" He lifted his hand to thump it down on the bed-clothes, then thought better of it. "You were misused by a villainous man. If it were in my power to kill Hendon Tolly, I would, but I am not a swords-man. I am a poet—and sometimes, I think, not much of that, either."

If he hoped she would disagree with him he was disappointed. "It is so . . . so hard to be alive," she said quietly. "A nightmare I cannot wake from. I sometimes think we are all Death's servants and he only lends us to the temporary service of other masters."

He hated when she spoke this way. "But you are safe now, Elan. Hendon Tolly is not even looking for you."

A little of the hardness came back to her face. "Oh, Matthias Tin-wright, you are a fool! Of course he searches for me. Not because he misses me, or even because he hates me—I could live with that—but because I *belonged* to him, and he does not let anyone steal from him."

"You do not . . ."

She held up her hand. "Please. It does no good to say such things—*you do not know*." Her expression changed again, became altogether more disturbing. There was nothing hard about her now—she looked abso-lutely defenseless, a soft-bodied thing with its shell torn away. "He has a mirror. He can . . . there are . . . there are things inside it. Things that . . . laugh . . . and . . . and talk. They know terrible secrets." A shiver ran up her frail chest, made her hands shake where she clasped them before her. "He made me look into it . . ."

Tinwright could not speak, could not even move when what he wanted most of all was to take her in his arms and protect her from the vile memories that troubled her so, but the sheer, haunted hopelessness in her voice made his limbs seem heavy and bloodless.

"He made me look," she said, whispering now. "He took me down into a basement room and held my head. It . . . it spoke to me. That thing spoke to me. *It knew who I was!* It knew things about me that no one should know, not even Hendon Tolly—not even my mother and father! I tried to run away but I couldn't. Whatever lived in there, it held me and it played with me like . . . like a cat who dandles a mouse, claps hold of it, takes off its paw, lets it run, then catches it up again. I . . . I . . ." She was weeping wholeheartedly now, but did not even raise her hand to wipe her face. "I do not want to live in such a world as this, Matt Tin-wright. A world that has such . . . filth, such terrible things hiding behind every looking glass . . . every reflection . . ."

Tinwright found his voice at last. "It was a trick . . . something he did to frighten you . . ."

She shook her head, tears still running down her cheeks. "No. He is frightened of it too. I think that was why he took me to it. It is like a beast in a cage. He thought to keep it as a pet, but it is demanding. He was going to let it feed on me. That is another reason he will not lightly let me go, Matt. I was going to keep the beast . . . occupied."

It was some time before Tinwright could calm Elan M'Cory enough for her to take a little cold broth and then fall asleep. It was a relief to see her put aside the worst of her cares and rest, but how long could he sit here and guard her? How much time could he take for these secret errands before someone in Hendon Tolly's court noticed his absences? The Inner Keep was packed with spies and sycophants, all of them fiercely jealous of their master's attentions—some of them even jealous of poor Matt Tinwright, who had never had a day's luck that didn't turn immediately into horse dung!

If Brigid won't come, I must find someone to help me with Elan. But who can I trust? Just as important, who can I afford? He looked down at the silver sturgeon, which barring a miracle on the order of Onir Diotrodos and the jars of beer, would have to last him for a fortnight. It seemed impossible. Anyone low enough to work for such wages would recognize Elan's status, sniff Tinwright's need for secrecy, and make him out as a prime candidate for blackmail. He needed someone with no money and few scruples, but who would not immediately turn around and stab him in the back, or who would at least wait a little while before doing so.

On the face of it, it seemed impossible. To his sorrow, though, Tinwright knew better.

There's only one person like that in all of Southmarch, he thought with a heavy heart. *My mother.*

But before he could hire her, he'd have to find her.

❦

For Briony, despite being surrounded by the comfort and pageantry of the Syannese court, the days crawled by. She had no cause to cause to complain about how she was treated—she was given accommodations suited to her station, a suite of chambers in the Broadhall Palace's long eastern wing with windows overlooking the river. She had also been gifted with serving maids and ladies-in-waiting and chests full of jewelry and clothes to wear, all chosen, she was told, by the king's favorite, Lady Ananka. Briony had been raised on nursery tales of jealous witches and evil fairies: before wearing any of the clothes she carefully searched them for poison pins.

The nobles of the court treated her with deference when they saw her, although in truth she did not leave her rooms very often at first. It was too strange for her, this world of not-this, not-that in which she found herself—not a real princess, but not a simple player among other players either (although at times she certainly felt herself to be playing a role again). It was hard to exchange pleasantries with the pampered, over-dressed folk of Enander's glittering court and not feel that by doing so, by biding her time, she was somehow betraying her own family and folk. But in a foreign court and without trustworthy friends she could only snatch at those few bits of news she could get from her home. The fairy-siege, she learned, still continued, but since it had taken on a more peaceful cast in the last months the Syannese people thought of Southmarch less and less. Tolly still reigned there as the nominal protector of the king's youngest child, Alessandros. And Briony herself was still a mystery— some people in Southmarch thought she had been kidnapped, perhaps even by the Autarch of Xis. Until recently, the rumor most believed in Tessis was that she had been killed and her body hidden, but her appearance at Broadhall Palace had taken some of the wind from that particular story's sails.

The four young women that the king's mistress Ananka had sent to wait on her (to spy on her, Briony felt certain) seemed nice enough, but she found it hard to talk to them, let alone trust them, even the youngest, little Talia, who was not even twelve years old. Briony had been so lonely those first weeks after Shaso's death and her escape from Landers Port that she had dreamed of just such homely pleasures as this, having her hair brushed, chattering of this and that, but either these young women were far more foolish than her favorite maids Rose and Moina had been at home or Briony had lost her taste for such conversation. Excited speculation about this ambitious courtier or that romance, pointed comments about who was aiming above his or her station, and the endless speculation about Prince Eneas and his romances and adventures did not much interest her. Briony had thought the prince impressive when she saw him, of course, but all she wanted was help for her people and her family's throne; she could think of no decent way even to approach him, let alone ask him for help. As for going to the king himself—well, Lady Ananka had already made it clear that she considered King Enander her private territory.

Marooned in her island chambers like a lost mariner, Briony found herself longing for something with more substance than Syannese court gossip and for better companionship than the ladies of the court could offer.

Then one morning Agnes, one of the ladies-in-waiting, came to Briony with great excitement in her pretty young face. "Your Highness, you will never guess who is here!"

"Here where?" But Briony sat up straighter. Was it the prince, come to see her on his own? If so, how could she lead the subject around to Southmarch and its needs?

"Here at the court," the girl said. "He just rode in last night—all dressed up in furs like a Vuttish merchant captain!"

"I can't guess." It wasn't the prince, that was certain, since he was already in residence. It must be some other noble, some legendary object of Syannese court gossip. If Perin himself came down to earth waving his holy hammer, Briony thought, all these people would talk about would be his shoes. And maybe whether or not he was wearing colors appropriate to the season. *Sweet Zoria, and my brother and I thought the nobles of Southmarch were shallow . . .*

Agnes was practically bouncing up and down. "Oh, but you should be able to guess, Highness—he is one of your countrymen!"

"What?" For an instant her heart leaped impossibly to Barrick, and then to Shaso, and even Ferras Vansen, all lost in different ways, but all lost beyond question. A sadness struck her then so swiftly and so deeply that for a moment she feared she might break into tears. It took her a long moment to regain her breath. "Out with it, quickly. Who is it?"

"His name is Jenkin Crowel!" The girl clasped her hands across her bodice as though she could barely control herself. "Do you know him?"

For a moment the name meant nothing to Briony—it had been so long since she had thought of any of those folk or the world she had shared with them . . . but then it came and the sadness turned to something more sour.

"Oh. Yes, I do. Brother of Durstin Crowel, Baron of Graylock, although I'm sure Durstin's more than a baron now since he's long been one of Hendon Tolly's most determined lickspittles." The thought of the Crowels made her want to kick something over. "Why is Jenkin here?"

"He is the new envoy here at Broadhall from your brother Alessandros."

Briony snorted. "Alessandros is less than half a year old. Envoy from the bloody-handed usurper Hendon Tolly, you mean."

The young lady's eyes widened. "Of course, Highness. As you say."

Briony did her best to control her temper. The treachery of the Tollys was not this girl's fault, even if she was one of Ananka's spies. "Thank you for telling me, Agnes."

"But what are you going to do, Highness? He has asked to see you."

"He has? Truly? By all the gods, these people must have solid brass . . ." She stopped herself. Using language appropriate among strolling players would only cause more talk about her here in Syan. The sourness in her belly became something worse, almost dread, but she felt a strong, hot surge of anger as well. "Very well. Yes, of course we will see him. If he is the Tollys' man we have much to talk about, he and I. But let me make some arrangements first."

After all, she had learned all the lessons she needed about the trustworthiness of Crowel's master. If she was going to talk to the man, she wanted King Enander's guards inside the room as well as outside.

Someone who knew neither of them might have thought that Jenkin Crowel was the one doing a favor and Briony the one gratefully accepting it. He brought two guards of his own and a thin, sour-faced cleric dressed in black, as though a contract were being negotiated.

Crowel himself was fleshy without being fat, with a ruddy face, prominent nose, and dimpled chin. He was dressed in what he obviously believed was the height of current Syannese style: when he made an elaborate bow his stiff pantaloons and frilly, oversized sleeves rustled and creaked.

"Your Highness, this is a delightful and most unexpected surprise! I could scarce credit it when I was told. Your people will be thrilled to hear that you are alive and well. How did you come here? I will at once send a message home of your survival that will put joy into the hearts of a grieving populace!"

Briony looked to her maids. All were sewing assiduously. Compared to this idiot, the childish obsessions and subtle cruelties of the Syannse court suddenly looked much better. Still, if that was the game Crowel wished to play, then Briony could have her sport as well.

"Ah, yes," she said. "I have missed my home so much, Lord Crowel. Tell me, how is my infant brother Alessandros? And my stepmother, Anissa? And of course, dear Cousin Hendon, who is taking such good care of all of them?"

He hesitated. "Is the steward . . . is Hendon Tolly truly your cousin? I, ah, I did not think the family relationship quite so close."

Briony waved her hand. "Ah, but the Tollys have always been closer than family to me. That is why I call Hendon 'Cousin.' Why, do you know, the night I left Southmarch we had the most illuminating conversation. Hendon told me all that he had planned for me and my family and the throne. I was touched that he had expended so much thought and effort on our behalf—oh, yes, touched. In fact, it has grieved me so terribly I cannot tell you that I still have not shown him my gratitude. But I have considered *very* carefully how Lord Tolly and his supporters should be rewarded, you may be sure. Yes, I have given it much thought, and I believe I have come up with a few rewards so unusual even Hendon himself cannot guess at them."

Crowel stared, his mouth slightly open. "Ah," he said at last. "Ah. Yes, of course, Highness."

"So when you write to dear Hendon, be sure and tell him that. As you will discover, I have many friends here in Syan, many powerful friends, and they all agree that such noble, loyal stewardship as his should be suitably rewarded."

Of all the hundreds of men and women living in the court of Enander, only a very few went out of their way to speak to Briony or seek anything beyond a passing acquaintance. One such was Ivgenia e'Doursos, the young daughter of the Viscount of Teryon, a small but important territory in the middle of Syan, south of the capital. The fact that it was she who reached out to Briony meant that she couldn't be trusted—the chances were too great that she was acting on behalf of the king's mistress—but Briony discovered she enjoyed Ivgenia's company anyway.

They met at one of the uncomfortable meals in the main hall, with dozens of tables and hundreds of servants, the room absolutely throbbing with the clamor of voices. Ivgenia was seated across from Briony, who had been put next to an older nobleman who drank too much wine and kept trying to look down the front of Briony's dress. Late in the meal he fell off his seat and had to be helped up by servants. The dark-haired girl leaned across the table toward Briony as the baron stumbled off to bed and, with a properly serious face, said, "We provincials have so much to learn from these sophisticated Tessians." Briony laughed so hard she almost choked on a piece of bread and their friendship began that night.

Ivgenia had been sent to the court to receive an education and she had certainly learned to pay attention to what was going on around her: she was a fountainhead of gossip and amused observation, her sensibility almost as dry as Barrick's. Ivgenia was an outsider herself, not because of her breeding, which was perfectly good, but because of her wit, a quality not much valued in Syannese girls, at least not in those young and pretty enough not to need it. Wit, as the popular saying explained, was a tool for ambitious men or ugly women.

Syan was in some ways more licentious than home—the women showed far more skin and the men far more leg than did the courtiers in Southmarch—but in others it was more conservative, perhaps because of the strong local influence of the Trigonate faith. The famous temple of the Trigonarch himself sat on a stony hill in the heart of Tessis, its towers looming even higher than Broadhall Palace, and the church's influence was everywhere. Everyone wore the Triskelion, and nearly every day seemed a holy day of some sort. And just as King Enander was flanked always on his left by Lady Ananka, he was companioned on his other side by the Trigonarch's most powerful priest, Hierarch Phimon, of whom it was said that the only ones who could get a word into the Trigonarch's ear more quickly were the three brother gods themselves.

"If you want to get something done around here, your Highness," Ivgenia said one day in Briony's chambers, "you really need to have the hierarch on your side. They say the Trigonarch will usually do as he asks. Maybe he would help you get your kingdom back!" Ivgenia, like everyone else in Broadhall Palace, knew at least a little of Briony's situation: a princess chased out of her own country was not the kind of thing that happened every day, even in a city as large and important as Tessis.

Briony felt a moment's chill—was she being manipulated? Was Ivgenia going to take what she said directly back to Ananka? "I'm certain Hierarch Phimon has better things to do," she said carefully. "I will wait until King Enander decides what he wishes to do about Southmarch. I am certain he will make a wise choice."

Ivgenia shrugged. "Just as well, Highness, since you're not the type who interests the hierarch anyway. They say that the only three kinds of people Phimon cares about are young boys with pretty voices, old women with lots of money, and trigonarchs."

"But, Ivvie, there's only one trigonarch!" Briony protested, laughing.

"Yes, that does make the last one a small category," said Ivgenia. "And you're not a young boy, although I heard you tried to pass yourself off as one. So you'd better find a way to get your hands on some money, Grandmother."

"Oh! You!" Briony threw a cushion at her. If Ivegnia was a traitor she was a very skillful one, and even having a false friend as entertaining as Ivegnia e' Doursos was far better than living in isolation. Still, each night Briony Eddon slept in Tessian luxury far from her stolen country, it took her longer to fall asleep.

"I've heard several people mention Kallikans again today," Briony asked. "What is a Kallikan?"

Several of the ladies-in-waiting made little noises of dismay, but not Ivgenia. "Do you want to see some? You'd find them quite interesting, I'm sure."

They were all leaving the Flower Meadow, the biggest marketplace in Tessis, and Briony was quite overwhelmed. The sheer size of the market was boggling—there seemed to be more folk here today, filing past the rows of stalls and blankets, than lived in all of the March Kingdoms, and the fabulous variety of goods on offer made Briony feel not just poor but ignorant: she hadn't heard of half the things for sale or half the places the things came from.

"Interesting . . . ?" she repeated slowly, turning to watch an oxcart piled high with gold-painted shrines. Greater Zosimia was only a few weeks away, a popular festival celebrating the end of winter. Back home it was mostly an excuse to drape vines and sprinkle dried flowers on the statues of the gods, but apparently the celebration here in Syan was much more elaborate. "I'm worried that if I see any more interesting things my head will swell up and pop like a bubble . . . but I suppose we could. Will our guards mind?"

Ivgenia looked at the four soldiers in blue tabards and rolled her eyes. "They're here to spy on you, not tell us where to go," she said. "They'll follow where we lead them."

Briony leaned closer to her friend. "Do you think that's true?" she asked in a low voice.

"What? That they'll follow, or that they're here to spy on you?" Ivgenia made a face. "All of them may not be spies, your Highness, but I can assure you that at least one of them is going back to the king's favorite and telling her where you went today. Might as well give them something to tell."

Her skirts held up so they would not drag in the muddy road, the dark-haired girl led Briony, the ladies-in-waiting, and the soldiers away from the market, but instead of heading back toward the palace they crossed wide, bustling Lantern Broad near Devona Fountain Square and turned down what looked to Briony like an ordinary narrow street, although judging by the line of rooftops it was higher than the streets on either side. Only when they had pushed their way through the eddying crowd did Briony see that the high street was actually a bridge across the river, lined on both sides with shops and houses.

"Over there," Ivgenia said. "On the far side of the Ester. They call it Underbridge."

"Who calls it that?"

"You'll see. Come on!" Ivgenia led Briony, the stoic soldiers, and the anxious girls into the flow of human traffic on the bridge. It was still cold, windy Dimene, less than two months since the beginning of the year, so where did all these people come from? Briony couldn't help wondering what the place would be like in Hexamene when the sun was warm and fresh fruits, vegetables, and flowers filled the market.

Still, the wonder of this daunting place made her miss her own home—humble Market Square (although she had seldom thought of it as humble before) and even Market Row, which seemed now to be a mere alleyway compared to most of the main roads of Tessis, let alone when placed beside the Lantern Broad, which was wide as a tilting yard, a street with great stone walkways in its middle so people could find a place to stand that was safe from the heavy wagons crowding the thoroughfare. In places people had even crammed small houses onto these raised walkways! Briony could scarcely believe her eyes—a road big enough to have houses in the middle of it!

But it wasn't home, of course. And more important, they didn't need her here, or even particularly want her.

On the far side of the bridge Ivgenia made the soldiers stop. She promised she and Briony wouldn't go out of sight and left the maids to entertain them—a task the girls preferred anyway, since they seemed to regard these Kallikans, whatever they were, as something faintly unsavory. Then Ivgenia led Briony down into a neighborhood of houses and shops so small that at first Briony thought it was something constructed for a royal child—an entire doll's street instead of just a single dollhouse. The tops of the doors scarcely came to her shoulders.

As Briony stood staring up and down the miniature road, wishing she could get on a stepstool to look into the windows on the upper floors, a woman less than half her size walked out of a house a few doors away to toss out a pan of slops, trailed by a pair of tiny children. The children saw Briony and Ivgenia instantly, and stared at them with unabashed interest, but it was only after the woman had finished shaking out the pan that she discovered she was being watched. Eyes wide, she stared back at the noblewomen for long moments, motionless as a startled mouse, then grabbed her children and scuttled back through her doorway and closed it behind her.

"If we'd been men, or had the soldiers with us, somebody would have rung the bell there." Ivgenia pointed to a temple tower, half-sized like everything else. "Then likely nobody would have come out at all. The whole street's full of folk just like her. Dozens and dozens."

"Funderlings?"

"Kallikans, silly! You wanted to see them."

"Back home we call them Funderlings. I didn't know you had them here." Briony shook her head: it all seemed quite dreamlike. "Isn't that strange—even a different name! Ours live in a big city of their own under Southmarch Castle. They made the place out of solid rock, with a very famous roof that looks like leaves and birds and . . ."

"The king and all, they made ours build here, up where everyone could see them," said Ivgenia. "They can be mischievous, you know. They steal."

Briony hadn't heard that said about the Funderlings back home—it was the Skimmers who were supposed to be unreliable, with their strange looks and strange language. "Do you have Skimmers too?" she asked.

But Ivgenia was already off, beckoning Briony to follow her down the narrow, winding street, deeper into the Kallikan neighborhood. Now the anxious guards came hurrying after them and Briony heard upstairs windows slamming shut, shutters rattling into place, as the little people made their secrets safe from the Big Folk.

* * *

By the time they got back to Broadhall they had missed supper in the great banquet hall. Ivgenia went in search of something to eat but Briony was tired. She was still hungry, though, so after a while she sent Talia, her youngest maid, down to the kitchens to ask for a bowl of soup and some bread while her other ladies helped unlace the tight jacket she had worn out to the market and remove her shoes and hose. The fire was roaring in the fireplace and she wanted nothing more than to sit in front of it and warm her chilled toes.

She had settled in, and might even have drowsed a bit, when a horrible clatter in the passageway outside made her jump. One of the maids ran to the door and peered out, then screamed.

Briony shoved past the terrified girl and discovered little Talia face-down in the hall in a puddle of spilled soup and broken crockery. When she turned the girl over her face was dark blue, her eyes staring as if in horror. Briony jumped up, fighting the urge to be sick. The little maid was obviously dead.

"Poison!" Briony's legs were trembling so badly she had to lean against the wall. The maids and other ladies stood huddled, wide-eyed, in the doorway. "Poor thing, she must have drunk a little of the soup on the way back. She said she was hungry. Oh, merciful Zoria—that was meant for me."

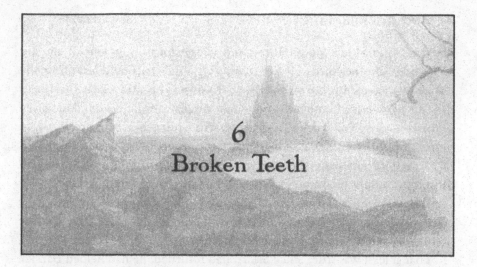

6
Broken Teeth

"The Book of Regret is a fairy chronicle which is claimed to contain the history of everything that has ever happened and of everything yet to come. According to Rhantys every page is of hammered gold and it is bound in pure adamant. Some old stories suggest the Theomachy, or Godwar, was fought over the theft of this book rather than the kidnapping of Zoria."

—from "A Treatise on the Fairy Peoples of Eion and Xand"

BARRICK HAD OFTEN CRITICIZED his sister Briony for her slovenly habits. She let dogs sleep in her bed even on warm nights, dropped her shoes wherever she took them off, and would cradle the muddiest, most disgusting creature in the world to her breast as long as it was a baby—whether puppy, foal, kitten, lamb, or chick. However, despite all the times Briony had driven her more fastidious brother into a rage, his strongest wish now was that he could speak to her again and apologize for saying that she was the most untidy thing that had ever lived . . . because now he knew better. No creature, not even some blind worm living in the very privies of Kernios, could be more disgusting than the raven Skurn, with his meals of frogspawn and festering mouse carcasses, his verminous, patchy feathers, and his constant smell of blood, rot, and ordure.

The big dark bird ate constantly, head bobbing up and down over some horror or other with the infuriating regularity of a waterwheel in a strong current. And Skurn ate anything and everything—bugs out of the air, droppings of other birds off the trees, slugs, and snails and anything else too slow to avoid his horny black beak. Nor was he a tidy eater: his breast was always covered with a drying crust of whatever he'd eaten last, often with some bits still faintly twitching. And his other habits were even more dreadful. Skurn was not careful about where he defecated at the best of times, but when he was startled he gave up all discretion: wayward droppings might splash on Barrick's shoulder or even into his hair.

"But us doesn't shit on you a-purpose," Skurn pointed out after one such accident when he was startled by a falling branch. "And as must be said, so far us's kept you clear of the silkins."

That at least was true. Since Skurn had returned, he had helped Barrick through Silky Wood with little contact from the creatures after whom it was named. A pair of silent stalkers had followed them for a while a few sleeps back, but had come no closer than the lower branches. Perhaps, Barrick thought with a touch of pride, word had spread of how he had dealt with their kin. (More likely, though, he recognized, was that they were simply waiting until more of them had gathered.)

He hadn't seen a sign of them at all yesterday or today, and had actually managed a few hours of sleep while the raven Skurn played sentry—or claimed he had, anyway: not only was Skurn self-serving, he was old. Once Barrick had actually seen him doze off midflight, lose control of his wings, and crack his head against a tree trunk, spinning to the ground like a clump of black leaves. As he hurried toward him, Barrick had been sure the raven had broken his neck.

Is it a heresy, Barrick couldn't help wondering, *to pray to gods whose existence you are confused about and whose kindness you certainly doubt, begging for the safety of a brute of a bird you do not even like?*

"I don't believe you know where you're going at all," he shouted at the bird. "We're going in circles!"

"No circles," protested Skurn. "All looks the same, this, 'cause un goes on and on."

"I don't believe you."

Between the mist, the thick trees, and the eternal twilight, Barrick had never been able to get a real idea of where he was or what this part of the shadowlands looked like, but they had been trooping through endless, indistinguishable forest so long that he was becoming desperate to see something of where he was. Thus, despite Skurn's strong disapproval, he began to climb uphill toward what he hoped would be a break in the trees and some kind of view.

"Stay away from high ground and low," said Skurn, fluttering nervously as he struggled to avoid the branches bending close overhead. "That's sense! Everybody knows of that."

"I don't." Barrick didn't want to talk: his arm was already aching and he wanted to save the breath he had for climbing.

Muttering darkly, the raven fluttered ahead up the slope but soon returned.

"Us thinks us knows this place, now. Tine Fay be here. They nest all hereabouts."

"Tine Fay? Nest?" Barrick shook his head. "Are they worse than the silkins?"

The raven lowered his head into his feathered shoulders, a corvine shrug. "Don't think so. In fact, they be somewhat slurpsome if un can separate 'em from they weapons . . ."

"So let me be, then."

"Not worse than them silkies, p'raps," the raven grumbled. "But us didn't say *nice*, either."

What might have been an hour later he was still toiling uphill, ignoring an arm that burned like fire as he dragged himself over fallen trees and through clinging undergrowth—worst of all the creeper whose vines were covered with tiny thorns and whose velvety black flowers bobbed at the ends of the largest stalks, big as cabbages. These creepers seemed to colonize entire hillsides and choke out everything else, even the smaller trees, growing so thick that he would have needed a scythe to cut through them, although even then it would have been hard, sweaty work. Wherever Barrick found the blackflower vines—and they were all over these hills—he could only turn and make his way around them. Still, one advantage of the eternal twilight was that just as full light never came, neither did full darkness. At least he did not have to fear night finding him exposed on the hillside.

But where did this twilight come from? Barrick understood that clouds and fog could cover the land and keep out the sun, but how could they hold light in the world after the sun had gone down for the day?

While they were keeping the shadowlands in twilight did they soak up the sun's rays like a dry rag in a puddle of water, so that light continued to leak into the sky long after the actual sun was gone?

What does it matter? It's more fairy magic. But it made him wonder about the gods, who from all he had heard seemed little different from men, at least in the ways they lived their lives. Perhaps Perin and Kernios and the others had not become the masters of mankind because they were gods— perhaps they were gods only because they had been powerful enough to make themselves masters of mankind . . .

Skurn dropped out of the sky and landed on his shoulder, making Barrick jump and curse out loud. "Quiet, now," the bird hissed in his ear. "Somewhat be moving in the trees ahead."

Heart beating fast, Barrick pulled his broken spear from his belt, then took a deep breath and stepped forward, pushing aside a branch to reveal a small clearing, a relatively bare patch on the hillside. There was indeed much movement in the trees and rustling among the branches, but the creatures swarming there were smaller than Barrick's smallest finger.

"They're . . . little people!" he said. "Like in the stories!"

An instant after he finished speaking a shrill horn call sounded from the greenery near him and a shower of sharp little objects came flitting down all around. Two or three stuck into the back of Barrick's hand; he cried out in pain and tried to shake the tiny arrows out of his skin but another shower of miniature barbs followed, stinging his face and scalp like horseflies.

"Stop it!" he shouted and turned again, but every direction he chose seemed to be full of prickling darts. At last he put his arm across his face and ran forward until he reached the first branch he had seen. As the tiny men scattered Barrick had a brief glimpse of chitinous armor like beetles' shells. He caught the branch before any but a few had escaped and shook it until little bodies were falling all around him. He caught as many as he could, perhaps half a dozen, and lifted the squirming but largely undamaged mass above his head as a shield. He heard shrill squeals in the trees above and the storm of miniature arrows suddenly stopped. "Yes, tell them to stop shooting at us, Skurn!" he shouted. "Tell them we mean no harm!"

"Us said to stay off high places," Skurn reminded him sourly, but after a moment Barrick heard the bird say something in a loud rush of trills and clicks. After a pause, Skurn spoke again—Barrick guessed that the voice of whoever was speaking for the tiny people was too quiet for him to hear. The raven's voice and the seeming silence alternated for long moments.

"Us thinks Tine Fay mought give us safe passage if you let loose those in your hand. Us told them you wouldn't keep more than two or three to eat."

"Three to eat? Three of what . . . ?" Barrick suddenly understood. "The gods curse you, you foul bird! We're not going to *eat* them!"

"Not for you," Skurn said, hurt. "Knowed you wouldn't. More like they were for me . . ."

"Listen to your foulness! These are people . . . of a sort, anyway. More than can be said for you." Barrick looked down. One of the tiny bark-clad men was struggling to cling to his sleeve, legs kicking above what must have been a terrifying fall. The little fellow's bird-skull helmet had tumbled off and his eyes bulged with terror. "For the love of the Three Brothers, they're even wearing armor!" While still keeping his head protected, Barrick moved his arm closer to his body so that the little fellow could gain the security of his tattered jacket.

"They armor shucks off easy enough," said Skurn. "And them is proper toothsome underneath. 'Specially they young ones . . ."

"Oh, be quiet. You are disgusting, bird. Not to mention that while you're talking like that up a tree, I'm the one who's going to get an arrow in my eye if anything goes wrong. Tell them I'm going to put them all down, if that's what they want, and not to let fly at me. Tell them that I'm going to let them *all* go, or by the gods, Skurn, I'm going to pull your tail feathers out."

While the raven relayed these words to the Tine Fay, Barrick slowly lowered his hands from his head and down to the ground. The little people, who from terror or pragmatism had stropped struggling, carefully slid to safety. He hoped he had not killed any, not because it shamed him—they had been shooting arrows at him, after all—but because it would make things more difficult now. That was a lesson of his father's: *"Don't rub your enemy's face in the dirt when you have him down,"* Olin had often said, *"not if you intend to let him up again afterward. Insults take longer to heal than wounds."* It had never made much sense to him before, since Barrick felt he was usually the one whose face was being rubbed in the dirt, but now he was beginning to understand it. Going through life was perhaps a bit like going through this horrible forest: the fewer things behind you that hated you, the less strength you had to use watching your back and the better you could worry about what was coming.

When the prisoners were all safe the rest of the Tine Fay slowly made their way down from the trees and from underneath the bushes in the clearing—perhaps a hundred in all. It was not only their minute size that separated them from true men, Barrick decided: their features were longer and stranger, especially their pointed noses and chins, and their limbs seemed in some cases as thin as spiders' legs. In most other respects, though, they were not much different than people many times their size. Their armor had been ingeniously constructed from bark, nutshells, and insect cases, and their spears were skewers of what looked like whittled bone. The looks on their faces were even those of a full-sized army in uneasy truce: as Barrick crawled toward them they all watched with fear and distrust, clearly ready to bolt back into the undergrowth if he showed any hint of treachery.

When Barrick was settled one of the Tine Fay stepped out from the crowd, his voice piping like a baby bird's. Despite this fluting tone he had a very martial look about him, his shield made from a shimmering blue-green beetle's shell, his little beard wound with ribbons, his head helmed in the skull of a toothy fish.

"He says that he respects the parley," reported Skurn, "but if you come to plunder the sacred gold from the hives of his people he and his men must fight you to the death anyway. Such is their oath to their ancestors, to protect the hives and the honey-horses."

"Hives?" Barrick shook his head. "Honey-horses? Is he talking about bees?" For a moment he could taste honey—nothing sweeter than sour berries had touched his tongue in months—and his mouth watered. "Tell him I mean them no harm," he said. "I am trying to make my way to Qul-na-Qar."

After a moment's ticking discourse, Skurn turned back to Barrick. "He says that if you doesn't mean to steal their treasure then they need to go back and keep an eye out for others who do." Skurn picked with his beak at his chest feathers, worrying out a flea. "They never stay long in the open—already they feel fretsome about being so long out of the shadows." Skurn cocked his head as the tiny chieftain spoke again. "But because you are honorable and they do not wish you to die horribly, they say go not near Cursed Hill."

"Cursed Hill? What is that?"

"Us has heard of it," the raven said gravely, "but heard nothing good. Us should be on our way."

But the chief wasn't done. He piped a few more times, pointing agitatedly at the bird.

"What's he saying?"

"Naught." Skurn was a study in disinterest. "Merest chitter-chat. Farewells and benedictions, like."

The chief's voice rose to a higher-pitched squeak. The Tine Fay seemed to have a very urgent way of saying farewell.

"Ah, well, tell them I say thank you, and . . ." Barrick's eyes narrowed. "Skurn, what's that under your claw?"

"What?" The bird looked into the air rather than down where Barrick was pointing. "Nothing. Nothing at all, Master."

If he hadn't already seen the minuscule man struggling weakly, the bird calling him "master" would have given it away. "It's one of them, isn't it? One of the wounded ones. Gods curse you, let that poor little fellow go or I truly will pluck out all your feathers—and have your beak off as well!"

The raven gave him a reproachful look as he lifted his scaly black foot. A half dozen Tine Fay hurried forward to carry their wounded comrade away. When they had him secure, the entire little tribe swiftly vanished back into the undergrowth.

"You are disgusting."

"He were already bad hurt," Skurn said sullenly. "Nothing much can they do for him—and see how plump he were!"

I withdraw my earlier prayers, Barrick silently told the gods. *I had no right to ask your help for a winged wretch like that.*

It was hard to make complete sense from the words of frightened imps as translated by a grumpy raven, but as best Barrick could discern he and Skurn were on a ridge that stretched a long way through the forest, but they needed to climb down it again to avoid the place called Cursed Hill. Why it bore such a name he couldn't tell. Skurn was sulking, now; the most the bird would tell him was that "folk what stray there come back mad or changed."

In any case, if he had understood the miniature folk correctly, once past the ill-omened spot they should only be a day or so away from safer lands beyond the silkins' territory.

Barrick hadn't relished the idea of being shot in the face by a hundred tiny arrows, but he was still sorry to see the Tine Fay go. As a child he had heard many stories of the little people, but had never thought to see them—it wasn't as if they were running around in the halls of Southmarch. Yet here they were and he had met them. It was just one more way in which his life had turned out to be even stranger than he had ever suspected it would.

Of course, he thought, *lately most of it has also been worse than I could have guessed.*

They continued to the top of the ridge and eventually found a rock outcropping that jutted a few feet above the trees so Barrick could make out something of the surrounding country. As Barrick climbed wearily up the rock he reminded himself that this feeling of time slipping away, while perhaps true in some larger sense, was mostly an illusion: the sun would not go down soon, no matter how dark the sky looked. It was true he would have to stop for sleep before too long, but it would not be in the dark. He would rise after a few hours, but the sun would not. Things were not going to change here.

And perhaps now Southmarch and all the March Kingdoms are like this, too, he thought. *Perhaps the Qar have dragged this blanket of shadow over all the lands of men. Perhaps this is all Briony and the others in Southmarch can see, too.* It was a dreary, disheartening thought.

He looked out over the rumpled, misty sea of treetops. The small folk had been right: he was on top of a long ridge that ran through the forest like a raised dike. On the horizon ahead of him, just at the point where the mists were thickest, a single large hill rose above both forest and ridge, a huge and solitary lump of green shrouded in plumes of fog; an outcrop of tall rocks ringed the hilltop like broken teeth. Perhaps because of the way it loomed above the sea of mist and yet had its own cloud of fog, the hill looked old and secretive, like a beggar so wrapped in rags he could not be distinguished from his background until he moved.

Barrick found he had no quibble with the Tine Fay's advice: he did not want to go anywhere near the spot called Cursed Hill.

*   *   *

He was exhausted but awake, staring up at nothing and wishing he could fall asleep. The old raven was huddled in his feathers close to Barrick's side, his snore a thin whistle. A flutter of rain was making the leaves bob above the prince's head, and beyond stretched the flat, gray blanket of twilight.

How long since I've seen the sun? he wondered. *Or the moon, for that matter? By the Three, how can these shadowland creatures live this way? They can't even see the stars!*

The stories said that the Twilight People had created the pall two centuries ago, pulled it over themselves like a blanket when their second attack on the world of men had failed—but why? Were they so frightened of the vengeance of humankind that they had chosen to give up the sun and the open sky forever—to put aside even night and day? He had seen the fairy folk on the battlefield; even with much smaller numbers than Barrick's people they had destroyed the human army. They certainly weren't cowards, either. Had their numbers been so much less or their warcraft so much more clumsy two hundred years ago . . . ?

Barrick was distracted from this thought by a movement in the branches high overhead. He lay still and kept his eyes narrowed as though they were closed. There! Something was creeping through the uppermost canopy like a huge, white spider—a silkin.

A second pale shape clambered silently out beside the first and together they crouched, staring down. It was all he could do to stay quiet. At last he pretended to yawn and stretch, as though he were just now waking up. The silkins went utterly still for a moment, then retreated back into the shadowy upper branches, but Barrick's heart did not slow down for a long time.

So they were still out there. What were the nasty things waiting for? Surely they could have no other reason to follow him than to seek a chance to attack, but he had already slept several times and they had done nothing. What were they waiting for?

Reinforcements, most likely.

A fine drizzle pattered on the leaves above him and occasionally drifted down to tickle his face, but it didn't matter: he wasn't going to sleep any time soon, anyway.

*   *   *

Barrick and Skurn had followed the bony ridgeline as long as they could, but now the hills were sloping downward, each a little smaller than the one before. The Cursed Hill loomed just ahead, blocking the sky like the dome of some great temple, silent and mysterious. Barrick did not much want to descend into the dark valleys where the trees blocked out most of what little light there was, but if that was how best to avoid such an ill-favored place, he thought, then the valleys it would be.

Even Skurn seemed to have lost his courage. "Smells worse, that mountain, as us gets closer," was the best he could explain. "Stinks of old days and dead gods—worse than Greatdeeps. Even the silkins don't go there."

Worse than Greatdeeps . . . Barrick shuddered and looked away. The horror of the tunnels and one-eyed Jikuyin, the dreadful king of those depths, would never leave him as long as he breathed.

So they started downhill under a damp drizzle, along wooded canyons that skirted the base of the high hill, the peak looming above them like a brooding giant. The darkness of the dells made Barrick feel much more vulnerable than he had on the heights of the ridge. Even Skurn, who ordinarily flew far ahead, disappearing sometimes for what seemed like an hour, now remained close to Barrick, moving forward only a few trees at a time and waiting for him to catch up. Thus, the raven was the first to notice they were being followed again.

"Three of them silkins," he hissed in Barrick's ear. "Just beyond trees there." He indicated the direction with his beak. "Don't look!"

"Curse them, they've found a friend." But he did his best not to let it frighten him. Half a dozen or more had come at him the last time and he had beaten them away—three would never be enough to overcome Barrick Eddon, master of the silk-slitting spear! Still, where there were three there could soon be more . . .

When will we get out of this gods-cursed forest? I cannot stand another day of this. But the memory of the long stretch of treetops beyond the Cursed Hill was fresh: Barrick knew they would not be under open sky anytime soon.

Skurn had flown a little distance ahead to hunt for a relatively safe place to spend the night. Barrick was getting hungrier by the moment. He had eaten little in the past few days but berries and a few bird's eggs drunk raw straight from the shell. Meat and a fire to cook it on seemed a fabulous luxury, something he could scarcely recall.

All princes should spend a year lost behind the Shadowline, he decided. *It would teach them to value what they have. By the gods, would it teach them!*

A movement in the near distance startled him. He looked up and saw something white vanish behind a tree, then glimpsed another pale smear moving a little deeper in the forest. *Closer than they were before,* he realized. *Maybe they think we've stopped because I'm hurt.* He picked up a rock and began to ostentatiously sharpen the point of his broken spear for the benefit of any observers. He had wrapped a piece of cloth torn from his sleeve around the handle to make it easier to hold, but he still wished mightily for a sword or at least a proper knife.

Skurn came fluttering down out of the trees, beating his wings as he settled to the ground near Barrick's feet. "Four of them," he gasped. "Oh, wings be smarting, us flew so fast to tell. Four, and carrying a net."

"I saw them," Barrick said quietly, gesturing with his thumb. "Over there."

"Over there? No, these be yon, just ahead. If you see'd some too, they be others."

Barrick made the sign of the Three as he sprang up. "Bastard things! They're trying to surround us." The helplessness he had felt in the woods at the edge of Kolkan's Field came over him like a sudden chill, that moment when he and his companions realized that the fairies had tricked them—that the Twilight People were not on the run, but had doubled back and were coming in from every side. The shrieks of terror from the men around Barrick as they had gone from hunters to hunted in a single breath would never leave him so long as he lived. "Go!"

He ran forward, angling away from where the raven said the four silkins were waiting with a net, but also away from those he had seen. A moment later Skurn flapped past him. "Many behind us!" the bird shouted.

Barrick took a look back. Half a dozen of the silk-wrapped creatures were scuttling along branches or speeding along the forest floor with that weird, hopping gait of theirs, half-insect, half-ape.

He turned back just in time to see another pair loom up before him out of the shadows between two gnarled old trees, spinning something like a fishing net. Barrick only had a moment to throw himself to one side—he felt the sticky edge of one of the strands drag at his arm for a moment as it brushed his skin. Skurn had to bank up sharply to avoid the net and disappeared into the upper branches.

More pale shapes glided between the trees, circling toward him. The uneven ground was treacherous so Barrick had to keep an eye on where he was running, but he thought he could count a dozen or more in just his brief surveillance. The creatures were trying to form a moving wall in front of him, falling back more slowly at the sides than before him: within a few moments he would be surrounded.

"No!" he shouted, and skidded to a halt, grabbing at a tree branch to keep from tumbling. For a moment his feet actually left the ground and the weight on his bad arm sent a bolt of fire through his elbow and shoulder all the way to his neck. Four or five more silkins he hadn't even spotted were clambering down from the trees—another dozen steps and he would have run right into them. "Go back, bird!" Barrick shouted, hoping Skurn could hear him, then he turned tail and ran back the way he had came, back up the slope. It was steeper than he remembered and he was running out of directions—time to start thinking about fighting. *"If you can choose nothing else,"* Shaso had always said, *"pick the spot to make your stand. Do not let your enemy dictate it to you."*

Shaso. For a moment grief and loss and even terror swept through him, not just at the thought of dying in the forest, but at the realization of how many things he would never know, never resolve, never understand.

Maybe when you die, you learn everything. Or maybe you learn nothing.

"Not that way!" Skurn was flying beside him, doing his best not to run into anything as he followed Barrick through the trees. "That way be Cursed Hill! Mind what the Tine Fay said!"

Barrick stumbled on a root but caught himself, kept clambering uphill. Well, why not? Hadn't the bird said that even the silkins did not go there? And if he had to make a stand, what better place could he find than in the open air, with one of those rock outcroppings at his back?

"Master!" called Skurn desperately as Barrick dug even harder up the slope. The raven fluttered down and crouched on a stone just ahead of him. "Master, it be death to climb that hill!"

"Do what you want," he told the bird. "I'm going this way."

"Don't want to leave you, but us will die for certain there!"

A moment later the ground had angled up so steeply that Barrick almost had to go down on all fours. He snatched at low-lying branches to pull himself ahead. He could hear the silkins rattling through the branches behind him and the growing murmur of their strange hunting song. "Go on! Fly, you fool bird!" he gasped. "If it's my time, I'm at least going to die in the open."

"Krah!" the bird croaked in frustration. "Be all Sunlanders such . . . such stubborn, pisshead idiots?" But he didn't wait for an answer. Instead Skurn unfolded his wings, flew up into the sky, and was gone.

7

The King's Table

"Kyros the Soterian cites as further evidence of the sacrilegious nature of the fairies' beliefs how closely their version of the Theomachy seems to follow the Xandian Heresy, portraying the Trigon as the enemies of mankind and the defeated gods Zmeos Whitefire and his siblings as mankind's benefactors . . ."

—from "A Treatise on the Fairy Peoples of Eion and Xand"

"I AM GRIEVED AND ANGRY to hear about this terrible thing, Highness," said Finn Teodoros. "This murder of your servant! Even in my captivity I have heard little else."

"It is far worse for the family of Talia, the little girl who died." Briony gave him a sad smile. " 'Highness'—it is strange to hear you call me that, Finn."

"Well, it must have been stranger for you during all that time you traveled with us, being called 'Boy' or 'Tim.' " He laughed. "Zoria in hiding, indeed!"

She sighed. "To be honest, I miss it. Tim may not have eaten as well as royalty, but no one tried to poison him, either."

"It truly is a shocking circumstance, Highness. Do you have any idea of who would do such a thing?"

She looked at the door of Teodoros' room, which Erasmias Jino had deliberately left ajar. She could see the colors of one of the guards outside. It would be foolish to say anything she didn't want overheard. "I know nothing except that a child died by poison meant for me. Lord Jino has promised he will find the culprit."

"Lord Jino?" Finn Teodoros chuckled ruefully. "I know him—a persistent fellow. He can be rather frightening. I'm sure he will get some result."

"Oh, Finn, have they treated you badly?" She had to fight the urge to put her arms around his rounded shoulders, but she was a princess again and it would not do. "I told them that you were a good man."

"Then, your pardon, Highness, but perhaps they do not trust your word, either."

She took a quick look at the door, then got up and quietly pushed it shut. *Let them open it again if they want so badly to listen.* "Tell me again," she said quietly, "we may not have much time—what did Brone want you to do here in Tessis?"

The playwright's expression was unhappy. "Please don't punish me for meddling in your family's affairs, Highness. I only did what Lord Brone told me—I swear I would not have served him if I thought anything evil was intended!"

"I doubt he made the choice as easy as that," Briony said with a sour grin. "I would guess he offered you payment for your troubles, but also threatened you if you would not consent."

Teodoros nodded his head solemnly. "He said we would never have a license to play in Southmarch again."

"Tell me what he wanted you to do."

Teodoros took a kerchief from his sleeve and mopped his shining brow. He had lost a little weight since the Syannese had imprisoned him but he was still a stout man. "I delivered letters here to the royal court, as you know, but I have no idea what was in them. I was also told to leave a message for Dawet dan-Faar in a certain tavern, and I did. The message said we would be at *The False Woman*—that I had news for him from Southmarch. But I never had a chance to talk to him. I don't know how he managed to get away from those soldiers . . ."

"I expect they let him go," Briony said. "I was a bit distracted at the time, but the whole thing had the look of a . . ." she put her finger beside her nose, " . . . a quiet understanding between Dawet and the guards." She shook her head. Spycraft—it was a maddening, sticky swamp. "And what were you to tell Dawet if you had been able?"

"I was to say that . . . that a bargain could still be made, but not only would Drakava have to return Olin, but also send a troop of armed men with him to prevent treachery by the Tollys who were trying to usurp the throne."

She felt a moment of shock. "A bargain with Drakava? Did he mean the hundred thousand gold dolphins or my hand in marriage? Was Brone offering me to Drakava—something my own father and brother had not done?"

Teodoros shrugged. "I have done errands for Avin Brone before now. He gives me only what I must have, usually a sealed letter. With dan-Faar he did not trust anything to be written down and told me no more than he needed to."

Briony sat back, hot blood rushing to her face. "Is that so? Perhaps the Count of Landsend has some plans of his own—secrets, even."

The playwright looked decidedly uncomfortable. "I . . . I . . . I do not know any more of what he wanted with the Tuani-man Dawet, I swear. Please do not be angry with me, Highness."

Briony realized that she had frightened Teodoros, one of the few people who had treated her like a friend when he didn't need to: the playwright was trembling and his forehead was beaded with sweat.

I truly am an Eddon again. Like my father, I often wish to be treated as if I were anything else but royal, but I forget that my temper can make others fear for their lives . . .

"Don't worry, Finn." She sat back. "You have done nothing to harm me or my family."

Teodoros still looked decidedly unhappy, but managed to say, "Thank you, Highness."

"But your service to Southmarch hasn't ended—I have more for you to do. I need a secretary. I can't trust any of the Syannese, but I need someone who can blend easily into the court—someone who has an ear . . . and a taste . . . for gossip."

Finn Teodoros looked up, his expression a mix of relief and confusion. "You surely don't mean me, do you, Highness?"

Briony laughed. "I was thinking of Feival, to be honest. He has played courtiers of both sexes, why should he not play one on my behalf? No, I have other plans for you, Finn. I want you and the rest of Makewell's Men to be my ears here in Tessis. Find out everything the people think, especially about Southmarch, any news of the war there or of the usurping Tollys." She stood. "I can't make decisions without information. Without sources of my own, I will hear only what King Enander and his hangers-on want me to hear."

"Of course, Princess—but how can I do your bidding? I am a prisoner!"

"Not for long. I will see to that. Be brave, friend Finn. You are my bondsman now and I will take care of you."

Briony went to the door and threw it open. "Players! Oh, but I am glad to be shut of them!" She said it loud enough for the guards to hear. "Take him back to his cell! I have grown weary of the company of professional liars."

❧

He bowed as he entered. "Good morning, my lady. Will you kill me today?"

"Why, Kayyin? Did you have other plans?"

It had become their customary greeting. It was not entirely facetious.

Lady Yasammez's eyes were closed. Her thoughts had ranged far and had only now returned to her in this foreign place, this Sunlander city beside the ocean—the same ocean as the black, sunless sea that beat against the rocks below Qul-na-Qar, but so different in aspect and feeling. Yes, the Mantle had changed things in only a few hundred short years, the great shroud that Crooked had taught them to keep them safe—but was it only the Mantle that had made things different? Hadn't something grown in the hearts of the people themselves—*her* people—that no longer loved the sun? She reflected on Kayyin as he stood before her with his strange, sad smile. Who of the Qar ever looked that way, wore that expression of fear and guilt and resignation that only a mortal could manufacture? *They are not so different from us as you might think—* Kayyin himself had said that to her once. At the time she had dismissed it as another way in which he was trying to enrage her, trying to force her to kill him and end this unnatural half-life of his. Then, later, she had come to brood on it. What if it were true?

Now, suddenly, as she thought about the dark surf rolling ceaselessly outside Qul-na-Qar, another thought came to her: what if the Sunlanders, the mortal insects who she had longed for years to crush, on whose swords she would gladly die if she had taken a great enough toll of her enemies first . . . what if the mortals were not merely like her people, but better? How long could a creature walk bent-backed before it could no longer straighten up? How long did cave animals continue to live as though one day they would return to the light before their eyes finally wasted away and their skins turned white as corpse flesh? How long could you live the life of an inferior beast before you *became* an inferior beast?

"You haven't yet made war, my lady," Kayyin said at last, breaking the silence.

"War?"

"You swore only days ago that you would destroy the mortal city before us. Do you remember? It was when you took those two women from Southmarch captive. You were most impressive, my lady, most frightsome. 'It will be a joy to hear the screams of your people,' you told them. But I cannot help but notice that here you sit, and the screams have still not begun. Could it be you have thought twice about this unreasoning hatred of yours?"

"Unreasoning?" She turned toward him, nettled. The fact of her annoyance was itself annoying—he lived only to goad her and she hated to satisfy him. But what he said now seemed odd, almost malicious. "It is only the persistence of reason that keeps them alive. Only a fool does not hesitate to do that which cannot be undone—and the plans I have for the mortals are of that sort. When the god is dead, the mortals will also die." She looked at him, allowed herself to blink once and once only, a signal of faint surprise. "Do you truly want me to attack them today, Kayyin? Do you want to hurry their end? I thought you had grown close to them."

"I want you to know your own mind, Lady. Much, I feel, will hinge on that."

"What nonsense are you talking?"

"Nonsense that was breathed in my ear before I knew myself again." Kayyin paused for a moment as if searching for words. "It matters not. But although you may not believe it, I fear for our people, O my Mother. I fear your decisions. I suppose that is why I ask you. Like a misbehaving child who waits for a parent to come home, I fear the punishment less than I fear the waiting."

"That is because you *are* a child, Kayyin, compared to me. When I decide to strike it will be swift and harsh and final. I will bring a power against this place that will kill everything that lives, even the birds in the trees and the moles in the ground."

For the first time he looked surprised, his face suddenly full of something like fear. "What? What would you do to them?"

"That is not for you to know, little turncoat. But because that destruction will be so complete, I will not begin until I am certain."

"So you admit you have doubts?"

"Doubts? Hah." She took Whitefire from where it lay in her lap and stood, stretching her long legs, then set the sword on her council table. The great hall that had once been the town's seat of goverment was empty even of ghosts. Her guards waited outside. Like Kayyin, they would be fitful and impatient at this long pause after their war had seemed all but won. Unlike him, they were soldiers, and would have the discipline to keep it to themselves. "Shall I tell you a story?"

"A true one?"

"You annoy me less than you think, but still more than is polite. Your father would have been ashamed—he was a creature of intense grace."

"Is that the story you would tell me? Of my father?"

"I would tell you of the Battle of Shivering Plain. Your father was unborn, but one of your ancestors, your great-great-great-grandfather Ayyam, was there. It was one of the last battles between the clans of Breeze and Moisture and their mortal allies. We fought for Whitefire against the treachery of his three half-brothers, the ones these idiot mortals worship.

"I was one of King Numannyn's three generals—Numannyn the Cautious as he came to be called. We had fought long in support of the great god Whitefire, battling for days against both demigods and armies of mortals, and our forces were tired. Night was almost upon us and the troops wanted nothing but to make camp before dark came. Whitefire's brother Moonlord had been killed and the moon had turned red and almost faded from the sky—the gods could fight without light, but it was harder for us. Numannyn, though, had a seer with him, and she told the king that under the cover of darkness a single man was escaping the field with a guard of several hundred mortal soldiers.

"'It must be someone important,' Numannyn said. 'One of the kings of the mortals, fleeing the battle, or perhaps a messenger from the mortals to the gods of Xandos. We must capture him.'

"'Your soldiers are weary,' one of the other generals told him. I did not dare speak then against the king's wishes, but I was also troubled. My warriors had been asked to give much already, and the next day threatened to be the bloodiest yet. Even the fiercest of our folk must rest sometimes.

"'Something about this speaks to me of ill omens,' the third general said. 'Can we not send a flight of Elementals to observe this refugee more closely? I smell a trap.'

"'If none of my generals will undertake this for me,' said Numannyn in anger, 'then I will take a company and go myself.'

"We were all shamed. As I was the youngest and the only one who had not voiced an objection, I felt bound to this service. I took my companions, the Makers of Tears, and we climbed onto our mounts and set out.

"We encountered the enemy crossing over the river Silvertrail at the base of the hills that ringed the great, icy meadow. As the seer had said, perhaps a hundred mortal soldiers were riding hard. They were strong and well-armed, but they seemed to have no other purpose except to protect a single litter carried by half-naked slaves. When we called to them to surrender they turned and fought, of course—we had expected no less. If the person in their custody was rich enough or important enough for such a large bodyguard we knew they would not give him up lightly. But for all their warlike strength and training they were only mortal soldiers and they had little more than us in sheer numbers. For us, it was like fighting strong but clumsy children.

"When we had beaten down the soldiers the slaves dropped the litter and fled. The mortal man who staggered out of it was small and dark-haired. I did not know his face, although something about him seemed familiar.

"'Do not harm me,' he said in a frightened voice. 'Let me go and I will make you all rich.'

"'What could you give us?' shouted my men, laughing. 'Gold? Cattle? We are the People—the true People. There is nothing you can give us that we did not give to you stone apes in the first place!'

"'Our king wants you, and so you will come!' others jeered. 'There is nothing else to say.' And they threw the prisoner roughly onto the back of a horse, his hands bound behind him.

"When we brought him before the king the prisoner spoke again, and although he still spoke pleadingly, there was something strange in his voice. 'Please, O Numannyn King, Master of the Qar, Lord of Winds and Thought, let me go and I will give you gifts. I do not wish trouble for myself or for you.'

"The king smiled coldly—it frightened me to see it, although I did not know why, but I had the sense that one has when a great stone begins to shift and tilt downslope. Something was happening, though I did not know what, and in a moment it would be too late to stop it.

" 'You can offer me nothing except what you know,' Numannyn said. 'And that you will give to me whether you want to or not. You belong to me now. Who are you and where were you bound?'

"The mortal looked down for a long moment as if ashamed or terrified, but when he looked up neither of these things were on his face. His eyes were bright and his smile was as cold and hard as Numannyn's.

" 'Very well, little king. I hoped only to leave this place and this incessant fighting, for which I am nowise fit, and return to my home atop Xandos. But you would stop me and interrogate me. You would make me a prisoner. Very well.' He lifted his hands. The guards nearest him drew their blades but the stranger made no other move. 'You wish to know my name? My servants call me Zosim, but you know me better as the first and greatest Trickster.'

"And it was indeed the god himself, wearing the form of a mortal man—even as he spoke he began to take on the true semblance of his godhood. He grew bigger and bigger. His eyes flashed and lightning played about his head. I was young and not as strong as I am now—I could not even bear to look straight at him as he revealed himself, so terrible was his aspect. And he was one of the least warlike gods! We had caught him trying to sneak away from the battle! But now he would fight. Now he would punish.

"His skin turned black as a raven's wing, his eyes red like coals. His armor, of a metal that was both red and blue, grew over him like moss on a stone until he was covered from head to foot. All of us, the king's servitors, stood gaping like birds entranced by a snake. One of his hands reached up and there was a whip of fire in it. The other reached out and caught up a rod of crystal. He began then to strike out—even the song he sang was terrible. You have never seen a god, Kayyin. A god in his battle array is the most frightening thing you can imagine. I hope my own long life will end before I ever see such a thing again. In fact, with a god like Trickster, a lord of moods and mysteries, his appearance itself was part of what made him so fearsome—our own terror made him greater.

"But do not misunderstand—his power was all too real. Some may say that the gods come from the same stock as we do—that they came at first from the same seed and bone, but what was different about them is what they could be, what they could control. Others say that they are another family of beings entirely. I do not know, Kayyin. I am only a soldier, and although I am old, the gods were old before I came into this world. But whether they are somehow our cousins, our fathers, our ancestors, never make the mistake of believing they are like us, because they are not.

"King Numannyn was among the first to die, split by Trickster's humming staff like a piece of wood chopped for kindling. The other two generals died defending him, as did many dozen of their soldiers, wailing like the callowest of mortals. If Trickster's own guards had not run shrieking in terror when he revealed himself they could have destroyed half our army, so terrible was the damage the angry god caused. But he had told the truth—he did not like war. When the first heat of his anger had cooled Trickster turned and walked away, shrinking as he did so like parchment in a candleflame until only his mortal disguise remained. None of the survivors made a move toward him. I doubt any of them even considered it.

"I had been beaten down in the first moments, my shield broken into flaming shards by Trickster's whip, my body flung away across the field by a chance blow from his gauntleted hand. I lay insensible for a long time and only awakened when your great-great-great-grandfather, Ayyam, was carrying me back to my troops. He was a warrior-servant to one of the other generals and had been wounded trying to save his master. He was loyal, and perhaps he went after me because he felt he had failed his general and his king.

"In any case, we became friends and in later days more than friends. We never spoke of the night we had met, though. It lay across both our thoughts like the scars of a bad burn . . ."

She paused then as if in a moment she might say more, but some time passed and she remained silent.

"So why do you tell me this tale?" Kayyin asked at last. "Am I supposed to take some instruction from my ancestor's loyalty?"

She looked up slowly, as though she had forgotten he was there. "No, no. You asked me why I do not destroy the mortals when I have told all the world I will. My beloved servant Gyir has died and the Pact of the Glass has come to nothing, as I feared it would. And so I will take down the mortals' castle, stone by stone if I have to, to get what I need. But that does not mean I will rush in, despite your impatience . . . and even despite mine."

He tipped his head, waiting to hear.

"Because the thing that dreams and suffers in uneasy sleep beneath that castle is a *god*, you foolish child. He is also my father, but that is of importance only to me." Yasammez's face was as pale and dreadful as a sky awaiting a thunderstorm. "Did you not understand anything of the story I told you? The gods are not like us—they are as far beyond us as we are beyond ladybugs clustering on a leaf. Only a fool rushes to disturb something that he cannot understand and cannot control. Do you understand me now? This will be our people's dying song. I wish to make sure that however it ends, we at least sing the tune we choose."

Kayyin bowed his head. After a moment, Yasammez did the same. A stranger wandering into that place might have guessed they were two mortals at prayer.

🍂

"Is that really what you're going to wear to meet the prince, Highness?" Feival asked disapprovingly. He was enjoying his new role greatly—*too* greatly, Briony thought: he was as much of a nag about her appearance as Auntie Merolanna or Rose and Moina had ever been.

"You must be teasing, Highness!" said her friend Ivgenia. "Why didn't you tell me? Is he truly coming here—Prince Eneas?"

Briony couldn't help smiling at the girl's reaction. Eneas was only a king's son, no different than Briony's own brothers—although, it had to be said, prince of a much bigger and more important court and country. Every woman in Broadhall seemed determined to treat him like a god. "Yes, he's coming." She turned to her other ladies. "And don't gawk at him when he arrives, you lot. Get on with your sewing." As soon as she said it, Briony wished she hadn't. It was the first time in the days since little Talia's terrible death that any of them had seemed interested in anything. "Or at least *look* as though you're sewing, please. Otherwise you'll frighten him off." She had an inkling that Eneas, like her brother Barrick, did not like being fawned over, although probably for quite different reasons.

When the prince appeared it was with an admirable lack of ostentation, without bodyguard or escort and dressed in what, for the court at Tessis, was very informal clothing, a plain although clean and well-made jerkin and doublet, the full, baggy knee-breeches that were now the style here, a traveling cloak stained from actual travel, and a wide flat cap that also looked as though it had spent too much time in the elements. Briony could tell that Feival was impressed by the prince's good looks, but disapproved of his ordinary attire.

"He must have closets the size of Oscastle," the young player whispered to her, "and yet he clearly never goes into them."

Eneas must be the only person in this whole court who isn't in love with his mirror, Briony thought. The combination gave him a serious, pleasing air as far as she was concerned: he was a man who put on clean and handsome clothes to visit a lady, but also had things to do, and so wore his workaday cloak and cap.

"Princess Briony," Eneas said, bowing. "Like everyone else, I was horrified to hear what happened to you here in the very heart of my father's kingdom."

"By sheer luck, nothing happened to me, Prince Eneas," she said gently. "However, poor Talia, my maid, had luck of a much different kind."

Charmingly, he blushed. "Of course," he said. "Forgive me. I can only guess at the sorrow her family will feel when they learn this news. It was a dreadful day for all of us."

Briony nodded. He took off his cap, revealing hair dark as dried cloves; it looked as though it had received some attention but no great trouble from a hairbrush. She gestured to the cushioned seat. "Please, sit down, your Highness. You know Lady Ivgenia e'Doursos, of course—Viscount Teryon's daughter."

The prince nodded to the girl, his face solemn. "Of course," he said, although Briony doubted he did remember her, even as pretty as Ivgenia was: Prince Eneas was famous for spending as little time at court as he could manage, which made his presence here today doubly interesting and more than a little flattering.

"How are you, Princess—in truth?" he asked when they were seated. "I cannot tell you the pang I felt when I heard of this terrible murder. That someone should feel he could do this, in our own house . . . !"

Briony had already decided that Broadhall Palace was not a great deal less dangerous than a nest of serpents, but she found it hard to doubt Eneas' sincerity. What had Finn said about him, back when they had first come to Syan, so long ago? *"He waits patiently. They say he is a good man, too, pious and brave. Of course, they say that about every prince, even those who prove to be monsters . . ."* To her sorrow, Briony felt she had met enough monsters now to judge, and she doubted this man would ever become one. He was rather charming, really, and certainly having him here in her chambers would make her the envy of almost every other woman in Broadhall, young or old.

"I am as well as can be expected," she said. "An enemy holds my throne. He tried to murder me, which is why I had to flee. He *did* murder my older brother Kendrick." She didn't know that for certain, of course, and Shaso had seemed to doubt it, but at the moment she was not testifying in the god-judged sanctity of the temple, but instead making a case to a potential ally. "And now he reaches out and tries to murder me here—or so I suspect."

"No." Eneas said it in shock and disgust, not negation. "Truly? You think the Tollys would commit such a foolish act here, under the king's very nose?"

The king's nose seems to be elsewhere just now, Briony thought but did not say. Living with the bawdy band of Makewell's Men had not made her more sweetly princesslike, but she had become much more practiced at dissembling. "I can only say that I was living here safely for some time, but within a day after Hendon Tolly's envoy arrived someone tried to murder me."

Eneas curled his big-boned hands into fists. He stood and began to pace. With his back to them, the sewing ladies could now gawk in earnest, and they did. "First of all, you will take all your meals from this moment from the king's table, Princess," he said. "That way you will receive the benefits of my father's own tasters. One of my own servants will bring your food to you when you do not join the others, to make sure that all remains safe." He paused for a moment, thinking. "Also, if it does not offend you, I will leave some men of mine to watch over your chambers. I must go away again and cannot properly look after your safety, but my guard captain will make certain you are safe both here and when you leave your chambers. Lastly, I will tell Erasmias Jino—a good man whom I trust—to keep an eye on your well-being at all times, and especially when I am absent from the court."

She wasn't sure she liked the sound of that (the sharp-eyed Lord Jino made her more than a little uneasy) but Briony knew better than to argue with this powerful, kind young man when he was trying to help her. She couldn't avoid a pang of sadness, though: the mention of a guard captain reminded her of Ferras Vansen—who, according to every source she had found, had disappeared with her brother Barrick after the disastrous battle at Kolkan's Field. In fact, she felt obscurely ashamed just now, as if she was letting this handsome prince make love to her instead of simply allowing him to help protect her—and as if she owed something to Vansen anyway, which she didn't. The very idea was foolish.

Still, the ache did not quickly leave her, and she fell silent for such a long while that Eneas began to look troubled.

Ivgenia, trying to rescue the moment, spoke up. "Where do you go this time, Prince Eneas, if I may ask? All the court misses you when you are away."

He grimaced, but Briony thought it was not directed at Ivgenia so much as the idea of people talking about him. "I must go south again. The Margrave of Akyon is besieged by Xixians in the south and I go with my Temple Dogs and the rest of the army we are sending to break the siege."

"And then will you relieve Hierosol itself, your Royal Highness?" Ivgenia asked.

He shook his head. "I fear Hierosol is lost, my lady. They say that only the innermost walls still stand—that even Ludis Drakava has fled."

"What?" Briony almost fell off her chair. "I had not heard this. Is there any news of my father, King Olin?"

"I am sorry, Princess, I have heard nothing. I cannot think that even a barbarian like the Xixian autarch will harm him, but I don't believe the Hierosol-folk would leave him to Sulepis anyway. Remember, they have not surrendered their city yet, and may hold out for a long time. Some nobleman will have taken Drakava's place, I think. Still, I wish I could give you better news."

Briony's eyes felt hot and full. Ordinarily she would have fought back the tears, but this was no ordinary time. "Oh, gods preserve my poor, dear father! I miss him so much!"

Feival leaned in with a kerchief. "You will run your powder like new paint in the rain, Highness," he told her.

Eneas looked uncomfortable. "I am sorry, Lady. Please, do not put too much stock in anything I say about your father or Hiersosol. The country is at war and little can be known for sure. It could be that Ludis, wanting a valuable bargaining piece like your father, has taken him with him in his escape."

Briony sniffed and let out a small, pained laugh. "I hardly think the idea of a desperate Ludis Drakava dragging my father across a battlefield is well made to cheer me up, Prince Eneas."

Now he looked even more discomforted. "Oh, by the gods' honor—truly, Briony, I mean Princess, I am sorry I even spoke . . ."

She didn't want to dangle him on the hook forever. "Please, Prince Eneas, don't worry yourself. You meant only kindness, and I have been deceived for so long by so many I thought friends that I can only thank you for telling me the truth. Now, please, do not let us keep you. I know you have much to do. Thank you for everything."

When a slightly confused Eneas had gone out, Briony daubed her eyes, waving away both Ivgenia's attempt to comfort her and Feival's attempts to repair her face. Pleading exhaustion and worry she sent them both away, though they were clearly dying to talk to her about Prince Eneas.

Briony was not suffering quite so much as she made it seem. She *was* miserable about her father, of course, and frightened, too, but that had been true for months—there was only so much terror she could feel, so much weakness and helplessness she could suffer. So she had made plans instead to do something about that helplessness, and now she had begun to put those plans into effect.

8
The Falcon and the Kite

"There are many reports of the fairies on the southern continent, or at least memories of them, from Xis all the way down to fabled Sirkot in the farthest stretch of the southern lands. It is also reported there are some forested islands in the Hesperian Ocean where the Qar still live, but this has not been proved."

—from "A Treatise on the Fairy Peoples of Eion and Xand"

PINIMMON VASH WIPED THE NIB of his pen carefully on the blotting paper and then drew the looping letter *bre*. He wiped the pen again before starting the next letter. It was more important to be accurate than swift.

The paramount minister of Xand was writing out his calendar.

Some of the other young nobles, scions of families at least as old as the house of Vash, had mocked him for spending so much of his youth on his letters. What red-blooded, true child of the desert would choose to sit cross-legged for hours, first sharpening pens and mixing ink and preparing parchment, then scribbling words on a page? Even if the words had been about something manly, like battle, it was nothing like actually fighting in one, and in fact the writing exercises in which young Pinimmon had been engaged often consisted only of copying household accounts.

Not that Vash had been unable to ride or shoot a bow. He had always been just good enough to escape the worst bullying, never finishing among the leaders at the feast-day games, but never finishing last, never embarrassing himself. Thus it was that his peers had ended with middling commissions in the military or been condemned to idleness on their family's estates while Vash had risen up beneath first one autarch then another, as scribe and accountant and bureaucrat, until he had reached the exalted position he held today, the second most powerful man in the world's most powerful empire.

In practice, though, that only meant that he was the secretary to the world's most dangerous madman.

Vash finished writing out his page and sighed. It was true these long days on shipboard had given him time to complete unfinished work, putting various political and economic affairs in order and answering his neglected correspondence, but even catching up with these tasks depressed Vash a bit: it felt as though he was preparing to die, readying his estate and selecting his bequests. He had been increasingly uncomfortable with his monarch for months now, but things had grown worse since the escape of the little temple girl whom Sulepis had bizarrely selected to be his hundred and seventh bride. Increasingly, the autarch seemed to be living in some realm that others like his paramount minister could only guess at but never enter—talking in disconnected sentences about odd subjects, often religious, and pursuing courses of action like this sea voyage north that Sulepis had not bothered to explain to anyone, but which would doubtless not have made sense even if he had.

Still, what was to be done? Many of the previous autarchs of Xis had been slightly mad, at least compared to ordinary folk. The generations of close breeding began to tell, not to mention that even the strongest and most sensible of men sometimes found it hard to deal with absolute power. A survivor of the reign of Vaspis the Dark had famously referred to living in that autarch's presence being as unnerving as sleeping beside a hungry lion. But Sulepis seemed different even from the most savage of his predecessors. He gave every sign of some serious intent, but nothing could make sense of his actions.

Vash clapped his hands and stood, letting his morning robe slide from his frail old body. His youthful servants scuttled forward to dress him, their handsome little faces serious, as if they were taking care of precious artifacts. In a sense, they were, because the paramount minister's power over them included the right to have them killed if they injured or displeased him. Not that he had ever killed anyone for displeasing him. He was not that type. A decade or so back he had even gone out of his way to choose boys with spirit, servants who would tease him or even occasionally pretend to defy him—knowing, mischievous, seductive boys. But as he passed four-score years Vash's patience had dimmed. He no longer wanted the once enjoyable, but now only strenuous exercise of bringing such servants into line. Now, he gave any new recruit only two or three whippings to reform. Then if they showed no signs of learning the silent obedience he had come to prefer he merely passed them to someone like Panhyssir or the autarch's current regent in Xis, Muziren Chah, someone who enjoyed breaking rebellious spirits and had no compunction about pain.

I have seen too much pain, Vash realized. *It has lost its power to amuse or even to shock me.* Now it just seemed like something to be avoided.

Vash pretended to meet Panhyssir by accident on the deck outside the autarch's huge cabin. The heavyset priest and an acolyte had apparently just opened the Nushash shrine.

"Good morning, old friend," Vash said. "Have you seen the Golden One today? Is he well?"

Panhyssir nodded, a movement that consisted largely of flattening the front of his several chins. In the greater informality of shipboard life he had stopped wearing his tall hat except during actual services; his head and wide face, now covered only by a simple coif, seemed curiously and obscenely naked. Panhyssir was, however, wearing a very impressive black robe. Instead of the autarch's falcon or the golden wheel of Nushash, though, it was embroidered with a flaming golden eye.

"What is that?" Vash asked. "I have not seen that mark before."

"Nothing," said Panhyssir airily. "A fancy of the Golden One's. He is sleeping in today with the little queens." These were his hundred-eleventh and hundred-twelfth wives, two young noble sisters, nieces to the king of Mihan sent to Sulepis as tribute. His interest in them, as opposed to the escaped temple girl, seemed of the ordinary sort. Ordinary for the autarch, in any case: the music of their shrieks had kept the ship's passengers from sleeping well the last several nights.

"Ah, good," Vash said. "May the gods send him health and vigor."

"Yes, health and vigor," repeated Panhyssir. Ready to move on, he gave Vash another little squish of his chins.

"Oh, I had just one question more, good Panhyssir. Do you have a moment? Could we speak somewhere out of the wind? These old bones of mine take the chill so, and I am not yet used to these northern waters."

The chief priest gave him a blank look but turned it into a smile. "Of course, old friend. Come to my cabin. My slave will make you some good, hot tea."

The priest's cabin was bigger than his, but did not have a window. After decades of doing the crucial social computations of court, Vash could not help considering what that meant, and was pleased to decide that it meant his own status had not dropped precipitously despite all the time Panhyssir had been spending with the autarch in the last half a year.

The high priest's cabin did have a chimney, which was good, since it meant he could have a small stove. An acolyte began making tea while Vash lowered himself onto a bench, consciously avoiding the usual game of trying to make a social near-equal sit first. He wanted the priest of Nushash in a good mood, after all: Vash was hoping for honesty, or something close to it.

"Now," said Panhyssir when the bowls of tea were in their hands, "what can I do for you, my dear old friend Vash?"

Vash smiled back, thinking of all the times he had toyed with bringing one of his kinsmen in from the country to put a knife in Panhyssir's eye. Court life made for both unexpected friends and enemies. Just now, he found himself thinking about the priest almost fondly. Panhyssir might be a self-serving dog, but he was one of the old crowd, and there were few enough left, especially after the carnage of Sulepis' rise to power. "It is the Golden One, of course," he said. "I worry night and day about how best to serve him."

Panhyssir nodded sagely. "As do we all, may the Lord of Fire protect him always. But how may I help?"

"With your wisdom," said Vash, and took a sip, deliberately slowing himself down. "And your trust. Because I would not want you to think I seek to pry into that which is unquestionably yours and yours alone."

"Go on."

"I mean of course your relationship with Golden One, and your counseling him in the ways of the gods. I do not wish to interfere in such an important stewardship, and of course I cannot even understand all the ways of the living god on earth, let alone the immortal gods in heaven."

Panhyssir was half-amused. "Granted, granted. To what end may I lend you my . . . wisdom?"

"I will be honest, old friend. That is how I show you my trust and good faith. We both know that there are many in our court who would seek to exploit any sign of weakness or doubt on the part of another minister—denounce him, perhaps, or simply seek to blackmail him."

"Terrible, these young ministers," said Panhyssir gravely. "They know nothing of loyalty or service."

"Just so. But I trust you, with your years of wise service, to recognize the difference between questioning the autarch's wisdom and a mere—and completely sensible—concern for his well-being."

Panhyssir was enjoying this. "You interest me, Vash. But then, in your zeal to serve, your thought always reaches far ahead of the rest of us."

Vash waved his hand, anxious to avoid a flattery contest, which in the Xixian court could last for hours. "I seek only the well-being of Xis and to do the will of the gods, especially mighty Nushash, who is king of all the heavens as the autarch is master of all the earth. But here we come to my question." He stopped and took another sip of tea, and for the first time felt the seriousness of what he was doing—the risk he truly was taking. "Where are we going, good Panhyssir? What does the autarch plan? Why do we take such a small force of soldiers so far beyond the reach of our mighty army into a strange northern land?"

Now that his doubt was spoken and could not be taken back, he swirled the tea in the bowl and watched the leaves eddy, the patterns as complex and beautiful as a poem rendered in fine script. For a moment Vash had a vision of a completely different life, one in which he had turned his back on power and wealth and had spent his time instead marking out in ink the delineations between earth and eternity, transcribing the words of the great poets and thinkers with no other goal than to make them as beautiful and evocative and true as they could possibly be.

But that Vash, disowned by his parents, would have starved by now, he thought, *so I would not be having this thought . . .* He realized his mind had wandered, even at this crucial moment, and marveled. *Truly, I am getting old.*

"Ah, yes, our journey north." The high priest frowned, not in anger or indignation, but like someone considering an interesting challenge. "What has the Golden One told you?"

Vash almost said "Nothing," but checked himself. That had the sound of exclusion to it. "Only this and that. But I fear I cannot understand him sometimes, his speech is so exalted and my thought is so humble. I thought perhaps you could explain it more fully to me."

Panhyssir smiled and nodded. *You self-satisfied toad,* thought Vash. *This is why you became a priest, isn't it? To be able to lord it over the rest of us, to say that you alone know the gods' wishes.*

"First of all," the chief priest said, "you must understand that the Golden One is a scholar as well as a ruler. He has located and read books of old lore whose names few learned men even know. I can honestly say that he has gone farther in the study of the gods and their ways than even I, the chief priest of the greatest god, have done."

Vash did not doubt that was true: Panhyssir was by no means a stupid man, but his enjoyment of power far exceeded his love of scholarship. "And all this . . . study? Somehow it draws us north, to some freezing, rain-swept, savage land—but why?"

"Because the Golden One has conceived a plan so audacious, so breathtaking, that even I can scarcely understand it." The priest patted his broad middle. "And there is only one place in all of Xand or Eion that it can be implemented—a castle in the tiny nation called the March Kingdom. The pagan king Olin's own country."

"But what plan, Panhyssir? What plan?"

"The Master of the Great Tent, our blessed autarch, is going to wake the gods themselves from their long sleep." The priest drained his tea and held out the bowl until the slave could come and take it from him. "And all it will cost is the northern king's life. A trivial price to pay to bring heaven to our corrupted earth, dear Paramount Minister Vash, don't you agree . . . ?"

Pinimmon Vash did not know what to think. As he slowly climbed the steps from the high priest's cabin to the upper deck, a wave of weariness rolled over him, heavy as the foaming sea itself. What could anyone do in the face of such folly, let alone one old man? Of course Panhyssir and his priests were perfectly satisfied with the autarch's madness—he jumped at their vaporous ideas like a cat chasing a piece of string. Was this the cause of the relentless expansion into Eion that had drained so many of Xis' assets and which left them with an army so large, hungry, and dangerous that it had to be kept constantly in the field to keep it from causing trouble at home? But if so, why then this sudden change of plan, first the costly attack on Hierosol and then this strange stab, like a conjuror's sleight-of-hand, into the far reaches of the northern continent?

Did the autarch and the priests truly believe the gods were waiting to be awakened at the northern king's castle? Or did they seek something less unlikely—some object of great power or great worth? But what could someone like Sulepis want that much? He was already the mightiest man in the world. Would he bankrupt Xis on such whims, throw every adult man into battle, perhaps destroy an entire generation, just to buy himself the imperial equivalent of a shinier sword or a grander house?

And my task—is it to aid this folly, or to try somehow to prevent it? But even if I decided to oppose the autarch, what could I do except die protesting? He is constantly guarded, even on this small ship, by tasters and servants and Leopard guards, and he is much younger and stronger than I am, even if I could by some chance get him alone. No, it was hopeless to think the paramount minister could do anything himself to harm the autarch, and any failed attempt would surely be punished by hideous torture before the inevitable execution. Vash thought of the fate of Jeddin, the autarch's former Leopard captain, and shuddered.

No, it would be senseless to rush into anything . . .

He found the foreign king enjoying the cool but bright sunshine on the foredeck, sitting on a bench with his hat off and the hood of his cloak thrown back. A dozen guards lined the rails on either side of him, and two more stood above him at the walkway around the opening to the gun deck. What was strange, though, was the northerner's apparent choice of companions: only a few steps from Olin Eddon sat the crippled scotarch Prusus, the curtain of his litter drawn back so he too could take the sun. The scotarch had been ill for the first days of the voyage, but even now that he was better he still looked on the verge of collapse, his head lolling and arms and legs twitching. Merely looking at Prusus irritated and frightened Vash. Choosing such a pathetic creature had been the first sign of the new autarch's alarming, incomprehensible ideas.

Vash turned back to the northern king. Whatever madness the Golden One had planned, it was clear it would mean Olin's death, so all conversation had to be undertaken with that in mind. It was like stroking an animal before sacrificing it—one did it only to calm the creature, because there was no value in developing a sentimental attachment.

Vash smiled. "Well, good day, King Olin. I trust you are enjoying the sun?"

"How can I not enjoy it when each time it goes down might be the last I see it?"

The paramount minister bowed his head in a good imitation of regret.

"Do not despair, your Highness. It could be that the Golden One will spare you. He is changeable, our great lord." Which he certainly was, but almost never to anyone's good.

Olin raised an eyebrow. "Ah, well, then. Why should I fear?" He turned back toward the horizon. He had gained color in these days aboard ship, his prisoner's pallor slowly turning brown. Even the faint reddish tones of his brown hair had begun to seem brighter and more fiery. Vash had to appreciate the irony. The closer he drew toward death, the more Olin Eddon began to look like a living man again.

"Is there anything you require?" Vash asked him.

"No. I am enjoying the wind on my skin, and for now that is enough. But you could answer a question for me." He gestured toward Prusus in his shelter. "I asked him, but the . . . scotarch, I believe you call him . . . is not much of a conversationalist."

"No, Highness, you are correct." *He is a pitiful freak who should have been put down at birth. Only a woman as rich as his mother could have got away with keeping him.* It was foolish to let it bother him, but having Prusus' watery, wandering eyes on him always made Vash fretful. "I will tell you what you wish to know, if I can."

"Very well. What *is* a scotarch? I gather that this fellow is, in some way, the autarch's heir."

"Yes, I can see how that might seem strange to you." Vash's legs were beginning to ache from standing so long. He moved to the opposite end of the bench from the northerner and sat down. "They say that it goes back to the old days of our people, when we lived in the desert and traveled in nomad clans. We would draw together once in a year around the *xawadis*, the place where the water never completely disappeared, a very holy spot, and we would choose a chieftain of all the clans—a Great Falcon. But we also chose a Kite, the high-flying vulture of the desert. This was usually an older clansman, responsible and wise and thought to be without ambition. He would go with the Falcon's clan and he would become Falcon if anything happened to the chief of the clans.

"Over the centuries, as we moved into the cities, the relationship became more subtle and more complex, and sometimes the Falcon and the Kite, now called Autarch and Scotarch, were almost at war with each other, each with his own adherents, clans, and armies. After the first Xixian empire collapsed, the surviving clan leaders came together in the place where the city of Xis now stands and made the Laws of Shakh Xis. The most important of these set out the roles of the autarch and scotarch. Or am I telling you things you already know, Highness?" he finished amiably.

"Oh, no, please continue."

"Good. So, the Laws of Shakh Xis set forth that the autarch shall always choose a scotarch, and that scotarch will never rule the Xixians unless the autarch dies, and then only until a council of the noble families can come together and approve the next autarch, who is almost always the heir of the autarch who just died."

"That doesn't seem too unusual," said Olin. "We have similar laws in some of the March Kingdoms."

"Ah, but it is when things are the other way around that the interesting part begins," explained Vash. He glanced quickly at Prusus, but the scotarch seemed to have fallen asleep; a thin line of drool connected his lower lip and his collar. "If the scotarch dies, the autarch also must step aside until the nobles can gather and decide whether he is fit to continue his rule. During that time, he no longer has the gods' protection. He may be deposed and executed by the nobles. It has happened more than a few times."

Olin raised an eyebrow. "If the scotarch dies, the autarch can be deposed? Why on earth would that be?"

Vash shrugged. "It was a way to make sure none of the jealous clans could grab at power. There is no point being a scotarch if you only seek power, because when the autarch dies, you rule only until a new autarch is chosen. And there is no point murdering an autarch, especially if you are an impatient heir, because the scotarch will step in and you may not rise to the throne."

"And each autarch chooses a new scotarch," said Olin, looking over to Prusus, who was snoring now but still quivered gently even in his sleep, hands waggling like poppies in a strong breeze. "But if the autarch is always at least temporarily deposed when his scotarch dies, would it not make sense to choose the youngest, healthiest scotarch you could find?"

"Of course, Highness," said Vash, nodding. "And in the past, autarchs have held great ceremonial games of wrestling and running and martial feats simply to find the healthiest, strongest candidates from among the noble families."

"But this autarch did not, obviously."

Vash shook his head. "The Golden One is unlike his predecessors in many ways, may his life be long." He lowered his voice a little so the guards couldn't hear him. "At the ceremony where Prusus received the

Kite Crown, his great majesty Sulepis said to us, 'Let any who doubt me watch whom the gods take first—this man Prusus, or my enemies.'" Vash sat up again. "So far many of the Golden One's enemies have left the earth, but Prusus still lives and breathes." He lifted himself off the bench, not without effort. He felt better now. Telling the story to the foreigner had clarified his earlier thoughts and worries. Surely it was the gods' duty to decide whether Sulepis was to be stopped, not Pinimmon Vash's. If heaven wanted the Golden One struck down or even just hindered, the gods had only to snap the slender reed that was the cripple Prusus' life. For the gods that should be no more difficult than swatting a fly.

"One more question, please," Olin said.

"Of course, Highness."

"If somebody—may the gods forbid—simply pushed Scotarch Prusus over the side, would the autarch then lose power?"

Vash nodded. "Others have had that thought. And it is possible."

"Possible? I thought it was the law of your country."

"Yes, but it is also well known that Sulepis is a law unto himself. Also, there is another reason no one has dared to try it, I suspect."

"And that is?"

"Whatever else happened, the murderer of a scotarch would be punished, and the punishment is a very cruel one—throwing a man's guts into a lion's cage while he is still alive and attached to them, if I remember correctly. Thus, no one ever murdered a scotarch even before Sulepis came to the throne."

"Thank you," said Olin. "You've given me much to think about, Minister Vash."

"I am pleased to have served you, Highness," he said, and bowed before turning back to his cabin. After an unexpectedly busy morning and the depressing company of a doomed man, Vash suddenly felt the need of a little food and sweet wine.

The man who never smiled stood in the doorway of the cabin. Pigeon, who in almost any other situation would have thrown himself in front of Qinnitan like a loyal dog, retreated behind her making little wordless noises of terror. Qinnitan did her best not to show that she felt much the same. "What do you want?" she demanded.

The unsmiling man glanced at her only briefly before letting his eyes roam around the small cabin, swelteringly hot despite the cool weather because its shutters had been nailed closed, foul with the smell of their unwashed bodies and the chamber pot, which was only emptied once a day.

"I am going into the town," he said at last. "Do not think to play any tricks while I am gone."

"What town?" That might at least give her some idea of where they were, how far they had sailed. She knew from the changes in the ship's motion and noises that they had dropped anchor and had been terrified for the past several hours that they had caught up with the autarch's ship. Perhaps something else was going on, though. She tried not to let hope get too strong a hold.

He didn't answer her question, but only took a last look around. "If I am not back by sunset, you will be given your meal by one of the crew. I have told them they may not kill you, girl, but if you play up or try any tricks they should feel free to torture the boy." He turned his pale, dead eyes on Pigeon. "That is why he is here. To make sure you do what you are told. Do you understand?"

Qinnitan swallowed. "Yes." He turned back to her. His eyes were as empty as those of the red and silver fish in the Seclusion's pools. "I would like to have a bath," she said. "To bathe myself. Surely even you don't plan to hand me over to the autarch stinking like this."

He turned away and stepped to the door. "Perhaps."

"Why won't you tell me your name?"

"Because the dead need no names," he said, letting the door fall shut behind him. She heard the latch fall heavily into place.

Somebody was talking to him in the passageway outside. It sounded like the captain—one of the autarch's best, from what Qinnitan had gathered from the few crewmen she'd been able to overhear. She had also gathered the captain wasn't happy taking orders from their kidnapper, whoever and whatever he was. She untangled herself from Pigeon and moved quietly to the door so she could put her ear against the crack.

" . . . But it cannot be helped," the captain was telling the nameless man. "Do not fear. We are a faster ship—we will catch the autarch's fleet within a few days."

"If it must be, it must be," their captor said at last after a long silence. A little emotion had crept into his voice—impatience, maybe even anger. "I will be back by nightfall. See that we are ready to cast off then."

Now it was the captain who could not keep the irritation from his voice. "A new rudder cannot always be fitted on the instant, even in a port town like Agamid. I can only do my best. The gods will always have their way."

"Not true," said their captor shortly. "If we fail to catch up to the autarch, even the gods will not be able to save you. That I promise you, Captain."

Qinnitan walked on her tiptoes back to the bed and climbed in next to Pigeon. The sheets were damp and the boy's skin was sweaty. Could he be catching some fever? She almost hoped so. It would be a good joke on the murderer who had stolen them if they both died of some workaday illness before he could deliver them to their fate.

"Sh," she whispered to the shivering child. "We will be well, my chick. All will be well . . ." But her mind was racing along like a cart rolling downhill. They were in Agamid the captain had said, and by the grace of the sacred bees of the Hive she recognized the name, a city on the southeastern coast of Eion, just north of Devonis. One of the girls in the Citadel's washroom had been from Agamid. Qinnitan turned her memory upside down now, but couldn't remember anything else the girl had said except that the port city had been claimed by both Devonis and Jael so long that the population spoke several languages. That did not help her. What she needed was a way to get off the ship while their enemy was away. If only she could think of a diversion . . .

"Do you trust me?" she asked the mute boy a few moments later. "Pigeon? Do you trust me?"

For a long moment he didn't seem to hear her, and she worried he might be too ill to do anything, let alone risk his life trying to escape. Then he opened his eyes and nodded his head.

"Good," she said. "Because I have an idea but it's a bit frightening. Promise you won't be too scared, whatever happens."

His thin hand came out from under the single threadbare blanket and he squeezed hers.

"Then listen. We only have one chance to make this work." And if it went wrong, one or both of them would die. She didn't say that, but Pigeon already knew it. They had been living on stolen time ever since the nameless man had dragged them up the gangway of the autarch's flagship.

Fever or fire, she thought. *Either way, I'll burn before I let the autarch touch me again.*

9

Death in the Outer Halls

"Goblins, especially the solitary larger sort, were still found in remote parts of Eion even after the second war with the fairies. A goblin was killed here in Kertewall in the March Kingdoms during King Ustin's reign, and its body was kept and shown to visitors, who all agreed it was no natural creature."

—from "A Treatise on the Fairy Peoples of Eion and Xand"

"I MUST CONFESS that I do not understand any of this, Chaven." Ferras Vansen shook his head. "Gods, demigods, monsters, miracles . . . and now mirrors! I thought witchcraft was a thing of poisons and steaming cauldrons."

The physician's smile looked a little forced. "We are not discussing witchcraft here, Captain, but *science*," he said. "The difference is one of learned men observing rules and sharing them with other learned men so that a body of knowledge is built up. That is why I need your help. Please tell me one more time."

"I have told you all I can remember, sir. I fell into the darkness in Greatdeeps. I fell for a long time. Then, it was as though I slept and dreamed. I can remember only snatches of that dreaming and I have told them to you. Then I walked out of darkness—and yes, I remember that part very firmly. I fell into the shadows, but I walked out on my feet. I found myself in the center of Funderling Town—although I did not realize it at first, of course, since I had never been there."

"But you were standing on the mirror, am I correct? The great mirror that reflects the statue of the god the Funderlings call the Lord of the Hot, Wet Stone—Kernios, as we Trigonates name him?"

Vansen was getting tired and couldn't understand why Chaven kept asking so many questions about the way he had returned to Midlan's Mount. Hadn't he explained it all that first day?

"I was standing on the mirror, yes. I didn't know the Funderlings had a different name for him, but it's clearly an image of Kernios. Now that I think of it, that's what that one-eyed monster Jikuyin planned in the first place—he wanted to open a door to the house of Kernios, whatever that might have meant. But I didn't think about it long because I quickly found I had other things to consider." He smiled a little. "A horde of Funderlings carrying all manner of sharp objects, for one thing. And if I remember correctly, *you* were the one leading them, Chaven, so there is nothing more I can tell you that you don't know already."

"It all makes a kind of sense," the physician said slowly, as if he had not heard the last bit at all. In fact, he had seemed to stop listening after Vansen mentioned the house of Kernios. "Perhaps there was another mirror within the darkness in the Greatdeeps mines where you fell," he mused. "Or something that acted the same way—we cannot even guess at all the knowledge the Qar still have, or that the gods once shared with them." Chaven began pacing back and forth across the refectory, one of the few places in the temple of the Metamorphic Brotherhood other than the sacred chapel itself that was big enough for the two men to stand upright and move freely. "And at the other end, a sacred place in Funderling Town—dedicated to the god under a different name, but dedicated nonetheless. As though a single house had a door that opened in Eion and another that gave onto sunny Xand!"

"Again, you've lost me, Doctor." Ferras Vansen could only spend so much time talking about such things, considering, pondering. He was a soldier, after all—his country was in danger and he ached to do something about it. "But please, do not waste your strength explaining. I am too simple for such things."

"You underestimate your own wit, Captain Vansen, as always." Chaven laughed. "The question is, have you convinced yourself? In any case, do not mind me. I have much to think about before I can make even the beginnings of sense out of this. The horrifying thing is that Brother Okros was one of the best men on just these matters, and I ache to share this with him and hear his thoughts even as a part of me wishes I could cut out his heart."

"I don't know him, I fear."

"Brother Okros? A traitor, a wicked traitor. I thought him a colleague and a friend, but it turns out he was in Hendon Tolly's employ all along." For a moment the physician seemed to be too full of emotion to speak. While he was wrestling with these feelings, the door opened and Cinnabar entered.

"Good day, gentlemen," he said, lifting his hand in salute.

Vansen had only spoken with him twice, but he liked the little man and understood why Chert spoke well of him. "It seems we must take your word for it, Magister Cinnabar—not that the day is good, but that it is day at all. I was a captive in the mines of the shadowlands before I came here—I haven't seen the sky for longer than I can remember." And he did ache to see the sun. He dreamed of it sometimes, in the way a person dreamed of a beloved relative who had died.

"That's because the people upground would be more interested in putting an arrow in you than letting you sniff the fresh air, Captain," said the Funderling leader cheerfully. "And that's hardly my fault, is it? Now, what I came here for was Chert Blue Quartz, but I see I've missed him."

"He's getting his family settled in upstairs," Vansen told him. "And Chaven and I have been talking about all kinds of things. I must confess, I had no idea of how much has been happening here in Funderling Town—hidden tunnels, Chert and Opal with their foundling son from behind the Shadowline, magical mirrors. To think I lived so long above such an exotic place without realizing it!"

"Mirrors again?" asked Cinnabar. "What is this talk of mirrors?"

Chaven spoke up. "Nothing. Mirrors are not important, Magister." Despite his earlier interest and all the questions that had quite worn Vansen out, Chaven now suddenly seemed to want to change the subject. "What matters is that we are very few here, trapped between the Qar outside the gates and the turncoat Hendon Tolly in the castle above us. And if they know about the Stormstone tunnels, as Chert suggested, the Qar may not remain outside the gates for long . . ."

Before the physician could finish what he was saying, the door opened and Chert Blue Quartz himself walked in, moving slowly as though he carried something heavy.

Which, in a way, he does, Vansen thought. Chert had been shoved to the forefront of many of their discussions, although he clearly did not like the responsibility. Still, he had impressed Vansen, who thought he saw a bit of his old master Donal Murroy in the Funderling, especially in the sour-sounding witticisms that did not do a very good job of concealing the little man's kind nature.

Cinnabar spread his arms. "Ah, here you are, Chert, my good fellow! Fresh from the table, no doubt. His wife is an excellent cook, did you all know?"

"With what those miserly monks give us Opal would be lucky if she could make stone soup," Chert said. "The Metamorphic Brothers regard enjoying one's food as a path to decadence." He rolled his eyes. "Nickel told me, 'Be grateful that you have crickets to roast. Our acolytes only get cricket mush once a week and consider it a feast."

Nickel himself came in a few moments later, frowning as usual. "I cannot get any work out of the brothers. They would rather gossip about Big Folk and fairies than see to the Elders' business."

"These are strange days," said Cinnabar. "Do not treat them too harshly, Brother Nickel."

The Quicksilver magistrate was the representative of the Guild's High-wardens, and it was the Guild, Cinnabar reminded him, who would decide whether Nickel would be promoted to abbot. Even Ferras Vansen couldn't help notice the quick change in the Funderling monk's demeanor.

"You are right, of course, Magister," Nickel hastily agreed. "Quite right."

Vansen caught sight of Chert Blue Quartz's expression of disgust and had to bite his lip to keep from laughing.

"So what you are saying is that it is *impossible* to defend Funderling Town?" Vansen asked.

"No, Captain," said Cinnabar. "But this is not a walled city like South-march above us. The closer in to Funderling Town, the more roads there are to defend. Dozens!"

"Then it's the temple itself we should be defending," said Chert suddenly.

"What nonsense is this, Blue Quartz?" Nickel didn't like Chert any more than Chert liked him, that seemed clear. "This is a holy place, not a battlefield!"

"A battlefield is where a battle happens, Brother Nickel," Cinnabar pointed out. "We are trying to prevent the Metamorphic Brothers' temple and Funderling Town from becoming battlefields. At least, that's what I think Chert is saying."

"More or less." The little man looked around as though he was suddenly uncomfortable with the attention. "But here we are. The ancient roads the fairy folk are mostly likely to use, the ones that cross beneath the bay from the mainland, pass the temple long before they reach the town. Not only that, those roads and the roads they connect with begin to fork just above us, so that by the outskirts of the town the original few passages have split into nearly a hundred more—far too many to defend."

"What about blocking them off?" Vansen asked. "You have stone and quite a lot of it, the gods know. In Greatdeeps I saw Jikuyin's slaves using gunflour . . ."

Cinnabar shook his head. "Blasting powder, we call it. Yes, we have that and stone, but it would take a year's worth of quarrying and ten times the men we have to block off all the approaches into Funderling Town. There are roads from the town that lead out to a half dozen different quarries, to freshwater pools, to a dozen outer neighborhoods, not to mention the natural caverns and tunnels we have not bothered to shape. We would have to seal every one of them." He sighed. "Chert is right. If the fairy folk make their way under the bay by the Stormstone roads, then we must stop them here, where we can reduce the number of entrances to a manageable few, or we will not stop them at all."

"You cannot mean to turn the temple into an army camp—!" Nickel began, but a loud knock on the door interrupted him as husky young Brother Antimony pushed his way in, face flushed. "Forgive me, masters, forgive me! It's just . . . some of the brothers . . . there's been . . . they've heard noises . . ."

Cinnabar raised an eyebrow. "What in the name of deadly rockfall are you talking about, lad? Noises? What noises? Where? And why shouldn't they hear noises?"

Antimony did his best to collect his thoughts. "At the Boreholes in the Outer Halls, Magister—a group of cavern cells connected by tunnels out beyond the farthest temple gardens. Several of the acolytes heard voices coming up from the depths and they sent someone to tell us."

"Why didn't they come to me first?" demanded Nickel.

Cinnabar waved his hand to quiet the older monk. "I am not certain I understand the concern, Brother Antimony. They fast, do they not, these acolytes? It is common to hear and see things when the stomach is empty for a long time."

Antimony bowed his head, but stubbornly went on. "They do, Magister. They fast, and they hear and see things. But several of them heard the same thing, voices whispering like the wind, and the voices were not speaking a tongue the acolytes could recognize."

Chert leaned forward. "Antimony, do these tunnels touch at any point on the Stormstone Passages?"

Antimony nodded. "Beyond the Boreholes, yes, of course, Master Blue Quartz. There is Blacklamp Row running below it, and beyond that the Stormstone roads begin."

"So if the fairies—the Qar—decided to make their way down from the mainland as we discussed, that is one of the ways they might come," Vansen said.

"And we have not even begun to secure the roads around the temple," said Cinnabar grimly. "Collapses and slides! How can we defend all our tunnels if the Twilight folk already mean to invade? The ways are too many! We might not do it with all of the upgrounders and all their horses and cannons."

"Nevertheless, someone must go to see these Boreholes, as you called them. Take heart—perhaps it *is* only the imagination of hungry monks. But we must go quickly, in case it is not."

"We Funderlings have no army, Captain Vansen," Cinnabar reminded him.

"You must have some who can fight." Vansen looked around. "Who were those who came at me when I first arrived? Most had only shovels and picks, but a few were young and fit and carried what looked like real weapons."

"The Warders of the Guild," said Cinnabar. "They are like sentries—no, they are more like reeves. They help to guard the guildhall and other important places and things. But it has been long since they have dealt with anything worse than ordinary crimes like theft and public drunkenness, or putting down the occasional public riot."

"It matters not." Vansen's heart was beating fast. Here was something he could *do,* a way he could truly help instead of merely answering Chaven's endless mirror questions. "They must have some training and they will at least have weapons. Send me a troop of these warders, as many as you can spare, and with the Guild's permission I will take them down to see who is whispering and spying out there."

"It will take hours to get a messenger to the Guild and back," Cinnabar said unhappily.

"Perhaps monks could accompany Captain Vansen," Chert suggested.

"They could not!" Nickel said, scowling. "They have taken sacred orders to serve only the Elders!"

"Truly? Would the Elders prefer to have the Qar living in the temple and frolicking in the Mysteries?" Chert asked him.

"Enough," declared Magister Cinnabar. "There are a half-dozen warders here who came with me as an honor guard for the Astion." The Astion was like the Eddon family royal seal, Vansen had learned, a disk of stone that showed the bearer was doing the Guild's official business. "They can go with Captain Vansen while messengers take a letter from me back to Funderling Town and tell the Guild of our fears and our need of more men."

"That sounds like a wise plan, Magister," Vansen said, nodding. "Can the monk who brought the news lead us back there?"

"He has run all day," Antimony told him. "He collapsed after he gave us the news. He is in the infirmary."

"We'll think of something else, then. Chert, can you help me to prepare for this? I know so little about your people and this place."

Chert gave an unhappy shrug. "Of course. Brother Antimony, would you find my wife and tell her I may not be back for the evening meal?" He watched the young monk go out. "Better him than me," Chert told Vansen quietly. "The old girl won't like it a bit."

Cinnbar presented the newcomer with the distracted air of a man walking a dangerous dog on a very short leash. "This is Sledge Jasper," he explained to Vansen. "He is the wardthane of the men you are taking. He wanted to meet you."

The newcomer was not much taller than Cinnabar, which meant he barely reached Ferras Vansen's waist, but he bulged with muscle so that he was nearly as wide as he was tall. His arms were long and his hands were as big or bigger than Vansen's own. Everthing about him seemed aggressive—his shaved head was round as a cannonball, and he had beetling eyebrows and a fierce bristle of whiskers on his chin.

The intimidating little fellow stared up at Vansen for a long moment. "Have you commanded men?"

"I have. I was . . . I still am captain of the Southmarch royal guard."

"In battle?"

"Yes. Most recently at Kolkan's Field, but not all my commands ended as disastrously as that, praise the gods." Vansen was amused by such harsh scrutiny, but he had waited a long time for Cinnabar to return and he was growing impatient. "And your warders—will they do what they're told?"

"If I'm there," Sledge said, still peering fiercely into Vansen's eyes. "They'll dig granite with their fingers if I tell 'em to. That's why I'm going along. The question is, who's in charge—me or you?"

Vansen wasn't going to be drawn into a pissing contest with this brusque little hobgoblin. "That's up to the magister."

"Captain Vansen is the leader, Sledge," Cinnabar told the wardthane. "And you knew that already."

Vansen suppressed a smile: he had suspected as much. "However, I do welcome your help, Wardthane Jasper. We'll be careful of your men's safety. We're only going to investigate some noises—I'm not expecting a fight."

Sledge snorted, crossing his thickly muscled arms across his barrel chest. "'Course you are—if you weren't, you'd be taking a troop of these temple fungus farmers with scrapers and baskets. The magister wants my warders, which means there's a good chance someone's going to get their faces pushed in."

"We'll see." He turned to Cinnabar. "I'll need a weapon, since I came here without one. Where are the rest of the men?"

"Waiting outside," the magister said. "We'll find you something by way of a fairy-sticker, then you can leave as soon as you want."

"Let me go and tell Opal goodbye, will you?" said Chert, rising.

"Why?" Vansen asked. "You're not going."

"But you wanted me to tell you . . ."

"I wanted you to answer my questions and you have. But as far as a guide for the tunnels, I've got permission to take Brother Antimony, a young fellow with an excellent knowledge of the place and no family of his own . . . unlike you. So shut your mouth, Master Blue Quartz, and for tonight at least, go back to your wife and boy."

Chert looked at him gratefully, struggling for words. Vansen did not linger long enough to let it become an embarrassment. Jasper's warders were waiting to meet him, men he would lead into danger and perhaps, for some of them, even to death. At this moment, the fact that they were half Ferras Vansen's size meant absolutely nothing.

It was as strange as anything in Greatdeeps, Vansen thought—no, stranger. To think that sights like these had been beneath his feet all the years he had been in Southmarch! The Cascade Stair was huge, a vertical tunnel in the shape of a great downward spiral, as though the stone had hardened around a whirlpool that had subsequently drained away. The bobbing coral-lights of the men winding down it in front of him looked like little stars bouncing in a thundercloud.

We have our own Shadowline right here, he thought. *But instead of two different lands side-by-side, it is two lands with one beneath the other, our Southmarch above and all this below.*

"Watch your step, Cap'n," growled Jasper. "Not so bad if you lose your footing here, but a little farther down you'd be falling for a long time. Better get used to looking where you're walking."

"Right." Vansen paused for a moment, propping the weapon Cinnabar had found him against the wall, a "warding ax" as the magister had named it, a one-handed battle ax with a knobby hammer on the poll, the opposite side from the blade. He reached up to straighten the piece of coral bound to his forehead in its little lantern, then picked up the ax again. The sickly, greenish yellow light was not very revealing— Funderlings saw much better in these dark places than he did. He wished he had a good old-fashioned flaming torch, but when he had mentioned it the Funderling wardthane had looked at him with disgust.

"Oh, they'd smell and hear *that* coming from a long way away, wouldn't they? Not to mention how fast it would eat up the air in some of the tight spots. No, Cap'n, you just leave the thinking to old Sledge."

But the Funderlings have fires, don't they? They have fires for cooking and for warmth—I've seen them! And what about their forges? Of course, from what Chaven had told him, they also had very elaborate systems to draw the smoke up out of Funderling Town, with lazily spinning fans like waterwheels that pulled the foul air upward and then puffed it out into the air over the stony hill on which Southmarch had been built.

Chimneys up where we live, was his bemused thought. *Roads that travel under the bay to the mainland, and others that tunnel down far beneath the water, if Chert Blue Quartz told me the truth. These Funderlings own more of this rock than we do!*

Near the bottom of the Cascade Stair, with the stone walls looming so far above them now that their little lights could not reach the top, Vansen and the others trooped through into a large open space full of pale stone columns that were wider at the top and bottom than at their middles. After walking for some time, they paused at last in front of a wall pierced by several stone tunnel mouths.

"They call this place Five Arches," Jasper whispered.

Brother Antimony prayed for a little while in a language Vansen didn't understand, words full of harsh *kah* and *zzz* sounds, as the dozen warders dipped their heads reverently.

"Beyond this," the acolyte said to Vansen when he had finished, "lies the Outer Halls. We go now from That Which was Built to That Which Grew."

This made no sense to Ferras Vansen, but he was getting used to that. "Are we far from the place . . . what was it called . . . where your monks are?"

"The Boreholes? We are not far now," Antimony told him.

"Close enough that we should keep our mouths shut," said Jasper, and reached out a long hairy arm to smack one of his warders sharply on the back of the head, silencing him midmurmur. "*All* of us," Jasper added sharply.

The young man who had been disciplined shot the wardthane a sulky look. For all Sledge Jasper's ferocity, Vansen was worried that the rest of the warders might not be up to the task if there proved anything to it.

"Just around this bend," Antimony whispered. "Let me go first and find someone who can talk to us. We should not disturb them more than we have to—they are on their Elder Walks, after all. That is what we call this time of retreat and prayer."

"You'll not go alone—you, Pig Iron," Jasper said to the warder he had chastised earlier. "Go with him. Keep him out of trouble and bring him back safe."

The one named Pig Iron looked pleased to have been given a suitably manly task: he puffed himself up inside his heavy cloak and lowered his short Funderling halberd, which was more like a spike-headed spear than like a proper halberd. Pig Iron had no helmet, no armor; but for the weapon, he might have been another monk.

How can we hope to fight anyone? Vansen wondered. *Our army is knee-high and dressed in wool.*

The pair trotted down the winding passage and were quickly gone from sight. Vansen, whose back was sore because he had been forced in so many places to walk almost doubled over, had what seemed scarcely more than a few breaths to rest before the two came clattering back.

"Dead!" Antimony's eyes were so big they looked like they might never fully close again. "All of them, in their cells!"

"How?" demanded Jasper before Vansen had a chance to speak.

"Couldn't tell," said Pig Iron excitedly, "But one of them was Little Pewter. I know him—he's no more than thirteen years old!"

"But what killed them?" Sledge Jasper demanded. "Was there blood?"

Ferras Vansen was a stranger and Jasper was their familiar leader: Vansen could understand why they might want to stick to that which was familiar, but confusion now might cost lives later. "Let me ask the questions, Wardthane," he said, softly but firmly. "Brother Antimony, what did you see? Just what you saw, not what you think might have happened. And let's keep it quiet."

Antimony took a deep breath. "The cells are side by side, only a few paces apart, and open to the outside. They are all still in the cells, slumped over like they died sitting up. Four of them—no, five. There were five, and the other cells were empty." He paused for a moment—Vansen could see him calming himself, collecting his thoughts. "The other cells, as far as we went, were empty. Perhaps a dozen. We turned back then."

"Was there any sign of what killed them? Were they cold?"

Antimony looked surprised. "No blood, but they were all dead. Their eyes were open, some of them! We did not touch them. We did not know who might still be out there, watching us . . ."

Vansen scowled. "It sounds very strange. If they all died like that, in their cells, they were not fighting back. They must have been surprised. But no blood? Very strange." To get a better grip on his warding ax he wiped his hands on his breeches. Chert's wife Opal had spent two days combining articles of Funderling clothing to make him a proper pair. "Let's go. Pig Iron, you lead for now, but when we get there I will go first." He turned to the others, who looked more than a little worried—

all except for Sledge Jasper, who was grinning in a bloodthirsty sort of way. "We will go silently from now on. If you need to speak, *truly* need to, then for the gods' sake, speak softly. If these are the Twilight folk, they are quieter, cleverer, and crueler than you can guess, and they can hear a whisper from a hundred paces." Even as he said it he felt a momentary pang of shame. Had not Gyir been his friend, of a sort? But he had lost too many of his men at Kolkan's Field and elsewhere to think of the rest of the Qar as anything but deadly enemies. "Do you understand me? Good. Jasper, you come behind me. Show your fellows how a man walks into danger."

Ferras Vansen wanted no part of losing untrained men (or at least men who were not soldiers) while trapped behind them, unable to help, so he was determined to lead the way as soon as he could. But there was a risk to that as well: if he got caught in a tight enough spot, they might not be able to help him even if they wanted to.

Like Murroy used to say, he thought, *if you can't be a soldier, hurry up and die so you can be a shield for someone else.* If Vansen got wedged in a tight spot it might give the others a chance to retreat and take word back to Funderling Town.

Still, it would have been nice to have a proper soldier's shield. Especially in the tight places, especially with all this darkness around them. Their quiet footsteps were beginning to sound like drumbeats to him. Surely the Qar had heard them coming long ago.

Vansen and his little troop stepped out of the narrow defile at last, into the open space of what Antimony had called the Boreholes, an underground chamber like a mountain valley, its sides scored with vertical creases that sloped upward into the darkness beyond the coral light. The great folds of stone between the creases were perforated with holes, some natural, some clearly chiseled out or at least enlarged by intelligent hands. Vansen could not see much in the thin, greenish light, but what he could see reminded him of the rockier heights of Settland where the old Trigonate mystics had hidden themselves away from the lures of daily life. But surely even the *oniri* would have found living in these heavy, lightless depths too hard to bear. Vansen had never thought you could miss the sky like a starving man missed food, but it was true. *Oh, gods in heaven,* he thought, *please let me live long enough to see the light of day again!*

Antimony pointed to the nearest fold of stone and its honeycomb of holes. For the first time, Vansen regretted the coral lamps. If they faced something that lived down here without light, or some of the many Twi-light folk who thrived in darkness, their own lamps, however dim, would make them into nothing but slow-moving targets.

Vansen stepped out in the lead now, skirting dark places in the floor that, as far as he knew, might be holes that would drop him into the center of the earth. As he drew nearer he saw that the closest cell was occupied, its inhabitant fallen halfway out, arms splayed and twisted. In the sickly light of the coral, the victim looked to be little more than a youth. Vansen moved forward and touched the Funderling acolyte's skin. It was warm, but he was otherwise limp as a rag, his eyes halfway open. He pressed his ear against the Funderling's chest, but could hear nothing. Dead, then, but for how long?

As Antimony had said, motionless forms filled several of the sparsely furnished cells on the bottom row, one of the bodies so small it made even Vansen's hardened heart ache in his breast. As Jasper and the other Funderlings crouched over Little Pewter, murmuring angrily, Vansen moved around the edge of the outcropping, wondering how many more cells might contain bodies, and how they had all died with no mark on them. Each dead man was in his own cell, which seemed to suggest that the catastrophe had struck them all at the same time, or else with extreme silence and swiftness.

The first cell in the next stony slope was empty, and Vansen was about to pass on to the next when his lamp showed him something he had not seen in the other cells—a hole at the back of the small space, leading deeper into the rock. He leaned closer. The floor of the cell, which in all the others he had seen so far had been kept scrupulously clean, was a mess of broken stone and dust. The hole in the back wall looked like something that had been done swiftly with a mallet and chisel. But why . . . ?

Vansen suddenly realized what he was seeing. He climbed out of the cell as quietly as he could manage and returned to where the others were waiting, most looking fearful now that their anger was spent.

"I think I've found the place they came through," he whispered. "Come this way."

Jasper was the first to follow him, with Antimony not too far behind, but the others hung back. Vansen felt a pang of renewed worry. These untrained Funderlings were not soldiers—they were nowhere near being reliable. He would have to remember that.

Sledge Jasper turned and glared at his warders, his face a grotesque mask in the light of their lamps. His men scrambled to their feet, but their reluctance still showed.

"It is a hole, dug through from the other side," said Antimony as he stared at the opening in the back of the empty cell.

"And not with Funderling tools, either," growled Jasper quietly. "Or Funderling knowledge. This is foul-looking work. See, the edges are ragged."

"The tunnels Chert spoke of—the Stormstone tunnels," Vansen said to Antimony. "Are we close to one?"

"I don't know. Let me think." Antimony stood up from examining the hole. "Yes, I think so, although we would never go through the Boreholes to reach it—there is a connecting passage much closer to the temple. But yes, it passes along behind this formation here."

"Then this may well have been done by the Qar," Vansen said. "Their invasion may already have begun. We must go through to the far side and see what is there," he told the warders. "We cannot report back to Cinnabar and the others without learning the truth. Follow me. Stay close together. And remember—silence!"

The low tunnel beyond the cell was an uneven path over scree and larger loose stones, sometimes through spaces so small Vansen was forced onto his knees and into the very real worry that he might become stuck. Once his coral lamp faltered, dimmed, and died, leaving him for some moments in near-total darkness until one of the Funderlings behind him passed forward a spare piece. At last the passage widened and he was able to climb to his feet; a few hundred stumbling paces later he stepped through another crude hole in the stone and, on the other side, could stand upright again.

As the Funderlings moved up beside him into the much wider space, the light of their combined lamps reached out and illuminated a passage half a dozen paces wide, a monument to careful workmanship and masterful craft whose ceiling, floor, and walls (except for the hole through which they had just come and the pile of debris beside it) were all finished with smoothly sanded stone.

"A Stormstone road," said Antimony with something like reverence. "I have never seen this one, so far even from the temple."

"The Guild is going to have to start keeping a better watch on them, as of this moment," said Vansen. "Someone has definitely broken through from here into the Boreholes. We must get back to Cinnabar and the others with this news."

He turned and led them back into the new tunnel, which seemed even more of a brutal, animalistic shambles now that he had seen good Funderling work. They had only gone back a little ways when a glimmer of light caught his attention. For an instant he thought that one of the other Funderlings had somehow got in front of him, but the part of the tunnel in which he stood was scarcely broader than his shoulders.

An instant later, the thing coming the opposite direction stood upright, blocking out the light behind it, and Vansen took a staggering step backward. It was manlike, but only just, bigger than he was and covered with leathery, scaly skin. Its eyes were sunk so deep under a shelflike brow so that they barely reflected the light of Vansen's lantern. He had only an instant to see that there was something in its brute face that was a little like the apelike servitors of Greatdeeps, then one of the massive fists, big as a sexton's shovel, swung toward his head. Vansen only just managed to get his ax up, but the sheer strength of the thing smashed the flat of his own weapon against his head so that he fell back, stunned, collapsing partway onto the Funderlings behind him as they shouted in terror and confusion.

"Aa-iyah Krjaazel!" someone screeched. "It can't be!"

"Deep ettin!" shouted Antimony. "Run, Captain, it's an ettin!"

But there was nowhere to run. The thing in front of him grunted, a deep sound Vansen could feel in his chest. He lifted his ax once more but as he did so a long, hollow stick appeared from behind the monstrous creature's shoulder, swaying like a serpent. A puff of smoke or dust came from the opening and suddenly Vansen could not breathe. He dropped his weapon and grasped his throat, trying to find the hands that strangled him, but there was nothing, only a growing red emptiness in his lungs. As he slid helplessly to the ground, Ferras Vansen felt his thoughts flicker out like a candle dropped down a well.

10
Sleepers

"There are several types of goblins according to Kaspar Dyelos. The smallest are called Myanmoi, or mouse-men, the middling are named Fetches, and then there are several which are as large as children and can live to be very old."

—from "A Treatise on the Fairy Peoples of Eion and Xand"

AT FIRST it was all Barrick could do to stay on his feet. The slope was uneven, vines and brambles grew in tangles between the trees, and every few steps a vast knob of pale, yellowish stone thrust out of the greenery like a broken bone to block his way. The silkins, however, did seem to be falling back: he could still see them in the trees behind him, white figures leaping from branch to branch like ghostly apes, but without the aggressive haste they had shown before.

The bird was right, he thought. *The silkins are just as afraid of this place as everyone else.*

Which probably did not mean anything good for Barrick himself, of course, except that he might get a chance to rest and think. The creatures would be waiting when he came back down and he still had no weapon to face them with but his broken spear. And where was Skurn? Had the bird finally deserted him once and for all?

The steep slope made his lungs and legs ache. When he no longer saw any of his pursuers he paused to rest, but could not stop thinking of their featureless, thread-wrapped faces and gummy black eyes and how they might be crawling silently through the trees to surround him, so after a short while he forced himself onto his feet and began to climb once more, searching for open ground and a better vantage point.

The slope became steeper. Barrick frequently had to use his hands on branches and outcroppings to pull himself up, which made his crippled arm ache even worse than his lungs, throbbing and burning until his eyes filled with tears. The hopelessness of his situation began to weigh him down. He was in a strange land—a deadly, unknown land full of demons and monstrous creatures—and all but alone. How long could he go on this way, without help, without food or weapons or even a map? Any bad fall would leave him helpless and waiting for death . . .

Barrick suddenly tripped and tumbled heavily onto his hands and knees—it hurt so badly he cried out. He sank forward onto his elbows, staring at the ground only a few inches away, eyes blurry with sweat and tears. There was something strange about that ground, he realized after a moment—something very strange indeed.

It had writing on it.

He straightened up. He was kneeling on a slab of the pale ochre stone. Symbols he did not recognize had been scratched deep into its surface, and although they had been polished almost to invisibility by wind and rain, it was unquestionably the work of some intelligent hand. Barrick hastily climbed to his feet. He looked up and saw that the crest of the hill was not as far away as it had seemed—perhaps less than an hour's climb even at his limping pace. He took a deep breath and looked around for any sign of the silkins—he saw nothing and heard only the wind sighing through the trees—then began to make his way upward once more. Even if he was going to die here on Cursed Hill, he thought, it would be nice to see a high place first. Maybe the gray skies would seem brighter up there—that would be something good. Barrick Eddon was sick at heart with mist and shadowy places.

As he struggled up the last heights he saw that some previous inhabitants or visitors had done more than simply carve symbols into the yellow stones: in some spots curves of outcropping rock had been used as makeshift roofs, with shelters built beneath them, although little was left of these but an occasional wall of loose stones gathered together and carefully stacked. As he neared the summit the yellowish outcroppings became more common, great knobs and curving stretches of stone to which the greenery clung like a rough blanket. The primitive structures also grew more complex, weathered lumps of the hill's smooth bedrock extended and connected by stacked boulders and even some crude wooden walls and roofs, but all empty and long since deserted, with no sign left of whoever had inhabited them except for the occasional antlike track of carved symbols across their surfaces.

Here in the evergreen highlands the mists were at least as thick and slippery as at the base of the hill, but the place was even quieter, missing even the very occasional bird noises he had heard below. Even though Barrick had not seen any sign of the silkins for what seemed an hour or more, the quiet oppressiveness of the place was beginning to unnerve him, making his plan to stay here seem utter nonsense. It was all he could do to continue climbing toward the highest ridge, only a short distance away now and nothing but pearl-gray twilit sky visible behind it.

He pulled himself up onto a prominence and saw that one last mound of stone, greenery, and muddy earth remained between him and the summit, and that the strangest dwelling of all had been built there, a dome of curving stone protruding at an odd angle from the trees and tangled shrubbery, with a huge oblong window gaping in the undergrowth near it. A stone path wound up the last stretch of hillside from the snag of creepers in which he stood, leading to a dark overhang just below the oblong window. The palisade of broken stones he had seen from so far away, the ones like broken teeth, jutted from the forested peak just above the odd dwelling.

Mist and fog hung over this strange place like one of the asphodel crowns children wore for the feast of Onir Zakkas. The vapors were not only thicker here than at the bottom of the hill, but also seemed a different color and consistency. Barrick stared for long moments before he realized that some of it was not mist at all, but smoke rising from between the trees along the very top of the crest.

Smoke. Chimneys. Someone lived in this godforsaken place. On top of Cursed Hill.

He turned, heart beating even faster now than in the midst of the arduous climb, but before he could take a step back down the slope a voice came to him from nowhere and everywhere, echoing softly in the skirl of wind along the hillside, but also inside his head.

"*Come,*" it whispered. "*We are waiting for you.*"

Barrick found he could no longer command his own limbs, at least not to take him farther away from the strange house on the summit, a house that awaited him like an abandoned well into which he might fall and drown.

"*Come. Come to us. We are waiting for you.*"

To his astonishment, he abruptly found himself a passive observer in his own flesh. His body turned and began to climb the promontory until his feet were on the stony path, then it walked on toward the stone dwelling like a cloud pushed by wind, Barrick watching helplessly from inside it. The oblong window and the shadowed overhang grew closer and closer. The last stretch of the hill's high peak loomed above him for a moment, then he passed beneath through the opening into darkness.

A moment later the dark gave way to a spreading, reddish light. Barrick recovered a little command of his own limbs, but only enough to pause for a moment, his heart hammering at triple speed, before the unwavering pull of what lay before him exerted itself again.

"*Come. We have waited a long time, child of men. We were beginning to fear we had misunderstood what was given to us.*"

The stony room rounded upward like a dome on the inside, a strange, pale, cavernous place five or six times Barrick's height, its uppermost point rife with incomprehensible carvings, scrawls, and swirls just visible through the black residue of smoke. The red light and the smoke both came from a small fire set in a ring of stones on a floor of rubble and dirt. Three hunched figures of about Barrick's own size sat behind it on a low platform of stone.

"*You are tired,*" the voice told him. Who was speaking? The shapes before him did not move. "*You may sit if that will ease you. We regret we have little to offer you in the way of food or drink, but our ways are not like yours.*"

"*We give him much,*" snapped another voice. It was almost identical to the first and equally bodiless, but with an edge to it that told him somehow it was a different speaker. "*We give him more than we have given any other.*"

"*Because that is the purpose to which we were called. And what we give to him will be no kindness,*" said the first voice.

Barrick wanted to run, wanted it badly, but he could still barely move. The raven had been right—he had been a fool to come here. He finally made his voice work. "Who . . . who are you?"

"*Us?*" the sharper, second voice said. "*There is no true name we could give ourselves that you would know or understand.*"

"*Tell him,*" spoke up a third, similar to the others but perhaps older and more frail. "*Tell him the truth. We are the Sleepers. We are the rejected, the unwanted. We are those who see and cannot help but see.*" The voice was like a ghost murmuring at the top of an empty tower. Barrick was shivering hard, but he could not make his limbs work to run away.

"*You are frightening the Sunlander child,*" the first voice said in mild reproach. "*He does not understand you.*"

"I am no child." Barrick did not want these creatures in his head. It was too much like the last moments before the great door of Kernios—the moments in which he had felt Gyir die. "Just let me go."

"*He does not understand us,*" said the weakest of the voices. "*All is lost, as I feared. The world has turned too far . . .*"

"*Be silent!*" said the harsher second voice. "*He is an outsider. He is a Sunlander. Blood means nothing beneath the Daystar.*"

"*But all blood is the same color under Silvergleam's light,*" said the first. "*Child, rest easy. We will not harm you.*"

"*You speak only for yourself,*" said the second voice. "*I could burn away his thoughts like dry grass. If he threatens me, I will.*"

"*Now it is you who should be silent, Hikat,*" said the first voice. "*Your anger is unneeded here.*"

"*We are scorned by all the world,*" said the one called Hikat. "*We nestle in the very bones of those who would destroy us as they hover at the edge of wakefulness. My anger is unneeded, Hau? It is you who are useless, with your impossible schemes and dreams.*"

"*When is the child coming?*" asked the trembling third voice. "*You spoke of a child?*"

"*The child has already come, Hoorooen,*" the first voice answered. "*He is here.*"

"*Ah.*" The weak voice let out something that felt like a sigh inside Barrick's head. "*I wondered . . .*"

"Why are you doing this to me?" Barrick tried again to turn and leave the domelike cavern but could not make his limbs do his bidding. "Are you all mad? I don't understand anything you're saying, not any of it. Who are you?"

"*We are brothers,*" began Hau, "*children of the . . .*"

"*Brothers?*" This was the one called Hikat. "*Fool! You are my mother—and he is your father.*"

"*I had a son, once . . .*" quavered Hoorooen.

The centermost of the three figures slowly stood. Its robes flapped open, and for a moment Barrick saw a glimpse of withered, sexless gray flesh. His heart stuttered and seemed to go cold in his chest; if he could have scrambled away from the firepit he would have. He had seen skin of that stony color on Jikuyin's cruel servant, Ueni'ssoh, but this creature seemed as dry and drawn as a mummified corpse.

"*But we are not that one, Barrick Eddon,*" said Hau as if the boy had spoken these thoughts aloud. "*We are not your enemies.*"

"How do you know my name?" It seemed more than impossible, here at the ends of the earth when he had almost forgotten it himself, and it terrified him. "Tell me, curse you—how do you know my name!"

"*He attacks us!*" Hikat cried. "*We must destroy him . . . !*"

"*Who is there?*" quailed Hoorooen.

"*Peace, brothers. He is only frightened. Sit, Barrick Eddon. Listen to all we have to say.*"

The thing that kept him from running now helped him to sit beside the fire. The rippling flames made the three figures seem to float before his eyes like something seen in the last moments of waking.

"*All of us were born long ago in the city called Sleep,*" Hau began. "*It is true that Hoorooen is the eldest, but that is all that can be said for certain. Even Hikat, the youngest, is so old now that we cannot remember when he came into the world.*"

"*She,*" said Hikat, but for the first time some of the edge of anger was gone and the voice sounded almost wistful. "*For some reason I feel I was a woman.*"

"*It matters not,*" said Hau kindly. "*We are old. We share blood. We were born to the people called the Dreamless, in the city called Sleep, but they cast us out . . .*"

Barrick felt a stirring of fear again. "The Dreamless!"

"*Hold until you hear all our story. Not all who walk beneath the darklights of Sleep are as cruel as the one you met, but we are different from all of them. We are the Sleepers.*"

"*They sent us away,*" said Hoorooen. "*I am the only one who remembers. We slept, and that frightened them. We dreamed . . .*"

"*Yes,*" said Hau. "*Among the Dreamless, we alone dreamed, and our dreams were no mere fancies but the true flickering of the fire in the void. In our dreams we saw that the gods would fall, and saw that the Dreamless would turn against their masters in Qul-na-Qar. We saw the coming of the mortals into the land. All this we saw and foretold, but our own people did not heed us. They feared us. They drove us out."*

"I have never seen the darklights," said Hikat angrily. "My rightful home was stolen from me."

"You saw them," Hau declared. "You just do not remember. We have all lost so much, waited so long . . ."

"I . . . I don't understand," said Barrick. "You . . . you are Dreamless? But I thought the Dreamless never slept . . ."

"Let me show you." The middle figure threw back its hood. As with the gray man in Greatdeeps, skin as fine and thin as silk clung to his gaunt features, but Hau's skin was also scored with a stitchery of innumerable fine wrinkles, so that he looked as though he were made of cobwebs. The biggest difference, though, was that where Ueni'ssoh's eyes had been unblinking, silvery-blue orbs, the creature who stood before Barrick had only more wrinkles of flesh beneath his brows, his sockets as empty as desert sands.

"You're blind!"

"We do not see as others do," Hau corrected him. *"Had we been like our unsleeping brethren we would have been blind indeed. But in our dreams we see more than anyone."*

"I am tired of seeing so much," said Hoorooen sadly. *"It never makes anyone happy."*

"The truth makes no one happy," snapped Hikat. *"Because all truth ends in death and darkness."*

"Quiet, my loves." Hau lowered himself back to the ground, then reached out to his comrades. After hesitating a moment, they both took the offered hand, so that the Sleepers were joined. Hikat and Hoorooen then extended their own hands on either side of the small fire. Barrick stared at the trio across the flames, not understanding, or not wanting to understand.

"Take our hands," Hau said. *"You have come here for a reason."*

"I came here because I was lost—because those silkin things were trying to kill me . . ."

"You came here because you were born," said Hikat, impatient again. The extended hands still waited on either side for Barrick to take them. *"Perhaps it began even before that. But you are here and that proves you belong. Nobody comes to the Hill of Two Gods without a reason."*

"There is a page for you in the Book of the Fire in the Void, said Hau. *Let us read from it."*

"Wait! There is another soul reaching out for you," said Hoorooen. *"A twinned soul that seeks you."*

Briony. That finally decided Barrick—by the gods, how he had missed her! He moved a little closer to the fire so he could reach the two proffered gray hands. The room was not cold but the fire didn't seem to give off any heat, even when he leaned so close, and its flickering light revealed little more than where the deepest shadows lay. Despite a sudden terror far beyond what the situation seemed to offer, he let his hands close on the dry, slippery fingers of Hikat and Hoorooen. A moment later his eyes slid shut without his willing it, and suddenly he was falling—falling! Plunging downward helplessly into darkness, limbs flailing . . .

But where *were* his limbs? Why did he seem to be only a single heavy thought, falling into the void?

He fell. At last, something other than darkness glimmered in the depths below him. For a moment he thought it was some vast, circular sea; a moment later it seemed an ornamental pond of silvery water, with sides of pale stone. Then he saw it for what it was—the mirror he carried for Gyir, but grown to great size. He had only a moment to marvel at this inversion, at the idea that he could fall into something that was even now in his own pocket, and then he plunged through its cold surface and out the other side.

He stopped moving. The mirror, though, still remained, but now it hung before him against a field of utter black, like a picture in the Portrait Hall back in Southmarch, and he could see his own face in it.

No, not his face: the features of the person there had changed somehow without him noticing, sliding like quicksilver into new positions, shifting color like the towers of Southmarch as the morning sun appeared and climbed into the sky. The face that looked back at him was black-haired and dark-skinned, very young but also very worried and pinched with weariness. Despite it all he thought her beautiful. It was *her,* truly her—he had never seen her so clearly! The face in the mirror was that of the dark-haired girl who had long haunted his dreams.

"You," she said wonderingly—so she could see him, too. "I feared you were gone forever."

"Truly, I nearly was." He could see and understand her better than ever before but their conversation was still much like a dream, with some things not even spoken but still understood and some things incomprehensible even after they had been said. "Who are you? And why . . . why can I see you now?"

"Does it make you unhappy?" she asked with a touch of amusement. She was younger than he'd thought she would be, still with a hint of childhood in her face, but although her gaze was clever and kind, something in her eyes seemed veiled, the effect of wounds survived but not forgotten. She seemed to be standing only inches away, but at the same time she shimmered and almost vanished as his eye moved, like something seen through thick mist, like something seen in a dream.

It's all a dream. He was suddenly terrified he wouldn't remember this dear, now-familiar face when he was awake again.

Awake? But he could not even remember where he was, let alone whether he could be dreaming. If he was asleep, where did his body lie? How had he come here?

"Tell me your name, spirit-friend?" she asked him. "I should know it, but I don't! Are you *nafaz*—a ghost? You are so pale. Oh, I hope if you are a ghost, you died happily."

"I'm not dead. I'm . . . I'm certain I'm not!"

"Then that is even better." She smiled; her teeth gleamed against the darkness of her skin. "And look—all your hair is fiery like my witch streak! How odd dreams are!"

She was right—the streak in her hair was as red as his. It felt like something more than mere kinship. "I don't think I'm a dream, either. Are you asleep?"

She thought about it. "I don't know. I think so. And you?"

"I'm not sure." But as soon as his thoughts began to slide away from the mirror hanging in blackness he began to fear he would never be able to find it again. "Why can we see each other? Why *should* we?"

"I don't know." Her look turned serious. "But it must mean something. The gods do not give out such gifts for no reason."

That seemed like something he had just heard or thought himself. "What's your name?" But he knew it, didn't he? How could she feel so close, so real, so . . . important, but still be nameless?

She laughed and he could feel it like a cool breeze across overheated skin. "What's yours?"

"I can't remember."

"Nor can I. It's hard to remember names in dreams. You're . . . you're just *him* to me. That pale-skinned boy with red hair. And I'm . . . well, I'm *me*."

"The black-haired girl." But it made him sad. "I want to know your name. I need to know it. I need to know that you're real, that you live. I lost the only other person I care about . . ."

"Your sister," she said, her face suddenly sad; then: "How did I know that?"

"Perhaps I told you. But I don't want to lose you, too. What's your name?"

She stared at him, her lips parted, about to say something, but instead she remained silent for a long moment. The mirror seemed to shrink against the darkness, although he could still see her soft thick eyelashes, her long, narrow nose, even the tiny mole on her upper lip. He was afraid that if he waited in silence too long the mirror would shrink and fall away from him. He almost spoke, but understood suddenly that if she did not think of her name now, if she did not tell him, she never would. He had to trust her.

"I used to be a Hive Priestess," she said at last—slowly, like someone reading from an old, damaged book. "Then I went to live with the other grown women. There were so many women! All together, all scheming and plotting. But worst of all was that we all belonged to . . . to *him*. The terrible one. Then I ran away. Oh, gods save me, I do not want to go back to him!"

Again he ached to speak but he knew somehow he should not. She had to find it herself.

"And I will not go back. I will stay free. I will do what I want. I'll die before I let him use me, either as a toy or as a weapon." She paused. "Qinnitan. My name is Qinnitan."

And in that moment he found a sudden strength, something that rooted him despite all the darkness through which he had come, rooted him in his own blood and history and name. "And I am Barrick. Barrick Eddon."

"Then come to me, Barrick Eddon, or I will come to you," Qinnitan said. "Because I am so afraid to be alone . . . !"

And then the mirror did fall away, spinning into darkness like a silver coin dropped down a well, like a bright shell tumbled back into the ocean, a shooting star vanishing into the endless field of night . . .

"Qinnitan!" But he was alone now in emptiness. He tried to feel again the strength and certainty that had given him his name, the knowledge of his own living blood, rushing through his veins hot as molten metal . . .

My blood . . .

Then he could see it like a river, a red river, stretching away in two directions. One way vanished into an impenetrable, silvery mist. The other way snaked a course back into darkness, but a living darkness full of movement and suggestion. It almost felt as though he could reach out and trace it with a finger, like a line of paint on a map, a line that meant movement, a road, a track, something that would lead him to . . . to . . .

Silver flashed, then flashed again, dazzling him. He fell into the hot red river and for a moment was certain it would destroy him, that it would boil away all that he was, even the name he had just recovered.

Barrick, he told himself, and it was as though he stood on the bank and called it out to another part of himself that was drowning in the crimson current. *Barrick Eddon. I am Barrick Eddon. Barrick of the River of Blood . . .*

And suddenly another face was there, congealing out of the redness just as the face of the girl had come to him out of blackness. It was a man, half-ancient, half-young, with white streaming hair and a bandage wrapped around his eyes, a face dimly familiar, as if seen once on an old coin.

Come quickly, manchild, the blind man said. *Soon it will all be moving too fast to change the course. We are rushing toward darkness. We are hurrying toward the end of all things.*

Come soon or you must learn to love nothingness.

And then everything around Barrick fell away into a greater darkness and he was falling too, tumbling once more through the unending black void, empty of all feeling and thoughts, touched only by a harsh, moaning wind and the dying whisper of the blinded man:

. . . You must learn to love nothingness . . .

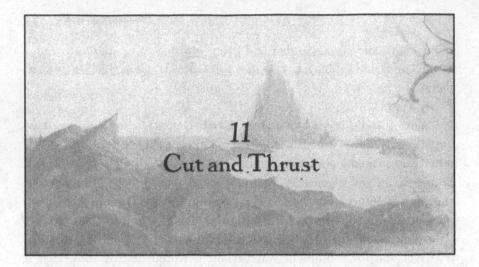

11

Cut and Thrust

"In ancient days Zmeos and his brother Khors stole Perin's daughter, Zoria. The war that followed changed the shape of the earth and even the length of days and nights. Almost all scholars agree that the fairies took the side of Zmeos, the Old Serpent. Because of this, the Trigonate Church still holds the Qar people 'cursed and excommunicate'."

—from "A Treatise on the Fairy Peoples of Eion and Xand"

"**P**RINCESS BRIONY," said Lady Ananka as the servitors cleared away the most recent course, "can you tell me how children are raised in the north?"

A few whispers and quiet anticipatory laughter ran the length of the royal table. Briony wished her friend was beside her, but Ivgenia had been assigned to one of the lesser tables at the other end of the hall and she might as well have been in another country.

"I'm sorry, Baroness, but I did not hear your question."

"How are children raised in the north?" the king's mistress asked. "Are they allowed to run wild there, as the Marchfolk allow their sheep and other animals to do?"

Briony smiled carefully. "Not all our animals run wild, Lady, but for those who live in areas where grass grows freely it only makes sense to take advantage of the bounty the gods provide."

"But it is the children I am interested in, dear," said Ananka with acid sweetness. "For instance, I was told that you were taught to fight with a sword and shield. Most exciting, I am sure, but to us it seems a little . . . uncivilized. I hope I do not offend."

Briony did her best to keep smiling, but it was growing harder. She had not expected the assault to begin quite so early in the evening—they had only finished the soup—but no one could stop this except the king, and Enander seemed much more interested in his wine and the conversation of an attractive woman on his other side.

It is like one of Shaso's knife exercises, Briony told herself. *Combined with playing one of Finn's invented parts. If I could do both of those, I can achieve this, too.* "How could you possibly offend, Lady?" Briony asked the king's mistress, letting no hint of irony into her words. "When you and His Majesty have so kindly given me a place here, as well as the priceless gift of your friendship?"

"Of course," said Ananka slowly, as if reassessing her strategy. Another flurry of whispers ran around the table. Those who had been deliberately ignoring Briony for social reasons were now regarding her openly, able at last to indulge their curiosity. "But I inquire because there is something else I wanted to ask. Something that I hoped you could . . . help me understand."

Whatever happens, do not be drawn into a battle, Briony told herself. *She has the high ground here and all the other advantages.* "Of course, Lady Ananka."

Ananka put a grave expression on her handsome, long-boned face. "Is it true that you challenged Hendon Tolly to a fight? A . . . swordfight?"

The whispers became something louder and more violent—laughs, gasps, expressions of disbelief and disgust. Women who had never done anything in their lives more strenuous than sewing stared at Briony as though she were some freakish example of the gods' displeasure—a two-headed ram or a legless cat. The looks on their faces ignited a flame of anger in Briony's gut, and for a moment it was all she could do not to stand up and sweep her crockery onto the floor.

Every night this woman tormented her. *Gods, I wish I had my sword now!*

"If you lose your temper, you will likely lose the fight." She heard Shaso's gruff voice as if he stood at her shoulder. *"The warrior who can keep his thoughts clear is always armed."* Briony took a breath. *"To play calm, you must remember calm."* That had been Nevin Hewney in one of his sober moments. *"Bring that feeling to your thoughts. Taste it like a piece of fruit."*

She thought of riding the wagon when they had first crossed into Syan, how the great expanse of the Esterian river valley had opened before her like the arms of a welcoming friend.

"I did challenge him, Lady," she said, her voice light. "I regret it now, of course. It was not seemly and it put a burden on my other guests." Nothing wrong with a small feint in return, though, was there? "No hostess should ever force her guests to participate in her own bad manners."

Another quiet chuckle ran around the table, but Briony fancied the laughter might have become a tiny bit more sympathetic.

"You put a sword to his throat, did you not?" asked Ananka sweetly, as though she too sought only to minimize an unfortunate moment.

"I did, my lady," she said. She was pleased to realize that much of her anger had passed through her like a storm. "I certainly did, and as I said, I am ashamed. But let us not forget, he is the man who usurped my family's throne. Imagine how you would feel if one of your loyal nobles," Briony turned with a smile, looking up and down the table, "turned out to be a traitor? Unbelievable, I know, but we trusted the Tollys, too."

For the first time she seemed to have Enander's attention. "Did you have no idea, then?" the king asked. "Did this Duke Hendon not live at your court?"

"The duke was his brother Gailon, Majesty," Briony gently corrected him. "And Gailon was, I must admit, a better man than I gave him credit for. Hendon killed him, too, as it turns out."

Now the whispers were unleavened by laughter. "Terrible," said one of the women, an old duchess with a wig like a bird's nest. "You poor thing. How frightened you must have been."

Briony smiled again, as shyly and humbly as she could. At the end of the table Ananka's face was set in a mask of polite sympathy, but Briony had no doubt that the baroness was none too happy with the way the conversation had slipped her reins. "Frightened—yes, of course. Terrified. But I did only what any young noblewoman would do when her father's throne was in jeopardy. I ran away in search of friends. Trustworthy friends, like King Enander. And again I thank him . . . and the Lady Ananka . . . for all they have done for me." She lifted her cup and bowed her head in the direction of Enander. "May the Three Brothers give you long lives and good health to equal your great kindness, your Majesty."

"His Majesty," echoed the others, and drank up. Enander looked surprised but not unhappy. Ananka was hiding her irritation well.

Briony considered it a victory on both counts.

After Briony had sent her maids away, she took out the note and studied it for the fifth or sixth time since she had received it the night before.

> *Come to the garden in the Vane Courtyard an hour after sunset on Stonesday.*

It had been sitting on her writing desk when she returned, a homely piece of twine around it instead of a wax seal. She did not recognize the handwriting but she had a good idea who had left it for her. Just to be on the safe side, though, she went to her chest and lifted out the boy's clothes she had worn while traveling with Makewell's Men. She had sent them to be cleaned, then packed them away—there was no telling when she might need them again. Even this, perhaps the greatest palace in Eion, felt like poor and unsafe shelter after the events of the last year.

Underneath the homespun garments was the sack with her Yisti knives. She rucked up her long skirts, not without a great deal of puffing and gasping as she bent across the whalebone stomacher, and was about to strap the smaller knife to her leg when she realized the foolishness of what she was doing.

What, shall I ask an enemy to wait while I roll around on the ground trying to reach past my petticoats for my dagger? What had Shaso said? *"Examine your clothes . . . find places you can keep them and draw them without snagging."* What would he have thought of her struggling red-faced to reach her leg?

She gave up and stood. She pulled on her mantle, then slipped the smaller of the two blades into her sleeve just as somebody knocked on her chamber door. Briony waited for a moment before remembering the maids were gone, Feival was out collecting gossip in the servants' hall, and she was alone. "Who's there?" she called.

"Just me, Princess."

She opened it but did not step aside to let her friend in. "Gods keep you, Ivvie. I don't think I'm going down to dinner."

Ivgenia looked at her clothes. "Are you going out, Snowbear?" The name was a little joke—her friend liked to pretend Briony came from the far, frozen north.

"No, no, I'm just cold." It was hard to lie to someone she thought of as a friend, but she could not bring herself to trust anyone in the court, even sweet, kindly Ivgenia e'Doursos. "I'm not feeling well, dear—just a little chill on my heart tonight. Please give the king and Lady Ananka my best wishes."

When Ivgenia was gone Briony found her shoes and slipped into them. It had been a dry week, which was good—it made the prospect of waiting out of doors more appealing. Still, as she walked quietly down the corridor she was already netted with gooseflesh.

The Vane Courtyard was named for an immense weathervane in the shape of Perin's flying horse. It stood atop a tall tower at one end of the courtyard, a monument that could be seen halfway across Tessis and was often used as the reference point in local directions. On the far side of the highest courtyard wall ran the Lantern Broad itself, the massive, ancient street that gave Broadhall Palace its name: Briony could hear the lowing of oxen, the scrape and thunk of cartwheels, and the shouts of peddlers. For a moment she wondered what it would be like to walk out of the palace and into that great street and simply follow where it led her—find a life that had nothing to do with courtly connivance or family responsibility, a life without monsters, fairies, traitors, or poisoners. If only she could . . .

"Hello, Lady," said a deep voice beside her ear.

Before the second syllable was finished she had whirled and snugged her knife against his throat.

"I gather you are not pleased to see me," said Dawet dan-Faar, his voice only a little thickened by the blade pushing against his gorge. "I am not certain why, Princess Briony, but I will be happy to apologize directly you remove your pretty blade from my windpipe."

"Did you enjoy yourself?" She lowered the knife and backed a step away. She had forgotten the smell of his skin and the quiet rumble of his voice and she did not like the way those things made her feel. "Sneaking into my rooms to leave a note? You men, you are all boys when it comes to it, playing at games of war and spycraft even when you do not need to."

"Games?" He raised an eyebrow. "I think what happened to you and your family shows that these are not merely games. Lives are at stake."

"Why? Because of other men." She slipped the knife back into her sleeve. "What will happen to you if you are caught here, Master dan-Faar?"

"In truth? Nothing that cannot be fixed, but I would prefer not to have to set my energies to such repairs if I can avoid it."

"Then let's go sit on the bench beneath that apple tree. It is mostly out of sight from the colonnades." She led him toward the bench and swept her skirts carefully to the side so she could sit down. She patted the wood a decorous distance away. "Here, sit. Tell me what has happened to you since I've seen you last. We had no time to talk at the inn."

"Ah, yes," he said. "The False Woman, with its grubby little proprietor. That was an unpleasant afternoon—they almost had me."

"Oh, stop." Briony shook her head. "I told you, these games bore me. Do you truly expect me to believe you escaped all on your own?"

He looked more than a little startled. "What do you mean, Princess?"

"Really, Master dan-Faar. What was it you said to the guard captain? 'I swear by Zosim Salamandros, you have the wrong man!' What, swearing by the Trickster god himself as a pass code and you think I could not guess? And then that . . . charade of an escape, conveniently out of everyone's sight? After spending months with a troupe of players, did you think I would not recognize sham and playacting? The guard captain let you go."

A smile tugged at the edge of Dawet's mouth, just visible in the torchlight. "I am . . . speechless," he said at last.

"I can even guess with whom you made that arrangement," she said. "Lord Jino, the king's spymaster—would it by any chance be him? No, you need not answer. The only real questions, Master dan-Faar, would be about your true relationship with the Syannese court. Secret envoy from Ludis Drakava in Hierosol? Or a double agent working originally for King Enander, but pretending to serve Drakava?"

"I am impressed, my lady," said Dawet. "You have been thinking, I see, and thinking carefully and well . . . but I am afraid you are not yet the mistress of intrigue you think yourself to be."

"Oh?" The air was growing cold now that the night had come on. She tucked her hands inside her sleeves. "And what have I missed?"

"You are assuming that I am your friend and not your enemy."

A moment later Dawet had clutched her two wrists through the sleeve and prisoned them together in the firm grip of a single hand. In the other hand he held a knife, longer and more slender than Briony's as he laid the blade gently against her cheek.

"You dastard! You . . . you traitor! I trusted you!"

"Exactly, my lady. You trusted me . . . but why? Because I admired you? Because my leg looks shapely in woolen hose? Yet I was your father's captor's man when you met me—poor grounds for friendship."

"And I treated you well when no one else would." Briony was trying slowly to tilt her balance so that she could kick Dawet hard in the leg, hoping it would hurt him enough that she could jerk free from his grasp and draw her own blade. She would rather have kicked him higher— Shaso had been most thorough in teaching her the best places to strike in close combat—but neither her angle nor her petticoats would permit it.

"Which matters not, my lady. I am trying to make a point, here." He leaned close, so that the thin blade of his knife was as near his face as hers. "You mistake men for moral creatures, as if each must measure up the good and bad done to him and then act accordingly, as though they were incorruptible judges weighing out a sentence."

Briony did her best not to tense. "Oh, I know men are corruptible . . . and corrupted . . . never fear."

She lashed out with her foot, hoping to surprise him. Instead, Dawet kept his hold on her wrists and hooked her leg with his, knocking her remaining foot from beneath her. Briony slid off the bench and would have fallen but Dawet held her up, so that she dangled between his hand and the bench like a deer carcass hung in front of a hunter's lodge. Her shame and fury almost exceeded her fear. "Let me go!"

"As you wish, Lady." He let go and she dropped the short distance to the ground.

Briony was up an instant later with her knife in her hand. "You! How dare you? How . . ."

"How dare I what?" His expression was flat, almost cruel, which was just as well. If he had smiled at her she might have tried to kill him. "Show you what a fool you are being? You are a very clever girl, Briony Eddon, but you are still only that—a girl. A maiden, even, I do not doubt. Do you understand what you have risked of your own safety and your family's fortunes coming here like this?"

The Yisti dagger wavered in her hand. "You . . . you do not mean to harm me?"

"By the Great Mother, Princess, do you think I am such a fool as to try to do injury to a white-skinned northern girl in a northern castle, within the hearing of a hundred armed guards or more, and not even put a hand over her mouth?" He shook his head. "Tell me I have not so far misestimated your intelligence, or you mine."

"You had a knife to my throat!"

"If I truly meant you harm, I would have disarmed you." He reached out, fast as Shaso himself had been, faster perhaps, and used his own blade to flip her dagger out of her hand. It spun into the darkness, disappearing into the shadowy garden border without a sound. "Now go find it. I will wait. That did not look the sort of knife anyone would like to lose."

When she came back, she had hidden the Yisti dagger in her sleeve again. "If it weren't for this wretched dress I would have had both knives out, and you would have had one of them in your shin, at the very least."

He grinned, but there was no mirth in it. "Then let us both be glad you didn't, for I feel pretty certain that things would not have gone so easily or happily as you suppose."

"But why did you do that?" She sat down again, much more warily this time, but Dawet did not make any movement toward her. "You frightened me."

"Good, my lady. That is the first thing I have heard since I met you here that makes me happy. I *want* you frightened. You are in terrible danger. Have you not realized that?"

She stared at him, doing her best to remember the lessons again, not of warcraft but of mummery. It would not do to let the tears well up. It would be altogether too . . . girlish. "Yes, Master dan-Faar, I have certainly realized that, most notably when someone tried to poison me three days gone, but I thank you for the reminder."

"Your sarcasm serves you poorly, Princess. You should thank me in truth for being honest with you when others would not or cannot." He reached out his hand and gently placed it on her arm. "In truth, I wish that were not my role. I would someone had given me a fairer, kinder part to play . . ."

This time he did not anticipate her strike. She moved so quickly that the point of her blade pinked the fat of his hand before he could pull back. He stood up, anger clouding his face, and yanked off his glove to examine the wound. It was not, Briony thought, a very serious spite. "You little . . . ! Why did you do that?"

"You are the one who counseled mistrust, Master dan-Faar." She was breathing hard and her heart was drumming. "You speak to me of how kind you are, how thoughtful, how you have my best interests in mind where no one else does. Very well. Start by answering this question, please—*what are you?* Are you an enemy with a soft spot toward me? Or a friend? Would you be my brother, or would you be a lover? I have spent my life at the center of public doings. I am not so flattered by your attention as to lose all sense of who I am and what I'm after, nor to forget that you seem to want to have things all ways at once." She stared at him. "Well, sir, what would you be to me?"

For a moment Dawet simply stared at her over his hand as he sucked on the place where she had pinked him. "Princess, I do not know. In truth, I am not certain I know who you are anymore. Your time in exile has changed you."

"Well, that should be no surprise, should it?" She once more tucked away her dagger. "If you decide you want to speak to me again—perhaps to give me some information I could truly use, like what you know of my father—you will know where to find me."

"Wait." Dawet lifted his hand to her as though conceding a wager. "Enough, Briony."

"*Princess* Briony, Master dan-Faar. We do not know each other so well, nor have you proved your friendship yet."

He drew back. "You are hard, Lady. Did I not warn you back in Southmarch that someone in your court meant you harm?"

"Come now. Without naming any names to me, what use was that? Of what ruler in all the world is that *not* true? You have not done me any unkindnesses, Envoy, but as far as I can see you have done me no services either, except to share the gift of your company." She unbent enough to give him a half-smile. "A gift not without merit, but hardly the stuff of undying loyalty."

He shook his head. "You have become a hard-shelled girl, Princess."

"I have stayed a living woman when many wished it were otherwise. Now tell me of my father or let us say farewell and get out of this cold night."

"There is nothing much to say. When I left Hierosol to come here he was still Ludis Drakava's prisoner. Since then I have heard the same rumors as you—that Ludis has fled, that your father has been given to the autarch, that Hierosol will fall at any moment . . ."

"What? Given to . . . to the *autarch?* I have never heard . . . oh, Merciful Zoria, say it is not true! What madness is this?"

"But . . . surely you have heard the tale. Many people here in Tessis are repeating it—Ludis traded him for his own escape, it's said. But do not fear too much, lady, it is only rumor so far. Nothing is known for certain . . ."

She hissed her anger. "Blood of the Brothers! Not one of these cursed Syannese has spoken a word of it to me!" She reached out and plucked a blossom from the branch near her head and held it for a moment. *No tears,* she reminded herself. She crushed it in her fingers and let the petals fall. "Tell me everything you have heard." The tears had ebbed without ever reaching her eyes. She felt a cold hardness in her breast, as though ice grew on her heart.

"As I said, Lady, these are only tales, much confused and . . ."

"Do not soothe me, dan-Faar. I am no longer a child. Just . . . inform me." She took a breath. The night seemed to bend close; the chilly darkness inside her rose to greet it. "I may have lost my family's throne but I will take it back, that I swear, and our enemies will suffer for what they've done. Yes, I promise that on the heads of the gods themselves." She looked up at Dawet's surprised face, just visible in the light from an open window above. "You are staring, man. Put the time to better use. Tell me what I wish to know."

12

A Good Woman, a Good Man, and a Poet

"It is said that a single king and queen have ruled the fairies since the days of the gods, an immortal pair who are known by many names, but most often called Eenur and Sakuri according to Rhantys, who was reputed to have friends among the Qar. Some stories even claim that these immortal rulers are brother and sister, like the monarchs of old Xis."

—from "A Treatise on the Fairy Peoples of Eion and Xand"

MATT TINWRIGHT HAD BEEN SEARCHING the inner and outer keeps for her a tennight or more, using almost every free moment when he was not at the court or tending Elan's slow recovery, so it was disappointing that he found her at last only a short way from his hired room near Skimmer's Lagoon in the outer ward. She had apparently gained a bit of a name for herself among those exiled from the mainland city, refugees who now lived in the most miserable conditions, crammed together in the besieged castle.

When he first saw his mother he did not immediately approach her, but instead followed the tall, bony woman as she walked down Staple Street from shop to dingy shop with a basket in her hand, apparently collecting food for the less fortunate. His mother, Tinwright thought grimly, never had any difficulty finding those she deemed less fortunate than herself. She could scent them like a hunting hound scents its quarry.

Still, he could not help noticing that despite the unarguable rectitude of her cause, she pocketed every fourth or fifth piece of food, loaf of stale bread, or whiskery onion, apparently for herself. She might insist on helping the less fortunate, even when they did not want her assistance, but Anamesiya Tinwright had always been just as firmly determined to help herself.

He approached her at last near the great temple in Market Square where she was shoving bits of food into the hands of the displaced folk living there in a sad camp of tents made from sticks and threadbare blankets. Watching her quick movements and her prominent, sharp nose, Tinwright could not help remembering what his father had called her in one of his less charitable moments—*"that damned interfering woodpecker."*

"If it does hurt your teeth," she was telling an old man as he walked up, "that is your own doing, not my good bread I give you for nothing."

"Mother?" said Tinwright.

She turned and looked at him. Her bony hand leaped to her breast and the wooden, almond-shaped Zorian vesicle she wore on a cord around her neck. "By the Trigon, what is this? By the blessed Brothers, is that you, Matthias?" She looked him up and down. "Your jacket is good, but it is dirty, I see. 'Let not your raiment be tattered and oiled,' as the sacred book says. Have they chased you out of the court, then?"

He felt himself flushing with anger and frustration. "It's 'tattered and soiled,' not 'tattered and oiled.' No, Mother, I am very well liked at the court. Kind greetings to you, too. I am glad to see you well."

She waved her hand toward the half dozen or so men and women crowding around her, all as tattered and soiled as could be. "The gods give me health because I give my best to others." Her eyes narrowed as she regarded the nearest old man. "Chew your food, you," she said sternly. "Do not bolt it down and then hope to cozen me out of more."

"Where are you living, Mother?"

"The gods provide for me," she said airily, which likely meant that she was sleeping where she could, as were so many other refugees from the mainland in this crowded, stinking city within a city. "Why? Do you come to offer me a bedchamber in the palace? Have you grown ashamed of offending the gods with drink and fornication and hope to climb back into their good graces by extending a little charity to the woman who bore you?"

Tinwright took a breath before answering. "You have always been fascinated with the idea of my drinking and fornicating. I wonder if it's entirely fitting for a mother to talk about such things so often."

He had the pleasure now of seeing her flush. "You are a wicked child—you always were! I speak only to point out your errors, with no thought for my own good. Of course it means I am always scorned, first by your father, now by you, but I will not hide when I know the gods' will is not being done."

"What is the gods' will, then, Mother?" Tinwright was close to walking away despite the desperation of his need. He should never have come near her. "Tell me, please."

"It is plain. It is time for you to give up this wasteful life you lead, Matthias. Wine and women and poetry—none of it pleases the gods. Work, boy—real, sober work—that is what you need. The sacred book tells us, 'He who does not work will have his eyes emptied.'"

Tinwright sighed. The sacred book was, of course, the *Book of the Trigon,* but his mother seemed to have access to a version no one else had ever seen. He was reasonably certain that the original injunction was "He who will not look will have his eyes opened," but it was useless to argue with her about such things. "May the gods testify, Mother, I did not intend that we should fight. Let us start our talk again. I came to tell you that I have a place for you to stay. It is not in the palace, but it is clean and wholesome."

She raised an eyebrow. "Truly? You would become a good son at last?"

He clenched his teeth. "I suppose, Mother. May we go so I can show you the place?"

"When I've finished here. A dutiful child will not mind waiting."

It was small wonder that none of her children had stayed long at home, Tinwright thought. He leaned against a column and watched as she finished doling out the rest of her hard bread and stern admonishments to the waiting poor.

The smile that had started to form on his mother's face when she saw the clean, well-appointed room suddenly went stiff as a dried fish when she spotted the sleeping girl. Her jaw dropped. "By the Sacred Brothers!" She made the sign of the Three on her breast so vigorously it might have been meant to protect her from a hurtling spear. "O my Heavenly Fathers and Mothers, defend me! What is this? What is this?"

"This is Lady Elan M'Cory, Mother . . ." he began, but Anamesiya Tinwright was already trying to force her way past him, back out the door.

"I'll have nothing to do with this!" she said. "I am a godly woman!"

"And so is she!" Tinwright tried to catch at her arm and received a backhand smack from one of his mother's large hands as she struggled to get away. "Blast and curse it, Mother, will you stop and listen to me!"

"I'll not share a roof with your doxy!" she screeched, still heaving against his restraining grip. Some of the passers by had stopped to watch this interesting show; other neighbors were looking down from upstairs windows. Tinwright blasphemed under his breath.

"Just come inside. Let me explain. For the love of all the gods, Mother, will you stop?"

She gave him a look of fury, her face deathly pale but for pink spots in her cheeks. "I will not help you kill this girl's baby, you fornicator! I know the folk of that court, with their wicked ways. Your father read books to you when you were young, no matter my warnings—I knew it would spoil you! I knew you would get airs above your station!"

"Gods curse and blast this whole muddle, Mother, you will *be quiet and listen!*" He dragged her back inside and closed the door, then leaned against it to keep her from escaping. "This girl is blameless and so am I—well, I have done nothing to her, anyway. There is no baby. Do you understand? There is no baby!"

She looked at him with astonishment. "What, have you done your foul deed already, killed one of the gods' innocents, and now you wish me to nurse her through it?"

He hung his head, praying for patience, although he was a bit uncertain as to who might be the best recipient for the request. Zosim, his own patron godling, was notoriously uninterested in that particular virtue, or in fact by virtue in general. In the end, Tinwright offered his prayer to the goddess Zoria, who was reputed to be good with things like this.

If she will even hear me, now that I have so long delayed her poem. But how could he help it when his muse, Princess Briony, Zoria's earthly avatar, had disappeared? *That was the beginning of my downfall. But I was raised up such a short time only! Zoria, surely I deserve a little pity?*

Whether it was the goddess' doing or not, after a moment he did feel a little calmer. Elan was beginning to stir as if she swam upward from great depths, her eyes still closed, her pale face troubled and confused.

"Listen carefully, Mother. I have rescued Lady Elan from someone who means her harm." He didn't dare tell her that the man he had saved her from was Hendon Tolly, the castle's self-appointed protector: his mother had a deep and unreasoning reverence for all kinds of authority and might march straight out and denounce them both. "She is sick because I had to give her a medicine to spirit her out of the palace and away from this man's clutches. She has done nothing wrong, do you understand? She is a victim—like Zoria, do you see? Like Blessed Zoria herself, driven out into the snows, alone and friendless."

His mother looked from him to Elan with deep suspicion. "How can I believe that? How can I be certain you are not making a fool of me? 'The gods help those who fill their own fields,' as the book says."

"*Till.* Till their own fields. But if you don't believe me, you can ask her yourself, when she awakes." He pointed toward the corner of the room and the tiny table set by. "There is a basin and cloth. She needs bathing, and . . . and it didn't seem proper I should do it. I will bring back some food for both of you, as well as some more blankets from the palace."

The idea of blankets from the palace clearly intrigued her, but his mother was not going to be convinced so easily. "But how long must I stay? Where will I sleep?"

"You can sleep in the bed, of course." He had opened the door and he was partway out already. "It is a big bed. Very nice, too. The mattress is full of soft, clean, new straw." He took another step back. He was almost out. Almost . . .

"It will cost you a starfish," she said. "Every week."

"What?" Outrage boiled up in him. "A silver starfish? What sort of mother tries to pickpurse her own son?"

"Why should I work without wage? If you do not wish to help me, your own blood, you can hire some girl from one of those taverns in which you've always spent your time."

He stared at her. She wore that look he hated, her flush of anger from earlier now turned to one of victory—the look that said she knew she'd get her way. Did the gods really speak to her? Could she somehow know that Brigid had sworn she would no longer help him, that he was backed into a corner with no escape, at risk of his very life?

"Mother, do you realize that if somehow the word gets out that the Lady Elan is here, the . . . the man who seeks her will have me killed? Not to mention what he will do to her, this poor innocent girl?"

She had her long arms folded across her chest now. "All the more reason why you should not begrudge me the pittance I ask. No price is too great to pay for this girl's safety. I cannot believe any child of mine would balk at such a small matter."

He stared at her. "I will not pay you a starfish every tennight, Mother. I cannot afford it. I will pay you two each month until she is well enough to leave. You will also be fed and have this room to call your own."

"I will have a room and bed to share, you mean. Share with this unfortunate woman, carrying the gods only knows what contagion, the poor thing. Two and a half each month, Matthias. Heaven will reward you for doing what is right."

He couldn't imagine heaven cared very much about half a starfish a month, but he needed her more than she needed him, and she had sensed it, as she always did.

"Very well," he said. "Two and a half every month."

"And to show earnest . . . ?" she asked, holding out her long hand.

"Earnest?"

"You want me to take care of her, do you not? What if I must go to the apothecary?"

He turned over his last starfish.

He walked beside the rickety piers at the northwestern end of Skimmer's Lagoon, kicking a lump of dried tar. The smell of fish and salt hung over everything. Despite the horror he had just called down on himself to buy freedom of movement, he was in no hurry to get back to the royal residence.

The woman I love, and for whom I have risked my life, loathes me as if I were vermin. No, not true—vermin she would hold blameless by comparison. I survive at court only by the goodwill of the very man I have cheated of his victim, and who will murder me without a thought if he ever finds out. And now I have been forced to pay my last money to hire my own mother—a woman I would gladly have paid even more money to avoid. Could my life be more wretched?

Matt Tinwright only realized later that in that very moment the gods had surely heard his provocative words and had begun to laugh. It must have been the richest jest they had heard all day.

"Hoi," said a large shape that had stepped out to block the walkway in front of him. "Hoi, what a surprise. I know you! You're the limpcod I owe a beating to."

Tinwright looked up, blinking. Standing before him were two big men dressed like dock roustabouts. Neither was the remotest bit pleasant to observe, but the nearest one had a pale, doughy face that struck him as sickeningly familiar.

Oh, heaven, what a fool I was to tempt you! It's that cursed guard from the Badger's Boots—the one who wanted to pound me into jelly for stealing his woman. The thick-bodied man wasn't dressed as a soldier now, though. Was that good? Or bad?

"I'm afraid you've mistaken me, sir . . ." he said, looking down as he stepped to one side. A hand as big as an Orphanstide ham shot out and curled in the collar of his jacket, stopping him midstride and holding him rigidly in place.

"Oh, I think not, neighbor. I think I know you well enough—though I didn't know who you'd be when we were sent looking for you. Now my question is, should we beat the guts out of you now and risk the silver we're to be paid for delivering you?" He turned to his almost equally ugly companion. "Do you think His Nibs'll still pay us if we bring this sack of shit in with a few broken bones?"

His comrade seemed to be giving it real thought. "The big man has a bit of a temper and I wouldn't want to cross him. He wanted this one alive, that's all I know."

"We can say he stumbled and fell into the wall a few times," suggested Tinwright's tormentor, grinning. "It won't be the first time one of our prisoners went and had a wee accident."

Prisoner? Big man? What was going on here? Until this moment, Tinwright had only felt the sickening anticipation of a beating. He had survived a few of those, although the thought terrified him. But this sounded like they actually planned something worse.

Tolly? Were they collecting him for Hendon Tolly? Had Elan's tormentor found out what he had done? Matt Tinwright's heart was suddenly beating so fast he felt dizzy and sick to his stomach. "Honestly, you have made a mistake." He tried to squirm away but the guard reached out his other big hand and buffeted Tinwright so hard on the head that for long moments he could see nothing but a glare of white light, hear nothing but a loud ringing sound, as if his head had become a giant bell tolling the hour. When his wits returned he was being dragged through the streets, his feet stumbling and scraping as the two men all but carried him.

"Anymore talk and I'll happily do that again twice as hard," said the pasty-faced one. "In fact, next time I'll just twist your stones until you shriek like a wee girl. How will that be?"

Tinwright stuck to silent prayer. Zoria heard from him, as did Zosim, the Three Brothers, and every other deity he could think of, including some he might have made up for his own poems.

Instead of them taking him toward the castle, though, it quickly became clear that the unpleasant men had some other destination. They frog-marched Tinwright down a succession of narrow streets, then across the bridge to the east side of the lagoon, finally arriving at a tavern on pilings that jutted right out over the water. The place had no name on it, only a long, rusted gaffing hook hung above the front door. It was dark inside, and when they first lifted him roughly across the threshold Tinwright felt as though he were being carried down into the frozen throne room of Kernios himself. He could not help noticing that it smelled more like something belonging to the sea god Erivor, though, as the cold, damp airs of the place rose and surrounded him, a miasma of fish and blood and brine.

All the tavern's clients seemed to be Skimmers. As he and his captors walked through the low-ceilinged main room the boatmen turned to watch with heavy-lidded, incurious eyes, like a pond full of frogs waiting for an intruder to pass so they could resume their croaking song.

Why have I been brought here? Tinwright wondered. *I know nothing of any Skimmers except that tanglewife. I have never done any of them harm. Why should someone here mean me ill?*

A tall but bent-backed Skimmer stepped out in front of them. He was old, to judge by his hard, leathery skin, and wore an actual shirt with sleeves, somewhat unusual among men who often wore no clothes on their upper bodies at all, even in cold weather. "What do you need, gentlemen?" he asked in a throaty voice. All the eyes in the room still seemed to be watching them, calm but intent.

The dough-faced guard did not bother to sound respectful. "We've got business in the back room, fish face. And you've been paid already."

"Ah, of course," said the old Skimmer, backing out of their way. "Go through. He's waiting for you."

The back room's door was so low that Matt Tinwright had to bend to go through it. His captors helped him, shoving down on his head hard enough to make his neck crack. When they allowed him to straighten up once more he found himself in a small room mostly taken up by a single large, bearded man sitting at a table of scarred wood.

"You found him, I see." Avin Brone's grin made Tinwright think of toothy wolves or hungry bears. "Coming out of his . . . bower of love, eh?"

Matt Tinwright, already terrified, almost gasped aloud. Did Brone know? No—he couldn't! He must think Tinwright was having some illicit assignation by the docks.

"Don't know about that, Lord," said the guard who had expressed interest in helping Tinwright fall against a wall several times. "We just waited on the street you told us and there he was."

"Good. Come see me later and you'll get your finder's fee. Sound work, men."

"Thank you, Lordship," the guard said. "Tonight? Shall we come tonight?"

"What?" Brone was already thinking of something else. "Oh, very well. Do you not trust me till Lastday?"

"'Course, Lordship. Just . . . we need things." Doughface turned to his companion, who nodded.

"Certainly, then." He waved his hand and the two men went out.

The little room was silent for an uncomfortably long time as Brone stared at Tinwright, looking him up and down like a butcher examining the carcass he was about to cut into chops. Matt Tinwright, knees trembling, couldn't help but wonder if this was some kind of trick being played on him. Now that the guards had been sent away was he supposed to make a run for it, try to escape? Was Brone seeking an excuse to kill him? No, that made no sense. The time Brone had threatened him was long past and much had changed since then. Avin Brone no longer ruled over Southmarch in all but name—Tinwright knew he had lost his post of Lord Constable months ago to one of Tolly's allies, the cruel Berkan Hood. The Count of Landsend's beard now contained far more gray than dark, and he looked, if anything, even stouter than before. Why should he still mean harm to poor Tinwright?

"Why am I here, my lord?" he at last found the heart to ask.

Brone stared at him a moment longer before leaning forward. His frowning eyebrows seemed like they might suddenly leap from his face and take flight like bats. He lifted up his hand, pointed his thick finger right at his captive. "I . . . don't . . . like . . . *poets.*"

It took quite a while for Tinwright to finish swallowing. "I-I-I'm s-sorry," he said at last. "I didn't mean to . . ."

"Shut your hole, Tinwright." Brone abruptly slammed his hand down on the table so hard it made the walls of the small room tremble. Tinwright had to acknowledge that he himself might have given forth a small, girlish scream. "I know all about you," the big man went on. "Cozener. Flatterer. Layabout and ne'er-do-well. What small success you have had comes from your having suckled up to your betters, and most of those were men like Nevin Hewney and his lot, who are the scum of the earth." Brone frowned hugely; if he had told Tinwright he was going to eat him alive, like a wicked giant in a children's tale, the poet would have believed it. Instead, the Count of Landsend's voice became quieter, deeper, throbbing with an anger that seemed to threaten worse things to come than Matt Tinwright could even imagine. "But then you came to the palace. Arrested. Involved with a criminal intent to take advantage of the royal family. And instead of having your head lopped off like the gutter-rolling traitor you are, you were given a gift fit for a hero—the patronage of Princess Briony herself and a place in the court. Oh, how you must have chuckled at that."

"Not . . . not actually *chuckled,* my lord . . ."

"Shut it. And how do you repay this astounding kindness? By kidnapping a high-born woman right out of the royal residence and keeping her as your prisoner! By the Three, man, the torturers are going to be staying up late every night trying to think up new ways to tear the flesh from your body!"

He knows! Tinwright couldn't help it—he burst into tears. "By all the gods, I swear it is not that way! She was . . . she is . . . Oh, please, Lord Brone, do not let them torture me. I'm a poor man. I meant only good. You do not know Elan, she is so good, so fair, and Tolly was so cruel to her . . ." He stopped in horror, thinking he might just have made things worse by denouncing the current lord of Southmarch. "No, I . . . she . . . you . . ." Tinwright could think of nothing else to say—his doom was utter and complete. He fell silent but for quiet whimpering.

One of Brone's bristling eyebrows crept upward. "Tolly? What does this have to do with Tolly? Speak, man, or I will start proceedings here myself and leave just enough left of you for you to gasp out your confession in front of the lord protector."

And Tinwright did speak, the words hurrying out of him with none of his usual pretense to cleverness, explanations and excuses bumping against each other and sometimes tumbling flat, like sheep hurried down a steep mountain path. When he had finished he sat wiping at his face, peering between his fingers at Brone, who was silent and thinking hard but still scowling fiercely, as if reluctant to let the expression leave his face because he knew he would be using it again soon.

"You are young, aren't you?" Brone asked suddenly.

All the usual objections rose to his lips, but Tinwright only licked his dry lips and said, "I am twenty, Lord."

The count shook his head. "I suppose some of the mistakes you have made are the same I might have made at your age." He shot Tinwright a glance. "But that does not include taking Elan M'Cory out of the castle. That is a capital offense, boy. That is the headsman's block."

Tears again filled Tinwright's eyes. "Oh, gods. How did I ever come to this?"

"Bad company," said Brone briskly. "To associate with playwrights and poets is to dally with thieves and madmen—what good can come of that? But perhaps all is not up for you—not yet. If the matter of Mistress M'Cory were to remain hidden from the lord protector, then you might yet survive to an honorable old age. But I would be taking a risk on your behalf, knowing and not telling. I would make myself an accessory . . ." He shook his head, grimly, sadly. "No, I fear I cannot take such a risk. I have a family and lands, retainers. It wouldn't be fair . . ."

"Oh, please, Count Brone." The big man seemed to be bending a little, leaning toward mercy. Tinwright did his best to make his words sweet and convincing. "Please—I did it only to save an innocent girl! I will do anything for you if you will spare me this terrible fate. My poor mother's heart would be broken." Which was a gross untruth, of course: Anamesiya Tinwright would probably be delighted to see her direst predictions come to pass.

"Perhaps. Perhaps. But if I am to take such a risk—to let you go when I know that you are guilty, and to cover up that guilt!—then you must do something for me."

"Anything. Shall I carry messages for you?" He had once heard rumors that Hewney and the others had performed such services for Brone. "Travel to a foreign court?" He could definitely think of worse fates than to leave his mother and his troubles and this entire grim city behind for a few moons.

"No, I think you shall be more use to me closer to home," said Brone. "In fact, I could use a man with access to Hendon Tolly and his inner circle. I have a number of questions I'd like answered, and you, Matty Tinwright—you will be my spy."

"Spy? Spy on . . . Hendon Tolly?"

"Oh, not just him. I have many questions and many needs. There is also a certain object whose whereabouts I need to know—it is even possible I'll ask you to obtain it for me. I suspect it is being kept in the chambers of Okros, the new palace physician. Do not look so worried, Tinwright, it is nothing particularly valuable—simply a mirror."

A mirror? Could it be the one Tolly had used to torture Elan? But only a fool or lunatic would go near such a thing . . . !

Matt Tinwright stared at the count with dawning horror. "You . . . you never meant to tell Tolly. He has cast you out! You only wanted a spy!"

Avin Brone sat back and twined his fingers together on his broad belly. "Do not bother your head with truth, poet. It is not your field of expertise."

Tinwright's heart raced, but he was angry now, angry and humiliated to have been played like such a lackwit. "What if I go to Tolly and tell him you tried to make me a spy in his camp?"

Brone threw back his head and laughed. "What if you do? Would you like him to hear my side of the story—the truth about Lady Elan? And even if trouble came to me as well as to you because of it, I have an estate happily far from Southmarch to which I can retire, and men to protect me. What do you have, little scribbler? Only a neck which will part for the headsman's ax like a fine sausage."

Despite himself, Tinwright lifted his hand to his throat. "But what if Tolly catches me?" He was almost crying again.

"Then you will be in the same situation as if I tell him what you've done. The difference is, if you do it my way, it will be up to you to keep yourself out of trouble. If *I* tell Hendon Tolly—well, trouble will find you very quickly, there's no doubt of that."

Tinwright stared at the old man. "You . . . you are a demon."

"I am a politician. There is a difference, but you are too green to understand it. Now listen carefully, poet, while I tell you what you must do for me . . ."

13
Licking the Needle

"It is said that in the earliest years of Hierosol, when it was still little more than a coastal village, a large Qar city called Yashmaar stood on the far side of the Kulloan Strait, and that trade between men of the southern continent and this fairy stronghold was one reason for Hierosol's swift growth."

—from "A Treatise on the Fairy Peoples of Eion and Xand"

*B*ARRICK EDDON. What a strange, strange name. For a moment Qinnitan could not understand why it ran through her head as she lay in the dark, over and over like the words to one of the prayers her father had taught her when she was a child. *Barrick. Barrick Eddon. Barrick . . .*

Then the dream came flooding back. She tried to sit up, but little Pigeon was sprawled against her, tangled with her, and it would be too difficult to pry herself loose without waking him.

What did it mean, that vision? She had seen the flame-haired boy several times in dreams, but this last time it had been different: although she could not remember everything they had said to each other, they had shared what she remembered as a true conversation. But why had such a gift been given to her, if it truly was a gift? What did the gods intend? If the vision came from the sacred bees that she had served, the Golden Hive of Nushash, shouldn't one of her friends from those days, like Duny, have come to her in dream instead? Why some northern boy she had never met or even seen in waking life?

Still, she could not put Barrick Eddon out of her mind, and not only because she finally knew his name. She had felt his despair as if it were her own—not as she sensed Pigeon's unhappiness, but as if she could truly feel the stranger's heart, as if the same blood somehow flowed through both of them. But that was impossible, of course . . .

Qinnitan felt Pigeon shift again and looked up into the blackness. She didn't even know what time it was, night or morning, since their cabin had no windows and the noises of the crew outside did not give much away: she hadn't yet learned the shipboard routine well enough to know the different watches by their voices and calls.

How she longed for some light! The sailors wouldn't let her have a lamp for fear she would burn herself up, which was foolish. Qinnitan did not care much about her own life—certainly she would give it up gladly if that was the only thing that would keep her out of the hands of Sulepis—but she would not sacrifice the boy while there was even a thin hope of saving him.

Still, a candle or lamp would make the long hours of the night go faster. She could only sleep so much—although Pigeon, it seemed, could sleep anytime and as much as he wished. But Qinnitan would have preferred to have something to look at when she could not sleep. Even better would be a book—Baz'u Jev or some other poetry, anything to take her mind away from her situation.

But that would not happen, at least not as long as their captor was in charge. He was cruel and clever and seemed to have no heart whatsoever. She had tried everything—innocence, flirtation, childish terror—all had left him unmoved. How could she hope to trick a man like that, a man of cold stone? But neither could she give up.

Light. The smallest things suddenly loomed so large when they could not be obtained. Light. Something to read. Freedom to walk where she wanted. Freedom from the terror of torment and death at the hands of a mad king. Gifts that most people scarcely knew they had, but which Qinnitan would value more than all the gold in the world.

But at the moment, she just wished she had a lamp . . .

An idea came to her then—horrifying, but impossible to dislodge once it had arrived. Pigeon moaned in his sleep and squeezed her arm as though he could sense what she was thinking, but Qinnitan scarcely noticed him. The ship rose and fell at anchor, its timbers creaking softly as she lay in the lightless cabin with the boy clutched to her, scheming how they would either escape or die.

❧

Daikonas Vo had been up before the dawn, as was his wont. He had never needed much sleep, which was a good thing: the house of his childhood, with its constant coming and going of male visitors and its drunken parties, had never provided much.

He had spoken with the ship's captain as well as the optimarch, the leader of the soldiers on the ship, waking them both in their cabins before the first light of dawn had touched the clouds overhead and impressing on them that it would be hard to say which would be worse for them if anything happened to the girl while he was gone—the wrath of the autarch or the anger of Vo himself. Neither man liked him, but then what man did? What was important was that he had the autarch's commission. Even better, he had seen the glimmer of fear in both men, better hidden in the captain's angry stare than in the optimarch's (who only outranked Vo himself by a few measures) but still there, still visible. He trusted that fear even more than he trusted their fear of the autarch. Sulepis was indeed fearsome, but he was far away. Vo was right here and he wanted them to remember that he would be coming back by nightfall.

He clambered up from the boat onto the dock and walked away without looking back, leaving the rowers to shake their heads and make the sign of pass-evil. Vo reveled in his unpopularity. It was one thing back in his own troop, when he had to live with the same men for years. He had not wished to provoke such enmity that they might all decide to band together and stab him in his sleep. But aboard ship, where he was outranked by several and had only his commission from the autarch to command respect, he wanted to keep them all at arm's distance. The greatest threat, after all, came not from obvious enemies but from purported allies. That was how people could be caught off guard. That was how kings and autarchs were assassinated.

Agamid rose up before him in three points, the trio of hills that were its fame, that looked down on the port city nestled in the foothills below the highest hill and that sprawled all the way down to the edge of the broad bay. Even at dawn the place was bustling, its roads full of wagons coming up from the docks toward the bazaar with the morning's catch of fish and the first goods from the trading vessels that had docked during the night. Oxen lowing, men calling to each other, children screeching and laughing as they were chased out of the way—it was exactly the kind of lively scene that made Vo wish some kind of massive ice storm would descend from the north and freeze everything, cover all the lands in a blanket of cold silence. That would be worth seeing! All these yammering, pop-eyed faces struck motionless like fish in an icy pond, and nothing to hear but the sweet, inhuman song of the wind.

Vo made his way from market stall to market stall, asking the owners where he might find an apothecary called Kimir, whose name one of the sailors had remembered from an earlier voyage and a bad case of the pox. Some of them were angry to be interrupted in their preparations for the day by someone who did not even mean to spend money, but a look into Vo's cold eyes quickly made them respectful and eager to help. At last he found the shop in a row of dark, vine-tangled houses a few hundreds steps up the first hill, at the back edge of the bazaar.

The shop itself was exactly what he had expected, ceiling cobwebbed with strings of hanging leaves, flowers, fruits, branches, and roots, floor covered with baskets, boxes, and clay pots, some of them stopped with wax or even lead. Beside the table against one wall stood a chest that was taller than a man and had dozens of tiny drawers, by far the most expensive piece of furniture in the room. Perched beside it on a stool was a lanky, bearded older man in a dirty robe who wore the black conical hat common in this part of the world. He looked up briefly from the contents of the drawer he was examining when Vo walked in, but did not otherwise greet his new customer.

"You are Malamenas Kimir?" Vo asked.

The old man nodded slowly, as if he had only just realized it himself. "So they say—but then, they say much that is untrue as well. How can I help you, stranger?"

Vo pushed the door closed firmly behind him. The old man looked up again, this time with mild interest. "Is there anyone else in the store?" Vo asked.

"Nobody else ever works with me except my sister," said Kimir, smiling slightly. "And she is older than I am, so if you mean to rob me or murder me I don't think you have much to fear."

"Is she here now?"

The older man shook his head. "No. Home with a bit of a pain in her back. I gave her a mild tincture of cowbane for it. Excellent stuff, but it promotes belly cramps and flatulence so I told her not to bother coming in." He tilted his head, stared at Vo like a bird viewing something shiny. "So. I repeat my earlier question, sir—how can I help you?"

Vo moved closer. Most people could not help shying back from Daikonas Vo when he approached them, but the apothecary seemed unmoved. "I need help. There is . . . something in me. It is meant to kill me if I do not do what my master wants. I am doing my best to serve him, but I fear that even if I do, he may not cure me."

Kimir nodded. He looked interested. "Ah. Yes, the kind of employer who might do such a thing to guarantee results from his underlings is not necessarily the sort you trust to be suitably grateful afterward. Is it by any chance the Red Serpent Root he forced you to eat? Did he say you had two or three days before the poison would kill you?"

"No. I have had this in me for months."

"Could it be Aelian's Fluxative? Did he warn you under no circumstances to eat fish?"

"I have eaten fish many times. There was no such warning."

"Hmmm. Fascinating. Then you must tell me exactly what happened . . ."

Daikonas Vo described what happened in the autarch's throne room, although he did not mention the identity of his master. As he described the death agonies of the autarch's cousin, Kimir's eyes widened and the old man began to grin a wide, yellow grin.

" . . . And then he told me that it was in my wine as well," Vo finished. "That if I did not do as he wished, the same thing would happen to me."

"And no doubt it will," said Kimir, rubbing his hands together. "Well, well. This is quite wonderful. This gives every sign of being the true *basiphae*—something I had never thought to see in my lifetime."

"I want it out," Vo said. "I do not care what it means to you. If you help me I will reward you. If you try to trick me or betray me I will kill you very painfully."

Kimir laughed shortly. "Oh, yes, I am certain you would, Master . . . ?" When there was no reply the old man stood. "No one would waste such an . . . encouragement as that on an unimportant servant with an unimportant task, and no one who could find, afford, and employ the *basiphae* would hire a clumsy servant. Oh, I am quite convinced you are a very good killer indeed. Sit here and let me inspect you."

As he seated himself on the stool, Vo lifted his hand.

"Truly, you need not say it," the old man told him. "I am quite certain something terrible will happen to me if I make you unhappy in any way." He touched the side of his nose. "Trust me—I have a long experience of secretive and dangerous customers."

Malamenas Kimir's hands moved quickly over Vo's belly, pushing and squeezing. The old man moved on to his face, pulling back his eyelids, smelling his breath, examining the color of his tongue. By the time he had finished asking Vo a series of questions about the quality of his stools, urine, and phlegm, an hour had passed and Vo could hear the temple bells ringing the end of morning prayers. His prisoners must be awake by now, which meant the little Hive bitch would be thinking of ways to make trouble.

"I cannot wait forever," he said, rising to his feet. "Give me something to kill this thing inside me."

The old man looked at him with shrewd eyes. "It cannot be done."

"What?" Vo's fingers stretched toward the knife in his waistband.

"There are limitations to violence, you know," Kimir said calmly. "But I do not aim to waste my last breath explaining them if you are going to kill me."

"Speak."

"Make up your mind."

Vo let go of the knife hilt. "Speak."

"Limitations to violence. Here are two. The only thing you could do to murder the *basiphae* creature inside you, although it is as tiny as a fern seed, would poison you, too. That is a limitation, is it not?"

"You said two. Speak. I do not like games."

The old man grinned sourly. "Here is the second. If you killed me, you would never have learned what I *can* do for you." He got up and walked to the tall chest, then began to search through its many drawers. "Somewhere in here," he said. "Fox's clote, no, herb of Perikal, no, Zakkas' wort, squill—ah! I had wondered where that squill got to." He turned. "Do you know, the last fellow in here who kept touching his knife the way you do wound up buying enough monkshood from me to kill an entire family, including grandparents, uncles, cousins, and servants. I've often wondered what happened to it . . ." Kimir stopped rummaging and pulled out a fat black bottle the length of Vo's index finger. "Here we are. Tigersbane out of far Yanedan. The farmers there use it to poison their spears when a tiger—a creature even larger and more dangerous than a lion—is stalking their village. It is made from a mountain flower called the Ice Lily. It will kill a man in moments."

Now the knife came out, although Vo did not yet leave his seat. "What nonsense is this? I don't want to die—do you, old man?"

Kimir shook his head. "The Yanedani dip their spears in the paste like eating chickpea butter with pieces of bread. For a man, even a mighty man like yourself, only the smallest, smallest amount is necessary."

"Necessary for what? You said this thing inside me could not be killed."

"No, but it can be . . . lulled. It is a living thing, not pure magic, and so it is susceptible to the apothecary's art. A very, very tiny taste of tigersbane every day will help to keep the creature . . . asleep. As a toad sleeps in the dried mud, waiting for the spring rains."

"Huh. And how do I know it will not poison me?" Vo waved the long, broad blade of his knife at the old man. "You will show me how much to take. You will take it first."

Malamenas Kimir shrugged. "Gladly. But I have not taken it in a while. I fear I will not get much work done this afternoon." He grinned again. "But I am sure in your gratitude you will pay me enough to make it worthwhile closing the shop for the day." He worried the stopper out of the black glass bottle, then began searching around the store for something.

"And how do you know I won't kill you when I have what I want, old man?"

The old man returned with a silver needle held between his fingertips. "Because this poison is very rare. You could go to a hundred places and not find it. If you let me live I will get more for you, and the next time you need it you will find it here. I do not know your name and would not tell tales on a customer if I did, so there is no advantage to you in harming me."

Vo stared at him for a moment. "Show me how much to take."

"Only a drop as big as you can lift on the point of this needle—never bigger than a radish seed." Kimir dipped the needle into the jar and withdrew it with a tiny ball of glistening, red-amber liquid clinging to the tip.

Kimir put it on his tongue and sucked it off the needle. "Once every day. But beware," he said. "A great deal more at one time will stop even a strong heart like yours."

Vo sat and watched him for some time, nearly an hour, but the old man showed little difference in his behavior. With Vo's permission he even began tidying his shop, although he seemed to work in a slightly lackadaisical way.

"It can almost be pleasant," Kimir said at one point. "I have not tasted it for a long time. I had forgotten. My lips feel a bit strange, though."

Vo was not interested in how the old man's lips felt. When enough time had passed that he felt sure no trick was being played, he took a slightly smaller quantity for himself and licked the needle clean.

"And this will keep the thing inside me asleep?"

"If you keep taking the tigersbane, yes," Kimir told him. "What you have there should last you until the end of summer. It cost me two silver imperials." Again that grin, like a fox watching a family of fat quail. "I will let you have it for that much, because you will be a returning customer."

Vo slapped the money down on the table and walked out. The old man did not even watch him go, so busy was he changing the arrangement of the drawers in his apothecary chest.

Vo felt a little odd, but no worse than after drinking a mug of beer quickly on a hot day. He would get used to it. It would not affect his alertness, he would see to that. And if it did, well, he would take an even smaller dose. There was still the chance that when he delivered the girl to Sulepis, the autarch would recognize his usefulness and reward him by removing the creature from Vo's innards. Who was to say that good things might not happen? If the autarch meant to rule two entire continents then he would need strong, clever men. He would find no better viceroy than Daikonas Vo, a man not bullied by his fleshy appetites like most of his brethren. A country of his own to rule would be an interesting experience indeed . . .

Vo stopped, aware that something was wrong, but not sure for a moment what it was. He stood on a promontory where the main bazaar road curved out and the hill dropped away on one side, giving a view over the harbor. The morning sun was now high in the sky, and the sky was cloudless . . . but clouds hung just above the water.

Smoke.

He stared. His feeling of near contentment abruptly fell away, replaced by anger and something that might even have been fear.

Down in the harbor, the Xixian ship—*Vo's* ship—was on fire.

✱

The sun had been up for an hour at least as far as Qinnitan could tell, and the nameless man seemed to have left the boat, or at least he had not come in to examine them with his empty expression, which was what he had done every other day, starting first about dawn.

So, gone . . . perhaps. If so, it might be the last time they would be out of his reach until he delivered them into the autarch's golden-fingered hands. If she was ever to try an escape, now was the moment.

She banged loudly at the door, ignoring Pigeon's look of concern. At last the bolt lifted and one of the guards peered in. She told him what she wanted. He frowned uneasily, then hurried off to get his commanding officer.

Two more officers came and went before the captain himself appeared, at which point she knew for certain that the nameless man was off the boat. It was obvious that the captain still feared him, though, from the anxious way he dealt with Qinnitan: clearly he knew little about her except that she was being taken to the autarch.

"I am a priestess of the Hive," she told him for the third time. "I must be allowed to pray to Nushash today. It is the Day of the Black Sun." She hoped the invented name sounded suitably ominous.

"And you think I am going to let you out on deck for that?" He shook his head. "No. No and no."

"You would bring bad luck down on your ship? Deny the god his prayers on this day of all days?"

"No. I would have to surround you with guards and to be honest, I dare not show so many men here in this harbor. We are not at home, after all." He realized he had said more than he should and scowled at her, as if it were Qinnitan's fault that he had a lax tongue. "No. You may pray until you are hoarse, but only in your cabin."

"But I cannot pray without sight of the sun. It is an offense against the god!" Now she said a real prayer, begging that he would think he had come up with the idea on his own. "I must have either a view of the all-conquering sun—or a fire. I have neither."

"A fire? Ridiculous. I suppose you could have a lamp. Or a candle. Yes, that would be safer. Would a candle be enough to keep the god sweet?"

"You mock the gods at your own risk," she said severely, but inside she was almost dizzy with relief. "A lamp would be sufficient."

"No, a candle. That or nothing, and I will take my risks with the gods."

Qinnitan did her best to look like a spoiled priestess used to getting her own way. "Oh, very well," she said at last. "If that is the best you can do."

"Tell the gods I did not hinder you," he said. "Be honest! You must always tell the truth to heaven."

After a feverish, frustrating wait, a sailor brought her a candle in a clay cup. It was a little thing, only slightly bigger than her thumb, its flame small as a fingernail. When they were alone again she set it on the floor and began to tear her blanket into long strips. Pigeon sat up, his eyes round, and made a questioning sign with his fingers. She smiled in what she hoped was a reassuring way. "I'll show you. For now, just help me. In pieces this wide."

When the blanket had been reduced to a couple of dozen strips, she pulled the water jug out from under the bed. She had been saving her water from last night, drinking only a few drops, and now she handed it to Pigeon. "Start pushing the pieces of blanket in this—like so." She shoved one in the jug and pulled it out, then wrung the excess water back into the ewer. "Now you do it. Just a few, then save the rest of the dry pieces."

While Pigeon, puzzled but willing, began to dip the scraps of wool, Qinnitan took a tiny perfume bottle she had been given by one of the other girls back in Hierosol. She pried out the stopper and poured it onto a piece of blanket she had saved for herself, then stood up to cram it into a crack between the planks of the ceiling. As the boy looked on in dawning terror, she lifted the candle up and held it to the perfume-soaked rag. A moment later a transparent blossom of blue flame sprang from it.

"Down," she told Pigeon. "Down on the floor. Hold this over your mouth—like so." She took one of the soaked strips of blanket and held it against his mouth. Like every other Hive priestess she had learned the story of the terrible fire some seventy years before, when the tapestries in the great hive rooms had caught fire and most of the bees—as well as many of the priestesses and acolytes—had been killed. Ancient Mother Mudry, a young woman then and the only person still alive in Qinnitan's day from that time, had survived the horrible conflagration because she had just come from the bath with wet clothes and wet hair, which she had pulled over her mouth. This had kept her alive long enough in the choking, blinding smoke for her to find her way to freedom. But now Qinnitan and Pigeon had an even more difficult task.

"We must stay alive until someone breaks down the door," she told the boy, speaking loudly so he could hear her through the muffling wet cloth. The flame was beginning to blacken the beams where the cloth was wedged and showed every sign of staying lit. When it got to the outer boards and the tar that made them waterproof she hoped the flames would be impossible to stop. "Stay down low, near the ground, and breathe only through the wet cloth. When it gets dry and you can taste the smoke, dip the cloth back in here." She showed him the jug. "Now lie down!"

O brave Nushash, she whispered, then realized that even though she had just set the blaze herself, praying to the god of fire might not be the ideal choice. Was the autarch not the child of Nushash, after all? Qinnitan was thwarting his will—perhaps Nushash would not take kindly to that.

Suya the Dawnflower. Of course—Suya had been stolen from her husband's side and forced to wander the world. She of all the gods would know and understand.

Please, O Dawnflower, Qinnitan prayed, clutching the shivering child beside her as smoke began to obscure the ceiling of the small cabin. Already she could smell it through the wet wool, but she wanted to save the water—only the gods knew how long they would have to wait. *Give us your help at this hour. Show me your grace and your favor. Let me protect this child. Help us to escape the people who would harm us. Show us your well-known mercy . . .*

Prayer finished, she closed her eyes tight against the stinging smoke and waited.

She shoved the scrap of blanket all the way down to the bottom of the jug, but it seemed to come out even more dry than it had gone in. The piece she clutched to her own face was bone-dry, too—all she could smell was smoke. Beside her, Pigeon was coughing hard, his tiny body shaking and straining in a way that made Qinnitan feel her heart would break. She could no longer see the door through the thick, coiling clouds of gray.

I don't mind dying, she told Suya and any other kindly gods who might be listening, *and I don't care what happens to me. But please, if the boy must die too, take good care of him in heaven. He is innocent.*

Poor Pigeon. What a dreadful life the gods had given him—his tongue taken, his manhood too, and then forced to run for his life simply for the crime of being in the wrong place when the autarch had one of his enemies murdered. *It isn't . . . isn't . . . fair . . . Poor . . .*

Qinnitan shook her head. She could see almost nothing now, and had to strain to get any breath into her burning lungs. Pigeon was barely moving. At the same time a booming pressure echoed through her, as if she were underwater and some ancient, sunken merchantman at the bottom of the ocean was tolling its ship's bell.

Boooom. Boooom. Boooom.

Qinnitan thought it was strange to be under the water. It hurt to breathe, but not in the way she would have guessed—and the water was so murky. Sand. Someone or something had stirred up the sand along the ocean bottom until it swirled in clouds around her, flecked with gold, with light, with little bits of starshine like the sky at night the dark the beckoning darkness . . .

Booom! And then something splintered and the water . . . the air . . . smoke . . . swirled and flames leaped above her and shapes staggered into the murky cabin—dark, shouting shapes that flickered with red light like devils capering on the floors of hell. Qinnitan could only stare and wonder what was happening as strong hands grabbed her and pulled her away from Pigeon. She was carried up the stairs outside the shattered doorway, jouncing like a saddle with a broken strap.

She found a little voice, but it was faint as a whisper. "Get the boy! Get Pigeon! Don't leave him behind!'

Before she could see whether the soldiers were bringing the mute child, she was dumped unceremoniously on the deck at the top of the stairs. Fire was everywhere, not just crackling in the deck but on the mast and even higher, flames capering in the sails and dancing across the rigging like wicked demon children. Some of the sailors were throwing buckets of water onto the blaze but it was like throwing pebbles at a sandstorm.

Another soldier dumped Pigeon beside her. The boy was alive, moving a little, but almost entirely insensible. She stared dully at the chaos for a moment, the men running, screaming, bits of flaming rope smacking down from above like the hell whip of Xergal, and then remembered what she had done. What horror her little candle had caused! Qinnitan struggled up onto her knees. No point trying to wake Pigeon: she would let the water do that job, or else finish the job the fire had just failed to do.

This time I'll die for certain before I let anyone take him again . . .

She waited a few more stuttering heartbeats until the men nearest her had their backs turned, then she lifted the boy's limp form as best she could and stumbled to the nearby rail. She leaned her back against it, heaved Pigeon up until his weight was across her shoulder and chest, then clung to him as his momentum carried them both over.

The fall took longer than she expected, time enough for her to wonder if dying in cold water would be better than dying in fire. Then they hit the water hard and green darkness closed around them like a fist.

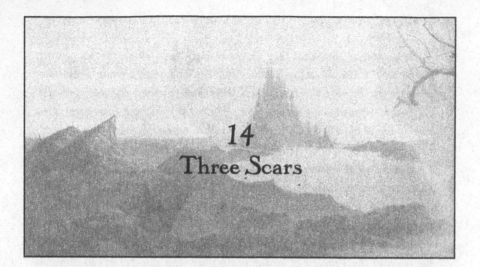

14
Three Scars

"Before the Vuts were driven out the lands now behind the Shadowline, the farthest northern outpost of men was the Vuttish city Jipmalshemm. In writings from that city there is much talk of a fearful place named 'Ruohttashemm,' the home of 'Cold Fairies,' which was also called 'the End of the Earth.'"

—from "A Treatise on the Fairy Peoples of Eion and Xand"

BARRICK EDDON FLOATED on the darkness like a leaf on a slow-moving river. The thoughts that made him took their direction from that flow: what they lost in complexity they gained in cohesion. It was peaceful, even pleasant, to be nothing, to want nothing, but the part of him that was still Barrick sensed that such peace could not last.

It didn't. Voices rose from the nothing—three voices entwined, three voices speaking as one, surrounding him with a tangle of words that only gradually came to reveal their meaning.

. . . Long ago, when the Dreamless broke away from their kin, it was because their own eternal wakefulness had driven them mad. The sleep of the People has always dulled the pain of their long lives, and even those highest and most long-lived, the Fireflower's children, can take a sort of rest and let their minds roam unfettered. But no such peace eased the pain of the Dreamless, trapped forever in the echoing cavern of their own thoughts.

So it came to pass that they turned against their fellows, turned against the rest of the People and went away into the wilderness to make new lives. In the forest beyond the Lost Lands they built a great city and named it Sleep, and even now no one can agree whether they named it in angry defiance of the People they had deserted or as the saddest of jests.

Nothing is more bitter than a family divided. As the years sped by the People and their unsleeping kin shed each other's blood and opposed each other's wills. Distance became enmity. The Dreamless ceased to venerate even those gods they had once loved, until the temples and sacred places of Sleep fell into ruin.

In all the rolling centuries since the sundering, out of all the Dreamless, the blood of the People has bred only we three who slumber as our ancestors slumbered. And in that slumber we dream far and clear.

Shunned by all, we were driven out of Sleep, but we were also unwanted in our ancestral halls, the House of the People. Thus we too went into the wilderness and have lived so long in the savage waste that we do not even remember the ways by which we came and could not find our way out again even if we chose.

Still we sleep, though, and when we sleep, we dream. In those dreams we see what is to be, or at least what might be—in any dream there are shadows and confusion, real foretellings mixed with false. But we know that we three were made different for a reason. We know that our dreams have meaning. And we know that no one else, mortal or immortal, has been given the visions that are vouchsafed to us.

We do not know who gives us the gift of these particular and heretical dreams, or why we were singled out and then doomed to wait so many centuries to use it. We do know that to ignore our gift would be to turn our backs on the one thing that holds all worlds and times together—the spirit of which the Book of the Fire in the Void *is word and thought—which is also the one thing that lends any hope of meaning to our own existence . . .*

These words, these thoughts, were Barrick's only companions in the void. The three speaking as one gradually unraveled into three separate voices once more, each with its individual character, but darkness still surrounded him: only the voices of the Sleepers kept him close.

"*What are we to do?*" asked the first voice, the kindest of the three. "*The story is unfolding but the characters have been misplaced or their entrances and exits mistimed.*"

"It was all bound to go wrong. I have said so." The sour one. Angry . . . or frightened?

"*Did we see this before?*" This one he remembered well, old and confused. The name . . . the name had been something like the wind blowing in a lonely place, a keening sigh. "*I do not recall it. I am cold and frightened. When the great ones come back they will be so angry with us all.*"

"*It is not for ourselves we do this, but for the story. Even the gods cannot destroy the story that we all are . . .*"

"*Untrue,*" said the sharp, angry voice. "*They can suppress it for so long that its shape becomes meaningless—until the tale has waited so long to come true that it becomes unrecognizable. The ending can be held off so long that it outlasts the world itself.*"

"*Only if we surrender,*" said the first Sleeper. "*Only if we refute our own dreams.*"

"*I wish I did not dream,*" said the old one. "*It has brought only sorrow. We had a family once, you know . . .*"

Hoorooen. That was the name of the ancient one with the querulous voice. Hoorooen. And the others had the same sound to them . . .

"*Quiet. It is time we think of what we can do. You heard the blind king. This little one, this young creature of the sun, must reach him soon or all is lost.*"

"*You struggle uselessly. Can the little mongrel fly? No. It is done, I tell you.*" Hikat, this one, Barrick remembered—a sound like an ax striking wood. Hikat. And the other was called . . .

. . . Hau. "*It is not done. There is a way. He can go by Crooked's road.*"

"*He does not know how—nor could he learn before years had passed.*"

"*I knew once,*" piped old Hoorooen. "*Did I not know? I think I did. I think I remember Crooked's roads and they were cold and lonely.*"

"*Cold and lonely they are, but there are other ways he might travel them besides his own strength.*" Hau spoke gently. "*There is a door in Sleep.*"

"*Ah!*" said Hoorooen. "*The darklights. I would like to see them again.*"

"*You are both fools,*" snapped Hikat. "*The city of Sleep means death, both to us and this mortal cub. There is no chance he could reach the door, or walk through it even if he found it.*"

"*Unless we help.*"

"*Even so.*" The one called Hikat seemed to take a certain joy in despair. "*What we can give him will only help him if he reaches the door—but he will never do so with an entire city full of deadly hatred against him.*"

"*There is nothing else to do. We have only this one chance.*"

"It will freeze up his blood," Hoorooen said gloomily. "If he travels those roads the void will drink away his life. He will become old and lost . . . like us. Old and lost."

"Nothing to be done—he must use Crooked's roads. There is no other way. But we will gift him with something of ourselves. Those are dangerous paths and we must prepare and armor him to survive them. Bring him toward us."

"It will diminish us—perhaps even destroy us. And he will only curse you for such a gift." Hikat sounded almost amused.

"It will almost certainly destroy us." Hau was sorrowful but resigned. "But the world and everything in it will curse us if we do it not . . ."

Barrick now found himself aware of his body again, then of the growing light of the fire and the dome-shaped room as well, and even the three Sleepers, but this perception did not bring freedom or even movement. The hooded Sleepers leaned over him as though they were mourners and he the corpse.

"We send him into dry lands," Hau said. "We must do what we can. But where? In what part of him do we pour our waters—our essence?"

"His heart," said Hikat. "It will make him strong."

"But it will also make his heart like stone. Sometimes love is all we have."

"So? It will give him the best chance to survive, you fool. Or would you betray the world you claim to hold so dear?"

"In his eyes," said quavering old Hoorooen. "So he can see what he will see in the days ahead and not be afraid."

"But fear is sometimes the first step toward wisdom," Hau replied. "To be unafraid is to be unchanging and unready. No, we will simply give our waters to him and his own being shall decide what to do with them. He is lame in one arm, out of balance—that is his weakest spot. We shall do it there, where he is already broken."

A uniform pressure moved over Barrick then, holding him motionless like a blanket of heavy armor links, but he could still feel the cool air of the room on his skin, the patchy heat of the fire. One of the three figures lifted an object up into the red light of the flames—a crude, ancient knife chipped from gray stone.

"Manchild," said the one called Hau, "let what we give you now, the waters of our being, fill you and strengthen you."

The pressure grew stronger on Barrick's left arm, the wounded place he had hidden from people's stares, had always tried to protect. Now he struggled again to protect it, but for all his desperate effort he could not move himself by so much as a finger's breadth.

"Do it swiftly," said Hikat. *"He is weak."*

"Not so weak as you suppose," Hau said, then something tore across the skin of Barrick's arm—a horrible, searing slash of pain. He tried to scream, to struggle free, but his body was not his own.

"I give you my tears," said Hau. *"They will keep your eyes clear to see the road ahead."* Something burned once more in the wound on his arm, salty and terrible. Another scream rose and fell deep inside him without ever breaking the surface.

The second shadowy figure took the knife, which rose and then came down again as another fiery spurt of agony pierced his arm. *"I give you the spittle of my mouth,"* Hikat growled. *"Because hatred will keep you strong. Remember this when you stand before the gods, and if you fail, spit in their faces for what they have taken from us all."* Again Barrick felt a drizzle of misery for which he was allowed no release of movement or sound.

The gods were punishing him, that was clear. He could take no more of such suffering. Even the smallest twinge of discomfort now and his head would flame and burst like a pine knot in a bonfire.

"I am dry as the bones on which we sit," quavered old Hoorooen. *"Tears and spittle I have none, nor any other of the body's waters. All I have left is my blood and even that is dry as dust."* The knife rose and fell a third time, biting into his mangled arm like a white-hot tooth. Barrick could barely think, barely hear. *"But the blood of dreamers may be worth something, in the end . . ."*

Something fell into his wound, powdery but also coarse and sharp, as though someone had stuffed tiny shards of glass into the bleeding place. The pain was everywhere and unendurable, as though biting ants swarmed over his exposed flesh. Wave after wave of suffering washed through him. Barrick drifted farther and farther away, as if he were flotsam carried on hot dark waves, but at last the hurt became a little less and he realized he was hearing voices again.

"You are stronger now—changed. We have given you all that we have left so that you might have a chance to give our dreams meaning. But now we are fading—we will not be able to speak to you much longer." For a moment, the hard voice of Hikat became almost gentle. *"Listen well and do not fail us, child of two worlds. There is only one way you can reach the House of the People and the blind king before it is too late—you must travel on Crooked's roads, which will fold your path before you so that you may step between the world's walls. To do that, you must find the hall in Sleep that bears his name."*

"Most of those roads are closed to you," said Hau, whose voice was more distant now than it had been. *"One only you might find and use in time, because it is close by. It is in the city of Sleep—the home of our own people. But know that the Dreamless who live there hate mortals even more than they hate the lords of Qul-na-Qar."*

"But even if our essences may enable him to survive the cold, dead places that Crooked traveled, still it will be for nothing." Hikat sounded angry again. *"Look at him—how will he cross Crooked's Hall? How will he open the doorway?"*

"That is not ours to know," said Hau. *"We have nothing left to give. Even now I feel the outer winds blowing through me."*

"Then it has all been for nothing."

"Life is always loss," murmured the old one. *"Especially when you gain something."*

Barrick found a little of his strength again, although the scalding pain still swirled through him like hot metal in a crucible. "What are you talking about?" he demanded. "I don't understand! Is this all a dream?"

Hau's voice was little more than a whisper now. *"Of course. But true, nevertheless. And if you reach Crooked's Hall at last, remember this one thing, child—no mortal hand can open the door there. It is written in the Book itself—no mortal hand . . ."*

"I don't understand you!"

"Then you will die, pup," said fading Hikat. *"The world will not wait for you to understand. The world will murder you and all like you. The Eon of Suffering will begin and you will all be punished for having left them outside in the cold so long."*

"Who? Leaving who outside?"

"The gods," old Hoorooen moaned. *"The angry gods."*

"You're telling me to walk into the city of the Dreamless?" Face certain death there just for a chance to fight against the gods themselves? It was utter madness. "How can I believe *any* of this?"

"Because we are the Sleepers, the dreamers," one of them murmured—it might have been Hau. *"And we have lived very close to them. Close enough to hear their dreaming thoughts, which roar in our ears like the ocean."*

"*Whose* thoughts? Do you mean the gods?"

"Look back as you leave." The voice was so faint he could no longer tell which one spoke. *"You will see. You will see them and perhaps you will understand . . . and believe . . ."*

And then Barrick's eyes were open and he was alone in the cave. The whispering shapes who had sat over him were gone. The fire was out, but a little light fell from the single oblong opening in the cavern wall. He looked down at his forearm. Three stripes of blood showed where the skin had been cut, but the wounds seemed largely healed, as if he had been lying there for days instead of hours. Had it all been a dream? Had he cut himself, hit his head, stumbled here, and fancied the rest while he lay in a swoon?

Barrick stood on shaky legs. He might have been dreaming, but he hadn't been sleeping—that seemed clear just from how weary he felt. He still desperately needed fire, so he limped forward to see if he could find a piece of smoldering wood, but to his amazement and disappointment the ashes were white and cold, as if nothing had burned there for years. He was about to turn away when he saw something half-buried in the ash and dirt beside the circle of stones. Barrick bent, favoring his injured arm, which did not hurt as it usually did. (In fact, it was cold and stiff but pain-less, as though he had soaked it a long time in a mountain stream until it had gone numb.) He scraped at the dirt and uncovered a ragged, ancient leather pouch, so long in the damp ground that the leather was almost as hard as stone. When he peeled it open a chipped piece of shiny black stone fell out; a little more work and he withdrew a crescent-shaped piece of rusted steel from the remains of the leather. Steel . . . and flint! He had found someone's fire-making tools! He could hardly wait to try it. Even if all the rest of this interlude had been no more than an exhausted dream, everything would be better now that he had fire.

He folded the remains of the leather sack around his find and tucked it into his belt. Barrick was exhausted and needed sleep, but he was reluc-tant to stay in this strange place any longer. If he had not dreamed the three strange Sleepers, perhaps they had only left for a while and would be coming back soon. They had not harmed him beyond whatever mys-terious thing they had done to his arm, but they had certainly held him prisoner and had talked madness to him about the gods and doorways and folds in the world.

And his arm . . . what had he dreamed about his arm? What had they done? He held up his left hand, which was not clenched as it usually was, as it had been for years, but instead was simply closed: with a little effort he could actually open it, something he had not been able to do in a long time. He was so startled by this that he laughed a little.

What happened here?

And there had been more: he had dreamed of the dark-haired girl again, and this time he had dreamed her a name—*Qinnitan*, and somehow that felt like a true thing. But if that dream had been real, what of the rest . . . ?

No, it was dangerous to think that way, Barrick told himself. Those were the sort of lies priests told people to keep them stupid—that the gods saw everything, that they had a purpose for everyone. Although now that he thought of it, that hadn't been what the Sleepers had said. Hadn't they suggested the gods themselves were the enemy? *"The Eon of Suffering will begin,"* one of them had told him, *"and we will all be punished for having left them outside in the cold so long."*

Barrick Eddon walked out of the domelike chamber into gray twilight. His eyes seemed to see subtleties in the dimness he had not noticed before—perhaps, he thought, because he had been so long in the dark cavern. Then, as he made his way down the path and off it and onto the raw stuff of the hillside, he remembered something else one of the Sleepers had said when he had asked whether they were really talking about the gods—the same gods Barrick knew. For most of his life Barrick had scorned his people's beloved *oniri*, the oracles and prophets who claimed to know the gods' will, but the strange Sleepers had said they heard the gods' very thoughts. How could that be?

"Look back as you leave," the quavering voice had told him. *"You will see. You will see them, and perhaps you will understand."*

Barrick did look back, but at the moment a fold of the hillside blocked the place he had been: all he saw were trees and glimpses of the butter-colored stone that dotted the hill. He shook his head and resumed hunting for a place to make camp.

A little later, when he had all but forgotten, he chanced to look back again, and this time he had descended far enough down the slope that he could see the whole crest of the hill.

"You will see them, and perhaps you will understand . . ."

The forms had been too harried to notice on the way up, and had been too close to see or blocked by trees before, but now they suddenly leaped to his eyes. Beneath the earth and greenery of the hillside loomed shapes the color of old ivory, but they were not outcroppings of stones, as he had thought. Rather they were half-buried . . .

Bones . . . ?

He had missed seeing it before because it was not one simple shape but two, wrapped together in a complicated way—two vast skeletons tangled in an embrace of love or death, giant bones which had perhaps once been buried, but which had been lifted up into the air by the living earth, a thin mantling of soil cloaking them like a shroud and providing the nurture of trees and vines. The tooth-shaped rocks on top of the hill *were* teeth, the immense jaw of a mostly buried skull, broken loose and exposed by wind and rain. The other skull . . . the other skull . . .

That's where I was, he realized, and a curtain of darkness threatened to fall over his mind and chase him away into the void. *With the dreamers . . . inside a god's skull . . .*

Barrick turned and fled down the hill—slipping and sliding, rolling more often than he ran, forced to vault over the branches that threatened to trip him, and which to his fevered thoughts seemed to be the fingerbones of the immortal dead, reaching up through the soil to snatch him and pull him down.

It might have been luck that he did not drop the flint and steel during that stumbling, terrified trip down the hill, or when he collapsed in weariness at the bottom. It might also have been luck that the first thing that found him there was not a silkin but something with a harsh, familiar voice.

"Thought you were dead!" After a moment, when he had not responded, something poked at his ear. "You don't be dead, do you?"

Barrick groaned and sat up. He ached all over from his numerous falls—except, oddly, his crippled arm, which still retained a stony numbness, although he could flex it now at least as easily as he ever could. "Skurn?" He opened his eyes. The black bird, head tilted to one side, stared at him with its fathomless black eye. "Gods, it is you." He let himself slump back, then sat up. "A fire! I can make a fire."

He scrambled to find enough dry leaves and grass to make a pile, then went to work, striking down at the crescent-shaped piece of metal with the flint. Once a few sparks fell onto the grass Barrick blew on them; after a little while he was rewarded with a curl of smoke and then a tiny, near-transparent flame. Relieved, he sat back and warmed his hands in front of the miniature blaze. "We must make camp somewhere nearby so I can build a proper one," he said.

"Not here." The raven lowered his harsh voice. "Here at the hill's bottom, silkins will find us."

Barrick shook his head. "I don't care. I have to rest, at least for a little while. I have climbed all the way to that hill's top today."

Now the bird tilted its head again, this time to inspect the boy. "Is that what you've been at all these last days? Climbing up hill and down hill like a Follower up a tree?"

"Days? One day at most, surely."

The raven examined his face carefully, as though he might be joking. "Days. But Skurn stayed. Skurn waited!"

Barrick did not have the strength to argue with a mad bird. He shielded the infant blaze with some stones, then went in search of a better place to camp—somewhere on good, natural stone, not the bony, yellowy stuff of the heights. Barrick wanted no more of any gods for a while, whether living or dead.

The heat of the fire was even more heartening than its light—it was wonderful to be warm again for the first time in longer than he could remember. After an hour or so the cold only lingered in his crippled arm, but even that was not a painful chill but a kind of absence, as if the organs of suffering had been somehow removed when he had gained his three parallel scars. They were all covered by scabs now and scarcely discomforting at all. His arm even seemed to have a degree of mobility it had not shown before, although Barrick could not tell whether that was because it could actually bend farther or just because it hurt less. The muscles were still weak, but it seemed a different kind of weakness, as though with more employment it would gain strength, like any ordinary limb long disused.

As a result he was in the best mood he had seen in a long while. Even in those first heady moments after he had escaped Greatdeeps and the monster Jikuyin, his happiness had been undercut by the loss of his two companions, Gyir and Vansen. Barrick knew he was still in great danger, perhaps with even more perilous times to come, but just now being warm and not in pain seemed a blessing as great as any that heaven could grant.

He stretched and yawned. "Tell me what you know about the city of Sleep," he asked Skurn, who was busy smacking a snail shell on a rock like a tiny blacksmith at his anvil.

The raven dropped the snail and turned toward him, feathers bristling around his neck like a courtier's ruff. "*Pfagh!* That be a foul name. Where did you hear such?"

"Spare me the warnings and the gloomy predictions, bird. Just tell me what you know."

"Us knows what any know and naught more. Night Men live there, who once were high among the Twilight folk until they fell into wicked ways, making foul allies and marrying only 'mongst theyselves and such. Then were they sent away. They made up their own city which they built in the dead lands down Fade River from here. None go there by their own will, it be said."

The idea that he would go to such a place seemed both frightening and amusing to Barrick—amusing only in that it was so clearly ridiculous. Follow the river Fade! It was like some bard's poem of fatal heroism. The Sleepers might have said a door in Sleep was his only way to reach the Qar king in his royal city, and it was true he had promised to take Gyir's mirror there, but that did not seem nearly enough compulsion to force him toward such an obviously murderous spot. What made them so sure he would do it? Why would any person who was not a half-wit go to such a place?

"Is that all you know, bird? How far away is it?"

"Us could fly there on five or six meals, like, but why would us?"

"I don't mean flying. How far for someone like me to walk?"

The raven dropped the snail shell again and hopped closer, examining Barrick carefully once more as though suddenly concerned that he was sharing the campsite with an imposter. "Just finished running up and down Cursed Hill, you did. Dost young master plan to visit every deathly spot in all the Twilight Lands, like pilgrim?"

Barrick grinned sourly. "What do you know of the gods, Skurn? Of what happened to them? Are they really gone from the world?"

Now the raven appeared truly agitated, hopping and flapping his way around the fire until he had found a stone to jump onto, as though he suddenly wanted to be a little farther off the ground. "Why yon strange questions? Us dasn't think too much about the ways of the gods, let alone speak on 'em. When they hears they names—even in dreams—they takes notice."

"Very well. No more talk." The pull of sleep was getting strong now, the fire like a warm blanket draped across his front, comforting, almost homely. "We can speak more on it tomorrow, when we set out."

"Set out?" The raven's voice had an unarguable touch of worry in it. "Set out where, young master?"

"For the city of Sleep, of course." Barrick almost smiled again. Was this how they had felt, those great heroes of old, Hiliometes or Silas or Massilios Goldenhair? As though they were part of some greater thing, tugged along through no choice of their own, helpless . . . but almost uncaring? It was a strange feeling. All of him, even his thoughts, seemed at this moment to be strengthened, yet as unfeeling as his arm. He looked down at the blackening blood on his skin, the three marks as though he had been clawed by some bird twice Skurn's size or more. What *had* the Sleepers given him?

Life is always loss, especially when you gain something, the old one had said. Did that mean they had also taken something from him? But what had he lost?

"You do not mean it, young master, do you? Not to go to such a place."

"You need not go, Skurn. This is my journey."

"But the silkins in the forest—and the Dreamless in that dreadsome city! They will freeze our blood and eat our skin!"

"You need not go."

"Then I will be lost here and alone."

Barrick fell silent then, but not out of pity for the bird. After he had slept he would wake. After he had awakened he would set out. He would walk until he reached the city called Sleep, then he would see what happened next—death or something else. He would go on like that until everything was over. It seemed simple, somehow.

But what had the Sleepers taken from him to give him such simplicity? And what had he lost . . . ?

Weariness took him then, pulling him down into darkness, carrying him away from the flickering fire to a place that mortals shared with gods.

PART TWO
CLOAK

15
The Soiled Dove

"Ruohttashemm, home of the Cold Fairies and their warlike queen Jittsammes, was reported to be on the far side of the Stallanvolled, a great, dark forest that covered a large area of Old Vutland."

—from "A Treatise on the Fairy Peoples of Eion and Xand"

EIVAL, DRESSED IN HIS NEW popinjay finest, was waving his hands behind the prince's head, urgently trying to signal something to her.

He's reminding me to get back to work, Briony realized. "Tell me again of how you led your men back from the south," she asked Prince Eneas.

"Yes, tell us again!" begged her friend Ivgenia.

"Surely you are bored with that story, ladies." To his credit, the king's son looked uncomfortable. "I have told it to you each time I have visited. The ending will still be the same if I tell it again."

"But it is such a good ending, Highness." Ivvie clearly would have been happy to listen to Eneas talk about anything, even in a language she didn't understand.

"But so many stories of fighting!" he protested. "Surely highborn ladies like yourselves would prefer more wholesome tales."

"Not me," said Briony with something near to real pride. "I was raised with brothers and trained to fight by Shaso of Tuan, as you may remember."

Eneas smiled. "I do, and I pray that one day you will let me question you about his tactics and methods of teaching. I envy you such a splendid, famous instructor."

"Such excellent schooling was wasted on me, I fear. I was never allowed to practice my fighting skills with any men save my brother, and for all my life Southmarch did not taste war, at least not on our soil."

"But that is no longer true, Princess—the men of Southmarch have just fought several battles against the fairies."

"Battles that did not end well." She allowed a hitch into her voice—it was not entirely manufactured. "Battles that took our finest men . . . and separated my beloved brother from me as well . . . perhaps forever." She smiled bravely. "So it is good to hear of happier results, like yours. It gives me hope. Please, Prince Eneas, tell your tale again."

Still standing behind the prince, Feival vigorously signaled approval: he himself had taught her that brave, tragic smile.

Eneas laughed and gave in with good grace. He was easy to like, this prince: almost any other man would have been only too happy to blow his own fanfare and rehearse his glorious deeds for Briony, her ladies, and Ivgenia. Gailon Tolly, the duke of Summerfield, although he had turned out a better man than Briony had thought him (at least by comparison with his murderous brother) had always been far too willing to speak at length about his own adventures hunting or riding, making it sound as though every ditch he jumped had been a triumph over Kernios the Soul-Taker.

"Our army crossed the border and stopped at the outermost of the Hierosoline garrisons," the prince said. "Our commander, Marquis Risto of Omaranth, had been sent not so much to fight on Hierosol's behalf as to see the lay of things and send back a recommendation to my father— that is why father had sent Risto, a shrewd, careful man. But nobody guessed that the autarch would strike so swiftly or with such numbers. At the same time as he brought a great force from the sea and launched his assault on the walls of Hierosol itself, the autarch also sent a second, smaller armada up the Kulloan Strait by night with oars muffled and sails furled. They had been led through the most dangerous part of the rocky strait by a traitor from Hierosol—a sea pilot who betrayed his country for gold." Eneas shook his head, genuinely puzzled. "How could a man do such a thing?"

"It is impossible to understand," said Ivvie, nodding vigorously.

"Impossible," echoed Feival, who was prone to be a little more involved in conversations than was proper for a secretary. "Disgusting!"

"Not all people feel as strongly attached to their countries as you and I do," Briony told the prince kindly. "Perhaps because their positions in those countries are not so secure and privileged as ours."

"Or perhaps they are just inclined to treachery by birth or blood," Ivvie countered. "There are peasants on my father's land who not only poach from our forests, they withhold taxes and lie to the reeve when the counting-out season comes, claiming they have more children than they do, or less land, anything to avoid paying my father what they owe."

Some of the other ladies made noises of polite agreement. They shared a general dislike of the people who dug the soil and harvested the crops, although, like their menfolk, they often spoke about them in a way that Briony found sentimental and false. She did not claim to know the life of a peasant herself, but she had experienced enough nights in cold barns or open fields while traveling with the players that she couldn't believe anyone would choose that life for the pastoral joy of it. Also, Briony had seen enough of the machineries of justice and taxes to know that the ills were by no means all on the side of treacherous peasants.

Still, it would do no good to start an argument: the people in this court already thought of her as odd, and it might also poison the prince's mood at a time when she was doing her best to make him like her.

Feival was glaring at her again, and she realized that her wandering thoughts had taken her away from Eneas describing how the Xixian invasion had caught the Syannese troops by surprise, forcing them to take refuge in a Hierosolian fortress.

"But if Marquis Risto and the others were under siege, how did you discover their plight?" she asked. "You must have told me, but I'm afraid I've forgotten." She hadn't, of course, but there was nothing wrong with applying a thin layer of helplessness to her appeal—not overdoing it, as she might have when playing the Miller's Daughter in a farce like *A Country Priest's Tale*, but giving it enough push that Eneas might think of her as a needy younger sister, someone whose interests wanted protecting.

"Because he was on a mission from my father, Risto was carrying pigeons to send messages back to Tessis. He had brought the last set from our frontier fort at Drymusa, and it was just good luck I had seen him there when he passed through. I decided to wait another fortnight with my men before leaving because I was curious to hear his report about the state of things in Hierosol."

"How clever of you, Highness," Ivgenia said.

Eneas gave her a look of gentle reproof. "It was luck, my lady, as I said. I had no idea that Risto would walk into a siege. Xis has threatened Hierosol for years, but none of us truly believed it was more than bluff, since it was easier for the Xixian autarchs to snatch prizes among the rich islands on the southern coast. In any case, word came, and I was there with a company of battle-ready men. Good fortune, as I said, was on our side."

"A blessing from the gods," murmured Briony.

Eneas nodded. He was known to be devout, and had quietly gifted several temples while his younger siblings were spending their own money on the pleasures of earthly existence. "Yes, a blessing indeed. Are you sure you wish to hear this all again?"

"Please," Briony told him. "We get so little firsthand news."

He gave her a wry look. "But I hear you have been out getting a good look at the world, both on your way here and since you have arrived, Princess Briony."

For a moment she was nonplussed, until she realized he must be referring to her trip out of the palace with Ivgenia. But why would something like that interest Eneas? Unless he was just interested in Briony in a general way, and had been asking about her . . . She couldn't afford to be too sure of herself, though: he might be interested in Ivgenia, after all—she was a pretty, vivacious young girl with a good family bloodline.

"I have found trouble for myself in all kinds of places, Prince Eneas," she told him, ignoring Feival's smirk. "I obviously require better advisers to keep me from mischief. I hope you will feel free to lend me your wisdom."

He smiled. "I would consider it an honor, Princess. But from what I hear you have done well and bravely on your own."

He really was quite handsome—there were no two ways about it. Briony was of several different minds about all of this. On the one hand, she felt like a traitor—a real one, not just one of Ivgenia's father's tenants trying to withhold a half-basket of barley to get through the winter. After all, she intended to use this man, not for his good or his country's, but for her own family's—to make up, in part, for her own failures. But there were several problems with such a plan. One was that Eneas might well be too clever to be manipulated, in which case she might alienate someone who could otherwise have become a true ally here at court. Second, the prince was not the kind of man of whom she could happily take advantage. By all accounts except his own (which tended toward modesty) Eneas was kind, intelligent, and extremely brave. He loved his father but was not blind to his own country's failings. He was also fiercely loyal to his friends, as everyone assured her. How could she set out to use her so-called womanly wiles to get her way—the very methods she had long despised when used by her stepmother Anissa or the other ladies of the Southmarch court?

But the need is great because the cause is so important, she told herself. *The lives of my people. My father's throne.*

Yes, and revenge against the Tollys, a sly little voice reminded her. *Do not pretend you do not wish that as well.* Not a noble motive, but one close to her heart. Hendon Tolly had taken almost everything from her. He and his brother Caradon deserved to die, preferably after much suffering and humiliation. Hendon had not just stolen her family's throne, he had made Briony feel helpless and weak, and for that alone she wanted him dead. Sometimes she felt as though she would never be strong again until Hendon had been punished for that crime.

"Princess?"

She lifted a hand to her mouth, embarrassed. How long had she been woolgathering? She dared not even look toward Feival, who must be beside himself. "I'm sorry, I . . ." Might as well use the chance when it was there. "I suddenly remembered . . . a painful thing . . ."

"It is my fault." He looked as though he believed it. "I should not have teased about your trip to the Flower Meadow market—that was cruel and thoughtless. I forgot utterly that was the day your young servant died. My deepest apologies, Princess."

Was that what they had been talking about—the market? She had entirely lost the thread. The simple thought of Hendon Tolly grinning that fox's grin of his as he bragged about how he had stolen her throne . . . "No, no," she said, recovering herself. "Not your fault, sir. Please, you hadn't finished telling us about the siege."

"Are you certain that you wish to hear my dry tale yet again?"

"It is not dry to me, Prince Eneas. It is like water to a parched throat. Go on."

He continued as Briony and Ivgenia and the other women listened intently, and even Feival kept forgetting that he was supposed to pretend he was working. Whether they were all fascinated by the prince's relief of the Hierosoline garrison and his escape back across the Syannese border with Marquis Risto and his men, or because Eneas was simply a fascinating man with an even more fascinating place in the world, the audience was no less rapt for it.

When he had finished his tale the prince stood and bowed and asked Briony's permission to leave her—a bit of southern court etiquette that amused her, as though the very presence of a noblewoman was like the pull of a whirlpool on a hapless swimmer, a death grip from which only the maelstrom itself could set the unfortunate free.

And what if I said no? she wondered even as he kissed her hand and bowed to Ivgenia and the other ladies. *What if I commanded him to stay? Would he have to do it?* What nonsense etiquette was! Something that had no doubt begun as a way to keep men from raping and killing, at least for short periods of time, had taken on such force that it could sometimes cause the most ridiculous confusions.

Ivgenia quickly broke the silence after Eneas had gone. "He seems to care for you, Princess Briony. That is the third time he has come to see you this week!"

"I am an entertaining oddity," she said, waving the idea away. "A princess who has traveled in disguise. I am like something in a story for children." She laughed. "I suppose I should be grateful I am not the subject of a more dreadful tale, a child abandoned in the woods or one who is mistreated by a cruel stepmother." Her own laugh ended quickly. Neither of those things were far from the truth.

"You make too much protest," Ivgenia said. "Doesn't she, ladies?" The others, maids and ladies-in-waiting, nodded their heads. "He has true affection for you, Highness. Perhaps it might become something more if you were not so stubborn!"

"Stubborn?" She had thought she was doing everything but throwing herself into Eneas' arms to keep his attention and good will. "How have I been stubborn?"

"You know perfectly well," her friend said. "You do not mix with the other folk at court except at meals. They think you too proud. Some say it is only that you have been so harshly treated, but others say . . . you must forgive me, Briony, but I will tell you the truth for your own sake . . . but others say that you think yourself better than the folk of the court."

"Better!" She was astounded. That the people of this grand, decadent court should think her too proud—it beggared her imagination. "I think myself better than no one, least of all these fine lords and ladies. I do not mingle because I have lost the art, not because I despise the company."

"There!" said Ivgenia triumphantly. "It is as I have told others—you feel out of place, but not above things. But truly, Briony, you must spend more time among the nobles here. They fall easily into gossip and Jenkin Crowel does you no favors in your absence."

The name of Tolly's envoy was like a splash of icy water. She had avoided the man for days and he had seemed to do the same with her.

"Ah, yes . . . you are no doubt right. Thank you for your concern, Ivvie, but I'm tired now and I'd like to lie down."

"Oh, my dear Briony!" Ivgenia looked miserable. "Have I offended you, Princess?"

"Not at all, kitten—I'm just tired, as I said. Ladies, you too may withdraw. Feival, stay for a moment so I can discuss some business with you."

When the others were gone, or at least discreetly out of hearing, she turned on the player. "Crowel does me no favors? What does she mean?"

Feival Ulian frowned. "You must know, Briony. He is the right hand of your enemy. What do you think he does? He works against you whenever he can."

"How?" Anger flooded her—anger and fear. Tessis was not her home. Briony was surrounded by strangers and some people clearly wanted her dead. She threw down her needlework—a clumsy, irritating affectation for her at the best of times. "What is he doing?"

"I have not heard any reliable news of his actual works." Feival had turned away and was admiring himself in a mirror hung on the wall, a habit of his that maddened Briony, especially when she was talking to him about serious things. "But he speaks against you—carefully, and never in general company, of course. He says a quiet word here, drops an offhand hint there . . . you know how it is done."

She did her best to bank the flame of rage: it would do her no good to let it overwhelm her. "And what slanders does Jenkin Crowel spread?" She had grown heartily sick of looking at Feival's back. "By Zosim's masks, man, turn around and talk to me!"

He faced her, surprised and perhaps even a little angry. "He says many things, or at least so I hear—he is not such a fool as to speak lies about you to me!" Feival scowled like a sulking child. "Many of them are just small insults—that you are mannish, that you like to go about in men's clothing, and not simply for disguise, that you are sour-tempered and a shrew . . ."

"More true than not, so far," Briony said with a grim smile.

"But the ugliest thing he will not say directly, but simply hint. He lets slip that at first everyone thought the southerner Shasto had kidnapped you . . ."

"Shaso. His name was Shaso."

" . . . but that now folk in Southmarch believe you were not taken against your will. That it was part of a plan you made to seize your father's throne, and that only Hendon Tolly being there prevented the two of you from carrying it off." He flushed a little. "That is the worst of it, I suppose."

"The two of us? My brother Barrick and I?"

"No. In the hints he lets drop, your twin brother was a victim too, sent away by you to die fighting the fairies. Your accomplice, claims Crowel, was that very southern general Shast . . . Shaso—the man who killed your other brother. And that he was . . . more than an accomplice . . ."

Briony's rage was so sudden and so powerful that for a moment blackness rushed into her head and she thought she was dying. "He dares to say that? That I . . ." Her mouth seemed full of poison—she wanted to spit. "His master Hendon did kill his own brother—surely that is what he is thinking of! He is telling people that Shaso and I were lovers?" She lurched to her feet. It was all she could do not to snatch up her sewing and run out to stick a needle in Jenkin Crowel's eye. "The infamous . . . pig! It is bad enough that he should insult that good old man who died trying to get me to safety, but to suggest that I would . . . that I would harm my own beloved brothers!" She was weeping now and could barely catch her breath. "How can he tell such lies about me? And how can anyone believe them?"

"Briony—Princess, please, calm yourself!" The player looked almost terrified by what he had unleashed.

"What does Finn say? What are people saying on the street, in the taverns?"

"It is scarcely discussed outside of court," he told her. "The Tollys are not particularly popular here, but it likely makes people wonder. Still, the king *is* popular and you are his guest. Most Syannese leave it to him to know what's best."

"But not here in the court, I take it."

Feival was trying to calm her now. "Most people in the court do not know you any better than do the drunken fools in the taverns. It is because you lock yourself away here like an anchorite."

"So you are saying . . ." She paused to get her breath, to feel her heart slowing a little. "So you are saying that I should get out and mingle with the others in Broadhall Palace more often? That I should spend more time with folk like Jenkin Crowel, swapping insults and telling lies?"

Feival took a breath and straightened, the very picture of a man who had suffered unfairly. "For your own good, yes, Princess. You should make yourself seen. You should show people simply by your presence that you have nothing to hide. Thus you will refute Crowel's lies."

"Perhaps you are right." The heated fury was receding, but what replaced it was something no less angry, only colder. "Yes, you are right. One way or the other, I must move to prevent the spreading of such terrible, terrible stories.

"And I will."

❦

The temple of Onir Plessos did not have enough beds for all the newcomers but the pilgrims were a sensible lot, happy enough just to find refuge from this year's cold spring rains. The Master Templar told them they could spread their blankets in the common room after the evening meal.

"Will we not disturb your other guests, or the brothers?" asked the leader of the pilgrims, a heavyset fellow of obvious good nature for whom the conducting of religious seekers and penitents had become, after so many years, more a business than a religious calling. "You have always been generous to me, Master, and I would not wish to gain a bad name here."

The Master Templar smiled. "You bring a respectable class of pilgrim, my good Theron. Without such travelers, our temple would be hard pressed to shelter and feed the truly needy." He lowered his voice. "An example of the kind I like less well, do you see that fellow there? The cripple? He has stayed with us for several tennights." He gestured toward a robed figure sitting in the sparse garden attended by a smaller figure, a boy of perhaps nine or ten summers. "I confess I had hoped that when the weather warmed he would move on—not only does he have a rank smell, he is strange and does not speak to us himself, but has the child speak for him . . . or at least pass along his words, which are usually full of doom and mystery."

Theron looked interested. The lessened nature of his own faith, or at least of his zeal, had not made him any the less drawn to the strong faith of others—the reverse, if anything, since just such strong faith had now become his livelihood. "Perhaps he is an oracle, your cripple. Was not the blessed Zakkas unrecognized in his own lifetime?"

The Master Templar was not amused. "Do not seek to teach piety to a priest, Master Caravaner. This fellow does not talk of holy things, but of . . . well, it is hard to say without you hear him yourself—or hear what the child says for him."

"I doubt we will have time," said Theron shortly, smarting a little from the priest's rebuke. "We must leave early tomorrow. There is at least one more snow coming to the Whitewood this year, and I would not be caught in it. The north has become strange enough these days without fighting the storms. I miss the warm springs we enjoyed here in Summerfield when the king was on his throne in Southmarch."

"I miss many things about those days," said the Master Templar, and on this safer ground the conversation continued for a while as the two men regained their old friendship.

The fire in the common room had burned low and most of the pilgrims had fallen asleep after a long, cold day's walking. Theron was having a quiet conversation with his wagoneer when the holy man—or so Theron was already disposed to think of him—limped slowly into the room, leaning on a dirty, sullen, dark-skinned child. The boy helped him to sit down by the hearth, close to the embers, and then took a cup from the beggar's hand and carried it off to fill it from the bucket.

Theron waved the wagoneer off to finish what he had to do before sleeping, then watched the frail holy man for a moment. It was hard to make out much of anything about him: his face was hidden by the long hood of his stained and tattered robe, his hands wrapped in dirty old bandages. The strange shape sat still as stone but for a faint trembling. As

Theron stared at the beggar he felt not an apprehension of holiness but of sudden dread. It was not that the man himself seemed particularly threatening, but there was something about him that suddenly made Theron think of old stories—not those of holy pilgrims, but of unquiet spirits and dead men who cannot rest in their graves.

Theron ran his fingers through the swaying, clicking collection of religious ornaments around his neck, some he had gained himself on his travels as a younger man to various holy sites, others given to him as gifts (or sometimes as partial payment) by the pilgrims he conducted. His hand lingered for a moment on a wooden dove, one of his favorites and long-since polished to a deep sheen by handling. It had come from one of his earliest pilgrimages, to a famous Zorian shrine in Akaris, and he found it particularly soothing to think of the White Daughter when he was troubled.

Theron felt a presence at his shoulder and looked up. It was the Master Templar. Theron wondered at this, since it was not the older man's habit to come down to the common room after evening prayers. "You do me an honor, Master," he said. "Will you share a glass of wine with me?"

The master nodded. "I will. I wanted to ask you a question and you said you had to leave early in the morning."

Theron was a little ashamed to be reminded of this, since he had said it in anger. He poured wine from his own jar into a cup and passed it to his friend. "Of course, Master. What can I tell you?"

"One of your travelers told me that King Olin's daughter is in Tessis—that she has been found alive. Is it true?"

"It is, as far as I can say—she appeared just before we left, or so everyone said. It was the talk of Syan in our last days there."

"And does anyone know what brings . . . what is her name? Buttercup?"

"Briony. Princess Briony."

"Of course—I shame myself. We do not hear much of doings at the court here and I grow forgetful in my age. Briony. Does anyone know why she is in Syan and what it means?"

Theron noticed that the hooded beggar near the fire had raised his head as if listening. He wondered if he should lower his voice, but then decided that was foolish: what he was saying was no secret, but news that would soon be on everyone's lips. Still, it would not be a wise idea to name the Tollys here in their own dukedom. "Some claim she escaped from . . . her enemies . . . and fled Southmarch. Others say no, that she fled after she was thwarted in her own attempt to take the throne with the help of a southerner—a black soldier who was once Olin's friend."

The Master Templar shook his head in wonder. "It is like the old days—the bad days of the second Kellick, when there were spies and plots everywhere."

"Do you remember that?" asked Theron, mildly surprised.

"Fool!" The Templar laughed. "A century and a half? Do I look so old?"

Theron laughed too, shamed by his own bad memory. The doings of kings and history had never been his strength. "My book learning is mostly forgotten . . ."

He was started by a figure at his shoulder and turned to find the hooded beggar looming there like the shadow of Death itself. For all that his back and legs seemed bent, he still stood as tall as Theron and must have been a powerful man once. The bandaged hands came up and a dry, scraping rustle issued from the darkness of the hood. Theron recoiled in fear, but for long moments the hooded man only stood silently.

"Where is the boy?" asked the Templar irritably. "Ah, there. Boy, come here and tell us what your master wants."

The boy, who had apparently been cadging food in the temple kitchen, duly appeared, still chewing on a lump of dough. Now that Theron looked at the child with more attention he noticed that not all the darkness of the black-haired boy's face was because of dirt or sun, that he had somewhat the look of a southerner himself, a color of skin usually only seen on the waterfronts of Oscastle or Landers Port. Yes, Theron thought, that was it: he had the look of one of those street urchins who lived like a harbor rat, by his wits and quickness.

"What is the cripple saying?" the Master Templar demanded.

The boy put his head close to the hood. It was impossible to hear any of the beggar's words above the crackling of the fire, but the boy stood up at last.

"He says that Death has turned loose of her for now."

The master shook his head in irritation. "Loose of whom? The princess? Tell him to go and find his bed and not disturb the talk of his betters." A moment later his expression changed. "No, that is unkind of me. The gods and *oniri* would not have us treat the afflicted so."

The boy was leaning close to the dark hood again. "He says that he knows death—that he dwelt for a while in Death's own house. But then he was let go again."

"What? He is saying that he lived in the house of Kernios?" The Master Templar clearly did not like this blasphemous turn the conversation had taken.

The boy leaned close to the hooded figure again. "And he says that since Briony has escaped he must find her."

"What nonsense!" said the house's master. "Take this beggar out to the stable, boy. I will not send the poor fool out into the cold but he must find someplace else to sleep tonight where he will not plague our guests." The priest waited, but although the boy apparently whispered these words to him the beggar did not respond. Theron was both interested and disturbed. "You are taking advantage of our charity," the Templar chief warned. This still produced no movement. "Very well, I will get some of the brothers to help me escort him to sleep with the horses and donkeys," he said, and strode briskly off across the common room.

The beggar was whispering to his young helper again.

"He wants to know if you are going north," the boy said to Theron.

The leader of the pilgrimage was confused: why should the old cripple want to know such a thing? "We go north through Marrinswalk, yes. This pilgrimage began in Blueshore and that is where we are returning."

The beggar pulled the boy toward him as if his next words could not wait.

"He wishes to go with you," the child said when the murmuring had finished.

Theron rolled his eyes. "I mean no disrepect to one whom the gods have already burdened," he said, "but the only members of our pilgrimage who walk are those who are young and fit—we travel fast. I have seen this man move. He could not keep up and we could not afford to wait for him."

The boy looked at him in puzzlement, although Theron thought what he'd said made perfect sense. Then the young beggar turned to look at his hooded master, who suddenly reached out toward Theron with his bandaged hand. Theron started back, unnerved, then saw something glinting there on the dirty linen. A gold coin.

"He will pay you for a place on one of the horses," the boy said after the hooded beggar had whispered to him.

"That . . . that is a dolphin!" said Theron, astonished. "An entire dolphin!" It was ten times as much as he had earned in fees from the whole of his caravan of pilgrims. The boy turned as the hooded one plucked at his sleeve, whispered to him again.

"He says to take it. The dead have no need of gold."

She was lost in the forest, but not frightened—not *too* frightened, anyway. The trees swayed but she felt no wind. As she passed they bent toward her, reaching with brushy fingers, but never touched her. The world was night-dark but she could see: a light moved with her, illuminating her path and surroundings.

Something scuttled across the track ahead of her, something silvery and swift, moving close to the ground. She changed direction, following it, and the path moved with her.

I'm dreaming, Briony realized.

The swift thing flickered before her again. It was both real and a shadow—she could feel it somehow watching her even as it ran before her. She knew it was trying to lead her somewhere important, that she needed to keep it in sight, but already she was falling behind. The trees grew thicker around her, the path harder to see. The silvery shape shimmered one last time, distant now, and then it was gone.

Briony woke with a sense of failure and loss far beyond the usual residue of dreams, but she could not stop to fret because she had missed something important. Her ladies were already bustling around her, urging her to hurry and get out of bed. Briony had an assignation to keep.

Dawet was wearing his usual black garb, but with a subtle difference: his clothes this time seemed more suited for courtly entertainment than going unnoticed in dark alleys and low places. His sleeves were slashed with brilliant red, the lining of his cloak the same bloody color, and his hose had also been picked out with vertical stripes of red and white.

"A new meeting place?" he asked her, looking around the Fountain Court.

"It is a little noisier here. Less likely anyone could overhear us." Briony eyed his attire. "You look less furtive than usual, Master dan-Faar."

He made a mock bow. "Milady is too kind. As it happens, I have a . . . meeting after ours."

"With a woman?" Briony didn't know why she should care, but it did rankle a bit.

Dawet's smile was, for once, neither knowing nor mocking. "I am your friend, I hope, Princess. Nothing more, perhaps, but certainly nothing less. For instance, I am not your servant. My trysts are my own."

Briony swallowed a retort, touching the Zorian vesicle hanging around her neck to remind herself of what was important. He spoke the truth: she had no right, and more than that, she had no sensible reason to take an interest in what Dawet did, and with whom, except where her own safety was concerned. "As long as we *are* friends," she said. "As long as I can trust you, Dawet. I mean this truly—I need someone I can trust."

He gave her an odd look. "You seem frightened, Princess."

"Not frightened. But I am engaged in . . . difficult matters. I am embarking on a journey. Once it begins I cannot turn and swim back to shore." She reached up again and cupped the vesicle in her hand, traced its oval shape and thought of the virgin goddess' own journey. "Will you help me?"

"What do you need, Princess?"

She told him. "Can you do that?" she asked when she had finished.

The look he gave her now contained both surprise and a hint of admiration. "Nothing easier. But . . ." He shrugged. "It will take payment. Such men as you want do not work for charity."

She laughed. It even sounded harsh in her own ears. This was difficult. It felt as though she truly was stepping out into the unknown. "I have money. Prince Eneas was kind enough to give me some—until my own affairs should be settled, he said."

"A prince indeed."

"Will this be enough?"

Dawet looked at the gold, hesitated a moment. The splashing of the fountain rose up to fill the silence. "More than enough," he said at last. "I will bring you back what remains." He stood. "I should go. There is time for me to put this matter in motion before . . . before my other business."

"Thank you, Dawet." She held out her hand. After a moment he took it and lifted it to his lips, but his eyes never left hers. "Why do you look at me so?" she asked.

"I had not thought to see this side of you, Princess Briony—not yet, at any rate."

She felt herself flush a little, but it would be hidden by the darkening evening. "So the Zorian dove now shows herself to be soiled, eh? Is that a disappointment?"

He laughed and shook his head. "Not soiled, no. Willing to protect herself, yes. Even the most pacific of Nature's children will do that." His face grew serious. "I had wrongly thought that old Shaso and his teachings had driven all the good sense from you."

"Yes, well, Shaso dan-Heza is dead."

The public attack on Jenkin Crowel, the envoy from Southmarch, a cruel beating at the hands of three unknown bravos, was the talk of all the court at Tessis the next day. Crowel had been surprised coming out of a favorite tavern by what had seemed at first merely a trio of unpleasant drunkards, but before more than a few words had been exchanged his two guards had been disarmed and beaten, then the assault had begun.

The attack itself was strange enough, although not incomprehensible, since Crowel was already known in Tessis for his love of gambling and his unpleasant temper. But what made it a subject of rapt speculation—for a short time, anyway, since the Tessian nobility never lacked for things to talk about—was what one of the battered guards witnessed as he lay on the ground.

Just before the attackers fled, one of the criminals had crouched beside the bloody, whimpering Jenkin Crowel, but the only words the wounded guard had been able to make out were, " . . . learn to keep your lies to yourself."

By the end of the week, though, when Crowel had proved remarkably close-mouthed on the subject, hiding his bruises and scars in his chambers and shunning all company, the denizens of Broadhall Palace moved on to newer and more interesting outrages.

16

In the Fungus Garden

"According to the Vuttish bards, the Qar themselves distrusted the creatures of Ruottashemm, even though they had kinship to them, and were in constant struggle with the Cold Fairies' queen, Jittsammes."

—from "A Treatise on the Fairy Peoples of Eion and Xand"

"ARE YOU SURE YOU'LL BE WELL?" Opal was twisting the hem of her cloak in her hands. She hated to be parted from them, of course, but she and Chert both knew it was the right thing for her to do. "You'll keep a close eye on the boy?"

"Do not fret so, my only love. It's but a few days." He put his arms around her and held her close. For a moment she fought against it. Opal did not like being confined, even by her husband—perhaps especially by her husband. Her father, Sand Leekstone, had once confessed that he found the women in his family a complete bafflement. *"Your Opal and her mother have been telling me what to do for so many years, I don't know what I'd do if I ever got my own way in anything—likely fall down dead."* Chert, never having expected anything when he married Opal except what he'd gotten, namely a wife who both loved him and argued with him equally fiercely, had only nodded and smiled.

"Few days?" she said now. "If you listen to the folk around here, the world might come to an end in a day or two—do you think that makes me any less worried?" But she was only protesting by rote—they had argued it all through and agreed; in fact, this trip had been mostly Opal's idea. Now that it was clear the threat of war was real, men were being mustered in Funderling Town and Opal had decided the women should also do their part: she was going back to enlist Vermilion Cinnabar and some of the other important women of the town to make sure the men called to fight would have what they needed, and to fill in for those called away from important jobs in the town. Chert was proud of her and knew she would do well. When Opal set her mind to something, it always got done.

"The world will not end while you are gone, my old darling," he told her now. "It wouldn't dare. Just promise me you'll stay with Agate as you promised—don't go back into our house. If you need something send someone else, in case it's being watched."

"How could it be watched without all of Funderling Town knowing?"

Chert shook his head. "You are thinking of soldiers—Big Folk. But I do not trust all our neighbors so far that I cannot imagine one of them taking some money to pass information to the Lord Constable if they see you back in our house. That is why we told no one outside the family where we were going."

"Now who thinks the world will end if he stops making it spin?" she asked, but he could tell from her voice that she wasn't angry. She squeezed him again, then let go. "Do keep a close eye on the boy."

"Of course."

"I wish I could take him."

"And if anyone is watching, what surer way to announce our presence? No, my dearest, he must stay here and you must hurry back to us."

Opal stood up to kiss his cheek and he kissed her back on the mouth, which surprised her and made her smile. She put the bag over her shoulder then and turned to where Brother Natron, a friend of Brother Antimony's, had been waiting a discreet distance away while they said their goodbyes. Natron seemed an intelligent and careful young man, which made Chert's mind a little easier, but he would have preferred the familiar and trustworthy Antimony, who was off with Ferras Vansen and some Funderling warders searching for incursions in the outer tunnels.

Worry suddenly clutched him. "Come back safe to me, my only love," he called, but Opal and the young monk were already up the trail and out of sight.

* * *

"Papa Chert, I need you to help me."

He could only stare at the boy in amazement—it was the first time Flint had ever called him anything like that. To make it even stranger, the boy had been largely silent for the last few days. Now, with Opal gone, he seemed to have gone through another of his odd, unsettling changes.

"Help you?"

Flint sat up and threw his legs over the side of the bed, then bent and scrabbled on the stone floor for his shoes. "I want to talk to the old one. The one who has the dreams."

Chert could only shake his head. "What are you talking about?"

"There is an old man here. He has dreams. Everyone knows him. I need to speak to him."

A dim recollection came to Chert. "Grandfather Sulphur? But how would you know that? You weren't here when Nickel told us about him."

Flint ignored this unimportant detail. "Take me to him, please. I need to talk to him."

Chert stared at this maddening, confusing, sometimes truly frightening child, remembering that moment which now seemed a lifetime ago when the sack had not yet been opened and Flint was still an unknown quantity.

And what if I had not opened it? What if I had taken Opal firmly by the arm and walked away—left it to be someone else's problem. Would things be different? Better . . . or worse? Because it was hard to avoid the idea that Flint's coming had something to do with all the other strange things that had seized their lives and the lives of everyone they knew, Big Folk and Funderlings alike.

He sighed. *In for a scrape, in for all the dig, as they say.* "Very well," he told the boy. "I'll see what I can do."

"I do not understand any of this," said Brother Nickel. The scion of a powerful Funderling family, he had only recently been elevated from acolyte to kainite, a common monk of the temple, but everyone, most definitely including Nickel himself, knew he was the abbot's handpicked successor, and he generally acted as though he had already taken up the ceremonial mattock. "Already your little group has upended all tradition and habit here. Women, children, big people, fugitives—we seem to be taking them all in. Were it not that Cinnabar and the Guild swear that the need is great . . ."

"But they do swear," said Chert. "Please, Nickel, just tell us where to go. We're grateful for your help but we don't want to steal anymore of your time than necessary . . ."

"Let you go off without supervision and . . . *interrogate* our oldest brother?" Nickel stood up. "I do not think so. I will take you to him myself. He is old and frail. If your questions upset him the conversation will end. Understood?"

"Very well, yes. Of course."

Chaven the physician, who had stood watching the discussion with some interest, cleared his throat. "I think I will come along, too—if that is acceptable, Chert . . . ?"

"Acceptable to *Chert?*" Nickel seemed far too dark a shade of red for a man of his comparatively young age. "What about the Metamorphic Brotherhood? No, by all means, let us take as many as wish to go! Perhaps we should simply declare a parade, as on the Day of First Delving—round up all the citizens, and lead a procession to the gardens to surprise the poor old man!"

"You perhaps exaggerate a little, Brother Nickel," said Chaven gently. "I am a physician, after all. Who better to have along if you worry about Grandfather Sulphur's health? And the child Flint has also been under my care. Yes, I think it is a very good idea that I come along."

Chert smiled, but he already felt weary and more than a little put out and the task had not even been begun. Why did it seem he was forever helping other people get their way?

"I have not been in this part of the temple," Chaven said as they zigzagged their way through a low-ceilinged cavern of twisted limestone shapes, following a path that Nickel alone could recognize.

"And why should you have been?" the Metamorphic Brother demanded. "Nothing of interest to your lot happens here. These are gardens and farms where we grow our food. We had almost a hundred mouths to feed here even before all of you started arriving."

And many more will be coming soon, Chert thought. *If you're lucky they'll be Funderlings, not fairies.* But he didn't say it aloud.

"Ah, but you see, I am interested in such things," said Chaven. "Any true man of science never ceases being a student. Please do not be so stern,

Brother Nickel. We are grateful you have taken us in. This is a time of war and stranger things. All good people must stand together."

Nickel snorted, but when he spoke again he sounded a bit more civil. "That is the road to the salt mine. The mine is small, but it gives us enough for our own use as well as to trade with the city above."

Flint alone seemed uninterested in the cavern and its grotesque fixtures of living stone. His face had resumed its usual placidity: he stared straight ahead like a soldier marching toward a life or death battle.

Who are you, really, boy? Chert no longer felt certain he would understand even if someone told him. *What are you?* In any case, the answer did not really matter. What mattered was that his wife loved the boy and he loved his wife. What he felt for Flint himself was harder to put into words, but as he looked now at the serious child with his shock of almost white hair he knew he would do whatever he could to keep the boy safe.

"Down here." Nickel gestured to a side passage.

Chert could smell the garden's pungent air of mold, moisture, and animal manure long before they stepped through the opening. The cavern was lit only by a few torches and scarcely brighter than the corridor. Chaven, still not entirely used to the dim light in which Funderlings lived, stopped and held out his hands like a blind man; Chert took his elbow.

The fungus garden was surprisingly big, a natural high-ceilinged cave that had been further shaped by the hammers and chisels of the Funderlings. Most of the effort had gone into clearing the middle of the floor, which was now crammed full of low stone tables, but the walls had also been thoroughly worked, incised with deep grooves to make rows and rows of shelves.

Every table on the wide floor was laden with trays of black dirt, each tray pockmarked with little pale dots. The alcoves had also been stuffed with manure and soil: thousands of delicate fanlike fungi were growing along the walls, from floor level to five or six times a Funderling's height, where monks on ladders tended the crops. Chert had just begun to wonder which of robed shapes was Grandfather Sulphur when he noticed a bent, bony old man perched on a stool near the center of the room, examining one of the trays with a rock-crystal seeing glass. Flint was already walking toward him, much to the distress of Brother Nickel.

"Here, now! You must let me speak to him first . . ." Nickel hurried after the boy and Chert trotted behind the two of them, fearing it might turn into an actual wrestling match. Flint was half a head bigger now than any of the Funderlings except Brother Antimony, so Chert wasn't worried the boy would be hurt, but they were all guests of the Metamorphic Brotherhood: it would be a bad idea to start a brawl.

"Chert?" called Chaven from behind him. "Where have you gone?" The physician let out a squeal of pain as he banged his shin against one of the stone tables.

Chert reluctantly turned and went back to help Chaven. It was too late to catch up to Nickel and Flint in any ease.

"Ah, there you are." Chaven clutched at his arm. "I will be better in a moment—my eyes do not take to darkness as well as they did when I was younger . . ."

By the time they'd made their way across the dim room Flint was waiting beside the old man's stool, his face once more expressionless, as though he had gone away somewhere inside his own head. Brother Nickel was talking to Sulphur, a tumble of words of which Chert heard only the tail end.

" . . . strange times, of course—you heard of the visitors, Grandfather, didn't you? This is one of them. He wishes to ask you something."

The old monk looked from Nickel to Flint, then back to Nickel again. Sulphur's face was gaunt, the wrinkled skin hanging slackly as though with age his skull had shrunk. His eyes, although clearly almost blind with cataracts, were squinting and suspicious. "Wishes to ask something . . . or wishes to take something?" The voice was cracked and dry as a sandstone cliff.

"I have told them very strongly that they can only . . ." Nickel broke off, staring. Chert was staring too. The hood of the old man's robe was quivering, as if one of his ears was trying to detach itself from his head. A moment later a grotesque little face popped out of the hood beside his cheek, so that everyone except Flint gasped and took a step back in surprise.

"Ha!" said Sulphur. "Iktis, down." He flapped his hand in his lap and the slender, furry little animal crawled out of his hood and down his arm. It settled on the monk's lap and turned to watch them all with bright eyes. It was a fitch, what some upgrounders called a robber cat. Some of the richer Funderlings had them in their houses to hunt mice and voles, but Chert had never seen one kept as a pet. "So, what does this child want of me?" Sulphur demanded.

Flint did not hesitate. "You have dreams," the boy said. "Frightening dreams of the gods. Tell me about them."

The old monk straightened up. The fitch chattered indignantly, clinging as a man in a storm might hang onto a pitching raft. "What could you know of my visions, *gha'jaz?*" Grandfather Sulphur's voice was a hoarse growl—he seemed fearful as well as angry. "Who are you, an upgrounder child, to demand the gods' words from me?"

Nickel and Chert both began to speak at the same time but Flint calmly ignored them both. "I am a friend. Tell me. Your people need you to tell me."

"See here, child . . ." Nickel began again, but Sulphur was ignoring him too. For a moment it seemed to Chert that everyone else in the great, musty room had vanished except for the old man and the pale-haired boy. Something passed between them—a language without words, like the tiny, all but invisible seeds of the mushrooms themselves, which passed through the air like a cloud of unseen spirits.

"The tortoise," said Grandfather Sulphur abruptly. "It began with the tortoise."

"What?" Nickel put his hand on Flint's shoulder as if to pull the boy away. "Grandfather, you are tired . . ."

"The tortoise came to me in a dream. It spoke to me of the coming times—the time when evil men will seek to destroy the gods. Of the catastrophe they will bring down on the Funderlings. It was *truth,* that dream—I know it. It was the Lord of the Hot Wet Stone himself."

"The tortoise . . ." said Chaven slowly, distantly, as if speaking to himself. Something in the physician's voice put the hairs up on the back of Chert's neck. "The tortoise . . . the spiral shell . . . the pine tree . . . the *owl* . . ."

Flint would not be distracted. "Tell me, Grandfather, what were you to do? What did the Lord of the Hot Wet Stone ask of you?"

"This is blasphemy," Nickel sputtered. "This . . . upgrounder, this *gha'jaz,* should not be asking about such sacred things!"

But Grandfather Sulphur did not seem to mind—in fact, Chert thought the old man seemed to be warming to the subject. "He said I must tell my people that Old Night is coming and that this sinful world will end soon. He came to me in many dreams. He said to tell the people that there is nothing they can do to resist his will."

"He told you not to fight against the will of the gods?" Flint asked. "But why would your god say such a thing?"

"Blasphemy!" said Nickel. "How can he ask such questions of Sulphur, who is the select of the Stone Lord himself?"

Chert put his hand on the monk's arm. "Brother Sulphur is not afraid to speak to the boy, so let them talk. Come, Nickel, these matters are beyond either of us—but you must see that these are extraordinary times."

Nickel could barely stand still. "That does not mean I should allow a . . . a mere *child* to do as he pleases in our holy temple!"

Chert sighed. "Whatever he is, I have known for a long time that my Flint is no 'mere child.' Isn't that right, Chaven?"

But the physician did not reply: he was listening raptly to the old man and the boy.

"You have always dreamed of the gods." Flint was telling more than asking.

"Of course. Since I was younger than you, child," said the old man, not without satisfaction. He lifted a spotted, clawlike hand. "When I had but two years I told my parents I would be a Metamorphic Brother."

"But these dreams are different," said Flint. "Isn't that true?"

The old man leaned back sharply, as though he had been struck. His milky eyes narrowed. "What do you mean?"

"The dreams of the tortoise—the dreams that brought you the god's own voice. You have not had dreams like *that* all your life—have you?"

"I have always dreamed of the gods . . ." the old man said, blustering.

"When did they change? When did they become . . . so strong?"

Again a long, silent communication seemed to pass between Flint and the old monk. At last Sulphur's lined face went slack. "A year ago or more, just after the season of cold. That is when I first dreamed of the tortoise. That is when I first began to hear His voice."

"And what came to you just before the dreams began?" Flint spoke as gently as if he were the priest and the old man some hapless, troubled penitent. "You found something, or someone gave something to you—isn't that true?"

Chert could not help being disturbed by this newest face of the child in whom he and Opal had put so much of their hope. What had been done to this boy behind the Shadowline? More important, was he even a boy, or some kind of Twilight dweller that only *looked* like a child? What kind of serpent had they taken to their breasts?

"Yes, what?" said Chaven with an edge of hunger in his voice. "What came to you?"

Sulphur waved his hand. "I do not know what you mean. I am tired now. Go away." In his lap, Iktis the fitch grew anxious; chittering, the creature vanished up the old man's sleeve.

"That is enough!" said Nickel. "You must go now!"

"No one will take it away from you," said Flint as if no one else had spoken. "That I promise, Grandfather. But tell the truth. Even the gods must respect truth."

"Leave now!" Nickel looked like he meant to grab the boy and drag him away, but Chert squeezed the monk's arm hard and held him back.

The old man's silence grew so long and deep that for the first time they could hear the squeak of ladders being moved on the far side of the room and even the murmur of whispered conversations between the other Metamorphic Brothers, who had not failed to notice what was going on at the center of the garden. Sulphur looked down at his own hands, knotted in his lap.

"My little Iktis found it," he said at last in a voice so quiet everyone but Flint leaned forward. "He brought it to me, dragging it all the way. He loves shiny things and sometimes he goes as far up as the town. I have had to send back many a woman's bracelet or necklace with the brothers who go to market. Sometimes Iktis even goes upground. And sometimes he goes . . . deep."

"Can you show it to me?" Flint asked him. "I promise no one will take it from you."

Again the silence thickened. At last Sulphur reached into his thick robe, which was frosted with mold along the crest of every wrinkle. Iktis, still hidden in the old man's sleeve, loosed a twitter of protest as Sulphur withdrew a shiny thing that hung around his neck on a braided ratskin cord.

"It is my seeing-glass," he said. "I knew it was meant for me the moment I saw it."

It was the thing he had been holding when they first saw him, a small, thin shard of crystal in an irregular silvery metal frame that had clearly been built around the crystal's natural shape and decorated with intricate little carvings even Chert's strong eyes could not quite make out. The metal was not one that he recognized, and neither was the style of the metalwork or even the crystal itself, although it was hard to be certain in the poor light of the fungus garden.

Chaven took a deep breath. "That is Qar work," he said dreamily. "Yes. The voice of the tortoise. A cage for the white owl. Yes, of course . . ."

"And when the little animal brought you this," said Flint, as calm as ever, "then the dreams of the Lord of the Hot Wet Stone began."

"But I have always dreamed of the gods!"

"Just let me . . ." Chaven reached out his hand toward the oblivious Sulphur; the physician's breath was sawing in his throat, his eyes staring like a sleepwalker's. "Yes, let me . . ." His voice had grown hoarse, a loud whisper. "I must . . ."

Chert had seen this before, if only briefly: Chaven's mirror-madness was upon him. He knew as surely as if it had been planned that in another moment the physician would snatch the crystal away from the old man and chaos would follow. In the end they would likely be sent away from the temple, their last and best hiding place.

Chert kicked Chaven in the shin, right on the same spot the physician had struck so painfully on one of the stone tables a short while earlier. The physician let out a shriek and began to hop up and down, trying to grab at this new wound. A moment later he fell, knocking over a pile of tools. Startled and suspicious, the old monk slipped his shard of crystal back into the safety of his moldy robe.

"What is going on here?" Nickel shouted. "Have you all gone mad?"

"Chaven hit his leg again," said Chert. "Nothing more. Help me get him back to the temple—the poor fellow's bleeding from the shin. Flint, you are needed too. Thank Grandfather Sulphur for his help and let's go."

The boy looked at the old man, whose face had gone stony and secretive again. Flint did not say anything to him, but turned and walked out of the garden, leaving Chert and Nickel to follow with the hopping, whimpering physician propped between them.

The first thing Ferras Vansen saw was a pale, yellow-green star hovering in the darkness above him. It was strange a star should move in such a lively manner: not only was it swooping back and forth across the darkness in a series of loops like a browsing bumblebee, it seemed to be *talking* to him as well.

Stars don't talk. Ferras Vansen was fairly certain about that. *Stars don't . . . bumble, either.*

" . . . Are you . . . ?" asked the star. "Can . . . hear . . . ?"

He was a bit disappointed: he had expected that if a star ever did speak to him it would have more important things to say. Weren't stars supposed to be the souls of fallen heroes? Had they all hung in the sky so long they had become simpletons, the way Vansen's father had in that dreadful last year of his life?

For a moment he wondered if he was dead himself and had somehow made his way into the heavens—not that he had done anything to deserve a hero's place—but thinking of his father made him wonder if death could be so . . . fuzzy, so confusing. It didn't seem likely.

" . . . He . . . more water now . . ." said the star.

Vansen tried to focus on the moving light. He soon realized a strange thing: he could see something beyond it—beyond the star! And not the black curtain of night he would have expected, but something that looked like a face. Could it be the great god Perin Skylord himself, inspecting Vansen's fallen soul? Or was it Kernios, the keeper of the dead? A trembling cold moved over him at the thought of that grim god. But if it was Kernios, he looked familiar. In fact, the god of the underworld looked like . . . Brother Antimony . . . ?

Vansen finally recognized that the yellow-green glow he had been staring at so blearily since his senses had returned was only the coral lamp bound to Antimony's forehead.

"I'm . . . not . . . dead?" His mouth was dry as sand. It was hard to make words.

"He's speaking sense again," said Antimony with clear relief. "No, Captain Vansen, you're not dead."

"What happened?" A memory rose up like a dark cloud. "We found them. Those things . . ."

"They used a kind of poison," Antimony said. "A powder they blew through a tube, as our ancestors used to do. We were fortunate it did not kill you. Also, you blocked the way so the rest of us were not harmed by it." He helped Vansen to sit up, then gave him some water. The other Funderlings crouched nearby, bald Sledge Jasper and his fellow warders. To Vansen's uncertain eye they all seemed to be present. "Is everyone alive?"

"All of us, thank the Earth Elders," said Antimony. "And look!" He pointed to a huge lump of darkness lying against the tunnel wall, something big as a horse. "One of the deep ettins—we killed it!"

"I did most of the killing," said Jasper with pleasure. "Let's speak the truth, Brother! Put my pointy bit right in its eye."

"What is it?" said Vansen. He crawled toward the massive corpse, then wished he hadn't: it gave off a smell so rank and musty that it made his eyes water. "You said . . . ettin?"

"*Krja'azel,*" said Antimony, the word so strange and harsh on his tongue that the kindhearted young Funderling suddenly seemed a different kind of creature entirely. "Something we have not seen since my great-grandfather's time, and even then rarely."

"But those were wild," said Jasper. "This one fought beside the fairies."

"And what is this under it?" asked Vansen, holding his nose. At first he had thought it was some sort of fin at the back of the thing's neck, but now he saw that what protruded there were stubby little fingers. He tried to move the ettin, but the thing was several times his own weight.

"One of its masters," said Sledge Jasper. "The ones with the powder-pipes. We saw them all rush past in their hoods when you fell, but when I spiked that thing in the eye, this one must have been caught underneath it."

Vansen began to shove at the stinking Scraper. "Could he still be alive?"

The wardthane's laugh was unpleasant. "You don't know how long you've been knocked senseless, do you?"

Antimony came to help him, and after watching with grim amusement for a while as they struggled, Jasper and his men joined too. At last they all managed to roll the deep ettin's corpse away. The figure under it was smaller than Antimony, and the weight of the creature that had fallen on it had pressed its face into a distorted death mask, but it was still plain even to Vansen what it was.

"By the gods," he said, "I think it's a Funderling!"

"Earth Elders protect us," Antimony said in a breathless voice. "One of our own?"

"No such thing," Sledge Jasper snapped. "Look. Look at his hands. Do I have hands like that? Do you?" The small corpse had broad, square fingertips and the nails were as long and thick as a mole's claws.

Vansen looked at the twisted, gape-mouthed face, the lower half of which was covered in a beard as thick and unkempt as black moss. "I've seen people like this before. In Greatdeeps, behind the Shadowline."

"By the Pool's Light, he's right," said Antimony softly. "It's a drow." He made a sign on his forehead and breast. "Now I have seen everything. A drow in Funderling Town."

"What is a drow?"

"They are our . . . relatives, Captain," Antimony told him. "Long ago, they followed the Qar into the north, but I did not know any still survived."

"I've seen more than a few," said Vansen. "These must have come down from the Shadowlands with the fairy army."

"This is bad," Jasper said. "Very bad. They are just as clever in the ground as we are. If it comes to a fight, we could baffle the upgrounders . . . but drows?"

"More important," Vansen told them all, "whether it is these drows they send or others—although I will pray they send no more ettins—the fairies have finally begun their attack on Southmarch itself. Or at least on the tunnels down here. But why now, when they could have attacked any time? There must be a reason! Why should they abruptly end what you've told me has been a long time of quiet, almost of peace?" He stared up the tunnel as though he could see all the way to the councils of the fairy folk and discover what he burned to know. "By all the gods, *why now?*"

"No one can understand the ways of the Old Ones," Jasper said. "And now they send our own lost cousins against us." He straightened up, glaring down at the bearded corpse. "I will gladly kill Funderling Town's enemies—I will wipe their blood on my breeches and laugh—but I will not take much pleasure killing drows. "

"Hold now, hold," said Antimony thoughtfully. "Yes, this all seems bad—but perhaps there is some good fortune here, too. We will find it hard to hold off this Twilight army for long, even with Captain Vansen's help. We do not have the men, the weapons, or the training. They will soon overrun us."

"I must have missed the part where you explained our good fortune," Vansen said.

Antimony smiled a little. "Simply this. If we can talk to no one else on the other side, we should be able to talk to our own cousins, however distant they might be." He looked to Vansen. "Do you see my meaning?"

"Ah. Ah, yes, I think I do." Vansen's estimation of the young monk rose even higher. "Which means we must capture one of these . . . drows . . . alive." He frowned. "But what of this one?"

"We will bury him properly," said Antimony. "Under stone, as we do our own. Help me make a cairn."

"A cairn?" Jasper almost shouted. "For this? But he . . . he was . . . !"

"Properly. Under stone." The young monk spoke with such cold conviction that even Sledge Jasper, taken aback, could only nod. "If his kin come back, it will show them we still hold to the old ways—that whatever the Twilight folk have told them, we are still one people."

17
Fish Heads

"Rhantys wrote, 'Far larger than a man is the Ettyn, a murderous ogre with thick clawed hands like a mole who makes his home in the earth.' It is known that during the second war against the Qar ettins undermined the defensive walls of Northmarch castle, which led to the defeat and destruction of that city, now lost behind the Shadowline."

—from "A Treatise on the Fairy Peoples of Eion and Xand"

FOR A LONG TIME after she had caught hold of the piling Qinnitan could do no more than cling to it while the breakers dragged her up and down against the pier's armor of barnacles. The salt water made her dozens of scratches and cuts burn like fire, but she had strength enough only to hang on and try to catch her breath. When Pigeon's arms began to slip from her neck she nearly let go of the slimy wooden pier to hold onto him, but she was terrified the current would drag them both away under the dock and she wouldn't be strong enough to find another safe haven.

"Wake up!" She choked and spat green water. "Pigeon! Hang on to my neck!"

The boy made a guttural noise of exhaustion and renewed his grip as well as he could. She had been fortunate her foot had touched him when she had first risen to the surface after plunging off the ship, and fortunate again that a piece of flaming mast had missed them when it hit the water a few moments later, just as she surfaced with the boy.

Another wave, small compared to open ocean but still far beyond her power to resist, flung Qinnitan against the piling again. When she opened her eyes several new cuts crisscrossed her arm, a net made of little streaks of red that disappeared as another wave splashed across them.

People were shouting and thumping across the planks above her head and the smoke of the burning ship was beginning to creep along the water. It was hopeless to stay here, only a matter of time until she lost her grip or the smoke overwhelmed her again. She was already rasping at every breath like a cart with a broken wheel. She had never been so exhausted in all her life.

There. A crude ladder of some kind hung down to the water on the far side of the dock. She hoped it was a ladder, anyway—it was a hundred yards away and her eyes were stinging from seawater and blood. She thanked Nushash and the Hive that she had spent lots of time in the deep bathing pool at the Seclusion and had learned how to swim a little. Still, she couldn't swim that far with one arm.

"You must stay on my back and hold on no matter what," she told Pigeon. "Can you hear me?" She waited until she heard him grunt. "Don't let go, even if I go under the water for a moment."

As she pushed away from the pillar, aiming for the distant ladder, the boy wrapped his arms around her neck. She couldn't breathe, and she floundered until she managed to yank his arms down so they were across her collarbone. Qinnitan had gone four or five strokes and was beginning to find a rhythm that allowed her to keep Pigeon mostly on her back when she saw the first triangular fin cut the water in front of her. A moment later she saw a second. Her limbs seemed to grow cold and heavy.

Sea-wolves. Not the thick bodied, axhead sharks of the Xixian canals but something sleeker and longer, pale gray and as slender as a knife blade. For a moment she paddled in place, afraid to go forward and afraid to go back, but the fins were moving away from her instead of toward her. Qinnitan prayed that they were after some other quarry.

Within moments of the disappearance of the first two she saw several more moving in wide loops as though not so sure of their destination as the first pair. Bodies in the water, Qinnitan realized with a horrible pang, sailors from the Xixian ship, wounded and dead—men she had killed by setting the ship on fire.

She couldn't think about any of it, not about the sailors and soldiers, not about the sharks. Pigeon was clinging to her back and his arms were tightening around her neck again as he began to understand why she had stopped swimming. In another moment terror might steal away his resolve—he might let go or even begin to fight her. She had heard sailors on her voyage to Hierosol talk about the hopelessness of struggling with a frightened, drowning man. She began to swim again, as quickly as she could.

Something rough as tree bark brushed against her leg as a pale shape slipped past her. She gasped and swallowed some water, but the fin was moving away. It was only a small shark, not half her length. She thrashed forward, but she felt as though the strength was leaking out of her like grain from a burst sack. Where was that ladder? Qinnitan did not even know which direction she had been swimming. The planks were gone from above her head so she must be out from beneath the pier, but where was she?

Pigeon was sliding from her back again. She caught him with one hand, but it all seemed pointless, remote. They sank into the water and green darkness was all around. She clutched the child as tightly as she could and kicked hard with her last strength, but they barely seemed to move upward. At last, just when she felt she could hold her breath no longer her face broke the surface for an instant, but even the air she gulped did not bring life back to her legs and arms. She slipped back under, exhausted.

Something grabbed Qinnitan by the hair, yanking so hard and so unexpectedly that she opened her mouth and swallowed water again. A moment later light burst all around her and she felt her body strike or be struck by something heavy. A shark. A shark must have her. The end . . . but where was Pigeon . . . ?

The weight of the boy fell on top of her. She was lying on something hard. A moment later Pigeon rolled away, coughing and gasping, but Qinnitan couldn't see anything except the watery mess she was vomiting up onto the planks of the pier.

Out of the water. They were out of the water.

Her stomach convulsed again but nothing more came out. She coughed and spat. A hand thumped her on the back and a little more water trickled out onto the wet boards. She was dimly aware of the smell of smoke and of people shouting and running not far away, but no one was near them except their rescuer. She reached out blindly until she found Pigeon. His skinny sides were heaving as he brought up his own bellyful of seawater but he was breathing. He was safe. She had saved him. Qinnitan let herself collapse onto her side. She could see a little of the sky now, gray-black with smoke, and the dim shape of their savior, the sun behind him so that he was only a dark shadow looming over them like a mountain, a benevolent god who had reached down a mighty hand and plucked them back into life. She tried to thank him, but she could force no words out of her burning, salt-scoured throat, so instead she lifted up her hand to touch his arm.

He knocked her hand aside. "Stupid little bitch." It was only after a moment that she realized he had spoken Xixian, her own language. Qinnitan threw up her hand to block the sunlight, dazzling even through the smoke.

Their rescuer was the nameless man, the autarch's stone-faced servant, but he was not stone-faced now: his features were twisted into a look of almost deranged fury.

"Do you see this?" He grabbed Pigeon's wrist and slammed the boy's hand down near Qinnitan's face so hard that although he was barely sensible, Pigeon still gasped in pain. The nameless man slapped the boy so hard that Pigeon's eyes fluttered open, then slowly widened in horror as he saw who had him. "Watch!"

In a single movement as swift as a serpent's strike the man pulled a long, broad knife out of his waistband and snapped it down on the boy's hand with a meaty *thok* like the sound of her mother cutting fish heads on the family table. Blood sprayed in Qinnitan's face, and the tips of three of Pigeon's fingers bounced away. The boy shrieked, a wordless noise so horrid that Qinnitan screamed too, helpless and disbelieving.

"Next time it will be his whole hand—and his nose!" The nameless man slapped Qinnitan so hard that she thought he had broken her jaw. As Pigeon rolled on the planks, gurgling and clutching his ruined hand, red wetness drizzling onto the dock, their captor pulled a cloth from his pocket and tied it roughly but tightly around Pigeon's fingers to slow the bleeding.

"Now get up, you little dung flies, and no more noise or playing up from either of you." He jerked Qinnitan onto her feet, then kicked at the whimpering Pigeon until the child staggered upright, his face gray with pain. "Because of you two, we have to find another boat."

"I never expected to be king."

Pinimmon Vash stiffened in surprise and fright at these words. He hadn't thought to hear anyone talking at all, let alone making such a unique declaration.

It was Olin's voice, of course—but to whom could the northern king possibly be speaking? The autarch was still in bed in his cabin, yet the foreigner was speaking as though to Sulepis himself. Vash's skin went cold: if he had failed to note and plan for the autarch's movements correctly then many of the things the paramount minister did each day (and especially what he was doing this very moment) were little more than elaborate forms of suicide.

Terror swept through Vash like a sudden fever. He scrambled back from the hole he had selected for eavesdropping, looking wildly from side to side although he was clearly the only person in the small locker. *Fool!* he chided himself—what was happening on the other side of the spyhole was all that mattered. Was Olin Eddon really talking to Sulepis? How could Vash have miscalculated? Only moments ago he had delivered the parchment bearing his morning report to the autarch's cabin and had been informed by the body slaves that the Golden One was still asleep.

He could hear Olin again. "It was not that I was unsuited for it, or afraid of the responsibility," the northerner was saying, "just that I did not imagine it would happen. My father Ustin was as healthy as a bull, my brother Lorick, the heir, was only two years older than me, and I had always been sickly, prone to fevers and to long, bedridden weeks. The physicians told my father and mother I would likely not survive to see twenty years. It was a weakness of the blood, they said—one to which many of my line had been prey . . . had been . . ."

Olin hesitated for so long that at last Vash moved back to the spyhole again to try to make sense of things. The discovery of this locker had been fortuitous—it was much less exposed than his previous eavesdropping spot—but it was hard on his old bones to force himself into the narrow space, and it would be almost impossible to get out of it quickly if he heard someone coming. Still, he had decided it would be worth it, especially if it helped him understand what the autarch was planning. Those who let Sulepis surprise them seldom lived long—or happily.

But if I was wrong and Sulepis finds me here, this locker will be no more than an upright coffin.

Vash still could see nothing from his angle, including to whom if anyone the northerner spoke, so he took his eye away and put his ear against the hole instead. He would bring a dark cloth next time to cover the inside of the hole—if he lived. That would make it less likely anyone would notice his presence.

"In any case," King Olin at last continued, "my illness and the health of my father and brother made it unlikely I would ever sit the throne. Instead of just tilting and hunting and other active sports, my youth was also spent with books, in the company of historians and philosophers. Not that there is anything wrong with learning to defend yourself! I made sure my own children would at least be able to acquit themselves well in a fight."

Who *was* he talking to? Surely the autarch would never stay silent so long. Could it be Panhyssir, the high priest? Vash felt a fizz of helpless jealousy at the thought. Or perhaps it was the antipolemarch Dumin Hauyuz, the commander of the soldiers aboard and the highest ranking military man in the autarch's party. It had to be one of them—certainly the king of a foreign nation would not speak so openly to anyone else.

Or had his captivity simply driven the man mad—was Olin talking to himself?

"Many people were wrong, of course," the northerner said. "My ill-ness has not shortened my life—at least not so far. My father did live a long time, but collapsed in apoplexy when he heard that my brother Lorick had fallen from his horse while hunting and was not expected to survive. My father did not regain his senses, but he did not die, either. As it turned out, neither of those strong men would die easily.

"It was a black time for my mother and little better for me. My father had never had as much time for me as for Lorick, but that was as it should have been, because my brother was being prepared to rule—who could have guessed the gods had such tricks in mind? But my father had been kind to me in his way, and now I had to watch them both clinging to life, unable to pull themselves out of the half-death in which they were immersed.

"My father died first. There was a party in court—led by the Tollys, the most powerful family after ours—who wanted to crown Lorick even as he lay senseless and dying, and then Lindon Tolly would rule in his name. My youngest brother Hardis was already married to one of the Tolly women, so they wished only to keep me off the throne long enough to find some way to put Hardis on in my place when Lorick at last succumbed to his injury. We had just enough allies in the court to resist this, but only barely. Southmarch lived in stalemate for almost a year.

"Hardis was young and easily led, and maybe even jealous of his older brothers, but I do not believe he understood that Lindon's plans to put him on the throne would have required my death. Hardis was no fool, but I'm sure it was easier for him not to wonder why the Tollys made so much of him. Or perhaps he simply felt sure, as everyone else had all my life, that I would not live to manhood.

"As it happened, I outlived them all. My poor brother Hardis died ten years ago of a fever after having spent his life more or less a prisoner of the Tollys, although he always pretended he was happy in Summerfield Court and had no wish to see his old home. Poor Hardis.

"Back in the year of succession, Lorick died at last and the puppet show ended, but not without several times almost tearing the kingdom apart. I was crowned and the Tollys had to be content with keeping what power they had.

"Curse my foolishness! I should have routed them out like a hive of wasps. I saw the danger of your country to Eion long before any of my fellow monarchs, starting with this autarch's cruel father, but I did not see the dangers in my own house."

There, thought Vash, relieved but still bewildered, and took his first full breath in some time. Clearly the man wasn't speaking to Sulepis himself—but what else could he be doing? Had the autarch given Olin a secretary? Was the foreign king dictating a letter to his family?

The northerner's voice rose. "And that is what I hate even more than the Tollys' treachery—my own stupidity. I left enemies behind me when I departed and then, even worse, I allowed myself to be tricked and imprisoned by that swine Hesper of Jellon. All of this may have cost our family the throne we have held for centuries, but it has cost me far more than that . . . it cost me my oldest son, my brave Kendrick, and perhaps my other two children as well." His voice became halting. "Ah, sweet Zoria and all her oracles—may the gods rain curses down on those who helped me to betray myself and my kingdom!"

For long moments after that Olin did not speak, but even without seeing the man Vash could tell he had only fallen silent, not gone away.

"I tried to prepare all my children to rule so that they would not find themselves surprised and unready as I had been, should the gods decide to set any one of them on the throne. And I loved them all, as a father should, even if I perhaps did not love them all equally.

"They were the last thing I had of my wife Meriel. She suffered greatly giving birth to the twins and did not recover, becoming weaker and weaker until she passed a month later. It tore my heart out of my breast. I banished the physician who attended her even though it was not his fault, but I could not bear to see the man's face when my dear wife was dead. She had been the one thing that made me think perhaps my own poisoned blood could be saved. When Kendrick was born, so fat and fit and laughing, it seemed that her sweetness had undone the sour strain of my lineage.

"I was a fool.

"She was lovely, of course, my Meriel, but not simply because her skin was milky and her lips were red, as the bards would have it. There were many other women in the March Kingdoms that might have been called more beautiful, and it would take a poet, which I am not, to tell you what exactly it was that made her so fair, but it was something in her eyes. All her life, until the moment those eyes last closed upon this world, she had the look of a child. Not innocent, not foolish or simple, but straight—straight as an arrow's flight. She looked out at the world without judging, or at least without hurrying to judgement. She could not flatter but she was always kind. She did not lie, but neither did she speak rash truth when it would bring pain for no reason . . ."

Again Olin paused. For the first time Vash was listening with real interest: the foreigner spoke well, as a king should. Some of the autarchs Vash had served had liked poetry, but none of them had spoken it or written it with any facility. In his younger years, the paramount minister himself had occasionally written a few lines, but no one had ever seen them.

"In fact," Olin continued, "Meriel was what I often thought a goddess might be like, if that goddess was kindhearted, for she was not above the pain of others. Ah, that she should have been taken from the world instead of me, with my tainted heritage and my doting self-regard! When she died the castle put on mourning and would not take it off, every servant and every courtier. That is true. They had to be told by the priests after a year had passed to doff their mourning clothes, that to mourn beyond the official time was to insult the gods! Can you imagine? We all loved her. The worst thing that ever happened to my children, far worse than us losing the throne or even Kendrick's death, was that they did not know their mother, the sweetest woman who ever lived. I thought I did not deserve her—I could not believe that she could be mine.

"She was not, of course. The gods reminded me of that . . . as they are wont to do."

Olin laughed then, a sound so painful that even Vash (who had heard the shrieking, pleading ends of dozens of men's lives, many of those executed at his own orders) had to fight the urge to stop his ears with his hands.

"I do not know what I mean to say," the king began again at last. "I started out to tell about my family. It has been nearly a year since I have seen them. Kendrick is dead, likely at the hands of the Tollys, but perhaps killed by some other. My brave son—he wanted only to do what was right. He would grow so angry when others broke the rules, even his younger brother and sister! They would play at hide-and-seek with him, then hide somewhere they had promised not to go and laugh at him when he found out. He could never make himself play the way they did, but instead would try to convince them that when the rules were broken the game was spoiled. Kendrick would have been a fine king—with my other son as his chancellor, perhaps, to remind him not to trust others to obey the rules just because Kendrick himself did. Because Barrick, if he still lives, may the gods protect him, lives in a very different world.

"Barrick was always troubled, always querulous, but after the first time the affliction struck—my affliction, passed down to him like the waters of a fouled river—he ceased to trust in the goodness of Fate entirely. And who could blame him? When he was young the sickness took the same course as it did in me. He would fall to the floor in fits of rage, choking, trembling, scarcely able to breathe, and struggle so that two strong men were needed to check him even though he was but a child. I grieved, of course, that I had brought this curse into his life, but I felt I could teach him how I had survived, the way I locked myself away when I felt the fits coming upon me. But then his sickness changed and found a different path.

"In Barrick, it became something that no longer made him rage and flail like a madman, but instead which slowly poisoned him on the inside. His view of the world became darker and darker, as when an eclipsing moon divides the earth from the sun. In my foolishness I thought at first that when his outward fits stopped it meant that he was getting better—that he was somehow fighting off the curse that had so polluted my life. I was wrong, but by the time I understood that, he had crawled so far into the shadows that I could no longer reach him. He was witty, clever, yet so crippled by my own poisoned blood that I think only his love for his sister kept him alive.

"For he did love her, and Briony loved him. They were twins—did I say that?—and their hearts beat as one from the moment they came into the world, born in the same hour. Perhaps that had something to do with their mother's death. Ah, gods, I no longer know! It has been so long, yet the pain feels as fresh as when I cut myself with my shaving blade yester morning.

"And here is another shameful confession—I loved Briony most of all. No, let me say *love,* not loved—please, may the gods grant that she lives! I loved Kendrick's honor and kindness and his dutiful nature, and I loved him because he was my firstborn. I love Barrick despite all the pain I gave him and he gave me . . . but I love Briony with such comfort and certainty that I cannot express it. She contains all that is best in me, and much of what was excellent in her mother. To think that such a powerful love should have failed her so completely—that I should have failed *all* of them so utterly . . ."

Again the northern king fell silent. When he spoke again his voice was quite different, somber and almost without feeling.

"I have bored you long enough. I thank you for indulging me. I think I will go and walk up and down the decks of my prison a little while and listen to the gulls."

The paramount minister of Xis heard Olin move, followed by his guards, the footsteps slowly growing fainter. After he was gone, no one else moved or spoke. Had he been talking to the guards, or to empty air after all, addressing only the cloudy spring sky? Vash slid himself out of the pantry as carefully as his stiff old bones would permit and hobbled down the stairs to the deck, then climbed back up to where Olin had been. The king had indeed left—Vash could see the top of his head at the far end of the ship, where he leaned on the rail under the wary eye of several soldiers—and there was no sign of the autarch or Panhyssir or Dumin Hauyuz or any other rational being. The only soul on the deck was the halfwit scotarch Prusus lolling in his chair, hands and head jerking, a thread of spittle dangling from his chin. For a moment Prusus the

Cripple seemed to look back at him, but as Vash walked toward him the scotarch's stare rolled vacantly, as though the paramount minister had suddenly disappeared from his view.

Pinimmon Vash stopped in front of the quivering shape and looked the scotarch up and down, thinking . . . wondering . . .

The world has slipped its mooring, Vash thought. *Yes, the world I knew has drifted out of familiar waters. Where it goes now, only gods and madmen can guess.*

❦

"Something is following us," Barrick whispered.

"Aye." When the raven spoke quietly he was hard to understand, all rasp and whistle. He fluttered down onto a stone and clung to the mossy surface, then lowered his head between his shoulders and fluffed himself bigger. "Silkins," he croaked. "Saw them when us flew over trees. Five nor six, us guesses."

"Let them come." He feared them, but Barrick also felt strangely sure he had not come so far and survived so much to die at the hands of these spindly thread-covered monstrosities. He felt strong—weirdly so, as though something powerful bubbled inside him like the foam on a mug of beer. It almost made him want to laugh out loud.

"Let them? Kill us both, they will—or worset, take us back to they hanging nests and put they grubs in our bellies." The raven flapped up into a tree branch several paces ahead. "Seen it happen to Followers, I have. Not even dead when the younglings hatch . . ."

"They won't do it to me. I won't let them."

The black bird shuddered and puffed up his feathers again. "Did you take a bump to the head when you climbed so long on that dire hill? Not at all the same since then, you."

Barrick couldn't help smiling. It was true, although he wasn't certain why. He *did* feel different—stronger, more certain . . . better. Even the constant dull ache in his crippled left arm, a pain that had plagued him for most of his life, was now gone: the only discomfort was an occasional prickle of the skin, as though he had slept on it.

Barrick held the torch near his forearm. The scars the Sleepers had made were all but gone, only three white stripes remaining that looked years old, although it had been no more than a day or two since he had descended from Cursed Hill. Even his hand, the loathsome crab-claw he had always tried to hide, now looked scarcely different from his other hand. What magic had those blind things done to him? It seemed they had brought him only good, but a nagging memory reminded him that they had spoken of a price . . .

Barrick tripped on a root and stumbled badly before regaining his balance. The ground was slippery from the mist that cloaked the twilight forest. A healthy arm wouldn't keep him from falling and hitting his head.

"Surely us must find a place to be safe, Master," Skurn said in a wheedling voice. "To rest. Tired, you are, and tired makes mistakes, as our old mam always said."

Barrick looked around. He had been walking for what seemed most of a day, following the raven's recollection of the best route toward the city of Sleep and its fearful inhabitants, the ones Skurn called Night Men. It wouldn't hurt to stop and rest, especially if a group of silkins were following. He could roast the roots he had dug that morning, which would at least make them seem a little more like actual food: he had discovered several things that grew here which he could eat and keep down, but cooking them definitely helped.

"Very well," he said. "Find me a place with a rock I can put at my back."

"Wise you are, so wise. Us will find a helpsome spot." The raven flapped heavily up through the canopy of trees and out of Barrick's sight.

The thing was, Barrick reflected as he chewed, roasting these pale, soggy roots made them taste more like food, but it didn't make them taste like good food.

"Couldn't you find us an egg or something?" he asked. "A bird's egg?" He had learned that it was important to be specific.

The raven turned toward him, the legs of some crawler he had pulled from under a log still wriggling in his beak. He tipped back his head to gulp it down, then shot Barrick a look of reproach.

"Hasn't Skurn looked and looked? Didn't us offer you the best us found, not even keeping none back for ourself?"

The "best" had been a large, soft grub the size of Barrick's thumb, pale and waxy as a candle and leaking greenish fluid where Skurn's beak had crimped it too fiercely. He had thanked the raven for his generosity and given it back.

"Never mind. These roots are fine." He laid three more pieces of wood that had been drying on the flames, then began to sharpen the head of his broken spear with a round stone. He could not get over the strange pleasure of having two arms that did not hurt.

"Tell me another tale," Barrick said after a while. "What happened to Crooked after he threw the gods into his grandmother's lands?"

"Great-grandmother's," the raven said, looking around as though something else toothsome might be crawling by. "It were his great-grandmother, Emptiness. She taught Crooked all her tricks of coming and going."

Find Crooked's Hall, the Sleepers had told him. Crooked's Hall, Crooked's roads, Crooked's doorway—did they actually expect Barrick to travel as the gods traveled? "So what happened? Did he become the king of the gods?" But Crooked, who until now had always been Kupilas as far as Barrick knew, was just a minor god, wasn't he? The *Book of the Trigon* talked of Kupilas only as the clever patron of blacksmiths and engineers. *And physicians,* he remembered. *Chaven had a statue of him in his house.* "What happened after he killed Kernios?"

"Is us a Night Man, full of secrets?" the bird said with a touch of indignation. "Do us know all the Firstborn know? Anyroad, Crooked didn't kill nobody—he threw the Earthlord and them others into the place where they sleeps forever."

"But what happened to Kupilas? To Crooked? What happened to him?"

Skurn shrugged, a motion where he lifted his feathers in a ruff around his neck and wiggled his head. "Don't know. Him were hurt bad by Earthlord's spear. Dying, some say. Don't know any more of the story, us. Mam never told it."

And Barrick had to be content with that.

He was half asleep and drifting when he felt something poking at his hand, something sharp and hard. A beak.

"Hist!" The raven crouched beside him, spotted feathers all a-prickle so that he looked more hedgehog than bird. "I hear somewhat . . ."

Barrick sat up straight but stayed silent, listening. He gradually became aware that something sharp was poking into the back of his neck, and this time it wasn't Skurn. He swatted at it but could not dislodge the painful thing from his skin. An instant later something else dropped down from the branches and caught the meat of his right arm—a thorny branch, bent like a hook, on the end of a strand of pale silk.

Before he had time to think several more strands came whipping down from the shadows above him. A few only flailed past him and then snapped away, but two more caught in his ragged clothes and pulled tight, like the thorny barbs already snagged in his neck and arm. Small, sharp pains bloomed all over him.

"They come, Master!" Skurn shrieked, flapping up into the air just as another barb shot out and swung through the spot where he had been. "Silkins!"

Now Barrick could see them, thin gray-white shapes scuttling through the upper branches above his head, casting down their weighted, thorn-hooked barbs to entangle him. He tried to reach into his belt for his broken spear but one of the creatures yanked on a silk strand hooked in his arm to keep him from reaching the weapon. Barrick grabbed the silk and pulled back hard until it slackened and he could grab the spearhead. He leaned out with his left hand and swept it up to cut through the strand imprisoning his arm, saying a silent prayer of thanks he had sharpened the edge. It took longer to work loose the thorny branch in his neck, and when he brought his hand away his fingers were smeared with blood.

Two of the maggoty things came tumbling out of the trees, silent as ghosts in the twilight, swinging their silks like horse-trappers as the dark wet spots of their eyes gleamed with reflected twilight. Barrick ducked under a flailing silk rope and felt the barbed hooks catch and tear at his scalp. He tore them loose from his head just as the creature leaped forward. Its strange, boneless limbs folded around him, and although it weighed little, the force was still enough to knock him off his feet. He fell and rolled, the silkin clinging to him until they both tumbled to a stop, Barrick's right arm pinned beneath his own body. A strand whipped around his neck and pulled tight. For a moment, with only his useless left arm free, he knew he would die.

But his left arm wasn't useless any longer. He reached up and caught the strange, slippery-but-sticky thing on his back and dug in his fingers. The strand around his neck tightened for a moment, but then he had tugged the thing loose and dragged it down onto the muddy forest floor.

I'm strong! He could have shouted it—he could feel it in him like a joyful flame. *Strong!*

Barrick was not able to get a solid grip on his attacker but as it rose up into a crouch he lunged forward and shoved the creature backward into the campfire even as another pale, half-human figure leaped down onto his back.

A horrible, whistling shriek went up from the one that had stumbled into the fire. The burning silkin staggered out of the firepit, pale yellow flames running up its legs and torso, the blackness beneath its mummifying threads beginning to ooze and bubble as the fire took it. Within a few heartbeats it was blazing like a torch, filling the twilight with shrilling screams so high in pitch that Barrick could hardly hear them.

The way to survival suddenly seemed clear. He leaped toward the fire, dragging the second silkin with him, and grabbed a burning piece of wood. With the broken spear in one hand and the flaming brand in the other he turned on the silkin clinging to his ankles and shoved the fire into the creature's featureless face until it sizzled and bubbled. Piping in agony, it pulled free of him and leaped away, blindly tearing at its own head before striking a tree trunk. It lay twitching for a moment, then crawled away into the undergrowth, rolling and lopsided as a drunkard.

Barrick grabbed the spearhead tight and beat his hand upon his breast. "Come on, then!" he shouted at the ghostly shapes still swarming in the trees above. "Come and get me!"

Two more jumped down, then a third. Skurn came out of nowhere and snatched with his talons at the one nearest Barrick, which gave him a moment to swipe the torch against it. He narrowly missed singeing the bird, who flapped up again, cawing in alarm. The silkin's wrappings did not catch, but Barrick stabbed at it again with his blade and spilled its black ooze, then turned and shoved the flame up against the next one even as it lurched forward. For long moments he could not tell how many of the silkins surrounded him, or how he was faring, but he could smell the ghastly, salty stink of the things as they burned. He began to laugh as he slashed with spearhead and torch, striking at everything that moved. From the corner of his eye he saw Skurn beating his way up into the air, looking for safety. Barrick only laughed louder.

An hour might have passed, or only moments—Barrick couldn't tell. The last moving silkin was at his feet, trying to hold in its slow-dripping innards where Barrick had slashed its belly wide open. In a fever of glee-ful rage Barrick dropped his spear and grabbed at the creature's head, his fingers compressing the silk-wrapped ball as if it were a rotten melon. He pulled it upright, then shoved the torch into its gaping, sticky eye.

"Die, you filthy thing!" He held it down with his foot until it was burning too hot to stand over it. Three more of the creatures lay motion-less and oozing at his feet, and nothing else moved in the trees.

Barrick lifted his hands before him, staring. He had known he would win—he had known it! What a marvel it was to have two strong arms, to be like anyone else! He kicked the smoldering corpse of the silkin and turned his back on it.

I have been given a gift. And what have I paid for it? Nothing.

He no longer felt any pain. Even the old miseries and the old losses—his sister, his stolen father, his murdered brother—troubled him no more; he had hardly thought of them in days. Just as the pain of his arm had gone, all his painful feelings had vanished, too.

When Skurn at last found the courage to come down again from the trees, Barrick was still laughing quietly.

Because I am whole for the first time, he thought. *The real Barrick Eddon, at last.*

18
King Hesper Is Unwell

"Most ettins are scaled all over like a lizard or a tortoise, and are often called 'Deep Ettins' because of their constant delving, but it is said that some have a smooth furry pelt that allows them to travel swiftly through tunnels other ettins have already excavated. These 'Tunnel Ettins' are also said to be blind."

—from "A Treatise on the Fairy Peoples of Eion and Xand"

"I'M AFRAID I DON'T UNDERSTAND, Golden One." Pinimmon Vash looked up. He had lowered himself onto his old, aching knees: when the autarch was in one of his unpredictable moods, he had found the conservative approach was safest. "I thought we were bound for . . . I have forgotten the name of the place. Your . . . guest's little kingdom in the north."

"Southmarch. And so we are." Sulepis stretched out a hand to admire the spread of his long fingers, each one tipped in gold as bright as the honey of Nushash's bees. "But first we are paying a visit to another ruler. May I not pass the time as I wish, Paramount Minister Vash? Surely life is too beautiful to be always hurrying!" The autarch smiled his lazy, crocodilian smile.

"May you . . . of course, Golden One! It goes without saying! Even the stars in the sky pause to know your plans." Vash squeezed himself a little closer to the floor, despite the pains sparking in his shins and hips. "We all live only to serve you. I just wished to . . . to know more of what you planned . . . so that we might better accommodate your needs." He tried to laugh, but instead of a knowing chuckle it came out as a shaky wheeze. "May you! You play a trick on your oldest and most dedicated servant, master! I would die to serve your smallest wish."

"I would like to see that." Sulepis' laugh was much more convincing than Vash's had been. "But not this morning, I think. Arrange boats to go ashore and bearers for the tribute. And tell the antipolemarch he may stand his soldiers down—I will take only the bearers, my carpet servants, and you. Oh, and I think King Olin might find the visit amusing too. Four guards should be enough for him."

"No soldiers?" Vash realized he was questioning his monarch again, but surely even the autarch was not so mad as to enter a foreign court with only four guards. "I am old, Golden One. Did I mishear you?"

"You did not. Tell Dumin Hauyuz that as long as his men remain on the ship and we remain ready to sail, he may otherwise do as he pleases."

"For which he will be profoundly grateful, Golden One, I have no doubt." Vash tried to back out of the cabin without standing up, but he quickly realized he no longer had the flexibility for it. After he had slid himself far enough backward, he clambered slowly to his feet and backed out of the presence of the inscrutable, incomprehensible living god on earth.

It seemed that the entire population of Gremos Pitra, capital city of Jellon and Jael, had lined up along the steeply rising road between the harbor and the palace to watch the strange procession. It was a small procession, as Sulepis had directed, with the autarch himself leading the way (except during the moments when the carpet slaves dashed in front of him to lay out the next section of cloth-of-gold carpet so that his sacred feet never touched the ground). Vash walked behind him, trying manfully to move onto the next piece of carpet each time before the sweating slaves snatched up the old one to carry it ahead of the god-king once more. The paramount minister was so terrified that one of the onlookers might do something untoward—what if one of them threw a rock at the autarch?—that his stomach ached.

Olin and his guards came next, walking on ordinary earth as ordinary men should; they were followed by the silent priest Vash had seen on the ship but whose name he did not know. The man had the dark, weathered skin of the deep-desert tribes and was covered with flamelike tattoos, and though he was not old his eyes were gray with cataracts. He carried a staff that clicked and jingled with the dangling skeletons of a dozen serpents. Everything about the priest made Vash fretful; he had been grateful during the voyage that the man had largely stayed belowdecks.

The snake-priest was followed by several dozen muscular slaves, each one carrying a huge tribute basket on his back—heavy baskets, too, from the frozen, uncomfortable grimaces of the men carrying them.

The onlookers crowding along the road watched and whispered in dull astonishment, both at the appearance of the tall southern god-king in his gleaming, golden armor and the almost complete absence of soldiers guarding him. Vash clearly was not the only one to be surprised that the famous enemy of all Eion should walk unarmed through a hostile city.

Pinimmon Vash did not find much chance to pray these days but he prayed now.

Nushash, I follow your heir. All my life I have been told the autarch carries your blood. Now I follow him into terrible danger in a hostile country. I have waited upon three autarchs and have always done my best to serve the Falcon Throne. Please do not let me die here in this backward land! Please do not let the autarch die under my protection!

He blinked dust from his eyes. At least the scotarch Prusus remained upon the ship, protected by Xixian soldiers. Even if the worst happened the ancient laws would be observed; the Falcon Throne would not go unfilled.

But Prusus is a cripple, Vash thought. *A drooling lackwit.* Still, it was said that some of the previous autarchs, especially those who reigned before the Ninth Year War, had not been much better. Tradition was what mattered. The scotarch would only rule until the council of noble families met and a new autarch was approved. Sulepis had several sons by several mothers. The line would not die.

The paramount minister was startled out of these gloomy thoughts by a stirring in the crowd. The Golden One's procession had reached the outer gates of Gremos Pitra and a party of armed soldiers stood waiting for them. Vash hurried forward as fast as his aching legs would carry him. The autarch could not speak directly to underlings. Surely things were not as topsy-turvy as that—not yet, in any case.

"I am Niccol Opanour, gate-herald of Gremos Pitra and of his majesty, Hesper, king of Jellon and Jael," said the leader of the soldiers, a fox-faced man with a short beard and the look of a good gambler. "State your business with King Hesper and his court."

"Business?" Vash had been carefully schooled by the autarch in what to say. "Surely a great king like Sulepis needs no petty excuse to stop and greet a fellow monarch? We bring your master gifts from the south—a gesture of goodwill. You would not make my monarch stand in the road like a tradesman, would you? You can see we come with no soldiers. We are at Hesper's mercy."

Which, as most of the other kings of this northern continent could attest, was as much as to say "hopeless." Hesper was only merciful for gain, a friend to other rulers only when it suited him, and everyone knew it.

Gate-herald Opanour frowned. "I mean your king no disrespect, but we were not told to expect this. We are not prepared. As it happens, King Hesper is . . . unwell."

"That is a pity," said Vash. "However, I feel certain that the gifts we bring him will cheer him somewhat." He hadn't spoke the Hierosoline tongue of the north in a long time, and was pleased to discover its subtleties hadn't entirely escaped him. He beckoned forward one of the sweating bearer slaves, then swept away the top of the man's basket. "See the generosity of Xis."

The handful of soldiers leaned forward in their saddles and their eyes grew round as they saw the gold and gems that filled the basket.

"That . . . this is most impressive," the gate-herald said. "But we must still ask our king for his permission . . ."

The autarch himself suddenly stepped forward, making the carpet slaves scurry to get another length of cloth-of-gold in front of him before his sandaled foot touched bare ground (which would reputedly cause the world itself to totter and collapse). The horses of the Jellonian soldiers shied away as though Sulepis was a kind of creature they had never seen before—as in fact he was, Vash thought: he was beginning to think the world had never seen anything quite like his master.

"Please say one thing to these men of Jellon for us, Paramount Minister," Sulepis said in Hierosoline. His voice seemed pitched softly, but it carried a long distance. "Remind them that even a benevolent king has limits. We have a warship full of long guns just outside the harbor, and several more will arrive by tonight." Sulepis smiled at the Jellonians and folded his arms across his breast, his golden armor clinking gently. "We come in peace, yes, but we would hate to see the spark of suspicion start a fire that would be hard to put out."

It was quickly decided that one of the soldiers should ride back to the palace to inform Hesper and the court that the autarch was coming.

The palace of Gremos Pitra was perched on a clifftop above the harbor, but in the years of peace the steep, narrow old path leading to it had been rebuilt into a series of wide, gentle switchbacks. Even Vash, old and sore as he was, did not find it too agonizing to climb from the harbor to the palace gates, but he still could not understand why so much time was being spent in such an odd exercise.

The gates swung open as they approached and the full panoply of Hesper's power appeared, guards on every parapet and a hundred more on either side of the entrance. The autarch walked serenely past them as though they were his own loyal subjects, looking neither to the left nor the right and walking in a measured but not overly slow pace so that the carpet slaves had to scurry to stay ahead of him. The procession crossed a formal courtyard rapidly filling with Jellonian courtiers and servants, those in back standing on tiptoe or trampling the hedges in their determination to get a view of the infamous Mad Autarch of Xis.

Many of the Jellonian troops filed into the great hall behind the parade of basket-hauling slaves, so that the autarch's party was hemmed in on all sides by armed soldiers wearing ceremonial green tabards bearing the blue rooster and golden rings of Hesper's Jaelian clan. The king's tall, canopied chair stood at the far end of the high-ceilinged room, surrounded by dozens of courtiers gaping at the new arrivals, too fascinated even to whisper among themselves. Vash squinted—it was a long room—trying to make out the small figure slumped in the huge covered chair, which looked more like a sack of clothes to be washed than a man. As the herald had suggested the king of Jellon looked old and ill, his skin pale, his eyes blue-ringed and sunken. He was dressed all in white, which had the unfortunate effect of making him appear to be a corpse wrapped in its burial shroud.

Sulepis strode toward him, the carpet slaves hurrying to prepare the way, and then stopped a few yards from the steps leading up to the chair. Vash thought his master might become angry at being forced to stand beneath a less powerful monarch, but if he was, the autarch showed no sign of it. The Jellonian guards fidgeted nervously with their weapons, but their ruler held up a shaking hand.

"So," Hesper said hoarsely, "the much feared Emperor of the South. You are younger than I supposed, sir. What do you want?"

"I am told you are not well," Sulepis said in a simple and matter-of-fact tone. "It is kind of you to rouse yourself to meet me."

"Kind?" Hesper straightened up a little. "You threatened me with your warships if I would not see you. Do not be absurd." His voice, which should have been forceful, had been robbed by his weakness of all but petulance. Still, Vash could see that he had once been a formidable man.

"Perhaps you are right," said Sulepis. "Perhaps we should put away our masks. I did not come only to give you gifts—although they are very fine gifts indeed." He waved his golden fingers toward the slaves, who still held their baskets high on their shoulders, as though the floor of the throne room were too dirty a place to set such down valuable objects. "But also to tell you that I am displeased with you."

"Displeased with me?" Hesper shook his head irritably. Vash could not stop looking at the man. The king of Jellon was not even sixty years old— much younger than Pinimmon Vash himself—but looked like he had lived a hundred years or more, and hard years at that. "Am I a child that I should care about such things? I am displeased that you disturb my rest. Say your piece and be gone."

"You promised me something, Hesper." The autarch spoke with the stern but loving tone of a disappointed father. "You had something I wanted—something I specifically asked you to acquire for me—but you sold it to someone else instead."

The courtiers began to murmur. Even without knowing what his master intended, Vash guessed they would have much more to wonder about before too long.

"What are you babbling about?" Hesper demanded, but he had the look of a guilty man caught in a lie.

"But you see," Sulepis said, "I have obtained it despite you." He clapped his hands and his guards pushed King Olin forward. The courtiers murmured more loudly, but it was clear most of them did not recognize the ruler of the March Kingdoms.

"What . . . what . . . ?" Hesper stuttered. "What foolishness is this . . . ?"

"I think the one who promises something to me and then does not keep his bargain is the foolish one," Sulepis said calmly. "I told you I wanted Olin of Southmarch. I gave you gold to show my goodwill. You kept my gold, Hesper, and then you sold Olin to Ludis of Hierosol. That is not the way to make me look kindly on you."

Vash was beginning to feel truly frightened. Hesper might be old and ill, and Sulepis might have warships outside the harbor, but at the moment the Xixians were surrounded by armed enemies and the harbor was a mile away. Why was Sulepis provoking a confrontation? Had he taken the idea of his own godhood too seriously? Did he honestly think that the Jellonians would not dare to touch him, let alone hack him to pieces where he stood? Perhaps the autarch believed that these northerners were like his own people, bred with a hundred generations of reverence for their god-king.

"Well, King Olin?" Sulepis certainly appeared as comfortable as if he stood in his own throne room surrounded by worshipful subjects and his own Leopard guards. "Have you nothing to say to your betrayer now that you stand before him at last? This is the man who took you from your family and sold you like the merest beast."

Olin looked from Sulepis to Hesper, then cast his eyes down again. "I have nothing to say. I am a prisoner. I am not here of my own will."

Hesper tried to stand but could not, and subsided gasping into the huge chair. He pointed at the autarch. "Do you think to humiliate me in front of my own subjects? You may rule a million blacks, but here in Jellon you are nothing but a fool dressed like a golden peacock. You pushed yourself upon me. You are no guest and I owe you no safety." He tried to say something else, but a long spasm of coughing prevented him. When he could again speak, his voice rasped like a loose cart wheel. "I do not know whether to ransom you or simply do away with you."

"All will proceed as heaven plans it," the autarch said, smiling. "Olin, are you certain you have nothing else to say? I have given you a chance to confront your enemy."

Vash was feeling a terrible pressure in his bladder and his heart was beating so fast he feared he would swoon in front of all these foreigners.

"Hesper has done me wrong," said Olin, "but it is you who brought me here like one of your tribute baskets—something to show off your wealth and power. I will not play your game, Sulepis."

"Enough," said Hesper, and coughed again. "I . . . I have . . ."

"It is too bad you do not understand all I am doing for you, Olin," said the autarch. "Lifting you from an ignoble fate to the most heroic end there could be. And this as well . . ." He turned back toward the throne. "Hesper, you have been ill a long time, I think—almost a year, I would guess. It began when you passed Olin to Ludis Drakava, did it not?"

Hesper's eyes bulged with pain and frustration as he tried to stop coughing. A little spray of red decorated his white robes. One of his servants stepped forward with a cup but Hesper waved him off. "Ill, yes," Hesper said at last in a breathy whisper. "And deserted in my need by that whore I had smiled upon and lifted up from nothing. Betrayed me, she did—left me for that cur Enander!" He paused then and looked around, as confused as though he had just woken up. A moment later he blinked and wiped red spittle from his chin. "It matters not," he said. "But I will live long enough to see *you* sent screaming down to hell, Xandian."

"You still do not understand, do you?" Sulepis smiled. "You are dying, Hesper, because you have been poisoned—I reached out all the way from Xand to accomplish it." He grinned, which only made him look more predatory. "You see, it is worse than you thought. Not only did Ananka leave you, she took my gold and poured death into your cup before she went." The autarch ignored the gasps and cries of the Jellonian courtiers as he turned from the wheezing, pop-eyed king of Jellon back to Olin. "Now you see how you have been avenged," he told his prisoner. "And King Hesper learns the price of betraying a living god."

Hesper recovered enough breath to flail his hand toward Sulepis and shout, "Guards!" but even as the first of the soldiers stepped forward— more hesitantly than Vash would have expected for men facing unarmed slaves—the autarch raised his hand high and they all stopped as though Sulepis were their king instead of blood-drooling Hesper.

"But wait!" the autarch cried and then began to laugh, a sound so strange and unexpected that even the armored soldiers flinched. "You still have not seen the gifts I bring!" Sulepis flicked his fingers.

The bearers lifted their baskets high above their heads and dashed them on the floor. Gold and jewels spilled out onto the tiles, but not only treasure: from each broken basket a cloud of black wasps rose like a moaning whirlwind, each wasp as big as a man's thumb; a moment later, even as the screams began, hundreds of poisonous hood snakes crawled out of the ruined baskets as well. The snakes immediately slithered off in all directions, striking at anything that moved including many of the helpless bearer slaves. Already the great hall was a chaos of shrieking courtiers and servants struggling to escape. Many held their hands over their faces to defend against the wasps only to stumble into a tangle of serpents and fall screaming to the floor, where they thrashed helplessly until the creatures' venom silenced them at last.

Vash was too astounded to do anything but stare at the horror around him, but wasps were snapping past him like sling stones and the first of the angry snakes had almost reached the place where he cringed by the autarch's side.

"A'lat!" called Sulepis.

The dark-skinned priest stepped forward and raised his rattling serpent-staff, then rapped it on the floor and shouted something Vash could not make out. A moment later the air around the priest seemed to grow as shimmery as a heat-mirage, then the strange blur stretched out and swallowed up the autarch and Vash and Olin Eddon and the guards as well.

It was like being covered by fog: Vash could still see the jerking, staggering shapes of courtiers and soldiers but they had become remote and hard to make out, like shadow puppets held too far from the screen. Still, the priest's spell, if that was what it was, had done nothing to diminish the sounds in the great hall, which only became worse as the gurgles and groans of the dying began to supplant the screams of the living still struggling to escape.

"A'lat," said the autarch, "I believe some smoke would add to the scene and make our exit even more impressive." He spoke as calmly as if he were deciding what kind of trees should be planted in the gardens of the Orchard Palace. "Vash, it will be rather confusing when we go out— please remind the carpet slaves that they must pay close attention."

Vash could only watch, slack-jawed with amazement, as the dark priest A'lat lifted a round object the size of a small cannonball and rubbed it with his hands while singing a few quiet words until the ball began to billow persimmon-colored smoke. The priest rolled it across the floor toward the doorway leading out of the great hall, then the autarch and his carpet slaves stepped after it.

The door to the courtyard was open and the garden itself was littered with bodies, some moaning and twitching, some silent. Some of the courtiers had even gone so far as to climb trees to escape the hood snakes, and could be seen clinging to branches with one hand while they tried to swat away angry wasps with the other, but their screams and the corpses lying at the base of some of the trees with shiny black insects still walking on their faces told a tale of futility, even through the blur of the priest's spell. The magical fog seemed cover the autarch wherever he went, like the royal awning slaves held over him on particularly hot days. The Jellonian guards still trying to reach the throne room and protect their own monarch rushed past the little procession as though they could not see it.

Vash had seen hood snakes before, although never in such numbers, but he had never seen anything like the huge wasps, creatures that seemed to have no other desire than to sting anything that moved and keep stinging it until motion ceased. Even in the midst of such madness and death he could not help wondering where they came from.

When they reached the gate, Sulepis told the priest, "More smoke, I think. It will serve to distract the multitude." The autarch then waited calmly as his guards winched open the massive portcullis and unbolted the outer door. A'lat rubbed another of his smoke-fruits into life and held it in his hand as he led Sulepis and the hustling carpet bearers out through the palace gate. The people who had lined the road before had lost all order and were now blocking the autarch's passage.

A'lat ignited a second smoke ball and held one high in each hand. The Jellonians shrank back, crying out in fear and amazement. Sulepis raised his hands.

"The great god of fire has destroyed your wicked king!" he shouted and some in the crowd cried out, while others fell into murmuring, confused talk. "He has sent doom down on Hesper from heaven itself— stinging insects, fierce serpents, lions, and dragons! Run! Run and you may yet be saved!"

Even as the Jellonians stared, some drawing away but some starting forward in anger and distrust, the first swarm of wasps issued from the open gate of the palace, flew past the autarch and his party as if they were not even there, and fell upon the nearest of the people in the road like a cloud of death. The screeching of these victims set many of the others running, and a moment later a dozen huge snakes wriggled out of the gate into the sunlight and the crowd dissolved into mindless terror just as the courtiers inside had done. The autarch's party walked down the road toward the harbor, the carpet slaves scuttling back and forth to keep the golden path always stretching before their master.

"Lions and dragons?" Vash looked around worriedly.

"The tale of what happened here will grow in the telling," the autarch said. "I merely add a few details to make the eventual history richer."

Olin Eddon had the bloodless look of a man living a nightmare, and staggered a little as he walked. His guards moved closer to help keep him upright.

"Is Hesper dead?" Vash asked.

"Ah, I hope it is not so." Sulepis shook his head. "I would like to think he will pass his last month or so before the poison kills him dwelling on what it means to cheat me and knowing that I will come back at my leisure and devour his little country like a sweetmeat." He paused and turned to gaze back at Gremos Pitra, an expression of great serenity on his long face. "After this, the people of Jellon will crawl to me on the day I return. They will beg to become slaves of Xis."

"Not everyone in the north will beg to become slaves," Olin said darkly. "You may find that many would rather die than bend their knees to you."

"That too can be arranged," the autarch told him. "Now come, all of you—step lively. It has been a busy morning and your god-king is hungry."

🌿

Qinnitan was still reeling when the nameless man dragged her out into the sunlight and began to lead her across the docks. Poor Pigeon limped beside them, his hand dripping blood through the makeshift bandage, his little face emptied by the shock of what had happened.

How could it be? How could all she had suffered and survived have given them only that few moments of freedom? Were the gods utterly evil?

Spare us, great Nushash, she prayed. *I was a priestess in your sacred Hive. I have only tried to do what was right. Heavenly bees, protect us!*

But there were no bees, only smoke and flecks of burning sail wafting on the wind. The ship that had brought them here was all but gone, only a bit of its burning forecastle still above water, the mast long since burned black and collapsed. Hundreds of people crowded the waterfront, shouting bits of the story to each other, staring as survivors were pulled from the water by men in small boats.

Some of them were innocent sailors, she thought suddenly, *like the men on Dorza's ship. Some of them might have been good men. Dead because of me . . .*

It did no good to think about it—no good to think about anything.

She was being taken to an unimaginable punishment at the hands of the autarch and her only hope of escape had proved futile. Even if she were to dive into the water, this nameless, relentless killer would only dive in and pull her back out again. Perhaps if she swallowed as much water as she could . . .

But that would leave Pigeon alone, she realized. *This monster would give him to the autarch to be tortured . . . killed . . .*

Suddenly a horrifying pain stabbed at Qinnitan's arm. She shrieked and staggered a step or two, then fell to her knees. For a moment she thought her captor had grabbed her elbow and broken it, but he was on the other side, holding the other arm. He tried to yank her back upright, but her limbs were as limp and boneless as wet string.

Blackness swam before her eyes and she hung her head, thinking she might vomit. The pain in her arm was growing fiercer, as if a sliver of the burning ship had been driven into her like a nail into soft wood, as if the joint in her arm were being carved with a sharp knife.

"Gods! Stop this!" she cried, or thought she did, but she was tumbling down into blackness and could not be certain of anything any more.

Shadows moved around her, eyeless things murmuring words she could barely hear.

"*Tears . . .*" whispered one.

"*Spittle . . .*" said another.

"*Blood . . .*" quavered a third in a voice so low she could scarcely make it out.

Her arm burned as if the bone had become a white-hot poker. The darkness swung around her in a wild dance, and for a moment she saw the face of the red-haired boy . . . Barrick! . . . but he clearly did not see her, although she tried to call to him. Something covered him and kept her from him—a frozen waterfall, a cup of glass—and her words could not travel to him. *Ice. Solid shadow. Separation . . .*

Then the world wheeled back into place around her, the cry of seagulls and the shouts of people on every side snapping into place like the last piece of a wooden puzzle. The hard, gray planks of the dock were beneath her hands and knees. Somebody was pulling her roughly to her feet, but she was not ready and almost fell again; only the strength of that powerful, iron-hard arm held her upright. The pain in her own arm was fading but she was still breathless with its memory.

"What are you playing at?" her captor, the nameless man, shook her hard. He looked around as though someone might notice, but no one on the dock was near enough to hear, even if they would have cared. *We must look like a father with two willful children*, she thought. *Behaving badly.*

Something struck her then—not more pain, but a realization: if she continued to walk this path there was no hope. She could feel it, feel things closing in, possibilities withering, so that only death stood at the end of the road—death and something more, something worse. *It's waiting*, she realized, although she did not know what *it* was. Something hungry, that was all she knew for certain, and it was waiting for her in the darkness at the end of her journey.

Qinnitan regained her balance and waited until the man took his hand off her to grab at Pigeon, then she turned and ran as fast her unsteady legs would carry her, straight toward the edge of the dock, not slowing even at a shout from her captor. The planks were wet and she almost slipped and tumbled into the water, but managed to stop herself by grabbing at a post. She held onto it, swaying, then raised her hand as the man began to walk toward her, dragging Pigeon behind him.

"*No!*" she said with as much strength as she could muster, the word a harsh croak in her sea-roughened throat. "No. If you take another step before you hear me out, I'll throw myself in. I'll swim for the bottom and drink in so much ocean I'll be dead before you reach me."

He paused, the look of rage on his unexceptional face changing to something else, something colder and more calculating.

"I know I can't get away from you," she said. "Let the boy go and I'll do what you want. Try to bring him along and I'll kill myself and you can take my body to the autarch instead."

"I make no bargains," said the nameless man.

"Pigeon, run away!" Qinnitan shouted. "Go on, run. He won't come after you. Run far away and hide."

The boy only stared at her, the shock of his injuries changing into something much more heartbreaking. The man still held his wrist. Pigeon shook his head.

"Go!" she said. "Otherwise he'll only keep hurting you to make me do what he wants. Run away!"

The nameless man looked from the boy to her. He bent and picked up a piece of coarse rope that lay in haphazard loops on the dock like an exhausted snake. "Tie one end around your waist and I will let the boy go." He flipped a coil of the rope toward her.

"Pigeon, move back," she said as she bent to pick it up, but the boy only stared at her, his face full of helpless misery. "Move back!" She turned to the man. "When he is at the edge of the dock by those steps, I'll tie it around my waist. I swear as an acolyte of the Hives of Nushash."

The man actually laughed, a harsh rasp of amusement. Something was different about him, she realized for the first time—something odd, as though he had lost a bit of his stony outer armor. He was still terrifying, though.

The man nodded. "Go ahead, then." He called over his shoulder to Pigeon. "Run, child. Once I see that rope tied, if you are still on the dock I will cut off the rest of your fingers."

Pigeon shook his head again, violently, but Qinnitan thought it was less in negation than in desperation. "Go away!" she shouted. A few people at the other end of the dock turned, their attention finally distracted from the fire in the harbor. "I cannot live with your suffering, Pigeon. Please—it's the best thing you can do for me. Go!"

The boy hesitated half a dozen heartbeats longer, then burst into tears and turned and ran away across the broad dock, his bare feet banging on the planks. Qinnitan considered throwing herself into the cold green water again, but whether it was the horror of nearly drowning earlier or the feeling that she had somehow changed what lay before her, if only a little, she tied the rope around her waist and then let herself be pulled toward the nameless man. Pigeon, she was relieved to see, was no longer in sight.

The only person left in this world who loved me, she thought. *Gone now.*

Qinnitan let the man lead her off like an animal going to holy sacrifice, away from the sparking chaos of the harbor and back into the shadowed alleys that ran between the narrow buildings clustered beside the docks of Agamid.

19

Dreams of Lightning and Black Earth

"One Deep Ettin killed with hot oil and dragged from its tunnel at Northmarch was more than twice the height of a man. King Lander later brought the bones back to Syan as a trophy. The monster's hand was said to have been as large as Lander's great shield."

—from "A Treatise on the Fairy Peoples of Eion and Xand"

SHE WAS DIGGING DESPERATELY through dark earth, but every time she caught a glimpse of her twin brother's pale, sleeping face he sank farther into the soil and out of her reach.

Once or twice she actually managed to touch his garments before he slid deeper into the ground, but no matter how hard she worked or how fast she threw aside the dirt she could not catch up to him. Barrick seemed alive but unaware of her, writhing as though trapped in a frightening dream. She called to him over and over but he wouldn't or couldn't answer.

She touched something at last and her fingers curled in the damp cloth of her brother's shirt, but when she braced herself and pulled up hard, what appeared out of the black loam like the cap of a mushroom was not her brother's pallid features but those of Ferras Vansen. Shocked and startled, she let go, but as the soldier disappeared back into the dirt the earth beneath her abruptly collapsed as well. She fell down into smothering, gritty dark.

She was in a tunnel, bits of white roots worming down from the rocky soil above her head. A flash of silver now appeared ahead of her—just a glimmer, but enough for her to recognize the thing she had chased before . . . in another . . .

When? She couldn't remember. But she knew it was true, and knew that the silvery thing had eluded her once more. She was determined it would not happen again. Still, although she scrambled after it as quickly as she could, she was not meant for traveling on all fours while the thing she chased clearly was: it remained always a turn ahead of her, giving her only glimpses of a pale, fluttering, brushlike tail.

Then she stumbled and bumped against the wall. The tunnel fell in on her and Briony Eddon woke up.

She shook her head, disconcerted to find she was wearing a heavy headdress—why would she wear such a thing to bed? Briony opened her eyes to find herself in her sitting room. Her ladies were sewing and talking quietly among themselves. She had fallen asleep sitting up, in midday, and probably drooled on herself as well like some ancient crone.

Her friend Ivgenia was watching her with a little smile on her face. Briony hurriedly wiped at her chin. "How terrible I am, how rude!" she said, sitting up straight. "I must have dozed off. Why do you look at me so, Ivvie? Did I say something terrible in my sleep?"

"Oh, Highness, no." The smile widened. "Poor thing. Too many late nights."

"You're teasing me. It was only one late night—and it was the last night of Greater Zosimia. You are the one always telling me I should go out and be seen by the people of the court."

"And you *were* seen. And you even danced! No one will ever again criticize you for holding yourself aloof, my dear."

"Danced?" Briony winced a little. She had intended no such thing, but the revelries had come at the end of a long, tiring day and she had clearly taken at least one cup of wine too many. "You make it sound terrible. Did I make a fool of myself?"

Ivvie smiled again. "You attracted much attention, but it was the sort many of the other girls envied, I think."

"Stop. You are cruel."

"We shall see. Your secretary has a few things for you to look at."

"What?" She really did feel terribly thick-headed. These nights of poor sleep and strange dreams—forests, digging, dark tunnels full of roots—were clearly taking a toll on her. Still, that was no excuse for playing the fool.

Feival Ulian had been standing in the doorway with his arms folded on his chest. He had taken to court life very quickly: no other secretary or cleric in Broadhall dressed so well or so colorfully. "Have we finished our little beauty nap?" he asked. "Because there are several messages awaiting your reply—and a few other things as well." He rolled his eyes. "One of the packages is addressed to 'The Lovely Dancing Princess'—I suppose that's you."

"Oh, dear. You'd better let me see it." She took the small fabric-covered box from Feival. "What is it?"

Ivgenia giggled. "You goose! Open it and find out."

"Is it a gift? It says it's from Lord Nikomakos." She fiddled it open and drew out a small velvet bag.

"He's an earl's son—the one with the yellow hair you spent so much time dancing with last night." Ivgenia laughed. "Surely your Royal Highness didn't drink so much wine that you can't remember him at all?"

"I do remember. He reminded me of Kendrick, my . . . my brother. But he wouldn't stop talking about his hawks. Hawk, hawk, hawk . . . Why should he send me . . ."—she lifted it out of the bag—"Zoria preserve me, why should he send me a gold bracelet?" It was a lovely thing, if a trifle gaudy, the kind of ornate work that she seldom wore by choice—a twining white rose, the blossoms picked out in pale gems. "Oh, merciful goddess, are those *diamonds?* What does he want from me?" She was horrified—she would never drink wine in public again. Instead of sounding out the nobles who might be sympathetic to her family's cause and could help put gentle pressure on King Enander, as she had meant to, she had apparently made a spectacle of herself to shame the worst provincial.

"Are you really such an idiot, Highness?" Ivvie demanded.

"I mean, certainly I know what he wants, and I suppose I'm flattered, but . . ." She stared fretfully at the bracelet. "I must send it back." She thought she could actually *hear* Feival pursing his lips in disgust. "Are all of these gifts from him?"

"From him and others," her friend said.

"Then I must send them all back."

"Truly? All of them?" Ivgenia held out a large parcel wrapped in cloth. "Even this one from Prince Eneas himself . . . ?"

Briony took it and opened it. "It's a book—*A Chronicle of the Life of Iola, Queen of Syan, Tolos, and Perikal.* Of course—the prince and I spoke of her the other day."

"How romantic," Feival said with a certain asperity.

"So are you going to keep it?"

"It is a very thoughtful gift, Ivvie—he knows I am interested in such things. Iola lived in secrecy for several years when young because her family had been usurped during the War of Three Favors."

"Which means you want to keep it, Princess. What of the bracelet? Do you still mean to send it back?"

"Of course. I hardly know the man."

"So you will keep a book and send back a jeweled bracelet? Do you wonder why half the court thinks you have set your cap at Eneas and the other half thinks you mad?"

It stung. There was something in what Ivvie said, of course—Briony did have some feelings for the prince, and it had been clever of him to give her such a gift instead of something merely pretty. Eneas understood that she was not like other girls.

Which made what she planned to do to him even more terrible.

"What about these others? There are half a dozen more letters and gifts." Ivgenia held out a carved wooden box. "This is pretty."

"I don't want any of these." Briony shook her head. "You open it."

"Truly? May I keep what's in it . . . ?"

"Ivvie! You are terrible! Very well, I might as well know—what is it?"

"It's . . . empty," said her friend, but her voice sounded odd. "Oh. I've hurt myself. On the clasp." Ivgenia held up her finger to show Briony a single drop of blood like a carnelian bead. A moment later the girl swayed and then fell heavily to the floor.

Briony didn't like the formality of Broadhall's Great Garden at the best of times, but today it felt utterly barren and oppressive.

It wasn't the size, although it covered many acres, but the tamed, controlled nature of the place. None of the hedges or ornamental trees were taller than a person's head, and most were far shorter; between them lay only geometric arrangements of low box hedges and careful, concentric flower gardens. You could stand in any part of the gardens and see almost all the rest, including who shared the garden with you. Perhaps the Tessians liked it that way, but she preferred a little more solitude, especially now, when it felt like malicious eyes watched her everywhere she went. The much smaller residence garden back home had several little hills and stands of tall trees that effectively divided the space into many separate locations—a world in miniature, as her father had once called it. (He was talking sourly of how parts of it had been allowed to go to seed, but what he said was still true.)

"I am sorry to keep you waiting, Princess." As Eneas emerged from the back of the scriptorium Briony had a momentary view of a legion of beetle-black scribing priests sitting side by side at the long tables, hard at work. "And even more sorry to keep you waiting at such an unhappy time. There is no way I can express my sorrow and shame that such things should happen in my father's court—and twice! Please, how is the Lady e'Doursos?"

"She will live, thank the gods, that is what the physician told me . . . but she will be a long while getting better." Briony fought back tears for what seemed like the hundredth time in the last few hours. She was so tired she felt as though she were made from frail glass. "It was a near thing. I sat up with her all the night as she passed in and out of her fever. I thought many times we would lose her, but it seems the sharpened piece of the clasp only barely pierced her, or it might have been the poison was weak." Briony still could not guess who had tried to murder her this time. Surely Jenkin Crowel had been frightened out of trying such tricks again, but if it hadn't been the Tollys' envoy then who could be behind it?

"We must praise the Three Brothers for that blessed bit of good fortune, then." Eneas offered Briony his arm. "Will you walk with me? I am mightily tired of the sound of pens scratching. I have been sending letters to every garrison between here and Hierosol about the autarch's attack. A damnable amount of work." He colored a little. "Not that I had to do all the copying myself, thank the gods!" He was speaking swiftly now, as though afraid to let silence fall. "I must get one of those writing machines the pamphleteers and poets use—or stamping machine, I suppose it should be called, for they work by stamping out letters and words as a royal seal stamps signs into wax. It would certainly speed the giving of orders to our field commanders . . ." He shook his head. "Listen to me, prattling on when you have just survived an attack on your life!"

"An attack that harmed me not at all."

He frowned. "You say that as though you wish it had succeeded."

Briony shook her head, although even such small movements felt nearly beyond her strength. "I don't wish that, Prince Eneas, of course I don't. But I feel terrible that others should suffer on my behalf."

"You are an admirable woman, Briony Eddon. I promise that I will do everything I can to keep you safe. I will send more of my guards. There are no more loyal men in all Syan."

"I'm sure of that, Highness," she said. "But even the finest soldiers are scant protection against poison."

He seemed more upset than Briony was herself. "Still, we must do *something*. This is an outrage, Princess—a deadly insult to my father's name and throne. Here in our own court!" He turned then, stopping them in the middle of the path, and took her right hand in both of his. "And it is especially disheartening to me, Briony Eddon, because I hold you in such high regard. There is nothing I would not do for you."

She blinked. His hands were warm. He had taken his gloves off.

"Surely you are not surprised." The prince looked troubled. "Was I so foolish as to be completely wrong when I supposed you might also have some feelings for me?"

Briony held her breath for a moment. She had been working toward this moment for weeks, but now she was confused. Eneas *was* admirable, kind, and clever. Everyone knew he was brave. And, as she looked at him now, she saw his strong, even features and knew that although he was no godlike beauty, any woman would be glad to have him even were he not the prince and heir of mighty Syan. But he was. And she needed his position and his power desperately to save her people, her family's throne. So why did she suddenly feel confounded and tongue-tied?

"I have struck you silent, Princess. You are not the type to be silent in the presence of men. I fear that I have offended you in some way."

"No. No, your Royal Highness—Prince Eneas—you have done me great honor." For a moment her imposture and the truth of her heart were so close she could not tell one from the other. "I think a great deal of you. I think you are the most admirable man in this whole great kingdom . . ."

He gently tugged his hand away from her, disguising his unhappiness a little by pushing his dark hair back from his forehead. " 'But,' you are about to say. But there is someone else to whom your heart has already been given—maybe your troth even plighted in the temple."

"No!" But it wasn't completely untrue—she *did* have feelings for someone else, as confusing and inappropriate and even ridiculous as those feelings might be. But that person could not save her kingdom. Eneas could—if any human agency could perform such a task. "No, it's not that. It's just that . . . I cannot let myself have feelings for anyone, even someone like you, though you are the dream of any sensible woman. I cannot." She tried to pull away, caught in the moment like a leaf scudding on the wind.

"But why?" Eneas would not let her go. He was strong. He would be masterful for anyone, she sensed—especially any woman—who wanted to be mastered. "Why can't you let your heart lead you?"

She had planned just such a moment—imagined it almost gleefully, as a hunter might dream of the moment the stag stood exposed and unaware on a hillside, breast vulnerable to the killing shaft. Now that it had come, though, it filled her with unease. How could she take advantage of a good man this way, even to save her family's throne? How could she pretend to love him just to gain his help?

Even worse, what if she was not pretending?

"I . . . I must think," she said. "I had not expected anything like this. I had hoped to find allies here in your father's court against my family's enemies, the usurping Tollys. I had not expected to find . . . someone I could care for. I must think." She looked off across the ordered rows of the garden. Distant figures acted out their own dramas, too far away to be recognized—each of them, herself included, as helpless in their actions as characters created out of air and smoke by Nevin Hewney or Finn Teodoros, ideas committed to paper and performed for the price of a night's food and lodging. How had she come to such a strange pass? Was she the player or the thing being played?

"Of course," Eneas said at last. The prince could not disguise the heaviness of his words. " 'Of course I will give you time, my lady. You must be true to yourself."

She should have slept like the dead that night, but instead she rolled and tossed through more nightmares of tunnels collapsing and dirt always beneath her fingers. This time there was no silvery shape to lead her, and the longer the dreams went on the farther down into choking darkness she went.

At last she found herself in a deep place, so deep that she understood somehow she had dug out on the other side of the world, that what lay beyond the small patch of ground on which she stood was the empty blackness of a sky with no stars, a blackness into which a single misstep could send her tumbling forever. And there, at the center of that dark otherness, she found her brother.

He was pale, senseless, as he had been before. He lay stretched before her as Kendrick had lain while the servants prepared him for burial, but Barrick was not dead. She did not know how she knew it, but she did.

The three shapes that crouched over him were no servants or funerary priests but something else entirely—dark, eyeless shadows singing wordless songs as they moved their hands above him. Then one of them lifted Barrick's crippled arm up to the emptiness of its face and her brother began to fade.

Tears, one of the shapes whispered, and the echo was swallowed by the damp, dark earth all around.

Spittle, said another.

Blood, said a third.

She tried to call to her twin, to wake him and warn him about what these terrible specters were doing, but she could not. She felt the change spreading through Barrick like flame, a train of fire from his arm to his head and heart that was also a spreading, burning agony through her own body. She tried to throw herself forward, but some invisible hand held her back.

Barrick! Her cries seemed all but silent. *Barrick! Come back! Don't let them take you!*

And at the last, just before the thing of cobweb shadows that had been her brother grew too dim to see, Barrick opened his eyes and looked at her. His stare was empty, utterly dead and empty.

She woke up choking on her own tears, feeling as though the most important part of her had been cut out with a dull knife. For long moments she could only lie on her bed sobbing helplessly. *Barrick* . . . Would she truly never see him again? The dream had felt so terrible, so final. Had something happened to him—something bad? Was he . . . ?

"Oh, gods, no . . . !" she moaned.

Briony dragged herself up. She could not even bear to think of the possibility. These dreams—the nightmares—they were stalking her as though she were their prey. Would she never sleep again without seeing some parade of horror? So tired that she could barely set one foot in front of the other, she stumbled to the chest she had brought with her from her time with the players, the locked box with the clothes she had worn and the few small objects she had picked up on her journey south.

Briony opened the lid and began digging through it, scattering the boy's breeches she had worn and the pamphlets that had been handed to her, not even knowing what she sought until her fingers closed on it and she felt the fragile bird's skull and the tiny dry flowers.

Lisiya's charm in her hands, she crawled back across her dark chamber and into bed. She held the charm tightly to her breast and tried not to think of the dream-Barrick's dead eyes. One of the maids whimpered a little in her sleep, and that was the last thing she remembered before the dark took her again.

She was in the forest once more, but this time she could see the thing she had been chasing so long. It was a fox, black on the underside but tipped all over its back with silver, and silver on its tail and sharp face as well. As it sped away it looked back at her, teeth bared in a grin that might have been fatigue but seemed more like mockery. Except for a thin ring of orange, the creature's eyes were as black as its belly.

The fox leaped over the roots effortlessly, but even in her dream Briony could not move with such liquid ease. She must have stumbled, for she found herself falling forward, the trees suddenly turned into whirling torrents of black. For a moment she thought she was back in the terrible, crumbling earth, but then she passed through that spinning darkness into a forest glade. The silvery fox had stopped running and now crouched with its back to her in front of an ancient tumbled altar of stone.

Briony staggered up and fell to her knees. Things seemed curiously painful for a dream: she could feel twigs and rocks digging into her skin.

"Who . . . who are you?" she gasped.

The beast turned. This time there was no question: its grin was one of mockery and disgust. The fox shook its head. "I said it before and I'll say it again—I fear for the breed."

The little animal hopped lightly up onto the ruined altar and lowered its muzzle to sniff. Thunder rumbled distantly. "Look at this," the fox said, and there was something familiar in the creature's voice that cut through the fog of Briony's dreaming thoughts. "Is this what people think of me, that my sacred places are left untended even *here?* Even in the dreamlands?"

"Lisiya?" Briony whispered. "Is that you?" But as soon as she said the name she knew it was true.

The fox turned; a moment later the black and silver beast had vanished and the old woman sat upon the altar, her gnarled bare feet dangling as if she were a child. "Lisiya Melana of the Silver Glade, do you mean?" she said with more than a trace of irritation. "Bad enough you summon a goddess and then fail to meet her, but to forget her name as well . . . !"

"But . . . but I did not summon you."

"You most certainly did, child. Three nights running, although I could barely hear you the first few times. Weak as a newborn kitling's, your voice was, but finally tonight I could hear you well enough to find you." Thunder boomed again above the forest, as though mirroring Lisiya's irritation.

Briony could not shake off the feeling that she was misunderstanding something. "I . . . I dreamed of you—or at least of chasing you. Through the forest. And through tunnels in the earth. But I did not see you before, only your . . . tail."

Lisiya levered herself off the edge of the altar and dropped to the ground; Briony almost cringed, afraid the demigoddess' bony old legs would snap like twigs. It was strange to feel so awake and yet to know she was dreaming! Other than a light-headed feeling such as came upon her when she had more wine than she should, she felt quite ordinary.

"Come along, child. I suppose it doesn't matter why you summoned me. In your heart you must have known you needed my help." Briony followed the demigoddess past the altar, out of the clearing, and into the trees. Thunder boomed again and a faint shimmer of lightning lit the sky overhead. "Restless," Lisiya commented, but did not explain.

In many ways the journey through the forest was as dreamlike to Briony as the pursuit of Barrick through the crumbling earth, but it was maddeningly ordinary as well. She could feel every step, every breath, even a moment of discomfort when she scraped her arm against the trunk of an oak tree.

"Where are we?" she asked at last.

"At the moment? Or in some larger sense?" Lisiya was laboring along at a good pace and Briony had to hurry to keep up. "We are very close here to the lands of the dreaming gods—all the old gods that Crooked sent to sleep. Your kind call him Kupilas, of course. Even we didn't always call him Crooked—that came after the three brothers and their clan tortured him. When Crooked was born he was named Brightshine—a son made by the dawn and the moonlight—you can guess why he was thought a beautiful child. No wonder he hated his uncles so much for what they did to him, let alone the tricks and cruelties and even murder they performed on the rest of his family."

There was a brief pause as lightning whitewashed the sky for a moment, but before Briony could ask any more questions, Lisiya began again as though she had.

"We are not on Crooked's roads here—a mortal cannot pass through them safely—but we are traveling in some of the lands that those roads traverse—do you see? Such roads belong to his great-grandmother Emptiness, of course, but she gave him safe conduct to travel them, and he made much of that freedom."

Before Briony could ask Lisiya to start over because she hadn't understood a word, the demigoddess abruptly stopped.

"So here we are," Lisiya said. "Now you can tell me what you need."

They stood before a small, rough house made of unfinished logs, its roof thatched with leafy branches. A crash of thunder shook the air and for a moment turned the house as flat and pale as one of Makewell's Men's painted backgrounds. Shoots of green grass grew between the dead leaves on the ground, but the house itself looked old and long deserted.

"Don't just stand there gawking, child. Follow me." Lisiya bent and clambered through the low door.

The rain was coming down now like arrows, but the hut was dry and surprisingly warm inside. Briony settled onto a fur rug, one of many that covered the dirt floor. Still, though, for all its homely comforts, it did not quite seem natural: every time Briony stared at anything very long it seemed to grow farther away in a way that made her feel a bit dizzy. She jumped as the thunder crashed again, rattling the walls.

"Not just restless," Lisiya said with a disapproving frown. "More like a sleeping bear smelling spring. Quick, girl, we may not have much time. Tell me what's troubling you."

Briony told her of the dreams, first those of her brother Barrick, especially the most recent and most frightening one. She still could not remember the way his eyes had looked without a chill on her heart.

"I can give you scant help there, I fear," Lisiya said after a long

moment's silent thought. "Your brother is hidden to me—whether because of where he is or the company he keeps, I cannot say. Still, something tells me he is not dead."

"Praise the gods! As long as he is alive, there's hope," Briony said—and
meant it. Her heart already felt lighter. "Thank you."

"You thank a goddess with a sacrifice," Lisiya said. "Honey would be
nice—clover or apple blossom make my favorites—but a pretty stone will
also do. You can leave it on one of my altars . . ." She looked up, suddenly
distracted.

Briony did not want to tell the demigoddess that she had never heard
of an actual altar to Lisiya—not in the waking world, anyway. "I will.
May I ask you another question?"

Lisiya slowly returned her attention to Briony. "I suppose. But swiftly,
child. The weather is growing strange."

Briony quickly told her of the dilemma—how her kindly feelings
toward Eneas seemed likely to destroy her plan to enlist his aid. "He's a
good man! A truly good man. How can I do such a thing to him? Even
for a good cause?"

The demigoddess cocked a draggled eyebrow. "But he is a man, for all
the things you say—a grown man and a prince. He will make his own
choices—to be with you or not, to do what you wish or not. Have you
promised him, 'Help me and I will marry you'—or even, 'Help me and
I will take you to my bed'?"

"Of course not!"

Lisiya laughed sourly. "You needn't act so disturbed, child. You are a
woman in all but name now, I see, and if it were so terrible an act I think
there would be a parcel fewer of mortals in the world."

"No, I didn't mean . . . well, I did, but . . . in any case, I am a
virgin!"

"It's a common enough condition, child. Nothing to brag about."

"But that's . . ." Briony took a breath as a flash of lightning made light
burst in through every crack in the hut walls and ceiling. A few moments
later thunder boomed again, so close it seemed right overhead. "That's
not what I mean! I mean that I would give anything, even my maiden-
hood, if it would save my family. I would even give it falsely! But I don't
want to give it falsely to . . . to a man who is truly kind. Whom in other
circumstances I could truly care for." She shook her head. "Is there any
kind of sense to that at all?"

Lisiya's expression softened. "Yes, child. But I do not think you tell me all the truth."

"I did . . . !"

"I think you already care for him. What is his name?"

"Eneas, the prince of Syan. But . . . but it is really another that I care for. At least I did—I am no longer certain." Briony started to laugh, then suddenly felt like weeping, but the laugh bubbled out anyway. "He and Eneas could not be more different, except that they are both kind men. He has no connections, no expectations—he is a commoner! And I do not even think he still lives. He went away a long time ago and almost everyone who went with him is dead."

"Your problem is like an apple on a high, thin branch," the demigoddess said, "—a branch that is too high to reach from the ground, but too thin to climb out on to reach the apple. But sometimes such an apple can be plucked anyway—with help. You can climb up to stand on the base of the branch, and thus lower the apple enough that someone on the ground can jump up and pluck it . . ."

Briony was about to ask her what in the name of Zoria's mercy she was talking about with all this *apples* and *branches* nonsense when the brightest blaze of lightning yet burst in through the cracks, accompanied almost simultaneously by a peal of thunder so loud that Briony and Lisiya bounced like dried peas in a bowl.

Except it wasn't thunder, Briony realized in terror as she rolled on the floor, trying to regain her balance: what she heard was a voice, too loud and low to understand, raging and bellowing as if a giant stood just above the house, shouting from the depths of the biggest lungs in the world.

"Get out, child!" shouted Lisiya. "Now!" She grabbed at Briony's arm and yanked her toward the door. Now the dream turned completely nightmarish: no matter how Briony struggled and stumbled forward, the door that should only have been a step or two away remained out of her reach. Lisiya had vanished and the hut had become an immense black space cracked like a broken pot, lit only by flashes of jagged light.

"Lisiya, where are you?" Briony screamed.

"Here! Here!"

And then she could feel the old woman's hand again, the calloused skin wrapped tight around hers. She was yanked forward, a tumble into dark space through sudden winds, then out into light and the rain-lashed forest. The sky above was frantic with lightning, burst after burst blanketing the sky and turning the trees into snapping, dancing silhouettes. The thundering voice, still unintelligible and still terrifyingly close, pressed in on Briony from all sides until she thought the very weight of it would crush her skull like an egg.

"What is it?" she shrieked, holding her hands over her ears, an action that helped nothing.

"He is starting to wake!" Lisiya's faint voice was all but blotted out by the deep, wordless roar. "Run!"

"Who is?" Briony screamed, the force of the wind and thundering voice making her sway and almost fall.

"Run!" shouted Lisiya. "It is later than I imagined! I should have told you . . ."

"Told me what?"

"Too late. You must go to the Stone People . . . they must take you to you their ancient drum . . . their stone drum . . . !"

And then the demigoddess was gone. The air was full of whirling leaves and branches stripped from forest trees, all smacking at her like angry hands, scratching her, making her all but blind. In the momentary bright smears of lightning, though, she could see one thing, a huge dark shape looming high overhead, far above the trees, blotting out the sky.

Briony covered her head with her hands and ran and ran and ran, through falling trees and hurtling branches, through air that tightened and boomed with the roar of rumbling laughter.

She woke up without screaming this time, but covered in sweat, her heart beating so fast her chest hurt. She lay clutching Lisiya's talisman to her chest, praying for her brother and herself and all she loved. Briony was so tired that she felt older and frailer than the ancient demigoddess herself, but even after her heartbeat had slowed to its ordinary pace she could not get back to sleep until dawn had almost arrived.

20

Bridge of Thorns

"It is claimed most ettins now live in the underground city of First Deep, far behind the Shadowline in what once was West Vutland, but before the days of the Great Plague they are said to have lived at least as far south as the Eliuin Mountains of Syan, and in the Settish and Perikalese mountains as well."

—from "A Treatise on the Fairy Peoples of Eion and Xand"

IAM THE WORST SPY THE GODS EVER MADE, Matt Tinwright had to admit. *The first time someone asks me what I'm doing here I shall scream like a little girl and swoon.*

He had never been in this part of the royal residence as far as he knew; with its unfamiliar, echoing halls and ancient floor-to-ceiling tapestries full of staring beasts it might as well have been an ogre's cave in the deep forest, carpeted in the bones of unwary travelers. Doom seemed to lurk around every corner.

The gods curse you, Avin Brone, he thought for perhaps the hundredth time. *You are a monster, not a man.*

Tinwright had only risked a venture into this frightening territory because most of the household were out on the castle walls looking at some devilry the fairies had begun across the water. He had wanted to go and see for himself, of course, but knew he could not afford to miss this opportunity. So far Brone had scorned all information Tinwright had brought him, dismissing a list of mirrors to be found around the residence as "blithering nonsense" and threatening to have the poet skinned and made into a hat. While even Tinwright did not believe he was likely to wind up in a milliner's workroom, he had no doubt that the Count of Landsend was losing his patience: every word of the man's last shouting denunciation had shivered him to the very center of his bones.

But now he had been wandering the residence halls for over an hour. He had been forced to tell several curious servants that he was lost, making up false errands to explain his presence, and each time his feeling of dread had increased. What if he was caught? What if they brought him to Hendon Tolly and he had to look into those horrible, piercing eyes and try to lie? He would never manage. Matthias Tinwright had learned long before that although he could write poems about heroes like Caylor, describe in stirring words how they stood before the direst foes with faith in their hearts and a smile on their lips, he was no hero himself.

No, I will tell my captors everything, he promised himself, *long before the first red-hot iron nears my skin. I will tell them Brone made me do it. I will beg for my life.*

Gods help me, how did I find myself in this evil trap?

Tinwright walked beneath an arch and paused, staring up at the faces lining the walls. He was in the royal portrait gallery—but how had he strayed so far? The kings and queens looked down on him, some smiling but most dour and forbidding, as if disturbed to find this callow interloper in their midst. The earliest, brought from Connord with Anglin and painted in the crude style of the early Trigonate era, seemed no more human than the beasts from the tapestries, all staring eyes and stiff, mask-like features . . .

Now, suddenly, he could hear voices in the passage outside the hall. Tinwright looked around in panic. He was caught in the middle of a large room—by the time he reached the far side and the door the speakers would see him. Did he dare hope it was only more servants and try to brazen out yet another encounter? The voices, getting nearer by the moment, sounded loud and authoritative. His heart raced even faster.

There. The wall was open just across from him—a stairwell. He dashed across the stone flags and up onto the bottommost step just as the men he had heard swept into the room, their voices suddenly growing and echoing beneath the tall ceiling. Tinwright crouched, shrinking back against the stairs so that he could not be seen, although it meant he himself could not see who had entered.

" . . . Have found something in one of the old works—Phayallos, I believe—that refers to such things. He called them Greater Tiles because of their size, and believed that they were—how did he put it?—'*Windows and Doorways, although few can cross their thresholds.*' " Tinwright could almost recognize the voice—he was certain he had heard it before, hoarse with age, breathy but sharp-edged.

"Which tells us little we don't already know," said the other. Tinwright shrank even farther back into the shadows of the stairwell and held his breath in fear. The second voice belonged to Hendon Tolly. "Look at all these cow-eyed fools!" Tolly was obviously speaking of the Eddon portraits. "Generations of kings no better than shepherds, content to tend their little pasturage."

"They are your ancestors, too, Lord Tolly," the other man observed respectfully.

To Tinwright's continuing horror, the pair had stopped in the middle of the great chamber, not far from where he crouched. *Why did I hide? Idiot! There's no way to pretend innocence now if they catch me!*

"Yes, but not my ideal," said Tolly. "Great Syan to the south has been weak for a century, beautiful to see but rotten inside. Brenland and the rest are little more than peasant villages with walls around them. With only a little determination we could have ruled all of Eion." Tinwright could hear him spit. "But things will change." A deeper tone entered his voice—something cold and harsh. "You will not fail me, will you, Okros?"

"No, Lord Tolly, fear not! We have solved most of the riddles already, except for the damnable Godstone. I begin to believe it doesn't exist."

"Didn't you say this Godstone was not absolutely necessary?"

"Yes, my lord, as best I can tell, but I still would like to have it before we attempt . . ." The physician cleared his throat. "Please remember, these are very complicated matters, sire—not like readying a siege engine. Not a matter of simple engineering."

"I know that. Do not treat me like a fool." The dangerous chill in Hendon Tolly's voice deepened.

"Never, my lord!" Tinwright had seen Okros Dioketian around the residence, a brisk, unsmiling man who seemed always a little contemptuous of those around him, though he masked it with etiquette. But he did not sound contemptuous now—he sounded terrified of his master. Tinwright could sympathize. "No, my lord, I say it only to remind you that there is much still to do. I am laboring all hours of the day and night to . . ."

"You said we must employ the charm at Midsummer or miss our chance. Is that not right?"

"Yes . . . yes, I did say . . ."

"Then we cannot wait any longer. You must show me how it is all to be done, and soon. If you cannot . . . then I will find another scholar."

Okros did not speak for some time, moments in which he had clearly struggled to master his shaking voice. He had not been entirely successful. "Of course, Lord Tolly. I . . . I think I have pieced together most of the ritual now—yes, almost all! I merely have to deduce what some of the words mean, since Phayallos and the other ancient scholars are not always in agreement. For instance, there is one who says most emphatically that for the charm to be successful, 'the Tile must be clouded with blood.'"

Hendon Tolly laughed. "I do not think we should have any trouble with that—a few less mouths to feed in this gods-blasted anthill of a city would be welcome." His voice grew fainter as he began walking again. Tinwright said a silent prayer of thanks to Zosim that he would not have to crouch in hiding much longer: his back and buttocks were beginning to ache.

"But I cannot help wondering what that means—'clouded'?" Okros sounded like he was following after. "I have checked three translations and they all say something like it. Clouded, fogged, never smeared or anointed. It is a mirror, lord. How do you cloud a mirror with blood?"

"Oh, gods," said Tolly in evident frustration, "slit a few virgin throats I suppose. Isn't that what those ancients always want? Sacrifices? Surely even in this blighted city we can find a few virgins—there are always children, after all."

Even as the horror of what Tolly was saying sank in, it abruptly became clear to Tinwright that the voices were coming back toward him once more—that Hendon Tolly had reversed his direction and was approaching the staircase where Tinwright was hiding. Without even taking the time to stand up, he turned and began to scramble up the staircase on his hands and knees. When he got to the first turn he pulled himself upright and hurried on, trying to match speed to stealth. He could still dimly hear Tolly and the physician arguing below him, but only a word here and there: to his measureless relief, they did not seem to be following him up the stairs.

" . . . Phantoms . . . lands that do not . . ." Okros was faint as wind around the castle's turrets. " . . . we *cannot* chance the . . ."

" . . . Gods themselves . . ." Tolly was laughing again, his voice rising in glee. "The whole world will fall to its knees, *shrieking* . . . *!*"

As he reached the top Tinwright tumbled out of the doorway and onto the landing above, his fear no longer just that of being caught. Something in Hendon Tolly's voice had changed—those last words had sounded like the cry of something not quite human.

For a long time he stood by the stairwell, trying to breathe silently as he listened for the sound of footsteps on the stairs, but he no longer heard even the voices. Still, Okros and the Lord Protector might only have moved to the next room. He would wait a long while to make sure it was safe to go down. Tolly terrified him at the best of times, but to hear the man talk so blithely of blood sacrifice—and that laugh, that terrible laugh . . . ! No, he would stay until nightfall if necessary just to make sure he avoided the master of Southmarch Castle.

At last, feeling the need to stretch his legs but not yet ready to venture downstairs, he took a quiet walk along the upstairs hall, past the open doors of storerooms now being cleared out to provide more accommodations for highborn refugees. At the far end of the hall a window faced south across the garden toward the gate of the inner keep. In fact, from the small mullioned window Tinwright could see all the way to the stretch of bay where the causeway had once joined mainland Southmarch and the island castle. The far shore looked strange somehow. Tinwright stared at it for a long moment before he remembered the fearful conversations he had heard during the morning, courtiers whispering that after a long, quiet time the fairies were up to some devilry.

"*Strange noises,*" some had said, saying they had been wakened in the dark of night. "*Chanting, and singing.*" "*Fog,*" others had claimed, "*a great fog rising up everywhere. Not a natural one, either.*"

Tinwright saw that a vast cloud of mist did indeed lie along the bay front on the mainland side, and at first he thought the dark, slowly moving shapes in the murk were plumes of black smoke, that the fairy folk had lit huge bonfires on the beach, but though mist itself eddied in the wind, the dark tendrils did not. Something . . . something was *growing* out of the mist. But what? And why?

Tinwright shook his head, unable to make sense of it. After several quiet months it had almost become possible to forget that the Qar were still there, malicious and secret as a fever. Was the long, fretful peace over?

Trapped between the fairies and the Tollys, he thought. *Might as well slit my throat now.*

Matt Tinwright decided he had hidden long enough—it was probably as safe to go down now as it would ever be. Avin Brone would want to know what he had heard here. Tinwright also had a responsibility to another, equally frightening authority.

"She is most unsatisfactory, this girl," his mother proclaimed. "I bring her good food from the marketplace and she turns up her nose at it. Does not the book say, 'The poor must be sausaged?'"

Solaced, he almost told her—but what was the point? Trying to tell his mother anything was like talking to a statue of Queen Ealga in the castle gardens. A very loud statue. "Are you not eating?" he asked the patient.

Elan M'Cory was propped up in the bed. Her color had come back but she still had the sagging look of a child's rag doll. Tinwright did his best to ignore a flash of annoyance that the young noblewoman was still in bed. She wasn't well. She had been poisoned—albeit lovingly. She would be well when she was well. "I eat what I can," Elan said quietly. "It's just . . . I don't mean to be ungrateful, but some of the things she brings back . . ." She gave a limp shudder. "The bread has *beetles* in it."

"Not beetles, only ordinary wholesome weevils." Anamesiya Tinwright clicked her tongue in disgust. "Not as though they were alive and walking around, either. Baked in—a bit crunchy, like a nice roasted pine nut."

Elan's shoulders quivered and she brought her hand to her mouth.

"Of course, Mother, I'm sure it's perfectly good, but Lady M'Cory is used to a different sort of fare. Look, here is a Brenlandish two-crab piece—no, a pair of them." He had been writing love notes for a court that, with summer approaching and the Qar still beyond the gates but quiet, had been full of a sort of fatal giddiness. Also, Brone had given him a silver starfish for his information about Okros and Hendon Tolly and had barely shouted at him at all, so Matt Tinwright was feeling unusually well-fixed. "Find Elan some nice bread made with good flour. No weevils. And a piece of fruit."

His mother snorted. "Good luck to you. Fruit? You've been living with the nobs too long, boy. Do you know how many people are sleeping in the streets? How hungry they all are? You'd be lucky to find a single wormy apple left in all Southmarch."

Elan looked beseechingly at him.

"Well, just try to get her something nice to eat, Mother—the best you can come up with for those two coppers. I'll sit with Lady M'Cory until you come back."

"Oh? What about me? What kind of son sends his mother off like a Kracian pilgrim without so much as a crab for herself?"

Tinwright did his best not to roll his eyes. He pulled another coin from his pocket. "Very well. Buy yourself a mug of beer, Mother. It will be good for your blood."

She looked hard at him. "Beer? Are you mad, boy? Zakkas' Ale is good enough for me. I'll put this in the gods' offering bowl to take a little of the stink of your sinful life off my hands." Then, before he could even try to snatch his copper back from its journey to oblivion, she was out the door and gone.

He turned to the bed. Elan's eyes were closed.

"Do you sleep?"

"No. I don't know," she said without opening them. "Sometimes I wonder if I did not truly die when I took the poison, and all this is but a phantom of my expiring thought. If it *is* the true world around me, why can't I care? Why do I only want it all to go away and let me fall again into dreamless darkness?"

He sat on the end of the bed and wished he dared to take her hand. Despite the fact that he had saved her from Hendon Tolly and that she belonged to no one now if not to him, Tinwright felt that in some way Elan had become more distant than ever. "If your expiring thought can manufacture a gargoyle like my mother out of pure imagination, then you are a more skilled poet than I will ever be."

She smiled a little and opened her eyes, but still would not look at him directly. Somewhere in the upper stories he could hear a baby crying. "You are droll, Master Tinwright, but you do your mother wrong. She is a good woman . . . in her way. She has done her best to keep me comfortable, although we do not always see eye to eye on what is best for me." She made an unpleased face. "And she pinches pennies most severely. The dried fish she brings . . . I cannot even tell you what it smells like. It must be caught where the residence privies drain into the lagoons."

Tinwright could not help laughing. "You heard her. She saves money so that she can sneak her extra coins into the offering bowls whenever she gets the chance. For a woman so holy, she seems to feel the gods are as stupid as unruly children and must be reminded constantly of her devotion."

Elan's face changed. "Maybe she is right and we are wrong—certainly the gods do not seem to be paying much attention to their mortal children. I would not dare to call the gods foolish or stupid, Master Tinwright, but I must say I have long wondered if they are too distracted to keep order here."

The idea was interesting. Tinwright felt a sudden urge to consider it— to think of what could take the gods' attention away from their human creations, leaving men to suffer and wonder without guidance. He might even make a poem of it.

Something like "The Wandering Gods," he thought. *No, perhaps "The Sleeping Gods"* . . .

The door banged open so suddenly that Tinwright jumped and Elan let out a cry of surprise. Anamesiya Tinwright pushed the door shut again behind her with an even louder thump, then fell to her knees on the board floor and began to pray loudly to the Trigon. The infant upstairs, startled by the loud noises, began to cry again.

"What is it?" Tinwright knew, with a sinking heart, that it must be something bad: his mother usually spent more time preparing a clean place to kneel than she actually did praying. "Mother, talk to me!"

She looked up; he was shocked to see her familiar, bony features so pale. "I had hoped you would find time to repent of all your wickedness before the end," she said in a hoarse voice. "My poor, straying son!"

"What are you talking about?"

"The end, the end. I have seen it coming! Demons sent to destroy us because we've angered the gods." She bowed her head once more in prayer and would not be interrupted no matter how many questions he asked.

"I'll go and see what this is about," he told Elan.

Tinwright made sure the door was locked behind him, then went out into the street. At first he followed the anxious throngs who seemed headed to the edge of the harbor, the nearest part of the city's outer walls, but after a moment he turned against the flow and struck out toward Market Road Bridge, which crossed the canal between the lagoons. If it was something happening across the water in Southmarch Town, he would be able to see it just as well from the outwall behind The Badger's Boots, a tavern near the end of North Lagoon where Tinwright had spent many a night with Hewney and the others. The alleyway that ran behind the place was not well known, which was why he and his drinking companions had found it a good place to take tavern whores.

As he walked east he listened to fragments of conversation from the people who passed him. Most of them had only heard rumors and were on their way to see what was happening for themselves. Some were terrified, babbling prayers and shouting imprecations, but others seemed only slightly more concerned than if they had been on their way to the Zosimia festivities.

"A sign!" many said. "The earth itself is against us!"

"We'll throw them back," others cried. "They'll learn what Southmarch men are like!" Some of the arguments became fistfights, especially if those who disagreed were drunk. The sun behind the high clouds had scarcely passed noon, but far more people than usual seemed to have started their drinking early.

Was this what it was like when the gods fought their great war? Matt Tinwright wondered. *Did some mortals go to the battlefield only to watch it happen, caring not that the world might end?*

It was another strange, interesting thought—the second in one day that might make a poem. For a moment he almost forgot that whatever he was on his way to look at had reduced his dragon of a mother to raw terror.

But what could it be? All I saw was mist and smoke. And why should that frighten so many?

He slipped past the Boots, which was even louder than normal with the sound of argument and lamentation. For a moment he strongly considered just going inside and drinking up the rest of the money Brone had given him—after all, if the world was ending, might it not be better to sleep through it all? As far as he knew, nothing in the *Book of the Trigon* actually forbade being drunk on the Day of Fate.

Ah, but what if he had to wait a long time for judgment? At a moment of universal catastrophe there would doubtless be huge crowds wanting to be judged, as when the king gave away grain in times of famine. *Not even drunk, then—by that time I'll be sobered up, with a dry mouth and throbbing skull.* Gods—it was bad enough to face Brone's bellowing with a clear head: how much worse to stand before Perin himself, lord of the storms, whose very hammer was a thunderclap!

When he reached the alley behind the tavern Tinwright made his way up the hill to the base of the looming wall, then inched his way along the top of the berm toward the abandoned guardpost. To his surprise, he found that at least a dozen other locals had apparently had the same idea. One of them, a grim-faced young man wearing a leather apron, even leaned down to help Tinwright up the broken steps so that he could join them.

They had an unimpeded view of the north end of mainland South-march. Most of the activity, though, seemed to be happening at the mainland city's nearest end, on the beach beside the remains of the ru-ined causeway. The murk Matt Tinwright had seen earlier had spread and he could see glimmers in its depths, flashes of light that looked less like the flicker of flames than the steady glow of smelted metal. But what he had thought were pillars of weirdly frozen black smoke were not smoke at all.

Monstrous black trees had sprouted from of the murk, their branches like gnarled fingers, as though a dozen giant hands reached out of the mist toward the city walls on the far side of the narrow stretch of bay. The clawlike limbs were bent almost sideways, clearly growing out over the water and toward the castle where Tinwright and the others watched in stunned, frightened silence.

"What are those gods-cursed things?" someone asked at last. A young man who should have been too old to cry began to do it anyway, deep, wracking noises like a consumptive cough.

"No," was all Matt Tinwright could say as he stared across the water. The things, the trees or whatever they were, had doubled or even tripled in size since he'd seen them from the residence window. But nothing in the world grew that fast! "It can't be true." But it was true, of course.

No one spoke after that, except to pray.

❧

The fog was unsettling enough—it came from everywhere and no-where, making the world outside their prison as daunting as the dim, lifeless fields surrounding the great castle of Kernios in the tales Utta had been told as a girl—but it was the noises that made her most uncomfort-able: deep groans and creaks shivered her bones, as though some vast ship a thousand times bigger than any human vessel was sailing past their win-dow, mere inches away but invisible behind the thick, cold mist.

"What *is* that dreadful sound?" Utta began to pace again. "Have they built some kind of—what are those things called . . . siege engines? One of those monstrous towers to bring against castle walls? But why would the fairies be pushing it back and forth along the beach all night? The noise gave me such terrible dreams!" In one, her family, years lost to her, had stood at the rail of a long, gray boat begging her to come aboard and join them, but even in the dream Utta had known from the dullness of their eyes that they were all dead, that they were inviting her to join them in a voyage to the underworld. She had woken up with her heart beating so swiftly that for a moment she had feared she was truly dying.

"Sister, you are sending me mad with your walking back and forth!" Merolanna complained. When they had first been prisoned in this abandoned merchant's house facing Brenn's Bay the older woman had spent days cleaning, as though each fleck of dust she wiped away lifted them a little farther beyond the power of the fairies and their dark mistress. But the opposite was true, of course: the more the duchess cleaned, the harder it was to ignore the fact that when the tidying was done they would still be prisoners. And now that the place was as neat as Merolanna could make it the older woman seemed to have fallen into a torpor of misery. She scarcely got out of the chair most days, although she seemed to have strength enough to complain about Utta pacing or making what Merolanna considered to be an undue amount of noise.

Blessed Zoria give us both strength, Utta prayed. *It is our predicament that makes us pick at each other this way.*

Not only had they so far avoided execution, but they had been housed in a spacious building with three floors and had been given the materials to make quite acceptable meals. Still, there was no doubt they were prisoners: two silent guards, strange and threatening as demons out of a temple carving, stood always outside the door. Another waited on the roof, as Utta had discovered one day to her horror when she had decided to take advantage of a little sun to lay out some clothes to dry. The unnatural creature had jumped down onto the balcony as she emerged with a bundle of damp things clutched to her breast, frightening her so badly she had thought she would fall down dead.

This fairy had been different than the other guards—less like a man and more like some kind of shaved ape or smooth lizard, with claws protruding through the ends of his gloved fingers, a misshapen nose and mouth like a dog's muzzle, and amber eyes that had no pupil. The fairy guard had grunted so angrily and waved his leaf-shaped knife at her so vigorously that Utta had not even bothered to show him the harmless chore she had planned, but instead had simply scuttled back inside.

What do these creatures think we are going to do? she had wondered that day as she staggered back down the stairs to the main living chamber. *Leap from the balcony and fly away? And would he have killed me to stop me doing so?*

She felt uncomfortably certain he would have.

"Why do they hold us?" Utta demanded as the unsettling noises continued. "If that woman in black hates our kind so much—their queen or whatever she is—why doesn't she simply kill us and have done with it?"

Merolanna made the sign of the Three on her bosom. "Don't say such things! Perhaps she intends to ransom us. Ordinarily I would say no, never, but I would give much to be back in my own bed, and to see little Eilis and the others. I am frightened, Sister."

Utta was frightened too, but she didn't think they were being saved for ransom. What could the bloodthirsty Qar possibly want in trade for a dowager duchess and a Zorian nun?

Somebody knocked on the doorway of the main chamber, then the door swung open. It was the strange half fairy, half man who called himself Kayyin.

"What do you want?" Merolanna sounded angry, but Utta knew it was a cover for her fear at this unexpected arrival. "Does your mistress want to be sure we're suffering? Tell her the house could be draftier—but only just."

He smiled, one of the few expressions that made him look almost entirely human. "At least she cares enough to imprison you. She thinks so little of me that I am allowed to run free, like a lizard on the wall."

"What is going on out there, Kayyin?" Utta asked him. "There have been the most terrible noises all morning but we can't see anything except this fog."

Kayyin shrugged. "Do you truly want to see? It is a grim thing. This is a grim time."

"What do you mean? Yes, we want to see!"

"Come," he said with the air of one surrendering to folly. "I will show you."

They followed his silky progress up the stairs and out onto the balcony on the highest floor, which Utta had shunned ever since the reptilian guard had driven her away. The fog still billowed here, but from this height they could see how low it hung, like a down comforter thrown haphazardly onto a bed. The creaking noises seemed even louder here, and for a moment Utta was so taken by the view—the great cloud of mist, and beyond it the bay and the distant towers of Southmarch Castle, her unreachable home—that she forgot about the monstrous guard. Then he swung down from the roof above them and dropped onto the balcony.

Merolanna shrieked in surprise and terror and might have fallen to the ground had Utta not supported her. The guard waved his wide short sword and snarled—it was hard to tell if he spoke a strange language or simply made threatening noises. His teeth were as long and sharp as a wolf's.

Kayyin, though, was unmoved. "Begone, Snout. Tell your mistress I brought these ladies out for some air. If she wants to kill me for that, she may. Otherwise, take your leave."

The thing stared at him with brightly furious eyes, but there was more to its expression than simply that of an angry animal.

What are these creatures, Utta could not help wondering, *these . . . fairies? Did the gods make them? Are they demons or do they have souls as we do?*

The creature snorted what sounded like a warning, then it scrambled back up to the roof as swiftly as it had descended and was gone from sight.

"Oh, that gave me a dreadful turn!" Merolanna detached herself from Utta's grasp, fanning her face with her hands. "What was that horror?"

Kayyin seemed amused. "A disciple of the Virtuous Warriors clan—cousins of mine, in fact. But he knows I am not to be touched, and my shadow seems to cover you two as well." He sounded as if he hadn't been completely certain the creature would obey him, which made Utta wonder how close they'd just come to being sent back . . . or worse.

"How could you call such a monstrosity your cousin?" Merolanna was still fanning determinedly, as though trying to disperse not just air but also the unpleasant memory. "You are nothing like it, Kayyin. You are almost like . . . like one of us."

"But I was shaped to be so, Duchess." Kayyin bowed his head. "My master knew I would be long among your kind, so he gave me a gift of changing to make me . . . it is hard to explain . . . soft like bread dough, so that I could take on the semblance of that which was around me. So I remained for years—a poor copy, but sufficient—until I was awakened again."

"Awakened to do what?" It was the first Utta had ever heard of all this. She had thought Kayyin merely an accident of nature or congress between the tribes of fairy and man.

Kayyin shook his sleek head. Now that Utta's attention had been drawn, she could not help thinking that there was indeed something strange about him, a lack of distinctive characteristics. She could never remember what he looked like when he was not around. "I do not know the answer myself," he said. "My king wished to prevent war between your race and mine if he could, but I do not think I have done much to make that so. It is a puzzle, to be honest." He cocked his head. "Ah, there—do you hear? It is beginning again."

He moved toward the balcony railing and Utta moved with him. She could hear it now, too—the deep, creaking sounds that had plagued them all day. Beneath their balcony, hidden deep in the roiling fogs, a dull light flared and abated but never quite died, as though down on the hidden beach below someone had lit a massive bonfire of blue and yellow flames.

"What is it? What are your people doing?"

"I am not certain they are my people anymore," said Kayyin with an odd, sad smile. "But it is the work of my lady's eremites, of course. They are building the Bridge of Thorns."

"Blessed gods!" murmured Merolanna. Utta turned to see a vast black *something* appear slowly out of the murk, like the tentacle of some awesome sea creature. In the moments before wind swirled the mists back around it again, she could make little sense of it. A plant, she realized at last—some kind of monstrous black vine as big around as a peasant's cot and covered with thorns long as swords. A breeze from the invisible bay tugged at the mist again; this time she could see not just the nearest branch but several more in the foggy depths, all twining upward. The terrible rumbling, screeching noise, so low and loud that it made the very timbers of the balcony they stood on quiver in sympathy, was the sound of the thing growing—growing up from the shore beneath them, stretching out like greedy fingers toward Southmarch Castle on the far side of the water.

"The Bridge of Thorns . . ." she said slowly.

"But what is it?" Merolanna demanded. "It makes me sick just to see it. What is it?"

"They . . . they will use it to attack the castle," Utta told her, fully grasping it all only as she said it. "They will climb the branches like siege ladders, across the bay and over the castle walls. They will clamber over it like ants and kill everyone. Isn't that right?"

"Yes," Kayyin said. He might have been a little sad about it. "I expect she will indeed kill everyone she finds. I have never seen her so angry."

"Oh!" said the duchess. For a moment Utta was afraid the older woman would fall again. "Oh, you monster! How can you . . . just *speak* of it, as though . . . as though . . ." She turned and stumbled back into the room. A moment later Utta heard her make her way slowly down the stairs.

"I should go with her," Utta said, hesitating. "Is there nothing anyone can do to talk your mistress out of this terrible attack?"

"She is not my mistress, which is a small part of the problem—instead, the king is my master, and if there is one thing Yasammez hates it is disloyalty, especially from family."

"Family?"

"Did I never tell you? Lady Yasammez is my mother. The birth was years and years ago and we have been long estranged." His bland face reflected nothing deeper than the interest of someone with a mildly diverting tale to tell, but Utta could not help feeling there was a great deal more behind his words—there *must* be. "I am by no means the only child she ever had, but I am almost certainly the last one living."

"But you said once you thought she would execute you one day. How could a mother do such a thing to her child?"

"My people are not like your people—but even among our people, Lady Yasammez is a strange and singular case. The love she bears is not for her own offspring, but for her sister's. And though she carries the Fireflower, unlike all others in our history, she carries it alone."

Utta could only shake her head in confusion. "I do not understand any of this. What is a Fireflower?"

"The Fireflower. There is only one. It is our great lord Crooked's gift to the Firstborn, because of the love he felt for one living woman—Summu, my mother's mother. And it is the legacy of the children he bore with her." He saw her expression and paused. "Ah, of course, your people know Crooked by a different name—Kupilas, the Healer."

In other circumstances Utta would have dismissed his words as the babble of a madman, and certainly there was a quality in Kayyin's dull, unexcited tones that made him seem deranged, but she had met the terrifying Yasammez; that, and watching the thorny results of the great magics the dark woman had put into effect made it hard to dismiss such things out of hand. "You are saying . . . that your mother Yasammez was fathered by a *god?*"

"That is your word, not mine—but yes. In those distant days the ones you call gods were the powerful masters, but your people and mine served them and were sometimes bedded by them. And at times true friendship and even love ripened between the great ones and their short-lived minions. Loving or not, though, some of the unions resulted in those you call demigods and demigoddesses, in heroes and monsters."

"But Kupilas . . . ?"

"What Crooked truly felt for Summu no one can know, since they both are gone now, but I do not think it would be wrong to call it love. And the children that they made together were like no others—they became the rulers of my race. All whom Crooked fathered had the gift called the Fireflower—a flame of immortality like the gods themselves carried. In Yassamez and her twin Yasudra it burned fiercely indeed, and it still burns in Yasammez, because she has never surrendered it to another. In fact, none of Summu's three firstborn children—my mother, Yasudra my mother's twin, and Ayann their brother—allowed their gifts to be diluted.

"Yasammez has kept her own Fireflower through the lonely centuries, and it has made her the longest-lived and perhaps most powerful of our folk. Yasudra and Ayann did not keep it to themselves as she did, but instead passed it to the children they made together—the kings and queens of my folk. Thus the Fireflower was kept pure in their blood . . ."

"Wait, Kayyin. Are you saying that your first king and queen were brother and sister?"

"Yes, and all the royal line since then have descended from that single pair as well, from Yasudra and Ayann, with each generation maintaining the purity of the Fireflower."

Utta had to think about this strange idea for little while before she could speak again. "So . . . do you have this Fireflower too?"

He laughed, seemingly without anger. "No, no. My mother Yasammez has never diminished her own gift by sharing it, which is why she has lived so long. None of her children have been allowed the Fireflower. Instead she has made it the duty of her endless life to watch over her sister

Yasudra's line. And now her sister's descendant, our queen Saqri, is dying. In revenge, Yasammez planned to go to war to destroy your kind, but my master the king forced a bargain called the Pact of the Glass. Apparently, though, that bargain has now failed, so Yasammez is free again to make war against your hated people."

"Hated? But why? You said revenge. Why is she so anxious to destroy us?"

"Why?" Kayyin's expression was impossible for Utta to read. "Because it is you humans—and most particularly, the humans of Southmarch—who are murdering our queen."

21
The Fifth Lantern

"In former days the name 'drow' was given to all Funderlings by people of the northwest, especially those who lived near them in Settland. However, the name is generally used now only to mean those small, stoneworking peoples who live in the lands of the Qar behind the Shadowline."

—from "A Treatise on the Fairy Peoples of Eion and Xand"

F ERRAS VANSEN KEPT HIS HAND on Jasper's shoulder as they stepped out of the tunnel, even though it forced him to lean at an uncomfortable angle. By the broadness of the echo, they must have reached the cavern called the Great Dancing Chamber, but of course he had no way of knowing for certain. Vansen felt like a child or a cripple— how could the Funderlings see in this blackness? And how could he hope even to fight alongside them, let alone lead them, when he was all but blind in places where both the Funderlings and their enemies could easily find their way? How he longed for the moment he could unshutter his lantern!

"The air feels loose here." Sledge Jasper's mouth was almost touching Vansen's ear. "But the far end's stubbed, so there must be an upthwart hole—but there isn't. It makes no sense to me."

It made no sense to Vansen either, but that was because he wasn't a Funderling—the chief warder might as well have been speaking ancient Ulosian. "Stubbed? Upthwart? What does any of that mean?"

"Quiet!" Jasper whispered.

Vansen had only an instant to wonder at that before Jasper grabbed his arm and yanked him forward and down onto his knees. A moment later metal clattered violently against stone behind them: something fast and sharp had flown past them and struck the wall where they had been standing an instant before.

"What is it?" he hissed as loudly as he dared. "What's . . . ?"

"A trap!" He was jerked again, downward this time as Jasper dropped onto his belly. The Funderling's grip was astonishingly powerful considering he was no bigger than a child. "Keep your head down!"

"I'm going to uncover the lantern," Vansen said. "Get some idea of what's going on . . ."

"Not near your head!" growled Jasper. "In fact, don't do it near any of us." The other Funderlings in the little troop were just now crawling up from behind them. Vansen stretched out his arm and set the lantern down a little way above and to the side of where they lay on the uneven floor. What kind of room was this? They called it the Great Dancing Chamber, but it felt more like a gravel quarry than a ballroom. He flicked up the shield and the lantern's glow spilled out, suddenly giving form and depth to what had been an endless, frightening blackness.

He barely had time to draw his hand back before several arrows whined through the spot where his fingers had been. One struck the lantern a glancing blow; the cylinder of metal and hard sea-glass was knocked spinning onto its side but the light did not go out.

Vansen risked raising his head for a quick look. A handful of moving shapes, some holding short bows, were scrambling for cover at the far end of the chamber like rats surprised in a storeroom, their shadows gigantic and spidery in the light of the single, dim lamp.

Ferras Vansen had not planned on facing arrows—the narrow underground passages had seemed to make them an unlikely weapon—but here he sat in a classic infantryman's nightmare, pinned down by a force he could barely even see with no way to fight back other than a hopeless frontal assault. It was pure luck that he and the Funderlings had not been slaughtered where they stood: they had apparently caught the Qar by surprise. Now all they could do was wait and hope that Cinnabar and the rest of the Funderling Town reserves would come as they had promised. But how to keep them from walking into the same trap?

"Simple enough," said Sledge Jasper after hearing Vansen's whispered concerns. "If there's a vein of drumstone between here and the Brothers' temple we'll have no problems, Longshanks—that's how we talked in the mines and even sometimes farther, but those were the old days. Anyroad, we'll just keep hammering on it until someone hears us. But whatever you want to say likely ought to be short and sweet."

Drumstone. That was a new one. Vansen raised his head again and peered across the chamber to where the enemy crouched behind what looked like a forest of stony towers, most of which stretched no higher than a tall Funderling. One of the Qar saw his movement well enough to snap off a shot: the arrow hissed past him and shattered against stone; a broken piece caromed off and dug into his hand. Vansen grunted in pain and sucked at the blood. "How about two words?" he asked Jasper. " 'Help' and 'trap.' Short enough for you?"

They sent a pair of men back to the seam of drumstone that crossed the road they had followed to the Dancing Chamber. The warning worked. Cinnabar and his troop of two dozen men came swiftly but carefully into the great cavern, carrying slings and other long distance weapons, and despite the inexperience of these new fighters, many of whom did not even have the rudimentary exposure to violence the warders had, they managed to help Vansen and Jasper chase the dozen or so armed Qar back out of the Great Dancing Chamber. The victory cost them: two Funderlings were killed, one of them a warder named Feldspar, so it was a somber group that headed back toward the Metamorphic Brothers' temple.

Vansen and Cinnabar walked behind the men carrying the bodies. Ferras Vansen was doing his best to divide his attention between complicated thoughts about the day's losses and lessons and the need to watch for low ceilings. He had been living with the Funderlings long enough that they sometimes forgot he was twice their height and couldn't see as well as they could, and thus didn't warn him when a low threshold was coming.

"I wish I had known of this drumstone before," he said.

"There are only a few small veins connecting parts of Funderling Town," Cinnabar said. "It was pure luck Jasper had seen that seam. The greatest use of drumstone was over longer distances, but we almost entirely stopped using it over the last hundred years or so as we lost touch with other towns and cities."

"Still, what a wonderful thing, if I understand Jasper correctly—to be able to signal over a distance underground! Have the . . . the Big Folk, as you call us, ever known of this?"

Cinnabar laughed. "I can assure you they did not. You'll forgive me if I say we thought it more likely to be something we needed to protect ourselves against your people than to aid them."

"Fair enough. And I promise I will keep the secret—the gods know I owe you and your folk that much and more. But it seems to me another example that you Funderlings have misplaced your trust when you ask me to lead you. Even were I as veteran a commander as you suppose—which, I assure you, I am not—I still know too little about this underground world in which we fight. The Qar reaching that chamber before us caught me completely by surprise. How did they do it?"

Cinnabar's amiable, weathered face showed surprise even in the thin light of Vansen's lantern. "But Jasper says he told you. The road should have been stubbed there, but he knew by the smell of the air that a second opening had been made, so that means there must be a new tunnel up-thwart the stub-end at the far side of the Great Dancing Chamber . . ."

"There, you see? I still don't understand." He raised his hand. "No, do not explain it to me now, Magister—there is too much to do. But when we return and have our council, I need you and Chert and the others to help me learn. We must find a way to remedy my ignorance before I get us all killed."

The Funderlings and the two Big Folk were grouped around one of the large tables in the refectory of the Metamorphic Brothers' temple, a place that had become the seat of the Funderling War Council, as Vansen had come to think of it—mostly because only the refectory and the chapel were large enough for many to sit down together.

In the previous days Ferras Vansen had sometimes viewed his involvement with these little men and women as almost amusing, as if he had been asked to lead an army of children, but that had ended long ago with the first assault by the Qar. Anyone who still doubted the seriousness of their situation need only descend to the deep, cold room beneath the main altar where the bodies of the two fallen Funderlings, Feldspar and Schist, lay waiting for their burial cairns to be built.

Vansen looked across the table at Jasper, Magister Cinnabar, and Brother Nickel. Nickel's power within the Brotherhood seemed to grow stronger by the day: there had been no confirmation yet that he would be the next abbot, but the other monks seemed to take it as a given. Chaven was also at the table—the only other person Vansen's size—but the physician seemed fretful and preoccupied. Beside him sat Malachite Copper, another important Guildsman, tall and slender for a Funderling, who had brought a contingent of volunteers down from the town to help defend the lower tunnels. Although the cavern-dwellers had no lords as such, Copper was the closest thing Vansen had seen down here to what he would have called a noble. Judging by his clothes, he was certainly the richest of them all. Young Brother Antimony rounded out the group: Vansen had been told that Chert Blue Quartz and his strange adopted son were off on some private errand and could not be present.

"I must beg your pardon," Vansen told the others. "I simply cannot accustom myself to the way you talk—*upwise, thwart, sluiced, scarped, stubbed*—I cannot understand it, not swiftly enough to lead men into battle. I am used to fighting on solid ground that spreads like a blanket before me, but here I find the blanket is wrapped around my head. I think you should give this task of leadership to someone like Cinnabar or Copper."

"I do not like to fill my head with details." Malachite Copper spoke lazily, as though it was almost too much effort to finish what he was saying. "I will have enough to do with leading my own scrapesmen. No, not me."

Cinnabar also shook his head. "As for me, I have not the knowledge of fighting, Captain Vansen, but I will do my best to help you to think as we think."

"But how can I learn all your people know? These drumstones, Stormstone's tunnels—I do not have time to become a scholar, even had I the wit for it!"

"Likely none of us is fit to perform the job entire," Chaven said. "If we want to survive we must work together and try to forge a single martial leader from among our disparate parts—a patchwork soldier, as in the old tale of King Kreas."

"Still," said Copper, "even if the mighty Stone Lord himself were to come out of the deeps to lead us, we would need more men than we have. Cinnabar, my dear, you must send a message to the Guild telling them to send every able-bodied fellow who can be spared to fight—sadly, we cannot pull the workers from the few jobs Hendon Tolly has given us without causing suspicion. That may bring us as many as a thousand. Until then we have less than two hundred all told, four pentecount at the outside, and only a few of those capable fighters. How many Qar wait on the far side of the bay?"

Vansen shook his head. "We never knew when we fought them—that was part of the hardship, that they could make their numbers and positions so confusing. But judging by what I saw of them marching, long ago, I guess they still muster several times our numbers."

"And from what you say, we could not hope to outfight them even if we matched them man for man," Cinnabar said.

"The March Kingdoms could not defeat them with many thousands, including hundreds of veteran fighters, cannon, and armored cavalry. But we were overconfident." He smiled sadly. "We will never be so again."

"Is there any chance the upgrounders—I mean your people, Captain Vansen—might help us? Surely Hendon Tolly does not want the Qar roaming free beneath his castle!"

"No, but first you would have to convince him," Vansen said thoughtfully. "That might be done . . . but then even if he agreed to help you he would never simply give you back Funderling Town afterward. Once he knew of the Stormstone tunnels and everything else belowground, he and his soldiers would be here to stay."

Malachite Copper broke the long, morose silence. "But the fairy creatures must fight us down here," he pointed out. "Surely that should be to our advantage, if we can only improve our numbers."

"Don't forget they have Funderlings of a sort among them," said Cinnabar. "And other creatures of the deeps as well, like ettins, some of which we only know from old stories . . ."

"So it is hopeless. Is that what you are saying?" Nickel stood up. "Then we must all prepare to meet our maker. The Lord of the Hot Wet Stone will save us if he sees fit—if we have pleased him—but if not, then he will do with us as he wishes. All this warlike posturing is for nothing. The Nine Cities of the Funderlings will be emptied but for dust and shadows."

"We do not need that kind of talk," Cinnabar said angrily. "Would you terrify our people into recklessness? At the very least, Nickel, think of our wives and children. Ah, but I forgot—you Metamorphic Brothers do not have time for such trivialities!"

"We do holy work!" Nickel shouted and the argument began in earnest, even Copper joining in, but Ferras Vansen was no longer listening.

"Enough," he said. When they did not heed him, he raised his voice, deeper and stronger than any of theirs. "*Enough!* Shut your mouths, all of you!" Everyone in the room turned to stare at him in surprise. "For the sake of the wives and children you mentioned—for all of our sakes—stop this squabbling. Brother Nickel, I heard you say 'the Nine Cities of the Funderlings'—what does that mean?"

Nickel waved a dismissive hand. "It is only an expression—it means all the Funderlings together, not just those here in Funderling Town."

"So there are other Funderlings? Where? Magister Cinnabar, you said something to me earlier about towns and cities, but I thought you meant ordinary towns, Firstford and Oscastle and the like."

Cinnabar shook his head. "I understand your interest, Captain Vansen, but if you are envisioning thousands of Funderlings sweeping in to save us from all over Eion, I'm afraid I must disappoint you. Some of the so-called cities are long gone, and little remains of most of the others—those that are in reach, that is. Two of them are behind the Shadowline and one is on the southern continent Xand."

"But are there still Funderlings who live outside of Southmarch?"

"Some, of course. Even long after our days of glory there have been Funderlings living in most of the biggest cities, working in stone and forging metal for the Big Folk, but their numbers have grown smaller and smaller. Here too. Just a hundred years back we were nearly twice as many as now." Cinnabar shrugged. "There is still a good-sized settlement in Tessis and another in the quarry mountains of Syan—between them they might have as many Funderlings as here. And I've heard some still live in our old city of Westcliff in Settland, although it is scarcely more than a village now. Perhaps another thousand of us are scattered around the other cities of Eion. At year's end we usually come together for the great festival called the Guild Market, but I do not think we will survive here long enough to be able recruit any help at market." He shrugged. "Have I anticipated your idea incorrectly, Captain?"

"No, you have hit it squarely, Magister." Vansen frowned. "But I would still like to know if these drumstones will speak as far as Syan."

"They used to," said Malachite Copper. "But the stones have long since fallen silent between here and there."

"You said there are as many Funderlings in Syan as here," Vansen said to Cinnabar. "Perhaps they will help us. Doubling our numbers would certainly keep us alive a good deal longer."

Cinnabar nodded slowly. "I suppose we can't afford to overlook even so unlikely a chance. In the old days there was a train of drumstones between here and what the Big Folk call Underbridge, the Funderling settlement in Syan. Unless the ground has shifted badly I see no reason they shouldn't still suffice."

"Forgive me," said Malachite Copper, "but I really must ask a question. What good is it if we could even bring five times the numbers we have now from somewhere else? We still would have too few to defeat the Qar, if everything I've heard today is true. What then is the point? It will take weeks for help to come from Underbridge—until Midsummer at least, even if they choose to send it, which I doubt. But even if they come, what real difference could it make?"

"You're right," Vansen told him. He had been thinking, in his slow, careful way, and he could see no other road forward. "It is true—we cannot defeat the Qar. They are fierce fighters, but they also have a terror and madness on their side like nothing I have ever seen or felt. But I do not intend to beat them."

Brother Nickel snorted in disgust. "Then why do we not simply surrender now? At least then we will be choosing the manner of our deaths."

Copper scowled at him. "Be quiet, you burrowing, slithering priest! I for one would gladly choose to die with a war hammer in my hand, not slapping my head and begging the Earth Elders for forgiveness!"

"Gentlemen . . . brothers," said Cinnabar, spreading his arms. "This is not right . . ."

"Stop. You did not let me finish, Brother Nickel," Vansen said loudly. He wished that convincing the others, as difficult as it would be, was the hardest part of what he envisioned. "I do not intend to defeat the Qar because, as I said, we *cannot* defeat them. We cannot even hope to hold them back for very long. But I know a little of what they want here, and I may know some things even their leader does not yet know—important things." Still, even the mere thought of the Qar's dark lady made him weak with fear—he had seen her in so many of his nightmares, visions left in his head by Gyir's thoughts like shadows cast on the wall of a cave. He was terrified to face her, but what else could he do? He was a soldier, and he had given his loyalty to these folk as completely as he had to the Eddon family and their throne when he first became a royal guard. "Here is my plan," he announced as the others at last fell silent. "I intend to make peace."

"Peace!" barked Copper. "With the Twilight People? With ettins and skinshifters? That is madness."

Vansen's smile was grim. "If so, then madness is the only thing that can save us."

❧

An isolated sliver of moon hung in the sky as they crept out the side door of Chaven's observatory beside the old walls. Chert had not smelled open air for weeks and for a moment the sharpness of it was almost overwhelming. He took a couple of reeling steps, light-headed, before finding his balance. The night seemed . . . so *big!*

Flint did not seem to notice. He looked briefly to either side and then trotted down the steps. At the bottom of the stairwell he turned to follow the road beside the wall, headed directly toward Skimmer's Lagoon as though he could see it. Chert could not suppress a shiver of fear. How did the boy *know* things like this? It made no sense—in fact, it refuted good sense entirely.

Still, sensible or not, if Chert lost the boy he would catch the rough side of Opal's tongue for certain. He hurried after him.

"Where are we going?" he whispered as Flint led them along Sheeps Hill Road at the base of the New Walls, past what seemed like a single endless encampment of refugees huddled around miserable little fires. A few of these looked up to watch the pair go past—Chert could only hope they thought he was a child, too. He grabbed Flint's arm. "Get back in the shadows, boy!"

Citizens of Funderling Town were banned from being aboveground in Southmarch by night, in large part because of Chert himself, so not only did he have a price on his head, the mere fact of him being a Funderling would be enough to get him dragged to a cell in the stronghold. Either way, if the guards got hold of him, he was doomed.

What am I doing? How did I let myself get talked into this? Opal would have my skin if she knew. He had a sudden moment of terror—what if his wife came back to the temple while he was gone? What would he tell her? She would scorch him! *But I suppose if I'm alive at that point for her to scorch, I'll already have my joists in,* he thought glumly. *Might as well not borrow trouble.* "Flint, where are we going?" he asked again.

"Across Market Road Bridge, turn toward the guard tower, then stop at the fifth lantern."

"And how do you know that? Who told you?"

The child looked at him as though Chert had asked him why he kept filling his lungs with air. "Nobody told me, Father. I saw it."

As they approached the bridge Chert did his best to hide his face from everyone who passed. Market Road Bridge was a short, high-arching span that crossed the canal between the outer keep's two lagoons. Where the canal crossed a muddy field to join with the North Lagoon it made a small estuary, usually the home of many birds, but in this time of privations and with so many hungry folk packed into the castle, most of the birds had long since been caught and eaten. The torch on the bridge had gone out; the little patch of water and grass and sand lay silent and almost invisible on either side, even to the Funderling's keen eyes, as though they passed through a void between stars.

On the far side of the bridge they stepped off the road and onto a small, almost invisible path of rough logs along the edge of the water. They proceeded along this dark track until they reached the dim glow of a fish-skin lantern hung from a pillar at the canal's edge. Continuing on and passing four more lights brought them to a largely empty section of Skimmer's Lagoon, but the last light, the fifth lantern, shone on more than just black water and the dockside path: a rickety gangway made of boards and rope stretched out from the pool of lantern light onto the dark lagoon and toward a dark, uneven shape pricked with a few smaller, reddish lights, like a campfire that had burned to embers. Small waves patted at the edge of the walkway near their feet.

"What are we doing here?" Chert whispered. "How do you know this place? I will go no farther without some answers, boy."

Flint looked at him, face pale in the fish-skin glow. Chert was suddenly frightened, not by the boy himself but by what he might say, what changes it might bring. But Flint only shook his head.

"I can't give you answers, Father—I don't know them. I saw this place when I was asleep and I knew I had to come here. I know what I must do. You will have to trust me."

Chert stared at the small face, so familiar and yet so unknowably foreign.

"Very well, I'll trust you. But if I say we leave, we leave. Understood?"

The boy did not reply, but turned and headed down the swaying gangway.

The barge at the end of it was low but wide, its deck a clutter of cabins and outbuildings—it looked more like the floor of a storage room than any seaworthy vessel. Lights flickered in several of the tiny windows, but Flint headed unerringly toward a patch of absolute darkness on the side of the barge; by the time Chert caught up with him the boy had already rapped twice on the cabin door there.

The door opened a crack. "What do you want?" a quiet voice asked.

"To speak with your headman."

"And who is it wants to speak with him?"

"A messenger from Kioy-a-pous."

Chert stared at the boy. Kioy-a-pous? Who or what was that? And what in the name of the Earth Elders was going on?

The door swung open, spilling amber light. A Skimmer girl stood there, waiting for them to enter. Chert had never seen one of her tribe close up. Her solemn face looked just like some of the ancient carvings he'd seen beneath Funderling Town, which made no sense—why would the old Funderlings have carved pictures of Skimmers?

The girl led them down a long, dark passage. Chert could feel the ship continuously moving beneath his feet, a most distressing sensation for someone who had lived all his life on stone. She took them into a low, wide cabin where half a dozen Skimmer men sat around a table whose height reflected the close-hanging roof: all the Skimmers sat on the floor, their knees bent and high. As they turned toward the newcomers the men's large, wide-set eyes and hairless faces made them look like a gathering of frogs in a pond.

"My father, Turley Longfingers," the girl told Flint and Chert, gesturing toward one of the men, "He is the headman of our people here."

"What is this, Daughter?" Turley seemed upset by this sudden intrusion—almost shamefaced, as though he and the others had been caught planning something wicked.

"He says he comes as a messenger from Kioy-a-pous," she said. "Don't ask me more, for I can't tell you. I'll bring some drink." She shrugged, then made a sullen little curtsy to the men and left the cabin.

"Why declare yourself with such a name, young one?" Turley said. "You have the stink of the northern king on you—old Ynnir Graywind. We do not serve him or his dying master. Too many broken promises lie between our peoples. We are the children of Egye-Var, Lord of the Seas, so what do we care for Kioy-a-pous? What do we care for the one called Crooked?"

Flint reacted very strangely to the Skimmer's words: for the first time since he and Opal had found the child in a sack beside the Shadowline he saw a look of fury cross the boy's face. It was a moment's expression only, a flash like the white smear of lightning across a dark sky, but in that instant Chert found himself truly afraid of the child he had brought into his home.

"Those are old ideas, headman," Flint told the Skimmer, his anger gone again, or at least invisible. "Taking the side of one of the Great Ones against another—that is a strategy from when the world was young and mortals had no part but that which the Great Ones allowed them. Things have changed. Egye-Var and the rest were banished for a reason, and you and the other inheritors would not like it if they came back to reclaim what was theirs."

"What do you mean?" the Skimmers' headman asked. "What have you come to tell us?"

"It is not what I have come to tell you that is important, it is what I need to ask," the boy said with invincible calm. "Take me to the keepers of the Scale."

The chief of the Skimmers was so startled he actually leaned back as though this odd child had struck him, his mouth working uselessly for a moment. "What . . . what do you speak of?" he demanded at last, but it sounded like weak bluster.

"I speak of the two sisters, as you already know," Flint said. "Many things may depend on this. Take me to them, headman, and do not waste more time."

Turley Longfingers looked helplessly at the other Skimmer men but they seemed even more taken aback than he was, their eyes bulging with anxious surprise.

"We . . . we cannot do it," their chief said at last. Resistance was gone. His denial was an admission, not a refusal. "No shoal-mooted man may visit the sisters . . ."

"They need to go and my Rafe isn't here," said the headman's daughter. "If you cannot take them, Father, I will."

If Chert thought Turley Longfingers would rage at the girl, hit her or drive her from the room, he was wrong. Instead he sounded almost apologetic. "But, Daughter, this is not a day to approach the sisters . . . not a shriven day, no salt has been sprinkled . . ."

"Nonsense, Father." She shook her head as if he were a child who had made a mess. "Listen! This child speaks of things no outsider knows, let alone any landlegged child. He speaks of *the Scale!* As if we did not already know that a time of change is upon us."

"But, Ena, we do not . . ."

"You may punish me later if you wish." She stood. "But I am taking them to the drying shed."

This finally opened the floodgates: the other Skimmer men all began to talk at once, arguing, hissing, vying for Turley's attention, pointing their long fingers at the chieftain's daughter as though she had walked into the room naked. The noise swelled until Turley flapped his long hands for silence, but it was not his voice that stilled them.

"Take us, then," said Flint. "We have no time to waste. It is less than a turn of the moon until Midsummer."

"Follow me, then." Ignoring the looks of outrage and open befuddlement from the Skimmer men, the girl drew a shawl from a hook on the wall and draped it around her shoulders. "But walk carefully—some of the way is dangerous."

To Chert's surprise, the girl led them no farther than the floating dock attached to the stern of the ramschackle barge. The moon had vanished somewhere behind the castle's outer walls and the night was so dark that but for the dull sparkle of stars when the wind blew the clouds aside, they might have been in one of the deepest tunnels of the Mysteries.

Ena pointed to a rowboat bobbing beside the dock. "Get in."

Chert thought there could be nothing more frightening than getting into a boat, with only air above him and water beneath him. He quickly found out he was wrong.

"Now put this on," Ena told them, handing Chert and Flint a length of cloth each. "Tie it over your eyes."

"Blind ourselves??" Chert was almost choking. "Are you mad?"

"If you do not, I will not take you. The way to the drying shed is not for landleggers, even those who claim to serve Kioy-a-pous."

"Please, Father," Flint said. "All will be well."

Oh, certainly, Chert thought. *Why not? Perhaps when we fall in the boy will charm the sharks, too, like one of the holy oracles.* With great reluctance, he tied the stiff, salty rag over his eyes; a moment later he felt the boat beginning to move. *What truly happened to this child behind the Shadowline—and when he went to the Shining Man?*

The Shining Man. Chert could not help thinking of how the boy had lain at the great figure's feet. Like the rest of his people, Chert had been taught that the Shining Man was the image of their creator, the Lord of the Hot Wet Stone. During the Mysteries it had even been hinted to him and the others crossing into adulthood that the great crystalline shape was somehow alive—that the power of their god lived inside it. So why had the boy struck off on his own to find it? And what had he done with that strange mirror—the one that Chert had later risked execution to deliver to the terrifying Qar woman? And just as important, what in the name of the Earth Elders was the boy up to now? Flint had questioned ancient Brother Sulphur until the old man had flown into a rage, and now he had demanded—and been permitted!—access to some treasure of the secretive Skimmers. Sisters, scales—Chert had no idea what any of it might mean, but he knew for a certainty that he had no more control of events than a man caught at the top of a rockslide: all he could do was hang on and pray . . .

These thoughts and a hundred more flitted through his mind as the oars creaked and the waves splashed gently against the side of the boat. At some point they passed through a long tunnel, with echoes bouncing off the stone. When the echo dropped away again the water, which had been as mild as one would expect on a lagoon inside the castle walls, suddenly began to rock the boat so strongly that Chert began tugging at his blindfold in panic.

"Don't!" said Ena. She sounded breathless, as though she was working hard. "Keep that cloth on you or I'll turn us around."

"What's happening?"

"Never you mind, Funderling. Just sit back."

Chert felt Flint reach over and squeeze his arm, so he reluctantly left the rag across his eyes. What was going on? Were they on the open sea? But how would they have got out through the harbor and past the harbor chain? What about the besieging Qar? It didn't make sense.

At last, after what seemed an hour or more on the water, the last half tossing and pitching in a very queasy way, Chert felt the prow of the boat bump up against something solid. The girl jumped out and helped them both up onto a dock, and from there onto dry land.

"Keep the eye-cloths on," she said. "I'll tell you when to take 'em off."

At last Chert heard a door open and he and Flint were led through, guided by Ena's careful, rough-skinned hands. Immediately his lungs and nostrils filled with harsh, salty smoke.

"You can unbind your eyes now," she said.

When he stopped coughing, Chert did. They were standing in what looked like some kind of upgrounder barn. A great fire roared in a stone pit in the room's center, flames twice as tall as Chert painting everything a dull red-orange. On either side of the fire long poles stretched from one end of the high-ceilinged, rectangular room to the other, supported every few paces with thicker, rough-hewn wooden pillars. On the poles hung hundreds of splayed fish carcasses.

"By the Elders, it really *is* a drying shed," Chert murmured, then found himself coughing again from the smoke. His eyes were already stinging painfully.

"Oh, who's there, who's there?" The voice, though quiet, seemed to speak right in his ear. He jumped and whirled around but saw only Ena and silent Flint—for all he could tell, it might have been the split carcasses of the fish that spoke. *"Dear, dear, we seem to have frightened Papa Sprat."* The invisible voice laughed, a cracked bray. *"Come here to us, darlings. Nothing to fear in the drying shed—unless you're a fish. Isn't that right, Meve?"*

Chert hesitated, but Flint was already walking toward the fire. As he made his way around the firepit Chert saw two small shapes sitting on a bench near the flames. One of them, an old Skimmer woman, rose as Flint approached. She was tiny, barely taller than Chert himself, and although all of the fisher-people had a little of the frog in their looks, this ancient creature was like one of the entombed toads or mudskippers the Funderlings sometimes discovered in the foundations of buildings they were excavating—a withered, seemingly lifeless creatures that nevertheless would recover if dipped in water, though it had been sleeping in the clay for centuries.

"Good evening," said the ancient Skimmer woman. "Gulda I am, and here is my sweet sister Meve." Gulda gestured to the other figure, even smaller than she, huddled in a coarse robe with the hood pulled close, as if even beside the fire Meve felt uncomfortably cold. "She talks not as much as she once did, but what she says is wise—is that not right, my love?"

"Wise," croaked the other woman without looking up.

"And greetings to you, Turley's daughter," Gulda said to Ena. "You can wait with your sea-pony. The great ones have naught to say to you tonight, although doubtless they will another time."

"Another time," Meve echoed in a dry rasp that suggested she had been in the smoky shed for a very long time indeed.

Ena looked disappointed but did not argue. She made a curtsy to the sisters and walked to the door.

"You are the keepers of the Scale," suggested Flint when the girl was gone.

"And why wouldn't we be?" Gulda's leathery, pop-eyed face seemed almost merry, although there was an edge of irritation in her voice. "Given the lore by our mother, we were, and she by hers, stretching back since keels first ran on ground here—who else would keep it and polish it and know its secrets?"

"And the god speaks to you through the Scale," said Flint, as though the sentence made absolute sense. It certainly must have to Gulda, because she nodded sharply.

"When he sees fit."

"When he sees," added Meve, nodding gently, as if too violent a motion—even coughing, which Chert himself was doing again—might shake something loose. How old were these creatures?

"The god has been speaking much to you of late," said Flint.

For the first time, Gulda hesitated. "Yes . . . and no . . ."

"No," said Meve. "Yes."

"He speaks to us." Gulda shook her head. "But sometimes it seems as though the dreams have changed him. He seemed not so angry before as now. As though something had come into his sleep and pained him."

"Sleep and pain," added Meve.

"Perhaps he remembers how he left the world," said Flint, each word taking him further away from Chert, who was feeling as though there was nothing solid in the earth to stand on anymore. "Perhaps he finally remembers."

"Aye, could be," said Gulda. "But still he seems changed."

"And what does the Lord of the Green Depths say to you?"

Gulda peered at him for a while before answering. "That the day of the gods' return is coming. That our lord wants us to do everything we can to help him come back to us."

Flint nodded. "To help Egye-Var come back. But you said he seems different when he speaks to you these days."

Gulda nodded. "Closer, like. And never so angry before, even in our grandmothers' days. Hot, not cold. Impatient and hot and grasping, like a thirsting man."

"Thirst," Meve said, and then began to struggle slowly to her feet. She swayed as she rose, a tiny, brittle bundle like a dried bird's nest, all mud and sticks. Gulda went to help her but Meve swatted her sister away with a tiny, trembling hand. When she turned back to them, Chert saw her eyes were white with pearl-eye—she was almost certainly blind.

"Dreams . . . changed . . ." she rasped, thrusting her hand at Chert as though he had stolen something from her. "Hot. Hot sleep! Cold time. Angry!"

He shrank back but Flint stepped forward and took her bony fingers in his own. The tiny old woman was shaking all over as though with a fever.

Her sister hurried to comfort her. "Oh, there, my love, my sweet, there," she said, kissing the sparse white hairs on her sister's head. "Don't fear. Gulda's with you. I'm here."

"Fear," said Meve in a rasping whisper. "Here."

"What's here, my love? What's here?"

The little old woman spoke so softly Chert could barely hear her. "Angry . . ."

Ena, Longfingers' daughter, brought them back to the fifth lantern on the estuary path and let them take off their blindfolds again. Chert was glad to have his sight back, but he had been even happier just to escape the salty, smoky air of the drying shed.

"So, did you find what you were looking for, little man?" the girl asked Flint.

"I don't know," he said. "I am touching unfamiliar things in the dark, trying to make out their shapes."

"A strange one, aren't you, boy?" The Skimmer girl turned to Chert. "I remember now who you are—Chert of the Blue Quartz."

Chert, who had thought the long night of strange surprises was over, stared at her. "How do you know me?"

"Never mind that. Better not saying. But you're a friend of the Ulosian, Chaven, aren't you?"

Even if she had helped them in some way—and since Chert had no idea what Flint had been doing, he couldn't even say that for certain—he was not such a fool as to tell a near stranger anything about the fugitive physician. "I used to visit him. That is common knowledge. Why?"

"I have a message for him. We helped him and he promised us payment. Days of work we gave him and because he has not paid us our due it makes my father look foolish in front of the others. If you see him, tell him that—the Skimmers want their payment."

As Chert and Flint made their way through Chaven's house toward the hidden door and the tunnel to Funderling Town, they heard noises—footsteps and what sounded like distant, ghostly voices. Chert's superstitious fright quickly gave way to a more straightforward terror when he heard the voices more clearly and realized that some of Hendon Tolly's guardsmen were in the house looking for them.

They must have been watching the place, he thought, fighting down panic. *But we stayed in the shadows—perhaps they are not sure we came in. Earth Elders, let it be so!*

Chert knew the place better than did any guards, at least the lower levels, and they managed to get out the door at the bottom of the house before any pursuers caught them. Once outside, Chert jammed the door closed with shards of rock and hoped that if the guards found the door behind the tapestry on the other side, they would think it had been sealed off long ago. But it meant that Chaven's observatory was being watched carefully. The place was no longer safe.

We are running out of ways to escape Funderling Town, he thought as he followed the boy back toward the temple. *Or even just to see the sky. Soon we will be like those rabbits trapped in their run by hunters. Stormstone's worst fears for our people are coming true.*

22
The Patchwork Man

"The Dreamless are another tribe of Qar, claimed by some to be related to the Cold Fairies. All that is known of them for certain is that in the days of the Theomachy or just after they left the other Qar and went to make a home for themselves called the City of Sleep."

—from "A Treatise on the Fairy Peoples of Eion and Xand"

THE MANY RIVULETS that Barrick had seen or even crossed as he made his way down from the heights around the Cursed Hill now began to join together, streaks of dull silver snaking through the gray-green moorlands in the perpetual twilight, one emptying into the next and then the next until they had swollen into a single cataract too wide to cross, whose thunder was always in his ears.

"This must be the river Fade." Barrick paused to rest a moment on a high, rocky part of the bank as the water foamed past beneath him. A cloud of mist wet his clothes but for once he did not mind being damp. "Does it stay like this all the way into Sleep?"

"Not so much," said Skurn as he fluttered from side to side, unwilling to land on the wet rocks. "At bottom of hills it goes a bit more calm, like, and a good bit wider—you'll see it. But it follows all the way to that bad place, yes. Are you different minded now?" he asked hopefully.

Barrick shook his head. "No, bird. I must go there." The whole venture was foolish, of course, and almost certainly doomed to fail, but a curious, unfamiliar sort of bubbling in his blood was leading him on. He felt inexplicably certain he would find solutions to his problems when he needed them.

Is this what it feels like to be well, he wondered, *worrying about no one save myself, and not much about me?*

Part of it was having a healthy body: his arm, which for most of his life had felt like it was not part of him except for the pain it caused, no longer bothered him. More than that, it felt as strong as his other arm, although he could tell by some small experiments that it wasn't. The muscles were shrunken from long disuse and he could not squeeze a stick as hard as he could with his healthy hand; still, the transformation was remarkable.

"I am changed," he said to the twilight sky. "I am saved."

"Pardon?" Skurn, who had been exploring ahead, flapped down to land on Barrick's shoulder. His odor was worse than usual, if such a thing were possible.

"Nothing. What have you been eating?"

"Fish. Found it on the rocks down there. Leaped out, it did, missed the water coming down. Been softening in the air for days. Very beaksome indeed."

"Get away from me. You stink."

"Be no posy thyself," said the bird in a hurt tone as he flapped away.

The moorlands were covered with green but desolate meadows, empty lands that showed every sign of once being inhabited, although by whom Barrick could not have guessed: stone ruins overgrown by grass and brambles dotted the lonely fields, cottages of almost every size, from stony lean-tos built into the sides of the hills, some of which looked big enough to house fabled Brambinag and all his family, to delicate miniature villages whose tallest buildings barely reached Barrick's waist, constructed of bark and grass and river-smoothed stones. Had he not already met the Tine Fay he would have thought these structures were like his sister's doll house, built only to amuse children. But why would the little people leave a civilized existence to move into dangerous Silky Wood and live like savages such a short distance away? What had driven them out of this green place, along with all the others who had lived here, leaving behind only these quiet, sad remains?

*   *   *

"How far?" he asked Skurn yet again. It was his third day in the meadow and his new sense of confidence was beginning to fade into the unrelenting sameness of following the river down from the moors and into these empty meadows. The wind blew almost continuously here, making Barrick feel as if he was trudging uphill even on the most level ground, and his tattered clothes did little to keep him warm.

"To the Night Man city? The bad place?" Skurn shook his shiny head in weary disapproval. "Fearsome far, still. Days and days walking."

Barrick frowned. What had the blind king said in the dream the Sleepers had given him? *"Come quickly, child. We are rushing toward darkness."* Time was growing short, that was clear . . . but what was the darkness the fairy-king feared?

Not everything about the river meadows was bleak. Unlike the tangling forest, these lands were at least open to the gray sky of the shadowlands, so that for the first time in a while Barrick could watch it through the course of the day. It remained in perpetual twilight, but it was not as unchanging as he had thought: the clouds moved as the wind rose and fell, and the sky itself darkened and lightened from a pearly, pale fog-color to the harsh, bruised hues of thunderstorms. Flights of birds winged overhead, too far away to see clearly, but apparently as natural as those he remembered from more wholesome lands. And the river, although slower here than in the heights behind him, was still lively enough that for nearly the first time since crossing the Shadowline Barrick could actually see himself moving forward, making progress.

Sometimes it was almost like being back in the lands of sunlight. Despite the lack of full darkness or bright light, both banks of the Fade were full of life. In low spots the river spread out into the meadows, creating marshes full of pale nodding reeds like thin bones; in other places drooping willows dangled branches in the water like women washing their hair. Swollen black frogs full of high-pitched, questioning noises fell silent as he went by, then resumed their piping when he had passed. Occasionally something larger rattled invisibly in the reeds, and once he saw a huge stag look up from where it had been drinking at the river's edge, dark but with a magnificent rack of silvery antlers, its silence and calm gaze making it hard for Barrick to believe it was only an animal, so impressive that despite his almost constant hunger it didn't occur to him until the beast was long gone that he could have tried to kill it.

There was also life in the river itself, from little shoals of glittering fishes that filled the backwaters to larger things he could not quite see, visible only as spiny backs breaking the surface or as long shadows slipping through the water.

Still, all of this life did him little good as far as filling his stomach. He discovered after a cold, wet hour or two wading in the river that the shiny fish were too swift to catch, and the closest he came to any of the birds haunting the marsh was uncovering an occasional nest of small, oddly colored eggs. Those and the edible roots and reeds Skurn suggested were Barrick's only fare. Although he now had fire, being able to cook food meant little when he had no food to cook. And after what must have been a week or so following the river through the apparently unending grasslands, even Barrick's healed arm began to seem unremarkable. It was hard to rejoice over being able to move an arm freely when his stomach always ached from hunger, and though the fingers that had once been crimped like a bird's claw now miraculously moved, they were still red and raw from the endless cold wind.

When the trees growing beside the river began to spread out into the surrounding land, first in small copses, then into larger stands of birch and beech interspersed with clumps of evergreens and other trees he did not recognize, Barrick at first found it a relief. It seemed a little warmer under the canopy of leaves, and it certainly held back the worst of the wind. But it also made it harder for him to make his way forward while staying next to the river, and it brought back uncomfortable memories of the silkins as well. Did the pale, hideously wet-eyed creatures live in this new forest as well? Or might something even worse make its home here—snakes or wolves or creatures no mortal had ever survived to give a name to?

Skurn was even less help than usual. As the woods began to grow thicker he was often distracted by the prospect of new and interesting meals, and although some of these benefited Barrick as well, especially the greater abundance of bird's nests, others—such as some spotted gray slugs the raven declared "sweetish and softly slurpsome"—were of no use to him at all. He was hungry enough to try one bite of the quivering thing, but nothing on earth could have induced him to take a second.

So it was that after days of walking through the empty lands toward Sleep, it was a wet, weary, unhappy, and very hungry Barrick Eddon who met the patchwork man.

*   *   *

Rain was pattering heavily on the leaves above his head, loud enough to be heard even over the rushing of the river. Barrick had struggled with damp kindling for a long time before finally getting it to light, and had just got the fire burning well enough to continue on its own when he heard a sound and saw an upright shape moving through the reeds near the river's edge some distance away. The intruder was not making much attempt to conceal itself—in fact, it was making a rather considerable amount of noise—but the hairs lifted on the back of Barrick's neck and he rose to a crouch, pulling the broken spear from his belt.

He stayed in this position, silent and alert, as the thing stumbled nearer. It seemed oblivious to Barrick's presence—unless, he reminded himself, it was trying to trick him. He held his breath and did not move as it emerged from the reeds and turned its grotesque head toward him. For a moment it seemed his worst fears had been made flesh—the thing was some sort of monster, a shambling heap of strange colors and waving fronds.

Barrick had already scrambled onto his feet, uncertain whether to attack it or run away, when he realized that what he had supposed was its head was only the hood of a cloak pulled low against the rain. The fronds were its tattered clothes, the colors surprisingly gaudy and bright, so that the strange figure seemed more like something out of a religious procession than any forest wild man.

Skurn dropped down onto his shoulder, startling Barrick badly. "Not right," the bird said in a quiet, anxious rasp. "Seen naught like that before. Don't go near. Us doesn't like it."

The thing had spotted their fire and hurried toward them, arms waving, shouting meaningless words in a scratchy voice: *"Gawai hu-ao! Gawai!"*

Barrick sprang back a step, brandishing his spearhead. "Stop!" he shouted. "Skurn, tell it some fairy-talk! Tell it to stay back!"

The tatterdemalion figure stopped and pushed back its hood, revealing a pale, mud-streaked face that Barrick could not help thinking looked rather ordinary, not to mention as human as his own. "What . . . what did you say?" the newcomer asked. "Is that sunland speech?"

It was a moment before Barrick remembered that was what the shadowland folk called the other side of the Shadowline. "Yes," he said, but kept his weapon leveled toward the newcomer. "Yes—that's where I'm from. You speak my tongue?"

"I do! I remember it!" The stranger took a few more staggering steps toward him. "Oh, by the Black Hearth, and you have a fire—all blessings on you, sir!"

Barrick waved him back with the spearhead. "Stop there. What do you want? And who are you?" He examined the odd figure. "You don't look like a fairy. You look like a man."

This startled the stranger, who wrinkled his face into a comical squint as he considered. He certainly had none of the exaggerated boniness of the Qar. His face was straw-thin and dirty, with grime in every wrinkle, and his hair was a wet tangle festooned with twigs and leaves. Still, though he had more than the usual number of missing teeth, he didn't look much older than the prince himself.

"Man? A man?" The fellow nodded slowly, his multicolored rags swaying. "That's a word. Yes, that's a word."

"Where are you from?" Barrick looked around in case the grimy creature might have confederates standing by to jump out and rob him, but there was no sign of anyone else nearby.

"From . . . yes, from the sunlands," said the stranger at last—slowly drawing it out, as if he had come up with the answer to a nearly impossible puzzle. "But I don't remember it well," he added sadly. "It was so long ago."

"What is your name?"

The patchwork man showed a sickly smile. "Master calls me 'Pick.' "

Barrick stepped back and let him approach the fire. Pick scuttled past him and squatted, holding his hands up to the low flames, his entire body wracked with shivers.

"What do you want?" Barrick asked at last. "Are you lost? Or do you mean to try and rob me?"

The one named Pick cowered as though he'd been slapped. "No! Please, do not hurt me, I beg you. I have been looking so long for someone who can help me. It is my master, my poor master!"

Every nerve and muscle urged Barrick to walk away from this ragged madman—Skurn had already flapped into the air, as though the man's folly might be infectious. "What are you talking about?"

"One of the blemmies fell out of the boat. I tried to help, but I fell too. I nearly drowned! I have been trying to find help for hours. But my poor, sick master . . ."

"Blemmies?"

"Just come." Although he was still dripping wet, the patchwork man now leaped up from the fire and began trotting back toward the river, turning every few steps like an eager dog to see if Barrick was following. "Come and you will see!"

Skurn hovered over Barrick's head making dire predictions as he made his way down to the wide bank of swaying reeds and the path Pick had already trampled through the weeds and mud. "Enough, bird," Barrick said at last. "Do something useful. Fly ahead and see if the fellow's waiting for me with a club or something."

The raven appeared a few moments later. "He's standing looking out at the water, waiting, like. There's a boat out there, but us don't like it—there be somewhat fierce wrong with it."

When Barrick reached Pick's side he saw that the smaller man was, as Skurn had said, standing on a patch of trampled weeds staring out at a place where the river widened into a calm backwater. At the center of it, a long stone's throw away from the bank, a black boat was being rowed in slow circles by a strange, hunched figure.

It took Barrick a moment to make sense of size and distance. "The one rowing is a big, big man. Is that your master?"

Pick looked at him as though Barrick had said something utterly mad. "That's the other blemmy. He's only got one oar."

"Still, he could pole his way back to shore," Barrick suggested, wondering what kind of half-wit rowers Pick's master had hired. "Tell him that."

"He's . . ." The patchwork man wiggled his hand beside his head. "Can't hear," he said at last.

"Oh, for the love of . . ." Barrick looked out at the hunched figure and the long, circling black boat. "Then just swim out and show him."

Pick was pulling strands of river-weed out of his hair. "Can't swim. Almost died when I fell in, but I found a place where the bottom was shallow, praise the Betweens."

Barrick looked at him, then turned back to the river. "Anything in that water I should know about? Anything with big teeth, for instance?"

"I got out," Pick said. "But I thrashed around a long while first."

Barrick cursed silently under his breath and waded in. Halfway out the muddy bottom fell away beneath his feet and he had to begin swimming. As he neared the slow-moving boat he expected the rower would turn toward him, but instead the man only stayed in his odd, bent-over position like someone who had gone dizzy, but meanwhile his wide back flexed and the thick arm plied the single oar in its lock, over and over.

The rower finally noticed him when Barrick's fingers closed on the wooden gunwale of the boat and he began to pull himself on board. He had only a moment to note that both the boat and the rower were even larger than he had guessed from the shore, and that a long, pale figure lay underneath a small tent on the deck, then the massive rower turned to look at him, still without raising his head.

That was because he had no head, Barrick saw—only two wide, wet eyes on his chest. With a shriek, Barrick jumped back into the water, almost hitting his head on another oar which was floating there. He dipped under the surface and then came up again. In his sudden fright he swallowed more than a little of the green water.

"Gods in heaven, what kind of demon is that?" he spluttered.

"No demon!" Pick called from the reedy bank. "Just a blemmy! It will not harm you!"

If he had been on dry land it would have taken Barrick a much longer time to work up the courage to approach the boat again, but he could not tread water forever. The creature turned to him as he crawled onto the boat once more, but otherwise did not react. Its broad arms continued plying the single oar, steady as the paddles of a millwheel, and the boat continued to circle the backwater in wide, lazy loops.

When they passed close enough to the other oar, Barrick scooped it out of the water and offered it to the blemmy, trying not to look too hard at the dull, unblinking eyes in its chest or the empty place between its shoulders where a neck and head should be. The creature did not seem to see it, but when Barrick slid the oar back into the lock the blemmy clutched it without hesitation and began plying both oars together. The boat headed out toward the downstream current.

"How do I make it head for land?" he shouted. "Does the cursed thing have ears?"

"Put your hand on it and say, *'s'yar'!*" Pick shouted back. "Loud, so it can feel you!"

Barrick put his hand on the blemmy's shoulder, which was overlarge but otherwise natural to the touch, and said the word. The monster shipped one oar until the little boat had swung around to face the bank, then began rowing with both oars again. Within moments the boat's thin black keel ran up onto the muddy reed forest and Barrick leaped out.

When the boat would go no farther the blemmy merely stopped rowing, its eyes staring from its chest at Barrick and Pick with no more curiosity than a cow in a field.

The patchwork man scrambled up onto the boat and folded back the tent, then kneeled beside the unmoving figure. His excitement gave way within moments to quiet weeping. "He is worse! He will never live to reach Sleep!"

Barrick tried not to look startled. "Your master is . . . from the city of Sleep?"

"Qu'arus is a great man," Pick said as if Barrick had suggested otherwise. "All of the Dreamless will mourn him."

"Kyow-roos." Barrick tried it on his tongue. "And he is one of them? One of the Dreamless?"

Pick wiped his eyes but it was useless: the tears kept flowing. "Yes—he saved me! I would be dead were it not for his kindness. And he almost never beat me . . ." He collapsed onto the silent figure's chest, his body heaving, as Barrick climbed back into the boat, stepping gingerly around the silent blemmy to get a look at Pick's master.

Although he had been half expecting it, it was still a shock to see the silky gray skin and gaunt features so similar to the demigod Jikuyin's murderous pet wizard, Ueni'ssoh. Pick's master was in the grip of some delusional fever but too weak to move much. His staring eyes, which rolled from side to side, fixing on nothing, had the same weird hue as Ueni'ssoh's—bluish-green as Xandian jade, with no trace of white. Faced with this monstrous reminder of Greatdeeps, it was all Barrick could do not to plunge his blade into the creature's heart, but the tattered servant clearly felt differently: when Pick looked up at Barrick his eyes were red and his face wet with tears.

"The other servants ran away when Master was struck down. I could not tend to him and control the blemmies. Come with me. Help me! Together we can get him back to Sleep."

"Us don't want that!" squawked Skurn from the high stern of the boat, flapping his wings in agitation.

"Quiet, bird." Barrick looked from scrawny servant to dying master. There had been a moment when he was fighting against the silkins and everything seemed clear: he was meant to do this. Like Hiliometes or Caylor he would find solutions to every difficulty. Here was one such solution—a boat to take him into Sleep and an adviser who would help him to pass unnoticed in that alien place. Perhaps the Sleepers had over-estimated the dangers—perhaps these days there were many mortals like this Pick living among the Dreamless.

Still, the idea frightened him. It seemed too simple to be safe, like a scrubbed and shiny carrot sitting in the middle of a loop of string near a rabbit den—but perhaps that was what it felt like to be touched by destiny. He took one last look at the blemmy, shuddered a little, then nodded.

"Very well," he said. "I'll come with you. For a little while anyway."

The proper number of oars now clutched in its massive fists, the headless blemmy propelled them down the river. The moderate current did much of the job, but the strange creature proved to see better than Barrick would have guessed, guiding the long boat around obstacles with a nimbleness quite different from its helpless circling in the backwater. While Pick tended to the gray man, who had fallen into a more peaceful sleep, Skurn sulked on the tall stern of the boat or flapped along behind.

"You said your master was struck down," Barrick asked the patchwork man. "What happened?"

"We were attacked by bandits in the Beggar lands." He dabbed at his master's gray skin with a wet rag. "Rope Men, they're called. Looked ordinary enough at first, but they were starveling thin—like eels with legs—and never closed their mouths. Yellow teeth long as house nails." The man in the colorful, ragged motley shivered. "One of the master's guards was killed first, then another of them Rope Men sh–shot Master with an arrow. One of the other servants and I . . . w–we pulled it out . . . but then the arrows killed the other guard and the rest of the servants went overboard to get away from them, but they never came up again. It was terrible! The blemmies were rowing fast, though, and the Rope Men were on the bank, so we got away, but the other servant had been shot in the back with an arrow painted like a snake. He died. Master . . . M–Master got worse and worse . . ." Pick had to break off. Embarrassed by the man's weepiness, Barrick turned away and watched the reedy shoreline sliding past until Pick could resume. "That was three sleeps ago by the master's hour-box. Then we hit a rock and the other blemmy fell out into the water and drowned. You saw the rest."

Barrick frowned a little. "How could one of them drown? They've got no mouths."

"They do, down low on their bellies. They even make noises when they're hurt or frightened—a sort of scratchy whistling . . ."

"Enough." Barrick didn't want to think about it—it was too unnatural. "And what will happen when we get to Sleep? Your master's dying—we both know that. What will happen to you . . . and to me, for that matter?"

"We will . . . be safe, I'm certain." The man called Pick said this as though he had never actually thought of it before this moment. "Master was always good to me. And there are the *wimmuai*—he has always taken care of them as well. He lets them die of old age!"

"Wimmy-aye? What are those? Some kind of animal?"

Pick ducked his head. "They are . . . they are men like you and I. Bred and raised in Sleep, offspring of folk captured over the years at the Shadowline. Master usually has a dozen of them at one time."

Slaves, in other words. Human slaves. But that was no real surprise—Barrick had never for an instant supposed that mortals would enjoy the same privileges in Sleep as the Dreamless themselves.

Qu'arus spoke in his sleep, a murmured gabble that had the sound of words in it but was no more intelligible to Barrick than the sighing of the wind.

"However did you come to serve such a creature?" Barrick asked.

Pick looked up, his face tight with suffering. "I was . . . I was lost. He found me. He showed me kindness and took me into his service."

"Kindness? This . . . thing? I cannot believe that."

The other gaped. "But he was . . . he is . . . !"

Barrick shrugged. "If you say it is so." His memories of the other Dreamless, Ueni'ssoh, were of a heartless monster. Could this creature really be so different, or might the man named Pick simply be addled by his experiences behind the Shadowline?

"Hungry," Skurn said suddenly. The raven launched himself from the stern of the boat, then flapped heavily away over the rushes lining the river and toward the forest.

What ails that bird? Barrick wondered. *He has not said a word before that since I can't remember when. On most days I cannot have a moment's peace from his yammering.*

It became clear as Barrick's time on the river stretched into what must have been days that Skurn was not just being quiet but actively avoiding company: he spent much of his time in the air, but even when he returned from his solitary flights he tended to perch atop the stern, a curving piece of black-stained wood taller than Barrick, and silently watch the river and bank sliding past.

Perhaps it's the blemmy that he doesn't like, Barrick thought. *The gods can testify it's ugly enough to frighten anyone.*

The blemmy was indeed ugly, but also very strong, accommodating sudden changes in the river current or avoiding rocks with little more than a flick of an oar. Barrick could only imagine the difference when two of the headless things were rowing together—it must be a very swift craft indeed.

In a rough part of the river, as the blemmy steered the boat between two large rocks visible only by the foam they made on the water's surface, Barrick almost lost Gyir's mirror. As he leaned with the boat's sudden change of direction the leather pouch fell out of his shirt and bounced off the bench. His left hand, his once-crippled hand, shot out and snatched it from the air like a hawk taking a sparrow.

For long moments he stared at it, amazed by what his wounded arm could now do, but also chilled by the idea of what had almost happened. He was a fool to be so careless with the mirror—it was his purpose now. He scoured the boat until he found a spare loop of the surprisingly slender anchor cord and sawed off a piece with his broken spear. He poked a hole in the pouch big enough to accommodate the cord, pushed it through and knotted it, then looped it around his neck before hiding it in his shirt again.

Other boats soon began to appear on the river, mostly small fishing skiffs manned by one or two ragged Dreamless. Barrick saw a few houses and even some small settlements begin to appear along the banks, presumably owned by these same gray-skinned folk. But some craft were a good bit bigger than their own, barges with wide, bruise-purple sails or even long galleys rowed by half a dozen blemmies or more.

"Are we close to Sleep?" he asked Pick after one such craft had surged past them, leaving them rolling in its high wake.

"A day away—no, a little more," the tattered man said distractedly. His master was still alive, but only barely, and Pick almost never left his side.

Later that long, gray afternoon Qu'arus swam up from his slumbers again, but this time once his gleaming eyes opened they stayed that way, watching everything, although his body remained limp.

"Here, Master, have some water," the patchwork man said, squeezing his cloth over Qu'arus' mouth.

"Pikkhh," the gray man rasped, using the sunlander tongue for the first time; his harsh accent made him hard to understand. "I not see you . . . !"

"But I'm here, Master."

"I feel . . . my home . . ."

"Yes. We are close, Master," Pick told him. "We will reach your house soon. Stay strong!"

"The end comes soon now, little Pikkhh," the Dreamless whispered, a fleck of pinkish spittle at each corner of his ashen mouth.

"Don't fear, Master, you will survive to see your home."

"Not the end . . . for *me*," Qu'arus breathed, so quietly that even Barrick bent down to hear better. "I care . . . little that. The end for all things. I feel it . . . feel it comes closer. Like cold wind." He sighed and his eyes fluttered shut, but he spoke one last time before sleep took him again. "Like wind from land of dead."

Qu'arus woke several more times as the day passed, but Pick said his words were almost all nonsense. He did not move much of anything besides his mouth and his eyes: the dying Dreamless seemed to watch them both with a kind of frightened yearning, as though waiting for them to cure or kill him. Barrick could not help thinking of the head of the Trigonate oracle Brennas, which was said to have remained alive and speaking for three years in a box after the Xandians had executed him.

After a while Barrick made his way past the giant blemmy, who was grinding away at the oars with his usual silent determination, and clambered up into the front of the boat to look for Skurn. He hung onto the high prow to keep his balance as he scoured the distance for some sign of the raven. Something dark was indeed on the horizon, but it was far bigger than Skurn.

"What is that—a storm?" he asked Pick. It seemed to hang too close to the earth, a great blob of darkness spread across the river, thick and black at the bottom but growing fainter higher up until it blended into the twilight sky like a puddle of ink leaching into a blotter.

Pick shook his head. "That's Sleep," he said.

"The city? Truly? But it's black—like thunderclouds!"

"Ah! Those are the darklights. The people of Sleep do not like the brightness of this twilight world under the Mantle. The darklights make a night for them to live in."

Barrick stared at the blotch on the horizon, which seemed to wait for him like a spider squatting grimly in its web. "They make *more* darkness? This gods-cursed forever twilight isn't gloomy enough for them?"

"The Dreamless love the dark," Pick told him seriously. "They can never have enough."

The raven finally returned. He landed on the railing of the small boat and stood silently, grooming his mottled pinfeathers in a disinterested way.

"Do you see that up ahead?" Barrick asked him. "Pick says it's Sleep."

"Aye, us seed it." The raven picked at something invisible. "Us flew there."

"Is it a city or just a town? How big?"

"Oh, a city, it be. Fearful big. Fearful dark." Skurn tipped his head sideways to stare at Barrick. "Didn't listen to us, did you? Now you and us both goes there." The raven let out a whistle of disgust, then hopped away down the rail toward the stern. "It be a bad place, that Night Man city," he called back. "Good thing us has got wings. Too bad some others here hasn't."

23
Guild of the Underbridge Kallikans

"Shivering Plain, one of the last great battles of the Theomachy, was also the last time it is known that fairies and mortals fought on the same side, although it is said that far more Qar than men were in the battle, and that far more Qar died there as well."

—from "A Treatise on the Fairy Peoples of Eion and Xand"

"I HAVE CHOSEN what gifts seemed best." Dawet still wore his traveling cloak, as though he had only clambered down from his horse a few moments ago. He and Briony had met in the River Garden this time, whose damp air made it one of Broadhall Palace's less visited spots. "The wars to the north and south mean that many things are in short supply, especially for such unusual folk. I'm afraid it cost more than a few crabs, as the saying goes."

"I hope I gave you enough." Briony had now spent almost all the money Eneas had loaned her.

"It sufficed, but I have none left over to give back."

She sighed. "I cannot thank you enough, Master dan-Faar. So many people owed me allegiance but failed me . . . or were taken from me. Now here I stand with only one friend left." She smiled. "Who would ever have guessed it would be you?"

He smiled back, but it was not the most cheerful expression she had ever seen him wear. "Friend, yes, Princess—but your only one? I doubt that. You have many friends and allies in Southmarch who would speak for you—aye, and do more than speak—if you were there."

She frowned. "They must know by now that I live. Word must have spread, at least a little. I have been living here openly for months."

Dawet nodded. "Yes, Highness, but it is one thing to know your sovereign lives, another to risk your life for her in her absence. How can even your most loyal supporters know whether you are coming back? Distance makes things uncertain. Get yourself safely to Southmarch and I daresay you will find more than a few partisans."

She nodded, then offered him her gloved hand. "I have no money left to pay you, Master dan-Faar," she said sadly. "How long can I keep relying on your friendship when I cannot repay it?"

He kissed the back of her hand, but kept his brown eyes fixed on her as he did so. "You may rely on the friendship no matter what, my lady, but do not assume that I am the worse for the current imbalance. Tell yourself that I am simply gambling—something I am well known for— by performing a task here, a small chore there, none at more than slight disadvantage to myself, but each carrying the possibility of great remuneration later on." He let go of her hand and made a mocking bow. "Yes, I think that would be the best way to look at our admittedly . . . complicated . . . relationship."

His smile had much of the tiger grin she remembered from the old days, and for a moment Briony found herself quite breathless.

"That said," he continued as he straightened up, "you will find your tribute in a room above this tavern near Underbridge—" he handed her a scrap of parchment—"along with two discreet men who will transport it for you." He bowed. "I hope that serves your needs, my princess. To be honest, following your adventures is nearly payment enough. Can you tell me why the Kallikans?"

"It is the gods' will."

"If you truly do not wish to tell me . . ."

"That is not a polite evasion, Master dan-Faar. A goddess spoke to me in a dream—well, a demigoddess . . ." He was smiling at her. "You do not believe me."

"On the contrary, my lady," he said, "I believe that things are happening that are without precedent since the days of the gods. You and your family are clearly in the midst of them. Beyond that, I reserve my secret heart even from you, Lady."

"That is fairly spoken."

"And with that I must leave you." He brushed a few flecks of night-dew off his breeches. His scabbard thumped against the bench. "I do not know when we will meet next, Highness. Other duties call me."

"You are . . . you are leaving the city?" The moment of panic this brought caught her by surprise.

"I am afraid I am leaving Syan entirely, Princess."

"But you . . . you are my only real ally, Dawet. Where are you going?"

"I cannot tell you," he said. "I beg your pardon for my secrecy, but a lady's good name is at stake. Still, be assured this is not the last time we will see each other, Princess. I do not need to believe in anything very strange to feel certain of *that*." He took her hand as she stood, suddenly full of confusion and discomfort. "My thoughts will be with you, Briony Eddon. Never doubt yourself. You have a destiny and it is far from fulfilled. That you may trust when you can trust nothing else."

He raised her hand to his lips and kissed it for the second time; a moment later he had turned and slipped away into the shadows of the garden path.

"I still do not quite understand what you are doing, Princess Briony," said Eneas as they made their way along a narrow road that ran parallel to Lantern Broad. So far they had attracted much less attention than they would have on the great thoroughfare, which was certainly what Briony wanted. Still, it was impossible to go out into Tessis with the heir to the throne, his guards, and a pair of oxcarts without drawing a crowd.

"Then you do me the greatest possible compliment by trusting me." As soon as she had said it, Briony worried that she sounded like she was trying to charm him. *He is a good man, after all—I owe him something more than just the ordinary round of courtly pleasantries.* "In truth, I've told you all I can. If I say any more you'll no longer fear I might be mad—you will be convinced of it!"

Eneas laughed. "I swear there is no such thing as a workaday conversation with you, Briony Eddon! Because of that alone I would have been happy to accompany you anywhere. As it is, I have only been asked to go to a part of my own city that I confess I do not know well. Underbridge has long had a name for its strange folk and stranger happenings."

"The folk are strange if height is your only measurement," she told. "But if they are anything like our Funderlings at home, Highness, I believe them to be honest citizens—as honest as any other men, that is."

Eneas nodded. "An important qualification. But let us not curse them too quickly even with the crimes of bigger men—perhaps dishonesty, like the price of fish and meat, increases with greater weight."

Briony could not help laughing.

As was his wont, Dawet dan-Faar had admirably prepared the ground for their visit: when they reached Underbridge the Kallikans immediately opened the gates of their guildhall and invited the company inside, oxcarts and all. Inside it was dark and the ceilings were low. A group of small grooms came forward and took the oxen off to the stable and began to unload the carts. In its own way the Kallikans' hall was as much a world of its own as Broadhall Palace—although smaller in all ways, of course.

A group of armor-clad Kallikan guards now arrived to lead them into the hall itself, bearing what looked like ceremonial digging-sticks.

"Your pardon, lady . . . and sir," said one of them, bowing. "Follow us, please."

This courtly little fellow reminded her suddenly of the day of the wyvern hunt back in Southmarch and the Funderling man her horse had almost trampled. That had been the day when everything had first begun to go really wrong—the day they had come back to the message from their father's captor asking for Briony's hand in marriage. But what she remembered now about that day was something else . . . something about her lost twin.

Oh, Barrick, where are you? It hurt to think about him, although scarcely an hour of any day went by that she didn't. The underground dreams had ended, but she still missed him as fiercely as ever.

On the day of that long-ago hunt Shaso had saved them from the Shadowline monster and Kendrick had been dragged out from beneath the carcass of his horse, miraculously unhurt but for a few scrapes and bruises. Many courtiers and huntsmen had run to attend to her older brother, but Briony had been more concerned about her twin and his crippled arm. Still, when she tried to help him Barrick had turned angrily away from her and Briony had demanded to know why he always fought against the people who loved him.

"When I'm fighting to be left alone it means my life is worth something to me," he had told her. *"When I stop fighting—when I don't have the strength anymore to be angry—then you should worry for me."*

Oh, sweet and merciful Zoria, she prayed now, *wherever he is, please let my brother still be fighting! Let him stay angry!*

The Guild of the Underbridge Kallikans, as Dawet had named them, had already assembled in the main hall to wait. The little people watched with careful and mostly silent attention from rows of benches as Briony and the others entered, which only added to the sense that she and the prince were performers in some unusual masque. In keeping with the citizens of Underbridge, the room was small and the ceilings were low. In the center of the closest bench sat a very round little man with an enormous fuzzy beard and a tall hat. As the guards showed them where to stand, this imposing figure raised his hand.

"Welcome, Princess Briony of Southmarch," he said in the same broadly understandable accent as ordinary-sized Syannese, which was a relief—she had feared the Kallikans might speak some language of their own. "I am Highwarden Dolomite."

She made a careful curtsy. "Thank you, Highwarden. You are kind to give me an audience on such short notice."

"And you are kind to bring us such splendid gifts." He smiled as several of the guards came forward to give him the manifest. *"Two dozen Yisti pick-heads,"* he read, giving a little whistle of appreciation. "Those are the finest anywhere, sharp as glass, strong as the very bones of the earth! And fifty hundredweight of Ulosian marble." He shook his head, impressed. "Rich gifts indeed—we have not had such fine stuff to work for over a year! We are impressed by your generosity, Princess." He looked to the other Guildsmen on either side before turning his sharp eyes back to Briony. "But what, if we may wonder, is the cause of such kindness? Even our own folk outside Tessis do not come to see us in these days, let alone bring us fine gifts."

"A favor, of course." Briony had danced this little dance of teasing flattery and hard questions a hundred times before. "But such wise folk as you knew that already."

"Indeed, we guessed." Dolomite smiled carefully. "And we of course will be very interested to hear what necessity has brought such an important woman to our humble hall. But, first, here is something else we do not know." The highwarden looked straight at Eneas, who still wore his traveling cloak. "Who is this man who stands beside you so silent and watchful? Why does he remain hooded under our roof like an outlaw?"

A couple of the prince's guards made angry noises and would have drawn their weapons but Briony saw Eneas calm them with a whispered word.

"You . . . you mean . . . you don't know . . . ?" Briony silently cursed her own stupidity. Dawet had not told the Kallikans about her companion, though she had explicitly asked him to do so. Accident—or a purposeful bit of meddling?

"No. Why should we?" Dolomite asked.

"Because he is your lord!" one of the prince's guards shouted, his outrage overcoming even his master's injunction to silence. A startled murmur ran through the watching Kallikans. "This is Prince Eneas—son and heir of your king, Enander!"

Zoria save me from my own stupidity! Briony was horrified by what she had done. She should have introduced Eneas first—no, she should never have brought him. She had let her own weakness drive her, inviting a strong man to accompany her instead of simply getting on with things herself. And now the gods alone knew what would happen.

Eneas pulled back his hood, prompting the Kallikans to more gasps and murmurs, loud as a covey of flushed birds. Several of them got down from their benches and prostrated themselves; even the highwarden removed his tall hat and began to clamber down from his chair to bow to the prince.

"Forgive us, Highness," he cried. "We did not know! We meant no disrepect to you or your father!"

Briony was a little sickened to see the change that had come over people who only moments before had been calm, careful, and subtle. "This is my fault!" she said.

"No, it is mine," countered Eneas. "I thought to stay out of this and let Princess Briony do what she needed to do. I should not have hidden my face from my father's subjects. I ask your pardon."

All of the Kallikans were relieved by the prince's words. Some were even nodding and smiling as they made their way back to their seats, as if the whole thing had been an amusing, if slightly frightening, jest.

"You are very kind, Prince Eneas, very kind." Dolomite looked anxiously between Briony and Eneas. "Of course, we will do whatever the princess asks of us, Highness."

Now Briony felt heavy and sick in the pit of her stomach. By bringing Eneas she had forced the Kallikans into a position where they had no choice but to do her bidding. That was a way to get what one wanted, but not a way to make real allies.

"I tell you in all honesty," she said to Dolomite and the other

Kallikans, "I asked the prince to accompany me only because he is one of my few friends here in Syan and I could not leave the court without some kind of escort."

"Surely the big folk in Broadhall palace do not think us a danger to noblewomen?" piped up a particularly wizened little Kallikan sitting next to Dolomite. He almost sounded flattered by the thought.

"I am certain you would be dangerous to Syan's enemies," Briony said. "But it was not your people I feared. One of my countrymen was attacked in the streets of Tessis only a short time gone, so my friends here do not want me to travel without a companion even in the city."

"And what better companion for a young woman than our famous prince?" said Dolomite. "We are ashamed not to have recognized you, Prince Eneas."

"And I should have made myself known to you immediately, Highwarden Dolomite, but I am glad we have met at last. I have heard your name spoken well of before, and from men I trust."

"Your highness is too kind." Dolomite looked as though he might swell up and start booming with pride like a frog during the spring floods.

Briony let her breath out all the way for the first time in a while. Despite mistakes, they had crept past the first obstacle. "Let me waste no more of your time, Highwarden," she said. "Here is what I've come to ask. Please, can you show me your oldest drum?"

"Drum?" The smile on Dolomite's face began fading—he looked genuinely surprised and confused. "Our oldest . . . drum?"

"That's all I know. I was told by . . . by someone important to ask for it."

The silence gave way to another series of murmured conversations, including several of the Kallikans in the front row around the highwarden, but the common tone seemed to be one of confoundment.

The little wrinkled fellow next to the highwarden suddenly began wiggling his fingers in agitation. "Ooh, scarp me, I've just had a thought," he began, then frowned so hard that his face almost curled away into his beard and vanished. "But no, that's foolish! . . . it wouldn't . . . would it . . . ?"

"By the Earth's Eldest!" sputtered Dolomite, "Would you be good enough to share your idea with us, Whitelead?"

"Just . . . I thought . . ." The old Kallikan waggled his fingers even faster beside his face, so that he looked like a river mudfish; at last he noticed what he was doing and stopped. "That . . . perhaps what she means . . . this drum . . . could it be . . . the *drumstones?*"

At these words even the last few whispers trailed off and the hall fell completely silent. All eyes turned toward Briony in astonishment.

I must make the very gods despair, she thought. *What have I done now?*

❧

The days were getting long, Theron Pilgrimer noted with satisfaction: even hours past the evening meal the sun settling into the hills beyond the river was still high enough to turn the whole length of the Pellos bright copper. That boded well for his desire to reach Onsilpia's Veil, the most important pilgrimage site in the north, well before the Midsummer Penance Festival began—and that would mean satisfied customers. He had been leading these pilgrim caravans since he was a young man, but for all Theron's experience things could still catch him by surprise. For that reason, he had guided this caravan far to the south of Brenn's Bay. He wanted nothing to do with the mad things he had heard about Southmarch, besieged by fairy armies, its royal family scattered to the winds.

He had just finished discussing food supplies with Avidel, his apprentice, when the cripple's boy appeared. "He wants to talk to you," the boy told him.

Theron cursed quietly under his breath and looked around for the tattered, ill-omened figure of the beggar. But no, Theron reminded himself, he should call the man by a different name: you couldn't very well name someone a beggar who was paying you an entire gold dolphin to join your pilgrimage for a fraction of its journey.

Theron followed the boy to the low hill where the cripple stood waiting, well away from the rest of the caravaners. The hooded man, whose blackened, bandaged face Theron had never seen properly, didn't show the least signs of interest in his fellow travelers except to share their fire and the meals they ate out of the communal pot. He spoke only through the boy, and that seldomly, so it was surprising he should ask to speak with Theron now.

The cripple seemed to be gazing out across the rolling land toward the broad sweep of the Pellos. Distant as an ant on a branch, an ox towed a barge from a path along the bank and several small rowboats bobbed in the backwater at the bend of the river as Silverside fishermen cast out their nets.

"Lovely evening, eh?" Theron said as he approached. He was looking forward to getting into his bedroll and paying his respects to the flask of wine hidden in his travel chest. It was not that the other pilgrims would disapprove, but rather that as long as it was hidden he didn't have to share it. He would not be able to fill it again until they reached Onsipia's Veil, which was still days away.

The hooded man waved his bandaged hand and his child servant stood on tiptoe to hear his muttered words. "How far away is Southmarch?" the boy asked.

"Southmarch?" Theron frowned. "At least a tennight, riding most of the day. For a group like ours, closer to a month. But of course we aren't going anywhere near it."

The bent man murmured again and the boy listened. "He wants you to take him there."

"What?" Theron laughed. "I thought your master was just crippled in his body, not simple-minded, but it seems I was wrong! We talked of this when he first joined us back at Onir Plessos. This caravan is not going to Southmarch nor anywhere near it. In fact, this is the closest we shall come." He waved his hands. "If your master wants to strike out on his own I will not stop him, of course. I will even pray for him, and all the gods know he will need it, and so will you, child. The lands between here and there are said to be full of not just the usual cutpurses and bandits, but worse things—far worse." He leaned toward the boy. "Goblins, they say. Elves and boggles. Things that will steal not just your money but your very soul." Theron straightened up. "So if he has sense to go with his money, he will stay with us until we reach the Veil. I know he keeps what's wrong with him a secret, but I have my guesses. Tell him there's a leper house there that treats its wards with true kindness."

The boy listened to another flow of whispers from the hooded depths, then turned to Theron again. "He says he doesn't have any leppersy. He was dead. The gods brought him back. That is no illness, he says."

Theron made the sign of the pass-evil, then remembered his position and changed it into the sign of the Three. "He talks nonsense. The dead do not come back. Only the Orphan, and he was the gods' favorite."

Both Theron and the child waited for some reply from the hooded man but he stayed silent, looking out across the darkening valley and the murky silver ribbon of the Pellos.

"Well, I can't stand here forever," the caravan master said at last. "Nice to talk with you and all," he added, remembering the exorbitant fee the man was paying. "If you haven't had any of the turnip stew, I recommend it. Few pieces of mutton in there, down at the bottom—don't make a fuss and nobody'll notice. But I should be on my way. Still a great deal to be done." Including, he suddenly remembered, exhuming his wine flask from his travel chest. The thought gave him a warm feeling. He might not be as devout as he had once been, but he was still doing the gods' work. Surely they looked on him with favor—surely they wanted only good things for Theron the pilgrimer, son of Lukos the potmaker. Look how high they had already raised him!

The cripple pulled something from his robe and held it out, waggling his clublike, bandaged hand until the boy took it from him. After a whispered instruction the child brought it to Theron.

"He says it is all he has left. You may have it all."

Theron stared at the dirty-faced boy for an uncomprehending moment, then took the sack. It was heavy, and by the time he tipped its contents into his palm Theron's hand was shaking, not from the weight but from his sudden realization of what he would see.

Gold coins. At least a dozen. And silver and copper to the amount of another two or three dolphins. He looked up in astonishment, but the crippled man was staring silently out across the valley again, as if he had not just put a sum great enough to turn someone like Theron from a comfortable but hardworking caravan master into a gentleman of leisure with a house, land, livestock, and several servants.

"What is this for? Why does he show it to me?"

"He says he must go to Southmarch," the boy said after a short, whispered convocation. "That is why the gods have brought him back. But he cannot go without someone who knows the way—he cannot find the way, even . . . even with me." The boy scowled as he said it; clearly the words stung. "His eyes are still seeing the world of the dead as much as the world of the living. He fears he'll get lost and arrive too late."

Theron realized his mouth was hanging open, like a door someone had forgotten to close. He shut it, then immediately opened it again. "Late?"

"After Midsummer. Then he will be too late. On Midsummer's Night all the sleepers will awake. He heard this when he was in the gods' lands."

The caravan master could only shake his head. When he spoke his words bumped against each other. "L–let me . . . understand, boy." He had never imagined holding so much money in his hands and doubted any of the other pilgrims had, either. They were all good, gods-fearing folk as far as he knew, but he didn't want to test their honesty too harshly. "Your master wishes to pay all this money . . . for *what*, exactly?"

After a short conversation with the hooded shape, the boy said, "To get to Southmarch. To be led there, and protected along the way. To be fed and to have a horse to ride." He turned back at some urgent murmuring from the crippled man. "Not just Southmarch, the country, but Southmarch Castle. In the middle of the bay."

Even with this incredible bounty in his hands, Theron still hesitated—not at the idea of deserting the pilgrims, but at the prospect of crossing the lands to the north, full of unknown dangers, and traveling right into the midst of what was said to be a war between the Marchfolk and the fairies out of legend. The weight of the gold in his hand, though, made a powerful argument.

"Avidel!" he called. "Come here!"

Theron slid the coins back into the sack and tied it to his belt with an extra knot, just to be sure. His apprentice was about to become a caravan master.

❧

The procession that moved down the corridors behind the Guild Hall was a large one. Briony, Eneas, and the prince's guards were led by Highwarden Dolomite and several other guildsfolk—including, Briony was pleased to see, at least one Guildswoman—and wrinkled little Whitelead, who it turned out was a sort of priest. Whitelead was accompanied by two huge acolytes—huge by Kallikan standards, in any case—who walked behind him carrying an object made of pots and sagging leather pipes, the whole thing steaming gently. When Briony asked politely what it was, Whitelead cheerfully told her it was a ceremonial replica of the Sacred Bellows.

"Sacred Bellows?"

"Ah, yes." Whitelead nodded vigorously. "The god used it to create all earthly life."

"Which god?"

He looked at her gravely for a moment, then smiled and winked. "I'm not allowed to say it out loud, Highness . . . but the Syannese celebrate him every year during the Kerneia." He winked again, even more broadly, just to make certain she understood.

The strange parade wound its way down what seemed at first to be only a series of corridors behind the Guild Hall, but Briony soon noticed that the bends and turns were not tight enough to be confined within the space of a normal sized building, even a large one. Also, in many places the passage sloped down at a distinct angle.

Eneas had noticed also. "How far does this go, I wonder?" he said quietly to Briony. "Some of my ancestors tried to prevent the Kallikans from digging in the stone underneath Tessis, but it seems they did not do a very good job of stopping them. They must have been at this for years!"

Indeed, it was clear that the walls, which near the Guild Hall had been paneled in dark wood, were now naked stone, beautifully polished and carved, sometimes inlaid with many different types of rock, work Briony could tell even by lamplight was exceptional.

"By the Three Brothers," Eneas said wonderingly after they had walked even farther, "have they burrowed all the way to Esterian?"

"Don't say anything to them!" Briony pleaded, then felt ashamed. "I'm sorry—I have no right to tell you how to treat your subjects, but it was me who forced them to take us here. I would hate to think I've repaid them with trouble."

Eneas laughed, but he did not seem happy. "Fear not, Princess. I will not make myself a troublesome guest, but it does set me wondering. If the mild Kallikans can flout us so, right under our noses, what other surprises will I find on the day it becomes my task to put Syan's house in order?"

Staring at his face, so sharp and intent in the lamplight, Briony was taken again by a strange, contradictory impulse.

Ferras Vansen. Were you real? Did I see what I thought I saw—did I see your feelings as clearly as I felt I did? What if it was only a phantom of my own mind? And even if not, she asked herself, what about this man, Eneas, this good man struggling to be fair? He cared for her—he'd said so—and he was exactly what Southmarch needed just now . . . It was too much to think about. Her feelings were as confused as the bubbles in a boiling kettle, first this one rising, then that one, then both at once and a dozen more.

At last, after long walking and many turns, and after descending what

Briony guessed must be at least a dozen fathoms beneath the Guild Hall, the procession reached a place where the corridor widened out into a sort of broad staircase with shallow steps clearly cut for Kallikan feet that led to a door in the far wall decorated with carved designs that stretched weirdly in the flickering lamplight. Briony could see an image of a man riding a fish and another tying a vast serpent into a complicated knot, but most of the carvings were harder to make out.

Several of the Underbridge folk sprang forward and banged on the metal of the door with sticks. After a long wait, the great portal swung open, revealing more lamplight inside. Highwarden Dolomite stepped forward and led them all through the doorway.

Even as the last of them stepped through into a room only slightly smaller than the great hall outside, and the door clanked shut behind them, a group of Kallikans in black robes like Whitelead's appeared from a passage at the back of the room, scuttling and slipping on the polished stone floors as they hurried forward, as though on an icy lake. They prostrated themselves before the highwarden and the priest, and then one rose and made a series of ritual gestures, although with a certain anxious haste. He was almost as small as Whitelead but a great deal younger, very thin, and his eyes bulged in his face as though he was terrified.

His eyes only grew wider as he finished his ritual and looked up from Dolomite and Whitelead to the others who stood watching. He goggled at Briony, Eneas, and the prince's guards, all towering over the Kallikans like ogres; for a moment Briony thought the little man might faint dead away. "Oh, Great Anvil," he said at last to Dolomite, "Great Anvil of the Lord, how did you know? How did you know?"

The highwarden stared at him for a long moment, then snorted in annoyance. "How did I know *what*, Chalk? What in the name of the Pit are you babbling about? We're here to use the drumstones. The prince of Syan himself has commanded it!"

Chalk looked at him in surprise, then back at the imposing visitors before suddenly bursting into tears.

When Chalk had composed himself he led them all back into the inner recesses of what was clearly some kind of temple, although the Kallikans were very reluctant to talk about it.

"It's just . . . well, we haven't had a message through the stones for decades—not since my father's day," Chalk explained, "and that was when he was nearly a boy! So you can imagine, Great Anvil, that when we heard . . . well, I was just on my way to tell you and the others!"

"Hold your tongue a moment, man, you are making my head ring," said the highwarden. "Are you saying that someone else has been using the drumstones?"

"Who could do that without authority?" demanded Whitelead, his little beard bristling like the ruff of an angry rooster. "We will have him in front of the Guild immediately!"

"No, no, my lords!" said Chalk so miserably Briony feared the little fellow would start weeping again. "The drumstones *spoke!* They spoke to us! For the first time since my father's day!"

"What? What do you say?" demanded Dolomite, truly surprised for the first time. The revelation sent a flurry of whispers and gasps through all the other assembled Kallikans. "Who speaks to us?"

Chalk pushed open the door to a final chamber, darker than any of the others. A great circle of smooth but otherwise unworked stone dominated the high wall before them, the space around it filled with other kinds of stone cut in fantastic shapes. "The folk of Lord's House—our kin in Southmarch."

Briony could not stay silent any longer. "Are you saying that you've had a message from the Funderlings in Southmarch? For the love of the gods, what did they say?" A kind of giddy excitement almost but did not quite overcome the chill that swept over her. As Dawet had reminded her, strange things were happening—more of them every moment. She had dreamed a demigoddess and her dream was taking shape in the waking world.

Chalk looked to his masters for approval before speaking. "The others . . . the ones in Southmarch said . . . it is hard to put it exactly in ordinary speech, because the drumstones speak in a tongue of their own—our old tongue, but shorter of speech." He furrowed his pale forehead, staring at his hands as he did his best to remember correctly. "The message was, '*A Highwarden of the Big Folk has come back alive from the Old, Dark Lands. He leads us now. Outside the walls, the Old Ones oppress us and we cannot hold out long. We call on you to honor our shared blood and our shared tale. Send help to us.*'" He looked up, blinking his large eyes. "That was more or less the whole of it."

Briony shook her head. "But what does it mean? 'Highwarden of the Big Folk'—Big Folk is us, yes? That's what you call us. But we have no

Highwarden, only a king." Her heart suddenly beat faster. "Do they mean my father? Has my father come back? Where are the Old Lands?" Her pulse was racing, but Dolomite was shaking his head.

"I do not think it means your father, Princess—everyone knows he is held in the south, in Hierosol. The Old Lands are what we call the country that lies behind the Shadowline. The lands of those you call the fairy folk. The Qar."

For a moment she felt only disappointment, then it came to her suddenly, startling as a sudden blare of trumpets. "A Highwarden of the Big Folk has come back from the lands ruled by the fairies?" Her heart began speeding again. "My brother—it can only mean my brother, Barrick! He has come back to Southmarch! He has come back! Oh, praise Zoria!" And to the tiny man's surprise and terror, she suddenly bent and kissed little Chalk on the head. Prince Eneas laughed, but the rest of the Funderlings were quite astonished. "Quickly, quickly!" she said to Dolomite and Whitelead, "Can we send a message back? Tell them I am here—tell them I must speak with my brother!"

With the permission of their leaders, Chalk and his comrades got out ladders and long striking-wands, objects that had obviously been used only for ceremonial purposes for some time (and not even that very frequently as suggested by how hard it was to find some of them—Chalk started sniffling again, this time in mortification, as the temple was ransacked for the last ladder, which had been used to refill a ceiling lantern and not returned). At last everything was in place. Chalk sat by Briony's feet with a tablet of clay and a stone stylus as he wrote down her message and did his best to translate it into words the drumstones could carry.

Underbridge to Lord's House, Hail! We hear your words and praise them! Our Highwarden and Hierophant attend. Also a Highwarden Mother of the Big Folk of Lord's House, who comes here but seeks her brother there. Please drum to us his words. We greet you, brothers, and will try to help you, but must know more.

"Highwarden Mother?" asked Briony as Chalk relayed these words to his underlings, who then began to beat at the circle of stone set into the wall as though it were a true drum, their stone-headed, wooden wands plinking and plunking a strange, arrhythmic music. "It seems a touch confusing."

"They have no word for 'princess,' it seems," said Eneas, amused. "I wince to think what they would call me."

When the message had been drummed and then drummed a second time, they waited, but although they stood—and then, after a long while, sat down where they could find places to do so—no message came back.

"Either they are gone," said the hierophant, "which seems strange when they had just sent a message to us, or something has broken the chain of drumstones. We will try to drum to them again tonight, and send word to you in the castle if we hear anything."

"You are very kind," said Briony, but the dizzying happiness of only a little earlier was fading. Perhaps she had been wrong about what the message meant. Perhaps the Kallikans themselves were wrong somehow about receiving it at all.

"Come, Princess," Eneas told her. "It's time to go back now."

She allowed herself to be led back through the maze of corridors toward the real world and the late afternoon sun.

24
The Failure of a Thousand Poets

"The Book of the Trigon states that the Godwar took place during the time of the Xixian Sea-Kings, many centuries before the founding of Hierosol. The battle of Shivering Plain is also the first mention in history of the legendary queen Ghasamez (or Jittsammes as the Vuts call her), who led an army to fight on the behalf of Zmeos and the other rogue gods."

—from "A Treatise on the Fairy Peoples of Eion and Xand"

"THEY'VE BROKEN THROUGH! The Twilight folk have broken through!" One of Sledge Jasper's warders fell through the doorway of the drumstone chamber, bleeding and staggering like a drunk.

Ferras Vansen leaped to his feet so quickly he almost knocked over the monk beside him. Luckily, the Funderling had just finished pounding on the drumstone wall with what looked like the ramrod for a cannon and Vansen's message had been sent out into the earth—and more important, he hoped, to the Funderlings of Tessis. "Where have they broken through?" Vansen demanded. "And how many of them?"

Two of the other temple brothers were now holding up the bleeding guard. "Just above the Festival Halls," gasped the wounded man, "but they're almost to the temple cavern. Wardthane Jasper and the others have fallen back to the narrows in front of the Curtainfall, but they ... will not last long ... you must ... must send ...." The man wobbled and his head sank.

"Leave him with the older Brothers to be cared for," Vansen said, "and if he is well, let him rest a while and then send him back—we need every hand. Where is Magister Cinnabar?"

"Cinnabar took a troop of warders to look at a suspicious cave-in below Five Arches," said Brother Nickel. "He will not be back for hours."

"Then I need someone else. I need men to go with me to the Festival Halls. I cannot find my way around without a Funderling guide." He had learned from harsh experience that any tracking skills he possessed meant nothing in these lightless tunnels. He turned and surveyed the drumstone chamber. "In fact, we need all these men, Brother Nickel. Half our guards or more are out of the temple, as well as Copper and most of the men he brought. If the Qar break through, we shall be separated from them and under siege."

"These are religious men, not fighters," said Nickel angrily, waving his hands at the half-dozen fearful-looking Brothers listening to the argument. "In any case, it is their task to listen for the drumstones—especially now, when we have just sent messages! What if our kin in Underbridge or Westcliff reply to us?"

"Then leave one, preferably someone too lame to fight. Send me all the rest and tell them to bring any weapon they can find—hoes and shovels from the gardens if there is nothing else. They must meet me in front of the temple as quickly as they can—we have no time to lose."

It was a ragged crew, there was little doubt of that: Ferras Vansen had only a dozen men, most too old or too young, and none of them looked as if he had ever raised a hand to fight before. Vansen had the armor the Funderlings had made for him, but none of his volunteers had anything to protect themselves but the mica goggles, leather helmets, and thick blousy jackets they wore for digging in the wet and dangerous depths.

"Nothing to be done about it," he told himself, but his heart was heavy. When had troops like these ever won a battle? They were sacrifices, not soldiers. "Where is Chert Blue Quartz?"

"Here," the Funderling said from the doorway of the temple. The small man hurried down the stairs. "What do you need, Captain?"

Vansen leaned close so only Chert could hear him. "Someone must hurry to Cinnabar below Five Arches. Tell him that if he and his men don't come quickly we are lost—the Qar have broken through above the

Festival Halls. But do not go yourself, do you understand? I need you to stay and make sure Copper and any others who come back are also sent to help us as quickly as possible. It must be you, Chert—I do not trust these priests to understand the danger."

Chert frowned, considering. "I'll send someone after Cinnabar right now, Captain, I promise. But it will be hours before he can reach you at the Stair, even if he starts when the messenger finds him."

"Can't be helped." Vansen shook his head. "Ah, I almost forgot. Go to Chaven and ask him . . . no, lean closer, I must whisper it to you."

When Vansen had finished Chert looked at him with wide eyes. "Truly? Poison?"

"Quiet, I beg you! I am afraid so."

"Then we must pray that the Earth Elders are sleeping no longer—that they will wake and help us."

On an impulse, Vansen thrust out his hand for the small man to clasp, surprising Chert more than a little. "Farewell, Master Blue Quartz. I hope I will see you again, but if the gods wish otherwise, take care of your family—and watch out for that boy of yours, especially. I wager he will play an important part before this is all over."

Chert nodded. "And be thrifty with your own life, Captain Vansen. We need you. Don't sell yourself for the first nuggets out of the seam."

Ferras Vansen had no idea what that meant, but he squeezed Chert's hand once more, then turned and motioned for his ragtag troop to follow him.

"The Earth Elders protect you!" Chert called after him, and several of the older brothers gathered on the steps echoed him, their voices dry and whispery as mice scuttling in a hay barn.

Chert found one young acolyte who seemed to have more sense than some of his fellows. "Go find Magister Cinnabar down below Five Arches," he said to the youth. "Tell him the fairies have broken through near the Festival Halls and Vansen needs every man he can get. Go, lad, and hurry."

A furious Brother Nickel was waiting as Chert passed the chapter house on his way to find Chaven.

"What do you think you are doing?" Nickel demanded. "You cannot give orders to my acolytes. I was given the authority during this crisis. *I* act for the abbot, not you!"

"Captain Vansen is in charge of defending this place and all of Funderling Town," snapped Chert. "Cinnabar and the guild told you so. The Qar have broken through and Vansen needed a message sent. There wasn't time to find you and ask your approval."

Nickel scowled, but seemed unable to find a response. "Just don't get too big and shiny, Townsman Blue Quartz," he said at last. "It was you and your mongrel son who started all this trouble—little people, fairies, outsiders in our Mysteries. Some others may have forgotten that but I haven't. And now I'm told your monstrous child has caused even more trouble for me." Nickel stuck a bony finger in Chert's face. "If it is as bad as I suspect, I will see him sent back to Funderling Town—and you, too, no matter what the guild and your Captain Vansen say." The monk stamped off like a man intent on crushing every insect in his path.

Chert was in a hurry to find Chaven the physician, but it sounded as though the boy had got himself onto some kind of scree slope again. Could the errand to Chaven wait? He did not want to leave the boy to be bullied or worse by Nickel—the monk was clearly developing a grudge against him. And what if the monk frightened the boy off somewhere? What if Flint fled the temple entirely? It was too dangerous now for the child to be outside on his own.

"Fracture and fissure!" Chert smacked his hands together in frustration: Vansen's errand would have to wait, at least for a while. He set off after Brother Nickel.

The loud voices seemed to be coming from the library and they sounded angry indeed. As Chert crossed the front hall he had a sudden premonition of what he would find there.

To his sorrow, he turned out to be right: Flint stood in the middle of a crowd of furious, dark-robed monks, half a head taller than most of them and as serene as a tall stone in the middle of a rushing river. The boy's eyes met Chert's for a moment and then continued roaming the walls as though he were sizing up the stone before carving a stringcourse.

"What's going on here?" Chert had to struggle to keep his temper. He knew the boy was unusual—it made his stomach churn sometimes just to think of how carelessly he and Opal had brought the child into their lives—but had never seen a scrape of harm in him. The Metamorphic Brothers were acting as though they had caught a thief or murderer.

Brother Nickel turned toward him, face flushed. "This is beyond all bounds, even for you, Blue Quartz," the monk said. "This child walked into the library—the greatest library of our people left in the world!—and began to put his hands on the texts! His filthy hands!"

Despite his own rage, Chert was shaken: trespassing in the library was no simple prank. It was worse even than entering the Mysteries, because the books in the library—some of them ancient prayers scratched into fragile slate in letters so shallow that they had become almost entirely unreadable, or etched on parchment-thin sheets of mica—were rare and easily damaged. The great Funderling library in Stonebeneath, a settlement that for centuries had lain beneath ancient Hierosol, had been destroyed along with most of the city in the floods of four centuries earlier, along with almost half of the lower city's inhabitants, and the library had been lost completely. The dreadful toll of the Stonebeneath Floods had been taught to Chert since he had been big enough to walk—the single greatest tragedy of Funderling history. No wonder the monks were so upset.

"Flint," he said as calmly as he could. "Did you go into the library? Did you handle the books?"

The pale-haired boy looked as if Chert had asked whether it was good to eat when you were hungry. "Yes."

"Do you see?" Nickel cried. "He feels no shame! He breaks into the Mysteries like an invader and then, not content with that outrage, comes to play his wicked tricks in the very heart of our people's memory."

Chert struggled for composure. "I'm sure with all those clever words you truly will be abbot one day, Nickel, but let's not completely lose our heads. Flint, why did you do it?"

The boy now looked at him as though he were actually a bit surprised, something Chert had scarcely ever seen from him. "I needed to learn something. I went to look at the oldest books. It's important."

"What? What did you want to learn?"

"I can't tell you." He said it with such clarity that Chert knew arguing would be useless. The assembled brothers were no longer just murmuring, but crowding forward as though they meant to lay hands on the boy and administer punishment. Chert stepped in front of Flint and held up his hands.

"He didn't understand. He doesn't mean harm, but he . . . he's different." He was ashamed to capitulate to the monks so easily, but there was no time to waste. "I'll take him with me. You won't have any more trouble with him—I promise that on my honor as a Guildsman. Just . . . just go about your business."

"How can we trust you?" Nickel demanded. "You have let him run wild, let him meddle in the affairs of holy men . . . ."

"This temple and Funderling Town are under attack," Chert said loudly. "And you know it as well as I do, Brother Nickel. We all have far more to fear than this boy—you should be organizing these men to defend the temple, not to attack a child. Now, will you let me go? I am very sorry Flint touched the books but it looks like no harm was done. I'll take him with me and he'll get into no further mischief. Please, let us all remember what's important now."

Nickel was scowling, but one of the other monks said, "Antimony told me that Chert Blue Quartz is a good man."

"He's right about defending the temple, that's certain," said another. "If Chert gives his word, perhaps we should allow him this one chance."

"Thank you." Chert looked around. The anger on the faces of the other monks had begun to fade like the disappearing sheen of water as it dried on a rock face: talk of an attack had reminded them of the true danger. Nickel, though, did not look satisfied. "Come along, Flint," Chert told the boy. "Say you're sorry and we'll be going—I have important errands for Captain Vansen." He grabbed the boy's hand and pulled him away from the library.

Flint did not say sorry, of course, but Chert hoped that in the racket of the monks beginning to argue among themselves they hadn't noticed the boy's silence.

He found the physician upstairs in his small dormitory cell and told him what Vansen had asked. Chaven thought about it for a moment before saying, "I think that the best solution in the short run would simply be to tie a cloth soaked in water across their faces. Anything more complicated will take me some time."

Chert stood, amazed at his own stupidity. "Cloth—water! By the Elders, I have been so preoccupied it is like I did not even hear Vansen. If there is one thing we Funderlings have, it is dust masks! With a little stuffing around the edges they should keep out the fumes of the Qar's poison dust." He began to pace. "In fact, the craftsmen who do the near-work, as we call it, the sanding and polishing, even wear hoods with mica over the eyes. What a fool I am!"

"Do not condemn yourself," Chaven told him. "We are all much distracted. Is there anything else I can do for you? If not, I have a few matters of my own . . ."

"Yes, yes, I'm afraid there is." Chert grabbed the boy. "Keep an eye on this young scamp for me—I must try to find some dust masks for Vansen. Even now he and Jasper's men are trying to keep the Qar out of the Festival Halls, if you haven't heard. But don't let this fellow out of your sight! He has been up to all kinds of outrage and mischief according to Brother Nickel. And especially keep him away from the library."

Chaven seemed to notice the boy for the first time. His round face relaxed into a smile, but Chert fancied he saw something else there, too, something more . . . calculating? "Ah, Master Flint, I hear you have been up to all kinds of interesting things since I saw you last. A visit to the Skimmers, was it? And now the library. Perhaps you can tell me about all of it while we keep each other company."

Flint was persuaded into the room with the bad grace of a cat being coaxed down off a high place.

"Remember," Chert said as he went out, "you can't let him out of your sight!" The physician waved a hand in acknowledgment.

Chert's search of the small forge where the temple smith repaired tools and other simple household objects turned up two fire-hoods, one of which the temple smith himself was wearing, pushed back on his bald, sweating head. The large-armed monk objected angrily to giving up either of them, but Chert asserted Vansen's guild-given authority and grabbed the unused hood, then scampered out before the smith lost his temper entirely.

In the temple undercroft he found some heavy cloth dust masks, the remains of an old rebuilding project. There were only a dozen, but he thought they might at least keep those in the front safe against the fairy poisons. He was about to go when he saw something else, a stone chest with a heavy wooden lid. Chert opened it and stared for a while at the wedge-shaped iron objects carefully stacked inside.

Why not? he thought to himself, and carefully lifted one out and tucked it into his belt. It was heavy and it dug into his belly, but Chert tightened his belt and decided it would have to do. He replaced the lid on the stone box, then cut some cord from a loop hanging from a peg on the wall before closing the storeroom door.

He put water in a bucket for the dust masks and hurried back across the temple and out the front hall, pleased to see that the monks seemed finally to have understood the danger: half a dozen of them were dragging the most valuable statuary inside, and the temple's ancient iron siege doors were being swung into place. Chert doubted the temple had ever been besieged—certainly it hadn't happened within his memory—but the Funderlings' native dislike of windows and other such upground fripperies would serve them in good stead now. As with most large Funderling buildings, the temple's air and water came in by ducts from other parts of the great limestone labyrinth beneath Southmarch and its storerooms were kept full of food even in lean times. An enemy would find it hard to drive them out quickly.

Chert met two of Sledge Jasper's warders on the far side of the Curtainfall. One was all but senseless and being dragged by his comrade, who was bleeding in a half-dozen places.

"Go back!" the upright warder said, gasping. He shook blood out of his eyes. "The wardthane and the big man, the upgrounder, are surrounded. The fairies made a cloud of blindness around them. They'll reach the temple any moment—they'll kill us all!"

Chert could get nothing else of use from the man and let him drag his wounded fellow toward the temple. Terrified by the thought of what lay ahead, he wondered for long moments whether he should not follow them back, but the sloshing bucket in his hand, carried so wearyingly far already, helped him make up his mind. Captain Vansen was in trouble. Only Chert could help him, at least until Cinnabar showed up with more men.

By the time he had gone another few hundred steps he could hear shrieks of pain and anger in the distance and his heart was pounding faster than a craftsman's hammer.

Forgive me, Opal, he thought. In that moment he missed his wife so fiercely that it felt like a hole, like cold wind blowing right through him. *Forgive me, my old darling, I'm doing it again.*

❦

Ferras Vansen was in the middle of a waking nightmare—strange shapes, guttural cries, and mad shadows cast by the flickering light of torches. Vansen, Sledge Jasper, and five of the remaining warders had barricaded themselves as best they could in the narrow hallway between the last two of the Festival Halls in an effort to keep the attackers from breaking through—at least two or three dozen Qar, he felt sure, although it was hard to tell in the darkened passages. He doubted the fairies had expected so little resistance or they would have sent more than this scouting party. But the number of invaders wasn't important: if Vansen and the others failed, nothing would remain between the Qar army aboveground and the temple caverns.

And then they will be through into Funderling Town, Vansen thought, wiping at his stinging eyes. *Innocents—women and children.* And from there the fairy folk would find it easy enough to break through into the castle above.

Five of us. And even if we somehow stop them for a while, there's no guarantee they won't send reinforcements pouring down from above. Vansen did his best to catch his breath, squatting behind the barrier of rocks Jasper and his men had thrown across the narrow passage to give them protection from the occasional arrow that came hissing out of the hall beyond. *But why so much effort to take the underground part of the castle? They've lost near a hundred of their fighters here in the past days.* The battle had gone on for hours today, but the Funderlings and Vansen had the advantage of defending narrow tunnels: they had killed far more than they had lost. *The Qar must know that the gates of Funderling Town can be shut on the castle side, sealing it off from the rest of Southmarch.* Did they honestly think they could sneak through without resistance? It made no sense.

He wiped at his eyes again. The invaders, primarily the ugly little imitations, the drows, had almost filled the far chamber with the choking dust they blew out of tubes, a weaker mixture than they had used on the acolytes in the Boreholes, but still enough to make it hard for Vansen and the others to fight. Even in small amounts it not only filled their eyes with tears but made their heads reel and their chests hurt with every breath. Vansen prayed that Chaven could come up with something, although there was scant chance it would do them any good now. The Qar were too close to breaking through.

Vansen took a breath and coughed, his throat stinging. "Could we get more of your people here to wall off this passage completely?" he whispered to Sledge Jasper.

Jasper started to speak, then ducked his bald head as an arrow snapped past overhead and rattled away behind them. "Can't do it, Captain. Anything we could throw up that fast they could pull down. Those are drows—likely they know near as much about stone as we do."

"Perin's Hammer," Vansen swore bitterly. "What a place to die!"

Jasper laughed, a harsh bark that turned into a cough. "None better, Captain. With the earth herself beneath you and around you."

"Ho, Thane." One of the Warders was peering over the makeshift barrier, taking advantage of the lull between arrows. He turned to Jasper, eyes wide and white in his dust-smeared face. "I think they're coming at us again."

"Out of arrows," said Jasper, rising to a crouch. "Now they're going to try to finish the job. Up and show them, boys—if we die, we die like stonecutters!"

Vansen put off standing as long as possible. The corridors were low for him anyway, and the thin cloud of the poison dust still hovering in the air was less overwhelming behind the barricade.

He climbed to his knees and peered through the angle where the makeshift barrier met the corridor wall. Not all the Qar could see as well in the dark as the drows and Funderlings, and he was grateful for that: some of the attackers carried torches, which allowed Vansen to make out what was going on. He couldn't imagine what it would be like to fight for his life in total blackness.

The torches were bobbing and fluttering now, but their light was mostly blocked by the dark shadows of advancing Qar. They knew Vansen and his defenders had no arrows: they were not afraid of making themselves targets.

They're just going to rush us and rely on numbers, he realized. *All or nothing.*

"Fight for your homes!" he bellowed, rising himself until he filled the passage almost to the top. "For your people and your city!" Then the enemy came rushing toward them, howling and shouting, and Vansen could not think anymore.

Ferras Vansen stood gasping, his eyes stinging not from the Qar's poisons but from his own blood, which streamed from a cut on his forehead. Their enemies' first rush had failed—the attackers had dislodged several rocks from the makeshift wall, but Vansen and the warders had killed several of them and their bloody corpses now fouled the Qar side of the barricade, making it harder for the attackers to keep their footing. However, when the bodies got high enough—if Vansen and his men lived long enough to pile more bodies—the invaders would simply climb over the stone wall on a ramp of their own dead.

"They're coming again, Captain." Sledge Jasper's face was covered with cuts and dirt, an ugly mask that made him look even more grotesque, like a wicked troll out of some old myth. "I can hear them getting nearer."

Vansen wiped his eyes and lifted his warding-ax again. He wished he had a short sword or a stabbing-spear. The ax was useful for keeping the enemy at arm's length, but its weight was wearing him down. The Funderlings must be stronger than they looked: two of the warders were still using theirs, although Jasper was carrying a pair of sharp rock picks instead, one in each hand.

"I'm ready." Vansen wiped blood from his face and flicked it away. "Let them come."

"You're a good man, Captain," Jasper said abruptly, eyes on the darkness beyond the barrier. "I had you wrong, I confess. You're nearly a Funderling yourself, if a scrape on the tall side. I don't mind dying with you at all."

"Nor I you, Wardthane." Vansen wished he had something to drink. They had finished the last of their water skins an hour before and his mouth was dry as the Xandian desert. "But first let's take a few more of these unnatural things with us . . ."

Jasper's reply was lost in the roar of the attack. A small, dark shape leaped up onto the top of the barrier, then quickly fell away again, howling, guts spilling from a blow of one of the warders' axes. Two or three more figures swarmed up to take its place, one of them thrusting a blazing torch into Sledge Jasper's face so that he had to lean back to avoid being burned. Vansen slammed the blade of his weapon into the torchbearer, piercing what felt like leather armor and skin, although it was impossible to tell if the blow was mortal or not. A moment later he and one of the other warders were wrestling with another of the shapes which had come scrambling over the top, a drow with a long, pointed knife that sliced Vansen's forearm below his chain mail and almost reached his face before he tightened his hands on the attacker's arm. He squeezed as hard as he could and heard a thin shriek above the tumult as the drow's wrist broke in his grip. The creature dropped the knife, but before Vansen could pull it to him and snap its neck the drow fought its way free and fell to the ground on the defenders' side of the barrier.

Something large now loomed up before him, blocking the torchlight. Jasper bent and clubbed the drow beneath their feet with one of his picks. Vansen felt it go limp, but his attention was almost entirely taken by the thing before him, one of the huge ettins. The creature's rumbling growl shook his bones. Vansen brought his ax down hard on its head even as it reached for Jasper, but the ax bounced off the plated skull without doing any discernible damage. Ignoring him, the ettin closed one of its huge, bearlike paws around Jasper, lifting the small man off the ground and bringing him toward its maw. Vansen grabbed at its heavy arms but it knocked him away, flinging him against the corridor wall like a child throwing a doll. He slid to the floor. He was struggling to get back onto his feet to help Jasper when a flash of lightning and booming crack of thunder turned the entire passage into skull-shattering day—a second of the brightest bright light and a piercing, painful thump of sound that felt like two giant hands clapped over his ears, and then Ferras Vansen knew no more.

🍂

A thousand artists could never paint such horror, Matt Tinwright thought as he cowered in a doorway. A thousand poets, all of them a thousand times greater than himself, could never tell it all. Southmarch was under attack. Many of the buildings around Market Square were aflame, but no one was trying to put them out. At least a dozen bodies lay within Tinwright's view, arrows jutting from their backs. The air was full of smoke but he could smell something else as well, an unfamiliar odor, sweet yet nauseating as decaying flesh. It made his eyes burn and his throat and chest ache.

Dozens of strange armored shapes continued to fire arrows down into the square from atop the huge thorny black trunks that had grown across the water and over the wall. Other invaders had already clambered down on ropes and had slaughtered dozens of other hapless Southmarchers before Durstin Crowel and his guards had managed to push them back. Small knots of fighting had spread all over the square, men and monsters hacking each other in a strange near-silence: even the screams of the wounded and dying seemed muted, as though the smoke hanging in the air somehow muffled the cries.

Hendon Tolly was here in Market Square, too, and fighting fiercely, his black surcoat with the red boar clearly visible across the square, the black plume in his helmet waving like another puff of smoke. The castle's lord protector stood high in the stirrups of a great warhorse, swinging a sword and shouting to his companions as they milled around him in the chaos of the fight. They had driven most of the attackers back into the shadows of the giant thorns, shadows that grew larger as the sun dropped down behind the western walls, but they could not make the Qar retreat and more of the fairy-warriors were now swarming across from the mainland on the thorn bridges.

Another thin shout went up from the castle folk who were struggling, like Tinwright, to get away from the fighting. A vast shape on a heavy battle charger had just come clanking into the square with another troop of soldiers, these armored and caparisoned in the crimson and gold of Landsend. It was Avin Brone, up and fighting despite his age and illness, looking a little like a teapot in his rounded cuirass, his beard halfway down his chest. The old man swung an ancient two-handed sword as he rode into the knot of fairies around Hendon Tolly with his men close behind, forcing the enemy to break and scatter. A few of the Southmarch folk cheered to see it.

Still, it seemed all but hopeless. Tinwright knew he should be fighting, but he had no weapon and no knowledge of how to use one. In any case, he was terrified.

I'm a poet! And a coward—I know nothing of war! I should never have come back! But Elan M'Cory and Tinwright's mother had left everything behind here when they fled to the safety of the inner keep, including the money he had given them—money Matt Tinwright could not afford to lose. *But now I shall be dead for the sake of a couple of starfish. Why wasn't I born rich . . . ?*

More Twilight People were dropping from the huge black trunks like beetles tumbling out of a rotten log. For a moment it seemed the newcomers might overwhelm the couple of hundred Southmarch soldiers, but whatever else his faults, Hendon Tolly was no coward: he and several of his men held the attackers off as Berkan Hood, the lord constable, rounded the rest of the defenders into some kind of order and began to back them away across the square in slow retreat, shields raised so that the fairy arrows bounced harmlessly away.

"Fall back!" came Brone's muted voice. "Fall back to Raven's Gate!"

Some of the noncombatants had realized what was happening and were running along the arcades at the edge of Market Square, urging all who were hiding there to flee over Market Road Bridge to the inner keep before the guards closed and secured the gate.

Can it be? Tinwright's heart felt as heavy as lead. *They are surrendering the outer keep entirely?*

A moment later he realized that if he didn't move quickly he would be part of what was surrendered. The colonnade along his side of the square was blocked with abandoned carts and other rubbish left behind by the terrified residents when the attack began; Tinwright had no choice but to wrap his arms over his head and run across the open cobbles as fast as he could, positive that any moment he would feel the horrible pain of the arrow that would take his life.

A few missed shots skittered across the stones beside him, but he reached the crowd on the bridge and ducked past a wagon some fool was trying to bring across as soldiers screamed and tried to shove the creaking cart back off the bridge. Protected for a moment by the bulk of the thing, Matt Tinwright joined the panicky crowd as they struggled over Market Road Bridge and up the hill toward the gate to the inner keep, packed so close together that he could smell the sharp, ugly stink of other people's fear.

25

Into Sleep

"It is said that the fairies known as the Dreamless go abroad only at night, and that they steal the dreams of mortal men because they have none of their own. It is also said that the Dreamless make pets from the ghosts of mortals who have died without a Trigonate blessing and use them for a hunting pack."

—from "A Treatise on the Fairy Peoples of Eion and Xand"

THE CLOUD OF DARKNESS covered a sizeable portion of the sky above the river by the time Barrick began to see the first bridges across the Fade, signs of the approaching city. At first he didn't even realize the asymmetrical shapes were bridges because they seemed to be jagged slabs of natural stone eroded by wind and water. As he saw more of Sleep he came to realize that this was the way of the Dreamless: their most careful constructions looked like preposterous accidents, with scarcely a straight line to be found anywhere.

The Fade itself was becoming busier, too, although all the boats and ships they saw, small or large, rowed by gray-skinned Dreamless or headless blemmies like the one laboring in their own craft, seemed to pass in funereal silence. There was no question, however, that the occupants of the other boats noticed Barrick and Pick: even the humblest Dreamless fisherman stared at the Sunlanders as though they had never seen anything so odd and so unpleasant in their long lives.

"Why do they look at us like that?" Barrick whispered. "Like they hate us?"

Pick shrugged, then lifted his bowl over the side to get more water for his master. "They do not love our kind, of course."

"But you said there were many of us kept here as servants."

"Oh, yes, Master keeps many. Not all are wimmuai, either. Some came from the Sunlands like you and I."

"Then why are the Dreamless staring at us?

Pick paused as he was crawling back under the tent on the deck. "I'm sure they are only staring at our boat because it belongs to Qu'arus. Perhaps they wonder why they do not see him—he is well known to many in Sleep."

After that the man in the patchwork clothes returned his attention to his dying lord and would not answer anymore questions.

Soon they reached the first of the darklights, a beacon atop a high-backed bridge that appeared to be a cauldron steaming out pure blackness—not a cloud, like smoke, but something thinner and less tangible, a stain that spread across the gray day. It stretched across them like a shadow as they neared the bridge and then slid past it. Barrick felt a chill seize his heart.

As the labyrinth of the city began to grow around them the gloom grew deeper. They passed more and more darklights, perched atop bridges or leaking from sconces on rough walls. The world became darker and darker, as though night had finally fallen over the shadowlands, but it was a curious sort of night that stretched in pools from the darklights instead of arising everywhere and equally: for a long time twilight still hung over their heads, gray sky glaring through the spaces between the somber darklights as distinctly as bright noon. Soon enough, though, there were no more spaces: the twilight had vanished altogether, hidden behind a curtain of inky darkness.

And with full dark came the Dreamless themselves, spilling out like termites from a split log, although at first Barrick could barely make out anything more than dim shapes moving through the streets of Sleep on either side of the river and crossing the bridges overhead, figures gray and indistinct as ghosts. As his eyes became more used to the darklights he could see them better. The color of their skin seemed always the same, but the Dreamless themselves were as different as the Qar he had seen at Kalkan's Field: some of them could have easily passed for human, but others were so disturbingly formed that Barrick could only thank the gods for the robes they wore. He also could not help but feel every single one of the Dreamless was watching him.

The River Fade became a wide, stone-sided canal, its edges entirely covered with docks and buildings, some of them so tall that Barrick could not see their tops above the murk of the darklights. As they slid deeper into the city, the blemmy still tirelessly plying the oars, Barrick felt as though he was being swallowed by something.

The Fade soon began to split into a series of lesser waterways. The blemmy steered down first one, then another, as if it knew exactly where it was going. The smaller the canals, the fewer passersby, until at last Barrick could see nothing else moving in this part of the bleak stone city except their own boat.

They had reached an area of silent marble buildings that were almost impossible to see clearly through the darkness. Huge willows lined the canal bank, long limbs swaying in the breeze, but the entire neighborhood seemed otherwise as lifeless as a mausoleum. The blemmy slowed the boat and then brought it to a stop at an ornate dock jutting several yards out into the water. While Barrick crouched in the stern, surprised by the sudden end to their journey, a crowd of shadowy figures drifted toward them out of the darkness, filling the dock while making no more noise than cats—almost a dozen Dreamless men and women dressed in black. Then one last figure came down the dock and the others made room for her. When she reached the end of the pier she stopped, her hands extended before her as though she walked in her sleep. Pick had folded back the tent. She stared down at Qu'arus where he lay in the bottom of the boat. Barrick thought at first that the Dreamless woman wore some kind of cowl, but then realized that the top of her hairless head was covered in plate, like the shell of a beetle. Her features were slender and mobile—her face looked nearly human but for her corpselike pallor—but much of her exposed skin was covered in bony carapace. He could not be certain because of her strange, Dreamless eyes, but he thought she had been crying.

When she spoke her voice was soft, though the language itself was harsh. The brief words could have been either a blessing or a curse for all that Barrick could understand them.

Pick looked up at her with a strange sort of satisfaction on his face. "I have brought him home, Lady."

She stood silently for a moment, then turned and moved back up the dock, her filmy black garment billowing around her ankles like mist. Several of the others lifted Qu'arus from the boat with Pick's help, then carried him along the dock after her, then up the steps toward what Barrick now saw was a great, dark house.

"Come inside quickly," Pick whispered. "It will be Repose soon—the skrikers will be out." After this incomprehensible warning he hurried up the dock after his master's body. Another servant, whose gray skin was as wrinkled as a wasp's nest, had tied a rope around the blemmy's waist and led it off through the willows and around the side of the squat, stony house. Barrick looked down at the place where Qu'arus had lain and saw for the first time that a gray wool cloak had been folded beneath him, no doubt by Pick to protect his master from the hard boards of the deck. Barrick lifted it and something fell out of the cloak and back into the boat with a clatter, making him look around in fear, but he was alone on the dock. The thing that had fallen was a short sword in an unadorned black scabbard. When he drew it Barrick saw with approval that its edges were sharp as a shaving razor, the kind of weapon he had not had since he had fought the Qar with Tyne Aldredge. He wrapped it back up in the cloak, then looked around for a place to hide them both. Something rustled beside him and he jumped, so startled that he almost dropped both objects into the river.

"Not going in, us hopes," croaked Skurn, tucking his wings. "Not into a Night Man house."

"What else am I going to do? At least I might learn something about where Crooked's Hall might be. Maybe I'll even get something to eat that won't have too many legs."

"As you wishes, then." The raven leaped up onto the rail of the slowly rocking boat and turned his back on Barrick. "Stay out here, us will. Not for us, a nasty mazy place like that."

Like much of what Barrick had seen of the city of Sleep, the house of Qu'arus was as intricate as the interior of a seashell, a succession of mostly windowless hallways, the stone walls sometimes rough, sometimes smooth, but always damp. Moss grew on the gray stone and in certain corners water dripped to the floor to be carried away down shallow sluices, but the moss also grew on white marble statues of incredible delicacy, and the water gurgled down hallways next to sumptuous carpets that bore tangled yet beautiful designs in stark black and white. He could see all of this only because of the small, pearlescent green hemispheres set low in the walls and along some of the passageway floors, which Barrick assumed at first were some kind of luminous stones, but soon realized were actually mushrooms.

He caught up with the servants carrying Qu'arus' body in the main hallway. The house was unpleasant, the near-silence disturbing, and the darkness oppressive. Had it not been for the changes the Sleepers had somehow made in him he would have been beside himself with unease—nothing could make him like this house: after only moments inside it he wanted badly to get out again. Still, he knew almost nothing of the city outside, let alone where he needed to go. What was it the Sleepers had told him?

"There is only one way you can reach the House of the People and the blind·king before it is too late—you must find Crooked's roads, which will fold your path before you so that you may step between the world's walls. You must find the hall in Sleep that bears his name."

Pick had not heard of a place called Crooked's Hall, but perhaps some of the other servants might know of it. He hoped so—Barrick couldn't imagine interrupting the mourning of the stony-faced lady of the house to ask directions.

In the past he might have despaired, but now he felt the new strength in his crippled arm, the way it moved without pain. He thought, *Anything is possible. I am a story now, like Anglin the Islander, and no one can say what the ending will be—not even these unsleeping monstrosities . . .*

"Come with me!" Pick had turned away from the others and was tugging on Barrick's arm. "We'll go to the servant quarters. You will be less obvious there."

"Less obvious? I thought they were used to Sunlanders."

Pick hurried him down a spiraling hallway. "Things are . . . strange here. Different than I expected."

"The master of the house is dead. What did you think to find, a celebration?"

They coiled around and down, passing through a garden of pale fronds, dozens of plants that looked as though they should grow at the bottom of a stream. It might have been the light of the mushrooms, but nothing in the house seemed to have any color.

"In here," said Pick, opening a heavy wooden door and hurrying Barrick through into a huge, low-ceilinged room. The air had a curious, sour stench, but for the first time in Sleep he found himself in something like natural light—the red and yellow flicker of a large fire burning at the center of a wide stone expanse surrounded by what looked like an empty moat. Confined by this stone ditch, draped over logs and perched on piles of stones, were a dozen or more huge black lizards, each the size of a hunting hound.

"By the Three, I thought you said servants' quarters!"

Pick pulled at his arm again. "We share the fire. The Dreamless do not care for too much warmth and light. See?"

At the far side of the wide chamber something close to a dozen man-shaped figures sat huddled together in the shadows. Like his guide, they all wore clothes made of rags and patches, and for the first time Barrick realized that Pick did not dress that way by choice: the human servants had clearly been given household rags and had made their own clothes from them. Despite the stinking heat of the room he felt a chill. "I thought you said Qu'arus valued his Sunlanders."

"He did! No other Dreamless will even have them."

Barrick whirled on the tattered man. "You told me our kind were common here."

Pick looked frightened. "In the house of Qu'arus, we are."

"You lied to me."

"I . . . I did not tell you all the truth. I was afraid to return alone." He lowered his voice. "Please, don't be angry with me, friend."

Barrick could only stare at the man in astonishment. He wanted to strike the miserable creature, but reminded himself that things could have been much worse: at least he had happened onto perhaps the one house in all Sleep where he could enter without being murdered.

One of the figures along the wall stirred. "Who's that with you, Beck?"

Barrick raised an eyebrow. "Beck? So you did not even tell me your true name?"

" 'Pick' is how Master says it—that is what he calls me. I did not lie."

"Who have you brought?" the man in the corner asked again. "Come where we can see you."

The man apparently called Beck made his way over to the others. As they whispered among themselves, Barrick shook his head and followed. The other sunlanders sat on loose straw, which they had piled together in one place to make a sort of nest. Except for the one who was talking with Beck, the rest looked as though they were half asleep, their eyes empty, their faces slack; a few looked up incuriously as Barrick approached but the rest did not even raise their eyes.

"Ah, the water flows thinner now, I see," said the bearded man beside Beck. He looked Barrick up and down from beneath long, straggling brows. "And the birds fly farther."

"What is that supposed to mean?" Barrick demanded, settling down into the straw. The stranger had a long, wispy gray beard and the lines in his face looked as deep as if they had been carved with a knife in soft wood.

"That the gods see all." The old man nodded briskly. "All they see will be."

"Finlae used to be a priest," Beck said. "He knows a lot of things."

"I know too much," Finlae said. "That is why the gods shot an arrow into my brain to set my thoughts on fire. Because I saw their tricks and sang the stories for the people. I warned them. But they laughed and threw stones and bones. Stones and bones!"

Barrick shook his head. Small wonder that Beck had lied to bring him back—the company of this old madman must become rather unfulfilling after a while. He looked at the other servants—or slaves, to put the right name on it—and saw little in the way of intelligence in their staring eyes. If they had been bred like cattle, as Beck had suggested, then the breeder had done his work well. They seemed as stupidly placid as any barn full of milkers.

"Where is Marwin?" Beck asked.

Finlae shook his head. "Carrying jugs and jars up from the cellar. All day the lady was weeping, but only I could hear it. And now they prepare the feast. To send the master's soul to the other side on tears and smoke." He turned and fixed Barrick with his weirdly bright eyes. "You have traveled sleeping to the between. He will travel sleepless to the beyond."

Barrick let his head ease back against the wall and closed his eyes. All he wanted to do was rest, perhaps sleep for a few hours, and then leave this den of madmen behind. Nothing here would help him—certainly not Beck or the demented old creature named Finlae.

He came struggling up out of the darkness when he felt a touch on his face—his hand, his injured hand, shot up and grabbed. Somebody—Beck, he realized, it was Beck—whimpered with pain.

"Don't . . . hurt me."

"Why did you touch me?"

"I . . . I know you."

He opened his eyes wide. Beck was cowering down on the straw. Old Finlae had fallen asleep. "What are you talking about? Of course you know me—I came here with you."

"I know you . . . from before. What is your name?"

He narrowed his eyes. "Why should I tell you?"

"I know you! I have seen you before. We have . . . I think we have met. In . . . in the *before* . . ."

He realized he was still squeezing Beck's fingers in his own, hard enough that the other man was grimacing in pain. He let go. "In the before? You mean before you came here?" It was possible, he supposed. It was not as though he had been unknown in the world on the other side of the Shadowline. And what harm was there in admitting it now? "My name is Barrick. Barrick Eddon. Do you still think you know me?"

A look of nothing less than gratitude swept across the other man's face. "By the gods, yes! I remember! You are . . . you are the prince! By the Three, yes, you are the prince!"

"Not so loud! Yes, I am." But it was strange—he did not feel much like it. In the past, for all his unhappiness, he had never doubted that he was the son of a king. Now it seemed to be someone else's life, a story he had heard but never lived himself.

"You and your sister . . ." Beck flapped his hands in excitement. "You spoke to me. You asked me questions. After the first time . . ." His face fell. "After the first time I saw the Twilight folk."

"If you say so." Barrick had no recollection of the man.

"Do you truly not remember? My name . . ." he paused, squinting. Clearly he had not summoned the memory in some time. "My name is Raemon Beck."

The name meant nothing to him, but Barrick liked it better that way: he wanted no more reminders of the past. He could remember quite a bit from what Beck called "the before"—names, faces—but the memories were distant and curiously flat, with little feeling attached to them, like the diminished ache of a very old wound. Even thoughts of his sister, which seemed as though they should mean more, seemed instead to be something that had been stored so long it had lost all savor. And Barrick was more than content to leave things that way.

"What are those creatures?" he asked suddenly, pointing at the black lizards, which lay clustered around the flames in the center of their pit like Kernios' slaves in the underworld. "Why are they here?"

"Salamanders—fire lizards. They are Master's pets. He likes . . . he liked to feed them."

Better than he fed you, I'll wager, Barrick thought but did not say.

Raemon Beck had more questions about how the prince had crossed the Shadowline, but Barrick would not be drawn into idle talk and eventually Beck gave up; soon the only sound was the crackling of the fire and old Finlae's thin snoring.

In his dream—for it must be a dream, he realized, even though he did not remember falling asleep—the lizard's eyes were as bright as the flames around it. The black-armored creature sat not beside the fire but *in* it, crouched in a split log that burned and blackened in the depths of the blaze.

"*Who are you that comes here without Tile or Pool?*" it asked him in a voice like music.

"I am a prince, son of a king," he told the creature.

"*No, you are an ant, son of another ant,*" the salamander lazily informed him. "*An insect with the gift of a little power coursing in your veins, but still an insect for all that. Hurrying here and there, soon to die. Perhaps you will see my return. That will be a glory that might lend your small life some meaning.*"

He wanted to curse this cruel, arrogant creature, but the lizard's stare held him prisoner, as helpless as if he truly were the small, creeping thing it had named him. His heart felt cold in his chest. "What are you?"

"*I am and I always was. Names do not matter to my kind. We know who we are. It is only your kind, with blinkered senses and swift lives, who insist on the tyranny of names. But no matter what your wise ones believe, you cannot command something simply by naming it.*"

"If we matter so little, why are you talking to me?"

"*Because you are a curiosity, and although I do not have long to wait now, I have been forced to remain idle for longer than I would like. I am bored, and even a crawling ant can provide amusement.*" Its tail whipped a little from side to side, knocking up a spray of sparks. The crackling of the fire seemed to be getting louder—Barrick could barely hear the last of the salamander's words.

"I would kill you if I could," he told the creature.

The laugh was as beautiful as the voice, singing and silvery. *"Can you kill the darkness? Can you destroy the solid earth or murder a flame? Ah, you entertain me most graciously . . ."*

But now the noise of the blaze had become as loud as someone else speaking—no, more than one person. The fire spoke with several voices, the tongues of reddish light leaping up and enveloping the black lizard completely.

" . . . When a poor man is trying to sleep," one of the voices said. "Burbling and bubbling."

"Shut your mouth, Finlae," Beck said.

"But why would they want to do that?" said a voice Barrick hadn't heard before. "They do no harm . . ."

Barrick opened his eyes. Raemon Beck and ancient Finlae were talking to a third man, a large fellow with his hair chopped in uneven swathes like hastily-cut hay.

"You misheard," Beck told the newcomer, then saw Barrick sitting up. "This is Marwin."

"I *knew* someone named Marwin," the big man said slowly. He had an accent a little like what Barrick had heard of Qu'arus. "That's all I said. Could be it was me, but I can't remember."

"Exactly," Beck said. "Your memory is bad and your ears aren't much better, so you must have been mistaken about what you heard just now."

The new man turned to Barrick. "I'm not. Mistook, that is. They were talking about them lizards—Master's sons and Master's brother, they were talking to the mistress. 'Then get rid of them,' she says. 'I can't stand the way they smell or the way they talk.' Then the menfolk went to get clubs and spears."

"See?" said Beck. "Marwin is a dullard and he gets everything wrong. Why would she say that? Lizards can't talk."

For an instant Barrick remembered something about a talking lizard—had it been a dream?—then the hairs on the back of his neck began to tingle. "You heard them say 'lizards'?" he asked.

Marwin shrugged his wide, sloping shoulders. "They said, 'o hasyaak k'rin sanfarshen'—that means 'animals in the cellar.'" He looked around the broad, firelit chamber, frowning. "And this is the cellar."

"You fools." Barrick scrambled to his feet, his heart suddenly thumping in his chest. "They are not talking about some filthy lizards—they're talking about us."

"They would not hurt us!" Beck's dirty face had gone quite pale. "Master loved us!"

"Even if he did, your master is dead."

"When I came out of the trees he sang to me with his eyes," Finlae said.

"I don't doubt it—but I don't care," Barrick said. "Help me out of here, Beck. The rest of you may stay and die if you wish."

"But I'm so *tired*," said Marwin like a cross child. "I've been a-working all the day. I want to sleep."

"Tired, yes." Finlae scratched his bearded chin. "The days are long since Zmeos was banished . . ."

Barrick did not have the time or strength to waste. He grabbed Raemon Beck by the collar and dragged him to his feet. "Then enjoy your sleep. I fear it will be a long one."

Beck still looked befogged as Barrick dragged him toward the door, as though he couldn't quite understand what was happening, but Barrick did not bother to explain it to him again. The huge black lizards did not even stir as they went by, but Barrick suddenly remembered the fiery gaze of something he had seen in a dream and hurried Beck past them as quickly as he could.

"*Can you kill the darkness . . . ?*" the thing had asked him.

"Which way?" he whispered when they were in the corridor. Beck didn't answer immediately, but Barrick heard what he thought might be soft footsteps coming toward them down the passage so he pulled the tattered man in the opposite direction. "The boat!" he said into Beck's ear. "Take me to the boat."

Raemon Beck finally seemed to understand the situation. He shook off Barrick's hand and began to lead him through the house's underground corridors. As they hastened down a long hall lined with closed doors, each one marked with a different symbol, a dreadful, raw shriek echoed past them, a sound of terror and pain. Beck stopped as though he had been stabbed to the heart. Barrick shoved him forward.

"That's your loving master's family at work behind us," he said. "Faster! Or we will be next."

Whimpering quietly now, Beck led them out of an unmarked door and into a wide wooden building that was dark but for a single row of the glowing mushrooms. For a moment Barrick was badly startled by what looked like a man waiting on the walkway in front of them, but it was only one of the blemmies. The creature, which had been shackled to a post with a heavy chain and left standing, turned to watch them go by but made no move to stop them. Its wide, dull eyes glinted in the mushroom light; the little round mouth low on its belly puckered and stretched as though the monstrosity were trying to talk. For all Barrick could tell it might have been the same creature that had rowed them to the house of Qu'arus in the first place.

"This . . . this is the boathouse," Beck told him. "But I do not know how to open the river door."

Barrick remembered the cloak and sword he had left in the front of the house. "Is the other boat still out there? The one that brought us?"

"Master's skiff? It could be." Beck was clearly terrified, but doing his best to think. "With everything else that's happening they might have left it to sit there until morning."

"Then let's go look. Can we get there from here?"

For once Raemon Beck didn't waste any time arguing. He led Barrick out of the boathouse and into the greater darkness outside the house, into the darklighted copse of willows that grew along the riverfront. As they rounded the side of the house and sprinted for the dock Barrick thanked whatever gods had chosen to bless him for once that the Dreamless made their houses without windows. He and Beck had a chance to escape before Qu'arus' kin could guess where they'd gone.

It was not to be. Just as he found the cloak and sword Barrick heard voices from around the side of the house: somehow, the Dreamless had found their trail. He hurried out onto the dock, Beck now running right behind him. The black boat still floated there.

"Thank the gods, thank the gods, thank the gods," Barrick murmured. He untied the boat and slid the oars into the oarlocks as quickly and quietly as he could. A faint green glow was bobbing through the willows toward them—most likely a lantern being held by the searchers. Now two more joined it.

"It's the middle of Repose," Beck said frantically. "The skrikers . . . !"

"Curse you, shut your mouth and get in if you're coming!" When the man still hesitated Barrick began to shove the boat away from the dock with his hands. This helped Raemon Beck make up his mind. He jumped awkwardly into the skiff, setting it pitching so badly Barrick cuffed him on the head in anger even as he struggled to keep the man from tumbling overboard.

"Get down, you fool!" he hissed. With Beck huddled near his feet, Barrick dipped the oars into the water and began rowing as quietly as he could. The shadowy mass of the house of Qu'arus and the flickering lights of their pursuers slid away behind them.

Barrick didn't stop or even slow until they had followed a series of branching canals far enough that even the darklights began to fade and the twilight to reassert itself. As he leaned on the oars catching his breath, exhausted but marveling at the new strength of his formerly crippled arm, he saw that Raemon Beck was weeping.

"By the Three, man, you can't be sorry to leave those people," he snapped. "They would have killed you! They've probably already done for your friends." He himself felt almost nothing in the way of regret. He would never have been able to herd Finlae and slow-witted Marwin out of the house in time. They would have all been caught and Barrick's own mission would have failed. A simple choice. "Beck? Why the tears? We're out."

The man looked up, his thin, dusty face streaked by tears. "Don't you understand? That's what frightens me! We're out!"

Barrick shook his head. "You make no sense."

"It's Repose. The time when all the Dreamless shut themselves inside their houses."

"All the better. How long does it last? We might find Crooked's Hall before they come out again . . ."

"You fool!" The man's eyes filled with tears again. "The skrikers are out—they're a thousand times worse than any Dreamless!" He reached out and grabbed Barrick's arm. "Don't you understand? It would be better if we were back in Qu'arus' house, beaten to death by his sons, than for the Lonely Ones to find us." He stared out over the water. "It would be better if we had never been born."

PART THREE
PALL

26
Born of Nothing

*"It is said that perhaps the most powerful among the many tribes of the
Qar are the Elementals, although no mortal man has yet seen one.
They are few in number, according to Ximander, Rhantys, and others,
but said to be as invisible as the wind and capable of tricks no other
fairy can play . . ."*

—from "A Treatise on the Fairy Peoples of Eion and Xand"

PRINCE ENEAS LEFT HER when they reached the front doors
of Broadhall Palace. "I hope you will forgive me," he told Briony.
"I have duties to my troops and we are later than I had thought we
would be."

"Of course. Thank you so much for coming with me, your Highness.
I hope I did not cause you too much trouble or offense."

His expression was indeed a bit troubled, but he did his best to smile
before he bent to kiss her hand. "You are a most unusual woman, Briony
Eddon. I do not know exactly what you have brought to us, but I can
sense things here in Tessis will never be the same."

Oh, dear, she thought. "I only wish to do my best for my family and
my people."

"As do we all," the prince said. "But your path seems a bit stranger
than most." He smiled again; this time it seemed more genuine. "Stranger,
but also more interesting. I would like to speak more of this and . . . other

matters soon. Will I see you at supper tonight? Perhaps we could walk in the garden afterward and talk."

"As you wish, Prince Eneas." But what Briony really wanted was some time on her own—time to think. Could her brother really be alive, or was she making too much of a strange message in the Funderlings antiquated drum language? But if it was true, then what was she doing here in a foreign land? She should be at his side, ruling Southmarch or fighting against the Tolly usurpers. Dawet dan-Faar had been right: the Eddon family could expect no loyalty from their subjects unless the people could see that the Eddons were loyal to them. But did she dare to go back without an army, simply because of a single, confusing message?

Of course not—too much is at risk for such foolishness. I must be patient. But it was hard, of course, and even more so now that there was a chance Barrick might be waiting for her in Southmarch.

"It's not enough to think you're a leader," her father had always said—*"you must think like a leader. You must honor the people who risk their lives for you— honor them every day, in your thoughts and your deeds."*

The memory made her feel ashamed. She had not been to see Ivvie all day—the friend who had almost died for Briony's sake. She was exhausted and didn't want to go just now, but a leader could not dishonor a sacrifice like that.

Ivgenia e'Doursos had been given a room of her own for her recuperation, a small, sunny chamber in the southern wing of the palace. Briony suspected that Eneas had ordered it so, and although she feared too many obligations to the prince, she was grateful for this favor.

Ivvie was pale with dark circles under her eyes and a tremor in her hands when she reached up as Briony bent to kiss her. "It is so kind of you to come, Highness."

"Nonsense." She sat down beside the bed and took one of the girl's cold hands in her own. "Lie back. Do you need anything? Where is your maid?"

"She is fetching me more cold water," Ivvie said. "Sometimes I am cold myself, but then other times I feel so hot it is as though I am burning up! She mops my brow and that helps a little."

"I am so angry that I let this happen to you."

Ivgenia gave her a weak smile. "It is not your fault, Princess. Someone was trying to kill you." Her eyes grew wide. "Have they caught him yet?"

Of course, it could just as well be a her, Briony thought. "No. But I'm certain they will find the villain and he will be punished. I only wish it had not happened to you." Briony did not want to speak too much about it for fear of making the girl feel unwell again, so she steered the conversation in another direction, telling Ivvie of her strange trip to meet the Kallikans. By the time Briony had finished the girl's eyes were wide again.

"But who would ever have guessed! Tunnels down into the earth? The same place that I showed you?"

"The same," Briony laughed. "I am beginning to learn the truth of the old saying about oracles in ragged robes."

"And they truly had a message for you from your home in Southmarch? What was it?"

Briony suddenly felt she might have said too much. "Perhaps I exaggerated a bit when I said it was for me. In truth it was almost impossible to tell what it might have meant—I cannot even remember all the words. Something about the Old Ones. I was told that it meant the fairy folk who have besieged the castle—those monsters attacking my home. I can scarcely stand to think about it."

"Your Highness must be in anguish to be so far away from your family and your subjects! That's what I told those stupid women."

"What women?"

"Oh, you know, Seris, the duke of Gela's daughter, Erinna e'Herayas—that group who are always hovering around the Lady Ananka. They came to see me." Ivvie frowned. She looked as though the visit had tired her already. "They were talking and talking about everyone—this one is so fat she has to have three maids to pull her stays tight, that one will never take her hat off because she's beginning to lose her hair. Most unpleasant. They know you're my friend so they didn't say anything foul about you—or at least they didn't come right out and do it—but they were saying that you must be happy to be here in such a civilized place, so far away from all those dreadful things happening in Southmarch. They also said of course you'd want to stay here as long as you could, especially when Prince Eneas himself is paying you such attention."

Briony realized she was grinding her teeth together. "All I think about is getting back to my people."

"I know, Highness, I know!" Now Ivvie looked worried, as though she had done something wrong. Briony fought down the urge to walk out of the girl's sickroom and go straight off to pick a fight with Lady Ananka and her little witches' coven. Instead, she steered the conversation back toward milder matters.

When Ivgenia's maid returned with a pail of water, puffing and muttering and looking quite sorry for herself about having to carry it so far, Briony stood and kissed Ivvie good-bye. She met the prince's physician on the stairs, a bony older man with a brisk, distracted air who was stopping to look in on Ivgenia. "Ah, Princess," he said, bowing. "May I trouble you for a moment?"

"What is it? She is getting better, isn't she?"

"Who? Oh, young Mistress e'Doursos, yes, yes, never fear. No, I only wanted to ask you about Chaven Ulosian. You were his patron, I understand. Do you know his current whereabouts?"

"I have not seen him nor heard anything of him since the night I left Southmarch."

"Hmmm. Pity. I have sent several letters but they are never answered."

"The castle is besieged," she pointed out.

"Oh, certainly, certainly. But ships are landing—other letters have got through. I heard from an old friend there, Okros Dioketian, only a month past."

Briony dimly remembered Okros, a colleague of Chaven's who had treated her brother during his fever. "I am sorry I cannot help you, sir."

"And I am sorry to trouble you, Highness. I hope Chaven is well, but I fear for him. He was always very reliable in the past when I needed an answer from him, very prompt."

By the time she had returned to her own chambers, Briony was full of frustration with her lot and itching to take some action. She burst in on Feival so abruptly that he jumped with a squeak and dropped the letter he was reading on the floor. "I want Finn," she announced.

Feival swept up the sheets of paper. "Want him for what? Zosim's fire, you gave me a start."

"Hurry and send for him. I want to talk to him." She glared at the letter. "What's that? Another admirer for me? Or a threat of death, perhaps?"

"Nothing you want to bore yourself with, Highness." He slipped the pages into his sleeve and stood. He was wearing a beautiful green doublet of slashed silk with gold underlining, and looked every inch the young Tessian nobleman. "I'll fetch him. Have you eaten? There's some chicken under a dish and some good brown bread. There might be some grapes left, as well . . ."

But Briony had begun pacing back and forth and was no longer listening.

"Does everyone in this cursed city think I have my eyes set on marrying the prince?" she demanded.

Finn looked at Feival. "What have you said to her?"

"Nothing! She came back in this temper."

"Do me the courtesy of talking to me, not each other." Still, she stopped pacing and sat in her chair facing Finn, who perched anxiously on the small bench that was ordinarily the resting place of diminutive ladies-in-waiting. "What do people think?"

"Of you, Highness? To be honest, your name is not much on the tongues of the Tessian groundlings, at least on the streets of the neighborhood in which you have so kindly lodged us. Southmarch is much discussed, of course, but that is because of the siege there and the presence of the fairies. The latest news is that the fairies have finally begun their siege in earnest—that they are trying to breach the walls—may the gods protect Southmarch!"

"May they hear all our prayers, yes." Briony made the sign of the Three. "But that is what the message from the Funderlings suggested—that the Qar were no longer content to sit and wait." She felt a momentary lift of her spirits—if the message had been right about that, then perhaps Barrick really had returned!

Finn nodded. "But there are always fools—even now some folk in Syan still do not believe the fairy folk have come back—they dismiss an entire war as exaggeration."

Briony scowled. "I wish they could see what I saw on Winter's Eve, my last night in Southmarch—or hear the stories the soldiers told . . ." Thoughts of that night always troubled her, but of all the strange things that had happened it was something much smaller that tugged at her memory now.

That doctor today talked about how reliable and prompt Chaven is. But that night, he came back after having been gone most of a tennight, without explanation. Where was he? Was Brone right to suspect his loyalty? Why would a man disappear in the middle of such dire happenings and not come back for days . . . ?

"Pay no attention, Highness," Finn was saying. "Such people are fools, we all know it. But you asked us to keep our ears and eyes open so I tell you all we have heard."

"And how about you?" Briony asked, turning to Feival. "You spend a great deal of time out and about in the castle—sometimes I do not see you for hours. I hope my wayward secretary is doing more than simply following the handsome young page boys."

She thought it was to Feival's credit that he still had the grace to color a bit. "I . . . I hear many things, Highness, but as Finn says, so much of it is simply the babbling of fools . . ."

"Do not explain it to me, please, simply relate it. What are the courtiers saying?"

"That . . . that you are determined to have Eneas as your husband. Those are the more . . . honorable rumors." He rolled his eyes. "Truly, Highness, it is all rubbish . . ."

"Continue."

"Others say that you have your sights set on a . . . a higher target."

"What does *that* mean?"

"The king."

Briony bounced up out of her chair, her wide skirts nearly sweeping the dishes and cups from the low table. "What? Are they mad? King *Enander?* What would I want with the king?"

"They ask, what more certain way to get your throne back than to . . . to flaunt yourself to the king? Forgive me, Briony—Highness—I am only saying what I hear!"

"Go . . . on." She was squeezing the fabric of her dress so hard that she was ruining the velvet.

"Feival is right," Finn said. "You should not concern yourself with such dreadful gossip . . ."

She raised her hand to silence him. "I said, *go on*, Feival."

He looked strangely angry at having to pass on this news. "Some of the folk of the court are suggesting that your idea from the first was to take Lady Ananka's place, to use your youth and your position to catch the king's eye. And there are uglier rumors, many of which you have already heard. That you and Shaso tried to steal the Southmarch throne.

That your brother Kendrick's death was . . . was your fault." He wrapped his arms across his chest like a furious child. "Why do you make me say such things? You know the poison people can spout."

Briony threw herself back down in her chair again. "I hate them all. The king? I would sooner wed Ludis Drakava—at least he is an honest villain!"

Finn Teodoros clambered from the bench and kneeled beside her, not without difficulty. "Please, Highness, I beg you, mind your words! You are surrounded by spies and enemies here. You do not know who might be listening."

"Murder my sweet Kendrick?" She was fighting tears now. "Gods! I wish I were the one who had died instead!"

After Finn Teodoros left Feival seemed almost as agitated as Briony herself. He went to the writing desk and sat for a while staring at the household accounts, but soon was up again and tidying things that didn't need to be tidied.

Briony, who had finally begun to calm a bit, was not in the mood to watch Feival Ulian march back and forth across the small sitting room. Between her confusion over Eneas, the Funderlings' message, Ivvie's illness and a dozen other matters she had more than enough to trouble her peace. She was considering going out to walk in the palace gardens and enjoy the last bit of evening light when Feival came and sat down across from her.

"Highness, may I speak with you? I truly must say something." He took a breath. "I think . . . I wish . . . I think you should leave Tessis."

"What? Why?"

He straightened his stockings. "Because it is too dangerous for you. Because twice someone has tried to kill you. Because the people here in court are liars and traitors—you can trust no one."

"I trust you. I trust Finn."

"You can trust no one." He got up and began to walk around the room, picking up and replacing things he had already moved several times. "Because everyone has a price."

Briony was astonished. "Are you trying to tell me something about Finn?"

He turned, his face red with what looked like anger. "No! I am trying to tell you that this place is a nest of serpents! I know! I hear them talk every day—I see what they do! You are too . . . too good for this place, Briony Eddon. Go away. Don't you have family in Brenland? Go to them instead. That's a small court—I've been there. People aren't so . . . ambitious."

She shook her head. "What are you talking about, Feival? If I didn't know you, I'd think you had lost your mind. Brenland? My mother's family? I've scarcely even met them . . ."

"Then go somewhere else." Feival turned back to her, his face distraught. "This is a terrible place."

He went out then and shut himself in the tiny room, little more than a closet, where he had his bed. He would not explain what had upset him so, and by the next day seemed too embarrassed even to discuss the incident.

❧

Qinnitan awoke dizzy and unhappy and sick to her stomach. Half a tennight had passed since she and the nameless man had left Agamid and her life had settled into a familiar round of misery.

Her ankle was tied to a short length of rope knotted around one of the cleats on the boat's rail. She could stand up and stretch, and sit awkwardly on the gunwale to urinate, but if she let herself fall overboard she would only dangle helplessly a little way above the water until someone pulled her back. Now that Pigeon was gone and her captor could not compel her with the boy's life, he was making certain she could not kill herself. He was going to give her to the autarch alive, whether she wanted it or not.

Her tormentor had allies now, as well. The survivors of the fire, decimated and now without a ship, were waiting in Agamid for the rest of the autarch's fleet to arrive, so her captor had been forced into other arrangements. This fishing shallop he had hired came complete with a dour captain named Vilas and his two thick-bodied sons. All three of them were burned brown by long exposure to sun, but still somehow gave the impression of dampness and stickiness, as if they had crawled from under a tidepool rock. They also shared a family trait of a single thick eyebrow and seemed to speak only gutter Perikalese, a language that her captor could understand but which sounded to Qinnitan like they were constantly clearing their throats to spit. Except for leering at her whenever the nameless man was looking away, the three fishermen seemed utterly uninterested in her: the fact that she was clearly a prisoner did not bother them in the least.

So Qinnitan had little to do as the coastline bobbed past but watch and wait . . . and think. As she gnawed the piece of tack one of Vilas' sons had tossed her as offhandedly as if she had been a dog she wondered how long she had until the nameless man handed her over to the autarch. Agamid was days behind them but the Jellonian headlands were still out of sight ahead. Where were they going? If they were following the autarch, why was Sulepis traveling so far north? Surely he would gain more from conquering vast Hierosol with all its treasure and its control of the northern side of the Osteian Sea. Why would the most powerful monarch in the world sail all the way north to the forested hinterlands of Eion?

For that matter, why had the autarch gone to such trouble to take Qinnitan from her family in the first place? It had never made any sense, never once. Why choose a girl for a royal wife whose father was a petty priest? Why do nothing with her or to her except for some kind of bizarre religious instruction?

And why had the northern king Olin taken an interest in her as well? He had been a kind man, but that alone should not have made him single her out from all the other girls working in the Hierosoline stronghold.

Hold a moment. Qinnitan stood, suddenly full of excited thought, but within two steps she had come to the limit of the rope that bound her. She swallowed her frustration, determined to hang onto the thought. The autarch had chosen her for something that she had never understood. Now he was heading north, up the coast of Eion. The foreign king, the prisoner, had thought he recognized something in Qinnitan—a resemblance, had he said? Was that where the autarch was going—to the land of the foreign king, Olin? Was that where everyone was headed?

It still made no real sense, but for that moment, out on the featureless, trackless ocean and surrounded by enemies, she felt as though she had touched something true.

With nothing to do and little to eat Qinnitan did not sleep well. At night she often huddled in her thin blanket for hours, trying to push away imaginings of what the autarch had in store for her as she waited for the blessed release of sleep. In the mornings she kept her eyes closed long past the time she was completely awake, listening to the keening of seabirds and praying to fall asleep again, to flee back into oblivion for even a short time, but it seldom happened. Often she woke while even her captor was still asleep, only Vilas or one of his sons on duty at the tiller.

After a few days of watching her nameless jailer Qinnitan came to realize he was a creature of patterns: he woke up every morning at the same time, just as the first coppery light of dawn was bleeding up from the eastern horizon. Then, directly after waking each day he put himself through a series of stretching movements, going from one to the other with the predictability of the great clock in the Orchard Palace's main tower, as though he were made of wheels and gears instead of flesh and blood. Then, as Qinnitan watched through slitted eyes, pretending to be asleep, this pale, unexceptional man who held her life in his hands would take a small black bottle out of his cloak, pull out the stopper, then dip what looked like a needle or a tiny twig into the bottle before withdrawing it and licking whatever he had drawn out. The container would then be stopped with great care and bottle and needle would disappear into his cloak once more. He would then generally eat some dried fish and drink a little water. Morning after morning the stretching rituals and the bottle continued, unchanged.

What was in the black glass container? Qinnitan had no idea. It looked like poison, but why would a man take poison by his own choice? Perhaps it was some powerful physic. Still, even though she could make little sense of it, the ritual was something to think about—to think about long and carefully. With nothing else left to her she had begun to hoard ideas like a miser hoarded coins.

Qinnitan lay silent, eyes closed, but she had grown so sensitive to changes in the hour and temperature that she could feel the first warmth of approaching morning push gently against her chill face.

How could she escape from her captor? And, if that failed, how could she end her life before he gave her to the autarch? She would welcome even as horrid a death as Luian's—the strangler had at least been relatively quick. It was what the autarch's servants would do to her while she lived that terrified her . . .

Her thoughts were interrupted by the quiet clink of the stopper being pushed back into the black bottle, and then by the even more surprising sound of her captor's voice.

"I know you are not asleep. Your breathing is different. Stop pretending."

Qinnitan opened her eyes. He was staring at her, his own eyes strangely bright, glittering as though with some secret jest. As he tucked the bottle away in his cloak the wiry muscles moved like snakes beneath the skin of his forearms. He was horribly strong, she knew that, and quick as a cat. How could she hope to get away from him?

"What is your name?" she asked for perhaps the hundredth time. He watched her, his lip minutely curled in amusement or contempt.

"Vo," he said abruptly. "It means 'of.' But I am not 'of' anything. I am the end, not the beginning."

Qinnitan was so startled by this little speech that for a moment she could think of nothing to say. "I . . . I don't understand." She struggled to keep her voice calm, as if it was nothing unusual for this silent killer to divulge something about himself. "Vo?"

"My father was from Perikal. His father was a baron. The family name was 'Vo Jovandil,' but my father disgraced it." He laughed. There was something wrong with him, she thought, something strange and feverish. Qinnitan was almost afraid to continue. "So he cut off his last name and went to war. He was captured by the autarch and became a White Hound."

Even to Qinnitan, who had lived much of her life in the isolation of the Hive and the Seclusion, the name of the autarch's troop of northern killers was enough to make her heart skip a beat. So that was why a white man from Eion spoke such perfect Xixian. "And . . . and your mother?"

"She was a whore." He said it offhandedly, but he turned his gaze away from her for the first time, looking out at the gleam of sunrise spreading across the horizon like a burning slick of oil. "All women are whores, but she was honest about it. He killed her."

"What? Your father killed your mother?"

Now he turned back to her, his eyes dull with contempt. "She asked for it. She struck him. So he beat her head in."

Qinnitan no longer wanted to keep him talking. She could only raise shaking hands as if to keep such things away from her.

"I would have killed her, too," Vo said, then got up and walked across the gently rocking deck to talk to the old fisherman Vilas, who was minding the tiller.

Qinnitan sat crouched down against the stiff, chill breeze for as long as she could, then clambered along the bench to the rail where she vomited up the meager contents of her stomach. When she had finished she lay with her cheek against the cold, wet wood of the rail. The coastline itself was almost invisible, shrouded by fog, so that the boat seemed to travel through some lonely place between worlds.

Something had definitely changed. In the following days Vo grew positively conversational, at least compared to what he had been. As the shallop crept northward along the coast it became his habit when he finished his morning ritual to talk to her a little. Occasionally he even mentioned places he had been and things he had seen, tiny fragments of his life and history, although he never again spoke of either of his parents. Qinnitan did her best to listen closely, although sometimes it was hard: this man Vo seemed to make no distinction between a meal he ate and a man he killed. There was nothing friendly in his talk, nothing of ordinary interaction. It seemed instead a kind of compulsion that came upon him when he had finished licking the needle, as though whatever lurked inside the poison bottle made him too ecstatic to remain silent. The fever never lasted long, though, and often he was angry and resentful with her later on, giving her less food or treating her roughly for no reason, as though she had tricked him into speech.

"Why do you say all women are whores?" she asked quietly one morning. "Whatever the autarch told you of me, I am not that. I am still a virgin. I was training to be a priestess. The autarch plucked me out of the Hive and put me in the Seclusion."

Vo rolled his eyes. The iron control that usually governed his every action seemed to grow slack during that first hour of the morning. "Whoring has nothing to do with . . . coupling," he said, as though the word tasted bad. "A whore sells who she is for protection, or food, or richer things." He looked Qinnitan up and down with blank disinterest. "Women have nothing else to offer but themselves, so that is what they sell."

"And you? What do you sell?"

"Oh, never doubt I am a whore, too," he said and laughed. He clearly did not laugh very often—it sounded awkward and angry. "Most men are, except those who are born with wealth and power. They are the buyers. The rest of us are their sluts and catamites."

"So you would be the autarch's whore, then?" She put as much scorn in her voice as she could muster. "You would hand me over to him, to be tortured and murdered, just to earn his gold?"

He stared at his own hand for a long, silent moment, then held it up before her. "Do you see this? I could snap your neck in a heartbeat, or drive my fingers through your eyes or between your ribs to kill you and there is nothing you could do to prevent me. So *I* own *you*. But here in my gut is something that belongs to the autarch. If I do not do what he commands it will kill me. Very painfully. So *he* owns *me*." Vo stood, swaying a little as swells rolled the boat, and looked down at her vacantly, his feverish mood beginning to fade once more. "Like most people, you waste your time trying to puzzle out the meaning of things.

"The world is a ball of dung and we are the worms that live in it and eat each other." He turned his back on her, pausing only to add: "The one who eats all the others wins—but he is still the last living worm in a lump of shit."

27

Mayflies

"Some scholars believe that the Elementals may be some other kind of creature entirely, less natural even than the fairies themselves."

—from "A Treatise on the Fairy Peoples of Eion and Xand"

FOR LONG MOMENTS Ferras Vansen could only sit and stare into the near-darkness trying to understand what had happened. He was weak and queasy and his head was ringing like a bell, a single continuous chime. Chert Blue Quartz stood over him, mouth working broadly, but Vansen could hear no sound.

Deaf, he thought. *I'm deaf.* And then he remembered the thunderclap that had knocked him from his feet, a crash louder than anything he had heard since the blasting in the pits of Greatdeeps.

He pushed that nightmare memory from his mind and closed his eyes once more. Dizziness picked him up like a boat on a rough current and swirled him around and around. He was suddenly aware for the first time in days that he was really, truly *underground*—deep in a hole beneath the world, with an unimaginable weight of stone between him and the sun. If only someone would take a giant stick and poke a hole through it so he could see the light again, instead of being lost beneath it . . . lost, confused, baffled . . .

" . . . *Throw it farther,*" someone whispered. " . . . *Didn't know . . .*"

Vansen opened his eyes again. Chert was still talking but now he could hear him, although the small man sounded as if he were a hundred paces away. Still, it meant that his hearing was coming back.

The cavern was full of other Funderlings as well, living Funderlings, none of whom Vansen recognized until Cinnabar himself appeared beside him, dressed in armor of a type he had never seen before: the small man was covered with round plates so that he looked a cross between a turtle and a pile of discarded dishes.

"How is he?" the Funderling magister asked Chert. Where had Cinnabar come from? All Vansen could remember was that he hadn't expected to see him anytime soon. For that matter, it seemed strange to him that Chert Blue Quartz was here as well.

"I think he was deafened by the burst." Chert's voice still sounded muffled.

"I'm not deaf," Vansen said, but the Funderlings showed no sign of having heard him. He repeated it, trying to be louder. It seemed to work because both of them turned toward him at the same time. "My hearing is returning," he explained. "What happened?"

"It was all my fault," said Chert, his face creased in worry. "I found some of our blasting powder beetles in the storage hall—we use them to crack rock—and thought, well, I didn't have a weapon, and it might scare the Qar away, so I brought one. When I got here I saw they were all over you, so I lit it, came up behind, and threw the beetle as far as I could." He looked chagrined. "My arm is not as strong as it once was . . ."

"Nonsense!" said Cinnabar. "My men and I would never have arrived in time. Because of you, Master Blue Quartz, the fairies were reeling and confused when we arrived and they couldn't retreat fast enough. You saved Captain Vansen and quite possibly the temple as well!"

Chert looked surprised. "Really . . . ?"

Vansen suddenly remembered the last moments. "Where is Sledge Jasper? Is he . . . ?"

"Alive," Cinnabar assured him. "Ears ringing like yours, but he is not complaining—oh, no. Too weak to complain, in any case. Some of my men are bandaging him—he leaked a lot of blood, but he'll live. There is a fighter who would make the Elders proud!"

Vansen could not quite shake the feeling that he was buried beneath a millionweight of heavy stone. He could move, but every part of him seemed misshapen, unfamiliar, and his thoughts were sluggish. "You said this . . . beetle . . . was full of rock-cracking powder. Is it the stuff called serpentine or gunflour—the same black powder we use for cannons? Is there more of it?"

"Yes, there's more," Chert said. "Nearly another dozen shells in the storeroom, and probably more blasting powder as well. But we have no cannons down here, nor room to shoot them . . ."

A young Funderling in armor hurried up. "Magister Cinnabar, one of the enemy that was smashed up by the blasting powder . . . one of those drows . . . !"

"What, man? Chip it loose and let's have it."

"He's alive."

Strangely, Vansen recognized the captive. The dirty little man staring resentfully up at him was the one who had tried to stab him, and whose wrist he had snapped. Indeed, the shaggy creature was cradling that arm, which was swollen and bruised.

"Can we speak to him?" Vansen asked.

Cinnabar shrugged. "My men have been trying to. He refuses to answer. We know nothing of what tongue he speaks—he may not even understand us."

"Then kill him," Vansen said loudly. "He's useless to us. Cut off his head."

"What?" Chert was shocked. Even Cinnabar looked taken aback.

Vansen had been watching the prisoner carefully: the little man had not flinched, had not even looked up. "I do not mean it. I was just curious whether he was only pretending not to understand. We must think of a way to make him tell us what he knows about his mistress' plans."

Chert still looked suspicious. "What does that mean? Torture?"

Vansen laughed sadly. "I would not hesitate if I thought it would save your family and my people aboveground, but the answers given by a man under torture are seldom useful, especially if we cannot speak his tongue well. But if you think of any other ways, let me know. Otherwise, I may begin to change my mind."

Magister Cinnabar gave directions for the prisoner to be taken back to the temple, then hurried off to supervise the other tasks he had assigned. Those of his reinforcements not gathering up bodies or helping the wounded had already been sent to repair the breach the Qar had made into the Festival Halls.

Vansen rubbed his aching head. He wanted nothing so much as to lie down and sleep. He had been exhausted long before Chert's bursting shell had nearly deafened him, and although his wounds had been washed and bandaged while he was senseless he ached mightily all over. He wanted a drink of something strong and at least an hour in bed, but he was the commander here, more or less, so it would have to wait.

"You said you had a dozen more of the gunflour beetles and more powder," Vansen said to Chert.

"That's what we have at the temple. We have more in Funderling Town, much more. We use it to break up stone when we must work fast—when we are not given time to do things in the old, proper ways . . ."

Vansen had learned more than he really wanted to in the past month about the good old days of wet-wedging and sand-polishing. "Let us talk to Cinnabar about it, then," he said hurriedly. "Perhaps we can prepare a welcome for next time that will make the dark lady and her soldiers think twice about coming into our home uninvited."

❦

Chert did his best to get Vansen to rest—the captain was ribboned with cuts and still clearly not hearing very well—but the big man would not be dragged away from the battlefield, so Chert returned to the temple alone. The Metamorphic Brothers had already heard news of the battle and almost all of them wanted to ask Chert about it, including many who seemed to think of him as a kind of hero. In another time he might have enjoyed the attention but now he was too frightened and weary to want anything but to get back to his room. He had seen some of the Qar forces, however briefly, and he knew there were thousands more of them besieging Southmarch aboveground. He had caught a very small number of these attackers by surprise with a blasting beetle, but next time there would be no surprise. The drows might even have rock-cracking powder of their own.

Chert was almost back to his room when he remembered Flint, whom he had left with the physician. Wearily he turned back up the corridor, but when he got to Chaven's room and rapped on the heavy door nobody answered. When he tried it, the door was not locked or even latched. He pushed it open, suddenly fearful.

Chaven lay stretched full-length on the floor as if he had been stunned with a club; there was no sign of Flint. For a terrible moment Chert thought the physician was dead, but when he kneeled beside him he could hear Chaven moaning quietly. Chert found a basin of cold water and a cloth and splashed water across the physician's broad, pale forehead.

"Wake up!" He did his best to shake Chaven, who was twice his size. "Where is my boy? Where is Flint?"

Chaven groaned and rolled over, then struggled until he could sit by himself. "What?" The physician looked around his room as if he had not seen it before. "Flint?"

"Yes, Flint! I left him with you. Where is he? What happened?"

Chaven looked blank. "Happened? Nothing happened. Flint, you say? He was here?" He shook his head slowly, like a weary horse trying to dislodge a biting fly. "No, wait—he *was* here, of course he was. But . . . but I do not remember what happened. Is he gone?"

Chert almost threw the wet rag at him in exasperation. He quickly searched the small chamber to make sure the boy was not hiding somewhere. He did not find him, but in one corner of the room he discovered a small hand mirror and a stump of candle lying on the floor. He smelled the wick. It had only recently been extinguished.

"What is this?" he demanded of the confused physician. "Did you get up to some of your mirror tricks with him? Did you frighten him into running away?"

Chaven looked both affronted and anxious. "I can't remember, to tell the truth. But I would never hurt or frighten a child, Chert—you should know that."

Chert remembered the boy's cries of terror the last time the fat physician had tried out his mirror-magics. "*Pfah!* He's gone, that's all I know. Have you no idea at all where he might be? How long he's been gone?"

But Chaven was mystified—and useless. He could only look from one corner of the room to another, rubbing his eyes as though the light in the dark room was too bright.

Chert was hurrying through the halls when he suddenly remembered the library. Flint had already got them both into trouble for going there once. What more likely place for him to end up this time?

To his immense relief he found the boy slumped in what seemed like ordinary childish sleep at one of the ancient tables, his head cradled on an irreplaceable book, a centuries-old collection of shallow carvings on sheets of mica thinner than parchment. As Chert lifted the boy's head to slide the pages from beneath him he glanced at the antique writing. He could not read it—it was too old, too strange—but it reminded him of the scratchings he had seen on the walls deep in the Mysteries. What was the boy doing with it? Did he have any sense of what he was up to? Flint acted sometimes as if he was ten times his true age, but at others he seemed nothing more than the child he was.

"Wake up, boy," he said gently. He could forgive almost anything as long as he didn't have to tell Opal he'd lost their child. "Come, now."

Flint lifted his head and looked around, then closed his eyes again as if to go back to sleep. He was far too big for Chert to carry—he was taller than his foster father, now—so Chert had to pull on his arm until the boy got to his feet and reluctantly allowed himself to be led out of the library and back across the temple to the room they shared. For once they seemed to be in luck: Vansen was apparently keeping Brother Nickel and the other monks busy with the temple's defense. Flint's return to the library had apparently gone undetected.

"Why did you do that, boy?" he demanded. "The brothers said to stay out of there—what were you doing? And what happened in Chaven's room?"

Flint shook his head sleepily. "I don't know." He walked on in silence for several paces, then suddenly said, "Sometimes . . . sometimes I think I know things. Sometimes I do know things—important things! And then . . . and then I don't." To Chert's astonishment, the boy abruptly burst into tears, something Chert had never, ever seen him do. "I just don't know, Father! I don't understand!"

Chert wrapped his arms around Flint, hugging this strange creature, this alien child, feeling the boy shake with helpless sorrow. There was nothing else he could do.

He had just got Flint settled in bed when someone rapped at the door. Wearily, Chert got up and opened it to reveal Chaven, wide-eyed in the dark hallway.

"Did you find the boy?" he asked.

"Yes. He is well. He went to the library. I have just put him to bed." He stepped back, beckoned the physician to enter. "Come in and I'll see if I can find us some mossbrew. Do you remember what happened?"

"I cannot," said Chaven. "In truth, I came to bring you a message. Ferras Vansen has sent to say that they have learned how to speak with the Funderling they captured."

Chert lifted an eyebrow. "*I* am a Funderling. That murderous creature is a drow."

Chaven waved his hand. "Of course, of course. Your pardon. In any case, will you come? Captain Vansen asked for you."

He shook his head. "No. I must stay with my boy. Too many things have called me away from him. Besides, there is nothing I can do there to help Vansen. If he truly needs me I will come to him tomorrow." He smiled sourly. "Unless the Qar murder us all before then, of course."

The physician didn't know quite how to take this. "Of course."

When Chaven had left Chert went to look in on the boy. Flint's face was slack in sleep, mouth open, his tousled hair lighter even than citron quartz. *What did all that mean?* Chert wondered. *He knows, but he doesn't know?*

As always, Chert could only wonder at the strange thing he and Opal had brought into their lives, this changeling boy . . . this walking mystery.

Utta pulled at the older woman's arm, trying to hold her back, but her efforts had little effect. Together they slid and slipped in the mud of the main street. Kayyin made a languid move to help them, but they regained their balance.

"I will not be stopped, Sister." Merolanna was breathing hard from the exertion and the cold. Before the Bridge of Thorns had begun to grow the days had actually turned warm, but since the beginning of the monstrous project the entirety of the coastline around Southmarch had been shrouded in chill wet mist, as if summer had entirely passed them by and they had tumbled straight into Dekamene or even later.

"Kayyin, help me," Utta begged. "The dark lady will kill her."

"Perhaps," the Qar said. "But, see—we are all still alive. My mother seems to have lost a bit of her bloodlust in these sad, late days."

"Are you mad, Halfling?" Merolanna said. "Lost her bloodlust! She is killing our people this moment! I can hear the screams!"

Kayyin shrugged. "I did not say she had become a different person entirely."

Merolanna strode on, determined, smacking away Utta's hand when the Zorian sister tried to slow her. "No! She will hear me. I will not be stopped!"

"If Snout and his fellow guards had not been called to the siege," Kayyin said cheerfully, "you would not have gotten out the front door."

Merolanna only showed her teeth in an expression that on someone other than a respectable dowager might have been called a snarl.

The collection of docks and harbor buildings facing the castle's drowned causeway had become a scene of nightmarish chaos. Creatures of dozens of different shapes and sizes hurried back and forth through the fog as the vast, creaking, treelike branches of the Bridge of Thorns loomed over all like the deformed bones of a collapsing temple. Merolanna, mud now spattered halfway up her skirt, did not flinch from even the most grotesque creatures that appeared out of the murk, but stamped along like a determined soldier, headed for the black and gold tent standing by itself at the center of things.

She is brave, Utta thought, *I cannot take that away from her. But the one she seeks is not some ordinary mortal to be cowed by an irate old woman. If what Kayyin said was true, the dark lady herself is older than we can imagine—the child of a god. And sweet Zoria knows that she is angry and vengeful beyond our understanding as well.*

If it had not been for the strangeness of the last year, the mad things she herself had seen, Utta would have dismissed the Qar's talk of gods and Fireflowers and immortal siblings as nonsense . . . but no other answers fit what she had seen and what was all around her this moment! For Utta Fornsdodir, who thought of herself as an educated woman, one who despite her calling could glean the difference between the important truths in the old stories and the superstition and silliness of some of the tales themselves, it had been a shocking and even disheartening time.

Yasammez stood before her tent like a statue of Nightmare, all in spiked black armor, an ivory-white sword hanging naked and unsheathed at her belt. She was watching something Utta could not see in the clouded heights of the thorns and did not turn even when Duchess Merolanna stumbled to a halt in front of her and slowly, painfully, lowered herself to her knees. A thin shrieking that might have been the wind wafted over the silent tableau, but Utta knew it was not the wind. Inside the walls of Southmarch castle, the fairies were killing men, women, and children.

"I cannot take this cruelty any longer!" Merolanna's voice, so firm only moments ago, now had a hitch that was more than fear, Utta sensed: something about dark Yasammez was enough to make the words stumble in anyone's throat. "Why are you murdering my people? What have they done to you? Two hundred years since the last war with your kind—we had all but forgotten you even existed!"

The face of Yasammez turned slowly toward her—an emotionless mask, pale and weirdly beautiful despite the inhuman angles of its bones. "Two hundred years?" the fairy-woman said in her harshly musical voice. "Mere moments. When you have seen the centuries flutter past as I have, then you may talk of time as if it meant something. Your people have doomed mine and now I am returning the favor. You may watch the ending or you may hide yourself away, but do not waste my time."

"Kill me, then," said Merolanna. The hitch in her throat was gone.

"No, Duchess!" Utta cried, but her legs suddenly felt wobbly as spring rushes and she could not move closer.

"Quiet, Sister Utta." The duchess turned back to the angular shadow that was Yasammez. "I cannot simply watch my people die—my nieces and nephews and friends—but I cannot hide from it, either. If you understand suffering as you say you do, end mine." She bowed her head. "Take my life, you cold thing. Torture does not befit a great lady."

Yasammez looked at Merolanna and something like a cold smile played across her face. For a long moment they stood like characters in a play, by appearance a terrifying conqueror and a helpless victim or an executioner and condemned prisoner—but it was nothing quite so simple, Utta realized.

"You should not speak to me of suffering," Yasammez said at last. Her voice was still rough and strange, but lower, softer. "Never. Were I to bring your loved ones here one by one and execute them in front of you, still you should not speak that word to me."

"I don't know what . . ." Merolanna began.

"Silence." The word hissed like a red-hot blade thrust into cold water. "Do you know what you and your wretched kind have done to my people? Hunted us, murdered us, poisoned us like vermin. Those who survived driven into exile in the cold lands to the north, forced to draw the mantle of twilight over themselves like a child hiding beneath a blanket. Yes, you even stole the sun from us! But, cruelest jest of all, you pushed our race to the brink of destruction and then also snatched away our last chance at survival." The pale face tilted forward, black eyes slitted. "Torture? If I could, I would torture every one of you soft mortal slugs, then burn the fat from your bodies while you screamed. Mounds of your charred bones would be your only monument."

The dark woman's hatred was like an icy blast of wind down a mountainside. Utta could not help herself—she let out a little noise of terror.

Yasammez turned on her as if she had noticed her for the first time. "You. You call yourself a servant of Zoria. What beside sentimental nonsense do you know of the white dove—of the true Dawnflower? What do you know of the way her father and his clan tormented her, killed her beloved, then handed her over to one of the victorious brothers as if the goddess of the first light was nothing but a spoil of war? What do you know of the way they tortured her son Crooked, the one you mayflies call Kupilas, until he was willing to give up his own life to rid the world of them? For thousands of years he has suffered to keep the world safe, agonies you and even I cannot imagine. Then think of this—you call him a god . . . but I call him *Father*." Her face, the mask of rage, suddenly went as slack as the features of a corpse. "And now he is dying. My father is dying, my family is dying, my entire race is dying—and you talk to me of suffering."

Utta's legs buckled at last and she sank down into the mud beside Merolanna. In the moment's hush she could again hear the cries of Yasammez' victims across the bay, a chorus of terror that sounded like nothing so much as the screeching of distant seabirds.

The dark lady turned her back on them. "Kayyin, take these things away from me, these . . . insects. I have a war to fight. Tell them the story of how their kind stole the Fireflower and murdered my family. After that, if they still want to die, I will be happy to accommodate them."

28
The Lonely Ones

"In the tome known as **Ximander's Book** *it is written that one family of the Elementals did join forces with the Qar long ago, and that they are called the Emerald Fire. According to Ximander they are a sort of royal guard to the king and queen of the fairies, like the Leopards of the Xixian Autarch."*

—from "A Treatise on the Fairy Peoples of Eion and Xand"

"**T**HE REPOSE . . . SKRIKERS? I don't understand." Barrick took up the heavy oars again and began to row. The weird murk of the darklights lined the river like an arbor of old trees, dense along the bank and stretching high on either side until it finally began to thin far above their heads. "It makes no sense," he growled at Raemon Beck, struggling to keep his voice to a whisper. "Why would the Dreamless shut themselves away for hours each day when they do not sleep? And if everyone's inside, why would they have these skriker things guarding the streets? From what?"

Beck had dried his eyes, but he looked as if he might burst into tears again any moment; the man's weak, puffy face made Barrick angry. "The Dreamless are fairies," Beck said quietly, "and except for my master they aren't kind ones. They trust no one—not even their own kind. As for the Repose, it is their law to lock themselves in, and that is what the skrikers see to. My master Qu'arus used to tell me that his people had to shut themselves away because too much wakefulness made their hearts and their thoughts sick. Before the Law of Repose many of them grew so damaged and secretive that they slaughtered their own families or their neighbors. There still are places where you can see the black ruins of estates that burned to the ground centuries ago with the family and all their servants inside, turned into funeral pyres by those who had grown tired of living . . ."

Barrick felt a disturbing moment of kinship with the Dreamless. How often had he dreamed of his own home in flames? How often had he wished for some disaster to end his pain, little caring who else might be harmed?

He rowed as quietly as he could, but the city was still as a tomb; every splash seemed certain to draw attention. The small waterway they were on came to an end, leaving them no choice but to move into a larger branch of one of the main canals. Three or four other boats were visible on the water, albeit distantly, but Barrick pulled hard on the oars and they managed to slip quickly across the wide waterway and then back onto one of the smaller side streams.

It was tiring to go so fast, though: the boat was twice as big as the sort of two-man skiffs used in Southmarch. Barrick found himself thinking of the headless blemmy that had done the work before—he wished they could have brought one of the horrible things, just to spare himself this backbreaking labor.

Barrick soon discovered that if he kept the skiff away from the dark-lights along the edge of the canals he could actually see fairly well, but the effect was still disturbing: out in the middle of the larger waterways was something like the shadowland twilight he had grown used to, but the banks seemed swaddled in inky black smoke. To see anything of what they were passing he had to move in close, until they were within the penumbra of the darklights and his eyes became accustomed to the deep shadow. But he had no idea whether they could be seen in turn or who might be looking at them.

"We need a place to hide," he told Beck. "Some place no one will find us while we decide what to do next."

"There is no such place," Beck said bleakly. "Not here. Not in Sleep."

Barrick scowled. "And you do not know where Crooked's Hall is, ei-ther. You are as useless as a boar's teats . . ."

At that moment something dropped on them out of the blackness, as though the darklights themselves had spat out part of their essence.

Raemon Beck threw himself down, pressing his face against the deck, but Barrick recognized the clot of shadow and its method of entrance.

"I didn't expect to see you again, bird," he said.

"Us didn't expect to see you, neither . . . not alive, like." The bird bent to groom its chest feathers. "So, how went your guesting with those kindly blue-eyed folk?"

Barrick almost laughed. "As you can see, we've decided to move on. The problem is, Beck here doesn't know where Crooked's Hall might be. We need somewhere to go where we can be safe from the Night Men. And the others . . . what did you call them, Beck? Skrikers?"

"Quiet!" The patchwork man looked around in anxious terror. "Do not name them here where the banks are close by! You'll summon them."

Skurn, who had been standing on one leg at the bow of the boat while he picked something out of his toes, shook himself and fluttered a little closer to Barrick. "P'raps us could fly up and try to see somewhat for you," he said offhandedly. "P'raps."

Barrick couldn't help noticing the overture of comradeship. "Yes, that would be good, Skurn. Thank you." He looked at the pitchy clouds of blacklight along the banks. "Find a place where the darkness is not so thick—an island, perhaps. Unused. Maybe wild."

The black bird flapped upward in a spiral and then leveled out, flying toward the nearest bank.

"My stomach is empty," Barrick said as he watched the raven disappear. "If we take a fish from this water will it poison us?"

Beck shook his head. "I don't think so. But there is already food in the boat. I doubt anyone touched it after we brought my master home. With so many lost on our hunting trip and my master wounded we did not eat it all—a good deal of dried meat and road bread should be left." He crawled forward and found a large waterproof sack folded underneath the foremost bench. "Yes, see!"

The food had a strange, musty taste, but Barrick was far too tired and hungy to mind. They shared a handful of dried meat and two pieces of bread as hard as boot-leather that reminded Barrick of the brown maslin loaves back home.

"And you are truly Prince Barrick!" Raemon Beck had recovered his spirits a bit. "I cannot believe I should see you again, my lord—and here of all places!"

"If you say so. I do not remember our first meeting." In truth, Barrick didn't much want to remember. It was nothing to do with the man in the ragged clothes. He had felt such relief at being separated from all that he had left behind—his past, his heritage, his pain—and he was in no hurry to bring any of it back.

Beck haltingly told him of how his caravan had been attacked by the Qar, he the lone survivor, and how after telling his story he had been summoned to a royal council and then had been sent back again to the same place along the Settland Road. The tale took a long while—Beck's memory had been addled by so much time behind the Shadowline, a stay even longer than Barrick's—and every name he recovered was a victory for him but gave Barrick only pain.

"And then your sister told the captain . . . what was his name? The tall one?"

"Vansen," said Barrick flatly. The guardsman had fallen into blackness defending Barrick's life after Barrick himself had cursed him many times. Was there to be no end to this parade of wretched, useless memories?

"Yes, your sister told him to take me back to where the caravan was attacked. But we never reached it—or I never did. I woke up in the night surrounded by mist. I was lost. I called and called but no one found me. Or at least none of the ones that I traveled with found me . . ." Raemon Beck broke off, shuddering, and would say no more about what had happened to him between that time and the time he was taken in by Qu'arus of Sleep. "He treated me well, did Master. Fed me. Didn't beat me unless I deserved it. And now he's dead . . ." Beck's shoulders trembled. "But I do not think your sister, bless her—forgive me, Lord, I should say Princess Briony . . . I do not think she meant me any harm. She was angry, but I don't think she was angry at me . . ."

"Enough, man. Leave it." Barrick had heard as much as he could bear.

Beck lapsed into silence. Barrick sat hunched in the robe that had cushioned Qu'arus on his dying journey and took up the oars again, rowing just enough to keep them in the middle of the quiet, backwater stream while they waited for the raven's return. The canal was narrow and the houses rose up on either side, scarcely distinguishable from the rough stony cliffs out of which they had been carved, only recognizable as dwellings by the occasional tiny window and the huge, gatelike doors in the walls above the waterline.

Doors, he thought. *More doors in this city than I can count. And all I have to do is find the right one.*

Skurn dropped down out of the dim sky and spread his wings to land on the boat's tall stern. It was easy to forget how big the bird was, Barrick thought—its wingspan nearly matched the spread of a man's arms. The raven did not speak at once, but picked and pruned at his feathers. It was clear Skurn wanted to be asked.

"Have you found us anything? A place to go?"

"Mought be. Then again, moughtn't."

Barrick sighed. Was it any wonder he was mostly alone in the world and preferred it that way? "Then please tell me," he said with exaggerated courtesy. "Afterward, I will thank you fulsomely for your kind service."

Pleased, the raven fluffed himself and stood straighter. "Happens that this is what Skurn has found—a skerry off the great canal, midstream. Trees and such, and only ruins. Us didn't see sign of naught on two legs."

"Good," said Barrick. "And I do thank you. Which direction?"

"Follow us." The raven flapped up again.

As Barrick paddled after the slow-flapping shape, Raemon Beck suddenly said, "Not all the animals here talk. And sometimes even with the ones that do, you're better off not to listen." He shook himself like a wet dog, beset by some evil memory. "Especially when they invite you back to their houses. It's not like one of those children's tales, you know."

"I'll do my best to remember that."

The island was much as Skurn had described, a small, overgrown knot of stone in the middle of one of the large canals, far enough from the darklights that it basked in a pool of twilit gray. Some immense structure had once stood among the dark pines, taking up most of the small island, but little remained of it now except a few crumbling walls and the circular ruins of what might have been a tower.

There was no beach to be found, and nothing left of the dock that had once served the island except a few bleached piers that looked enough like great ribs to make Barrick think uneasily of the Sleepers and their bone mountain. They moored the boat to the closest of these and waded to the rocky shore through water up to their chests; Beck and Barrick were both shivering by the time they reached dry ground and crawled into the shelter of the pines.

"We need a fire," Barrick said. "I don't care if anyone sees it or not." He got up and led Beck through the thick growth until they reached the remains of the stone tower. "This will at least hide the light of the flames," he said. "There's nothing we can do about the smoke."

"Use these," said Beck, bending to pick deadfall from the ground. "It's a good wood and they'll put off less smoke than green branches."

Barrick nodded. So the man wasn't useless after all.

With a small fire burning, Barrick finally settled back to warm his hands and realized that Skurn was gone. Before he had too much chance to think about it the bird came back, flapping down through the upper branches before hopping the rest of the way from limb to tangled limb. Something dangled in his beak, a dark bundle that he dropped with great ceremony.

"Us thought you would be hungry, like," the raven announced.

Barrick examined the almost eyeless corpse, a creature like a large mole but with longer and more delicate, fingered paws. "Thank you," he said, and meant it: he was painfully hungry. Except for the few morsels he had shared with Raemon Beck he hadn't eaten in what seemed like days.

"I'll do for that," Beck said. "Have you a knife?"

With some reluctance, Barrick produced Qu'arus' short sword. Beck examined it for a moment and raised an eyebrow, but said nothing. The merchant bent to the task of skinning and gutting the creature while Barrick stoked the fire, and he gave the entrails and hide to Skurn without asking. The raven gulped them down, then hopped onto a stone and began to groom himself.

"So what do you know of this city?" Barrick asked as their dinner roasted on a pine-skewer over the open flame. The smell was most distracting, musky but appetizing. "Where are we? How is the place shaped?"

Beck wrinkled his dirty face in thought. "I know little, to be truthful. The only time my master took me out before the hunting trip was on a ceremonial visit to the Duke of Spidersilk. He brought several of his mortal servants—just to put out the duke, or so it seemed." A sad little smile flickered on Raemon Beck's lips. "We had to go far into the city, and he pointed things out to me along the way. Let me think." He picked up a pine twig and began to draw with it in the dark, damp soil. "It has a shape like this, I think." He scratched an awkward spiral.

"*K'ze-shehaoui*—the River Fade—that is what they call the great canal," he said, tracing this main line. "But there are other waterways crossing it all the way in." He drew other lines across the main line. The shape began to look like one of the halved chamber shells the priests of Erivor wore upon their breasts as an emblem of their god.

"But where are we?" Barrick asked.

Raemon Beck rubbed his face for a moment. "I think the house of Qu'arus must be somewhere here," he said, jabbing with his stick about halfway along the outermost spiral. "Master was always proud that he lived outside the heart of the city, separate from the other wealthy, important families. And *this* spot is probably somewhere near here." He poked again, scratching a larger mark on the second and third spirals. "I couldn't guess how far we've come exactly, but I know that part is full of islands."

Barrick frowned. He pulled the meat from the fire, then set it on a clean rock and began to cut it into two portions, an awkward process with a blade so big and a meal so small. He left Beck's on the rock and began to eat his own share with his fingers. "I need to know more. I have been set a task."

"What kind of task?" Beck asked.

Even the unfamiliar human company and the comfort of a hot meal was not enough to induce Barrick to share all his secrets with someone who was after all nearly a stranger. "Never mind that. I need to find a certain door, as I said, but I have no idea where it might be except for the name Crooked's Hall. What else can you tell me? If you don't know Crooked's Hall, is there a famous door somewhere in Sleep? An important gate? Something guarded?"

"Everything is guarded," Beck said grimly. "What is not watched by the skrikers is in the houses of the Dreamless, clutched tight."

"You mentioned some fellow your master took you to see—the Duke of Spiderwebs, was it?"

"Spidersilk. He is tremendously old. My master said he was one of the oldest in the city, second only to the members of the Laughing Council."

Despite himself, Barrick blinked. "What sort of name is that?"

"I don't know, my lord. Master hated them. He said someone should suck the last of the juices from them and then we could all begin again. He also said that laughter should have a sound, but I do not know what he meant."

Barrick was growing impatient with all the history. "This Spidersilk—

where is he? Could we reach him? Could we make him tell us what we want to know?"

Raemon Beck stared in abject horror. "The duke? No! We cannot go near him. He would destroy us without lifting a finger!"

"But where did he live? Can you at least tell me that?"

"I'm not certain. Somewhere near the heart of the city. I remember because we passed many of the oldest places as we reached the middle of Sleep, some of them burned and others fallen down into ruins, some of them so surrounded with darklight that I could not see them even from a short distance. My master pointed out many things—such strange names!—the Garden of Hands was one, and a place called Five Red Stones, the Library of Painful Music—no, Pitiful Music . . ." He took a breath. "So many names! Syu'maa's Tower, Traitor's Gate, the Field of the First Waking . . ."

"Hold," said Barrick, suddenly intent. "Traitor's Gate? What was that?"

"I . . . I don't remember . . ."

Barrick reached out and grabbed Beck's arm with his left hand, and only realized that he was hurting him when he heard him whimper. He let go. "I'm sorry," he said, "but I must know. Think, man! What was it, this Traitor's Gate?"

"Please, Lord, it was . . . it was one of the places so dark I could not see it. But Master said something . . ." Beck squinted his eyes, clearly trying hard to remember, all the while rubbing the arm Barrick had squeezed. "He said it was a *hole*."

"A hole?" Barrick had to restrain the impulse to grab the small, dirty man again and shake him this time. "Is that all?"

"I know it sounds strange, but he called it a hole . . . what did he say? A hole that even the gods could not . . . could not . . ." His face brightened. "That even the gods could not close."

Barrick's heart was beating fast. He had heard enough talk of Crooked's roads to know this was something he could not ignore. "Show me how to find it."

Beck's look of satisfaction evaporated. "What? But . . . my lord, it's in the heart of Sleep—in the district of Silence where only those who are called may go. Even my master would not have set foot there without being summoned by Spidersilk . . ." He jumped at a loud clacking noise, but it was only Skurn cracking a snail shell against a rock.

"My master was very clever," Beck said. "If he wouldn't go there by himself, neither should we. You do not know these creatures, Prince Barrick—they've no souls, no kindness at all! They will skin us just to amuse themselves, with less concern than I gave to this coney!"

"I will not force you to go with me, but I cannot let the chance pass." Barrick wiped his hands on his ragged clothes and began smoothing out a place to lie down. "I must see this place, Beck. I must find out if this . . . hole that even the gods can't close is what I'm looking for. I have a task, as I said." He reached into his shirt to touch the mirror in its bag. "You are free to do what you want."

"But if you leave me, I will be caught! A runaway servant—and a Sunlander!" The man's eyes filled with tears. "They will do terrible things to me!"

Some of the coldness had returned to his heart: Barrick was suddenly tired and did not want to listen to this weak fellow's weeping—he could almost feel himself hardening like clay becoming brick. He lay back in the hollow between two pine roots and rolled the hood of Qu'arus' cloak behind his head as a cushion. "I cannot make your decisions for you, trader. I have responsibilities beyond shepherding one man." He closed his eyes.

It should not have been easy to fall asleep with Beck sobbing quietly only an arm's length away, but Barrick had scarcely slept in the house of the Dreamless—would not have said he slept at all, but for the memories of that strange lizard-dream. The world quickly slipped away.

In his dream he stood on a hilltop, an oddly featureless place the color of ancient ivory. A crowd of people had gathered on the slope below him, their staring faces like a garden bed of unusual flowers. He could recognize some of them instantly—his father the king, Shaso, his brother Kendrick—but some of them were less familiar. One might be Ferras Vansen he realized after a moment, but at the same time it was an older man with a gray-shot beard and thinning hair—a Vansen who could never exist because the guard captain had died in Greatdeeps, falling into endless darkness. Most of the rest were strangers, some in antique-looking dress, others as weird and misshapen as any of the creatures he had met in the demigod Jikuyin's slave cells: the only things the strange assembly seemed to share were their silence and attention.

Barrick tried to speak, to ask them what they wanted of him, but his mouth would not form the words. His face felt numb, and although the muscles of his jaw and tongue twitched, something kept them from moving freely. He reached his hand to his lips. To his horror, he felt nothing there but skin, stiff as old leather. His mouth was gone.

Barrick? Is that you?

Someone spoke from behind him, the achingly familiar voice of the dark-haired girl—Qinnitan, that was her name—but he could not answer her no matter how he tried. He struggled to turn toward her but could not move, either—his body had become as numb and hard as his face.

Why won't you talk to me? she asked. *I can see you! I have wanted to talk to you so long! What have I done to anger you?*

Barrick strained until his vision swirled, trying to make his stony muscles move, but it was useless. He might as well have been a statue. The expectant faces still gazed up at him but some of them began to change, showing impatience and confusion. He stood looking down as the sky darkened and rain began to fall, cold drops that he barely felt, as though the very flesh of his body had become something thick and stiff as tree bark. He heard Qinnitan's voice again but it grew fainter and fainter until at last it was gone. The crowd began to disperse, some clearly enraged by his inaction, others merely puzzled, until he stood by himself on the bare hilltop, dripping with rain that he could not wipe away.

"Prince Barrick, if you truly . . . ah!" Raemon Beck, who had only shaken Barrick once, was startled to feel Qu'arus' blade pressing against his neck.

"What is it?"

Beck swallowed carefully. "Could you . . . could you please not kill me, my lord?"

Barrick withdrew the blade and slipped it back into its scabbard. "How long did I sleep?"

Beck rubbed his throat. "It's always hard to tell here, but the quarter bell rang a short time ago. We do not have long before Repose is over and the Dreamless are out on the canals again." Pale and with dark circles under his eyes, the young merchant looked as though he had not managed to sleep at all. "If you truly mean to look for this place, we should go."

"We? Does that mean you are going with me?"

Beck nodded miserably. "What choice do I have, my lord? They'll kill me either way." His mouth pursed as he struggled with his composure. "For the first time in a long while I was thinking of my children and my wife . . . thinking of how I will likely never see them again . . ."

"Enough. That does neither of us any good." Barrick sat up, stretched. "How much longer will this Repose last?"

Beck shrugged miserably. "I told you, the quarter bell rang. That means three-quarters of it is gone. I do not even know how to judge time anymore, Prince Barrick. An hour? Two hours? That is all we have."

"Then we must try to find the center of the city before then. What of these skrikers? Will they interfere with us on the river?"

"Interfere?" Beck laughed, the sound hollow as a rotten log. "You do not understand, my lord. The Lonely Ones are not sentries or reeves like we had back in Helmingsea. They will not 'interfere'; they will turn the marrow in your bones to ice. They will pluck out your heart and swallow it whole. If you are on the water and you hear their voices calling to you, you will drown yourself to get away from them."

"Stop talking in puzzles—what are they?"

"I don't know! Even my master was afraid of them. He told me his people should never have brought them to Sleep. That's what he said— 'brought them.' I don't know if they found them or bred them or summoned them like Xandian demons—even the Dreamless speak of the skrikers only in whispers. I heard one of Qu'arus' sons tell his brother they were like white rags caught on the wind, but with the voices of women. The Dreamless also call them 'the Eyes of the Empty Place.' I don't know what that means. May the gods help me, I never want to find out." He was all but weeping again.

"Stop this blubbing. Here, look at your map." Barrick squatted over the spiral the merchant had drawn. "We don't dare go straight down the big canal, especially if Repose is ending soon, as you say. You must help me find our way to the center by smaller waterways."

"The small canals—it's all darklight," Beck said. "You can't see anything. Some of them are blocked with water gates—we're blind, they'll still be able to see *us* . . ."

Barrick groaned in frustration. "Still, there must be a way to get there, even if we have to go right down the middle of the biggest canal . . ."

"Like a snail shell," Skurn said suddenly. The bird lifted his head from where he had been pecking through the fractured, sticky remains of just such an object. "Seen that, us has. From above."

"Yes. We want to get to the center, but Beck says we can't go down the smallest waterways without being noticed."

"Us could find a way," Skurn said. "Island to island, where the dark don't reach."

"Then do it," Barrick told him. "Do it, and I promise I will catch you the biggest, fattest rabbit you ever saw and I won't take even a bite myself."

The bird tipped his head sideways to look at him, black eyes alive with reflected firelight. "Done," he said and spread his wings. "Keep up best as can, then."

Before getting back into the skiff Barrick stopped to extinguish the fire, but before he kicked the sandy dirt over it he took a pine bough, sticky with sap, and held it in the flames until it caught.

"That's real fire!" Beck said when he saw it. "Put it out!"

"It's dark as night out there. I'm not going to feel my way through this cursed city on hands and knees. Besides, if the Dreamless don't like twilight, maybe they'll be scared of actual fire."

"They hate light, but they're not afraid of it. And they'll see it from far away. If we carry that, we might as well go shouting at the top of our voices for the skrikers to come and find us."

Barrick stared at him, trying to sift the man's sense from his fearfulness. At last he threw the torch into the river; a wisp of smoke drifted after them as they slid away from the island.

Barrick had not liked the gloomy city before, but as they worked their way deeper and deeper into the heart of Sleep he liked it even less. It might be a less forbidding place when Repose had ended and the streets were full again, but it was hard to imagine it ever being cheerful, or even ordinary. The waterways, with their high, leaning sides, docks like crooked teeth, and bridges hanging close overhead, seemed almost intestinal—as though the city were some great, mindless creature like a starfish, absorbing them slowly into itself. The houses, even the largest, seemed cramped and secretive, with small windows like the foggy eyes of blind men. Barrick also saw little in the way of public places, at least that he could recognize as such, only the jagged bridges and occasional barren open spaces which looked less like squares or markets and more as if the buildings that had once stood there had vanished without being replaced. Worst of all, though, was the aura of brooding silence that hung over the dark maze. Its residents might be called Dreamless, but instead of perpetual wakefulness every building Barrick and Raemon Beck passed seemed a sort of nightmare construct, a hard shell hiding a seed of slumbering malice in its depths, as though Sleep were not a city at all but a mausoleum for the uneasy dead.

They had just slipped out of the security of one of the midcanal islands and were rowing across an open space toward another skerry of rocks, trees, and twilight when the last bell of Repose rang, a dull reverberation that Barrick felt in his bones more than heard in his ears.

"They will be coming out now," Beck said quietly, but he was struggling to stay calm. "Someone will see us."

"If you keep twitching and jumping that way someone will certainly notice. Sit still. Look as though you belong here." Barrick pulled his own hood farther down over his face. "If you don't have something to cover your head with, lie down."

Beck found a piece of patched sailcloth and wrapped it around himself. "It is just that I know these folk. They are cruel, the Dreamless—cruel for no reason! They are like boys pulling the legs off flies."

"Then we'll have to make sure they don't get hold of our legs, won't we? Now where did that cursed raven get to . . . ?"

Barrick was still looking for Skurn as they passed beneath a place where several ancient bridges seemed to cross over and under each other at different heights, like the thorny branches of a rose bush, connecting a series of crumbling ivied, tile-covered towers on either side of the shadowy canal. A smear of grayish movement along one of the bridges caught Barrick's eye, as if someone up there was waving a handkerchief at him. He glanced up. Something looked back down at him. He could barely see it through the guttering darklights but he felt its gaze like a claw of ice tightening around his heart.

"What are you doing?" Beck whispered urgently. "You dropped the oar!"

Barrick heard his companion splashing as he dragged the oar back into the boat, but it might have been happening on the far bank. "Where . . . where did it go?" he said at last, barely able to speak the words. "Is it still up there?"

"What? What are you talking about?"

"Its eyes—they were red. I think it was alive, but . . . but it . . .

wasn't . . ." His mouth was dry as sand, dry as dust, but he swallowed anyway. "It *looked* at me . . ."

"Gods help us," Beck moaned. "Was it a skriker? Oh, Heaven save us, I don't want to see it . . . !" He pressed his face into his hands like a frightened child.

At last, his heart rabbiting, Barrick worked up the courage to look again. The tangle of bridges was falling away behind them, and although for one chill moment he thought he saw something pale fluttering on the highest bridge, when he blinked and looked again it was gone. Still, he could not push the memory of it from his mind, although he could not say exactly what had frightened him so.

Like white rags caught on the wind . . .

The city seemed to be stirring back into a hushed, morbid sort of wakefulness. Barrick saw shapes moving in the darklit shadows, but they were all so heavily cloaked and wrapped that it was hard to make out anything more than their movement. Most of them were solitary, walking slowly along the sides of the canals or occasionally crossing overhead on one of the curiously high bridges, often bearing darklight torches so that they traveled in a small cloud of moving blackness. Barrick now wanted nothing more dearly than to escape this place as quickly as possible. What kind of unnatural things were these Dreamless? Did they truly hate the light so much, or was there something more to the practice? He was suddenly grateful that Beck had talked him out of carrying real fire.

Following Skurn's slow-flapping lead, they crossed the widest part of the Fade and slipped into a narrow waterway that curled in on itself like a dead centipede, twisting through a seemingly forgotten section of town that, despite its proximity to the center of Sleep, seemed almost completely empty and abandoned, half the buildings in ruins, several of them nothing but charred rubble. Raemon Beck sat up in the bow of the boat, his face tense with attention and fear. "This is it," he said. "Master took us here—I remember that tree." He pointed to a gnarled and ancient alder growing on its own small, stony island, its trunk deformed by wind and time, branches reaching up and spreading over the center of the canal like the hand of a drowning giant. "I think Traitor's Gate was nearby."

"I hope so," Barrick said, squinting. There were fewer darklights in this area, only an occasional brand spreading inky darkness from a canal-side sconce, but they still cast enough shadow to make it hard to see details of what was on the shore. A moment later he sat up and pointed. "Is that it?"

Whatever it had been once, the stone structure was now little more than a ruin, its outer buildings collapsed and the remaining high walls overgrown with trees and creepers. It looked like one of the tombs in the cemetery outside the Throne hall back in Southmarch, except that this tomb would have sufficed for a dead giant.

"I . . . I think that's it," said Beck, his voice dropping to a whisper. "Oh, Heaven protect us, I didn't like it then and I don't like it now—what my master said of the curse frightened me."

"What are you talking about? You might have told me before." Hills, ruins—was there nothing in these benighted shadowlands that *wasn't* cursed?

"I didn't remember." Beck's eyes were wide and staring; his hand, which he held up as if to shield his eyes from the nonexistent sun, shook badly. "Master said that this place was forbidden ground—and that all the people of these lands, Dreamless and Dreaming, were cursed too because of what Crooked did to the gods." He pawed at his face. "I can't remember anymore—I was new here then. Everything was so strange . . ."

Barrick felt a cold contempt wash over him. Words—words! What use were they to anyone? "I'm going in. You may stay here if you wish."

Raemon Beck looked around wildly. "Please don't, my lord! Can't you see how bad it is? I won't go in there!"

"That is your choice." As the boat grounded softly against the rotting wooden dock, Barrick stood up, making the boat pitch so that Beck had to grab the rails. Skurn was nowhere in sight, but he would surely see the boat and know where Barrick had gone.

Beck didn't say anymore, but when Barrick climbed carefully onto the pier, which quivered but held, Beck got up to follow him, face pinched with misery and fear.

"Be sure to tie up the boat so it doesn't float away." Barrick had an ugly feeling they might want to leave suddenly.

When he stepped into the trees, away from the single darklight torch that burned on a post near the edge of the canal, Barrick could see the building better. It was larger than it looked from the canal and the land around it was wider and deeper than it had first appeared. The place seemed measurelessly old, its pale, vine-latticed walls scratched with deep gouges—writing, or mystical incantations perhaps, but as crude as if they had been made by an immense child. Every soft step they took across the leaves and fallen branches seemed to rattle like a drumroll. As Barrick picked his way through the undergrowth toward the great stone ruin, past gigantic blocks of stone that had broken loose and tumbled from the walls, he was coldly satisfied to hear Beck scuffling along behind him, whispering miserably to himself.

A black something came rushing through the trees toward him.

"Run!" shrieked Skurn as he dove past. "Coming!"

Barrick stood for a confused moment after the bird was gone. Then he saw a pair of pale shapes coming toward him from the ruins, sweeping over the uneven ground like windblown leaves.

"Skrikers!" choked Raemon Beck. He turned to run back toward the boat, but tripped and fell face first into a clot of brambles.

The creatures moved with terrible swiftness, loose garments rippling and flowing like mist, faces invisible in the depths of their hoods as they leaped or slithered over obstacles they barely seemed to touch. They crossed a hundred paces of distance so quickly that Barrick only had time to yank Raemon Beck to his feet before the first of the things was upon them. Without thinking, he swung Qu'arus' sword at the thing's head, or at least where its head should be. It leaned back, hissing like a startled snake, and he caught a glimpse of a face—red eyes and a cobweb of dull scarlet veins on corpse-white skin. Then the thing laughed. It was a terribly, lonely wheeze of sound, but worst of all was that the inhuman voice was unmistakably female.

Barrick's legs felt stiff and weak as wax candles, as if any moment they would break beneath his weight. The other pale thing floated to the side, trying to get behind him. Barrick staggered back a step and let go of Raemon Beck, who crumpled to the ground with a whimper of resignation. The boat was several dozen paces behind them but it might as well have been miles. The billowing shapes moved closer, their ragged voices twining in a cracked chant of hunger and triumph.

The skrikers were singing.

29
Every Reason to Hate

"The fairies' only remaining city is in the far north of Eion, north even of what was once Vutland. Ximander calls it 'Qul-na-Qar' or 'Fairy Home,' but whether those are the names the fairies themselves use is unknown. The Vuts called it 'Alvshemm' and claimed it was a city with towers as numerous as the trees in a forest."

—from "A Treatise on the Fairy Peoples of Eion and Xand"

THE SUN HAD ALMOST SUNK to the horizon and the lamps were being lit all over Broadhall Palace. Briony was on her way back from visiting Ivvie, who was feeling better, if not quite well—the girl's hands still shook badly, and she could take nothing into her stomach stronger than clear broth—when she was met in the hall outside her rooms by two armed and helmeted soldiers wearing the royal Syannese crest. The guards' air of tense expectancy was such that for a moment she feared they meant to kill her. She was relieved, but only a little, when one of them announced, "Princess Briony Eddon, you have been summoned by the king."

"I would like to go and change my clothes, first," she said.

The guard shook his head. His expression gave her a cold feeling in the pit of her stomach. "I am sorry, Highness, but it is not permitted."

She ran through all the possibilities as they escorted her toward the throne room. Could it be her meddling with the Kallikans? Or had something about Jenkin Crowel's injuries been whispered in the king's ears? That would be easy enough to deny—Dawet was too clever to leave any loose ends.

As she walked across the great throne room between the two tall men she could not help wondering if the covert glances from the courtiers betrayed the same squeamish sort of fascination they might have felt for a famous criminal.

Oh, sweet mistress Zoria, what trouble have I caused now?

King Enander and his advisers were waiting for her in the Perin Chapel, a high-ceilinged room much longer than it was wide. The king sat on a chair with the great altar behind him, at the feet of Perin Skylord's monstrous marble statue. The god held his great hammer Crackbolt, its massive head resting on the floor just behind the chair occupied by the Lady Ananka, the king's mistress, who was one of the last people Briony wanted to see. Equally loathsome was the presence of Jenkin Crowel, the Tollys' envoy at the Syannese court, although it suggested she had guessed right: one of the bully-boys had probably talked. Crowel smirked at her; his giant white neck ruff made him look like a particularly ugly flower. It was all she could do not to go to him and slap his pink, insolent face, but she struggled for calm and found it. She had learned a few lessons since Hendon Tolly had provoked her almost to madness at her own table.

She dropped to her knee in front of King Enander and looked down at the floor. "Your Majesty," she said. "You summoned me and I have come."

"Not hastily," said Ananka. "The king has waited for you here a long time."

Briony bit her lip. "I am sorry," she said. "I was with Mistress Ivgenia e'Doursos and your messengers only just found me. I came as soon as I heard." She looked up to the king, trying to gauge his mood, but the expression on Enander's face was a disinterested mask that could have augured anything at all. "How may I serve you?"

"You claim to serve King Enander?" said Ananka. "That is strange, since none of your actions show anything like it."

Whatever was happening here, it was obviously bad. If Lady Ananka was to serve as her inquisitor the cause would be lost before Briony even knew what was at stake.

"We welcomed you to our court." She saw now that Enander's face was flushed as though he had been drinking heavily for this early hour of the day. "Did we not? Did we not open our arms to you as Olin's daughter?"

"Yes, you did, Majesty, and I am most grateful . . ."

"And all I asked of you was that you not bring the intrigues of your . . . troubled homeland into our house." The king frowned, but it seemed as much in puzzlement as anger. Briony felt a moment of hope. Perhaps it was a misunderstanding—something she could explain. She would be contrite, grateful. She would apologize for her youth and headstrong ways, trot out whatever nonsense the king wanted to hear like Feival performing a soliloquy of girlish innocence, and then she could go back to her chambers for some blessed, necessary sleep . . .

A movement at the corner of her eye caught her attention. It was Feival himself, who had come so quietly into the great chapel that Briony had not even heard him. She was relieved to see at least one familiar face.

"You were extremely generous to her, my lord," said Ananka. Was Briony the only person who could hear the venom dripping from the woman's tongue? What good was beauty—a mature beauty, but beauty nonetheless—if it cloaked such a viperous soul?

Please, merciful Zoria, Briony prayed, *help me to keep my temper. Help me to swallow my pride, which has landed me in trouble so many times.*

"So if all that is true," said Enander suddenly, "why have you betrayed my hospitality and betrayed me, Briony Eddon? Why? Common intrigues I could understand, but this—you have struck at my very heart!" The pain in his voice was real.

Betrayed? Briony suddenly felt icy fear envelop her. She looked up at Enander but the king would not meet her eye. "Majesty, I . . ." She found it hard to form words. "What have I done? May I know? I swear I have never . . ."

"The list of your crimes is long, girl." The high collar of Ananka's elaborately beaded dress made her look like a Xandian hood snake. "If you were of common blood, any one of them would have you in the House of Tears. Lord Jenkin, tell the king again what she did to you."

Jenkin Crowel, still with a thin purple shadow beneath one eye, cleared his throat. "Within a few short days of arriving in your gracious court as a legitimate envoy, King Enander, I was set upon by thugs in the public street and beaten almost to death. As I lay in the dirt in a pool of my own blood one of the ruffians leaned down and told me, 'That is what happens to those who stand against the Eddons.'"

"That's a lie!" Briony shouted. It was, at least in part. After she had become convinced that Crowel had poisoned her little maid in an effort to kill Briony herself, she had instructed Dawet to hire some bully-boys to give Crowel a taste of his own cruelty, and then say to him that next time he tried any dangerous tricks his payment would be worse. No mention could have been made of the Eddons because Dawet would never even have hinted to those men who they were actually serving.

"I know what I heard," Crowel said, doing his best to look both suffering and noble. "I thought I was dying. I thought they were the last words I would ever hear."

"You are as much a liar as your master." Briony forced herself to take a breath. "Even if I were behind such a terrible thing, would I have them use my name?" Just the sight of Crowel's doughy, self-satisfied face fanned the rage inside her until its flames billowed. "If I was taking revenge for the treachery your master has shown my family, then the name Eddon would be the last thing you would hear all right, you pig, but you would never have got to your feet again!" Enander and the others were staring at her, Briony realized. She swallowed. "I am innocent of this charge, King Enander. Would you take the word of this . . . this upstart over the daughter of a brother king?"

The king narrowed his eyes. "Were this the only accusation against you, and the only witness, you would have some case to make, Princess. But there is more."

"I am innocent of any wrongdoing, Majesty. I swear. Call on your witnesses."

"Is it not as I told you, Enander?" said Ananka in a tone of triumph. "She plays the innocent so well. And yet she plotted nothing less than to steal your son and your throne!"

Enander's throne? Oh, gods, that was treason. Even princesses might be put to death for treason, and not quickly. It was all she could do to force out the words. "I have no idea what you are talking about, Lady Ananka—I swear my innocence in front of Perin and all the gods!"

"You tried to entrap Prince Eneas, girl. Everybody knows. You made up to him, played the blushing virgin, all the while trying to lure him to your bed and bend him to your will! And that was only the beginning of your plot!"

"This is a dreadful lie!" Briony cried out. "Where is the prince? Ask him yourself. Our dealings were always honorable—which is more than I can say for what you do to me here!"

"He is beyond your reach," Ananka said with obvious satisfaction. "Beyond your lies and cozening. Eneas has been sent away from Tessis this very hour, with his soldiers. The glamour you have drawn over him will do you no good."

Briony was struggling so hard against her anger the room seemed to have gone dark except for the figures of the king and his consort. She stumbled a little as she turned to Enander. "Majesty, your son has done nothing wrong and neither have I. We have a friendship—nothing more. And I want nothing from him or you except help for my people, my country . . . your allies!"

Enander looked troubled. "That . . . that is not what I have heard."

"Heard from whom?" Briony demanded. "With respect, King Enander, Lady Ananka does not like me, that is clear, although I have no idea why . . ." But even as she said it she saw a look of amused complicity speed between Ananka and Jenkin Crowel and realized that the king's consort had more than a stepmother's interest in the proceedings. *She has made some bargain with the Tollys,* Briony thought. *The bitch has some plan of her own.* Even her flaring rage could not melt the chill settling deeper inside her as she realized how thoroughly matters were set against her here in Syan. "But . . . but that is hardly enough for judgment," she finished. "Call back your son. Ask him."

"My son has the care of the realm to think of," said Enander. "But as I said, there are other witnesses. Feival Ulian, step forth and tell us what you know."

"Feival . . . ?" Briony stared, astounded. "What does that mean?"

The young player at least had the grace, or skill, to look troubled as he stepped out and kneeled before the king. "It . . . it is difficult for me, Majesty. She is the daughter of my king, and for a long time we traveled together and were friends . . ."

"Were? I *am* your friend! What are you saying?"

" . . . But the things she has done will not stay locked inside me any longer. It is all true—she has spoken of it often in front of me. She has had one thought, and that was to make Prince Eneas love her so that through him she would eventually gain control of the throne of Syan. First she brought me in, and also put the other players to work as her spies—I can show you the accounts. And then she set her cap at the prince. She did her best to make love to him at every opportunity, full of sweet promises, leading him on while all the while confessing in private that she did not care for him, but only the throne of Syan."

Briony gaped, then clambered to her feet. One of the soldiers caught her arm and held her in place. "Sweet Zoria, Feival, how can you do this to me? How can you tell such terrible, baldfaced lies . . . ?" But then she saw as if for the first time the rich clothes Feival wore, the jewelry she had not given him but had not bothered to wonder about, and realized that she had been outmaneuvered since she had first set foot in the court of Tessis. Ananka had found a weak reed and bent it to her own purposes. "It is none of it true, King Enander!" Briony said, turning to the throne. "It is . . . it is a conspiracy, and I do not understand the reason for it—but I am innocent! Ask Eneas! Bring him back!"

The king shook his head. "He is beyond your reach, girl, as my lady said."

"But why would I do such things—why would I need to trick Eneas? Your son cares for me! He has said so himself . . ."

"See?" In her triumph Ananka almost rose from her chair, but thought better of it. "She as much as admits her plan."

"But I turned him down, even though his representations to me were all honorable! Ask him! Do not condemn me on the word of a single treacherous servant without hearing what your own son has to say! My maid and my friend have both been poisoned in this castle—do you not see that someone here is trying to destroy me?"

"Tell the rest, Ulian," Ananka said loudly, interrupting her. "Tell the king what this scheming creature said she would do after she tricked the king's son into marriage."

Briony started to object again, but the king held up his hand for silence "Let the servant speak."

Feival could not meet Briony's eye. "She said . . . she said that she would do whatever she must to see Eneas put on the throne in his father's place." He sighed, and although it might only have been at the guilt of telling such a gross lie, the young player seemed to be growing increasingly uncomfortable with his role.

Briony could only shake her head helplessly. "This is all madness!"

"And the rest," Ananka commanded. "Be not afraid. Tell the king what you told me. Did she not say that she would use witchcraft to hasten the succession if necessary?"

Briony's legs seemed to turn to water. One of the soldiers had to catch her to keep her from falling to the floor of the chapel. Witchcraft—against the king's life? Ananka did not simply want her banished, she wanted her dead. "Lies . . . !" she said, but her voice sounded feeble.

Even Feival seemed stunned, as though this was a depth of treachery even he had not expected. "Witchcraft?"

"Tell him! Tell the king!" Ananka seemed ready to shake it out of him.

Feival swallowed. "I . . . to be honest, my lady . . . I do not . . . remember that . . ."

"He is no doubt frightened to talk about it, Majesty." Ananka said to Enander. "Frightened to say it in front of the girl herself—afraid she will put some curse on him." The king's mistress settled back into her seat, but the look she gave Feival suggested that his new mistress was less than happy with his performance. "But you can see what sort of plot we have uncovered—what danger you and your son were in!"

Enander shook his head. Was it drink that made him flush so, or something else? Was Ananka poisoning him as well?

"These are terrible things you are accused of, Briony Eddon," the king said slowly, "and were your father not also a friend to us I would be tempted to pass sentence this moment." He paused for a moment as a quiet hiss of frustration escaped the woman beside him. "But because of the long years of brotherhood between our nations I will deal with you as carefully as if you were one of my own. You will be confined to your chambers until I can investigate this matter in the depth it deserves." He took a shaky breath. "This is as hard for us as it is for you, Princess, but you have brought it on yourself."

"No!" Briony was shaking with fury, barely able to contain herself. Treacherous Feival, cruel Ananka, even the swine Jenkin Crowel—behind those careful masks, they must all be laughing at her! "Will you again let Jellon betray my family, King Enander? Are you so blind to what goes on in your own court?"

Many of the others gasped at Briony's words, but the king only looked puzzled. "Jellon? What nonsense is this? Have you forgotten what country you are in?"

"Jellon! Where Hesper sold my father to the Hierosoline usurper, Ludis Drakava! And now this woman has come from there, schooled in treachery by her lover to bring down my kingdom—and perhaps yours as well! Can you not see? Nothing comes from Jellon but lies and betrayal!"

"You are distraught, young woman." Enander looked old and tired. "Jellon is our ally, too, and they bring much to the world. The Jellonians are very good at weaving, you know."

Briony stared at him. The king's thoughts were more than slow, they were hopelessly muddled—there was no point in further arguing. She struggled to keep the misery from her face—at least she would not let that cow Ananka see her weep. "You wrong me," was all she said, then turned and walked out of the chapel, praying that her legs would bear her. Guards silently moved in on either side of her. She would not be walking alone anymore, that was clear.

In the throne room outside, the king's counselor Erasmias Jino approached her. "I apologize, Princess," he said quietly. "I was not aware any of this was planned."

"Neither was I. Which of us do you think was most surprised?" She let the guards lead her away.

❦

Sister Utta could not make herself stand, although the storm that raged in her thoughts demanded some physical release. She wanted to run as far and as fast as she could to escape this impossible talk, or to throw things clattering to the floor until the noise and chaos wiped away everything she had just been told. But still it went on, the tale of how the mortals of Southmarch had destroyed the Twilight People's royal family.

"It cannot be." She looked imploringly at Kayyin. "You only do this because your dark mistress wants to torment us. Such horrible tales—admit they are all lies!"

"Of course they are lies," Merolanna said angrily. She would no longer meet the fairy's gaze. "Wicked lies. Told by this . . . this evil changeling to make us fearful, to destroy our faith."

Kayyin spread his hands in a gesture that looked like resignation or abandonment. "Faith does not enter into it, Duchess. My mistress Yasammez ordered me to tell you the truth and that is what I did. I owe her nothing but my death so I can assure you I would not lie on her behalf, especially about this, the greatest tragedy of my people." His expression grew distinctly colder. "And now I recall some of the ways in which I am *not* one of you, no matter how many years I played the counterfeit. My people do not run from the truth. It is the only reason we have survived in this world . . . this world that your kind have made."

He turned and walked out of the room. Utta heard his light footfalls for a moment on the stairs, then the house was silent again.

"Do you see?" There was an edge of triumph in Merolanna's voice—a feverish edge, Utta thought. "He knows we have seen through him. By leaving he fairly admits it!"

After days and days of shared captivity, Utta no longer had the strength or even the inclination to argue. After all, if Merolanna needed to believe such things to keep up her spirits, who was Utta to take them from her? But even so, she couldn't be entirely silent.

"As little as I wish to admit it, much of what he said . . . well, it does ring in accord with the history of my order . . ." she ventured.

"But certainly!" Merolanna was briskly tidying up a room that needed no such efforts. "Don't you see? That is the cleverness of it! They make their lies plausible—until you consider what they are actually saying. Oh, no, it was not those monsters that came out of their shadowy country and attacked *us!* All of the gods-fearing people of the March Kingdoms—we lured them out, then betrayed and slaughtered them! Can you not see how foolish it is, Utta? Really, I despair of you. My husband told me of such madnesses when he came back from the wars in Settland—you have been a prisoner so long you are beginning to believe your captors."

Utta opened her mouth, then shut it again. *Patience,* she told herself. *She is a good woman. She is frightened. And I am frightened, too.* Because if what Kayyin had told them was a lie, as Merolanna so fervently believed, then the Qar were completely mad. But if it was the truth . . .

Then they have every reason to hate us, Utta thought. *They have every reason to want to destroy us all.*

The fury that was boiling inside Briony began to die down on her way back to her chambers, as if someone had taken a lid off a cooking pot. She did not have time for anger, she reminded herself: her life was at stake. At any moment they might put her in a cell, or remove her to some country estate to live as a prisoner. Ananka might even talk the besotted old king into believing that witchcraft nonsense if she had long enough to work at him. Briony's own word—the word of a king's daughter!—had meant nothing to Enander. Instead, he had sat back like the great fool he was and let his whore manipulate him . . .

Calm, she told herself. *What was it Shaso used to say? Even as you are defending, you must be attacking. You cannot simply react to what is given you. A warrior must always act, even if only to plan the next move.*

So what was the next move? What assets did she have? Dawet was gone on some errand of his own. The money Eneas had given her was mostly spent. Well, Zoria would provide for her, she told herself . . . but Zoria had to be given a proper chance. Briony had come to this city with nothing but her freedom. She would be happy to leave it in the same condition.

It was obvious by their embarrassed expressions that her ladies-in-waiting had heard the news. No surprise: gossip traveled fast in the Broadhall Palace. Still, it was painful to watch them try to decide how to treat her. Had they known about Feival's treachery all along? And how many of them were also Ananka's spies?

Of all her ladies-in-waiting, only Agnes, the tall, thin daughter of a country baron, even came to meet her when she entered. The girl looked Briony over carefully. "Are you well?" She sounded as though she truly cared about the answer. "Is there something I can get you, Princess?"

Briony glanced at the other young women, who turned away and busied themselves with a variety of aimless tasks. "Yes, Mistress Agnes, you can come and talk with me while I put on some other clothes. I have been in these all day."

"Gladly, Princess."

When they were in her retiring room Briony quickly began undoing the clothes she had been wearing. As Agnes helped her out of the dress and into a heavy night robe Briony watched the girl. She was a little younger than Briony but much the same height, and although she was thinner, she was fair-haired like Briony, too—which would count for a great deal.

"How much do you know of what happened to me this afternoon?" Briony asked.

Agnes colored. "More than I like, Princess. I hear that Master Feival has gone to the king and told him lies about you." She shook her head. "If they would have asked me, I would have told them the truth—that you are blameless, that you acted only honorably with his highness, Prince Eneas." She looked startled. "Do you want me to tell them, Princess? I will do it if you wish, but I fear for my family . . ."

"No, Agnes. I would not ask that of you or the other girls."

"The other girls are cowards, Princess Briony. I fear they would not tell the truth, anyway. They are afraid of Ananka." She laughed ruefully. "*I* am afraid of Ananka. Some say she is a witch—that she has the king under a spell."

Briony scowled. "Well, I can show her a little conjuration of my own—but only if you'll help me."

Agnes finished tying the belt of Briony's robe and looked up at her solemnly. "I will help you, Princess, in any way the gods will allow. I think what they are doing to you is terrible."

"Good. I believe we can manage this without any harm to your reputation here at the court. Now, listen . . ."

The first time she sent Agnes out, Briony went to the door with the girl so that the guards could see her in her night-robe. *Modesty be cursed*, she thought. *A warrior has no modesty.*

"Hurry back," she told Agnes loudly enough for all to hear. The soldiers turned to watch the girl hurry by, but Agnes was not the kind to draw much attention from men. She was carrying a note to the king full of the sort of pleading and vows of innocence that could be expected from someone in Briony's position, but the guards did not even bother to ask her errand, let alone read the letter.

Idiots, Briony thought. *Well, I suppose I should be glad they think so little of me here.*

While Agnes was gone, Briony went through the chest that contained the few things she had brought to the court at Tessis. She made a bundle of what she wanted and wrapped it in a traveling cloak, the poorest one she could find, a simple, heavy, unembroidered length of dark wool left behind by some visitor and never claimed.

Perhaps it's one of the prince's, she thought. *Yes, I can imagine Eneas in just such a modest garment, leading his soldiers.* It was certainly long enough to belong to him.

Agnes soon returned and Briony sent her on another errand, this one taking a letter to Ivgenia e'Doursos. Briony wanted to let her friend know what happened, and had written to tell her she had been unjustly accused, but of course wrote nothing about what she was planning to do. She had learned she could not trust anyone, not even Ivvie—in fact, she was being forced to rely on young Agnes far more than she liked, but some things could not be helped.

Briony stood in the doorway again and made sure the guards saw her. "Push it under her door," she told Agnes. "Don't wake her."

Agnes smiled. "I'll be careful."

The other ladies looked irritated that they were not being sent on these apparently important errands. Briony put them to work getting her some food.

"Bread and cheese from the common store," she told them. "Lots of it. Let no one know it's for me. And some dried fruit. Medlars, too—wrap them in a kerchief or they shall get on everything. And what else? Yes, I'd like some quince paste."

"Are you very hungry, then, Princess?" one of the girls asked.

"Oh, famished. After all, it is hard work being betrayed."

The ladies went off with wide eyes, whispering behind their hands before they were three steps out the door. Briony noticed that one of the guards had gone somewhere. The other soldier barely looked up as the two young women hurried past.

When the bread and cheese and the rest had been brought back, Briony took it to the retiring room where no one could see, unrolled her bundle, and hid the food in the center of it. "You may go to bed now," she called to the women. "I am going to wait for Agnes. I am not yet sleepy."

Disappointed in their hope to see more eccentricity—or perhaps to see Briony eat the entire mound of supplies they had brought back—the ladies-in-waiting went to the retiring room to prepare for bed. A short time later Agnes came back.

"Thank all the gods," Briony said. "I was beginning to fear something had happened to you."

"There were people in the hall and I did not know whether you wanted me to be seen or not," Agnes told her, "so I waited until they were gone. Have I done wrong?"

"Merciful Zoria, you have done nothing of the kind! Why didn't I discover you before?" She gave the girl a quick kiss on the cheek. "There is one more thing. Give me your dress."

"My dress, Princess?"

"Quiet! Not so loud—the others are just in the retiring room. We must be quick. Then take this robe and put it on."

To her credit, young Agnes did not waste time asking questions. With Briony's help she got the dress off, and as she stood shivering in her shift Briony draped the night-robe around her.

"Now help me," Briony told her.

When she was laced into the dress, Briony took Agnes to the chest. "It goes without saying that you may have any of my dresses you choose," she said. "There are several in the big chest. But I want you to have something else. Here. The fool who gave this to me did not get what he wanted for it, but he gave it to me nevertheless, so it is mine to give to you." She took out the expensive bracelet Lord Nikomakos had sent her as a love gift and clasped it around the girl's wrist.

Agnes' eyes grew wide, then a tear welled up in the corner of each. "You are too kind to me, Princess!"

"No. You still have one more job to do and it is not an easy one. You must convince the king's men when they come for me—it may be tonight if something has made them wonder, or it may not be until sometime tomorrow—that you did not know what I was doing." She frowned. "No, that will not work—you are too clever a girl. You must convince them that I frightened you into keeping quiet."

Now it was Agnes who frowned and shook her head. "I will not blacken your name, Princess Briony. Leave it to me—I will think of something."

"May the gods bless you, Agnes! Now, when we get to the door, come halfway out and no farther—and keep your face turned away from the guards."

Just as they opened the door, Briony said loudly, "Hurry, girl! You must go to her and come back quickly. I want to go to sleep!"

There was only one guard, and as Briony hoped, he only straightened up long enough to see the two familiar shapes—the woman in the robe bidding her servant go out one last time—before leaning back on the wall again.

"Princess running you near to death, is she, my lady?" he called as Briony trotted past with the bundled cloak clasped to her breast.

"Oh, yes," she said—but in a murmur only she could hear. "It's true, I am quite beside myself tonight." A moment later she had turned into the adjoining corridor.

* * *

She retraced the route she had traveled with Eneas, stopping in the stables long enough to don the boy's clothes she'd worn as a player. She thanked Zoria and the other gods that the cloak she had picked was a warm one: it might have been spring in Syan, but it was a cold night. She was also grateful that it was a market night and the palace's gates were open late as people went in and out. She buried the dress Agnes had given her in the straw and made her way out of the stables and through the gate to the town.

Briony headed straight for the tavern where the players had been staying. The Whale Horse was in a narrow street in a dark but active part of Tessis near the river docks; its sign depicted a strange sea creature with tusks curling from its mouth. Drunken men wandered past, singing or quarreling, some of them with women on their arms as drunk and quarrelsome as themselves. Briony was glad she was dressed as a man and she prayed that no one tried to make her talk. This looked like the kind of place where it might not go well for her even if she were thought a boy instead of a girl.

Nevin Hewney was sleeping with his head on a table in the tavern's main room. Finn Teodoros, in somewhat better condition beside him, still did not recognize her for a long moment, even after she whispered his name.

He leaned back as if to see her whole, then leaned forward again. "Young Tim . . . I mean Prin—"

Briony smacked her hand over his mouth so sharply that a less drunken man would have cried out in pain. "Don't say it! Is the company all here?"

"I sink tho . . . I mean, I think so. Big Dowan has gone to bed hours ago. I believe I saw Makewell chatting up a local merchant . . ." He goggled at her again, as if not sure he wasn't dreaming. "What are *you* doing here? And dressed . . . like that?"

"I'm not going to talk about it here. Round up Hewney and meet me in your room."

"Feival?" Teodoros went pale. "Is this true?"

"True? Do you think I would lie? He betrayed me!"

"I'm sorry, Highness, I just wouldn't have . . . that is . . . by the Trickster, who could have guessed?"

"Any of us, if we'd had any sense." Nevin Hewney sat up, dripping.

He had been dousing his head in a basin of water. "Always had a taste for the better things, our Feival. I said he'd leave us someday for a rich man . . . or even a rich woman. Well, he found one. And he doesn't even have to swive her."

"Hewney!" said Teodoros, shocked. "Not in front of the princess."

Briony rolled her eyes. "None of it is new to me, Finn, just because I went back to being a princess—only my clothes changed." She laughed sourly. "And look! I'm back in my old clothes again."

The fat playwright looked miserable. "What will you do now, Highness?"

"What will I do? No, it is what *we* will do—and what we'll do is leave tonight. Feival has named you all as my spies—said it in front of the king of Syan himself. There may be soldiers on the way here already."

Hewney grunted. "That little whoreson!"

Finn blinked. "The king's men?"

"Yes, you great fool, and be grateful I thought of coming to you. This way, at least you have a chance to escape. We'll make for Southmarch."

"But how? We have no money, no supplies . . . How will we get out the gates?"

"That remains to be seen." She took the last of the gold Eneas had loaned her from her pocket—a shiny dolphin—and tossed it to Teodoros, who for all his consternation caught it smoothly. "Take it and get on with things. I'll wait here while you round up the others. Are they close?"

Finn looked around. "Most of them. Estir's out somewhere. And tall Dowan went out, too. Bathed and shaved." He goggled. "I think he might have a woman!"

"I don't care, Finn, but we need them all back, and quickly."

"Me, I'm going to get a jug of wine to take with us," announced Nevin Hewney. "If I'm to die, may the gods forbid it's sober."

Finn Teodoros also stood. "May the gods watch over us all," he said. "It seems the life of a princess is never dull, and almost always dangerous. For once I am glad my veins run thick with peasant blood."

30
Light at the Bottom of the Stairs

"The Soterian monk and scholar Kyros believed strongly that the Qar were not things of flesh and blood but instead the unshriven souls of mortal men who lived before the founding of the Trigonate Church. Phayallos disputes this, saying that the fairies, 'while often monstrous, are clearly living creatures.'"

—from "A Treatise on the Fairy Peoples of Eion and Xand"

EVEN THE OPEN SKY felt dangerous, but people were gathering again in the little square in front of the Throne hall, setting up stalls, haggling over what someone had discovered in their root cellar or the morning's meager catch of small fish from the unguarded East Lagoon. Like everyone else, Matt Tinwright kept looking fearfully over his shoulder, but although the massive black trunks of the Twilight People's thorn bridge still bent above the castle's outer walls, the immense, bristling shadows throwing much of Market Square into darkness, the fairy folk themselves had truly left the outer keep.

Not left for good, though, Tinwright feared: from atop the walls they could still be seen through the smoke and mist, moving around in their camp on the mainland as though the slaughter of the last few days had never happened.

Nobody trusted this sudden peace because the retreat itself made no sense. The creatures had entirely overrun the castle's walls, a swarm of horrors like demons out of a temple fresco; despite the best efforts of Avin

Brone, Durstin Crowel, and even Hendon Tolly himself, the fairies had utterly routed the humans from the outer keep. Much of Market Square and the great Trigonate temple had been burned—parts of the neighborhood just southwest of the gate wall were still smoldering. The streets of the inner keep were now clogged with human wreckage, those without homes huddling against the walls in tents made from scraps of cloth, untreated wounded lying everywhere, so that it looked as though some great flood had crashed through the Raven Gate and broken against the throne hall, scattering flotsam on all sides. Tinwright had seen sights already this morning that would haunt his sleep for years—children still black with burns, beyond help but still pitifully crying, whole families ill or starving, slumped in a fevered pile outside shuttered houses, warmth and help only a few uncrossable yards away.

But then yesterday, after all this destruction, after bringing such horror to so many, the Twilight People had simply stopped their siege of the inner keep as though hearing a silent call and had begun an orderly retreat. They took nothing, not prisoners, not gold—the ruined but otherwise untouched Trigonate temple was now surrounded by Hendon Tolly's men to keep out looters—and disappeared back into the mist as though the entire siege had been nothing more than a murderously bad dream.

But whatever the reason, Matt Tinwright, like his fellow Southmarch citizens, had been given some breathing space—he could not afford to spend it wondering about the fairies and their incomprehensible motives. He had a family to provide for now, of sorts: Elan and his mother were staying with Puzzle's niece in Templeyard, a relatively quiet neighborhood in the southwestern part of the keep, but the pantries were bare and, in a household of women, the task of going out into the city for food had of course fallen to Tinwright. He hadn't wanted to be the one to do the marketing, but even the narrow streets of Templeyard were so full of refugees he feared to send any of the women out on their own. He was also terrified that his mother, full of self-righteous prattle as always, might say something in public that would give away who the girl she was caring for truly was.

So, as seemed to be his lot these days, he had been left with two bad alternatives, sending his mother out for food or going himself, and had chosen the one that seemed least dangerous.

It was strange, Tinwright thought as he made his way through the unsettled crowds, stepping over the helpless and trying to harden his heart against the pleading of injured men or mothers with hungry children. The soldiers who only a scant day earlier had been fighting on the walls against creatures out of legend were now forced to break up scuffles between hungry Southmarch folk. Just in front of him now two men were wrestling in the mud over a scrawny marrow grown in someone's window box. For a moment he considered making it the subject of a poem—how different from the usual matters!—but Matt Tinwright was serving so many masters that he had no time even to think these days, let alone write. Still, it was an interesting idea—a poem about people fighting over a vegetable. It certainly said more about the times he lived in than a love poem written for a courtier on the subject of a young woman's white throat.

He was on his way back from Market Square with a slightly moldy heel of bread rolled in his cloak beside a small onion and his most exciting find, a length of dried eel that had taken most of his shopping money. The eel stews his mother had made were one of the few happy memories of his childhood. Anamesiya Tinwright had only bought eels on the days the boats came back with too many and the prices were low, so the meal had been a treat that would bring both Matt and his father to the table early, hands and faces washed, mouths watering in anticipation.

I should see if I can find some Marashi pepper pods somewhere in this wreckage of a city . . . he was thinking when he abruptly found himself face to face with Okros, the royal physician, who had just stepped out of the doorway of a chicken butcher's yard.

"Oh! Good day, my lord," said Tinwright, startled, his heart suddenly drumming. *Does he know I know him? Have we ever actually spoken, or have I only spied on him?*

Okros himself looked, if anything, more startled than the poet. He had something under his cloak—something alive, it quickly became clear. Even as the smaller man tried to step past Tinwright, a bright, desperate eye and yellow beak popped out where Okros was trying to hold the garment closed at his neck. It was a rooster, and quite a handsome one from its brief appearance, with a red comb and shiny black feathers.

Okros barely glanced at Tinwright, as if it might hurt to look someone directly in the eye. "Yes, yes," he said, "good day." A moment later he was gone, hurrying back toward the castle as though possessing a chicken might be a crime against the throne.

Perhaps he is afraid of being robbed, Tinwright thought. *Some people here would kill for a smaller meal than that.* But the whole encounter seemed strange. Surely there were more birds to be found in the castle residence than down here in the ruins of the outer keep—and why should the physician seem so furtive?

As he made his way back up the hill toward the Inner Keep a memory floated just beyond Tinwright's reach—something from a book he had read, one of his father's . . .

The love of reading might have been the only gift the old man had given him, he sometimes thought, but it had been a good one: a nearly endless supply of books, mostly borrowed (or perhaps stolen, Matt Tinwright suddenly thought now) from the houses where Kearn Tinwright had been a tutor—Clemon, Phelsas, all the classics, as well as lighter fare like the poetry of Vanderin Uegenios and the plays of the Hierosoline and Syannese masters. Reading Vanderin had inspired young Matt with visions of a courtly life, a career of being admired by fine ladies and rewarded with gold by fine gentlemen. Strange that he should finally be living that life and yet be so cursedly miserable . . .

The thing that had been tickling his memory came to him suddenly—some lines from Meno Strivolis, the Syannese master poet of two centuries earlier:

And took she then the black cockerel
Laid it on the stone, took up her sharp knife
Let out the salt wine that Kernios drinks . . .

That was all—just a morsel from Meno about Vais, the infamous witch-queen of Krace, a few lines which spoke of a black cockerel like the one the physician had been hiding. Nothing else to it—but it *was* odd that Okros should come so far just to buy poultry. Better and fatter birds could be found in the residence henyard, surely . . .

But perhaps not birds of that particular color, Tinwright thought suddenly. More of the poem had come to him:

Always it is blood that calls the High Ones
From their mountaintops and hidden shadows
From their deep forests and ocean strongholds,

And blood that binds them, so they may be asked
To grant to a soliciting subject
Some gift, or ward 'gainst threatening evil . . .

The fear that had seized him when he bumped into Okros came back to him threefold, so that for a moment Matt Tinwright couldn't walk straight and had to stop in the middle of the narrow street. People shoved past him with angry words, but he barely heard them.

So it was she spilled the cockerel's blood
And prayed the ancient Earthlord give to her
Deathly power against her enemies . . .

Could that be the reason? Had Okros walked all the way down from the safety of the residence to the outer keep because he needed a rooster of just the right color for some kind of ritual? Did it have something to do with the mirror Brone wanted to know about?

Full of confused, fearful thoughts, but also afire with excitement that felt a bit like a fever, Matt Tinwright hurried back across the crowded, brawling inner keep.

His mother was predictably furious. "What do you mean you are going out again? I need wood for the fire! It is all well for you to come in here like some petty lordling, calling for eel stew, demanding that I break my back cooking. What devilry are you up to?"

"Thank you, Mother, and a good day to you, too. But I am not going out quite yet." He bent his head so he could go up the narrow stairwell without dashing out his brains.

Elan was sitting up in the large bed she was sharing with Puzzle's grand-nieces, working at a bit of embroidery. He was glad to see her stronger, but she still had the haunted look he had hoped to see banished from her face forever.

"My lady, are you alone?"

She smiled grimly. "As you see. The girls are visiting the neighbors', trying to cozen an extra blanket—their mother and yours are now sleeping on the couch downstairs, if you remember."

He did. The whispered struggles of the two older women crammed together on the narrow couch like two bad-tempered skeletons in a single coffin were the reason he was back sleeping with Puzzle in the crowded royal residence, unsatisfying as that was. "I saw Brother Okros in the market place. Do you know anything of him?"

Elan gave him a strange look. "What do you mean? I know he is Hendon's physician. I know he is full of odd ideas . . ."

"Like what?"

"About the gods, I think. I never paid much attention when he was at table with us. He would talk on and on about alchemy and the holy oracles. Some of it seemed blasphemous to me . . ." She curled her lip. "But blasphemy never bothered Hendon."

"Does he . . . have you ever heard that he is a magic-worker?"

Elan shook her head. "No, but as I said, I scarcely know him. He and Hendon would often talk late at night, at strange hours, as if Okros were working at some important task for him that could not wait. Hendon once had a man beaten almost to death for interrupting him during an afternoon nap but he never lost his temper with Okros."

"What did they talk about?"

Elan's expression had become something painful to see, and Tinwright suddenly realized he was making her think about things she did not wish to remember. "I . . . I cannot remember," she said at last. "They never spoke for long in front of me. Hendon would take him to another part of the residence. But I heard the physician say once that . . . what was it, it was so strange! Oh, yes, he told Hendon, 'The perfection has begun to change—it is telling a different truth now.' I could make no sense of it."

Tinwright frowned, thinking. "Could it have been 'reflection,' not 'perfection'?"

Elan shrugged. He could see the darkness in her eyes and wished he could have spared her this. "Perhaps," she said quietly. "I could not hear them well."

The reflection has begun to change, he thought. *It is telling a different truth now.* It made a sort of disturbing sense if they had been talking about the mirror Brone had mentioned. And Elan had mentioned the gods. Meno's poem spoke of a heartless queen sacrificing a black cockerel to Kernios so she could curse her enemies. Was that what Okros planned to do? That would be no ordinary sacrifice, but some kind of witchcraft instead.

He had to tell Avin Brone. Then, duty discharged, Matt Tinwright could return to the somewhat flea-ridden bosom of his family and enjoy a well-earned bowl of eel stew.

Brone motioned to a spotty young man who was leaning against a threadbare tapestry, cutting his nails with a gleaming knife—Tinwright thought he was probably one of the count's relatives from Landsend. "Bring me some wine, boy." He turned back to Tinwright. "Very well. Here are some coppers for your new information, poet. Now find Okros again—he is probably in the herb garden this time of day, especially with so many wounded in need of physic. Follow him wherever he goes, but do not give yourself away."

Matt Tinwright could only sit and stare, open-mouthed. "What?" he said at last, barely able to get the word out of his mouth. "What?"

"Don't gawp at me, you knock-kneed pillock," Brone growled. "You heard me. Follow him! See what he's up to! See if he leads you to the mirror!"

"Are you mad? He's a witch! He's going to cast a spell on someone, or . . . or try to raise demons! If you want him followed so much do it yourself, or send that pimpled lad."

Brone leaned forward across the writing desk on his lap, his doubleted belly spreading until it almost knocked over the inkwell. "Have you forgotten that I have your tiny little poet's jewels cupped in my hand? And that I can have them snipped off any time I wish?"

Tinwright did his best not to appear terrified. "I don't care. What are you going to do, report me to Hendon Tolly? I'll just tell him that you're spying on him. Your jewels will end up on a knacker's table next to mine, Lord Brone. Then he'll kill us both—but at least I'll still have my soul. I won't be carried off by demons!"

Brone stared at him hard for a long time, his mouth working in his bushy beard, which was now mostly gray. At last, something like a smile appeared in the hairy depths. "You've found a bit of courage after all, Tinwright. That's good, I suppose—no man should remain an unmitigated coward all his life, even a wastrel like you. So what are we to do?" Brone suddenly reached out, far faster than Tinwright would have guessed possible, and grabbed the collar of the poet's cloak so tightly that it threatened to strangle him. "If I can't report you to Tolly, I suppose the only thing I can do is throttle you myself." The smile had become something much more menacing.

"Nnnh! Dnnn't!" It was really quite painfully tight around Tinwright's throat. The Landsend relative returned with the wine and stopped in the doorway, watching the spectacle with interest.

"If you are no use to me, poet—even worse, if you have become a threat to me—then I have little choice . . ."

"Buh umm nuh uh thrt!"

"I'd like to believe that, boy. But even if you're not a threat, you're still no help to me, and in such hard times—such dangerous times—there's no need for you. Now, if you *were* to help me by doing what I ask, well, the crabs and starfish would keep coming—you must enjoy having a little money, eh, especially these days, with everything so dear and food so rare?—and I wouldn't need to rip your head off."

"Ull hlp! Ull hlp!"

"Good." Brone turned loose of his cloak and he fell backward. The Landsend youth stepped politely out of the way to allow Tinwright to collapse onto the floor where he lay gasping.

"But why *me?*" he asked when he had finally struggled back onto his feet, rubbing his aching neck. "I'm a poet!"

"And not a particularly good one," Brone said. "But what choice do I have? Limp around the residence myself? Send my idiot nephew?" He gestured at the youth, who was paring his dirty fingernails again, but lifted the knife toward Tinwright in a sort of salute. "No, I need someone who is allowed and even expected to be in the residence—someone too foolish to be feared and too useless to be suspected. That's you."

Matt Tinwright rubbed his aching throat. "You do me too much honor, Count Avin."

"There you go—a little spunk. That's good. Now go find out what's afoot and there'll be more in it for you—perhaps even a jar of wine from my own store, eh? How would that be?"

The idea of being able to drink himself into oblivion for a day or two was the first real inducement he'd heard to keep serving Brone, although not dying was a close second. He made a cautious bow before leaving, half worrying that his head would fall off.

"Do you know what I think, Mother?" Kayyin spoke as if in continuation of a conversation briefly interrupted, instead of after an hour or more of silence.

Yasammez did not look at him and did not reply.

"I think you are beginning to feel something for these Sunlanders."

"Other than to hasten your death," she said, still not looking up, "why would you say such a preposterous thing?"

"Because I think it is true."

"Have you any purpose other than irritating me? Remind me—why haven't I killed you?"

"Perhaps you have discovered that you love your son after all." He smiled, amused at this conceit. "That you have feelings as base and sentimental as the Sunlanders themselves. Perhaps after all these centuries of neglect and open scorn, you have found that you desire to make things right. Could that be, Mother?"

"No."

"Ah. I thought not. But it was entertaining to consider." He had been pacing; now he stopped. "Do you know what is truly strange? Having lived so long in the guise of a mortal—having lived as one—I find that in some ways I have become one. For instance, I am restless in a way none of our people ever has been. If I stay too long in one place it is as though I can feel myself dying the true death. I become impatient, discontented— as though the body itself commands my mind, instead of the other way around."

"Perhaps that explains your foolish ideas," Yasammez said. "It is not you, but this mortal guise you have taken on, that offers this nonsense. Interesting if so, but I would still rather have silence."

He looked at her. She still did not look at him. "Why have you withdrawn from the Sunlander castle, my lady? It was all but yours, and you have also nearly conquered the tiny resistance in the caverns beneath it. Why pull back at such a time? Are you certain you have not begun to pity the mortals?"

For the first time her voice betrayed something, a descent into a deeper chill. "Do not speak foolishness. It offends me that a child of my loins should waste the air that way."

"So you do not pity them at all. They mean less to you than the dirt beneath your feet." He nodded. "Why, then, should you ask me to tell them the story of Janniya and his sister? What purpose could there have been for that, unless you wanted them to feel something of our pain . . . of *your* pain, to be more precise?"

"You tread on dangerous ground, Kayyin."

"If I were a farmer pledged to destroy the rats that ate my crops, would I take the rats aside before passing sentence and explain to them what they had done?"

"Rats do not understand their crimes." She turned her dark eyes on him then, at last. "If you say another word about the Sunlanders I will pull your living heart from your chest."

He bowed. "As you wish, my lady. I will walk on the seashore instead and think about the enlightening conversation we have had today." He rose, then moved toward the door. Yasammez could not help noticing that whatever was mortal in him now, or whatever feigned it, had not entirely diminished his grace. He still walked with the insolent silkiness of his younger days. She closed her eyes again.

Only moments after he had gone out she felt another presence— Aesi'uah, her chief eremite. Aesi'uah would stand silently for hours waiting for acknowledgment, Yasammez knew, but it was pointless to make her do so: the elusive point that Lady Porcupine had been chasing through the labyrinth of her own long memory was gone.

"Has the time come?" Yasammez asked.

Her adviser's complexion, usually the soft, warm gray of a pigeon's breast, was noticeably pale. "I fear it is so, my lady. Even with all the eremites mingling their thought and their song, he has withdrawn beyond our reach." She hesitated. "We thought . . . I thought . . . perhaps if you . . ."

"Of course I will come." She rose from her chair, her thoughts heavier than her thick black armor. For the first time that she could remember she felt something of the vast weight of her age, the burden of her long-stretching life. "I must say farewell."

The eremites had taken a cave for themselves high in the hills above an empty stretch of windswept beach a short distance east of the city. Quiet and solitude were the walls of their temple, and they had picked a good place for both things: as Yasammez followed Aesi'uah up the rocky trail she could hear only wind and the distant creaking of seabirds. For a moment she was almost at peace.

Aesi'uah's sisters and brothers—it was not always easy to tell which was which—were all gathered in the dark cavern. Even Yasammez, who could stand on a hilltop on a moonless, starless night and see what a hunting owl could see, could make out no more than the dull glitter of eyes in their dark hoods. Some of Aesi'uah's youngest comrades, born in the years of twilight, had never seen the full light of the sun and could not have survived its bright heat.

Yasammez joined the circle. Aesi'uah sat beside her. Nobody spoke. There was no need.

In the dreamlands, in the far places where only gods and adepts could travel, Yasammez felt herself take on a familiar shape. She wore it when she traveled outside herself, both in the waking world and here. In the waking world it was as insubstantial as air, but here it was something more—a fierce thing of claws and teeth, of bright eyes and silken fur. The eremites, given courage by her presence, streamed behind her in an immaterial host like a swarm of fireflies. The Fireflower did not burn inside them as it did in her; without protection, they could only travel so far.

Aesi'uah had spoken the truth, though—the god's presence was weaker than it had ever been, faint as the sound of a mouse walking in new grass. Worse than that, she could feel the presence of others, not the other lost gods but the lesser things that had been driven out with their masters when her father had banished them all. These hungry things smelled change on the breeze of the dreamlands and sensed that the time might come when they could return to a world that had forgotten how to resist them.

Even now, one such thing sat in the middle of the path, waiting for them. The eremites flew up in distress, circling, but Yasammez paced forward until she stood before it. It was old, she could tell that by the way it shifted and changed, its form too alien to her understanding for her eyes and thoughts to order it properly.

"You are far from your home, child," it said to one of the oldest creatures that still walked upon the earth. *"What do you seek?"*

"You know what I seek, old spider," she told it. "And you know my time is short. Let me pass."

"You are rude to a neighbor!" it said, chuckling.

"You are no neighbor of mine."

"Ah, but soon I might be. He is dying, you know. When he is gone, who will hold me and my kind back?"

"Silence. I want no more of your poisonous words. Let me pass or I will destroy you."

The thing shifted, bubbled, settled again. *"You have not the strength. Only one of the old powers can do that."*

"Perhaps. But even if I cannot end you, it may be that I will hurt you so badly that you will be in no condition to cross over when the time comes."

The thing stared at her, or seemed to, because in truth it had no eyes that Yasammez could see. At last it slithered aside. *"I do not choose to contest with you today, child. But the day is coming. The Artificer will be gone. Who will protect you then?"*

"I could ask you the same." But she had wasted enough time already. She passed and the eremites followed her like a cloud of tiny flames.

Yasammez moved as swiftly as she could through places where the wind howled with the voices of lost children and through others where the sky itself did not seem to fit correctly, until she came at last to the hillside where the doorway stood, a solitary rectangle crowning the grassy peak like a book standing on its end. She climbed the slope and crouched before it, curling the tail of her dream-form around her, ears laid flat against her head. The eremites hovered, uncertain.

"He can no longer be heard on this side of the door, Lady," they told her.

"I know. But he is not gone. I would know if he were." She sent out a call but he did not answer. In the silence that followed she could feel the winds that blew through the icy, airless places beyond the door. "Help me," she said to those who had followed her. "Lend me your voices."

They were a long time then, singing into the endlessness. At last, when even the inhuman patience of Yasammez had nearly gone, she felt something stir on the edges of her understanding, a faint, small murmur like the dying breath of the Flower Maiden in the stream.

" . . . Yessss . . ."

"Is that you, Artificer? Is that you . . . still?"

"I am . . . but I am . . . becoming nothing . . ."

She wanted to say something soothing, or even to deny it altogether, but it was not the way of her blood to try to bend what was real into what was not. "Yes. You are dying."

"It is . . . long awaited. But those who have waited almost . . . as long as I have . . . are readying themselves. They will . . . come through . . ."

"We, your children, will not let them."

"You have . . . you have not the power." He grew fainter then, small and

quiet as a drop of rain on a distant hilltop. *"They have waited too long, the sleeping . . . and the unsleeping . . ."*

"Tell me who we must fear. Tell me and I can fight them!"

"That is not the way, Daughter . . . you cannot defeat strength . . . that way . . ."

"Who is it? Tell me?"

"I cannot. I am . . . bound. Everything I am . . . is all that keeps the doorway closed . . ." And now she could hear the immense weariness, the longing for the end of struggle that death would finally bring. *"So I am bound . . . to keep the secret . . ."*

His voice fell silent—for a time she thought it was gone forever. Then something came to her, wafting like a feather in a night wind. *"The oracle speaks of berries . . . white and red. So it shall be. So it must be."*

Surely there was nothing left of him now. "Father?" She tried to be strong. "Father?"

"Remember the oracle and what it says," he said, his quiet voice now slipping away into nothingness. *"Remember that each light . . . between sunrise . . . and sunset . . ."*

"Is worth dying for at least once," she finished, but he was gone.

When she was herself again, the Yasammez that breathed, and felt, the Yasammez that had lived each painful moment of her people's millennial defeat, she rose and walked out of the cave. None of the eremites followed her, not even Aesi'uah, her trusted counselor. Death was in her eyes and in her heart. No living thing could have walked with her then and every one of them knew it.

🌿

This was not how Matt Tinwright would have chosen to spend his evening.

He broke apart the last small piece of bread he had brought with him and soaked up the wine in his cup. Sops, when he could have had eel stew! Still, he was lucky he'd found the wine, and he did not feel the least bit sorry for whoever had set it down. He'd been hiding on the chapel balcony from the evening bell to what must now be almost midnight, keeping an eye on the door that led to Hendon Tolly's chambers, which was where the physician's apprentice said Okros Dioketian had gone. What could the man be doing in Tolly's rooms so long? More important, when he finally came back out, would he return to his own chambers so Tinwright could go and sleep? Surely Avin Brone didn't expect him to follow Okros into his bedchamber . . . !

He heard the creak of the door opening before he saw the movement. Tinwright crouched lower, his eyes just above the balcony rail, even though he was a stone's throw away and hidden by the shadowed over-hang of the small chapel.

As he had prayed, Brother Okros came out of the door, his slight frame and bald head instantly recognizable despite his voluminous robes, but to Tinwright's surprise he was not alone: three burly men in quilted surcoats bearing the Tollys' silver boar and spears walked behind the physician, and another man in a dark, hooded cloak went beside him. Just the cloaked man's graceful movements were enough to tell him who this was. Tinwright's heart was pounding. Okros and Hendon Tolly, going some-where together—he would have to follow.

He felt quite ill at the thought.

He had expected them to head for the physician's chambers, but any hope of remaining indoors was dashed when Okros led the little proces-sion out of one of the residence's side doors. Tinwright did his best to remain well behind, and when he followed them out he tarried a few moments in idle conversation with the door guards, speaking of his own sleeplessness and the need for some cool night air to cure it.

Cool night air, indeed, he thought as he hurried across the side garden, trying to find his quarry again by the light of the torches they had brought from the residence. In fact, it was bloody freezing. All he had was his woolen cloak over a thin shirt—no hat, no gloves, and not even a torch to keep himself from stumbling. Curse Brone and his wretched, bullying ways!

He found them again crossing the muddy main road that led to the armory and the guard barracks and began to follow them at a distance. One of the guards was carrying a large bundle wrapped in cloth, and another gingerly held a smaller package—could it be the cockerel? But why would they be carrying the rooster around at this time of the night, unless they planned to use it in some kind of sorcerous ritual? Tinwright felt his blood grow even colder than the night air had already made it.

A moment later, as the group of men turned away from the main road that led to the Throne hall and instead walked down a winding path beside the royal family's chapel, the poet's blood grew even chillier. Tolly and Okros were headed toward the graveyard.

It took everything he had to keep following. Tinwright had a horror of cemeteries and the overgrown temple-yard was one of the most fearful, with its strange old statues and its mausoleums like prisons for the restless dead. His fear of Avin Brone alone kept him moving—his fear, and a certain curiosity as well. What did Okros plan? Did he mean to invoke the gods here in this lonely place, at this haunted hour? But why?

The men stopped outside the door of the Eddon family crypt and Tinwright had to suppress a groan of horror. Hendon Tolly had a key around his neck. When the crypt door was open four of the men went down the stairs, leaving a single guard to stand sentry outside. The light of the torches dimmed as they disappeared below, but their sheen still glimmered in the doorway. Tinwright felt very glad that he was not in that house of death with them, watching the shadows jump and crawl along the walls.

The sentry, who at first stood erect and alert at the entrance to the tomb, after a while began to slump a little, and at last leaned back against the carved face of the tomb and propped his spear against the wall. Tinwright (who would never have imagined himself so bold) decided this would be a good time to creep closer and perhaps hear something of what was being said inside. Surely that would be worth a few extra starfish from Brone—maybe even a silver queen or two!

He moved in a wide semicircle beyond the torchglow spilling from the door of the crypt until he had almost reached the wall of the chapel. Tinwright could see the sentry's back, and the man's slack posture emboldened him to creep forward until he was only a few paces from the doorway. He crouched behind a monument that had been half-immured in ivy creeping down from the temple wall.

"*. . . But not that way,*" someone in the crypt was saying, the words thin but clearly audible—Tinwright thought it was Okros. "*It is not the sacrifice here that matters, but the sacrifice there.*"

"*You are tiring me,*" said another voice—one that Tinwright knew all too well. Suddenly his moment of foolish optimism was over. What was a poet doing here in the middle of the night, playing at being a spy? If Hendon Tolly caught him he would be flayed alive! Only the fear of making noise and alerting the sentry kept Matt Tinwright from turning and bolting back to the residence. He was shaking so badly now he could barely keep his balance where he crouched. *"And boring me,"* Tolly continued. *"It is not my best mood, leech. I suggest you do something to make me interested again."*

"I . . . I am trying, my lord," said Okros, plainly anxious. *"It is just . . . we must . . . I must be cautious. These are great powers!"*

"Yes, but at this moment I am the greatest power you know. Go ahead. Complete the sacrifice however you see fit—but complete it. We must find the location of the Godstone or we will have no hope of making the power serve us. If we fail this gamble, Okros, I will not suffer alone, I promise you . . ."

"Please, my lord, please! See, I am doing as you ask . . ."

"You are only poking, you fool. Have I promised you inconceivable riches just to see you poking at a reflection? Reach in, man! Make it happen!"

"Of course, my lord. But it is not so . . . so easy . . ."

And then, even as the physician's voice grew softer and Tinwright leaned forward to hear him better, a sudden shriek split the darkness, rising so swiftly and so terribly that it did not sound as if it could come from a human throat, then dropping just as quickly into a choking, gurgling noise for the length of a rabbiting heartbeat or two before it vanished beneath the sound of men scuffing and clattering up the stone stairs as they fled the tomb.

The first one out of the crypt was a guard who fell to his knees at the top of the stairs and began to vomit. The second ran past him, holding his own mouth with one hand and waving a torch in the other. The first got up, still spitting, and began to follow him across the temple-yard, the two of them running in awkward zigzags between the monuments.

The tall, hooded shape of Hendon Tolly appeared in the door of the crypt, the large cloth bundle in his arms. "Go back to the residence," he told the sentry, who stood now gaping.

"But . . . my lord . . ."

"Shut your mouth, fool, and get moving. Follow that idiot with the torch. We dare not be caught here. Too much to explain."

"But . . . the physician . . . ?"

"If I must tell you again to be silent I will quiet you for good and all with a slit throat. *Go!*"

Within moments they had vanished into darkness, leaving Tinwright gasping and trembling, alone in the shadowed cemetery. The door to the tomb still gaped. Light still flickered there.

Matt Tinwright did not want to go down those stairs—no man with his right thoughts would do such a thing. But what had happened? Why was the torch still burning there in the depths, despite the silence? At the very least, he should go and pick it up—he did not want to cross the cemetery again without light.

Tinwright would never after be able to explain why he did what he did. It could not have been bravery: the poet was the first to admit he was not a brave man. And it was not ordinary curiosity—no mere curiosity could have overcome that terror—although it was something like it. The only way he could explain it was that somehow he *had to know.* At that moment, in the dark temple-yard, he felt sure that nothing would be more terrifying than to wonder ever afterward what had happened down there.

He put his foot on the first step and paused, listening. The light in the doorway below him was little more than a smear of yellow. Matt Tinwright went carefully and silently down the dark stairs until he reached the bottom. He could see the niches on either side, like dark honeycombs, and the torch lying on the stone floor. That was all he needed, really, he suddenly decided—let wondering be cursed. The burning brand was only a few steps away. He could crawl to it while staying close to the floor so he would not have to look at any of the empty stone faces atop the sarcophagi . . .

He saw Okros just as his fingers wrapped around the torch handle. The physician was just to one side, sprawled on his back with legs spread and left arm outflung, a piece of parchment still clutched in his hand. His eyes were impossibly wide and his mouth stretched in a silent scream, the face of a man so terrified that his heart had burst within the walls of his chest. But what was most frightening of all was his right arm—or, rather, the right arm he no longer had: all that remained was a short, shiny length of bone jutting from Okros' shoulder like a broken flute, the flesh peeled back all the way to his neck, showing the red muscle beneath. Nothing else was left from his right shoulder down except little strings and wisps of flesh, like the torn threads of hemp that remained after a rope snapped.

Worst of all, there was no sign of pooling blood in that entire wreckage of flesh and bone—not a single red drop, as though whatever had torn his limb away had also sucked his flesh dry.

Tinwright was still on his hands and knees, heaving out the contents of his stomach, when he felt something cold and sharp against the back of his neck.

"Look, now," a voice said, echoing against the walls of the crypt. "I come back for a scrap of parchment and find a spy. Stand up and let me have a look at you. Wipe the vomit from your chin first, there's a good fellow."

Tinwright climbed to his feet and turned around as slowly as he could. The cold, sharp thing traced its way up from his neck, bent his ear in passing, slicing the skin so that it was all he could do not to cry out, then was dragged ungently along his cheek until it stopped just below his eye.

By a trick of the light the blade of the sword was invisible: it seemed as though Hendon Tolly held him prisoner with a length of shadow. The Lord Protector looked feverish, his eyes bright, his skin glittering with sweat.

"Ah, my little poet!" Tolly grinned, but it did not look at all right. "And who is your true master, then? Princess Briony, pulling your puppet strings all the way from Tessis? Or is it someone closer—Avin Brone, perhaps?" For a moment, the sword threatened to slip higher. "It matters not. You are mine now, young Tinwright. Because, as you can see, I have lost one of my most important liegemen tonight and there is much still to be done—oh, much and much. I need a man who can read, you see." He gestured toward the one-armed remains of Okros Dioketian. "Of course, I cannot promise the job is without dangers—but nothing half so dangerous as refusing me. Aye, poet?"

Tinwright had to nod very carefully with the sword blade so close to his eye. He felt numbed, helpless, like a trapped fly watching the spider step slowly down the web.

"Then take that parchment from Okros," Tolly said. "Yes, pick it up. Now walk out ahead of me. Fortunate poet! You will sleep at the foot of my bed tonight—and every night from now on. Oh, the things you will see and learn!" He laughed; the sound was as bad as the sight of his smile had been. "A short time in my employ and you will never again mistake your empty, sickly sweet notions for truth."

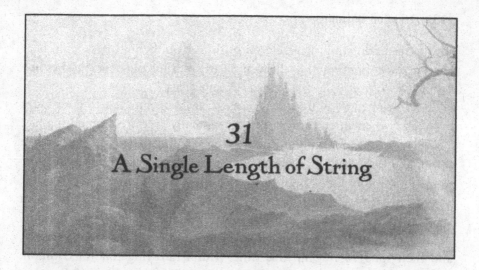

31

A Single Length of String

"Kupilas the Artificer, who figures only briefly in the many tales of the Trigon and the Theomachy, nevertheless seems to figure prominently in many of the Qar's stories. Some of their tales even suggest he eventually conquered the Trigonate Brothers—part of what Kyros calls 'the Xixian Heresy.' In Qar legends, Kupilas, whom they call Crooked, is generally a tragic figure."

—from "A Treatise on the Fairy Peoples of Eion and Xand"

BARRICK HAD ONLY AN INSTANT to draw his sword before the first of the skrikers was upon him. It came out of the darklight as if carried on the wind, pale robe flapping, ragged arms stretching wide. When he slashed at it his blade tore through cloth that seemed no sturdier than a rotting shroud. The pitch of its song changed but the eerie crooning did not stop as he jabbed at it again and again. He could not damage it—his sword touched nothing that felt like a body. Were these Lonely Ones nothing but billowing robes? Were they ghosts?

He was almost too frightened to think. The silkins had at least been real creatures, whatever they were made of—he could cut them and burn them. But he could not cut these skrikers and he had no fire.

Again and again the thing swept toward him and then whirled away, its rhythmic song winding in counterpoint around a fainter tune—so where, he suddenly wondered, was the second skriker? Barrick spun just as another undulating shape closed on him from behind. He could hear Shaso's voice shouting in his head as clearly as if the old man stood beside him: *"Don't let them fix you in place! Keep moving!"*

As he skipped away from this new attack, desperate not to get caught between two enemies, the first skriker suddenly produced something like a horsewhip, although it looked as though it was made of nothing more substantial than mist and cobweb. When it snapped the whip at him he jumped back, but the lash grazed his calf in an icy swipe of pain.

Now the two skrikers began to circle, trying to catch him between them again. Terror had a grip on him now, getting stronger by the moment: the second creature had also produced one of the strange lashes, and their song rose again, this time with a hurrying tone of triumph. What were these things made of? Why could he see nothing of them but their eyes, like spots of blood on the pale rags of their faces? They had to be more than air—but what were they?

As if it meant to answer his question, one of the skrikers lunged at him and for a moment its hood rippled open to reveal a nightmare face, bloodlessly white but for crimson bruises around the red eyes and a mouth like an empty hole—a female face without humanity or kindness, stretched into a shrieking mask.

That horrifying moment was almost fatal: as Barrick stood transfixed, the other creature caught him with the tip of its lash in the middle of his back. Pain crashed through him like a thunderbolt and dropped him to his knees. His sword clattered away, he didn't know where—the agony had all but blinded him. As he desperately sought the strength to stand the first of the skrikers slid toward him, raising its weapon. Instead of retreating toward the other creature Barrick threw himself forward and grabbed his attacker where its legs should have been. There was nothing there, or almost nothing—he felt rags and dampness and a crunching, brittle resistance like icy branches. Cold spread rapidly through Barrick's arms and within a moment he could feel the chill crawling into his chest, freezing his heart; it was all he could do to pull his arms free and roll to the side. As his fingers closed on his sword the things swept in on him, piping like excited jays, their song clotted with rapid clicking and slurring that might have been words.

Howling with disgust and fear, Barrick slashed and slashed with his sword, forcing the skrikers back a little way so he could climb to his feet, but his legs were so weak he could barely stand. He swayed, gasping for breath, unable even to keep the blade of his sword level. The situation was hopeless but he was determined to sell his life as dearly as he could.

Then, as the two things closed on him, eyes narrowed to bloody pinpoints and inhuman voices skirling in cold joy, something black whirled through the air and struck the nearest of the skrikers in the back. For a moment Barrick thought it was Skurn trying to help, but then the creature that had been hit straightened up and let out a weird *hoooo* of pain or surprise and Barrick saw that small black waves were lapping at its robes—black flames.

The second skriker had frozen in surprise, as if they were not used to being resisted. Barrick leaped forward and grabbed at it with both hands. Despite its seeming fragility it resisted him with surprising strength, but before it pulled free he was able to force it back just far enough to bring it into contact with its hooting, flapping companion. A moment later a blaze of shadow ran up its sleeves and onto its hood.

The first skriker was completely engulfed in dark flames, not singing any more, its voice a discordant, almost inaudible shriek. The waves of cold that came from it were too painful for Barrick to approach so he turned to the second one and waded into the chill, slashing away with his sword over and over until he felt the cloth ripping beneath his blows, great shreds of it coming away and tangling his blade. Now his foe was covered in black flames as well, its wordless voice shrilling louder and louder in what sounded much like fear, until it abruptly lost shape and fell away before him. For a moment Barrick grasped at several dark tendrils of something as slick and runny as melting suet, then the blackness flowed away into the ground and was gone and he held only empty, rotting robes that fell apart and ran through his fingers as dust.

He turned in time to see the other skriker thrashing for an instant in a haze of flickering, leaping darkness, then it fell in on itself with a huge pop and fizzle of ice-cold sparks and was gone, leaving nothing but a smoldering pile of clothes that dwindled away in a last flutter of shadow. But for the charred stump of its handle, the torch itself had entirely burned away.

For long moments Barrick could only stare, unsure of what had happened, dazed and aching. Then Raemon Beck stepped toward him out of the shadows of the trees, looking almost shamefaced.

"I . . . I went and got one of the darklights. I threw it."

Barrick let out his breath and sat down heavily. "You most certainly did."

He would have liked nothing better at that moment than to curl up and sleep, but it seemed unlikely they could burn away two of the city's guardians without anyone noticing. In truth, he realized, they might only have moments before more of the hideous things came. Groaning, Barrick struggled back onto his feet and led the reluctant Beck toward the massive stone wall and whatever lay beyond it.

They made their way cautiously through the wild tangle, following the wall until they found an arched gateway. The gate itself lay on the ground in lengths of rotted timber salted with bits of rusted metal: there was nothing to keep them out.

To Barrick's surprise, the courtyard beyond the gate was nothing but an overgrown field of grass like a sward around a manor house, although this greenery had not known the teeth of any grazing animals for some time—it was almost knee high, dotted with wild shrubs and netted with black creepers like veins beneath a man's skin. At the far end of this courtyard stood a wall with another archway and another collapsed gate.

"Let me go first and see what's here," Barrick said.

He had taken a few steps across the greensward when something grabbed at his ankles. He cursed and yanked his boot free, but when he put it down something clutched him again. The grass itself was twining around him, its blades probing the air like the lightning tongues of serpents, wrapping him in long stalks that continued to twist and climb up his legs.

"Stay back!" he called to Beck. "The grass—it lives!"

He hacked desperately at the stems, but for all the damage Qu'arus' sword did to them it might have been made of parchment. Some strands of grass now reached up to snatch at his hand as if it were trying to pull the weapon from his grasp. Behind him he could hear Beck shouting but could not make out what the man was saying.

The grass blades that had curled around his legs began to tug him downward, contracting like strips of drying animal hide. Barrick knew that if they pulled him to the sward he would never get up again. He was still slashing but still accomplishing nothing—a few of the strands parted, but for every one he cut two more seized him.

Then, just at his moment of greatest despair, an idea came to him.

Barrick shucked off the gray cloak he had appropriated and threw it out full length on the grass before him, then fell onto it, twisting as he did so, to land on his back in the middle of the garment. He could feel the grass squirming like clutching fingers beneath the cloth but the strands could not reach him through the heavy wool, which was pressed down by the weight of his body. Momentarily protected, he began to saw away at the grass imprisoning his feet. Hard, breathless work finally released him. For several moments he could only lie panting like a ship-wrecked sailor, his cloak a raft on an angry green sea; then, when he had a little of his strength back, Barrick began to crawl like a caterpillar across the length of the lawn. He moved the cloak with him, always keeping the heavy garment between him and the predatory grass. When he reached the far end and clambered off into the archway he took a swift look through it to make sure nothing else lay in wait for him there, then turned and threw the wadded cloak back to Beck. The cloak trick learned, Beck took less time to cross the greensward than Barrick had.

At last they huddled side by side in the archway, looking into the next courtyard. It was full of low-lying mist, but when Barrick looked closer he saw that the mist floated above a shallow pool of water that filled the courtyard as the other had been filled by grass.

"You will not try to walk through it, will you, my lord?" asked Beck.

Barrick shook his head. "I don't know what else we can do. But you don't have to come—I told you that."

The other man groaned. "What, turn back? After helping murder two of the Lonely Ones?"

"Ah, yes. That was clever," Barrick said as he threw his cloak back over his shoulders. "Burning them with their own darklight torch."

"No 'clever' about it, sire. I ran to grab something to fight with. The darklight was the first thing I saw."

For a moment Barrick almost felt warmth toward the man, even something like kinship, but that was a weakness he could no longer afford. He turned to examine the waiting pool.

The mist curled lazily above the water, but now he could see that it hid a row of cracked, ancient stones that rose just above the surface and led toward yet another arched gate at the far end. It was plain that they were stepping stones, but just as plain to Barrick that even so, crossing would likely not be as easy as it looked. He stepped out onto the first stone and waited an anxious moment for something to happen. When nothing did, he stepped to the next, sword gripped tight in his hand, eyes roving across the water for whatever fearsome creature might strike at him from the deceptively placid shallows. Still no menace emerged, so Barrick stepped forward again and Raemon Beck slowly followed him.

It was only as he reached the halfway point, beginning to hope that whatever might have once inhabited the pool was gone, that Barrick began to feel a weakness in his lower body, as though his legs were grain sacks and something had gnawed a hole in them. When he looked down he saw that the thin mist above the pool had thickened around his ankles and calves, foggy tendrils moving in a way that seemed to have little to do with any air currents he could feel. As he stared, and as the feeling of weakness began to spread, he thought he could see shapes in the mist, grotesquely deformed faces and clutching fingers. Everywhere the mists touched him he was getting cold. He took another step but his legs had grown so weak that he tottered and almost fell. He looked back helplessly at Beck, who was swaying under the same attack.

"Hurts . . . !" Beck moaned. "Cold . . . !"

"Don't fall!" Barrick was fighting to keep his balance; if he went into the water he knew he would not come out again, that the mist-faces would bleed his strength away.

That's it—they are bleeding us empty, like leeches . . .

The cold patches on his skin were spreading. His clothing did not seem to protect him from the heat-eaters at all, as if fever chills crawled through him—but these were on the outside, working their way in . . .

Warmer on the inside, he thought blearily. *We're all warmer on the inside. They want warmth . . .*

The idea was a mad one, but he knew he had only moments to do something. He lifted his left hand and slashed at it with Qu'arus' short sword. He barely felt the blade cut, as though he had plunged the arm in snow first, but blood welled in the crease of his palm and began to drip down his wrist. Barrick stretched out his arm, struggling to stay upright, and let the blood drizzle into the water.

Immediately the mists began to swirl faster, circling around the place where his blood was spreading pinkly through the water. The fog above the pool thickened, then it too began to turn a subtle rosy shade, like low clouds refracting the coming dawn.

"Move!" Barrick cried, but his voice was so weak he found it hard to believe that Beck could even hear him. He let more blood drip, then took a staggering step to the next flat stone. The mists swirled for a moment around the blood before moving toward him again. Barrick shook out more blood, but already the flow from his palm was beginning to slow. He cut himself in a different spot and let it drip into the water. Even the mist clinging to Raemon Beck's legs seemed to grow thinner as some of it wafted to the spot where Barrick's blood stained the water. Beck's first step was like a man waist-deep in mud, but the second came a little easier; after a few moments they were both lurching forward across the stepping stones toward the safety of the courtyard's far end.

By the time they collapsed into the archway, wheezing and shivering, Barrick had cut his arm in three more places. His entire arm and hand below his elbow were streaked and smeared with red, the few patches of clean skin as startling as eyes in a dark forest.

When Beck had caught his breath he tore off the ends of his tattered sleeves and began to wrap them around Barrick's wounds. The bandages he made were not the cleanest, but they stanched the blood well enough.

Barrick peered unhappily across the next courtyard. This one seemed even more innocuous than the others, a featureless stone close with steps at the far end leading up to what looked like a simple, closed door—but he knew better. "What's waiting for us this time, do you think," he asked sourly, "—a nest of adders?"

"You will defeat it, Highness, whatever it is." Something in Raemon Beck's tone made Barrick turn to look at him. Was that admiration he was seeing? Someone admiring the infamous cripple, Barrick Eddon? Or had the day's terrors simply injured the man's mind?

"I don't want to defeat it." Barrick could see Skurn circling high above their heads, far away from bewitched grasses and blood-drinking mists. One of them had some sense, anyway. "I want someone to come with a battering ram and knock it all down. I'm weary of all this."

Raemon Beck shook his head. "We must go forward. More skrikers will come to avenge their sisters and we will not surprise them the same way again."

"Sisters?" It made him feel ill. "They truly are women?"

"Not human women," Beck said grimly. "She-demons, maybe."

"Forward, then, as you say." Barrick knew there was a certain inevitability to what was happening: of course he couldn't go backward, anymore than he could go backward through life to repair the mistakes already made. He got to his feet, groaning. The numbness of the biting mist had worn off and he ached all over. What would the people of Southmarch think of their wretch of a prince if they saw him now?

Here I stand, he told himself, *the Prince of Nothing. No subjects, no soldiers, no family, no friends.*

Skurn dropped from the sky and fluttered down onto the paving stones on the far side of the archway. As the raven strutted back and forth only a few paces away, Barrick half expected something to reach up from between the stones and throttle the black bird, but either the lurking danger did not care about ravens or it was something more subtle.

"Happy now?" Skurn demanded. "Can't help wondering, us."

"Shut your snailhole, bird. I had to come to this wretched city. Now I have to do this as well. Nobody forced you to come along."

"Oh, aye, cast us out, 'course. All us did was warn you. Fair payment."

"Look, instead of scolding me like an old woman, tell me if you've seen anything. What's beyond this next courtyard?"

The raven eyed him. "Naught."

"Truly? Then what's on the other side of that door?"

Skurn squinted across the courtyard toward the ancient wooden portal, which was unmarked except for a corroded metal boss in the middle—a handle, perhaps.

"On other side? There *be* no other side."

"What are you talking about?" It was all Barrick could do to keep his temper. "Once we cross that courtyard and open that door, there has to be something on the other side—a building? Another courtyard? What?"

"Naught—us told you!" The raven fluffed his feathers in irritation. "Not even door. On far side be the outside of yon big wall. Then trees and whatnot. Same as the front, like. Nothing else."

Repeated questioning finally established that what sounded like a misunderstanding was in fact the truth: according to Skurn, who had flown over the site several times, nothing stood on the other side of that final wall with the door in it, and on the outside there was no sign that the door even existed. It was all some elaborate trick. Barrick slumped down in the archway, defeated, but Raemon Beck tugged at his arm.

"Come, Highness. Do not despair. We are nearly at the end." The man's patchwork clothing was now almost as badly torn and dirtied as

Barrick's own clothes, which he had been wearing for months. Barrick suddenly wondered what he must look like to someone else—what he must *smell* like.

Prince of Nothing, he thought again, and began to laugh. It took him so hard that for long moments he could do nothing but sit, bent double, wheezing.

"Highness, are you hurt?" Beck tugged again. "Are you ill?"

Barrick shook his head. "Help me up," he said at last, still struggling to catch his breath. He didn't even know why he was laughing. "You're right. We're nearly at the end." It was just that he had a different idea of what the end meant than Beck did.

Once on his feet Barrick did not pause—what use in waiting any longer?—but walked out of the arch and began to make his way across the cracked and crumbling stone flags of the empty courtyard. He did his best to hold his head up and walk forward bravely, although he knew that at any moment something would reach up from below or drop on them from the sky. But to Barrick's weary astonishment, no reaching hands clutched at him, no menaces leaped out of the shadows. He and Beck marched slowly but steadily across the stone courtyard until they stood on the steps looking up at the great gray door and its crude metal handle.

Skurn dropped onto Barrick's shoulder, clutching nervously with his claws so that Barrick squirmed in discomfort. He reached out toward the door, expecting that any moment something would happen to stop him—a noise, a sudden movement, an agonizing pain—but nothing like that occurred. His fingers closed on the rough, corroded metal of the handle, but when he pulled the door did not budge or even quiver. It might as well have been part of the wall.

Barrick wrapped both hands around the handle and pulled harder, ignoring the pain from his bandaged palm, but the door seemed as immovable as a mountain. He put his foot against the topmost step and leaned back, using his legs as well as his arms, but he might as well have been trying to heave the entire green earth onto his shoulders. Raemon Beck then put his arms around Barrick's waist and added his own weight and strength, but it still made no difference.

"Didst think on *pushing* yon great door, 'stead of just pulling?" offered Skurn.

Barrick stared at him balefully, then stepped onto the threshold and shoved as hard as he could. The door did not budge. "Happy now?" he asked the bird, then turned his back to the door and slid down until he was sitting on the threshold looking back across the gloomy, twilit courtyard, here in this place where no darklights burned.

"Pushed hard, did you?" Skurn asked.

Barrick scowled at him. "Try it yourself if you don't think so."

Skurn made a throaty sound of disgust. "Got no hands, does us?"

The raven's words poked at his memory. No hands. Barrick let his head fall back against the door—it felt as solid as the side of a granite cliff—and closed his eyes, but the thought remained elusive. He was so tired that the world seemed to tilt and pitch around him and he opened his eyes. Surely he had never been so tired in his life . . .

"Hands," he said abruptly. "It was something about hands."

"What?" Raemon Beck looked toward him, but the merchant's gaze was dull and hopeless. Barrick felt sure he was seeing an army of skrikers making their way across the courtyard of grass, then the courtyard of water . . .

"Listen," Barrick said. "The Sleepers told me something about this place—Crooked's Hall, if this is truly it. They said no mortal hand could open the door."

Beck barely seemed to have heard him. "We have to do something, my lord. More Lonely Ones will be coming soon!"

Barrick laughed, harshly, bleakly. What use was the knowledge even if it was correct? They were all mortal here, even Skurn. If it had been "no man's hand," perhaps the raven could have tugged the door open with his beak. Barrick snorted at the thought. Perhaps they should ask the skrikers to help them . . .

"Wait. *No mortal hand,* they said." He reached into his shirt and took out Gyir's mirror, then slipped its cord from around his neck. For a moment, feeling the mirror's substantial weight in his hand he had the strange sensation that it was a living thing he held, but he had no time for such thoughts—the idea that had just come to him was little to do with the mirror, but everything to do with the slender piece of anchor cord on which it hung.

Raemon Beck looked up from his exhausted slouch at the base of the steps. "What is that . . . ?"

"Don't say anything." Barrick leaned closer and threw the cord over the door handle, grabbing it with his hands on either side of the pouch that held the mirror. Then he pulled. Nothing happened.

Skurn flapped up into the air, circling once near Barrick's head.

"Them gray things. I see more by the river, coming this way," the bird announced. "Fast, like . . . !"

Barrick's fingers began to tingle. A moment later, a flicker of light ran the length of the string, so faint that only the dark shadows in the doorway made it visible. Without thinking he twisted his hands, one over the other, and pulled. The door swung outward with a deep rumble and an almost inaudible screech, as if the hinges were breaking free from centuries of rust. Barrick had to step back as the heavy door slowly swung past him, and Raemon Beck half-tumbled down the steps to the courtyard stones to avoid it. Skurn flapped his wings, hovering before the opening, but then suddenly spun in the air and vanished into the blackness beyond the doorframe as abruptly as if a great wind had caught him and swept him in.

"Hoy, bird!" Barrick flung out his hand toward the emptiness inside the door, but pulled back before his fingers passed into it. It was more than shadow, it was nothingness itself, like the black gulf that had taken Captain Vansen . . .

He felt a wind blowing past him, pulling at his hair, his clothes . . .

Raemon Beck only had time to tell him, "My lord, I'm afraid . . . !" then everything seemed to tilt up on edge and they both fell out of the world. Barrick couldn't scream, couldn't weep, couldn't think, could do nothing but tumble through the blackness, the cold nothing-at-all that already seemed to go on forever . . .

There was only void, without sound or light, without direction, even without meaning. Time itself had deserted this emptiness, if it had ever trespassed here at all. He waited a thousand, thousand years to breathe, and then a thousand more for his heart to beat. He was alive, but he was not living. He was nowhere, forever.

An age passed. He had forgotten everything. His name had gone long ago—his memories, too—and any purpose had vanished long before that. He floated in the between like a dead leaf in a river, without volition or concern and with no motion but what was given to him. The void itself might have rushed and surged like a cataract for all he knew, but because he was in it and of it, he felt nothing. He was a grain of sand on a deserted beach. He was a cold dead star in the farthest corner of the sky. He could barely even think anymore. He was . . . he was . . .

Barrick? Barrick, where are you?

The sounds fell upon his thoughts, stunning in their complexity. They were meaningless to him, of course—clumps of noise stopping and starting, artifacts of intent that could mean nothing to a leaf, a pebble, a cold spark whose light had guttered out. But still, the feeling of it tugged at him, quickened him. What did it mean?

Barrick, where have you gone? Why won't you speak to me? Why have you left me alone?

He thought of something then, or felt it, a mote of brilliance dancing before his eyes, a bit of light . . . a smear of fire. The brightness finally gave the void shape and as it did it gave him direction as well, *up* and *down, backward, forward* . . . The light emanated from a small, slender figure with dark eyes and darker hair—hair almost as black as the void itself but for one gleaming streak, the fiery smear that had caught his attention through the endless nullity. It was a girl.

Barrick? I need you. Where have you gone?

And then it began to come back to him, but in confused pieces, so that for a moment the black-haired girl seemed to be his sister, or maybe his betrothed. *Qinnitan?* He tried to call to her with all his strength. *Qinnitan!*

I am so lonely, she cried. *Why won't you come to me anymore? Why have you deserted me?*

I'm here! But although it seemed he was almost beside her, he could not make her hear him. *I'm here! Qinnitan!* She might as well have been on the far side of a thick, distorting window. They were alone in the void together, but they could not touch, could not speak . . .

Why? she cried. *Why have you forsaken me . . . ?*

Praise the ancestors. Another voice, another thought, suddenly intruded into the emptiness. *I have searched and searched. I thought you lost in the Great Between . . .*

Qinnitan clearly did not sense this presence any more than she heard or saw Barrick. Her voice was growing fainter. *Oh, Barrick, why . . . ?*

Come, the new voice said—a male voice. He had heard it before. *I will help you, child, but you must cross the gap yourself. It is late now—you must go directly through a dark time . . .* Then he could see it, a huge, pale shape on four legs, its head a complication of slender boughs like a young tree.

No, he realized, they were *antlers:* what stood before him in the endless dark, burning icily bright as a distant star, so that he could barely see Qinnitan beyond it, was a great white stag.

Follow me, it said. The very words seemed to glow with a pale lavender light of their own. *Follow—or have you already fallen in love with nothingness?* Something seemed to seize him then, a flash of white that lifted him loose from the void and pulled him away from the dark-haired girl.

No! He fought but could not overcome it. *Qinnitan, no, I'm here! I'm here!*

But she still could not hear him, and he could not fight this new force. A moment later she was slipping away, retreating into greater inclarity as though she sank beneath the surface of a muddy pond; the last he saw of her was a flicker of fire in the great black. Barrick felt as though his heart had been ripped from his breast and he was leaving it behind in the void.

Now he began to spin through alternations of heat and cold and flashes of light that pained and sickened him but did not entirely disperse the darkness. He was falling, he was flying, he was . . . he could not tell. The flashes of light came faster, the pulses of heat more frequently. Soon came sound as well—brief wordless hisses, groans, and then roars, as if the world of life and movement were crashing in on him like ocean waves and then receding just as swiftly.

I want to go back . . . ! But whoever had pulled him away from the dark-haired girl was no longer speaking to him, or at least Barrick could no longer hear his voice.

Qinnitan, I'm so sorry . . .

And then light and sound suddenly broke in like a river overflowing its banks, a flood of sensation that hammered at his thoughts until he could not think, only absorb. Madness surrounded him.

Faces big as mountains—faces that were mountains, vomiting out rockfalls—and faces like swollen thunderheads spitting lightning. Men that were storms and women that were fiery columns. Shadows riding horses that trampled tall trees beneath their hooves. The land itself riven and turned over, gouged into fresh valleys and mountains, the sky blazing with white light or popping and crackling as it filled with falling stars. Barrick could only cringe and whimper as it all thrust in upon him.

It was a war between gods, a war of giants and monsters, the maddest, strangest war that had ever been. The warriors became animals, became spinning winds or sheets of flame as they struggled with each other before the walls of a bizarre city, a rumpled hedgehog-hide of high, spiky crystalline towers that seemed to both loom and tremble, as though the sky itself pressed down on them. One moment the city seemed taller than any mountain, the next it was dwarfed by those who fought there, by both besiegers and besieged.

A battle was raging. Birds arrowed down from the sky in thousands, attacking a woman who seemed to be made of water, but who grew until she was a fountain higher than the black towers themselves. Bursts of blinding light revealed whole armies of skeletal soldiers that became invisible again when the light died. Stones swirled like windblown leaves, a snake made of bundled lightning squeezed the top from a mountain and set it tumbling down to shatter one of the castle walls. The hole was quickly patched by a swarm of insects all made from metal, huffing steam at every crack and joint.

In the center of everything three massive figures stared down upon the gates, their shapes indistinct even in the brightest glare except for the icy, star-bright gleam of their eyes. One of them held a massive hammer forged from some dull gray metal, but the other two held spears, one spear double-pronged and green as the ocean, the other as black as a hole in the ground.

Barrick knew those three, although it terrified him to admit it, even to himself.

The middle figure raised his hammer and what seemed like a storm of bright shadows rushed forward and flung itself against the walls of the great castle, fiery shapes, glowing shapes, changing shapes, their combined radiance so great that Barrick could scarcely make out what was happening. For a moment it seemed that the city, for all its size and magnificence, must simply burn away like a dry forest in a raging firestorm. Then an even brighter light began to burn like the rising sun and the attackers fell back from the walls in disarray.

Only two shapes came forward from the besieged city, but they drove back the attackers. One was a great sphere of blazing amber light, the other a chilly, blue-white glow that somehow remained visible even beside the greater golden brilliance. The shapes of two riders sitting proud and tall atop their mounts could be seen within these two powerful lights, each rider carrying a sword; it was impossible to tell whether the glow came from the figures themselves, from the blades they carried, or from the armor they wore, but faced with the bright radiance of the two the besieging army now scattered in all directions.

The roar in Barrick's ears became louder, so that his skull boomed and echoed as though a storm beat inside it. He could scarcely see for the blazing light. The three shapes on the hill spurred their mounts forward, rushing down the slope, the hooves of their monstrous horses not even touching the ground. They raised their weapons and the very sky seemed to crack open to bring unending darkness stabbing down at them all.

And then, suddenly, they were all gone—the fire-women, the air-men, the beautiful figures in their terrible anger, all the fighting and all the fighters ended and vanished in an instant. Only the castle itself remained, its pale, shining towers now toppled like trees after a winter storm, broken and scattered so that the pieces gleamed in the muddy ashes like droplets of molten gold on the floor of a forge.

Barrick had only seen the mad beauty that had preceded this ruination for a short moment, but as he stared at the destruction he found himself mourning what had been lost with every nerve of his being.

Then, without warning, he found himself plunging downward. The ruins of the castle were changing even as he rushed toward them: what had been gleaming gold, pale blue-green, or creamy white now grew back black and twisted, and what had been translucent became full of shadow. The castle that had been so marvelous was now only a dusty, deserted cobweb where a shining, rain-shimmering spider's net had once hung. The beauty was gone, but in some strange way it remained.

It was the same. It was completely different. And Barrick fell into it like wind blowing down a well.

He had only a moment to realize he was lying facedown on a floor of flat, polished, and carefully interlocked black stones. He heard strange skittering noises getting closer, and then, a moment later, the whisper of soft footfalls.

He opened his eyes to a nightmare. The faces pressing down on him were bestial, with rolling, idiot eyes and gaping fanged mouths. Only the shape of their heads was vaguely human. That was the worst part.

"Ah," said a voice behind him—a cold, unfamiliar voice. "Very good, my dear ones. You have caught a trespasser."

32

Mysteries and Evasions

"Another tribe of fairies described in **Ximander's Book** *are the Tricksters, Qar who seem to be the bargain-making fairies of many human legends. Only Ximander and a few other scholars claim to know anything about them, and since Ximander died before his book was read by any others, his sources are unknown and therefore his conclusions are untrustworthy."*

—from "A Treatise on the Fairy Peoples of Eion and Xand"

"IN TRUTH, it is not so strange at all," said Brother Antimony, warming to his subject. "The tongue the prisoner speaks is much like the old language of the *Feldspar Grammars.* You may not know this, but the *Grammars* were written on perfect mica sheets, each one shaped from a single crystal, and they contain stories of the Eldest Days found nowhere else . . ."

Vansen cleared his throat, interrupting the enthusiastic young monk. "That's all very well, Antimony, but we need to know what *this* fellow is saying *now.*"

He flushed so deeply that Vansen could see it even in the dim light that Funderlings loved so much. "My apologies . . ."

"Just go on, son," Cinnabar told him. "Talk to the prisoner, if you can."

The young monk turned to the trembling, scowling drow, who clearly thought he had been brought to the refectory to be tortured. Two Funderling warders stood behind the fierce little bearded creature, ready for trouble, but Vansen wasn't worried. He had seen many men being questioned and this one showed signs of the false, blustery courage that would collapse quickly.

"Ask him why they have attacked us here in our home," said Vansen.

Antimony uttered a halting string of deep, throaty sounds. Some of the other Funderlings looked bemused, as though it had a familiar ring, but to Vansen it was all noise. The shaggy-bearded drow looked up at the monk, resentment in every dirty line of his face, but did not answer.

"Ask him why they follow the dark lady." He struggled for a moment to remember the name Gyir had given her. "Ask him why the drows follow Yasammez."

This time Antimony's question made the drow stare in surprise. After a moment, he said something—short and clearly reluctantly given, but something.

Antimony cleared his throat. "He says that . . . Lady Porcupine, I think that is the name . . . that she will crush you. That she will have revenge against the Sunlanders. I think that is right."

Vansen suppressed a smile. Slogans—that was what you got from prisoners who did not actually know why they had been fighting. "I'm going to step to the back of the room, Antimony," he told the monk. "You and Cinnabar ask him some questions about why drows would take up arms against their brothers—against Funderlings."

He gestured as if in frustration and walked away. Cinnabar leaned in and began to ask questions, Antimony carefully translating. Vansen noticed that every now and then Cinnabar recognized one of the foreign words and repeated it. Vansen could not help being impressed by the magister's wits.

Thus he underscores the connection between them—see, drow, he is practically speaking your tongue now!

Vansen stood quietly in the background as Cinnabar continued asking questions, leaning heavily on the idea that the Funderlings were closer relatives to the drows than the Qar leaders they served, but still the prisoner would not tell them anything.

Ah, but if we have created even the smallest bit of sympathy or shame . . . Vansen thought. "Ask him what his name is."

Antimony looked surprised, but asked. The drow looked shamefaced, but grunted a reply.

"*Kronyuul,* he says—that is 'Browncoal' in the old tongue, I think."

"Good," said Vansen, still speaking quietly so as not to draw attention to himself. "Then ask Master Coal why exactly his Lady Porcupine wants our castle. What will she do with it if she gains it? Why does she waste so many drow lives to take this castle?"

After Antimony had translated the drow stared back at him, apparently at a loss for words. At last he began to murmur. It went on for some time. The young monk leaned close to hear, then straightened up.

"He says the dark lady is angry. The king of the Qar would not let her simply slaughter us wicked folk—he calls us something like 'sun-land-dwellers'—but forced her instead into some kind of a pact. The dark lady did her best to honor that pact, but it failed. Her . . . I do not understand the word he uses . . . her relative, her friend, something—it is a little like our word 'clansman' . . . was killed, and so now she says the pact is broken. She blames the fairy-king, but she is also angry because of her kinsman." Antimony sat back. "That seems to be all he knows—he is only a petty officer of the belowground army . . ."

Vansen's heart was suddenly beating fast. "Perin's hammer, I don't believe it. The pact? Did he say pact?"

Antimony shrugged. "Bargain, pact, treaty—the word is not precisely the same as . . ."

"Silence! No, I beg your pardon, but do not say anything for a moment, Antimony." Vansen did his best to remember. Yes, he thought, it all seemed to fit. "Ask him if he knows the name of the lady's kinsman—the one who was killed. The one whose death ended the pact."

The young monk, surprised by Vansen's vehemence, turned and passed the question along to the drow, who was looking less frightened and more puzzled every moment. "He wants to know if you are going to kill him," Antimony said after listening to the man's reply. "And he says that he thinks the kinsman's name was Storm Lantern."

"I knew it!" Vansen slapped his hand on the stone table, making the prisoner jump. "Tell him no, Antimony—no, we are not going to kill him. In fact, he is going to be set free to lead me back to his mistress. Yes, I will go and speak to her. I will tell her the truth about the Storm Lantern and the pact. Because I was *there*."

Haltingly, the monk translated Ferras Vansen's words to the prisoner. The small room fell silent. Vansen looked around. Cinnabar, Brother Antimony, Malachite Copper, even the drow—all were staring at him as though he had utterly lost his mind.

Chaven's bed still hadn't been slept in. In fact, there was no sign the physician had even been in his cell.

"He's not here," Flint said in his solemn, high-pitched voice.

"I know he's not," Chert growled. "We haven't seen him for days—not since he let you run off when he was supposed to be watching you. But I want to talk to him. Did he say anything to you about going somewhere?"

"He's not here," Flint said again.

"You're going to make my head cave in, boy." Chert led him out of the room.

"Captain Vansen isn't here," Cinnabar said. "He's preparing for a trip where he'll risk his life to do something I don't quite understand and which seems to have no chance of succeeding in any case." He sighed. "I hope you have some better news for us."

"I'm afraid not," Chert told him. "I found no sign of Chaven anywhere in the temple."

Cinnabar frowned. "That is very strange and worrying. He is under threat of death from Hendon Tolly, so why would he go upground into the castle, or even into Funderling Town?"

"Let us hope he has not gone off on his own somewhere and fallen," said Malachite Copper. "So much is dark down here, especially beyond Five Arches—we might never even find his body."

Brother Nickel was furious. "I told you it would make trouble—a stranger who is not even of our tribe wandering willy-nilly in the temple grounds and beyond! Bad enough that Chert Blue Quartz's child found his way into the Mysteries. What if this . . . upgrounder, this magician-priest, should do the same? What kind of misfortune might he bring down on us all?"

"Why should Chaven want to enter the Mysteries?" asked Chert.

"Why shouldn't he?" Nickel was so angry he could barely control himself. "It seems everyone thinks they have business in our most sacred places these days! Upgrounders, children, even the fairies!"

"Fairies?" Chert turned to Cinnabar and Heliotrope Jasper in confusion. "What does that mean? I've heard nothing of this."

"Jasper and his warders have stopped a few attempts to dig into tunnels beneath the temple levels," said Malachite Copper. "But that proves nothing—likely the fairies were only trying to find a way to take us unaware. Then after beating us, they could surprise the castle's defenders by appearing from the gates of Funderling Town, already well inside the castle walls."

"You are deluding yourself," said Nickel. "They seek the power in the depths." He glared at Chert as though the Blue Quartz family were somehow complicit in this vile plan. "They seek to control the Mysteries."

"Why? Why would the fairies want such a thing? What could that even mean?" Chert looked at Nickel's angry face and saw a flash of sudden fright there, like a child caught in an obvious lie. "Hold a moment. There is something going on here that I don't understand. What is it?"

"Tell him, or I will," said Cinnabar. "Chert's earned our trust."

"But Magister!" Nickel looked distraught. "Soon everyone will know the secrets . . ."

"The Guild granted me authority and I will decide, Brother. Besides, perhaps the time for secrecy is over." The magister sighed and slumped back in his chair. "Still, may the Earth Elders forgive me, but I wish this burden had passed to another generation."

Chert looked from face to face. "I don't understand any of this. Can someone please tell me what it's about?"

Despite his comparative youth, Nickel had the face of a much older man, and just now he looked as though he had bitten into the sourest radish in a harsh crop. "This is . . . this is not the first time . . . that the Qar have tried to get into the Mysteries. They have been there many times."

Chert could only stare. "What?"

"As I said," snapped Nickel. "They had been coming for as long as the Metamorphic Brothers have kept records. The elders of the brothers and of the Guild knew it and permitted it, more or less—it is a complicated story. But then it ended, and it has been a long time since they last came. Two hundred years and more."

Chert shook his head. "I still don't understand. What did they do in the Mysteries?"

"We don't know," said Cinnbar. "There is an old tale of some monks who snuck down into the Mysteries and tried to spy on the fairies—or the Qar, as the fairies call themselves—but the tale says that those men lost their minds. The fairies came only seldom—perhaps once a century at most—and always in small groups, which may be why it was permitted. The tradition was old when the first Stonecutter's Guild was formed seven centuries ago. They always came through the Limestone Gate from Stormstone's longest road, the one that leads to the mainland. They stayed only a few days and never took anything of value or harmed anything or anyone. For a long time our ancestors did not interfere, or so the story goes. Then, after the battle at Coldgray Moor, the Qar stopped coming."

"But if they had a way to gain entry, why didn't they just use it again this time?" Chert asked.

"Because we sealed the Limestone Gate after the second war with the fairies," said Brother Nickel with an angry sniff. "They proved themselves untrustworthy. That is why they've had to dig their way in from the surface. And that is why they try so hard to reach our holy Mysteries!"

Chert rubbed his forehead, as if to knead what he had just heard into a more sensible shape. "Even if that's true, it doesn't explain the *why* at all, Nickel. Does nobody know what they did down there, or why they were permitted in the mysteries in the first place?"

Cinnabar nodded. "In truth, it seems that in a past age the Qar helped to *build* the Mysteries—no, my apologies, Nickel, I do not mean to blaspheme. I meant to say they helped build the tunnels and halls in the depths, not the Mysteries themselves."

"Fracture and fissure!" Chert felt as though he had been struck by a rockslide, as though he were being carried down and away from everything he knew. "And I only learn this now? Am I the only person in Funderling Town who didn't know?"

"This is new to me, also," said Copper. "I do not know what to say."

"It is new to all of us, even me," Cinnabar said. "Highwardens Sard and Caprock called me to them before they sent me here and told me. Only the highwardens themselves and a select few chosen by the innermost circle of the Guild have known this. For Nickel it was the same."

"It's true," said Brother Nickel. "The abbot told me when he became ill. '*This is a young man's time,*' he said to me. '*I am too old to keep these secrets to myself any longer.*'" The monk scowled. "I have been given more generous gifts."

"'We do not keep Grandfather's ax because it looks handsome in the hall,' as the old saying goes," Cinnabar told him. "We are carrying the trust of all who came before us and all who come after. We must do what is right."

"Then we must pray to the Lord of the Hot Wet Stone that your Captain Vansen has not lost his mind," said Brother Nickel. "That he can achieve something more than getting himself killed. Otherwise, we may throw back another attack, perhaps two, but eventually we will fall and the Mysteries will be theirs."

"Not just the Mysteries," said Malachite Copper. "If we fall, then Funderling Town will fall, and then the castle above will be theirs, too."

"What are we doing, Father?"

It still seemed strange for the boy to call him that, almost as if the child were playing the part of a dutiful son in one of the Mystery Plays. "I am frightened for Chaven and I want to look for him," Chert explained. "But I am not going to make the mistake of leaving you alone again. By the Elders, I miss your mother!"

Flint looked back with calm eyes. "I miss her, too."

"Maybe I should send you to her in Funderling Town. It would keep you out of trouble—or at least keep you out of trouble in the temple."

"No!" For the first time the boy seemed agitated. "Do not send me away, Father. I have things to do here. I need to be here."

"What nonsense is that, child? What could you need to do?" Flint's certainty made Chert uneasy. "You're not going to go rummaging in the library anymore, do you hear me? Nor make any surprise excursions down into the Mysteries. As it is, the brothers have barely forgiven you or me."

"I need to stay in the temple," the boy said stubbornly. "I don't know why, but I do."

"Well, we can talk of it more later," Chert said. "For now you can come with me. But you stick by my side, is that understood?"

In truth, he was just as glad to have the boy's company. Chert was growing more and more worried about the physician, increasingly certain that Chaven had not simply wandered off somewhere. Either he had been taken by the Qar, which was a frightening thought, or he was in the grip of his mirror-madness again, which might lead to something even worse. Chert didn't plan to search anywhere very dangerous, although nowhere beneath Funderling Town would ever feel completely safe again after the last year's madness, but if several uneventful days had not passed since the last Qar attack he would not have dared bring the boy out of the temple. Even so, he had slipped both a stone pick and hand ax into his belt, and carried a greater than ordinary amount of the lamp coral.

Elders protect us both, he thought. *The boy from any harm, and me from Opal should anything happen to him.*

He missed his wife. Never in his life since the days he was apprenticing under old man Iron Quartz and had traveled with him as far as Settland had he been separated from her so long. It was not that he missed her in the same way he had when they were newly married, when to be apart from her felt like a bodily ache, when he could not be near her without touching her, teasing her, kissing her, and to be denied those things was torment; rather he missed her now as he would have missed a part of himself if it had been taken from him. He was incomplete.

Ah, old girl, I really do ache for you! I'll have to tell you that as soon as I see you, instead of being silly. I can't wait until I can give you the squeezes I've been saving. And I want to hear your voice, even if you're calling me foolish. I'd rather be mocked by you than praised by the Guild.

"She's a good woman, your mother," he said out loud.

Flint cocked his head. "She's not my real mother. But she is a good woman."

"Do you remember your real mother?" Chert asked.

Flint kept walking, but Chert had learned the boy had different kinds of silences. This was the kind that meant he was thinking.

"My mother is dead," he said at last, his voice as flat as a split slate. "She died trying to save me."

But despite this sudden, surprising assertion, when pressed Flint could not remember anything else. After a while, concerned that they were far enough from the temple now that quiet was better than unnecessary talk, Chert let the matter drop.

They searched the dark areas at the sides of the Cascade Stair and up as far as the tunnels on the level below the Salt Pool, then stopped to eat mushrooms and some smoked mole Chert had brought for a treat. They were thirsty when they'd finished so they walked a little way farther up the great stair to a spot where the sloping cavern was pierced by a natural sinkhole, a phenomenon the Funderlings called an "Elders' Well." Unlike the Salt Pool, which seeped in from the bay and whose surface was never any higher or lower than the sea itself, the Elders' Wells were full of fresh, sweet water that soaked down from rainfall on Midlan's Mount. In fact, it was these sinkholes that made life on the great rock possible for both the Funderlings and the Big Folk, who dug their own wells into these aquifers from the surface.

As he watched Flint kneeling at the edge of the pool, filling his hands and drinking with his usual fierce concentration, as though experiencing something he had never done before, Chert wondered at how the simplest things in life could be so complicated. Here, fresh water. Only a few hundred cubits above was the saltwater of Brenn's Bay. Only the limestone of Midlan's Mount kept the two apart, and if that ever changed—say, perhaps because of an earth tremor like the ones that occurred frequently in the southern islands, but never in Chert's memory here—then everything else would change, too: the bay would flood in and drown everything lower than the Salt Pool, killing all the monks and everyone else in the temple. Many of the deeper sweet water springs would become undrinkable.

And yet despite this precarious balance, life had gone on here, hardly changing, for century upon century. Chert, with the help of the Blue Quartz family tablets, could track his own line back nearly ten generations; some of the richer and more powerful families claimed they could name a line of a hundred ancestors.

But would the next generation be able to say the same? Or would they be reciting their Funderling history in some kind of poor scrape or burrow after a Qar victory had destroyed their ancient home? Would the Funderlings of days to come live wild in unshaped caves, as some of their more eccentric philosophers claimed their ancestors once had?

Chert realized with a little start that Flint had finished drinking and was standing just in front of him, staring with those calm, wide eyes. "Did you hear that?" he asked. "I thought I heard someone moaning."

"Could it be Chaven?"

The boy shook his head. "Too big. Too deep."

"Likely just earth sounds, then. Sorry, lad. I was thinking about water and stone—the kind of things an old guildsman like me tends to think about."

"This is shellstone," the boy told him solemnly, holding up a pale, irregular rock. "The kind of limestone with shells in it."

Chert laughed and stood up. "I'm glad to see you've been paying attention. Good lad."

Having found no sign of Chaven or anything else out of the ordinary in the halls around the Cascade Stair, Chert and Flint made their way down past the temple again and through the Five Arches gateway, then into the complicated web of tunnels that led down to the Maze. He was not going to go any closer to the Mysteries, of course—the last thing he wanted to do was run the risk of somehow losing track of the boy in those confusing depths—but if Chaven was lost somewhere in the deeps below the temple, this seemed the most likely place to look. The Maze was even more confusing, of course, but if the physician had made his way that far down Chert would need the help of the Brothers themselves to search it properly: he had not forgotten his own disturbing experiences in that benighted place.

Something like an hour later, Chert was standing at the fork of two tunnels and thinking it was probably time to give up and head back to the temple if they wanted to have a hope of supper when he noticed that Flint was no longer standing behind him.

He ran back down the tunnel, fear swelling inside him. "Flint!" he shouted. "Boy! Where are you?" Chert cursed himself over and over again as he searched every cross-track he had passed: everything Opal had ever said about him, even at her most uncharitable, was clearly true—he was an utter dunderhead. Bringing the boy right back to the place where he had already vanished once, a place where he had suffered through the Elders only knew what kind of terrifying times!

As he was exploring perhaps the sixth or seventh cross-track he found himself in a long corridor that dipped and twisted several times. After he had run for some time Chert began to feel he was wasting too much time down this one rabbit hole. He was just about to turn and make his way back to the main hall when the corridor opened in front of him. This wider space ended in a great crevice as wide as the Funderling's arm and three or four times his height, but he had only a moment to notice that before he saw the pale-haired figure lying crumpled in the shadows a short distance away.

"Elders preserve us all!" he cried and threw himself down on his knees beside Flint. To his immeasurable relief, the boy was breathing, and even began to stir as Chert pulled him a little way off the ground and awkwardly cradled him against his chest.

"Oh, child, what have I done?" Chert said. The boy twitched in his arms, just a little at first, but then harder. A moment later Chert felt something wet and warm against his neck and leaned back, searching desperately for a bleeding wound . . . but it was not blood that had run from the boy's face and splattered on him but something else. Flint was weeping.

"Boy?" Chert said. "Boy, what is it? Are you well? Can you hear me?"

"Dying . . ." he said. "Dying."

"You are not! Don't say such things—you will draw the Elders' attention!" He pulled the boy close to him again. "Don't tempt them—they must fill their hods with souls each day."

Flint groaned. "But I feel . . . Oh, Papa Chert, it hurts so!"

"Don't fear, boy. I'll get you back."

"No, it's not me. That is . . ." The boy struggled in Chert's arms so that he could barely hold him. "It's there. I felt it. There!" He pointed to the crevice at the end of the passage. "Dying!" he said, and moaned as if caught in the claws of some agonizing disease.

Chert let the boy down gently and crawled closer, letting the fragile beam of his lantern play over the crevice. "What do you mean? Is there something in there?"

"Something . . . something I do not . . ." Flint shook his head. He was pale, and in the lantern light Chert could see that beads of sweat covered his face. "It frightens me. It hurts. Oh, please, Papa, I'm dying . . . !"

"You're not dying." A shiver ran up Chert's back and neck. Long ago, in the Eddon family tomb, the boy had acted the same way, even before he had disappeared into the Mysteries. "It's a hole, boy, or rather it's a crevice where two big slabs come together. Why does it frighten you?"

Flint could only shake his head, his expression sullen and a little trapped. "Don't know."

Chert moved forward until he could look inside the crevice, but saw nothing by the pale, yellow-green light except more stone. The crevice was no wider than his two hands flattened side by side. "It seems ordinary enough to me . . ." he began, but then realized something about it did seem familiar. But how could that be? It was nothing but two great pieces of stone and the narrow space between them . . .

"That smell," he said suddenly. It was faint, but now that he'd noticed it the scent was as clear as the sound of a tap hammer ringing on crystal. "I've smelled it before . . ."

The memory when it came was as powerful as a blow—the dark, massive cavern of the Mysteries, the lake of gleaming metal and the Shining Man itself . . .

"By the Hot Lord," he swore, and did not even realize he had voiced such a fierce oath in front of the child. "That's where . . . that smell . . . ! In the cavern. The quicksilver pool. The Sea in the Depths!" He remembered that he had wondered at the time where the air escaped to, because quicksilver vapors were poisonous, but he and the boy—and, presumably, many monks over the years—had all come away from the Sea in the Depths alive. Also, now that he thought about it, quicksilver itself had no scent.

He leaned back to the crevice, sniffing. He could detect another smell as well—something of the sea, which must be air drifting down from the surface above—but it was the scent he identified with the silvery pool that was most noticeable. He would have to ask Cinnabar what it could be.

"Come on," he said to the boy. "Up now and let's go back to the temple."

Flint did his best, but he was weak and could hardly stand. He was too big to be carried on Chert's back, but Chert found that if he let the boy lean on him they could make slow but steady time. They would be late for supper, though. At another time that would have made him very bitter indeed, but the fright the boy had given him, coupled with the strange smell of the Sea in the Depths, had largely taken away Chert's appetite.

It made him think again about the strangeness of this little world beneath Southmarch—a world not only vaster and more complicated than the Big Folk living on the surface dreamed, but clearly more than even Chert and the other Funderlings realized. If the Sea in the Depths vented to the surface, as it must then the opening should be somewhere within the walls of Southmarch Castle. Nothing strange about that—the limestone of Midlan's Mount was full of holes, and there were many such cracks that kept air moving through Funderling Town and the depths, otherwise so many people could not have made their home there—but for reasons he could not even begin to guess, the knowledge that there was only air between the Shining Man and the surface of the world now troubled Chert's thoughts like an ache.

*   *   *

Getting past Five Arches seemed to do much for Flint's strength: by the time they were making their way up the lower Cascade Stair he was able to walk unsupported, although he was still short of breath and had to stop often to rest.

"I'm sorry, Father," he said during one such pause, "I was . . . I thought I was dying. But it also felt like someone I loved was leaving me—as if you or Mama Opal were going away."

"Never mind, Son. You'll feel better with some soup in you. No shame in any case—those are strange passages down there, everyone knows it."

As they approached the temple along the path through the ceremonial fungus gardens they saw a bulky shape standing at a point where two paths crossed, looking down at a lacework of white fungal strings that had been induced to grow over a frame in the shape of the sacred mattock. As they drew closer, Chert began to think he recognized who stood there.

"Chaven? Is that you? Chaven!" He hurried forward. "Praise the Elders, you're back!"

The physician turned, his face mild and smiling. "Yes, I am," he said, but with the air of someone who has only been out for a short walk.

"Where did you go?"

Chaven looked past him to the place where Flint had stopped in the middle of the path. The boy seemed in no hurry to come closer. "Hello, lad. Hmm, where did I go?" He nodded as though the question was a wise one, one that required proper thought instead of a rushed answer. "Out to the passages beyond Five Arches. Yes."

"We just came back from there. How did we miss you? Have you been back long?"

Still the mild, surprised look. "I was . . . you know, I cannot completely recall. I was looking into some ideas . . . some . . . thoughts . . . that I had." He frowned a little, in the way of someone who has just remembered an undone errand. "Yes, I had some thinking to do, and I just . . . wandered."

Chert was going to question him further, determined to get some better answers than this unsatisfying fare, when one of the monks suddenly appeared at the top of the path, waving both arms and clearly excited.

"Blue Quartz, is that you? Come quickly! We are invaded."

"Invaded?" Chert felt terror rise inside him. Would there never be any peace? Did this mean Vansen had failed?

"Yes," the monk said. "It is dreadful. There are women everywhere!"

"What? Women? What are you talking about?"

"Women from Funderling Town. The magister's wife and all, they just arrived. Dozens of them! The temple isn't meant for all these women!"

Chert laughed in relief. "Yes, you brothers are in for it now, you poor scrapers!" He turned to Flint. "That means our Opal's come back, too. Come on, boy."

As they followed the anxious monk, Chaven fell a few steps behind them as if still pleasantly distracted by his thoughts.

Flint leaned close to Chert. "He's not telling the truth," the boy whispered. He did not sound as if he disapproved, but instead simply reported dry fact. "Not all of it. He's hiding something important from us."

"I had the same feeling," murmured Chert. Up ahead, monks swarmed the colonnade in front of the temple like mice escaping a cat. "The same feeling. And I do not like it at all."

❧

So I'm back in armor again, thought Ferras Vansen with weary amusement as he adjusted the byrnie the Funderlings had given him, a chainmail shirt made from a surprisingly delicate series of barred links that was so light it scarcely needed any underpadding. *Ah, well, at least I didn't have enough time to grow used to freedom.*

"I packed some food, as you asked, Captain," said Brother Antimony. "Some bread and cheese and a couple of onions. Oh, and we are lucky—look!" The monk held out an open sack. "Old Man's Ears!"

For a moment Vansen's stomach threatened to crawl up his throat and leap out of his mouth. Then he realized that although the things in Antimony's bag did look like fleshy, shriveled ears, they were in fact some kind of mushroom. Still, they smelled very strange, dark and damp and musty; Vansen found it difficult to muster much enthusiasm. "Yes. Splendid."

"I still don't think this is a good idea, Captain," Cinnabar told him. "Let us at least send a dozen men with you. Jasper is up and around."

"Yes, take me, Captain." Sledge Jasper's bald head was so cut and bruised it looked like it had been carved from marble. "I'll do for some of those meadow-dancers. Yes, I wouldn't mind killing a few more at all."

"Which is why this isn't the mission for you," Vansen said. "I wouldn't waste our best fighter when I don't want a fight. They need you more here."

"But we need you here, Vansen," said Malachite Copper. "That is the most important truth."

"You must trust me, gentlemen—I can do more good this way. Would you rather have me here waiting to defend against another attack, or out making sure there are no more attacks?"

Cinnabar shook his head. "That is chop-logic—those are not the only two possible outcomes. You might be killed without any bargain made. Then we have neither a defender nor a peacemaker."

"Not a very cheerful thought, Magister, but I must chance the odds. I am the only person who can do this, you must believe me. And if I take too many men with me, I will not only leave your defenses compromised, but increase the chance my mission will be seen as an attack. My only hope is to speak to their leader, face to face." He turned to Antimony. "I admire the rope around the prisoner, Brother—we must certainly keep him tied to us—but I would rather see it around his ankle than his waist. If he tries to get away I want to be able to jerk him off his feet." He looked sternly at the drow, who, although he could not understand Vansen's words, could certainly understand his tone. The bearded little man cringed in fear, baring his snaggy yellow teeth.

They did not linger in the leavetaking: Vansen knew Cinnabar and the others did not agree with him, and he felt bad himself that he had to take Antimony, a very well-liked fellow. It was possible another of the Funderling monks might be able to translate, but he trusted young Antimony to keep his head in a crisis, and despite his own show of confidence he knew he had only a very small chance of achieving his goal without something going wrong.

The drow, who still seemed to fear some kind of treachery by his captors, trudged ahead on his short length of rope, leading them up into the Festival Halls, back to the spot where the Qar had broken through. Cinnabar's men had almost finished filling the space where the Qar had dug their way in, stacking rock so expertly that it was impossible to get past. Vansen was taken aback—he had forgotten that the breach was being repaired. How would they get to the Qar? Not by any surface route, that was certain: if the confused bits of news that had trickled down to Funderling Town and thence to the temple were true, aboveground the siege had turned into a full-bore invasion. He and Antimony would never survive an attempt to reach the Qar that way.

It would take hours to shift the stone again here—hours these Funderlings should be spending improving the defenses elsewhere instead of undoing and redoing their work. Ferras Vansen leaned against the wall, suddenly weary beyond words. Commander? General? He wasn't even fit for his old post as guard captain.

The drow looked the repairs up and down, then looked at Vansen. He said something in his harsh, gulping tongue.

"He says . . . I think he says there is another way to reach his camp from here," Antimony told Vansen.

"Another way? The Qar have another way into our caverns?" He stared at the little bearded man. "Why would he surrender that secret to us?"

"He is afraid if we turn back now the rest of my people will lose patience with him and kill him. He says the hairless one—Jasper, of course—was . . . making gestures." Antimony suppressed a smile. "Making it clear that he would be happy to wring this one's neck . . . or worse."

"I'll wager he was." Vansen nodded. "Yes, tell him we will let him show us the way."

"He asks only one thing. He begs you not to tell Lady Porcupine that he showed you a path you did not already know. He says that would mean an ending for him more terrible than anything even the hairless one could imagine."

33
Caged Children

"Rhantys, who claimed to speak with fairies himself, says that the Qar queen is known as the First Flower because she is the mother of the entire race. Rhantys even suggests her name, Sakuri, comes from a Qar word meaning 'Endlessly Fertile,' but the absence of a Qar grammar means this is hard to prove or disprove."

—from "A Treatise on the Fairy Peoples of Eion and Xand"

IT WAS NOT THAT PINIMMON VASH disliked children. He had always kept dozens of them as slaves, especially for his closest needs. All boys, of course—he found girls unsatisfying and inadequate. Still, he had young female slaves among his household as well. No one could claim he had anything against children. But it was the strange pointlessness of these particular children he found disconcerting.

Not to mention all the work it had caused him. It was one thing to deal with the autarch's ordinary moods, his sudden urges to eat bizarre foods or to hear some exotic style of music or experiment with some ancient, near-forgotten form of interrogation. That was well within the ordinary scope of Vash's job; he had performed such services for other autarchs before this one. In fact, he prided himself on his skill at foreseeing such requests and having at least the beginnings of fulfilling them at all times. But Sulepis made even his grandfather Parak, a man of wild appetites and fancies, seem as staid as the oldest and most constipated priest in the great temple. And now . . .

"Go ashore with a troop of soldiers," the autarch had told him when they made land at Orms, a city in the marshy Helobine country south of Brenland, and began trading with the locals to refresh the ship's supplies of fresh food and water. "Go some miles outside the walls—I do not wish to waste my time fighting with these people, and if I set my men on the city I will have to let them off the leash and then we will be here days and days. So take your men out to the countryside and bring me back children. Alive. A hundred should do . . ."

There had been no further explanation, of course, nor instruction: there seldom was with this autarch.

Seize one hundred children from their homes. Bring them back to the ship. House them, feed them—keep them alive and more or less well. But am I told why? No, of course not. Ask no questions, Vash. You may be the autarch's oldest and must trusted adviser, but you deserve no courtesies, he told himself sourly. *Just do as you are told.*

The paramount minister walked one last time around the section of the hold that had been boxed in with lashed staves to make a cage for the young prisoners. A dozen were housed here, the rest scattered out over several other ships. Feeding them was not the problem, Vash thought as he examined their pale faces, so confused, sullen, or blankly terrified. But keeping them alive— how was he supposed to do that? Already several of them were running at the nose and coughing. A cage in the hold was not a very warm place to house a dozen half-naked children, but would the autarch understand that if a sudden fever ran them through them and took them all? He would not.

No, then it'll be my head, Vash thought gloomily. He stared at a weeping boy and wished he could reach through the bars and hit the child to make it stop crying. *And even if I am lucky and manage to keep them alive for whatever madness he plans, what next? What next, Pinimmon?*

The autarch's parade of strange whims continued. They had started off from Hierosol in a single ship, but many more ships from the Xixian navy had caught up and joined them during the voyage, all loaded with soldiers. Now, after the fleet had skirted Brenland and passed through the Connord Straits, they landed in a shallow bay in the wild lands along the eastern border of Helmingsea. This was as much of a surprise to Pinimmon Vash as the order to capture one hundred children. He was increasingly convinced that his master was deliberately leaving him in the dark about the most important parts of this weird venture.

Stranger still, a troop of the autarch's fierce White Hound soldiers and their horses now went ashore in boats. They rode off west into the forest and had not returned when the autarch told the captain to weigh anchor. The fleet was still many leagues from Southmarch, their apparent destination, so Vash could not even guess at what mission the White Hounds had been left behind to fulfill.

"Let us be honest with each other, Olin," Sulepis said, "as men of learning and brother monarchs, if nothing else." Now that they were at sea again, sweeping along the coast toward their destination, the autarch was in an expansive mood. He was standing so near the railing—and the condemned northern king—that Vash could almost feel the anxiety of his Leopard bodyguards, who were watching the situation with the fixed, predatory stares of their namesakes. "Most of what we are told of the gods by priests, by the sacred books, is nonsense," he continued. "These are tales for children."

"Perhaps that is true for the tales of your god," Olin said stiffly, "but that does not mean I so lightly throw away the wisdom of *our* church . . ."

"So you believe everything your *Book of the Trigon* tells you? About women turned to lizards for spurning the gods' advances? About Volos Longbeard drinking the ocean?"

"The intentions of gods are not for us to judge, nor what they can accomplish if they choose."

"Ah, yes. On this we are agreed, King Olin." The autarch smiled. "You do not find the subject interesting? Then let me speak of more specific things. Your family has a certain invisible . . . deformity. A stain, as it were. I think you know what I mean."

Olin was clearly furious but he kept his voice even. "Stain? There is no stain on the Eddons. Just because you have the power to kill me, sir, does not mean you have the right to insult my family and my blood. We were kings in Connord before we came to the March Kingdoms, and we were chieftains before we were kings."

The autarch looked amused. "No stain, is it? Not of character or of body? Very well, then, let me tell you a little of what I have learned. If you still say I am wrong when I've finished—why, on my oath, I might even apologize. That would be entertaining, wouldn't it, Vash?"

The paramount minister had no idea what Sulepis wanted him to say, but his master was clearly waiting for an answer. "Very entertaining, Golden One. But astonishingly unlikely."

"But let me tell you a little of my own journey first, Olin. Perhaps that will give you some idea of what I mean. You will be interested too, Lord Vash. No one else in all Xis has heard this tale, except for Panhyssir."

His rival's name was like a hot coal dropped down his collar, but Vash did his best to smile and look gratified. At least the high priest was elsewhere; otherwise, the humiliation would have been even more excruciating. "I listen eagerly for whatever wisdom my lord wishes to share."

"Of course you do." Sulepis seemed to be enjoying himself: his long-boned face kept creasing in wide, crocodilian smiles and his unusual eyes seemed even more lively than usual. "Of course you do.

"I have know that I was not as other children since I was very young. Not simply that I was the son of an autarch, because I was raised with dozens of others who could claim the same thing. But ever since I was a small boy I have heard and seen things that others could not see. After a while I came to realize that I, of all my brothers, could actually sense the presence of the gods themselves. Truly, every autarch claims to hear the speech of the gods, but I could tell that even for my father Parnad these were empty words.

"Not so for me.

"But here was a strange thing! All of the other royal sons and I were the children of the god-on-earth—yet only *I* could sense the presence of the gods! Stranger still, I had no greater power than this one small gift. The gods had given me no greater strength than other mortals, no longer life, nothing! And clearly the same was true of my father as well, and all his other heirs. The autarch of Xis was nothing but an ordinary man! His blood was ordinary blood. All that we had been taught was a lie, but only I had the courage to acknowledge it."

Vash had never heard so much blasphemy spoken—and it was being spoken by the autarch himself! What did that mean? How was he supposed to react? Indifferent as he largely was to religion, except insofar as it was the steady heartbeat of Xixian court etiquette, still Vash could not help cringing, wondering if any moment the great god himself might not strike them all down with his fiery rays. Clearly, every worry he had entertained about the autarch's sanity had been justified!

"So I took it upon myself to learn more about it," Sulepis continued, "both about the blood of the gods and the history of my own family.

"At first I spent my days exhausting the great libraries of the Orchard Palace. I learned that before my ancestors swept out of the desert to take the throne of Xis the city had been ruled by other families who claimed kinship with other gods. The farther back I went, the more these ancestors were described as being close to godlike themselves. Was this because they were closer to their godly ancestors than we moderns are, so that the holy blood ran thicker in their veins? Or had the stories around them simply grown over the years? What if these ancient monarchs, self-proclaimed descendants of Argal or Xergal, had been no less mortal than the dull creatures being raised around me in the palace—no less mortal than my father? Parnad might be fierce and cunning, but I had long since learned that he had no wit for and no interest in matters of religion and philosophy.

"Some of the priests recognized in me what they thought of as a kindred spirit. They were wrong, of course—I have never been interested in esoteric knowledge simply for its own sake. A single mortal lifetime is too short for such untrammeled, undisciplined study. I had only one thought in mind. Without the truth I had no tool, and without a tool I could not reshape the world into something I liked better.

"In any case, the library priests began to tell me of books they had heard of but never read—for the first time I came to understand that there were writings that the libraries of the Orchard Palace did not possess, writings in languages other than our own, some of which had not even been translated into Xixian! Do you wonder why my Hierosoline is so good, King Olin? Now you know. I learned it so that I could read what the ancient scholars of the north had to say about the gods and their doings. Phayallos, Kofas of Mindan, Rhantys—especially Rhantys—I read them all, and searched for the forbidden books of the southern continent as well. I finally located a copy of *Annals of the War in Heaven* in a temple near Yist, where my several-times-great-grandfather had destroyed the last of the fairy cities in our land."

"There were Qar in your land?" It was the first time Olin had spoken for a while, and he sounded, Vash thought, as though he were interested despite himself.

"Were, yes. My ancestors took care of that." Sulepis laughed. "The Falcon Kings are not such sentimentalists as you northern rulers—we did not wait for a plague to destroy half our kingdoms before driving out the fairy vermin.

"My search for truth took me to many strange places in my youth. I unearthed cylinder-books from the serpent tombs of the Hayyids that cover the plains like the castings of desert ground-cats. I bargained with the *golya* at their desert fires, eaters of man-flesh who are also said to be shape shifters—they become hyenas under the full moon's light. They told me tales of the earliest days and showed me the stone carvings they had carried since the gods walked the earth. From them I learned the secret of the Curse of Zhafaris, the curse of mortality that the great god of all laid on humanity when his children turned against him.

"I even plundered the resting place of my own kin, the Eyrie of the Bishakh, where my desert chieftain ancestors had been laid to rest atop high Mount Gowkha, their mummified bodies resting on nests made from the bones of slaves, their fleshless faces looking east to where the Sun of Resurrection will rise. As the moon climbed overhead and the howls of the *golya* rose from the desert canyons below, I pried stone tablets from my forefathers' crabbed, dead hands in search of heaven's secrets even as my guards fled in terror down the mountain.

"But all I learned confirmed only what I already knew. The gods might be real, but their power was gone and no man had it, not even the autarchs of Xis. My line may have been fathered by holy Nushash, the lord of the sun himself, but I cannot make a light in a dark room without a lamp, nor light that lamp without a flint.

"But as I followed the ancient scholars down paths so dark and forbidding that even the library priests finally began to shun me, I learned that what was true of my own ancestors was not necessarily true of all people. Some families, I learned, had been said since the eldest days to carry the blood of the gods in truth, often through the *Pariki*, the fairies—the ones you know as Qar."

"I do not wish to hear any more of this story," Olin said abruptly. "I am weary and ill and I beg your leave to go back to my cabin."

"You may beg all you like," said the autarch with a look of annoyance. "It will not do you any good. You will hear this story, even if I must bind and gag you to obtain your collaboration, because it amuses me to tell you and I am the autarch." His expression changed into a smile. "No, I will make it simpler. If you do not agree to listen I will have one of our child captives brought to me and I will strangle it in front of you, Olin of Southmarch. What do you say to that?"

"Curse you. I will hear you out." The northern king's voice was so quiet that Vash almost couldn't hear him over the noise of the sea.

"Oh, you will do more than that, Olin Eddon," said the autarch. "You see, *you* have such blood in you—the blood that bestows the power of a god. To you it is worthless, a curse, but it means everything to me. And in only a few days now, when the final bell of Midsummer's Day tolls, I will take it for my own."

The last few hours of darkness before the Tessis city gates opened were terrible. Briony huddled on the floor of the company's wagon and tried to sleep, but despite her great weariness sleep would not come. Feival's treachery, the cruelty of Lady Ananka, and the mistaken, unfair, and foolish judgment of King Enander would not leave her head, the words these enemies had spoken buzzing in her head like blackflies.

And now I am a fugitive again, she thought. *What have I accomplished here in all this time? Nothing—no, less than nothing. Another city is barred to me and I have lost all hope of bringing any help to Southmarch from Syan.*

Finn Teodoros came quietly into the wagon. "Your pardon," he said when he saw she was awake, "just looking for my pens. Did Zakkas nip you, Princess? You look full of deep thoughts."

She frowned at the casual blasphemy. The oracle was the patron of both prophecy and madness and fits of either were sometimes called "Zakkas bites." "I'm fretful and I can't sleep. I've spoiled everything."

The playwright sat down beside her. "Ah, how many times have I said that myself?" He laughed. "Not as many times as I should have, I suppose—I seldom see what I've done wrong until much later. It's good you see it immediately, but don't let it carry you away."

"I wish I could sleep but I can't keep my eyes closed. What if they're waiting for us at the gate?"

"Waiting for us? Not likely. For you . . . perhaps. Which is why you will stay in the wagon."

"But someone may have remembered you. That Lord Jino is a clever man. He said he was sorry for what happened to me, but that won't keep him from doing his job. He'll have noted the name of the troupe."

"Then we will call ourselves something else," said Finn. "Now try to rest, Princess."

He went out, his weight on the small steps making the wagon bounce and sway, leaving her alone with the voices of her many failures.

★ ★ ★

By the time they rolled up to the city gates, Makewell's Men no longer looked much like a company of traveling players. The masks and ribbons and all other displays that had served as a flag of their profession had been hidden, and the players themselves were dressed in unexceptional traveling clothes. Still, for some reason they had attracted the attention of one of the guards and Briony was beginning to feel anxious. Had someone in the castle remembered the players after all?

"Where did you say you were going?" the man asked Finn for what must have been the third or fourth time. "I've never heard of it."

"The well of Oracle Finneth, in Brenland." Finn told him as calmly as he could.

"And these are all pilgrims . . . ?"

"By the Three!" Pedder Makewell had little patience at the best of times. "This is outrageous . . . !"

"Shut your mouth, Pedder," Teodoros warned him.

"You don't know of Finneth's Well?" Nevin Hewney stepped in front of Makewell. "Ah, that's a pity, a true pity." Hewney was better known for his writing than his acting, but here he stepped smoothly into the scene and began to improvise. "Young Finneth was a miller's daughter, you see, a chaste, pure girl. Her father was an unbeliever—this was back in the days when Brenland and Connord were mostly heathen, counting the Three Holy Brothers no different from the other gods." Hewney put on the rapt look of a believer—for a moment, even Briony, peering through a crack in the boards of the wagon, found herself believing his fervor. "And her father was ashamed that she went around preaching the sacred word of the Trigon, and denouncing him because he was living with a lewd woman without marriage in the temple, as is proper," Hewney went on, seizing the guard's elbow and leaning so close that the man flinched back. "So he and his lewd woman seized Finneth in her sleep and threw her between the stones of the mill, but the stones would not turn, you see, would not harm her. Then they dragged her to the well at night and threw her in to drown, but in the morning . . ."

"What are you babbling about?" The guard pulled his arm away.

"I am telling you of the Oracle Finneth," said Hewney patiently. "And of how in the morning the women of the village came to the well to draw water, but Finneth rose up from the waters, shining like one of the gods themselves, and spoke to them of the truth of the Three Brothers, of the Sixfold Way and the Doctrine of Civility to Domesticated Animals . . ."

"Enough, man!" groaned the guard, but just as it seemed he was about to send them on their way Briony felt the wagon bounce and heard the wagon's door rattle. She threw herself back on the ground and pulled the blanket up to her neck.

"And who is *this?*" It was one of the other gatehouse guards. He climbed into the wagon and stood over her. Briony moaned but did not open her eyes. "Why is this girl here?" he demanded. "Let me see you."

Briony felt his rough hand close on the blanket and pull it away. She brought her hands up to shield her belly and the bundle of rags stuffed under her threadbare dress.

"Please, sir, please!" said Finn. "That is my wife. We are taking her to the oracle's well to ask for a safe birth. None of our other children survived . . ."

"Yes," said Hewney from behind him. "My brother-in-law has suffered terribly. There is something wrong with his wife, the poor, corrupted woman—we think she is diseased. The last birth, a noxious black discharge came out of her with a stink like rotting fish . . ."

Despite her fear, Briony almost laughed as the guard backed hurriedly out of the wagon.

When the gates of the city were at last out of sight behind them, Briony emerged to sit on the steps of the wagon as it bumped down the Royal Highway, the broad river Ester shimmering beside it in the early morning sun.

"Civility to Domestic Animals?" she asked. "And *rotting fish . . . ?*"

Hewney gave her a superior look. "I knew a woman in Greater Stell who smelled like rotting fish all the time. She had her share of suitors, too, believe me."

"Not to mention a clutter of cats that followed her everywhere she went," laughed Finn. "Well done, Princess. I see you have not forgotten what we taught you." He clasped his ample stomach. "'Oh, my poor baby! Oh, poor me!' Most convincing."

Briony could not help laughing. It was the first time she had done so in a while. "Rogues, all of you."

"Which still makes players more honest than most noblemen," said Hewney.

Briony lost her smile. "Except for Feival."

Hewney's face turned grim as well. "Yes, except for him."

★   ★   ★

They made it all the way to Doros Eco that night, a walled town nestled in the foothills above the river. It was a cool, windy evening. As Briony huddled in her cloak and watched Estir Makewell tending the cook pot, she realized that for the first time in months she felt . . . free. No, not precisely free, but the heaviness that had seemed to press down on her every day in Broadhall Palace, the weight of other people's suspicions or expectations, was now gone. She was still worried, even terrified, by what had happened to her life and the people she loved, but here beneath the open sky, surrounded by people who didn't want anything of her she wasn't happy to give, she certainly felt a little more hopeful about things.

"Can I help, Estir?" she asked.

The woman looked at her with more than a little suspicion. "Why would you, Princess?"

"Because I want to. Because I don't want to sit and watch someone else do it. I've had that all my life."

Pedder Makewell's sister snorted. "And that's such a bad thing?" She pointed at a couple of carrots and a whiskery onion. "Make yourself happy, then. The other knife's over there. Chop those for me."

Briony spread a kerchief in her lap and began to cut up the vegetables. "Why are you here, Estir?"

The woman did not look at her. "What sort of question is that? Where else would I be?"

"I mean why do you travel with the players? You are a comely woman. Surely there have been men who have . . . who have favored you. Did none of them ever ask you to marry?"

The look of distrust returned. "As it happens, yes, though it's no business of yours . . ." She suddenly went a little pale. "Forgive me, Highness, I forgot . . ."

"Please, Estir, forget all you want. We were . . . we were almost friends, once. Can't we be that way again?"

Estir Makewell sniffed. "Easy to say. You could have me killed, my lady. One word from you to the proper folks and I'd be bunged up in a tower, waiting for the headsman. Or whipped in the town square." She shook her head, worried again. "Not that I think you'd do that, of course. You're a kind girl . . . a proper princess, that's what I mean . . ."

It was impossible to have an ordinary conversation with the woman. Briony gave up and concentrated on chopping carrots.

＊　＊　＊

As the days went by Briony began to fall back into the rhythms of life on the road. The players had the last of her money so they did not have to give performances, but they prepared sets and props and costumes for the plays Finn, Hewney, and Makewell intended to perform when they were back in the March Kingdoms again. To everyone's astonishment young Pilney, Briony's onetime stage husband, had fallen in love with the daughter of an innkeeper—*not* the treacherous Bedoyas, but the master of the Whale Horse—and had stayed behind in Tessis to marry and help his new father-in-law. Between this loss and the less charming defection of Feival Ulian, Briony found herself called on to stand in for most of the girls and youth parts. It was amusing and even enjoyable, but this time she could never quite rid herself of the knowledge that it was a temporary thing, that the world was much closer to her now than it had been on their trip into Tessis.

One obvious proof of that was the news they got in towns and from other travelers. On the trip south people had been talking about the events in the March Kingdoms, rumors about the fairy-war and the change of regime in Southmarch and about the autarch's siege of Hierosol. Now they still talked about the autarch, but the rumors were both more fearful and more confused. Some said he'd razed Hierosol to the ground and was marching north toward Syan. Others suggested that for some reason he'd gone to Jellon and attacked that nation. Still others had him sailing toward Southmarch, a tale that made no sense at all to Briony, but still filled her with dread. What would a monster like that want with her tiny little country? Could it be true? Was she hurrying toward an even worse situation than she already feared? Of course, the other rumors were just as troubling, if not more so: if Hierosol had truly fallen, where was her father? Was Olin even alive?

It was not surprising that Briony couldn't find as much joy in playing a part as she once had.

Hewney and Pedder Makewell came back from the town looking very discouraged.

"The king's soldiers have already been here as well," Makewell said, washing the dust of the road from his mouth with a gulp of sour ale. "We dare not go into town except in ones and twos."

Briony felt her heart sink. It was not that she had particularly wanted to walk into the small town—what would there be for her, anyway, an inn's common room where she would have to keep her face mostly hidden? A few market stalls where she might shop for some trinkets if she had any money to spare, which she did not?—but the knowledge that King Enander was hunting her so seriously, so soon, was disturbing. Worse still was the knowledge that if she were captured, Finn and the players would suffer badly for her sake.

A long shadow fell over her. "You look sad, Princess." It was Dowan Birch, the company's tallest member, doomed to play every ogre and cannibal giant in defiance of his true, sweet nature. Briony did not want to trouble him or the others with her fears—they all knew well enough what was going on.

"It is nothing. Why didn't you go into town with Pedder and the others?"

He raised his thin shoulders in a shrug. "If somebody is looking for Makewell's Men, they are more apt to remember me than any of the others."

She lifted her hand to her mouth in surprise. "Oh, Dowan, I am so sorry! I didn't even think of that. I have trapped you here, skulking in camp, just like I have trapped myself."

He smiled sadly. "It's just as well, truly. People always stare at me wherever I go and I am weary of it. I'm happy to sit here," he gestured around their camp with his impossibly long arm, "where nobody notices me."

"That's a very small dream, Dowan."

"Oh, I have bigger ones than that. I dream of a day when I can have a farm of my own . . . settle down with a good woman . . ." He blushed suddenly and looked away. "And children, of course . . ."

"Birch!" called Pedder Makewell. "Why are you idling when there is mending to do?"

He rolled his eyes and Briony laughed. "Coming, Pedder."

"I meant to ask you," she said, "how is it that you learned to sew so well?"

"Before I became a player I studied to be a priest, and lived with other acolytes in the temple of Onir Iaris. There were no women, of course, and we all had tasks. Some discovered themselves to be cooks. Some didn't, but thought they were," he said, laughing a little. "Me, I found myself to be reasonably skilled with a needle and thread."

"I wish I could say the same. My father used to say that I stitched like a woman killing spiders with a broom—poke, poke, poke . . ." Now Briony laughed, too, although it hurt to think of Olin. "Gods, how I miss him!"

"He still lives, you said. You shall see each other again." Birch slowly nodded. "Trust me. I often have such feelings and they are usually right . . ."

"You are going to have the feeling of losing your place in the world and having to beg for your meals," called Pedder Makewell loudly. "Get on with your work, you great stilting stork!"

"We had one like him in the temple, too," Birch whispered to Briony as he stood. "We poured a bucket of water over him one night when he slept, then swore that he pissed his own bed."

As she laughed the tall man started to walk away, then turned. A strange, distracted look had come over his face.

"Do not forget, Princess," he told her. "You *will* see him again. Be ready to say what you need to say."

Qinnitan finally learned her captor's first name, but largely by chance. She also learned something else that she hoped she could put to better use than any name.

Half a tennight or more had passed since she had dreamed of Barrick turning his back to her on the hilltop, and although she had dreamed of the red-haired boy again he never responded and each time he seemed farther away. The helplessness of her situation had begun to wear away at her resolve. She sat for hours each day watching the distant coastline slide past, struggling to think of some plan for escape. Sometimes other boats passed nearby, but she knew that even if she called to them no one would try to help her, and that even if someone did they couldn't outfight the demon Vo, so she kept her mouth shut. She had already cost poor Pigeon his fingers—why cause the death of an innocent fisherman?

On the night she learned Vo's first name she had lain brooding for a long time before falling asleep. Padding footfalls woke her in the thin, cold hours after midnight; she could tell by the step that it was Vo who paced the deck. She lay listening to him as he walked back and forth in a tight pattern of which her own position might have been the midway point. She wondered at the muttering that every now and then rose above the continuous slap and slosh of the waves against the boat until she realized it was her captor talking to himself in Xixian.

The thought of such an iron-willed man talking to himself was frightening enough: it betokened madness and loss of control, and although Vo terrified her, Qinnitan knew that if he remained in his right mind she would at least live until he handed her to the autarch. But Sulepis had put something inside him, and if that were hurting him badly, or if the drops of poison he took each day were somehow sickening his mind, anything could happen. So Qinnitan lay trembling in the dark, listening as he paced around the deck.

He seemed to be having a conversation with someone, or at least was speaking as though someone was listening. Much of his talk seemed a list of grievances, many of which meant nothing to Qinnitan—some woman who had looked at him mockingly, a man who had thought himself superior, another man who had fancied himself clever. All had been proved wrong, it seemed, at least in her captor's fevered mind, and now he was explaining this to some imagined auditor.

"Skinless, now, every one of them." His hissing, triumphant voice was so chilling that it was all she could do not to cry out. "Skinless and eyeless and weeping blood in the dust of the afterlife. Because Daikonas Vo will not be mocked . . ."

A few moments later he stopped a little distance away. She risked opening her eyes a little, but could not quite make out what he was doing: Vo's head was thrown back, as if he downed a cup of wine, but the movement lasted a moment only.

The poison, she realized. Whatever was in the black bottle, he was taking it at night and not just in the morning as she'd thought. Did he always do that? Or was this something new?

When Daikonas Vo had finished he staggered a little and almost fell, which was the strangest thing yet: she had never seen him anything less than dangerously graceful. He sat down on the deck with his back against the mast and let his chin sag to his chest, then fell silent, as though he had dropped into a deep slumber.

Learning his first name brought Qinnitan nothing. Hearing him talking angrily to himself merely left her even more frightened than she had been—he truly did seem to be going mad. But what stuck in her thoughts was the way his body so quickly grew slack and heavy after he put the poison to his lips.

That was indeed something worth thinking about.

34

Son of the First Stone

"Eenur, the king of the fairies, is said to be blind. Some say he took this
wound when he fought on the side of Zmeos Whitefire during the
Theomachy and was struck by a fiery bolt from Perin's hammer. Others
say that he gave his eyes in return for being allowed to read the
Book of Regret."

—from "A Treatise on the Fairy Peoples of Eion and Xand"

A FIGURE IN A PALE ROBE stepped forward out of the confusing shadows. The three beast-things retreated to swarm
around it like a huntsman's hounds, but these crouching, apish
creatures were nothing like hounds.

Barrick drew himself up so that he could defend himself but the
stranger only stood looking down at him with an expression that might
have been bemusement. At first glance Barrick had thought the newcomer a man, but now he was not so certain: the stranger's ears were an
odd shape and set too low on his hairless skull, and the shape of his face
was also unusual, with very high cheekbones, a long jaw, and a nose that
was little more than a low bump above two slits.

"What are . . . ?" Barrick hesitated. "Who are you? Where am I?"

"I am Harsar, a servant. You are in the House of the People, of course."
The stranger was speaking—his lips even moved—but Barrick heard the
voice in the bones of his head. "Was that not your destination?"

"I . . . I suppose it was. The king. The king told me to come here . . ."

"Just so." The stranger reached out a hand as cold and dry as a lizard's claw and helped Barrick to his feet. The three creatures capered around him for a moment and then went scampering out the door into the blue-lit hallway beyond where they stood, crouched and waiting. Barrick looked at his surroundings for the first time and saw that he was in a room decorated with intense but somber intricacy, surrounded by a forest of striped columns, far too many for any mere structural purpose. Set into the otherwise featureless black stone floor beneath him, a great disk of some glowing pearlescent material provided the only light in the large chamber.

"Am I still . . . ?" Barrick shook his head. "I must be. Behind the Shadowline?"

The hairless one cocked his head as if he had to consider the question. "You are still in the People's lands, yes, of course—and this is the People's greatest house."

"The king. Is the king here? I have to give him . . ." He hesitated. Who knew what intrigues existed among the Twilight People? "I need to speak with him."

"Just so," Harsar said again. He might have smiled—it passed like the flicking of a snake's tongue. "But the king is resting. Come with me."

The strange little creatures gamboled around their feet as they left the room with the glowing floor and stepped out into a high hallway, dark but for shimmers of weak turquoise light. Barrick was exhausted, breathless. He had reached his destination at last, he realized—Qul-na-Qar, as Gyir the Storm Lantern had named it. Even the compulsion that the dark woman had put upon him, which had subsided over time into a sort of dull, constant ache, was now satisfied. He had done it!

But what exactly have I done? With the need at last satisfied, uncertainty began to blossom. *What will happen to me here?*

Everything about the place was strange to Barrick's eyes. Its architecture seemed shapeless, every right angle subverted by another less explicable shape; even the dimensions of the passages shifted between one end and the other for no reason he could see.

The light was odd as well. At times they stepped into utter darkness, but then flagstones down the center of the floor gleamed beneath their feet. Most other places were lit by candles, but the flames were not all the ordinary yellow-white: some burned pale blue or even green, which gave the long halls the watery appearance of submarine caverns.

Barrick was also beginning to notice that everywhere he went he seemed to be surrounded by quiet noises—not just the breathy sounds of the little creatures scampering around Harsar's legs, but sighs, whispers, voices quietly singing, even the gentle fluting or sounding of invisible instruments, as though a host of ghostly courtiers hung in the air above their heads and followed wherever they went. Barrick could not help remembering an old Orphan's Day tale from his childhood, Sir Caylor with the bag of winds that had swallowed all the voices in the world, and how some of them leaked out as he rode and almost drove him mad.

"And only he returned to tell the tale . . ." Barrick thought. *That's how it ended.*

Remembering that famous tale of a lonely escape brought another thought. "Wait," he said. "Where are they? The others who came with me . . .!"

His slender guide stopped and gave him a mild but disapproving look. "No. You were alone."

"I mean they came through Crooked's Gate with me. From the city of Sleep. A man named . . . named Beck—and a black bird." For a moment he hadn't been able to remember the merchant's name: the last moments in Sleep seemed far away not just in distance but in time.

"I'm afraid I cannot help you," the hairless one said. "You must ask the Son of the First Stone."

"Who?"

The disapproval became a shade less mild. "The king."

They continued through the empty halls. Barrick was finding it hard to keep up with his guide's deceptively rapid pace, but was determined not to complain.

It was perhaps the strangest hour of his life, he would think later—this first time in Qul-na-Qar, this last time of seeing it with his old eyes, his old way of looking and understanding. The shapes of the place were like nothing he had experienced: the building was clearly orderly and logical, but it was a logic he had never encountered before, with walls abruptly bending inward or ending in the middle of a room for no clear reason, and stairs that led up to the high ceilings and then back down again on the other side of the room, as though built solely on the chance that someone might wish to walk high above the room. Some doors opened onto apparent nothingness or flickering light, others stood in isolation with no wall on either side of them, disconnected portals in the middle of chambers. Even the building materials seemed bizarre to Barrick's eyes: in many places dark, heavy stone was coupled with living wood that seemed to grow within the substance of the walls, complete with roots and branches. The builders also seemed to have exchanged random sections of wall for colorful streaks of gemlike, brilliantly glowing stuff as clear as glass but thick as slabs of granite, allowing views of what was outside but never clearly enough for him to make out more than a blur of shapes and shadows. And everywhere they went seemed deserted.

"Why isn't anyone here?" he asked Harsar.

"This part of the People's House belongs to the king and queen," the servant answered, giving his little pack of straying followers a stern glance until they trotted back to him. "The king himself has few servitors and the queen is . . . elsewhere."

"Elsewhere?"

Harsar began walking again. "Come. We still have far to go."

The empty halls and the chambers they traversed to get from one hallway to another were furnished, some of it quite ordinary to his eyes, some almost incomprehensible, but Barrick could detect a similarity between every piece, from the simplest to the most complex, a unifying vision behind them all that he could not fail to notice because it was so different from anything he had known, as if cats had made clothes for themselves or snakes had choreographed an intricate dance. Chairs, tables, chests, reliquaries—no matter how simple or ornate the pieces, they all had an obvious similarity he could not quite grasp, a disturbing shared subtlety. From a distance the carpets on the dark, polished floors and the tapestries hung on the walls seemed familiar enough objects, but when he looked more closely their dense, complex designs made him dizzy and reminded him uncomfortably of the living lawn that had guarded Crooked's Hall. And though some chambers had tall windows opening onto the twilight sky, and some were windowless, though some sparkled with a thousand candles and others had no candles or lamps at all, the light was much the same in all of them—that muted, watery, inconstant glow. Traveling through Qul-na-Qar was a little like swimming, Barrick thought.

No, he decided a moment later, it was more like dreaming. Like dreaming with his eyes wide open.

But of all the unusual feelings that swept through him as he walked

466   �֍   Tad Williams

this first time in the House of the People, the strangest was that Barrick Eddon felt as if he had at last, after a lifetime of exile, come home.

At last, just when he was beginning to stumble from weariness, his guide showed him into a small, dark room that was built to a more human scale than many of the others, a sort of retiring chamber with polished wooden chairs of smooth and simple (but still undeniably alien) shape. Its walls were filled with niches like a beehive. Each of these small compartments held what looked like a single statue carved from shiny stone or cast in metal, but Barrick saw nothing familiar in any of their shapes; he thought they looked chance-made, like slops left over from the construction of more sensible objects, lovingly collected from the forge floor and displayed here.

Harsar pointed to a bed, a simple thing in a simple wooden frame. "You may rest. The king will see you when he is ready. I will bring you food and drink."

Before Barrick could ask any questions, his guide had turned and walked out the door, his strange little troop leaping and capering around him.

At another time he might have explored the room, so homey and yet so strange, but he did not have the strength to stay upright another moment. He stretched himself on the bed and sank into its welcome softness like a shivering man climbing into a hot bath. Within a few moments sleep came and claimed him.

When he woke Barrick at first lay quietly, trying to remember where he was. His dreams had been subdued and sweetly peaceful, like distant music. He rolled over and sat up before he realized he was not alone in the room.

A man sat in a tall-backed chair a short distance away—at least he looked like a man, but of course he was not, Barrick realized, not in this place. The stranger's long, lank white hair was pulled close to his head by the blindfold over his eyes. He wore no other emblems, no crown or scepter or medallion of state on his breast—in fact his gray clothes were as tattered as Raemon Beck's patchwork had been—but something in his posture and solemnity told Barrick who this was.

Have you rested? The blind king's words sounded in Barrick's head, tuneful as water splashing in a pool. *Here, Harsar has left food for you.*

Barrick had already smelled the enticing scent of the bread and was scrambling off the bed. A plate filled with many lovely things was waiting on a small table—a round loaf, a pot of honey, fat purple grapes and other small fruits he did not recognize, as well as a wedge of pale, creamy cheese. He had already begun stuffing himself—everything tasted glorious after a diet of mostly roots and sour berries—when he suddenly wondered if it had been meant to share.

No, the king said when Barrick began to ask. *I scarcely eat at all these days—it would be like throwing an entire pine trunk onto a few dying coals and expecting it to burn.* The king let out a small laugh that Barrick actually heard with his ears, a gust wintery as snow tossed by a breeze, then did not speak again until Barrick had gobbled even the rind of the cheese and was wiping the plate with the last bit of bread.

So, he said. *I am Ynnir din'at sen-Qin. Welcome to the House of the People, Barrick Eddon.*

Barrick realized that he had never bowed or made any kind of obeisance to this strange, impressive figure, but instead had thought only of filling his stomach. Wiping his sticky fingers on his clothing, he lowered himself to his knees. "Thank you. I saw you in my dreams, your Majesty."

Such titles are not for me. And those my own people use would not be appropriate to you. Call me Ynnir.

"I . . . I couldn't." And it was true. It would be like calling his own father by his first name, to his face.

The king smiled again, a ghost of amusement. *Then you may call me "Lord," I suppose, as Harsar does. You have slept and eaten. One thing remains before our duties as hosts are complete.*

"What do you mean?"

If you step into the next chamber, you will find hot water and a tub. It does not take any great power of observation to know you have not bathed in some time. The king lifted his slender fingers, gesturing. *Go. I will wait here. I am still weary and we have far to walk.*

Barrick found the door set in the far wall and was just about to open it when he remembered something.

"By the gods, I almost forgot!" He hesitated, wondering if he had blasphemed by mentioning the gods in this place, but the king seemed not to notice. "I have brought something for you, Lord, a gift from Gyir Storm Lantern—something very important . . . !"

Ynnir raised his hand again. *I know. And you will complete your task, child of men—but not this moment. We have waited so long that another hour will mean* *nothing. Go and wash the dust of the road from yourself.*

The chamber beyond the door was not like anything Barrick had seen before, steamy and windowless but lit by glowing amber stones set into the wall. A stone tub full of water sat in the center of a floor of dark tile, and when he tested the water with his hand it was gloriously hot. He shucked off his ancient, tattered clothes for the first time in longer than he could remember and almost leaped in.

When he climbed out again some time later even his bones and blood seemed to glow with renewed warmth. He was startled to discover that his ruined clothes were gone and that other garments had been left in their place. How had that happened? Barrick was certain no one had come in or out of the room while he had bathed. He held up the new clothing to inspect it before putting it on—breeches and a long shirt of some silky pale material and slippers of soft leather, all beautiful but simply made.

As he left the bathing room he realized that if such fine things were freely available for strangers, the king's own tattered raiment was even more inexplicable.

Ynnir still waited in the same place, his chin on his chest as if he slept. It was doubtless a trick of the place's strange lights, but Barrick thought he saw a lavender glow flickering above the king's head, faint as foxfire.

As Barrick approached Ynnir stirred and the glow vanished, if it had been there at all.

Come with me now, the king told Barrick, turning his blind face toward him. *It is time to set our feet to the narrowing way, as my people say.*

Ynnir rose from his chair. He was taller than Barrick had expected, taller than most men, but his obvious natural grace was inhibited by what Barrick realized after a moment must be age or weariness, because he swayed for a moment and had to reach out and steady himself on the back of his chair.

Somehow blind Ynnir knew what Barrick was seeing and what he was thinking. *Yes, I am weary. I thought I had lost you in the Between, and I ex-* *pended much strength helping you find your way here—strength I could ill afford.* *But none of that matters now. We have waited long enough. Now we must go to* *the Deathwatch Chamber.*

As he walked with the tall king Barrick finally began to see some of the great castle's other inhabitants. It was hard to make out anything for certain in the dark, dreamy halls—the figures moved too quickly, or were visible only for instants before fading back into obscurity again, and what little of them he saw was often more confusing than if he had seen only shadows—but it was clear now that the castle was occupied.

"How many of your people live here, Lord?" he asked.

Ynnir walked a few more slow paces before answering. He lifted a hand and brought fingers and thumbs together as though holding something small. *Most have gone with Yasammez, but we were already far fewer than once lived here. A few stayed to serve me and to serve Qul-na-Qar itself, and some like the tenders of the Deep Library would never leave—could never leave. There are others like that, too—you saw Harsar's sons . . .*

"Sons?" For a moment Barrick didn't know what the blind king meant. Then he thought of the grotesque little monstrosities that had scampered around the servant's feet. "Those things?"

The First Gift does not always yield helpful changes, said the king, explaining nothing. *But all the children of the Gift are nurtured.* He made another gesture that had the resignation of a sigh. *All together I would suppose there are fewer than two thousand of my people left in all these many, many rooms . . .*

Barrick was distracted by the view from the hallway's high windows—his first clear view of what lay outside the halls. Qul-na-Qar stretched across the visible distance, a forest of towers in dozens of shades of shiny black stone that seemed to stretched on and on toward the horizon until the edges disappeared in mist. The spires themselves were a hundred different shapes and heights, but all seemed built to the same idea, simple shapes repeated over and over again until in aggregate they became somber starbursts of complex black and dark gray.

"Only a thousand or two . . . in all this?" Barrick was astonished—Tessis or Hierosol alone must be able to count a hundred times that number.

Most of them have gone to war, Ynnir told him. *Against your people, to be precise. I doubt any of those will return. The bitterness of Yasammez is too old, too deep . . .*

The name, and the sudden memory of the frightening, awesome woman in black, made Barrick stop and fumble in his shirt. "I have it . . . !" he said, trying to pull it free. "The mirror . . ."

Ynnir held up a thin hand. *I know. I can feel it like a burning brand. And that is what we are going to do—use it to restore the heat of the Fireflower. But do not give it to me yet.*

Thoughts were cascading through Barrick's mind, the newest dislodging the previous ones before he had a chance to examine them. "Why are we . . . why are you . . . ?" He paused, confused: for a moment, he had forgotten who he was—even *what* he was. "Why are the Qar at war with Southmarch?"

Because your family destroyed my family, the king answered with no discernible malice. *Although it could also be said that our family is destroying itself. Now please be silent, child. We have reached the antechamber.*

Before Barrick could even begin to make sense of what the tattered king had just said, he found himself stepping out of the dim but almost ordinary light of the passage and into a room that seemed carved from raw stone, with long streamers of pale rock stretching between ceiling and floor like cobwebs—this despite the fact that they were in the midst of the great palace. "What is this place?" he asked.

The king raised a hand. *No questions for now, child of men. I must go ahead of you and tend to the rituals alone—the Celebrants especially do not much like mortals. In any case, you are not yet ready to see such things—not with your own eyes and thoughts. Stay here and I will come back for you.*

The king stepped into a dark place along the wall and was gone. Barrick took a few steps forward to examine the spot Ynnir had disappeared. Was it a doorway? It looked like nothing but a shadow.

He waited in the stony chamber for what seemed like a terribly long time, listening to the quiet, empty voices that were everywhere in this place. The king had all but called him a murderer, or at least called his family murderers, yet he had treated Barrick like a welcome guest. How could that be? And the mirror that he had carried so far and through so many dangers—why hadn't the king simply taken it from him? If humans were Ynnir's enemies, why did he continue to trust Barrick with a prize for which the warrior Gyir had sacrificed his life?

Confusion and boredom at last overcame patience. Barrick went back to the place the king had disappeared and stood, listening, but heard nothing: if it was an open doorway then only silence was on the other side. He put out his arm and felt it go chill for a moment, but nothing impeded it, so he stepped forward himself into the cold shadow.

For an instant—just an instant—it was like falling into the doorway at Crooked's Hall again and he was terrified that he had done something fatally stupid. Then the light warmed to swirling gray and he could make out a white shape, fluttering and ragged, surrounded by a whirl of shad-

ows like a man beset by angry birds. The white figure was Ynnir, who
had his hands raised in the air and his mouth open, as though he were
calling for help, or . . . or singing. The black shapes whirled and darted.
Barrick caught a snatch of the wailing, otherworldly melody before he
realized some of the flitting shadows had left the king and were moving
toward him instead. Heart hammering, he stepped back into the cold
darkness once more, retreating into the empty stone chamber; by the
time he had reached it he was shivering and covered with clammy
sweat.

You must bow to Zsan-san-sis, Ynnir told him when he returned. _If he
had noticed Barrick's intrusion he had not mentioned it. He is much older
than me, at least in one sense, and his loyalty to the Fireflower is unquestioned._
The king laid a cold hand on Barrick's shoulder and guided him toward
the dark door.

The room on the far side seemed different this time, not a confusion
of grays but a shadowy depth, the only source of light a yellow-green
glow on the far side of the chamber. As the king led him forward Barrick
realized with a shock that the glow came from inside the hood of a dark,
robed figure waiting there like a statue. Then the hooded head lifted and
for a moment Barrick caught a glimpse of stark, silvery features—_a mask,_
Barrick thought, _it must be some kind of mask_—that leaked green light from
nostrils, eyes, and mouth. The thing raised its arm toward them as if in
greeting, and for a moment a six-pointed green star of light bloomed at
the end of its sleeve.

"This is Zsan-san-sis," said Ynnir, needlessly.

Barrick bowed as low as he could. It was much preferable to having to
look again into that weird, sickly gleam.

Words were spoken, or at least Barrick thought he heard whispers, not
words but hisses and quiet bubblings. Then the glowing, hooded thing
seemed to fold up into itself and disappear. The walls dissolved around
them, then the king led him forward once more into a place whose walls
and floor and ceiling were covered with faint but constantly moving
specks of colored light, so that the darkness seemed lit by a thousand
minute candles.

Despite the dazzle of it all, Barrick's eye was drawn immediately to the
figure at the center of the small, low-ceilinged room, a woman stretched
on an oval bed as if asleep. At first he thought by her paleness and stillness

that she was a statue, but as the king led him nearer Barrick's heart grew heavy and cold. She must be dead, this dark-haired woman with her strangely angular features, and his own arrival too late after all. The figure was a corpse, a beautiful, stern corpse, a queen lying in state.

"I am so sorry, Lord . . ." He took the mirror from its leather bag and held it out to the blind king.

She still lives. The king's thoughts were soft as snowfall. His long fingers closed on the mirror and he held it up before his face as though he examined it with his blind eyes through the strip of cloth that covered them. A small frown crossed his face.

Something is wrong, he said quietly. *Something is missing.*

Barrick's insides went cold. "My lord?"

The king sighed. *I expected more, manchild, even with the Artificer so close to his ending. Still, it does not matter. This age of the world comes down to what we hold here, whatever essence he has given us. We have no other choice but to use it and pray the flaw is not too great.*

The blind king breathed on the mirror and then laid it against the queen's breast.

For a stretching moment nothing seemed to change. The chamber's inconstant light flickered silently; the very air seemed drawn tight like a held breath. Then the queen's face contorted in what seemed a grimace of pain and she gasped as she pulled in air. Her eyes—black eyes, startlingly dark and deep—sprang open for a moment and her gaze slid from Barrick to Ynnir, where it rested. Then, like a drowning swimmer who has come to the surface for one last breath before surrendering forever, she seemed to fall back. Her eyes fluttered and slid closed once more; her hand, which had moved toward her breast as if to touch the mirror, fell back on the bed.

Barrick felt as if he might weep, but the pain was too cold, too stony for tears. He had failed. Why had he or anyone else thought it might end differently?

The king bowed his head and for long moments knelt in silence beside the queen. Then he reached out a hand that shook only a little and lifted the mirror from her bosom. He held it up as if to examine it, then, shockingly, tossed away the thing that first Gyir, then Barrick had carried for so long. As it clattered across the room the walls erupted into movement, and for the first time Barrick saw that the gleaming scales that covered walls and ceiling were shimmering beetles, each wingcase flashing rainbows like a puddle of oil.

It has given her a few more hours, perhaps days, but there was not enough of our ancestor in the mirror to wake her, Ynnir said heavily. *There is only one way left to me. Come, child of men. I must tell you of true and terrible things, then you must make a decision no creature of your race has ever been asked to make.*

Whether the gods were always here, or whether they came to these lands from somewhere else entirely, we cannot know. Even Ynnir's thoughts came slowly, as if with great effort.

The two of them had returned to the room where Barrick had slept, and Barrick realized for the first time that with all these miles of castle to choose from, the humble little chamber was the king's own retiring room.

They say they always existed. Ynnir paused to drink from a cup of water, a strangely ordinary thing to do. *None of us were alive so we cannot dispute what they say . . .*

"The gods say they always existed?" Barrick was not sure that he had understood Ynnir.

That is what they told our ancestors. In fact, that is what Crooked himself, the father of my line, told the first generation of the Fireflower, although even Crooked could not have known for certain. He was born here, of course, during the Godwar.

Born *here?* What did the king mean, Barrick wondered. And why was Ynnir bothering to tell him all this if the mirror had failed—if Barrick himself had failed?

But whatever their birth, their source, the king went on, *the gods were already here when the Firstborn arrived.*

"The Firstborn—is that what you call your ancestors?"

And yours, child. Because once we were all the same people—the Firstborn. But one part of that race had the First Gift—the Changing, as some called it. The part that would become our people came from a trick of nature and our blood that allowed us many different shapes, many ways of living and being, while the rest of our Firstborn fellows—those were your people—were immutable in their bones and skin. So as time passed the two tribes began to grow apart until they were quite separate, my people and yours, and in some cases did not even remember their shared root. But shared it was, and is—that is why some of us, especially of my family, look so much like your kind. We have changed, but mostly on the inside. On the outside we have kept much of our original seeming.

Barrick thought he understood, at least enough to nod—but what astounding sacrilege the Trigonate church back home would name it!

Forgive me for sending this all to you on the wings of thought, Ynnir said, but it tires me less than speaking the way your kind does. He sighed. By the time that the Moonlord and Pale Daughter ran away together to his great house, beginning the Godwar, our two peoples were no longer separated simply by the First Gift. Most of your ancestors were in the southern continent, living near Mount Xandos, worshipping Thunderer and his brothers. Most of my people had settled here in the north around Moonlord's stronghold, and as a result, when Moonlord and his kin were besieged by the Thunderer's clan, we took the side of Moonlord and Whitefire . . .

"Moonlord, Pale Daughter . . . I . . . I don't know who these people are, Lord . . ." Barrick said.

Not people—gods. And you know them well, just not by our names. Call them Khors and Zoria, then, and Zoria's father Perin the Thunderer, who angrily laid siege to the lovers' moon-castle. So Khors called for help from his brother and sister, Zmeos and Zuriyal, who came to his defense. My people cast their lot with them, and even those of my ancestors who were far away came to join them here.

For a long moment, as Ynnir sat gathering his thoughts, Barrick did not understand the meaning of what he had heard. "Hold, please, my lord. Your ancestors came . . . here?"

Yes, this place is far older than my people, Ynnir said. The castle in which you sit, or rather the castle that lies beneath and behind the castle in which you sit, was once the domain of the god of the moon himself, Khors Silvergleam. When next you see the walls and the tall, proud towers, look not to the black stone we have built with, but look for the gleam of the moonstone beneath. A careful eye will see it.

Barrick could only stare around him. This strange castle—was it truly Everfrost, the dark fortress of all the stories?

Even the most ignorant of your people knows how that battle ended, although they do not know all the reasons, Ynnir continued. Khors was killed, his brother and sister banished from the earth. His wife—Perin's daughter, Zoria—escaped and wandered lost until at last she was found by Perin's brother Kernios, the dark master of the earth. He took her into his house and made her his wife—whether she wished it or not.

But she had a child during the war, of course—clever Kupilas, fathered by the

Moonlord—and as he grew his gift for making things was such that although they mocked him and treated him brutally, Perin and the other Xandian gods took Kupilas back with them so they could have his skills at their service. He made many wonderful things for them . . .

"Like Earthstar, the spear of Kernios," said Barrick, remembering Skurn's tale.

Yes, and that particular weapon was both Crooked's glory and his doom, Ynnir said. *But we do not speak of that yet. Still, the doom of the Fireflower—that which overwhelms us even now—was built in the ruins of the Godwar. Crooked escaped his captors at last. He traveled the world, teaching both your people and mine, learning more than any other man or god ever learned about the art of making things. And during those years he also learned how to walk the roads of the Void.*

Barrick nodded, remembering another of the raven's strange stories. "His great-grandmother's roads."

Yes. And so he came at last and lived for a while among my people, here in the ruins of the moon-castle, and while he lived among us he fell in love with one of my ancestors, the maiden Summu. Those were days when gods and mortals shared the earth, and even had children together. But unlike most of his kind, Crooked—Kupilas—did not leave his offspring with only tales as a legacy. Summu had three children, two girls and one boy, and all of them were born with the gift we call the Fireflower. When Kupilas had gone on to fulfill his great and terrible destiny, it was discovered that his offspring were not as others of their tribe—life ran stronger in them. One of those children was Yasammez, the great dark lady you have met, who has lived all the ages since then, a life almost as long as that granted the gods themselves. Her brother and sister, Ayann and Yasudra, used the gift in a different way, although they did not at first know they had any gift to give. Although they lived no longer than those of our families usually do, a span that can be counted in a few centuries, their gift was not granted to them, but to their offspring.

Summu had been of the highest blood of our kind, so her eldest boy and girl, as was the tradition then and now, were married to each other to keep the line pure and strong. But these two, Ayann and Yasudra, passed the Fireflower along to their own children, and the gift it bestowed was that when Ayann and Yasudra were dead and their children ruled the People, their children had the parents' essence in them—not just their spirit or their blood, but their living essence and all their memories. The children then birthed children of their own, Ayann and Yasudra's grandchildren, and one day those two married and received the wisdom and thoughts of both their parents and grandparents. So it has gone ever since, the king and queen of our people each passing down all that he or she is to the next born. We are a living Deep Library, and so we have what we need to guard our children through the pain of the Long Defeat. The king nodded slowly. *You do not know what that means, do you, manchild? We call it the Long Defeat because we Qar are too few ever to contest our once-cousins the mortal men for ownership of this world, so we know it is our fate to diminish and eventually be supplanted by your folk—although, again, I speak too simply of complicated things.*

But here is where we come to the hard truths.

The Fireflower runs forever in Yassamez because she has not shared it. She has never taken one of her own blood for a lover, so she has not diminished the gift. Some say it is because she is selfish. Others call it the opposite, a sacrifice—they say she has accepted a painfully long life so that she may watch over the generations of her brother and sister's bloodline. But whatever the truth, Yasammez is what she is.

Those of us who received the Fireflower from our parents, and must pass it along in turn to our own offspring, have a more complicated path to walk. For one thing, each passing of the Fireflower, each passing of the memories of all the previous generations to the next, takes great strength. We cannot find such strength in ourselves alone—the cost is too great. There is only one place we can go to gain it. To Crooked himself—or rather, to the last trace of him remaining in this world.

This ultimate trace of the god stands beneath the castle your people call Southmarch, but which was once a doorway into the home of the Earthlord Kernios. It is the last true vestige of the terrible old days when all the gods walked the earth.

Most of your folk do not even know of it, but some who live in the depths beneath the castle do. They call it the Shining Man.

"I haven't . . . I do not know it, Lord."

But the drows of your family's castle do. They have worshipped and protected it for years without every knowing what it truly was.

"Drows?"

He waved his hand. *You call them "Funderlings," I think. It matters not, because now we are at the crux of things.*

For years the place you call Southmarch was occupied by men—warlords and petty nobles ruled it at the behest of other kings, and although we of the People's ruling family could not come there openly, we knew other ways to reach the Shining Man and gain the strength we needed to keep the Fireflower alive in our blood. My sister Saqri and I made the pilgrimage in the days of the empire in Syan. Our grandparents had been there when Hierosol ruled mankind. But then came the plague years and the humans drove us out of all their lands—lands which had been ours once, but in which we were now interlopers, objects of fear and hatred—and the most painful loss of all was the place you call Southmarch, where Crooked waited in the depths for us. We fought to keep our way to him open but were defeated, in large part by your ancestor Anglin, and forced to fall back to our lands in the north, where humans seldom walked.

Thus, when Saqri and I began to sicken with age, we could not pass the Fireflower to our son and daughter. A century went by and our plight became desperate. Yassamez, the elder sister of our entire line, counseled that we should make war on mankind to win back the castle, but I feared that we would lose such a contest and things would only be worse. My wife sided with our ancestress. For a long time our family was locked in dispute, until all of Qul-na-Qar was riven by it. At last, hiding their thoughts from their mother and from me, my son Janniya and his sister Sanasu set out themselves for Southmarch with only a small troop of household guards and retainers.

They were captured, though, and brought before Kellick, Anglin's heir, the ruler of the March Kingdom. Your ancestor Kellick saw Sanasu, my beautiful Sanasu . . . Here Ynnir stopped, and although his face did not change, the cessation of his quiet, calm thoughts in Barrick's head was as shocking as if the king had burst into tears. . . . *And he wanted her for his own,* he continued at last. *A mortal man coveted the one who would have become immortal queen of her entire people! And he took her, as a wolf takes a graceful deer, little caring what beauty is destroyed as long as his appetites are slaked . . .*

This time the pause was more deliberate. Barrick, in a sort of helpless dream, watched the king's pale face harden into something even stonier than before.

He took her. Janniya, her brother, her intended—my son!—fought for her, but Kellick Eddon had many men. Janniya was . . . killed. Sanasu was taken. The Fireflower could not be passed to the son and daughter. The end of the people was at hand.

Queen Sanasu . . . ! Barrick thought of her picture in the portrait hall, a face he knew well, strange, haunted eyes, fiery hair, and pale skin. *But she . . . was married to the king of Southmarch! Could she truly have been one of the Qar?*

In the wake of that terrible day, the king resumed, *Yassamez and others of course brought war to the humans, and for a while even recaptured the place where Crooked had destroyed the last of the gods, but Kellick took my daughter Sanasu and retreated farther into the domains of men until he could find enough allies to fight back. While we owned the castle again, Saqri and I did what we could to strengthen our inner flames, but we knew that without heirs we only delayed the inevitable. Eventually the humans overwhelmed us and forced us back out again, slaughtering so many of our folk that we gave a great deal of our remaining strength to creating the Mantle, a cloak of twilight that would discourage men from following us into our lands. And so we have lived these last years.*

Now the queen and I are both dying. I have loaned her what strength I could while we waited to see how this . . . he lifted up the mirror *. . . gamble called the Pact of the Glass played out. But it is not enough. She will not wake again. Unless I give her what little I have left of myself. Unless I give her my life.*

Barrick sat, shocked. "You would have to give your life for her? But that wouldn't help anything."

In any other situation that would be true, but the ways of the Fireflower are complicated and subtle. There might yet be a way to stave off the inevitable end of our line—at least for a little while longer. Perhaps that is what Yasammez thought when she sent you to me. I would like to think she had some intention other than to mock me.

"I . . . I don't understand, my lord."

Of course not—how could you? Your people have hidden the truth of what happened. But still, at times in your young life you must have wondered, perhaps sensed that something was . . . wrong . . .

Barrick was beginning to feel a chill now, as if fever was rolling through him. "Wrong with me? Are you talking about me?"

You, your father, and anyone else who has ever carried the painful, confusing legacy of the Fireflower as it burns in human veins. Yes, my child, I am talking about you. You are a descendant of my daughter, Sanasu, and the blood runs strong in you. In a way, you are my grandson.

Barrick stared at him. His heart was pounding so swiftly that he felt dizzy. "I'm . . . one of the Twilight People?"

No, you are less than that . . . and also more. You have the blood of the Highest in you, but to this hour it has brought you only sorrow. Now, however, it might make you the last hope of our ancient people—but only if you make a great sacrifice. You can let me pass the Fireflower itself along to you.

Barrick could not make sense of it. He stared. The king's calm face looked just as it had looked an hour earlier, before he had said these things which turned all the world upside down. "You . . . you want to give this Fireflower to . . . to *me*?"

To keep the queen alive a little longer, I will need to lend her my last strength.

If I can pass the Fireflower along to you—and it may not be possible—that legacy at least will survive. But even if you survive it, Barrick Eddon, you will never be remotely the same again.

"But if you do that, what . . . what will happen to you?"

For the first time in a long while, Ynnir smiled—a thin, weary tightening of the lips. *Oh, child, of course I will die.*

35
Rings, Clubs, and Knives

"The fairies killed in the great battle at Coldgray Moor were buried in a common grave. Although the local inhabitants shun the place and claim it is haunted by the vengeful spirits of dead Qar, and I was unable to locate the grave precisely, the general area is now a beautiful, flowering meadow."

—from "A Treatise on the Fairy Peoples of Eion and Xand"

THEY HAD TO STOP at the outskirts of Ugenion because the Royal Highway was blocked by a funeral procession bound for the temple in the city. It was clearly a rich man's leavetaking: four horses pulled a wagon bearing the black-draped coffin, and so many mourners followed it that Briony climbed out of the wagon and joined the other players by the roadside.

"But who has died?" Briony asked one of the mourners at the back of the procession, a woman carrying a long willow branch.

"Our good baron, Lord Favoros," the woman told her. "Not before his time—he had threescore years and more—but he lost his son to the autarch's cannibals and so he leaves a sickly wife and too young an heir, may the Brothers bless his line." She made the sign of the Three.

Briony found herself doing the same thing as she turned away.

"I have never heard of him," she told Finn Teodoros quietly as they stood watching the mourners file past. "But from the sorrow I see on these people's faces, he must have been a good man."

"Either that or you see sorrow because they have lost a known quantity for an unknown, in very uncertain times." Finn shrugged. "Still, I suspect you are right. I do not see too many herring-weepers in the crowd."

"Herring-weepers?" The picture it made in Briony's thoughts made her laugh. "What in the name of goodness are those?"

"Those who will walk in a funeral parade and cry loudly for a copper crab or two, or who can be hired in a group for a single silver herring. It would be a much-loved man indeed whose family did not have to hire at least a few herring-weepers."

They watched the end of the line as it moved slowly past, the children bearing candles, the wagons carrying bread, wine, and dried fish for the temple where the body would lie in state and the priests would pray night and day to ensure the deceased's rapid progress to heaven. When the last mourners had passed and the last interested onlookers had trailed after the slow parade, Briony and Finn climbed back into the wagon. Dowan Birch snapped the horses' reins and the wagon rolled up to the city gates with the rest of Makewell's Men following close behind.

Once they had negotiated a small but adequate bribe with the guards in the gatehouse they were allowed into Ugenion. They followed the funeral as it wound up the hilly main road toward the temple at the center of the town.

"He was a wealthy man, too, from the look of all this," said Finn as they had their first look at the entire procession spread out on the road before them. "But I have heard no word of funeral games, which is usual here even after the deaths of lesser men. Perhaps it is the fear of what is happening in the north."

"And the south," said Briony sadly. "Poor Hierosol." The jolting of the wagon sent her away from the window to sit on the floor. Where was her father this moment? Alive? A prisoner, still? If Hierosol collapsed, would the autarch be willing to ransom him? And what difference would that make if neither she nor Barrick had access to the Southmarch treasury?

Could it really be true that her twin had come back to Southmarch? That alone would make something good out of the darkest spring Briony Eddon had ever known.

"You look solemn, Princess," said Finn. "As if you knew the poor soul who is being carried to the temple."

"I'm just . . . it's all so uncertain. Everything. What will I do when I get to Southmarch? What if the fairies have already taken the castle?"

Finn turned away from the window. "Then things will be very different from when we left. You cannot try to outthink the Qar, my lady, because they are not like men. Please indulge me in believing this one thing to be true—I know a little of them, after all."

"Why? Did you . . . did you write a play about them?" She tried to make it a light remark, but her sadness and bitterness spilled through. "About their charming elfin magic and how they use it to kidnap and murder innocent folk?"

Finn raised his eyebrows. "I have of course used the Twilight folk as characters in my plays, and in many different ways. If I have erred in portraying them, I suspect it was on the side of making them more mysterious and fearful than they are, rather than using them as quaint purveyors of magic rings and reassuring rewarders of blockheaded virgins. But in fact, I gained my knowledge of them in a very odd and unusual way for a playwright—I studied them."

"What do you mean?"

"What I have said, Highness. No disrespect, but perhaps you would rather rest a little rather than talk. You seem to me a bit out of sorts."

She closed her eyes and tried to calm the anger that was bubbling in her, but she was not entirely successful. "I'm sorry, Finn. Don't go. I have good reason to be angry, though and so would you. Leaving out all of my innocent subjects they have harmed, my brother—my own twin!—is missing or dead and it is those creatures' fault. And they also took someone . . ." She hesitated, then wondered what she would have said about Vansen. "Someone I considered a friend. Like my brother, he never came back from Kolkan's Field. So I am not disposed to hear much good of these Qar."

"Fear not—I said I studied them, Highness, not that I became one. Lord Brone set me to finding out all that I could about the Peaceful Ones, as they are euphemistically termed. Paid me well for my work, too—more than I've made for any of my plays so far, whether they had fairies in them or not."

She laughed a little in spite of herself. "Tell me, then, Finn. What do you know about them?"

"I know that I do not understand them, Princess Briony. I also know that they have some great interest in Southmarch, but not why that is so."

"Because it stands in their way, does it not? Anglin, the founder of our line, was given the castle to be the first bastion against the Twilight People's return. We have held that a sacred trust ever since."

"And where did they first attack this time, Highness?"

She remembered pathetic young Raemon Beck. "Somewhere on the road to Settland. They destroyed a trader's caravan."

"And if that was where they began, why would they then travel a hundred leagues east from there to attack Southmarch? They could have gone west to Settland, a much weaker target, or if they wanted spoils they could have headed south into the Esterian Valley, full of fat merchant towns far from King Enander's protection. The northern end of that valley is twice as far from Tessis as the place they took the caravan is from Southmarch."

"What are you saying, Finn?"

"That what they have done makes little sense but for two possibilities. They came against us for revenge, pure and simple, or there is some other advantage they see to conquering Southmarch—and not the entire country, but only the castle itself. They destroyed everything they encountered on their march toward your family's stronghold, but they left Daler's Troth, Kertewall, and Silverside untouched."

"But why?" It was a moan: Briony did not need any new mysteries. As it was, she struggled just to live day to day with so many unanswered questions about her nearest and dearest. "Why do they bear us such hatred?"

He shrugged. "I don't know, Highness."

"Then find out. That is your calling from now on."

The fat playwright looked startled. "Princess . . . ?"

"If my father does not return—Zoria grant mercy that he does, but if he does not—then I must have help. I must understand the things my father and even my oldest brother spent years learning. It is obvious that the Qar will be one of the things I must try to understand. I know of no one else who knows even as much as you do, Finn. Are you my subject?"

"Princess Briony, of course I honor you and your family . . ."

"Are you my subject?"

He blinked once, twice, taken aback by her ferocity. "Certainly I am, Highness. I am a loyal Marchman and you are the king's daughter."

"Yes, and until something changes, I am the Princess Regent.

Remember, Finn, I count you a friend, but we cannot have things both ways. I cannot ever go back to being 'Tim' again. I will never be a mere player, even if for this moment I hide among you. My people need me, and I will do whatever I must to serve them . . . and to lead them."

His smile was weak. "Of course, Highness. I shall count myself honored indeed to be the Royal . . . what shall we call it? Historian?"

"You shall be *a* Royal Historian, Teodoros, that is certain." She was satisfied to see him wince, not because she disliked the round man, but because she needed him to understand how things stood now. "Whether there are others will depend on how well you do your job."

The wagon rolled to a halt and Briony heard raised voices. Worried, she patted at her knives, which she had taken to carrying in a bundle in her sleeve. A fair amount of time passed and still they sat unmoving; at last, Estir Makewell stuck her head inside the wagon.

"Why have we stopped?" Finn asked.

"Pedder and Hewney are talking to a reeve and two or three bully-boys," she said. "It seems the king's guards have been here twice in the last tennight, asking questions about certain travelers . . ." she cast a worried look at Briony, " . . . and so the reeves are stopping all the strangers they meet and asking their business, where they have been, and suchlike."

"Shall I come out?" asked Finn.

"You can, but I think my brother is managing fairly. Still, they may ask to look into the wagon. What will we say if they ask to see inside?"

"Let them, of course," Briony said. "Finn, give me your knife so I don't have to unwrap mine."

Both Estir and the playwright goggled at her.

"Oh, come! I'm not going to fight the reeves with it! I'm going to cut off my hair again." She took a hank in her hand and sadly examined it. "Just when it was beginning to look as it used to. But such vanity is of no help. I played the boy before, I will do it again."

By the time a red-faced man stuck his head into the wagon, Briony was wearing one of Pilney's old shepherd outfits, squatting on the floor at the feet of Finn Teodoros and mending the strap of one of the playwright's shoes.

"Who are you," said the reeve to Finn, "and why do you ride when the owner walks?"

"I might as well ask, who are you, sir?"

"I am Puntar, the king's reeve—you can ask any man hereabouts." He squinted at Briony for a moment, then let his eyes rove around the crowded wagon stuffed with costumes, taking in the wooden props and hats hanging from every open place. "Players . . . ?"

"Of a sort," said Finn quickly. "But if my friend told you he was the owner, he was lying—drunk, most likely." He gave Estir Makewell a stern glance before she could utter any outraged defense of her brother. "Poor man. He owned this enterprise once, but long ago gambled it away. Lucky for him that I kept him on when I bought it."

"And who are you?" the reeve demanded.

"Why, Brother Doros of the Order of the Oracle Sembla, at your service."

"You are a priest? Traveling with *women?*"

For a moment Finn faltered, but then he saw that the reeve was pointing at Estir Makewell, not Briony. "Oh, *her.* She is a cook and seamstress. Don't worry for her somewhat shopworn virtue, sir. The brothers are a pious, sympathetic lot—if you don't believe me, ask the bearded one we call Nevin to tell you something about the dreadful martyrdom of Oni Pouta, raped over and over by Kracian barbarians. The man weeps as he describes it, so carefully has he studied this and other lessons the gods give us."

The reeve now looked thoroughly confused. "But what . . . what are all these costumes? How can you be priests and yet be players?"

"We are not players, not truly," Finn said. "We are in truth on a pilgrimage to Blueshore in the north, but it is the work of our order to put on shows for the unwashed, acting out pious lessons from the lives of the oracles and the *Book of the Trigon* so that the unlettered can understand what might otherwise be too subtle for them. Would you like to see us portray the flaying of Zakkas? He screams most beautifully, then is saved by a winged avatar of the gods . . . ."

But the reeve was already making his excuses. Estir Makewell led him back out of the wagon, pausing to glare back at Finn before she went down the steep, tiny stairs.

"Did you make all that up?" Briony asked quietly when he was gone. "I have never heard such nonsense!"

"Then, like the oracles themselves, I was speaking with the tongues of the gods," said Finn in a self-satisfied manner, "because as you can see, he is gone and we are safe. Now, let us find a place to stop tonight and discover what pleasure this city has to offer."

"They are in mourning for their baron here," Briony pointed out.

"All the more reason, you will discover as you grow older, to celebrate the fact that the rest of us are alive."

It was not always possible for the players to convince local authorities that they were pilgrims on their way to Blueshore. In the larger towns they sometimes got out the juggling tools and let Hewney and Finn deploy the troop's collection of rings and clubs to earn a few coppers while the others gathered up local gossip and news of bigger events. Hewney was quite nimble when he was sober, but fat Finn was a revelation, able to juggle even torches and knives without harm.

"Where did you learn to do that?" Briony asked him.

"I was not always as you see me now, Highness," her royal historian said with a sniff. "I have been on the road since I was small. I have made my living in ways honest and . . . not so much. Most of my juggling I had from my first master, Bingulou the Kracian—he was the best I have ever seen. Men used to go straight to church after watching him, certain that the gods had granted a miracle . . ."

Two things they heard again and again wherever they stopped, in every town or city of the Esterian Valley: that the Syannese soldiers had not given up looking for them, and that strange things were going on in the north. Many of those they questioned, especially the traders and religious mendicants who traveled there frequently, spoke of a sort of darkness that seemed to have settled over the March Kingdoms—not just the weather, although to all it seemed grayer and cloudier than the season warranted, but a darkness of the heart as well. The roads were empty, the travelers said, and the fairs and markets that were always such an important part of the year were poorly attended if they were held at all. City dwellers were reluctant to travel, and those country folk who could do so had moved into the cities for safety, or at least huddled now in the shadows of their walls.

At the same time, though, not even those who had been there most recently, such as a tinker they met north of Doros Kallida, could describe exactly what was happening. Everyone agreed that the Twilight People had come down out of the mist-shrouded north, just as they had two centuries before, and had destroyed Candlerstown and several other cities as they moved on Southmarch. But the siege that had begun before Briony left home seemed to have been prosecuted for most of the time since in a most strangely offhand manner, with the fairies camped almost peaceably outside the walls for months, and no fighting at all between shadowlanders and men.

But more recently that had changed, the tinker told them, or so he had heard from other travelers he had met farther north. Sometime in the last few tennights the siege had resumed, this time in earnest, and the reports were horrendous and frightening, almost impossible to credit—giant tree-creatures pulling down the walls of Southmarch, the outer keep in flames, demon-things slaughtering the defenders and raping and murdering helpless citizens.

"By now it must surely be over, may the gods help them," the man said piously, making the sign of the Three. "There can be nothing left."

Briony was so miserable after hearing the tinker's words that she could scarcely speak for the rest of the day.

"These are only traveler's tales, Highness," Finn told her. "Do not take them to heart. Listen to a historian, one who searches such tales for truth—the first reports, especially if they are passed by people who were not there, are always far more grisly and exaggerated than what has actually happened."

"So how should that soothe me?" she demanded. "Only half my subjects dead? Only half my home on fire?"

Finn and the others did their best, but that night and for several days afterward, Briony could not be cheered.

And what if Barrick really did come back? she thought over and over. *After all that, have I lost him now forever? Have the fairies killed him?* She lay awake in the small hours, tormented. *If they have, I will see every one of those godless creatures slaughtered.*

"We have a problem," Finn announced as they sat eating their mutton stew. Estir had cooked it, making up for the paltry amount of meat with a generous helping of peppercorns they had bought in the last market, so although it was not as filling as it could be, it was at least warming.

"Yes, we do," said Pedder Makewell. "My sister spends all our money on spices and we are almost copperless again."

"You are a fool," Estir said. "You spend far more of our money on drink than I do on pepper and cinnamon."

"Because drink is the food of the mind," declared Nevin Hewney. "Starve the mind of an artist with sobriety and he will be too weak to ply his craft."

Finn waved his hands. "Enough, enough. If we are careful, Princess Briony's money should last us all the way home, so enough of your carping, Pedder—and you too, Nevin."

"As long as careful does not mean drinking water," Hewney said crossly.

"The problem is what the farmers we met today said," Finn continued, ignoring him. "You heard them. They claim that Syannese guardsmen are camped outside the walls of Layandros. Now, what do you think they are doing there?"

"Making friends with the local sheep?" Hewney suggested.

Finn gave him a look. "Your mouth is your greatest possession, old friend—even more valuable than your purse. I suggest you keep both tightly shut. Now, if you have all finished filling the air with the fumes of your ignorance, give some attention. The soldiers are looking for Princess Briony, of course—and for us. We have been fortunate enough to avoid capture so far, although we were nearly found out in Ugenion and one or two other places." He shook his head. "We may not be so lucky this time, I fear. These are Enander's trained soldiers, not the local boobs and strawheads we have cozened—I doubt I shall be able to convince them we are on pilgrimage."

Briony spoke up. "Then there is only one thing to do. I must leave you. It's me they're searching for."

"Spoken like the heroine of a tragic tale," said Finn. "But with all respect to your station, Princess, if you believe that you are a fool."

For a moment she bristled—it was one thing to be talked to in a familiar way, another to be called a fool by a commoner!—but then she thought of how poorly she had been served by flatterers and thought better of it. *I cannot have friends who will not tell me what they truly think. Otherwise they are not friends, only servants.*

"Why shouldn't I leave you, Finn?" she said. "I broke the king's law by running away—went against his express order. And I am certain the Lady Ananka has been poisoning his ear even more busily ever since. By now, I am probably guilty of the loss of the entire Syannese Empire . . ."

"You are certainly the one they are most interested in, my lady," said Finn. "But do not think for a second they are not searching for us, too. Why do you think we've so often made Dowan fold his long legs like a grasshopper and squeeze into the wagon with you? Because he is the easiest of us all for someone to recognize. Even if you were not with us, Princess Briony, they would not let us go. We would be taken, and then . . . persuaded . . . to tell all we know of your whereabouts. I doubt any of us would ever see freedom again."

A sudden misery washed through her, so strong that she could only put her face into her hands. "Merciful Zoria! I am so sorry—I had no right to do this to you all . . . !"

"It is too late to change that," said Hewney. "So waste no tears on us. Well, on Makewell, perhaps, who hoped for an easy life buggering orphan boys back in Tessis, but he was outvoted."

"I will not bother to answer such a ridiculous charge," said Pedder Makewell. "Except to say that my interest in boys is purely defensive, since they are the one thing I can be sure you haven't given the pox to . . ."

Finn rolled his eyes as the others laughed. "Gods, you are a crude lot. Have you forgotten that the mistress of all the March Kingdoms is traveling with us?"

"Too late to worry about her, Finn my old blossom," said Makewell. "She curses like one of us, now. Did you hear what she called Hewney the other night?"

"And without cause," the playwright said. "I simply stumbled against her in the dark . . ."

"Enough!" said Finn. "You all jest because you do not want to talk about what is before us. The Royal Highway is not safe. The king's men are waiting for us outside Layandros, and even if we manage to sneak past them, it is still several days walk to the Syannese border."

"So what do you propose, Finn?" Briony asked. "You sound as though you have a plan."

"Not only does she have better manners than the rest of you," the large man said, "she has more wit as well. But I suppose it would be hard *not* to," he added, glaring at Hewney and Makewell. "In any case, a few miles north of here is a small road which turns east off the highway. It looks like nothing much more than a farmer's track—in fact that is what it is for the first few miles. But after a while it joins another, larger road— nothing as large as what we've been on, but still, a proper road, not just a track—and passes through the edge of the forest. On the far side is a Soterian abbey, so that we will probably only have to spend one night in the woods, then will be welcomed, warmed, and fed in the abbey the next day."

"Through the edge of the Black River Forest?" said Dowan Birch. It was the first time the giant had spoken.

"Yes," said the playwright. "Of course." .

"I did not know it stretched so far west, that we could reach it in a day or less." His long face was troubled. "It is not a good place, Finn. It is full of . . . of bad things."

"What is he talking about?" demanded Pedder Makewell. "What sort of bad things? Wolves? Bears?"

But Dowan only shook his head and would not say more.

"We will be in it scarely a night," said Finn. "We are nearly a dozen and we have weapons and fire. We even have food, so we do not need to forage. We will stay together and all will be well—and more than well. Come, do you really want to chance our luck with the king's soldiers?"

Several of the others tried to get Birch to explain what he feared, but the big man would not be drawn. At last, for lack of a better plan, they all agreed.

They reached the fork in the road before the next morning's sun was high in the sky. A few other travelers shared the road with them, mostly local folk, and they all watched with surprised curiosity as the Makewell troop left the main road for the bumpy forest track.

For several days they had been passing through wilder and wilder country, but now it was suddenly ten times as apparent. The great expanse of the Royal Highway had meant that it passed mostly through open areas, and even when it didn't the very size of it meant the trees on either side were widely separated and offered little impediment to the sun. As soon as they turned east onto Finn's track the oaks and hornbeams suddenly seemed to shoulder in on either side like curious folk coming to see what strangers had entered their lands. Suddenly the sun that had been their companion for most of the journey was absent for long stretches. Gone were the occasional sounds of farmers calling to other travelers on the road, or summoning their straying sheep or cows back from some high place. Other than the noise of the wagon's wheels, the wind in the treetops, and the occasional muted trills of birdsong, the players' new route was all but silent.

Also, it turned out that Finn had not been entirely correct: the farmer's track, which is what it had looked to be when they left the main road, in places came to seem something much more chancy, more like a track for animals than people, so that the wagon often became stuck and required much work before it could be shifted and set rolling again. They had barely reached the outskirts of the forest when the hidden sun began to dip behind the western horizon and shadows stretched out across the world.

"I don't like it here," Briony said to Dowan Birch, who walked beside her. Because of the bad road and the absence of other travelers she and the giant had left the wagon and were walking behind it like everyone else, ready to push it out of the next ditch.

The place reminded her of something she could barely remember, her lost days after Shaso died and Effir dan-Mozan's house burned down. Something about the way the shadows moved, the way the uneven light made the trees themselves seem to be turning slowly after she passed, felt secretive, even malicious. Because of it, she had pulled out the talisman Lisiya had given her and had been wearing it for hours.

Dowan shrugged. He looked even more gloomy than Briony. "I do not like it myself, but Finn is right. What else can we do?"

"Why did you say . . . that there were bad things here?" she asked.

"I don't know, Highness. Things I heard when I was small." He looked hurt by her smothered laugh. "I *was* small once, you know."

"It wasn't just that," she said. "It was that, and . . . and . . . and you called me 'Highness.' I mean, look at you!"

He frowned, but wasn't entirely displeased. "I s'pose there's different kinds of highness, then."

"Did you grow up somewhere near here? I thought you were born in Southmarch."

He shook his narrow head. "Closer to Silverside. But we had many travelers coming from the country to the market in Firstford, which was over the river. My father used to shoe their horses, if they had them."

"How did you come to Southmarch, then?"

"Mar and Dar took the fever. They died. I went to my uncle, but he was a strange man. Heard voices. Said I was made wrong—I was getting big, then. That the gods took my parents because . . . I don't remember, truly, but he said it was my fault."

"That's terrible!"

Another shrug. "He was the one who wasn't right. His head, you see? The gods gave him nightmares, even in the daytime. But I had to run away or I would have killed him. I traveled with some cattle drovers up to Southmarch and I liked it there. People didn't stare so much." He colored, then looked up. "Can I ask something, Highness?"

"Certainly."

"I know we're going to Southmarch. But what are you going to do when we get there? If those Tollys still have the crown, you see? And if the fairies are still there. What will any of us do?"

"I don't know," she told him. That was the truth.

Just before dark they stopped and made camp. The players shared the meal with a great deal of boisterous noise, as though nobody wanted to listen too carefully to the sounds of the forest night around them, but what was more unusual was that they did not stay up late. Briony, squeezed in between the warm, reassuring bulks of Dowan and Finn Teodoros, rolled herself tightly in her cloak and clutched Lisiya's amulet to her breast.

A few times, as she floated in the river of dream, she thought she could hear the demigoddess' voice, faint and beseeching, as though Lisiya of the Silver Glade were being pulled away in another direction. Once she thought she saw her: the old woman stood by herself on a barren hilltop, waving at her. At first Briony thought the demigoddess was trying to get her attention, but then she realized that what Lisiya was trying to tell her was *"Go away! Go away!"*

She woke, shivering, in the nearly pitch-dark of midnight, with only the faintest light from the campfire embers to show her where she was. Her eyes were wet, but she could not remember anything in her dreams that should have made her cry.

It could not have been much after the middle of the day, when the sun should have been at its highest and brightest, that the world began to grow dark. A superstitious panic ran through the troop until Nevin Hewney pointed out what the rest of them should have realized immediately.

"It's a storm," he said. "Clouds covering the sun."

Despite the thickness of the trees around them, the forest did not seem like a place in which they wanted to weather a bad storm. Makewell's Men and their royal charge did their best to hurry ahead, hoping to reach the abbey, or at least high, dry ground before true darkness fell. The road was wider here, crisscrossed by some other forest tracks, which made

Briony feel hopeful for the first time in hours. Surely they must be near-ing a place where people lived!

It was Finn Teodoros, laboring along at her side, who first saw the faces in the woods.

"Hist," he said quietly. "Briony—Highness. Do not turn, but in a mo-ment look past me on my left. Do you see anything strange?"

At first she could make nothing out of the complex, meaningless pat-tern of light on leaves—the graying of the day only made it harder to tell what was light and what was surface—but then she saw a glint of some-thing a little brighter than what was around it. A moment later it resolved itself into a smear of orange fur and a bright black eye. Then it was gone.

"Sweet Zoria, what was it?" she whispered. "I saw . . . it looked like a fox. But it was the size of a man!"

"I do not know, but that was not the only one," Finn said. His usual lightness of tone was gone, his voice tight with fear. He walked forward, carefully looking only straight ahead, and whispered in Hewney's ear, then trotted a few more steps to talk to Pedder Makewell.

As she watched him, Briony saw another trace of movement in the dim, wavering light, this time on the far edge of the road, ahead of them and slightly to one side. Another strange, beastlike face appeared for a moment from behind a tree, then was gone, although for a moment she could have sworn it rose straight up into the air before it disappeared. Frightened, Briony stumbled and almost fell. Goblins? Fairies? Some outriders of the twilight army that had attacked her home?

Suddenly beast-men crashed out of the trees on either side, shrieking like demons.

"To me, to me!" Pedder Makewell bellowed. Briony saw him grab his sister and thrust her behind him, so that the wagon shielded her back. Makewell had a knife, but it was a poor thing, little more than a blade for cutting fruit and sawing over-tough mutton. Still, he held it up as though it was Caylor's Sighing Sword, and for a moment Briony almost loved the man.

"Together!" Finn Teodoros called. He had the wagon door open and was pulling out what arms they had, many of them little more than props. The beast-men had paused just inside the belt of trees and now were slowly advancing.

"Throw them down!" shouted the first of the things in a loud, angry voice. "Throw down your weapons or we kill you where you stand." It was with something like relief that Briony saw that he was no magical creature but only wore a half-mask. Several of the masked men had bows, the rest were well armed with spears and axes and even swords.

"Bandits," said Nevin Hewney in disgust.

The leader walked toward him, grinning beneath his crude fox face. "Watch your tongue. We are honest men, but what are honest men who cannot work? What are honest men whose lands have been stole by the lords, who know no law but their own?"

"Is that our fault?" Hewney began, but the bandit chieftain cracked him hard across the face with the back of his hand, knocking the playwright to the ground. Hewney got up, cursing, blood running between his fingers where he held his nose. Dowan Birch held him back.

"Bone, Hobkin, Col—you watch them," the leader said. "You others, take what they have. And chiefly search that wagon. Go to it, men!" At this his eyes, which had been flicking from one member of the company to another, lighted on Briony and widened. "Hold," he said quietly, but his men were already busily and loudly at work and did not hear him. He walked toward her where she stood beside Finn Teodoros. "What have we here? Young and fair . . . and passing for a boy?" He leaned toward her, his breath rank. He was missing most of his teeth, which made him seem older than he truly was. The two pegs in his upper jaw protruded below the rim of the fox mask, and for a moment it was all too much for Briony. She drove her knife up at his belly, but he was a man who had been living on the edge of things for a long time: her thrust came as no surprise. He caught her wrist and twisted it hard. To her shame, the pain made her drop the knife immediately.

The Yisti knife, had the bandit known it, was probably worth more than the rest of the players' possessions combined, but he had chanced onto prize he liked better and she had all his attention. "You are pretty enough in your way, girl," he said, pulling Briony close. "Did you truly fool these yokels? Did they think you a boy? You will be happy to know that Lope the Red is not so easily gulled. You belong to a real man, now."

"Let her be . . ." Finn began angrily, but the bandit cuffed him and the playwright fell heavily to the ground and then struggled to rise as Lope the Red shoved at him with his foot.

Briony stared at the bandit chieftain and suddenly recognized something in him. He was a beast, a thief and a bully, but he was also the strongest and the smartest of these men: if the world continued in the same mad fashion as it had of late, many such men would be rising up from the shadows, and some of them would make kingdoms for themselves.

This is the truth, she thought. *This is the ugly truth of my royal bloodline and every other. Those who can take power take it, then leave it to their children . . .*

Finished amusing himself with fat Finn, Lope pulled Briony close again. Then, as the bandit chief reached out a dirty hand to feel for her breasts beneath her loose shirt, he suddenly cried out in pain and staggered back a few steps, the knife which he had twisted out of Briony's hand standing quivering from his thigh.

"Bastard!" said bloody-faced Finn, hauling himself onto his knees. "I meant that for your stones!"

The rest of the bandits had turned at their chief's shout, and stood staring as he took a staggering step toward the playwright. "Stones? I'll have *your* stones off, if you even have any, you eunuch jelly." He waved his hand and two more of the bandits hurried forward, overcoming the struggling Finn in a matter of moments and throwing him to the ground, then pinning him there with the weight of their bodies. Lope the Red pulled the knife from his leg with a contemptuous shake of his head.

"In the meaty part. Ha! You are no fighting man, it's clear." He leaned forward. "I will show you how to use a knife on a man . . ."

"No!" shrieked Briony. "Don't hurt him! You can do whatever you want with me!"

The bandit laughed. "I *will* do whatever I want with you, trull. But first I will carve this one like a joint of beef . . ."

The air hummed and Lope the Red stopped for a moment, then slowly straightened up. He lifted his hand to his face and tried to take off his mask but found he could not: an arrow, feathers still trembling, had pierced his brow just above the eye and nailed it to his skull.

"I . . ." he said, then toppled backward like a felled tree.

"Take them!" someone shouted. A dozen armed men crashed onto the road from out of the trees. Arrows were buzzing in every direction, like furious wasps. One of the men who had pinned Finn to the ground leaped up in front of Briony only to fall back against her an instant later with three feathered shafts quivering in his chest and guts.

More arrows snapped past her. Men screamed like frightened children. One of the bandits clutched a tree as if it were his mother; when he fell away he had left it painted broadly with his blood.

Briony threw herself down on the ground and covered her head with her arms.

The Syannese soldiers dragged the last of the bandits' bodies onto the pile. "All here, Captain," one of the men-at-arms said. "Best we can tell."

"And the others?"

"One dead. The others only have a few small wounds."

Briony scrambled to her feet. One dead? Estir Makewell was on her knees, sobbing. Briony hurried toward her but one of the soldiers grabbed her arm and held her back.

Estir turned from the tall man's corpse and pointed in fury at Briony. "It's your fault—*your fault!* If not for you, none of this would have happened and poor Dowan would be living still!"

"Dowan? Dowan's dead? But . . . I didn't . . ." There was nothing Briony could say. Even the other members of the troop, Estir's brother, Nevin Hewney, even Finn, seemed to stare reproachfully at her from the spot where the guards had rounded them up.

The soldiers wore Syannese colors but an insignia Briony had never seen—a fierce red hound. Their captain stepped forward and looked her sternly up and down. His beard was long but carefully shaped; a bright white plume adorned his tall helmet. Briony thought he had the look of a man who thought himself quite elegant. "You are Princess Briony Eddon of Southmarch, late of our king's court in Syan?"

No point in denying it now—she had done enough harm. "I am, yes. What will happen to my friends?"

"Not for you to think about, Mistress," he said with a grim shake of the head. "We've been looking for you for days and days. Now come with me and don't make trouble. You're being arrested, you are."

36

Hunting the Porcupine

"The fairies who survived the second war with men and fled back into the north called down behind them—in an act of sorcery unseen since the days of the gods—a great pall of cloud and mist that men named the Shadowline. All mortal men who cross into those lands are now in danger of losing at least their wits if not their lives. The few who have gone and returned claim the whole of the north is now beneath the cover of that shadow."

—from "A Treatise on the Fairy Peoples of Eion and Xand"

I SEEM DOOMED *to be part of strange trios in strange places,* thought Ferras Vansen as they clambered up the curving track that Antimony called the Copper Ring. *First across the Shadowline with the heir to the throne and a Qar soldier with no face, now through the depths of the earth with two little people. I survived the first one . . . if only just . . .* But even now he was still dumbfounded by what had happened: why should he have fallen through a doorway behind the Shadowline and come out in the Funderlings' own halls beneath Southmarch?

There was no answer, of course. Perhaps the gods had a hand in it, although he wasn't certain about even that. The one thing that had become clear during this year of madness was that even the gods did not seem to be masters of their own fate.

Antimony and the grubby little creature known as Browncoal were arguing. The monk was a head higher—he was the largest Funderlings Vansen had met, the top of his head reaching the bottom of Vansen's ribs—but he could not match the drow's ferocity: the little man was snarling like a cornered cat. It was strange to see the two of them so close together, see both their similarities and differences, as though one were a wild pony, bristly and undersized, the other a handsome, stolid farm horse.

"What is all this about?" Vansen demanded.

Antimony scowled. "It is a trap or a trick. He wants to lead us up Old Quarry Way to Tufa's Bag, but I was there only yesterday. There is no way out of it! We call it a bag because that's how it is—you can only come out the way you came in."

Vansen looked at Browncoal, who was glowering like a badger who'd just been dug up. "Does he say why he wants to go there if there's no way out?"

"He says there is. And he says I'm a blind fool for thinking I know otherwise." Antimony balled his fists. If Vansen had been Browncoal's size it would have made him very nervous.

"Let's see where he leads us. If it's a trap, it's a rather strange way to go about it, leading us down a dead end. Besides, I'm sure he knows if he proves false he'll be the first to die." Vansen showed the sullen drow his ax. "But it wouldn't hurt to remind him of it."

Browncoal led them farther up Old Quarry Way until they had left all but the most occasional cross-passages behind them. The corridor took a distinctly downward slant; then, after a bit more silent trudging, they reached a fork.

Antimony pointed to the rightmost of the branching tunnels. "That's Tufa's Bag."

"And where does Old Quarry Way go from here?" Vansen asked, pointing along the other branch.

"Back up again until it finally connects with the Copper Ring on the far side of Funderling Town. That's one of Stormstone's roads."

"And why would somebody make a dead end here?"

"That was the original path of Old Quarry Way, but the digging proved too hard—there was no blasting powder in those days. They went this way instead," he said, gesturing to the left hand fork, "where the stone was softer."

Despite Antimony's distrust, Vansen allowed Browncoal to lead them both down the spur tunnel, which twisted and turned and grew low enough in places that Vansen had to get down on his haunches and move forward in an awkward crouch. At last they came to a slightly wider spot.

By the pale golden light of Antimony's coral lamp Vansen could see that the monk's summation seemed accurate: the corridor ended in an abandoned scrape and a pile of rubble. There was no way out.

Even as Antimony shook his head in dour satisfaction, Browncoal stepped forward, bent, and reached under one of the broken stones piled in front of the scrape. He grunted as he lifted; to Vansen's surprise a few individual rocks rolled away but the rest of the stones came up together in a single block. Vansen hurried forward and saw that one of the drows' round battle-shields had been covered with some kind of cement and garnished with stones so that anything except a very careful inspection would reveal nothing more than an innocuous pile of rubble.

"Perin's Hammer!" he said. "A secret door!"

Browncoal looked up them with a near-toothless grin of triumph, then slipped his legs into the hole revealed beneath. He pulled at the rope around his ankle until the length between him and Brother Antimony had gone taut, then dumped the rest of the coil down the hole before letting himself drop in after the rope. For a moment after the drow had disappeared Antimony and Vansen could only stand, staring, as the rope first went slack and then tight again.

"By the Elders," said Antimony in sudden shock, "he is down there by himself!" He tossed his pack over the edge of the hole and quickly followed. When he was gone, Vansen hesitated for a moment. He did not like the idea of letting himself down into something he could not see and did not know.

"Brother Antimony?" he called at the edge of the hole. "Are you there? Are you well?"

"Come down, Captain Vansen," the monk called up from what sounded like only a short distance below. "You can jump. The landing is easy, and down here there is . . . stay, you must see it for yourself. Wonderful!"

Vansen had his doubts, but was reassured to hear the Funderling. He dumped his pack in and then turned around and let himself drop, shielding his face with his arms.

His armor shirt didn't weigh much, but it still made his landing clumsier than the others': Vansen slid, stumbled, slid again, and just managed to turn around before his feet went out from him altogether and he landed on his tailbone in a pile of hard stones.

"By the Thunderer!" he swore, groaning as he got to his feet. "You call that an easy landing?"

"But look," Antimony said. "Is it not worth the tumble?"

Vansen had to admit it was—if you were a Funderling. The down-tilting passage at the bottom of the disguised hole opened out after a few sliding steps down a pile of tailings. The flickering golden glow of the coral revealed a huge cavern, its ceiling covered with strange, rounded pillow-shapes, each one almost as big as Vansen himself, so that he and the two smaller folk seemed to stand in the center of a motionless cloud. At the center of the room was a lake, lit by an odd, pearly light of its own. In the dim light the water was so still it seemed like crystal. As Vansen gazed down into depths no coral lamp could have reached he suddenly understood why the Funderlings believed that their creator god had arisen on the shores of such a pool.

"Is it not magnificent?" Antimony asked. "Who could have guessed this lay on the other side of Tufa's Bag? I could almost forgive this beast and his kind for trying to kill us, just for bringing me here. This is what it must have been like when my ancestors first explored the Mysteries!"

Vansen wasn't exactly certain what that meant. "It's certainly beautiful, but we must get moving."

"Of course, of course." The monk said something to Browncoal, received a reply, then turned back to Vansen with a pained smirk. "He says he is sorry he had to reveal this to me to save his own skin. He had hoped neither my people nor the Qar ever found out about these caverns so his people could claim them for their own. In that way, at least, he proves himself kin to us Funderlings."

The two little men led Vansen around the edge of the subterranean lake, which seemed almost as large as one of the lagoons in Southmarch Castle overhead. No matter where he looked down he could find no end to its depths, but from one or two angles he fancied he saw movement in the deepest shadows, although he told himself (and in fact hoped quite strongly) that it was only a trick of the lights he and his two companions wore.

Browncoal led them through the lake cavern and out the far end, where some ancient drainage had carved a sort of narrow valley down at an even steeper angle. They followed this low-ceilinged canyon, doing their best not to touch the delicate crystals like cone-shaped snowflakes that clung to the walls and disintegrated at the slightest touch. Antimony even wept after accidentally shattering one large and exuberant example that had sprouted sideways from the rock like a miniature tree, the trunk ramifying into ever more exquisitely narrow sprays of translucent stone. The drow Browncoal watched the unhappy monk in silence, his dirty face twisted in an unreadable grimace.

As the little company traveled deeper and deeper into the strange caverns Vansen saw things he could never have imagined—chambers hung with branching structures that might have been monstrous stag's horns, and caverns filled with chalky pillars that grew both upward from the floor and down from the ceiling, as if two pieces of bread had been spread with honey, pressed together, then slowly pulled apart. Often beauty and danger came together as the travelers made their way along narrow tracks or over slender bridgelike structures with pits of empty blackness yawning below them.

Who would have guessed that an entire world lurked here beneath the ground? Vansen thought as they passed pools with eyeless white crabs and fish that darted away from their intruding footfalls. In some of the larger caverns bats roosted in astounding numbers—once they disturbed such a dormitory and the shrieking, flapping cloud seemed to take a good part of an hour to clear the chamber, the little creatures were so numerous. But more often Vansen followed his guides through confined spaces where he often had to crawl on his elbows and knees, or even on his belly, wriggling like a snake through narrow holes so that soon every part of him had been covered in mud and grit.

Finally they halted in front of one such gap, a crevice so small Vansen did not believe even his companions could get through it. He put down his pack and crouched beside it, measuring. It was no wider than the cubit between his elbow and fingertip!

"I cannot fit through a space so small," he said.

The drow seemed to understand him; he said something in his guttural speech. "He says you must go," Antimony translated. "This is the last narrow passage." He frowned, listening. "Although he says that this is why they did not try to attack this way. It was too narrow for the . . ." He fell silent. "He calls them the Deepings—I think he means the giants we call ettins. They could not fit through this tunnel and it was too long to widen—someone would have heard so much work."

Vansen suppressed a shiver. "None of this matters. I will not fit."

"Then he says you must go back," Antimony reported. "There is no other way to reach the dark lady."

But Vansen knew that only he could speak to her—only he had a chance to end this before every living person in Southmarch, big and small, aboveground and belowground, had been slaughtered. "Very well," he said at last. "I'll try. Can you take my armor and my weapon?"

Antimony considered for a moment. "Not and carry the rest of the food and water through a narrow place. I am not that much more slender than you—Nickel says I eat enough for two or three Metamorphic Brothers."

Vansen did his best to smile at the monk's weak joke. "Then I must leave the armor—but I will push the ax in front of me. So how will we do this?" Vansen asked. "Should I go last?"

"No. If you are as necessary to this envoy as you say you are, I do not want to be stuck on the far side from Funderling Town, unable to go back but unable to pull you out. If aught goes wrong, someone must be able to return for help. And I am certainly not trusting that inbred creature to go first. If you did get stuck, that would be the last we saw of him. No, I'm afraid you have to lead the way, Captain Vansen. Our little friend will follow, and I will be last."

Ferras Vansen took off his byrnie and his padded undershirt—the change sent a chill through him so that his teeth chattered a little. He looked over to the drow, who was watching the proceedings with squint-eyed interest. "Don't let him hamstring me," he told Antimony.

"Don't worry about that, Captain," the monk said with a grim set to his jaw as he gathered the coils of the prisoner's rope. "If he tries to do anything he shouldn't, I'll pull the leg right off him."

"Yes, well, don't kill him," Vansen said. "We may still need him on the other side. Do I go in head or feet first?"

"Depends on if you want to travel in light or in the dark." Antimony pointed at the Salt Pool lantern tied around Vansen's brow. "No, you must go head first, Captain. Your shoulders are the widest part. Remember to lift your arms when you need to make yourself narrower. And do not fear—I will be behind you."

Vansen took a deep breath, then a few more, but he knew he could delay no longer. He crawled to the hole. How could he ever get himself into such a tight space?

"One arm up, one arm down if you can manage it," said the monk. "It will give you more choices of how to move, and it can make you even narrower."

Vansen pushed his ax into the tunnel and then crawled in after it. To his surprise he managed to shift his shoulders and torso through the first tight space. The tunnel opened up a little after that, although he still could not bring his arms down below his head, so he nudged the ax ahead and then wiggled after it like a snake.

A very slow, clumsy, and frightened snake, he could not help thinking.

Everything in Vansen revolted at the idea of forcing himself ever deeper into the earth this way. Even the warm, moist air he was breathing began to feel thin and inadequate. The tunnel was not, as he had half-imagined, a single smooth passage like the burrow of an animal—it had been created by the accidental spaces left between huge slabs of fractured stone. He began to think about tremors, those times that the earth shrugged like a sleeping giant. If it did that now, even the smallest shift, he would be obliterated like a grain of wheat caught between millstones.

Once, when the tightness of the passage around his chest kept him from filling his lungs all the way he had to fight a sudden and surprising terror. He could dimly hear Antimony talking behind him, encouraging him no doubt, but his own body and the drow behind him blocked most of the sound and the monk's voice was no more than a murmur.

Maybe he's not encouraging me, Vansen thought suddenly. *Maybe he's thought of something he forgot to tell me—that there's a pit or an even narrower spot ahead . . . or to watch out for snakes or venomous spiders . . .*

Stuck in a tight bend and trying to free himself, Vansen banged his head painfully on the wall of the tunnel. He felt a trickle of wetness on his head and assumed it was blood. A moment later his lantern flickered and went out, leaving him in complete and utter darkness.

His heart raced, tripped, and seemed for a moment as if it would not catch its rhythm again. He was choking—trapped in blackness and strangling! No air!

"Stop!" he growled at himself, although the sound was more of a gasp or gulp than actual words. Still, it was his own voice. There was air. The sudden terror that was making his heart pound and his head feel as though his skull was being squeezed in a monstrous fist was only that . . . fear.

What does darkness matter, anyway? he asked himself. *You can only crawl, moving forward an inch at a time, Vansen. You are a worm. Do worms fear darkness?*

It was a weirdly reassuring thought; after some moments his heart began to slow. He suddenly saw himself as a god might see him—a god with a sense of humor: Vansen was only a little creature where he didn't belong, crammed in a tunnel deep underground like a dried pea in a reed—the kind he used to blow at his brothers and sisters when they were children. The earth surrounded him, but it cradled him, too. There was nothing to do but go forward. When he stuck in the narrow places he would simply wriggle until he managed to free himself.

Forward. Only forward, he told himself. *No point in anything else.*

How the gods must be laughing!

Sweaty, shivering, with mud stinging his eyes and every joint trembling, Ferras Vansen at last crawled out of the far end of the crevice into a small cavern that felt as capacious and airy as the great temple in Southmarch after the tunnel. Browncoal crawled out behind him, followed by Antimony, who clutched the drow's rope like a child hanging onto a kite string. They ate and rested, unspeaking, and then when Vansen could stand without his knees shaking they made their way forward.

They encountered only a few narrow spots the rest of the way, and nothing like that long, throttling tunnel; at last, after perhaps an hour or two of steady upward movement they clambered up into a gallery that had clearly been worked by the hands of thinking creatures, with crude pillars of stone left to hold up the roof so that the long, low series of chambers had the feeling of a beehive or a garden maze. Vansen was just wondering who and what had created it when a spatter of arrows cracked off stones above them. Vansen and Antimony dove for cover, the monk yanking the drow's rope so hard the little creature flew off his feet and tumbled like a child's toy.

The attackers quickly found the range and arrows smacked against the rocks all around them. A chip of broken stone gouged Vansen's cheek. The drow Browncoal, crouching beside Antimony, began to scream at the unseen enemy in his guttural tongue.

"Tell me what he says!" Vansen demanded.

"I don't understand all the words." Antimony listened as the others shouted something back. Browncoal called out to them again, an odd tone of desperation in his voice. "Our drow is saying we come in peace to talk to the dark lady," he told Vansen quietly. "But the others—they are drows, too—say something about the rope around his leg. I think they do not trust him—they think we force him to tell lies for us."

"Cut the rope."

"What?"

"You heard me. Cut the rope, untie it, what you will. But let him go to them so they can see we speak the truth."

"Forgive me, Captain, but are you mad? What will stop them from killing us then?"

"Don't you understand, Brother? We cannot fight them. They have bows and we do not, and even now they may be sending for reinforcements. Let the drow go."

Antimony shook his head but did as Vansen ordered. When he realized what the monk was doing, Browncoal's eyes widened. When the rope fell off he began to inch away from his captors.

"Tell him to say to his fellows that we come in peace."

By the time Antimony finished translating the drow was already several steps away, raising his arms as he walked toward his fellows. One arrow snapped out of the shadows but by good fortune missed him. Browncoal stared balefully at the place from which the arrow had come and no more were launched.

"Now we wait," said Vansen.

"Now we pray," Antimony corrected him.

Ferras Vansen had time to address several different gods before Browncoal returned with a troop of his fellows, all dressed in leather armor and wearing almost identical expressions of suspicion. Despite Antimony's misgivings, Vansen surrendered his ax—the drow who was detailed to carry it looked like an ordinary man staggering beneath a side of beef. The drows used the rope that had bound Browncoal to tie Vansen and Antimony by the wrists. Then their former prisoner said something to them, sharp and short. Vansen did not need the translation, but Antimony gave it anyway, in a voice of weary resignation.

"He says, 'March.'"

They climbed steadily for another short while. As they went, squinting drows and other, stranger creatures appeared out of the darkness on all sides until a good-sized crowd followed them. Vansen began to feel like the leader of a religious procession, but couldn't help remembering that in some processions it was the beasts meant for sacrifice that were carried on the foremost wagons.

They finally reached a huge, high-ceilinged chamber like the inside of a domed temple. The narrow path wound up the outside of the cavern wall and had been widened in some place with wooden walkways fixed directly to the stone. A troop of full-sized soldiers waited there, alien faces stern and eyes bright in their dark armor, and Vansen thought at first they had reached their goal, but instead the guards stepped aside to reveal a massive armored figure sitting on a rock. For a moment Vansen thought it was the demigod Jikuyin and terror gripped him, but as the drows prodded him forward he saw that this new figure, although huge, was smaller than the monster that had held them prisoner in the mines of Greatdeeps, and less like a man as well. Its skin was covered with rough, scaly skin like a lizard's and its heavy-browed face seemed a crude approximation of human features, as if some creator god had hurried through its making.

Even seated, the thing looked down on them. As Vansen approached, the bright, surprisingly small eyes watched unblinkingly.

"Antimony," Vansen said quietly, "ask Browncoal to tell this creature that we come in peace to speak with the dark lady . . ."

"You shall not need Master Kronyuul," the giant said in a voice like stone dragged over stone. "As you see, I speak your tongue. The Lady Yasammez likes her generals to know our enemies well." His chuckle sounded like a hammer pounding slate. He rose, towering far above even his tallest guards. "I am Hammerfoot of Firstdeeps, war-chief of the ettins. You are assassins."

"No!" Vansen took a step back. "We come to parley . . ."

"Why should she parley with you? We will sweep you all away in days, both above and below the ground, and you know it. You come in desperation, hoping to kill our general. Do not worry! You will have your chance . . . but only if you kill me first."

"What?" Vansen took another step back. "Don't you understand? We come to parley!"

"Here, take up your weapon," Hammerfoot said. "Give him back his ax. I shall have none." One of the drows staggered forward with the Funderling ax. Vansen took it, in part out of pity for the creature who had carried the heavy thing some distance, but he did not lift it.

"I will not fight you," he told the giant.

"Come, even you Sunlanders are not such cowards, are you?" Hammerfoot rumbled, leaning forward until his immense, cracked-leather face was no higher than Vansen's own. "I will even let you strike first. Are you still afraid? Your ancestors were not so hesitant at Qul-Girah, where they killed my grandfather with buckets of burning pitch. Does only water run in the veins of their descendants?"

From childhood, and even after, when he became a soldier, Vansen's quiet calm and slowness to anger had often been mistaken for cowardice. Only his captain Donal Murroy had recognized the fire that burned inside, that Ferras Vansen was a man who would put up with nearly any provocation to avoid a meaningless fight, but would battle like a cornered animal when there was no other choice. Still, Vansen felt hot shame rush through him at Hammerfoot's taunts and the harsh laughter of those Qar who could understsand what the giant said.

"Take me to the dark lady," Vansen said again.

"Your path is through me," Hammerfoot said. "Is it because you have left your armor behind?" The ettin peeled off his giant chestplate and let it drop to the cavern floor with a noise like a temple gong. "Come, Sunlander, come and die—or are you completely without honor?"

"Captain!" It was Antimony's voice, fearful to the breaking point.

Everything in Ferras Vansen strained to take up the ax, to wipe the smirk off that great, leering face in a cascade of red—or whatever color a giant bled. He lifted the weapon, weighed it in his hands. Hammerfoot spread his massive arms to show he would not block the blow.

Vansen dropped the ax to the floor of the cavern. "I will not fight. If you will not take me to your mistress then you may as well kill me. I ask you only to let the Funderling monk return. Your Browncoal will tell you he came in good faith and only to translate."

"I make no bargains with sunlanders . . ." snarled Hammerfoot, raising his tree-stump fist over Vansen's head.

"Do not kill him, Deep Delver," a new voice called, icy as an Eimene wind. "Not yet."

"Elders protect us," Antimony murmured.

"Lady Yasammez!" Hammerfoot sounded surprised.

Vansen turned to see a small procession stepping down off the spiral track and onto the cavern floor. Leading it was someone he had never seen before but nevertheless recognized instantly. She was taller than Vansen himself and caparisoned in black plate armor. A long white sword, unsheathed and thrust through her belt as though it were merely a spare dagger, seemed to glow with a subtle light of its own. But it was the woman's face that arrested him, stony as a ritual mask, hard as a figure carved atop a tomb. At first Vansen saw nothing alive in that face at all but the eyes, brilliant as slashes of fire. Then the fiery gaze narrowed and the thin lips curved in a mirthless smile and he saw that it was indeed a face, but one without kindness or sympathy.

"So many visitors today," she said. "And all unwanted." She came closer. Even when he closed his eyes Vansen could feel her nearness like the approach of a winter storm. Beside him, Antimony let out a noise that might have been a whimper. "I suppose you hope to convince me that we should band together against the common foe."

Vansen blinked. Was she talking about Hendon Tolly? "I . . . I'm not . . ." It was hard to look at her, but it was also hard to look away. He felt like a moth circling a candle flame, hopelessly drawn and yet knowing the mere touch of it would scorch him to ashes. "I do not know what you mean, Lady."

"Then the world spins more strangely than even I thought," she said. "This small delegation here has come to inform me that the human creature known as the Autarch of Xis will soon enter the bay with a force of ships and men."

Vansen stared, seeing for the first time that it was not only armed guards who accompanied the Lady Yasammez: looking cowed and fearful beside her stood three hairless, long-armed folk.

"Skimmers!" Vansen was utterly surprised. "Are you from Southmarch?" he asked, but the hairless men only looked away as if he had said something shameful. Vansen turned back to the dark lady. "The Autarch of Xis is the most powerful man on the two continents. Why would he come here?" Vansen looked around. Even in this moment of ultimate danger, he could not help marveling at how the world he had known had been so thoroughly shattered and rearranged into *this*—fairy warriors, giants, Funderlings . . . and now, apparently, the monster of Xand was joining this mad Zosimia festival. "He has the greatest army in the world," he said loudly, as much for Yasammez' supporters as the dark lady herself. "Even the terrible Lady Porcupine cannot defeat him. Not without help . . ."

"*Fool.*" Her voice snapped like a drover's whip. "Do you think that just because my folk will soon stand between two human armies I must sue for peace?" She glared around the chamber as though daring any of her minions to speak. Clearly, from their blank faces and downcast eyes, none of them even contemplated it. "I would rather die in the mud of the

Hither Shore than make another pact with treacherous mortals!" She turned to the giant ettin. "This prattle is meaningless, Hammerfoot. Go on about your sport. Kill them quickly or slowly, as you choose."

Antimony cried out in fear, but Vansen took a step toward her, crying "Wait!" In an instant a dozen Qar bows were drawn and aimed at him. He stopped, realizing he could easily be killed before saying what he needed to say. "You spoke before of a pact, Lady Yassamez. I know of another one—the Pact of the Glass!"

She looked at him, her expression unfathomable. "Why should I care? It has ended—the Son of the First Stone's gambit has failed. There is nothing now not even this southern wizardling on his way here with all his warriors . . . that can prevent me burning this house of treachery to its foundations."

"But the Pact of the Glass hasn't ended!"

It might have been some trick of the shadows and the flickering torches, but for a moment Ferras Vansen thought he saw the dark lady become bigger, saw her silhouette grow and become spiny as a black thistle. "How dare you speak thus to me!" she cried, and he could feel the raging words clamoring in his head. He fell to his knees, clutching at his skull, almost weeping from the pain. "*My father is dead!* Kupilas the Artificer is dead! Despite imprisonment and solitude and pain you could not even imagine, he kept this world safe for century upon century . . . but now he is dead. Do you think I will bandy any more words with creatures like you—the destroyers of my family? Let this mortal autarch come! He will find nothing waiting for him but ruins. In my father's name and memory, and in the memory of all the lives you mortals have stolen from us, no living thing shall survive here and the gods will sleep on in exile forever!"

But as she turned away again Vansen dragged himself up onto his knees and reached toward her. His head was throbbing, and blood dripped from his nose and into his mouth, so that he tasted salt.

"Kill me if you wish, Lady Yassamez," he called, "but hear me first! I knew Gyir Storm Lantern. We traveled together behind the Shadowline. He was . . . he was my friend."

She spun and took two long steps back toward him, hand on the hilt of the white sword. "Gyir is dead." The words landed cold as hailstones. "And he was no mortal's friend. That is *not possible.*"

"I am more sorry to hear of his death than you know. I was there in

Greatdeeps with him in his last hour, and if we were not friends we were certainly allies."

The reptilian gaze fixed him. "I doubt that. But what does it matter anyway, little man? He failed me. Gyir is dead, and in a moment you will be too."

"You may be wrong, Lady. I think there is a chance that despite his death Gyir may yet succeed, and if he does, it will be because of a gift you sent to the king of the Qar—a gift named Barrick Eddon, prince of Southmarch."

Her hand curled more tightly around the sword's hilt. She was close enough, Vansen realized, to decapitate him with one swing. He bowed his head, resigned to whatever would happen next. "Gyir did not fail you, Lady, and if he died, it was doing your bidding. The pact could yet succeed."

He waited for the blow but it did not come.

"You will tell me all you know about Gyir Storm Lantern," she said at last. "You will live that long, at least."

37

Under a Bone-white Moon

*"**The Qar's Book of Regret** is not their only written record. It is said that they also have a collection of oracles called the **Bonefall** that has been kept since early times. Both are said to be part of some larger book or story or song called "**The Fire in the Void**", but no scholar, not even Ximander, can say for certain what that is."*

—from "A Treatise on the Fairy Peoples of Eion and Xand"

BRIONY COULD NOT STOP marveling at the size of the Syannese camp. She had expected a group of men waiting on horseback, perhaps as many as a pentecount of soldiers camped beside the Royal Highway. Instead, after reaching the road and riding on through the rain for perhaps an hour Briony and her captors reached a muddy meadow full of tents—hundreds of them, she felt sure, an entire military encampment crowded with foot soldiers, mounted knights, and their attendants. As they turned to look at her, curiosity plain in even the sternest faces, her stomach clenched. Would they execute her? Surely not—not simply for running away! But she couldn't get Lady Ananka's cold-eyed stare out of her head. Briony had learned early that when you were a king's daughter people might hate you without ever knowing you.

"*Remember, you are not quite real in their eyes,*" her father had often said. "*You are a mirror in which people, especially your own subjects, see what they wish to see. If they are happy then they will see you in that light. If they are unhappy they will see you as their persecutor. And if a demon is in them they will see you as something to be destroyed."*

If the gods only touched people in dreams, as Lisiya had said, then could they sow lies there as well as truth? Had an evil god set Ananka and the king of Syan against her?

Listen to me! she chided herself. *Isn't it bad enough that I take pride in the number of soldiers sent to shackle me and drag me back to Tessis? Now I flatter myself that the gods oppose me as well. Stupid, prideful woman!*

But whatever happened, she would give no one the satisfaction of seeing an Eddon weep and beg for mercy. Not even if she went to the headsman's block.

When they reached a large pavilion near the center of the camp the captain dismounted and helped her from the saddle with silent and ungracious efficiency. Now that she could see the emblem on his surcoat more clearly she saw that the red hound was almost skeletal, its ribs showing so clearly that they resembled a lady's comb. It sent a shiver across her skin.

The captain steered her past the sentries outside the pavilion. Once inside, he squeezed her arm hard enough to make her wince to stop her. At the center of the room several more soldiers, all in armor, were bent over a bed covered in maps. Nobody seemed to have noticed the visitors.

"Your pardon, Highness . . . ?" the captain said at last, clearly unwilling to wait to share his good news and receive his praise. "I have found her—the northern princess—and made her prisoner."

The tallest of the armored men turned and his eyes widened. It was Eneas, the king of Syan's son. "Briony . . . Princess!" An instant later he turned on the captain. "You have done what? What did you say, Linas—made her *prisoner?*"

"As you ordered, Highness, I found her and captured her." But the captain's voice, so firm and proud only a moment before, now sounded less certain. "You see, I have brought her . . . brought her to you . . ."

Eneas scowled and came toward them. "Fool. When did I ever say 'make her a prisoner'? I said *find* her." He extended his hands to Briony, then to her astonishment dropped to one knee before her. "I crave your pardon, Princess, please. I have confused my own soldiers and that is nobody's mistake but mine." He turned to the man who had brought her in. "Be glad you did not put her in irons, Captain Linas, or I might have had you whipped. This is a noblewoman and we have already treated her dreadfully."

"My . . . my apologies, Princess," the captain stammered. "I had no idea . . . I have wronged you . . ."

She did not like the man but she did not want to see him whipped. Or at least not too badly. "Of course, you are forgiven."

"Go now and tell the others to call off the search." He watched as the chastened captain hurried out of the tent, then turned to the other armored men, who were watching with amused interest. "Lord Helkis, you and the others may leave me. I would speak to the princess alone." He thought about it. "No, stay. I do not want this poor woman's reputation any further besmirched—she has suffered enough at the hands of my family, and quite unfairly."

The handsome young noble bowed. "As you wish, Highness." He retired to a stool in the corner of the pavilion. Briony felt almost as though she floated in a dream. One moment she had been wondering whether she would be executed, the next moment a prince was kneeling before her and kissing her hand.

"Please," said Eneas, "I cannot expect you to forgive my family, or even hope for such a thing—it is not deserved, in any case—but I can apologize again. I was sent away soon after we returned from Underbridge. By the time I found out what had happened and returned to Tessis you were already gone." He squinted at her. "This is strange, but I could swear that is my old traveling cloak you're wearing. Still, never mind."

The prince went on to explain how he had only learned the truth because Erasmias Jino had sent a messenger who had caught up to him as he led his troops south along the southern Kingsway, toward the border. Briony found herself wishing she could thank Jino, whose goodwill—or at least his loyalty to Eneas—she had clearly underestimated.

"When I read the letter, even though it was the middle of the night, I called my Temple Dogs to fold their tents and we turned back to Tessis," Eneas said.

"Temple Dogs?"

"You see them all around you. They are my own cavalry troop," he said with more than a little pride. "I picked each one of them. Do you remember how I asked you questions about Shaso and his teachings? The Temple Dogs are modeled after Tuani horsemen. Do not let Linas and his foolish error mislead you—they are the best Syan has, trained to move quickly and efficiently, both on the road and in battle. I am sorry you had such a bad first meeting."

Briony shook her head. "It was by no means all bad. They saved us from bandits." She remembered Dowan Birch's bloodless face and half-opened, unseeing eyes. "Most of us . . ." Her joy at having been spared turned into something cold and heavy. "Can we send for my companions, the players? They do not know what has happened to me. They probably think I am going to be beheaded or dragged back to Tessis." She stopped in confusion. "Am I going back to Tessis? What will happen to me now that I am your prisoner, Prince Eneas?"

He looked startled. "Never my prisoner, Lady. Never. Do not even think such a terrible thing. Of course, you are free to go where you will . . . although, yes, I pray you *will* let me take you back to Tessis. We can clear your name of these offensive, baseless charges. It is the least I can do."

"But your stepmother, Ananka, hates me . . ."

For a moment Eneas' expression hardened. "She is not my stepmother. With the grace of the gods my father will soon end this unseemly relationship."

Briony doubted it would be so easy. "Still," she said, "Two people close to me were poisoned by someone trying to murder me."

"But you would be at my side," Eneas said. "Under my personal protection."

The idea of letting someone as kind and strong and competent as Eneas take charge of her was certainly tempting—Briony had been on her own a very long time. Her father was gone, both her brothers were gone, and it would be such a relief just to rest . . . "No," she said at last. "I thank you, Highness, but I can't go back to Tessis."

He did his best to smile. "So be it. Still, whatever refuge you choose, Princess, I hope you will let me escort you there safely. That is the least I owe you for your harsh treatment in my father's court."

"Then take me back to the players—your captain knows where they are. And tell me everything you've heard and seen since we last spoke," said Briony. "But I think no matter what I hear, I'll still want the same thing—to go back to Southmarch. My people are in sore need."

"If that is your choice," said Eneas solemnly, "then I will take you there, though the legions of black Zmeos himself block my way."

"Please, don't talk about the gods, especially the angry ones," Briony said in sudden alarm. "They are too much with us already."

When it happened, it happened quickly.

Many days had passed as the fishing boat on which Qinnitan was a prisoner followed the coast of Syan into lower Brenland and into the straits that separated Brenland from Connord and the many smaller, rocky islands surrounding it. As a young woman who had spent most of her life in the Hive or the Royal Seclusion Qinnitan would have known none of this, but she had discovered that during the morning hours after he had swallowed his potion or whatever it was, Daikonas Vo would now sometimes answer questions. Clearly, something of his iron control was slipping, but Qinnitan did her best to speak to him only sparingly for fear of this unlikely spring of knowledge suddenly drying up.

Qinnitan had known for a few days that Vo was taking his physick every night as well as in the morning: he became more and more agitated as the afternoons wore away until he quieted himself with the potion a short time after dark. She did not understand exactly what this meant but she was grateful for the slackening of his attention, which allowed her time to think and saw through her rope with an iron rail.

For some time all she could see on the coast sliding past had been stony headlands, cruel cliffs with waves beating at them like beggars pounding on a bolted door. But today, as Vo paced the deck and old Vilas plied the tiller, his sons sitting at his feet like stones, the fishing boat slid past a last bulwark of hills. The rocky front suddenly dropped away to reveal a great, flat expanse of wet sand dotted here and there with massive round stones like the dropped toys of giant children. Beyond this wet tidal flat the land rose into grassy hills spotted with groves of white-barked trees; beyond lay a forest lay spread like a dark green blanket on the knees of distant hills.

Tonight, she decided: if it was ever to happen, it must be tonight. Soon the coastline might be all rocky cliffs again as it had been for days, stones against which even a good swimmer would be crushed and drowned. It had to be tonight.

It wasn't hard to stay awake, but it was very hard to remain still. She forced herself to keep her eyes closed as much as she could, fighting the urge to make certain that the moon she had just looked at a few moments before was still as bright.

Vo was mumbling to himself, a good sign. When she had last dared to look at him he had been scratching his arms and neck with his fingernails as he paced, and rubbing his belly as though it pained him.

" . . . Waking up," he said, then let loose a string of curses in gutter Xixian that would have made the Qinnitan of a year earlier blush and grow dizzy. "Tricked!" he growled. "Not asleep at all. Both of them! They knew! Did it to me!"

He stopped pacing at last and Qinnitan lay as still as she could, doing her best not to breathe. She risked opening her eye just a slit. Vo had his back to her and was licking the needle that he used to take his potion. To her surprise, he dipped into the bottle again, then lifted the needle to his mouth.

Licking the needle three times in a day! Was that good for her or bad? She thought for a moment and decided it could only be good. She found it even more difficult to wait now, but the gods were kind to her: after only a short while, Vo sagged down to sit on the deck.

Through half-shut eyes she watched until the moon had dropped behind the mainsail. Then, after taking a long breath and letting it out slowly, Qinnitan rolled over, snapped the last threads of rope, and crawled toward the shadowed figure leaning against the mast.

"Akar," she whispered, using the Xixian word for master. *"Akar Vo, can you hear me?"* She reached out and gave him a carefully measured shake. His head lolled. His mouth opened a little as though he might say something, which made her start back in alarm, but his eyes remained shut and no sound came.

She gave him another gentle shake and as she did she let her hand slide into his cloak. She searched until she found his purse and drew it out. It was heavier than she'd expected, made of heavily oiled leather. She shoved the bits of hard bread she had saved into it, then froze in terror for a moment as her captor stirred and mumbled. When he had once more gone still, she quickly tied the purse to the piece of cord she wore as a belt over her tattered, threadbare servant's dress from Hierosol. Her heart was beating very fast. Did she really dare to do this?

Of course she did. She could do nothing else. Now that Pigeon was gone she owed her life to no one. If she died trying to escape—well, that still would be better than what awaited her when she was given back to the autarch, of that Qinnitan had no doubt.

She reached into Vo's cloak again and found the bottle, pinching it carefully between finger and thumb to draw it out. For a moment she hesitated. If she drank it herself, all her problems would be over—at least all problems that troubled the living. The darkness inside the small glass container called to her, a sleep from which she would never have to awake—so tempting . . . ! But the memory of the young man named Barrick, her dream-friend, tugged at her. Had he really turned his back on her? Or had something happened to him—did he need her help? If she ended her life she would never know.

Decided, Qinnitan pulled out the glass stopper, sent up a prayer to the golden bees of Nushash that she had tended for so long, then upended the bottle over Vo's mouth.

She was almost undone by the thickness of the physic, which did not splash out like water but rather oozed like pomegranate syrup: it had barely begun to drip when he started to struggle. Still, she managed to pour at least a small spoonful into the back of his throat before he came awake and broke free from her, coughing and sputtering. He knocked the bottle from her hands and it skittered down the deck, but Qinnitan did not care. She must have given him dozens of times his normal portion—surely that would be enough to kill him.

She did not wait to find out, of course. Vilas and his dull, cruel sons were on the boat, the older of the two boys minding the tiller while the other two slept. In a moment even that dullard would notice the struggle. She dashed to the low rail and threw herself over it on the landward side. When the first shock of the cold water had passed, she rose to the surface and began to swim as best she could toward the dark, distant shore. When she had gone a little way she turned to look back toward the boat. She saw something dark go over the side and make a pale splash in the moon-lit water. Her heart flopped in her chest. Was Vo coming after her? Could it be that even a mouthful of poison hadn't killed him?

Perhaps he stumbled and fell over the side, she told herself as she quickly started splashing toward the shore again. *Maybe he's already drowned.*

Only a long stone's throw from the fishing boat Qinnitan was already cold and exhausted—at times it even seemed the water was pushing her away from the shore, as though Efiyal, the wicked old god of the ocean, was doing his best to defeat her.

I won't . . . she thought, although she wasn't quite sure what she was resisting and she was finding it hard to think. *Death? The gods? Daikonas Vo? I won't!*

She fought on, struggling and thrashing so that she knew they must be able to see her from the boat, but the boat did not come after her. Did that mean Vo was dead? Or that they felt sure she was beyond rescue?

It didn't matter. She could do nothing but what she was doing.

Water stung her eyes and threatened to fill her mouth. The moon hung above her like a giant eye, rippling as her head sunk beneath the water each time and then rose again. Her legs were like stone, dragging her down no matter how hard she kicked them against the grip of the ocean. And now the weariness seeping through her, which only a short while earlier had burned in her veins and lungs like fire, had begun to turn into something else—a killing cold that spread inch by inch until at last she could no longer feel her limbs, did not know up or down, living or drowning, whether it was the moon itself that hung above her or its reflection in the mirroring deeps . . .

Qinnitan's feet touched sand and smooth rocks, then lost them again. A few more jerking lunges and the shore was beneath her again, this time for good. Her feet touched the bottom and the water was only at her neck . . . then her breasts . . . then her waist.

When she could no longer feel the water Qinnitan dropped onto the wet stones of the beach and followed the moon up into darkness.

Qinnitan woke up shivering under a bone-white moon. She could see no sign of Vo or his boat, but she felt terribly exposed on the beach and the wind was cold and strong. She squeezed as much water as she could out of her sopping dress, then slowly began to make her way toward the hills, her bare feet so cold she scarcely noticed the sharp stones on which she trod.

Partway up the hill she found herself in a sea of long grasses that leaned this way and that in the wind, whispering like anxious children. Qinnitan was too tired to walk any farther. She got down on her knees and crawled a little, thinking in her exhausted, dreaming way that she was somehow tunneling to safety, that she would reach a place where no one could see her. Finally she let herself sink down into the deep, grassy murmur until she could no longer feel the burn of the wind and then the world escaped her again.

"I wish you had not cut off your hair, Princess," said Eneas as he helped her pull the mail shirt down over her head. "Although in truth such a mannish look will match more nearly with your current garb."

"People will do strange things when they are fleeing for their lives."

The prince colored. "Of course, my lady, I did not mean . . ."

Briony changed the subject. "This is very light—much lighter than I would have expected." In truth, the armor did not feel a great deal less comfortable than one of the formal dresses she had worn at court, let alone the stomacher and starched collar and layer upon layer of petticoats that she had been forced to wear beneath the dresses. The mail hung comfortably over a padded undershirt and dangled to almost her knees, but was slit on either side to make riding easier.

"Yes." The prince was pleased she had noticed. It was one of his more endearing qualities, Briony couldn't help feeling, that he was always happy when she showed interest in arms and armor—or at least more interest than other women would. "As I told you, it is modeled on the Tuani and Mihanni, fast desert riders like your teacher Shaso commanded. No longer can slow-moving knights trample an enemy at will. What the longbow made difficult during our grandfathers' day, guns will soon make impossible. Even the strongest armor can stop a rifle ball only from a distance, but it leaves its wearer ungainly on a horse, and helpless when he falls . . ." He colored again. "I am talking on and on. Let me help you with your surcoat." Eneas and his page slid the garment over her as she held out her arms, then Eneas stepped away, perhaps out of a sense of propriety, while the young page tied up the sides.

"There," said the prince. "Now you are a proper Temple Dog!"

Briony laughed. "And honored to be one, even if only for show. But is it truly necessary this soon?"

"Southmarch is a long way, Princess, and the north is unsettled and dangerous. Lawlessness has followed in the wake of the fairy army. Those bandits that Captain Linas and his men killed are by no means the only ones, and there are many others who do not love my father or Syan, even within our own borders."

"But surely no one will attack a troop this size!"

"I do not doubt you are right. But that does not mean someone might not fire on us from cover with a bow or a gun." He held out a helmet with a drape of mail at the neck. "And so you will wear this, too, Princess."

"May I at least wait to put it on until we leave the tent?"

He smiled at last. Briony had to acknowledge that Eneas was really quite good to look at, with his big open face and strong jaw. "Of course, my lady. But then you may not take it off again until we reach Southmarch. No, nor even then."

The prince had ordered his men to prepare for the journey north as he and Briony and his private guard rode back to where the players were still being held in uneasy custody by Syannese soldiers.

"Again we are rescued from a most unpleasant fate, thanks to you, Princess," said Finn Teodoros.

"A fate that wouldn't have threatened you were it not for me," she said. "I'll do what I can to make it up to you all. How do the others fare?"

"As you would guess," Finn told her. "Mourning Dowan Birch's death, of course. We all loved him, but I think Estir loved him more than the rest of us realized."

Briony sighed. "Poor Dowan. He was always so kind to me. If I ever have my throne again I will build a theater and name it in his honor."

"That would be kind, but I would not mention it yet, while the wound is so new." Finn shook his head. "I cannot tell you how my heart sank when they took you away, Highness—yet here you are! There is something epic in your adventures, I cannot help feeling, and I suspect I have only heard half of them from you."

"Teodoros may praise you to the heavens," said a voice behind her, "but don't expect it from me."

Briony turned to find Estir Makewell staring up at her, eyes red and hair draggled.

"Estir, I am so sorry . . ."

"Are you?" The woman seemed sunk into herself, but taut, like an animal poised to spring. "Truly? Then why didn't you ask to pay your respects to Dowan when you first came back?"

"I meant to . . ."

"Of course." Estir grabbed Briony's arm hard enough that it felt like a kind of assault. "Come, then. Come and see him."

"Estir . . ." said Finn Teodoros in a warning tone.

"No, I'll go," Briony told him. "Of course I'll go."

She allowed the woman to drag her across the road and back a few steps toward the beginnings of the forest where they had been waylaid.

The tall man's body lay on the ground, his face and chest covered in one of the bright costume cloaks he had worn as the god Volios.

"Here," said Estir. "This is what I have left of him." She twitched back the covering, revealing Dowan's long face, fish-belly pale. She had closed his eyes and tied his jaw shut with a length of cloth, but despite the soothing words people always said, the kind giant did not look anything like he was sleeping. He looked like a mere object now, broken and useless.

Like poor Kendrick, she thought. *One moment the blood was making a blush in his cheeks, the next moment it was only a drying splash on the floor. We are nothing when the life is gone from us. Our bodies are nothing.*

"Are you *weeping?*" Estir demanded. "Are you weeping for my Dowan? You have some nerve, princess or not. You have the pride of the gods if you can weep for him when it was you who brought this on him." She pointed at the giant's awful, empty face. "Look at him! Look! He was all I had! He was going to marry me when we had a little money! Now he's . . . he's only . . ." She swayed and then sank down to her knees, hitching and sobbing. "Kernios lead you s—safely and take you in, dear D—D—Dowan . . ."

Briony reached down to touch her shoulder; Estir knocked her hand away. "Don't! The others can fawn over you but this was your fault! You never cared for us at all."

"Estir," said Finn as he hurried to Briony's side, "you're being foolish. The princess had nothing to do with this . . ."

"She had *everything* to do with this," Estir Makewell snapped. "But no one else will say anything to her because she's a gods-cursed royal! What do I care? My lover is dead—the last chance I had! The last . . ." She fell forward again, sobbing as she lay her head on the corpse's chest. "Dowan . . . !"

"Come away, Princess," said Finn. "None of the rest blame you."

But Briony could not help noticing that none of the others had come to welcome her back, either—that Nevin Hewney and Pedder Makewell and the rest had watched from a distance, as though a spell had transformed her into something new and a little frightening.

"I will see that he has a good burial in Layandros," she told Finn. Briony looked to where Prince Eneas waited with his men, deliberately staying at a distance so that she could have this reunion with what he supposed—what she herself had supposed—were her friends. "That's the least I can do."

"I say again, do not blame yourself, Princess. The roads are bad these days and we have spent much of our lives traveling. This might have happened whether we journeyed with you or not."

"But you *were* traveling with me, Finn, and I didn't give you any choice about it. Without me, Dowan could have stayed behind—could have gone off to tend a farm with Estir."

"And caught the plague, or been gored by his own bull. I'm not certain I believe in the gods, but Fate is something else." Finn shook his head. "Our deaths will find us, Princess—mine, yours, Estir Makewell's—whether we hide from them or not. Dowan's found him here, that's all."

She could not speak for a long moment. The weight of all she had lost and all she had failed to do felt as though it were pressing down on her so heavily she could barely breathe.

"Th—thank you," she said at last. "You are a good man, Finn Teodoros. I regret involving any of you in my troubles."

Now it was the playwright's turn to fall silent, but it seemed a silence of consideration rather than emotion. "Come a little way aside with me before you leave us, Princess Briony," he said at last.

They retreated back across the road until they stood a goodly distance from Eneas and his soldiers but still in sight, and far enough from the grieving Estir Makewell that Briony could breathe again.

"If there is something you want, ask me," said Briony. "Dear Finn, you are one of the few people in this world who has done me nothing but kindness." She could not forget the imperiousness she had shown him earlier—it made her wince to think of how she had threatened him with her rank. "You will be my historian, as I said, but I hope you'll also still be my friend."

For the first time since she had met him he seemed at a loss for words, but once again it seemed something other than raw feelings that kept him silent. At last he shook his head as if to throw off some nagging annoyance. "I must speak to you, Princess."

"You puzzle me, Master Teodoros. Aren't we speaking?"

"I mean in honesty. True honesty." He swallowed. "You have suffered much for your people and risked even more, Highness. Listen to me now. Those whom you consider your friends and allies—well, some of them are not friends. Not at all."

Dawet had said much the same to her on that day so long ago, back in Southmarch. That felt like another world. "What do you mean? I do not mean to mock you, but I can scarcely think of anyone who *hasn't* betrayed my family's trust—the Tollys, Hesper of Jellon, King Enander . . ."

"No, I mean someone closer to you." His usual air of amused cynicism was quite gone. "You know that I have long served Avin Brone, both as a scholar and as a spy."

"Yes, and someday I will ask you to tell me what you can of those days, those tasks. Brone himself said that I was too trusting, that I needed to find my own spies and informants, but I confess I know little of the game . . ."

Teodoros raised his hand, then thought better of displaying impatience to a princess. "Forgive me, Highness, but it is Brone himself I am talking about."

It took a moment before she understood him. "Brone? Are you saying that Avin Brone is a traitor?"

His round face was full of pain. "This is difficult, my lady. Lord Brone has never been anything but just and fair with me, Highness, and neither has he ever said anything to me that suggested he was less than loyal to you . . . but he left me alone in his retiring room once, when one of his other spies was brought in unexpectedly from the South Road, wounded by an arrow . . ."

"Rule. His name was Rule," Briony said. "Merciful Zoria, I remember that night. I was there in Brone's chambers."

"And I was in a room nearby where the count does his business." Finn glanced around to make sure they were still out of everyone's earshot. "I am . . . I am a curious man, to tell you something that will not surprise you. By Zosim the Many-Faced, it is not my fault—I am a writer! I had never been left alone among Lord Brone's things before, and . . . well, I must confess that I took the chance to look at some of his papers. Some of them were things I could not make much sense of—maps of places I didn't know, lists of names—and others were simply reports about doings in Summerfield, Hierosol, Jellon, and other places, obviously reports from his many spies. But at the bottom of a pile in his writing desk I found a vellum cover with the Eddon blazon upon it, but without a seal to keep it closed."

"You know you should not have even touched such a thing," said Briony. "You could have been executed for that if someone caught you reading it." She said it almost lightly, but in truth she spoke only because she was stalling; she did not want to hear what he would say next.

"As I said, Princess, I am a writer, and as all know, that is another name for a fool. I stepped to the doorway to listen for anyone coming and then unfolded the cover. Inside was a list of people—those that I recognized were trusted agents of Lord Brone—who, at a certain time and at a certain signal, would kill or imprison the members of the royal family. There were also plans for consolidating power afterward and keeping the people pacified. And the scheme was in Brone's handwriting. I know it as well as my own."

"What . . . ?" She could not believe what she was hearing. "Are you telling me that Brone plans to murder us?"

Finn Teodoros looked miserable. "It could be that I am wrong, Highness. It could be that it was another report—some conspiracy that he had uncovered, and perhaps even thwarted, copied over in his own hand. Or something entirely different. I would not want to declare the count guilty on what I saw alone and have his death on my conscience. But I swear it was as I tell you, Princess. He had made a list in his own hand that looked very much like a plan of betrayal and assassination—a plan to seize the throne of Southmarch. I wish it were not so, but that is what I saw."

The clearing beside the road suddenly seemed as unstable as the deck of a ship. For a moment Briony feared it would spin away from beneath her and she would faint. "Why . . . why do you tell me this now, Finn?"

"Because you are leaving us soon," he said. "We will not be able to keep up with the prince's soldiers and in truth we wouldn't want to. We are not fighters, but there's fighting ahead of you, the gods know." Finn bowed his head as though he couldn't meet her eye. "And . . . because you have been kind to me, Princess. I am fond of you. As you said, I would like to think of you as a friend—and not simply because of the power that comes with being close to royalty. Once I could convince myself that I might be mistaken, that it was none of my affair. Now . . . well, I know you too well, Briony Eddon. Princess. That is the truth."

"I . . . I have to think." As alone as she had felt since her twin brother marched away, this was worse. The world, already a dangerous and confusing place, had now proved to have no center and no sense at all. "I have to think. Please leave me alone."

He bowed and went away. And when Prince Eneas came to speak to her, sensing something wrong, she waved him off as well. There was no comfort to be had in the company of other people. Not now, anyway. Perhaps never again.

38
Conquering Armies

"Some mortal men, it is said, still bear the blood of the Qar in their veins, especially in the lands around the legendary Mount Xandos on the southern continent and among the Vuts and others who once lived in the far north. How many bear this taint, and what the effect of it upon mortals might be, I can find no scholarly record."

—from "A Treatise on the Fairy Peoples of Eion and Xand"

OLIN EDDON STOOD AT THE RAIL. He was tethered to one of his guards, with two others standing close by. The autarch might not worry about what a desperate, condemned man might do, but Pinimmon Vash did, and he had finally ordered that some kind of restraints be kept on the northern king at all times. At the very least, Olin might throw himself overboard and spoil whatever purpose Vash's master had in mind for him. Why this didn't worry Sulepis, Vash had no idea, although the autarch generally behaved as though he were infallible. So far nothing had proved the Golden One wrong, but Vash knew from long experience that if something did go wrong, it would be considered his fault, not his monarch's.

"You do not look well, your Majesty," said Vash.

"I do not feel well." The northerner was more pale than usual, and his eyes were shadowed. "I have been sleeping poorly of late. I have many bad dreams."

"I'm sorry to hear it." What a strange dance the autarch had forced him into, Vash thought. Everyone on the ship knew that this man was doomed, and yet the autarch expected Olin to be treated not just with courtesy, but as if nothing were out of the ordinary. "It is good you have come out on deck. The sea air is reputedly good for many ailments of the spirit."

"Not for this one, I fear." Olin shook his head. "It will grow worse as I draw closer to my home."

Vash didn't know what to say—hardly knew from listening to their conversations whether either King Olin or his own master were entirely sane. He looked up at a castle on the rocky headlands. A flag flew from its tower, but it was too far away to make out anything but its colors, red and gold. "Do you know that place?"

"Yes—Landsend. It is the home of one of my oldest and most trusted friends." Olin's smile was more like a grimace—Vash could see the man was hiding some sharp pain, but whether it was physical or caused by a memory, he couldn't tell. "A man named Brone. He was, in many ways, *my* paramount minister, as you are the autarch's."

And I would wager you treated him better than Sulepis does me, whom he considers little more than a useful pet. Vash was surprised at his own bitterness. "Ah. Would you prefer to be left alone?"

"No, your presence is welcome, Lord Vash. In fact, I had been hoping we would find a little time to talk like this . . . just the two of us."

The skin on Vash's neck prickled. "What does that mean?"

"Merely that I believe that you and I have more interests in common than you might immediately recognize."

Did this fool think he could talk Pinimmon Vash into betraying the Autarch of Xis? Even had he not been frightened of his master—and the gods knew that Sulepis terrified him—Vash would never betray the throne. His family had been serving Xis for generations! "I am certain that we have many interesting things to discuss, your Majesty, although I cannot conceive of any common interests we might share. Sadly, though, I have just remembered several chores still to be done this morning, so our conversation will have to wait."

"Do not be so certain that we have no common interests," Olin said as Vash turned to go. "None of us can know all the truth. It is a truly strange world we mortals inhabit—that is both my greatest solace and my greatest fear."

*   *   *

The next time Vash encountered the northerner, Olin was brought to the fore of the ship to join Sulepis while the priests chanted and poured two golden seashells full of the autarch's blood over the side to purify the waves and to claim this new body of water for Xis. Other than the linen bandages around his forearms, Sulepis seemed almost bursting with health, and when Olin and his guards climbed onto the forecastle the contrast between the two could not have been greater.

"Vash tells me you are not well," the autarch said. "If it is the sea that does not agree with you, take heart—as you can guess, we will drop anchor in only an hour or two."

Olin did not reply. Instead of watching the spectacle of Panhyssir and his priests blessing the waters, he turned to look back at the rest of the great ship. Everything was being prepared for landfall, sailors and soldiers swarming over the deck, windlasses creaking as the army lifted out their equipment and prepared to debark. It was unusual and more than a little dangerous to begin unloading before the ship touched land: Vash could tell that Sulepis was in a hurry.

Ranged behind them up the bay was the rest of the fleet, almost half of the ships the autarch had brought to the northern continent, so that the golden falcons on their sails seemed to be flying across the water in a great flock. Hierosol's great outer walls had fallen in a few days. How long could the much smaller Southmarch hope to resist the power of Xis?

The northerner had doubtless been thinking the same thing. "You have brought an impressive force," Olin said, turning back to the autarch. "It reminds me of a bit of history. You are a well-read man, Sulepis. Have you heard of the Gray Companies who roamed these lands three centuries ago?"

The autarch spread his gold-tipped fingers as if to admire how they sparkled in the sun. "I have heard of the mercenaries, of course," he said. "Such things would not be allowed in my country. In Xis bandits are impaled on sharpened posts for all to see. My people know that I watch over them."

"Oh, I am certain of that," said Olin. "But looking at your fleet and the vast army it carries, I was reminded of the days of the Gray Companies, and especially the famous warlord Davos, called 'The Mantis.' "

The autarch seemed amused. "The Mantis? I have never heard of him."

"I think that is because you have studied my family's later history more closely than you have that particular period."

"Was he truly a priest, with such a name?"

"He owned the income of a mantisery, but that did not make him a true priest. Neither did he receive that name for his good deeds. In fact, there are some who say there was never a greater villain on the continent of Eion . . . but others might argue that."

Sulepis laughed with what seemed honest pleasure. "Oh, very good, Olin! Never a greater villain *until today* is what you mean."

The northerner shrugged. "Do you really think I would be so rude to such a thoughtful host?"

"Speak on. You have my interest."

"You will know how the Gray Companies sprang up here in the north during the chaos of the first war against the Twilight People. They roamed the lands in the years after Coldgray Moor—bands of soldiers with nowhere to go, fighting at first for any lord who would pay them, but turning at last to pillage and robbery for its own sake. The worst of these—and the most powerful—was the son of a Syannese noble family, Davos of Elgi. Because of the mantisery income, or perhaps because of the long, black cloak he wore, he gained the name 'Mantis.' In the chaos of those days Davos fought for many causes and plundered many cities, but a great warlord is like a man riding on a fierce bear—everyone fears him except the bear, and he must always remember to keep the beast fed. The Mantis was forced to continue his raids even when most of the wars that followed the Qar's withdrawal had ended. As more and more northern cities were despoiled, the starving survivors had nowhere to go but to follow their despoiler, so the armies of the Mantis grew and grew. At last he ruled over all Brenland and large stretches of Syan. His men also pillaged parts of my own country, roaming through Southmarch and Westmarch, robbing and killing, until the people screamed out to be saved from this terror. Helping them fell to my ancestor, King Anglin's granddaughter, Lily Eddon."

"Ah, yes," said the autarch. "The woman who ruled a nation! This name I have heard."

"She earned her fame. Her husband had been killed in a fight against one of the Mantis' fellow bandits and his son had died beside him. Lily was left to rule the country alone, and many of the frightened people argued that she should be deposed, that a warrior-knight should be elevated to the throne. But Lily was as much a warrior as any man in her court—Anglin's blood ran hot and strong in her. She would not be put aside.

"The Mantis had long admired Southmarch, and not just because of its young queen. The land was fertile and the castle was all but impregnable. Davos sent Queen Lily an offer of marriage. She had no husband and no son. The Mantis pointed out that he was rich and strong, and that if she married him his great army would be at the service of the March Kingdoms. Many in the Southmarch court urged her to accept this proposal. What other hope did they have?

"Instead, Lily sent a letter back to Davos Elgin, the black-cloaked Mantis—master, so it was said, of a hundred thousand bloodthirsty soldiers—which read, 'Queen Lily regrets that she will be unable to honor your invitation. She will be too busy killing the rats that are swarming across her lands.' And that is what she commenced to do." Olin glanced up. "Am I wearying you, Sulepis?"

"Not at all! You are amusing me and that is a rare treasure." The autarch leaned down toward the foreign king. With his bony, long-nosed face and troublingly bright, unblinking eyes, Vash thought Sulepis looked more than ever like a human hawk. "Please continue."

"Lily knew that the Gray Companies could not survive without plunder—they had already left destruction across all the other lands they had entered—so she sent her agents out to tell the people to retreat, not just in the Mantis' direct path but all around, even from places it seemed he did not threaten. She told the people to take everything they could and destroy all that was left behind. If they could reach Southmarch, she told them, she would protect them there. Then she sent out her armies, still full of hard, battle-worn veterans of the war against the Twilight People, to harass the Mantis' much greater force but never to confront him directly.

"Thus, as the mercenary armies trekked across the March Kingdoms they found the way deserted and scorched before them—no nobles to ransom, no valuables to steal, no food to eat. As they struggled on, the Marchmen appeared from out of nowhere, struck, then vanished like shadows, never killing many of the Mantis' soldiers but making them all fearful because of the unpredictability of their attacks. Sometimes they slit the throat of just one mercenary where he lay sleeping in the midst of a dozen comrades, so that when the others found him they would know it could just as easily have been any of them. Queen Lily's raiders killed the Mantis' men in a hundred different ways, subtle and otherwise, weakening the bridges, poisoning the mercenaries' water or rations, or simply setting fire to their tents as they lay sleeping. So many of Davos' sentries were murdered that finally the pickets insisted on huddling together in groups of three or four, which meant large stretches of the perimeter were left virtually unguarded.

"At last, with his unnerved men starting at shadows, Davos the Mantis staked everything on a swift and direct assault upon Southmarch Castle itself. The shores of the bay were full of rough dwellings built by those who had already fled Davos' assault but could not get into the crowded castle. As the mercenaries' march drew closer these refugees fled from them again, disappearing into the caves and forested heights of the headlands. Then, as Davos and his men marched down the main street, wary of ambush, they smelled the smoke and saw the first flames—the town along the shore had been set on fire. The mercenaries looked at each other fearfully. These people of Southmarch would rather burn their towns down again and again instead of ceding one inch to the raiders. Who could fight such madness?

"And then the Mantis' men at last saw the high walls of Southmarch Castle across the bay, and knew it would take them a year or more to overthrow such a powerful stronghold—a year of starvation, because the land had been made uninhabitable around them and their stores were empty. Even Davos' most loyal lieutenants, the men who had enriched themselves at his side and gone from bandits to magnates in his employ, now refused his orders. They had lost the will to fight. Many of the soldiers threw down their weapons on the spot and skulked away from the overwhelming sight of unconquered Southmarch.

"But Lily had kept only a token army inside the castle. The greater part of her forces had been taken by ship to the coast of Landsend to begin their ride south. So it was that as the Mantis' army was in its greatest disarray, with a quarter or more of its number deserting and the rest fighting among themselves, the army of Southmarch fell upon them.

"The Southmarch folk were much fewer but they were fed, and angry, and fighting for their own land. The mercenaries trapped on the beach put up only a short resistance before the Southmarch force split them in half. Those on one side were forced back against the waves of the freezing bay and either surrendered or were killed. Those on the other side did their best to follow their comrades who had fled earlier, but most were caught as they tried to climb the cliffs. The queen's archers picked them off like birds on a low branch, their bodies tumbling down the hillside in such quantity that in Southmarch we have for centuries called a disordered heap a 'mantis-pile,' although few these days remember where the term came from.

"The Mantis himself, Davos of Elgi, died in Brenn's Bay, trying to wade toward the castle with a dozen arrows in him.

"You see, the March Kingdoms have been invaded by Syan, by Hierosol, by the Kracians and all the mercenaries of the Gray Companies. We have been invaded three times by the Qar themselves. Twice we have driven them out with them suffering great losses, and we will drive them out again. And you, Sulepis, for all your power and certainty, will soon be only another name in the histories of my country—another failed invader, another man whose pride was greater than his sense."

Even though only Vash, the autarch himself, and Panhyssir spoke enough of Olin's tongue to understand all he had said, the northern king's tone as he finished his tale was enough to make many of those surrounding the autarch's litter look up at their monarch with foreboding, if not terror. This foreigner was insulting the Golden One!

At first Sulepis said nothing, but at last a smile stretched slowly across his angular face.

"Very good," he said. "Very good indeed, Olin. A story with a lesson in it! Although I think you could have trusted your audience to puzzle out the meaning without the last bit—perhaps a bit too much honey on the cake, if you take my meaning. Still, very good." He nodded as if taken with a new idea. "And your advice is excellent. It would certainly not be a good idea to sail all my ships and all my men into the bay at once, leaving myself open to whatever mischief these Qar have planned for me." He leaned down as if about to impart a secret. "So in a few moments we will disembark a good number of our soldiers and let them come upon Southmarch from the land while the fleet approaches on the water. What do you say, King Olin? Since it is your idea, will you accompany me? It may be your only chance to feel the earth of your homeland beneath your feet—or at least, to do so with the open sky above your head." He laughed, then called out to the captain of the flagship, "Prepare to make land!"

The autarch swept down from the forecastle and his servants scurried before him like ants. Pinimmon Vash had to follow the Golden One, of course—this early landing was news to him and he had much to do. When he looked back, Olin Eddon still stood in the same place, surrounded by guards, his pale, weary face empty of any expression Vash could recognize.

If he had wished to be completely honest, Pinimmon Vash would have had to admit that Olin Eddon made him uneasy. He had only ever met two types of monarchs, and certainly all the autarchs he had served had been either one or the other—those who were oblivious to their own shortcomings or those who were overwhelmed by them. Some of the most savage, like the current autarch's grandfather, Parak, had been of the latter sort. Parak Bishakh am-Xis VI had heard conspiracies in every whisper, seen them in every downcast gaze. Vash himself had barely survived his years in Parak's court, and had kept his head only by recommending—in the subtlest possible way, of course—other targets to the autarch's attention. Still, Pinimmon Vash had twice been arrested in those last, nightmarish years, and once had written his testament (not that if he had been executed Parak would have honored it: one of the incitements for an autarch to declare treason was that the traitor's goods were always forfeited to the throne).

The current autarch was of course the other sort, the sort that believed himself infallible. In fact, the young autarch's luck was so extravagant that even Vash had begun to believe that the success of Sulepis might have been ordained by Heaven itself.

But this northerner, Olin Eddon, was like no other ruler the paramount minister had ever met: in truth, his measured way of speaking and his quiet observation of what went on around him reminded Pinimmon Vash of his own father. Tibunis Vash had been chief steward of the Orchard Palace, a position from which he was the first ever to retire—all others before him had died in harness or been executed by dissatisfied autarchs. Even after Pinimmon had reached adulthood, and indeed even after he had been raised to the position of paramount minister, the highest position a nonroyal could reach, he had still felt intimidated in his father's presence, as though the old man could see right through what impressed so many others, could see through the robes of office to the trembling boy beneath.

"He has been dead ten years," Vash's younger brother had once said, "and yet we still look over our shoulder in case he is watching."

But Tibunis Vash had not been cruel or even particularly cold, just a reserved and careful man who always thought before he spoke and spoke before he acted. In that way this Olin Eddon was much like him. Neither of them ever rushed to speak and both of them seemed to hear and see things others missed. If there was a difference it was in the impression that each gave to an observer: Pinimmon Vash's father had seemed to sit above the turmoil of the busy and treacherous Xixian court, serene as the statue of a god in a temple garden. King Olin seemed bowed down beneath a great but secret sorrow, so that nothing else in life, no matter how wonderful or dreadful, could ever seem more than trivial. Still, though, despite his aura of defeat, there was something about the northern king that made Pinimmon very, very uncomfortable. So it was that as Olin stood beside him now on the rocky beach of the small cove where the boats had set them down, Vash felt that it was he, not the prisoner, who was subtly in the wrong.

"It will not be long," Vash said. "We will be moving before the sun has finished tipping noon."

Olin did not seem to care much one way or the other: the northerner did not even look at him, but went on watching the troops preparing for the march, some carrying jars and chests off the ships, others assembling wagons that had been in pieces in the hold, or harnessing teams of horses and oxen to pull those wagons. "Did you wish to have that conversation now?" he asked at last, still looking anywhere other than at Vash himself.

"What conversation?" Was the man truly so desperate, or just a fool? "Look, here comes the Golden One. Have your conversation with him, King Olin."

A hundred paces down the beach the autarch stepped from his gilded boat onto the backs of a dozen crouching body-slaves, and from there to the throne atop his litter, which the slaves then lifted and carried up the beach. The gold leaf that covered it glittered so brightly in the spring sun that it did in truth look like the sun's own chariot.

The commanders of the brigades now brought the soldiers, who had been waiting in the sun, back to attention. By the time they had marched out the supply train would be ready to move in behind them.

Vash was still on his knees when the litter stopped beside him. "Ah, there you are," the autarch called down to him. "I did not see you groveling in the sand. Stand up."

Vash quickly did what he was told, although he had to struggle not to groan out loud at the pain in his joints. It was mad that he should be here in the wilds of this uncivilized land, exposed to the gods alone knew what kind of chills and harmful vapors. He should be back in Xis overseeing the kingdom, dispensing wise justice from the Falcon Throne in the autarch's absence, as befitted his age and years of service . . . "I live only to serve you, Golden One," he said when he was on his feet at last.

"Of course you do." Sulepis, dressed in his full battle armor, looked up and down the beach at the waiting soldiers—several thousand fighting men and nearly an equal number of their supporters, with at least that many more remaining on the ships until they reached Olin's Southmarch. Vash knew that the northerners could not even comprehend the autarch's power, the size of his empire, let alone withstand it: the Golden One could easily summon an army ten times bigger than this if he needed it, while still leaving Hierosol under strong siege and his home in Xis impregnably guarded.

The autarch himself knew all this, of course: he had the expansive, grinning face of a man who watched something dear to his heart finally taking shape. "And where is Olin?" he called. "Ah, there. We agreed you would travel with me, so come sit at my feet. This is your country—I am sure there are many local features and quaint customs you can describe for me."

Olin looked sourly up at Sulepis atop the litter. "Yes, we have many quaint customs here. Speaking of such, may I walk? I find the long weeks on the ship have left me in want of exercise."

"By all means, but you will have to speak loudly so I can hear you from up here—a metaphor of sorts, eh? A caution against becoming too removed from one's subjects!" Sulepis laughed, a high-pitched giggle that made some of his bearers tremble, so that the litter actually rocked a little. Vash's heart climbed into his mouth. The autarch seemed to grow wilder and less predictable by the hour.

The drums thundered and the horns blew. The great army began to move out, armor gleaming in the afternoon sun so that the flashing wave caps seemed to have rolled across the beach and over the land for as far as the eye could see. Vash waited with Olin and his guards, Panhyssir and the other priests, and dozens of other courtiers and functionaries, all doing their best to crowd into the shadow of the autarch's raised litter.

"I don't believe I finished talking with you about the fairies," said the autarch as they reached the coast road and the ranks of men and animals turned and began to travel southwest toward Southmarch. "We were speaking of your unusual family heritage, Olin, weren't we?"

The northerner was breathing heavily after only a short climb up from the beach, and his face had gone from deathly pale to an angry red flush. He did not answer.

"So, then," Sulepis said. "The fairies—or the *Pariki,* as we call them in Xand—were driven out of most of our lands long ago, even the high mountaintops and deep jungles in the south. But when they had roamed our lands in the earliest days the fairy-people had sometimes coupled with the gods themselves. Sometimes fairies coupled with mortals as well, and sometimes those couplings made children. So even long after the gods were gone and the fairies driven out, the heavenly blood survived in certain mortal families, unseen and unsensed sometimes for many generations. But the blood of the gods is a strong, strong thing, and it will always make itself known again.

"In my studies I learned that your northern Pariki, the Qar, had never been completely driven out, and in fact still held much of the northernmost part of the continent. More important, though, I learned that they had shared blood with one of the royal families of Eion, and that what was even more interesting was that the Qar who had done so also claimed direct descent from the god Habbili . . . the one you call Kupilas, I believe? Yes, Kupilas the Artificer. You can imagine my interest at learning there were mortals living in the north with the blood of Habbili himself flowing in their veins. You know the family I mean, Olin—don't you?"

The northerner bunched his hands into fists. "Does it amuse you to mock the curse of the Eddons? The grim trick the gods played on us?"

"Ah, but my dear Olin, that is where you are wrong!" chortled the autarch. Vash had never seen the god-king in such a strange mood, like a perverse child. "It is no curse at all, but the greatest gift imaginable!"

"Still you mock me!" Just the tone of Olin's voice made the autarch's Leopards loosen their daggers in their sheaths. Vash was very glad to see they weren't planning to use muskets in such close quarters. The loudness of guns made him nervous, and he had once seen an undervizier's head blown off in an accident when the Leopards were trooping. "You have me prisoner, Sulepis—is that not enough? Must you taunt me, too? Just kill me and have done with it."

Vash had grown used to the way the autarch treated Olin as an amusement, how he took abuse and resistance from the northern king which would have had one of his own subjects tortured to death ages ago, but he was still surprised at the mildness of Sulepis' reaction.

"It *is* a gift, Olin, even if you do not know it."

"This gift, as you call it, likely killed my wife in childbirth. It made me throw my own infant son down a stairway, crippling him for life, and forced me many nights each year to hide myself away from my own family for fear I would hurt them again. In its grip I have even howled at the moon like your Xixian hyena-men! And that same curse that crawls through my veins, and in the veins of my children as well—and if the gods continue to hate us, will someday crawl like a poison through my grandchildren too—now grows stronger in me again with every hour as you drag me back to my home. Gods, it is like a fire inside me! I might have been Ludis Drakava's captive as well, but at least in Hierosol I was free of it, may heaven curse you! Free of it! Now I can feel it again, burning in my heart and my limbs and my mind!"

It was all Vash could do not to turn and run away. How could anyone speak to the Living God on Earth like that and survive? But again, the autarch seemed barely to hear what Olin had said.

"Of course you can feel it," Sulepis said. "That does not make it a curse. Your blood feels the call of destiny! You have the ichor of a god inside you but you have always tried to be nothing but an ordinary man, Olin Eddon. I, on the other hand, am not such a fool."

"What does that mean?" the northern king demanded. "You said there is no such curse in your family, that your ancestors and you are no different than other men."

"No different in blood, that is true. But there is a way in which I am *nothing* like any other man, Olin. I can see what none of the rest of you can see. And here is what I saw—your family's blood gave you a way to bargain with the gods, but you didn't understand that. You have never used this power . . . but I will."

"What nonsense is this? You said yourself you do not have the blood."

"Neither will you after it has leaked out of you on Midsummer's Night," the autarch said, grinning. "But it will help give *me* power over the gods themselves—in fact, your blood will make me into a god!"

King Olin fell silent then, his footsteps slowing until one of his guards had to take his elbow to make him move faster. The autarch, on the other hand, appeared to be enjoying the conversation: his long-boned face was lively and his eyes flashed like the golden plating on his costly battle armor. Earlier that year Vash had almost lost his head when he had been forced to tell the autarch they could not make his armor suit entirely from gold, that such weight would cripple even a god-king. He had learned then what was now becoming obvious to Olin—you could not reason with Sulepis the Golden One, you could only pray each morning that he would spare you for one more day.

"Come, Olin, do not look so offended!" the autarch said. "I told you long ago that I would regret ending our association—I truly have enjoyed our conversations—but that I needed you dead more than I needed you alive."

"If you think to hear me beg . . ." Olin began quietly.

"Not at all! I would be disappointed, to tell you the truth." The autarch reached out his cup and a slave kneeling at his feet instantly filled it from a golden ewer. "Have some wine. You will not die today, so you might as well enjoy this fine afternoon. See, the sun is bright and strong!"

Olin shook his head. "You will pardon me if I do not drink with you."

The autarch rolled his eyes. "As you wish. But if you change your mind do not hesitate to ask. I still have much of my story to tell you. Now, what was I saying . . . ?" He frowned, pretending to think, a playful gesture that made Vash feel ill in the pit of his stomach. Could it be true? Could the might of the heavenly gods really come to Sulepis—a madman who was already the greatest power on the earth?

"Ah, yes," the autarch said. "I was speaking of your gift."

Olin made a quiet sound, almost like a little sigh of pain.

"You know, of course, how your gift comes to you—the Qar woman Sanasu captured by your ancestor Kellick Eddon, the children that he fathered on her who became your ancestors. Oh, I have studied your family, Olin. The gift is strongest in those who show the sign of the Fire-flower, the flame-colored hair sometimes called 'Crooked's Red'—or 'Habbili's Mark' as it is called in my tongue. I suspect the gift runs in the blood of all of Kellick's descendants, even those who do not bear the outward signs. . . ."

"That is not so," said Olin angrily. "My eldest son and my daughter have never been troubled by the curse."

The autarch smiled with childlike pleasure. "What of your grandfather, the third Anglin? Everybody knows he had strange fits, prescient dreams, and that he once almost killed two of his servants with his bare hands although he was considered a very gentle man."

"You truly have learned . . . a great deal about my family."

"Your family has attracted much attention in certain circles, Olin Eddon." The autarch leaned toward him. "You must know that even though your grandfather Anglin showed every sign of this . . . tincture of the blood . . . he was not one of the red Eddons, was he? He had the pale yellow hair of your ancient northern forebears, just as your daughter and eldest son."

"You mock me. My daughter bears no taint," Olin said tightly.

"It matters not—she is of little interest to me," the autarch told him. "I have what I need, thanks to Ludis, and that is you . . . or rather, that is your blood. The one thing on which the oldest and most trustworthy of tale-tellers on both continents agree, as well as those alchemists and thaumaturges of my own land who performed secret experiments and lived to describe them, is that only the blood of Habbili—your people's Kupilas— can open a path to the sleeping gods. Why is that important? Because if the path can be opened, the sleeping gods that Habbili banished so long ago can be reawakened and released."

"You are mad," Olin said. "And even if such madness were true, why would you do it? If we have lived so long without them, why would you let them walk the earth again? Do you think even with all your armies that you could stand up to them? By the Three Brothers, man, even the tiniest drop of their diluted blood in my veins has turned my life topsy-turvy! In their day they threw down mountains and dug oceans with their bare hands! Why would you, loving power as you do, free such dreadful rivals?"

"Ah, so you are not entirely naïve," said the autarch approvingly. "You at least ask, *but if it were true, what next?* Yes, of course, I would be a fool to let all the gods go free. But what if it were only one god? And more important, what if I had a way to rule over and command that god? Would that power not become mine? It would be like having mastery over one of the ancient *shanni*—but a thousand times greater! Anything within the god's power would be mine."

"And this is what you plan to do?" Olin stared. "Such hunger for more power and wealth in one who already has so much is ludicrous . . . sickening."

"No, it is so much more. It is why I am who I am while other men, even other kings like yourself, are merely . . . cattle. Because I, Sulepis, will not surrender what I have when Xergal the master of the dead comes with his cowardly hook to take me away. What point conquering the earth if the bite of an asp or a piece of stone fallen from a column can end it in an eyeblink?"

"Everybody dies," said Olin. There was contempt in his voice now. "Are you so frightened of that?"

The autarch shook his head. "I feared you might not understand, Olin, but I hoped the magic in your own blood might make a difference. What is a man who settles for what he is given? No man at all, but only a brute beast. You ask what a man who already rules the world can possibly desire? The time to enjoy what he owns, and then, when he ceases to enjoy it, to tear it down and build something else." Sulepis leaned so far that Vash was terrified he might topple from the litter. "Little northern king, I did not kill twenty brothers, several sisters, and Nushash knows how many others to seize the throne, only to hand it to someone else in a few short years."

Somebody was shouting outside and the platform began to slow.

"So, we near your old home, Olin. It is true, you do not look well—it seems you were right about being close making you ill." The autarch laughed a little. "Still, that is another reason for you to be grateful to me. I shall make certain you do not suffer such unpleasantness for too much longer."

"Golden One, why have we stopped?" Vash asked. He had visions of some of Olin's people springing out of the woods in ambush.

"Because we are only a short distance away from the place where this coastal road comes out of the forest," the autarch said. "We have sent scouts ahead to determine where we should make our camp. It is likely we will have to dislodge the Qar, who have been besieging our friend Olin's castle for some months. Their army is small but they are full of tricks. However, Sulepis has some tricks of his own!" He laughed as gleefully as a young boy riding on a fast horse.

"But why are we even here?" Olin asked. "If you believe you must kill me to pursue your mad ideas, why come all this way? Simply to punish those of my family and subjects who still care for me? To taunt them in their helplessness?"

"Taunt them?" The autarch was enjoying this playacting. At the moment, he pretended to be insulted. "We have come to save them! And when the Qar are driven off and I am done here, your heirs may do what they please with this place."

"You came here to save my people? That is a lie."

Again the autarch refused to take offense. "It is not the whole truth, I admit. We are here because once this was the very place the gods were banished. Here, now buried beneath the buildings your kind made, lies the gate to the palace of Xergal—Kernios, as you northerners call him. And here Habbili fought him and defeated him, then pushed him out of the world forever. Here is where the ritual must take place."

"Ah," said Olin. "So as I suspected, it has nothing at all to do with anything but your own mad schemes."

The autarch looked at him almost sadly. "I am not greedy, Olin, whatever you think. When I have the power of the gods at my service I will not need to quibble over this castle or that castle. I will rebuild the heavenly palaces of Mount Xandos itself!"

Olin and Vash could only stare in amazement and horror, although of course the Paramount Minister did his best to hide his feelings.

A good part of an hour had passed as they sat motionless in the middle of the coast road. Olin had fallen into silence and the autarch seemed more interested in drinking wine and dandling one of his young female servants while he whispered in her ear. Vash was using the delay to look through his records—he would be hideously busy the moment they reached the place to make camp—when one of the autarch's generals came to the platform and asked for a word with him. After an exchange in which the general did not raise his voice above a whisper, the autarch sent him away. For a moment he was silent, then he began to laugh.

"What is it, Golden One?" Vash asked. "Is everything well?"

"Never better," said the autarch. "This will be even easier than I planned." He waved his gold-tipped fingers and the platform lurched into movement once more, the slaves carrying it groaning quietly as they began to walk. "You will see."

It was some time before Vash learned what his master meant. As they reached a bend in the road the slaves got up and pulled back the curtains, giving Vash a moment of panicky vulnerability, but a moment later he saw why they had done it.

On the coast side of Brenn's Bay, the mainland city of Southmarch was deserted. Much of it had been burned, or was still burning, but the smoke and the dancing flames gave the scene its only movement. There was not a living creature in sight anywhere nearby, and even the castle across the water looked empty, although Vash did not doubt that plenty of Olin's countrymen lurked inside, sharpening their weapons to shed Xixian blood.

"See?" the autarch said in triumph. "The shore is ours—the Qar have gone. They had no wish to be caught between our army and the bay. They have given up their claim to the Shining Man!"

Vash was distracted by a noise behind him, but the autarch paid it no attention. Sulepis was gazing over the scene with obvious satisfaction, as though this were not Olin's long-lost home but his own.

The noise, Pinimmon Vash realized after a moment, was King Olin praying as he stared out across the water toward the silent castle.

39
Another Bend in the River of Time

"Some claim that the Qar are immortal, others that their lives are only of greater length than those of mortal men. But which of these things is true, or what happens to fairies when they die, no man can say."

—from "A Treatise on the Fairy Peoples of Eion and Xand,"
prepared by Finn Teodoros for his lordship Avin Brone,
Count of Landsend

ALL HIS LIFE Barrick Eddon had prayed the things that made him different from others, his crippled arm, his night-terrors and storms of inexplicable grief, all the terrible legacy of his father's madness, would prove to have some meaning—that the truth of him was something more than simply a botched and meaningless life. Now his prayer had been answered and it terrified him.

I didn't save the queen. What if I fail with the king's Fireflower, too? What if it will not have me?

He stood on the balcony of the king's retiring room. A shower had just passed over the castle; the towers and pitched roofs jutted like tombstones in a crowded cemetery, dozens of different shades of damp, shiny black. In the short time since he had come the skies over Qul-na-Qar had always been wet, shifting back and forth between mist, drizzle, and downpour as though the ancient stronghold were a ship sailing through the storms.

Still, there was something peaceful about the place, and not just its near emptiness: the seemingly endless maze of halls had the quiet air of a graveyard, but one in which the ghosts had been dead too long to trouble the living. He knew things lurked in the shadows that should have terrified him, but instead he felt at home in this god's house full of uncanny strangers. In fact, it was odd just how little he missed anything that had been his before—his home in the sunlands, his sister, the dark-haired girl in his dreams. They all seemed very distant now. Was there anything worth going back for?

Barrick grew impatient at last with the shimmer of wet roofs and his own circling thoughts. He left the room and made his way down a steep stairway of cracked white stone and out into the covered colonnade beside a dripping, empty garden. Even the strange plants seemed muted in color, their greens almost gray, their blossoms so pale that their pinks and yellows could only be seen from nearby, as though the rain had leached most of their color. From down here the castle's many towers looked less like cemetery stones and more like the complexity of nature, full of abstract, repeating shapes—pillars and bars and chevrons of the sort human nobles used as heraldic symbols to mark their family name, but which were repeated here in endless patterns like the scales of a snake. The profusion of these basic shapes both lulled and confused the eye, and after walking for a while Barrick found even his thoughts growing weary.

Why have you given me a choice, Ynnir? he thought. *I've never chosen well . . .*

As if coming to answer him, a swirl of rustling leaves blew around the corner then eddied back as the king in his tattered robes stepped into the colonnade in front of Barrick, appearing from nowhere as though he had walked out of a fold in the air.

I can no longer bear to hear the weeping of the Celebrants, Ynnir told him, his thoughts fluttering to Barrick like the leaves falling on the path, *so I have brought my sister—my beloved—out of the Deathwatch Chamber. Whatever you choose, Barrick Eddon, I must give her my strength soon if I am to preserve her life. I sense that the Artificer has failed at last. My own strength is fading. Soon the gift of the glass will fail Saqri too and it will no longer matter what we do.*

Walk with me.

Barrick accompanied the tall king in silence as they made their way out of the wet garden and back into the echoing halls. As they walked, some of Ynnir's servants came whispering out of the shadows, creatures of many different shapes and sizes who fell in behind them and followed at a respectful distance. The strange faces peering at him made Barrick uncomfortable, but only because he knew they belonged here and he didn't.

"I don't know what to do," he said at last. "I don't know what will happen."

If you did, you would only be making a selection, not a choice. Ynnir stopped and turned to him. *Here, child. Let me show you something.* He reached up to the rag covering his eyes, touched it delicately with his long fingers. *As the years of my life passed and our people's plight became more and more grim, I turned farther and farther inward in search of anything that might save us. I lived almost every moment with my ancestors, with the Fireflower and the Deep Library, and traveled in my thoughts to places that have no names you would understand. I dove so deeply into what might be and what had been that I lost sight of what was before me. A century passed before I noticed that my wife, my beloved sister, was dying.* He undid the knot at the back of the blindfold, let the piece of cloth slide free. His eyes were white as milk. *Eventually I lost my sight in truth. I have not seen my beloved's face except in memory for longer than I can remember. I will never know your face, boy, except for how you look in the minds of others. All from trying to know all that will happen. All from trying not to make any mistakes.*

"I don't . . . I don't think I understand."

One of our oracles tells us, 'Rain falls, dew rises. Between is mist. Between is all that is.' Let that be your answer, manchild. Do not brood too much over what went before or worry too much over what is to come. Between those two is everything that matters—all that is.

Ynnir knotted his blindfold again and walked on. Barrick hurried after him, then accompanied the king in silence for a long while, thinking.

"Could you do this even if I didn't want you to?" he asked at last. "Could you force it on me?"

I do not understand. Could I force you to take the Fireflower?

"Yes. Could you give the Fireflower to me if I didn't want it?"

What a strange question. Ynnir seemed tired: he was even more slow in his movements than he had been in the first hours of Barrick's arrival. *I cannot imagine such a thing—why would I do that?*

"Because you need to do it for your people to survive! Isn't that a good enough reason?"

If you take the Fireflower, Barrick Eddon, that does not mean my people themselves will survive—only what they have learned.

"But could you force it on me?"

Ynnir shook his head. *It . . . I do not . . . I am sorry, child, but thoughts colored by your language will not carry the meaning. The Fireflower is our greatest gift, the thing that Crooked gave us that sets us apart from all others. Those who will carry it wait our whole lives for it, and we gain it only when our mothers or fathers are dying. Then, when we have it, we spend the rest of our lives contriving to pass it along to our heirs, the children of our bodies. To force you to take it—I cannot find the words to explain, but it is just not possible to my mind. Either you will accept it, and then we will see what comes, or you will not, and my people will continue to an end that no longer contains the Fireflower. And thus roll the days of the Great Defeat unto Time's sleep.* He stopped. *We have reached the hall where Saqri waits.*

The huge, dark doors were open. The king stepped through and Barrick went with him, but none of the creatures following them crossed the threshold. The hall was lit with many lights, but it was the darkness that lingered beneath the carved beams despite candles and lamps that made the strongest impression on Barrick—the darkness and the mirrors.

On either side of the hall, stretching so far that Barrick thought he must have fallen into a dream as he walked, the walls were lined with oval reflecting glasses in countless sizes, with as many different frames as there were mirrors. In each both light and shadow made a home, and in each they produced something different, so that Barrick felt he was seeing not reflections but windows which, though set closely side by side, opened into a thousand different places. He was confused and overwhelmed—but there was something more. "I have . . . I have been here before."

Ynnir shook his head, but did not reply for a moment. When he did, his voice sounded weaker than it ever had. *You have not been here, child. No mortal has . . .*

"Then I dreamed it. But I know I've seen it—the mirrors, the lights . . ." He frowned. "But it was full of shapes, and at the end of the hall . . . at the end of the hall . . ."

It had all been so overwhelming that until this moment he had not noticed the figure at the hall's far end. Now he and the king seemed to move toward her through a shimmer like that of the most blazing summer's day, though the hall itself was cool and even a little drafty. When they had come near enough, Barrick saw that the queen had been set in one of two stone chairs, her body slumped like a corpse; the other throne was empty. It seemed macabre for the king to have left her this way, both odd and disrespectful. He felt an urge to go and lift her upright, to hold her in a position that befitted a creature of such singular, helpless elegance.

"Why is she . . . my lord?"

Ynnir had stopped and lowered himself to his knees. At first Barrick had thought he was making some ritual gesture of respect or mourning, but now he realized that the king was fighting for breath. Barrick scrambled forward and tried to help him rise but the king was too long-boned and his weakness was too great. At last Barrick just crouched with his arms around him, astounded to feel actual muscle and bone beneath the ragged clothes. The king, for all his weird majesty, was only flesh after all, and he was dying.

The world, the shadowlands, even the mirrored hall shrank away in Barrick's mind and disappeared. There was nothing now but the king and himself and his choice. "Yes," he said. "I've decided, and I say . . . yes."

The king's breathing eased. *Still, you must be certain,* Ynnir told him at last. *Such a thing has never happened—receiving the Fireflower might kill you. And if it does cross to you, nothing will remove it from you but death. You will be a living memorial, haunted by the memories of all my kingly ancestors, until your last moment upon the earth.*

Now it was Barrick's turn to struggle for breath. "I understand," he was finally able to say. "I am certain."

Ynnir shook his head sadly. *No, my son, you do not understand. Even I cannot fully understand what Crooked gave us, and I have lived with it all my long life.* The king climbed to his feet, but when Barrick would have risen too, Ynnir shook his head and gestured for him to stay sitting on the floor. *But that was what had to be, and this is all as it must be too—Saqri, myself, you, and the threads of foolish choice and strange accident that bound our families together.*

"What do I have to do?" Fear swept over Barrick, not of the pain the Fireflower might bring him, but that he would fail Ynnir, that he would not be strong enough to receive what was given.

Nothing. An unusual glow filled the room, purple as the last evening light. A moment later Barrick realized that the glimmer was not so widespread as he had thought, but coming from very close—it surrounded Ynnir's head like a mist around a mountain. The tall king bent down and took Barrick's head between his hands, then pressed cool, dry lips against the young man's forehead just above and between his eyes. For a moment Barrick thought that the soft light had somehow seeped inside of him, because everything around him—Ynnir, the dusty mirrors, the ceiling beams carved like hanging boughs heavy with leaves and berries—had taken on that same violet glow.

"What?" He blinked. A bell was sounding—it must be a bell, it was so loud, so deep! "What do I . . ." The bell sounded again—but it could not be a bell, he realized, because it was silent. Still, he felt its tolling shiver down into his bones.

Sleep, child, Ynnir said, still holding his head. *It has already begun . . .*

And then Barrick could hear nothing except the slow sounding of his own thoughts, his heart beating as loud and strong as icy waters pulsing through the veins of a mountain, a pain like freezing fire, and his skull quivering with each echoing beat . . . beat . . . beat . . .

At last, exhausted from struggling, pierced by an infinite moment of agony, he fell away into a place of darkness and silence.

The hairless, manlike creature stood looking down at him, shadows cast by the flickering lamps swimming across his face. No, it was not just one creature, it was more, many more, all slightly transparent.

Something whispered to him then, a voice without sound, tickling at his thoughts: *Harsar so faithful servant but never to be completely trusted the Stone Circle have lost too much in the Great Defeat . . .*

Now the voice in his thoughts trailed away and the figure before him became only one shape again—the king's servant, Harsar. For a long, dizzy moment Barrick could not make sense of anything. What had happened? Where was he?

"Still in the Hall of Mirrors," Harsar answered him, though Barrick had not spoken. He could see the servant's mouth move, could hear Harsar's carefully uninflected voice in his ears, but he heard it in his thoughts as well, and what it said there was subtly different. "The First Stone sleeps. The Daughter of the First Flower asks for you."

The soundless whisper blew through him again: *Success she lives but we are fruitless we cast our seed on the wind just as we roll the bones.* It was nothing as simple as a voice in his head, but . . . an idea, quiet as grass stretching toward the sun. Barrick tried to sit up. Why was he lying on the ground? Why did his head feel like a sack overfilled with gravel and threatening to rip its seams, while all these thoughts *words ideas sounds smells* crackled in his head like pine knots bursting in a fire? He lifted his hands to his head to keep his skull from breaking open. After a moment the sensation faded, although his head still felt disturbingly full and the world around him seemed tenanted by ghosts of itself, as though he watched everything through poorly made glass.

"Come forward," Harsar said. "The Daughter of the First Flower . . ."

Saqri, Sister, Wife, Granddaughter, Descendant . . . the silent voices in his head murmured.

" . . . is waiting for you."

In the Place of Narrowing. The Crossroads Hall. Beneath the thorn boughs, as in the First Days, when the People were young . . .

Barrick's head felt like a beehive—it was all he could do not to raise his hands and swat at the swarming thoughts. "But what about the king . . . where is Ynnir?"

"The Son of the First Stone is in the Hall of Leavetaking," he said out loud.

. . . Has passed to the Heart of the Dance of Change, his thoughts said.

"Come," he said aloud. "She will take you to him."

Barrick could not speak anymore: it was all he could do to follow Harsar up the aisle while the new thoughts swirled like dust flecks in a windstorm—names, moments, glimmers that felt like memories, but were memories of things he could not remember seeing and did not entirely recognize. And with all these flecks of meaning bedeviling him, there was more: everything in the hall—the benches, the mirrors on the walls, the swirling tiled designs on the floor—seemed to have a kind of glow, a shine of *realness* unlike anything he'd experienced before. Even the most familiar objects of his own childhood had never seemed as much a part of him as the beams above his head, the dark, ancient wood shaped into prickly holly leaves and sinuous vines. Everything had a texture and shape that could not be ignored; everything had a story. And like everything else in Qul-na-Qar, the hall itself *was* a story, a great story of the People.

Then he saw her, waiting in her shimmering white robes.

Just the sight of her crashed onto Barrick like an ocean wave, battering all his senses, submerging his mind in memories he had never had before—a forest full of red leaves, a smooth shoulder, pale as ivory, her upright form on a gray horse with snow dappling her cloak.

Saqri.

Wind Sister.
Last of the line.
Beloved enemy.
Lost and returned.
Queen of the People . . .

The memories crowded in until there was almost nothing left of Barrick himself at all, but at the same moment something far more powerful and far more pure struck him as well, as if a beam of brightest light pierced his eye at the same moment that a silver arrow pierced his heart.

He swayed. He could not stand. He fell to his knees before her and wept.

Saqri was the most beautiful thing he had ever seen, so powerful and complicated that it hurt him just to look at her: one instant she seemed made of gossamer and cobwebs and dry twigs like a child's doll from a hundred years gone, so old and fragile that she might fall apart under the gentlest handling, then a moment later she seemed a statue carved of hard, gleaming stone. And her eyes—her eyes, so black and deep! Barrick could not look into them without his head reeling, without feeling as though he would fall and fall without ever touching bottom.

The queen looked back at him, her face as unmoving as a mask, a mask stranger yet more familiar than any face in the world. The smallest curve at the corner of her lips made it seem as though she smiled, but her eyes and his inexplicable memories told him that she did not.

"So this is what is left of my daughter Sanasu's precious blood?" She spoke aloud as if she could not bear to touch his thoughts. Her voice was without warmth. "This jest, this piece of strange lost material, this is what comes back to me at the end of days?"

He knew he should be angry but he did not have the strength. Just standing before her was too overwhelming. Was it her or the Fireflower that filled his head with colors and noise and heat? "I am what the gods made of me," was all he could manage.

"The gods!" Saqri let out a short sound that might have been a laugh or a sob, but her face did not change. "What have they ever made for us that did not turn its sharp edge? Even Crooked's greatest gift has been proved a torment."

Even the shadows seemed to draw back as if from a terrifying blasphemy. A part of Barrick recognized that what she said was spoken from the depths of an anguish he could not begin to understand. "I am sorry . . . if what I am displeases you, Lady. I didn't choose to come here and I didn't choose the blood that runs in my veins. Whatever my ancestors did to you, none of them consulted me."

She looked at him for a long time with eyes so dark and fierce he could barely sustain her gaze. "Enough," she said. "Enough of talking. I have a husband to mourn."

The queen came down from the dais as lightly as if carried on a breeze, her billowing robe barely seeming to touch the ground. As Barrick followed her back down the center of the hall a thousand fairy-queens and a thousand mortal princes surged toward the doorway, reflected in the mirrors on either side. Some of the Barricks even turned to look back at him. Some of the faces were nothing like his, but it was the expressions worn by some of those most like him that he found more disturbing.

They stepped out into the great chamber beyond the door of the Mirror Hall and found it thronged with fairy folk of a hundred different sorts, apparitions that were completely strange to Barrick's eyes, and yet somehow he recognized them all—*redcaps, tunnel-knockers, trows tall as trees*— and even knew that the place where they were waiting was known as the Chamber of the Winter Banquet. As the queen moved past with Barrick just behind her they joined in behind, the weeping women and the small men with animal eyes, the winged shadows and others with faces like unfinished stone, swelling the procession until it filled the corridors and extended back beyond Barrick's sight, a river of uncanny life.

He followed Saqri through a maze of unknown corridors, but names and ideas seemed to slide across them like a reflection on a still pond— *Sad Piper's Rest, the Groaning Solar, the place where Caution and Swimming Bird parted.* At last they moved out beneath the open sky, across a garden of stone shapes twisted as though in uneasy sleep where the rain spattered his face and wetted his hair. The sensation was something so old and so recognizable that for a moment the other thoughts fell away and he was simply himself again, the Barrick he had always been, before the Shadowline, before the Dreamers, before Ynnir's kiss.

What will become of me? He was not as frightened as he had been earlier, but it was hard not to mourn his losses. *I will never be that person again.*

On the other side of the garden—*Beetle's Wakeful Garden*, his thoughts whispered, *where Rain Servant held the King of Birds and told him how the world would end*—they passed into a vast room, dark except for a small ring of candles on the floor and empty except for those candles and the body that lay on a flat stone at the center of the ring.

Barrick's eyes filled with tears. He did not need to be told who this was. Now the chorus of whispers in his head served only to fog the clarity of his feelings. The one who lay before him had, in only a single day, become a sort of father to him—no, more than that: Ynnir had shown him nothing but forbearance and kindness.

The queen stood looking down at her husband's body. The blindfold was gone, Ynnir's eyes closed as if in sleep. Barrick took a few steps forward and then sank slowly to his knees, unable to carry the weight of the present moment any longer.

Son of the First Stone, the Leaping Stag, Clever Weakling . . . It was a chorus of whispers like the cooing of pigeons. *Traitor!—no, Crooked's Own . . . !*

Look at me, another voice said, sighing and distant. *So small. So lost in the moment!*

Startled, Barrick looked around. "Ynnir?" The voice had been the king's, Barrick was certain. *Don't leave me!* He cast his thought after the king's thoughts. The other memories, voices, ghosts, those countless shades and rags of understanding that haunted him now, all dispersed before his inquiry, but whatever of the real Ynnir had touched him was gone again.

"Old fool," the queen said quietly as she stared down at the king's pale, rigid face. "Beautiful, blind old fool."

The funeral of the Lord of Winds and Thought passed before Barrick's senses like a swollen, flooding river, the current crowded with objects that had become unrecognizable. In that dark, murmurous room shapes assembled around the king's body, weeping, singing, sometimes making noises and gestures that Barrick could not connect with any human emotion at all, then after a space they dispersed again. Some of these mourning gestures were as complex as plays or temple rituals and seemed to last hours, while others were no more than a brief fluttering of wings above Ynnir's silent form. Barrick heard speeches of which he could understand every word, but which nevertheless made no sense to him at all. Other mourners stood beside the king's body and uttered a single unfamiliar sound that opened up in Barrick's mind like an entire book, like one of the tales told by Orphan's Night bards that lasted from sunset until dawn.

And still they came.

Rats, a thousand or more, a living velvet carpet that swirled around Ynnir and then were gone; weeping shadows; men with eyes as red as embers; even a beautiful girl made of broomsticks and cobwebs, who sang for the dead king in a voice like settling straw—all came to say their farewells. As the hours crept by, as wind and rain lashed the rooftops outside and the flames of the lamps guttered in the death chamber, Barrick came to understand, not the full depths of what was being expressed in that room, but something of what it meant to be one of these people. He saw that the procession was more than the individuals and what they had to say, or the movements they made to show their grief. Instead it was a collection of shapes and sounds in time, each separate yet as connected to the whole as letters in a word or words in a story. Time itself was the medium, and somehow—this was only a gleam of understanding, like a tiny fish in a stream, and to grab for it was to see it disappear altogether— somehow the People, the Qar, lived in time in a way Barrick's mortal kind did not. They were both of it and outside it. They mourned, but they also said, *This is what mourning is, and how it should be. This is the dance and these the steps.* To make either less or more of it would be to lift it out of time, like lifting a fish from the river. The fish would die. The river would be less beautiful. Nothing else would change.

The candles at last flickered out. New tapers were lit, and this itself seemed but another part of the dance, another bend in the river. Barrick let it all flow over him and through him. Sometimes he found himself knowing before someone spoke, or sang, or presented their silent tribute, who they were and what they had brought. Other times he was lost in the strangeness of it all, as when he had been a child and had listened to the wind skirling around the chimneys and under the roof tiles of his home, overwhelmed by suggestions of meaning that he knew he could never grasp, by the eternal mortal frustration of being so small against the uncaring vastness of the night.

He surfaced at last out of a darkness full of dwindling song and shadow. The great room was empty. The king's body was gone. Only the queen remained.

"Where . . . where is he . . . ?"

Saqri was as still as the statue she resembled, gazing at the empty dais. "His husk . . . is being returned. As for the truth of Ynnir . . . he has chosen to give his last strength to wake me, and now he and his ancestors are lost to us forever."

Barrick could only stand, uncomprehending.

"And so we move a step closer to the end of all things," she said as she turned toward him, although she barely seemed to see him and spoke as though to herself. "What is your place in it to be, mortal man? What is written in the Book for you? Perhaps you are meant to keep a shadow of our memory alive, so that when we altogether vanish, still a dim, confused recollection might trouble the victors. Do we trouble you? Have you an inkling of what you have destroyed?"

So fierce, so bright—like a fire! a voice inside him whispered, but Barrick was too angry to pay it any mind.

"I have destroyed nothing," he told her. "Whatever my great-grandfathers did is nothing of mine—in fact, it has cursed me too! And I did not choose to come here—I was sent by your . . . porcupine woman, Yasammez." A little of his confusion suddenly fell away, as though someone had wiped a layer of grime from an old, shiny thing. "No, I *did* choose to come here, at least in part. Because Gyir wanted me to. Because the king called me, asked me . . . urged me. I didn't ask to be born at all, and I certainly didn't ask to be born with Qar blood burning inside me. It almost drove me mad!"

The expression on the queen's perfect, eggshell-delicate face did not change, but she was silent for a while.

"She did choose you, didn't she—my dear one, my love, my ancestor?" Saqri moved a step closer to him, lifted a hand and brushed his face. "What did she see?" Although she was no taller than Barrick and slender as a reed, it was all he could do not to shrink back from her touch. Her fingers on his brow, like her husband's kiss, were cool and dry. "Did Yasammez mean only to taunt him? She never cared for my husband—not as I did. She thought he was too lax a protector of the People, that he valued doing what was right over doing what was necessary."

But they are the same, something murmured in Barrick's thoughts.

The queen yanked her fingers away from his face as though she had been burned. "What trick is this?" Her hand shot out again like a striking snake, then flattened with surprising delicacy over his eyes, pressing firmly on the space at the center of his forehead. "What trick . . . ?"

A moment later she staggered back, the first less than perfectly graceful movement he had seen her make. Her eyes widened. "No. It is not possible!"

In this place of ancient knowledge and timeworn ritual, such obvious surprise frightened Barrick. "What? Why are you looking at me that way?"

"He is . . . he is in you! I feel him but I cannot touch him!"

Something that now lived inside Barrick was unmoved by her consternation, even amused. "He said he would try to pass the Fireflower to me."

"No!" She practically shrieked it, although he realized a moment later it was only the difference from her usual measured tone that was so startling. "You are a mortal. You are a whelp of the creatures who raped us . . . murdered us!"

We are all children of both the good and evil that has gone before us.

Ynnir? Is that you? Barrick tried his best to catch at the thought, but it was gone again. He realized that the queen was standing directly before him, her eyes so intent that it almost hurt to face them. She clutched his arm; her grip was astoundingly strong.

"What do you feel? Is he there, my brother . . . my husband? Does he speak inside of you? What of the Forerunners, do you feel them as well?"

"I . . . I don't know . . ." And then Barrick felt it swimming up from the depths and for a moment his limbs, his tongue, his head was not his own. *"We are here, all of us,"* said his mind and his mouth, but Barrick himself was none of it. *"It is not what we expected and many of us are confused . . . many others are lost. Never before has the Fireflower passed like this. It is all different . . ."* Then the alien presence fell away and Barrick commanded his own limbs once more—but everything had changed, he knew. Everything was different and it always would be.

The queen continued to stare at him but her eyes now seemed far away. Then she simply folded, her white robes rustling faintly as she slumped to the ground. Shadows coalesced from the corners and hidden places of the great chamber, servitors who had waited silent and unmoving all this time. They surrounded her, then bore her up and carried her away.

Barrick could only stand and watch them go, alone with the tribe of incomprehensible strangers who lived now in his blood and his thoughts.

Appendix

PEOPLE

A'lat—a Xandian priest

Anamesiya Tinwright—Matt Tinwright's mother

Ananka—from Jellon, first Hesper's, then Enander's mistress

Anglin—Connordic chieftain, awarded March Kingdom after Coldgray Moor

Anglin III—king of Southmarch, great-grandfather of Briony and Barrick

Anissa—queen of Southmarch, Olin's second wife

Antimony—a young Funderling temple brother

Argal the Dark One—Xixian god, enemy of Nushash

Ash Nitre—in charge of gunflour for Funderlings

Autarch—Sulepis Bishakh am-Xis III, monarch of Xis, most powerful nation on the southern continent of Xand

Avidel—Theron's apprentice

Avin Brone—count of Landsend, the castle's lord constable

Axamis Dorza—a Xixian ship's captain

Ayann—brother of Yasammez, Yasudra's husband

Ayyam—a Qar, ancestor of Kayyin/Gil

Azurite COPPER—aka "Stormstone", famous Funderling Highwarden

Barrick Eddon—a prince of Southmarch

Baz'u Jev—a Xandian poet

Beetledown— a Rooftopper

Big Nodule (Blue Quartz)—Chert's father

Bingulou the Kracian—Finn's first master

Bone—a bandit

Brambinag Stoneboots—a mythical ogre

Brennas—an oracle whose head was said to have survived his execution by three years.

Brigid—a serving-woman at the Quiller's Mint

Briony Eddon—a princess of Southmarch

Brother Okros Dioketian—physician-priest from Eastmarch Academy
Caradon Tolly—Gailon's younger brother
Caylor—a legendary knight and prince
Chalk—a Kallikan drumstone priest
Chaven—physician and astrologer to the Eddon family
Chert (Blue Quartz)—a Funderling, Opal's husband
Cheshret—Qinnitan's father, a minor priest of Nushash
Children of the Emerald Fire—a Qar tribe
Cinnabar Quicksilver—a Funderling magister
Clemon—famous Syannese historian, also called "Clemon of Anverrin"
Col—a bandit
Conary—propietor of the Quiller's Mint
Conoric, Sivonnic, and Iellic tribes—"primitive" tribes who lived on Eion
    before conquest by the southern continent of Xand
Daman Eddon—Merolanna's husband, King Ustin's brother
Davos of Elgi, aka Davos the Mantis—a famous mercenary, leader of a Grey
    Company
Dawet dan-Faar—envoy from Hierosol, late of Tuan
Dolomite—Highwarden of the Underbridge Kallikans
Donal Murroy—onetime captain of the Southmarch royal guard
Dumin Hauyuz—antipolemarch of the Autarch's expedition force to
    Southmarch
Duny—Qinnitan's friend, an acolyte of the Hive
Durstin Crowel—baron of Graylock
Earth Elders—Funderling guardian spirits
Eilis—Merolanna's maid
Elan M'Cory—sister-in-law of Caradon Tolly
Ena—Skimmer, daughter of Turley Longfingers
Enander—King of Syan
Eneas—Prince of Syan, son of Enander
Erasmias Jino—Marquis of Athnia, important Syannese official
Erinna e'Herayas—a Tessian courtier
Erivor—god of waters, AKA "Efiyal", "Egye-Var"
Ettin—a Qar giant
Ever-Wounded Maid—a character out of legend
Favoros—a Syannese baron
Favoros, Baron —Lord of Ugenion
Feldspar—Dead Funderling Warder
Ferras Vansen—captain of the Southmarch royal guard
Finlae—Settlander priest, slave in Qu'arus' house
Finn Teodoros—a writer
Finneth—Brennish oracle in Hewney's tale
Funderlings—sometimes known as "delvers", small people who specialize in
    stonecraft

Gailon Tolly, Duke of Summerfield—an Eddon family cousin

Golya—"eaters of man-flesh"

Grandfather Sulphur—a Funderling elder of the Metamorphic Brothers

Gray Companies—mercenaries and landless men turned bandits in wake of the Great Death

Gregor of Syan—a famous bard

Guard of Elementals—a tribe of the Qar

Gyir—a Qar, Yasammez' captain, AKA "Gyir the Storm Lantern"

Hammerfoot—a Deep Ettin, war leader of Firstdeeps

Harsar—Ynnir's counselor

Hasuris—a Xixian storyteller

Hayyids—an ancient people of Xand

Helkis, Lord—Prince Eneas' second-in-command

Hendon Tolly—youngest of the Tolly brothers

Hesper—King of Jellon, betrayer of King Olin

Hiliometes—a legendary demigod and hero

Hobkin—a bandit

Iaris—an oracle of Kernios, a semi-saint

Iola, Queen of Syan, Tolos, and Perikal—queen during the Syannese empire and the War of Three Favors

Iron Quartz—one of Chert's earliest masters

Ivgenia e'Doursos—the young daughter of the Viscount of Teryon

Jeddin—chief of the autarch's Leopard guards, also known as "Jin"

Jenkin Crowel—envoy from Southmarch to Tessis

Kallikans—Syannese name for Funderlings

Karal—king of Syan killed by Qar at Coldgray Moor

Kayyin—a Qar, Yasammez' son, AKA "Gil the Potboy"

Kellick Eddon—great-grandnephew of Anglin, first of Eddon family March Kings

Kendrick Eddon—prince regent of Southmarch, eldest son of King Olin

Kernios—earth god, AKA "Xergal"

Khors—moon god, husband of Zoria, brother of Zmeos, father of Kupilas

Kofas of Mindan—an Ulosian philosopher

Kreas, King—figure out of an old tale

Kupilas—god of healing, AKA "The Artificer," "Habbili," "Crooked," "Kioy-a-pous"

Lander III—son of Karal, king of Syan, aka "Lander the Good," "Lander Elfbane"

Lily—Anglin's granddaughter, queen who led Southmarch in time of the Gray Companies

Linas—a captain of Eneas' Temple Dogs

Lindon Tolly—father of Gailon, former First Minister of March Kingdoms

Little Pewter—a monk

Lope the Red—bandit chieftain

Lorick Eddon—Olin's older brother, who died young

Ludis Drakava—Protector of Hierosol

Luian—an important Favored in the Seclusion, previously known as "Dudon"

Lukos the Pot-maker—Theron's father

Makers of Tears—Yasammez's famous fighting legion

Malachite Copper—a Funderling leader

Malamenas Kimir—apothecary in Agamid

Marwin—another of Qu'arus' slaves

Massilios Goldenhair—a legendary hero (mentioned by Barrick)

Matthias Tinwright—a poet, aka "Matty"

Melarkh—a semi-legendary king of Jurr

Meno Strivoli—Syannese master poet

Meriel—Olin's first wife

Merolanna—the twin's great-aunt, originally of Fael, widow of Daman Eddon

Mesiya—moon goddess

Metamorphic Brothers—a Funderling religious order

Miller's Daughter, The—a character in "a Country Priest's Tale"

Moina—one of Briony's ladies-in-waiting

Nevin Hewney—a playwright

Niccol Opanour—Gate Herald to Hesper of Jellon

Nikomakos, Lord—son of a Syannese earl

Numannyn—King of the Qar at the time of Shivering Plain, known as "the cautious"

Nushash—Xixian god of fire, patron god of the autarchs, AKA "Zmeos," "Whitefire"

Olin Eddon—King of Southmarch and the March Kingdoms

Opal—a Funderling, Chert's wife

Panhyssir—Xixian high priest of Nushash

Parak—former autarch of Xis, grandfather of Sulepis

Pariki—Xixian name for Qar

Parnad—father of current autarch, Sulepis, sometimes known as "the Unsleeping"

Pedar Vansen—Ferras Vansen's father

Perin—sky god, called "Thane of Lightnings," AKA "Argal"

Phayallos—a philosopher and alchemist

Phimon—Hierarch of Tessis

Pig Iron—a Funderling warder

Pinimmon Vash—paramount minister of Xis

Pouta—an oracle, possibly invented by Finn Teodoros

Prusus—scotarch of Xis, sometimes called "Prusus the Cripple"

Puntar—a reeve

Purifiers—fanatics who banded together to punish Qar and others for Great Death

Puzzle—court jester to the Eddon family

Qar—race of non-humans who once occupied much of Eion

Qinnitan—an acolyte of the Hive in Xis, escaped bride of Autarch Sulepis

Qu'arus—a Dreamless

Raemon Beck—member of a Helmingsea trading family

Rafe—Skimmer, Ena's friend, Hull-Scraped-the-Sand clan

Rhantys of Kalebria—author of "Agony of Truth Forsworn"

Risto, Marquis of Omaranth—a Syannese nobleman and military commander

Rooftoppers—little-known residents of Southmarch Castle

Rope-Men—A people living in Beggar lands behind the Shadowline

Rose—one of Briony's ladies-in-waiting, a niece of Avin Brone

Rule—Avin Brone's informant

Saqri—queen of the Qar, AKA "The First Flower"

Sanasu—widow of Kellick Eddon, AKA "Weeping Queen"

Sand Leekstone—Opal's father

Sandstone—a Funderling family

Schist—dead Funderling

Selia—Anissa's maid, also from Devonis

Sembla—an oracle, possibly invented by Finn Teodoros

Seris—Duke of Gela's daughter, a Tessian courtier

Shanni—a type of Xixian spirit that grants wishes

Shaso dan-Heza—Southmarch master of arms

Silas of Perikal—semi-legendary knight

Silkins—shadowland creatures who "Speak not, nor go to market," per Skurn

Skimmers—a people who make their living on and around water

Sledge Jasper—the wardthane of Funderling Town

Sleepers—renegade Dreamless, AKA "Dreamers"

Snout—a Qar guard

Stone Circle People—a Qar tribe

Stone of the Unwilling—a Qar of the Guard of Elementals

Summu—Yasammez's mother, "bride" of Kupilas

Surigali—Xixian goddess, AKA "Zuriyal"

Sveros—old god of the night sky, father of Trigon gods, AKA "Zhafaris"

Talia—a young maid of Briony's in Tessis

Theron—leader of pilgrimages

Tibunis Vash—father of Pinimmon Vash

Tine Fay—very small Qar

Tricksters—a tribe of the Qar

Trigon—priesthoods of Perin, Erivor, and Kernios acting in concert

Trigonarch—Head of Trigonate church, chief religious figure in Eion
Turley Longfingers—a Skimmer headman, Back-On-Sunset-Tide clan
Twilight People—another name for the Qar
Tyne Aldritch—Earl of Blueshore, an ally of Southmarch
Ustin—King Olin's father
Utta—AKA "Sister Utta," a priestess of Zoria and Briony's tutor
Vais—legendary "witch-queen of Krace"
Vanderin Ugenios—classical poet
Vaspis the Dark—an autarch of Xis
Vilas—a Perikalese fisherman
Vo Jovandil—Daikonas Vo's family name
Volos Longbeard—a god
Warders of the Guild—the guardians of Funderling Town
Rocksalt—a Funderling
Yasammez—Qar noblewoman, sometimes known as "Lady Porcupine,"
    "Scourge of the Shivering Plain"
Yasudra—twin sister of Yasammez
Ynnir the Blind King—lord of the Qar, AKA "Ynnir din'at sen-Qin, Lord
    of Winds and Thought," "Son of the First Stone"
Zhafaris—Xixian name for Sveros, AKA "Twilight," father of the gods
Zmeos—a god, Perin's nemesis, AKA "Whitefire," "Nushash"
Zoria—goddess of wisdom, AKA "Suya," "Pale Daughter," "Dawnflower"
Zosim—god of playwrights and drunkards, AKA "Trickster,"
    "Salamandros"

PLACES

Agamid—a city north of Devonis
Akaris—an island between Xand and Eion
Badger's Boots—a Southmarch inn
Basilisk Gate—main gate of Southmarch Castle
Beetle Way—street in Funderling Town
Beggar Lands—territory behind the Shadowline
Black River Forest—a forest in northern Syan
Blacklamp Row—road outside Funderling Town that runs into Stormstone
    Roads
Boreholes—monastic retreat beyond the Five Arches
Brenland—small country south of the March Kingdoms
Brenn's Bay—surrounds Soutmarch Castle, named after legendary hero
    Brennas
Candlerstown—Daler's Troth town
Cascade Stair—in the Funderling Depths
Chapel of Erivor—Eddon family chapel

Cloud-Spirit Tower—a tower in Qul-na-Qar

Coldgray Moor—legendary battleground, from a Qar word, "Qul Girah"

Copper Ring—the outer road that leads to many of the Stormstone Roads outside Funderling Town

Deep Library—a place in Qul-na-Qar

Devona Fountain Square—in Tessis

Doros Eco—a town in Syan

Drymusa—a fortified town at the southern border of Hierosol

Eastmarch Academy—university, originally in old Eastmarch, relocated to Southmarch at the time of the last war with the Qar

Eion—the northern continent

Emberstone Reach—in the Funderling Depths

Esterian—city near Tessis

Fade, or "River Fade"—main watercourse in City of Sleep

Fael—a nation in the heartland of Eion

Firstdeeps—a place in Qar lands

Flower Meadow—biggest market in Tessis

Funderling Town—underground city of Funderlings, in Southmarch

Gremos Pitra—capitol of Jellon

Helobine—marshy country south of Brenland

Hierosol—once the reigning empire of the world, now much reduced; its symbol is the golden snail shell

Hive—a temple in Xis, home of the sacred bees of Nushash

House of Tears—dungeon in Broadhall Palace

J'ezh'kral Pit—a place out of Funderling myth

Jellon—kingdom, once part of Syannic Empire, now combined with Jael

Jurr—an ancient city-state in Xand

Kertewall—one of the March Kingdoms

Krace—a collection of city-states, once part of Hierosoline Empire

Landsend—part of Southmarch, Avin Brone's fief, colors red and gold

Lantern Broad—main street in Tessis

Layandros—a city in the north of Syan

Limestone Gate—part of the route from the Southmarch mainland into the Funderling Lord's House—Kallikan name for Funderling Town

Marash—a Xandian province where peppers are grown

March Kingdoms—originally Northmarch, Southmarch, Eastmarch and Westmarch, but after the war with the Qar constituted by Southmarch and the Nine Nations (which include Summerfield and Blueshore)

Market Road—one of Southmarch's main roads

Market Road Bridge—Bridge over the canal separating two lagoons in Southmarch

Market Square—main public space in Southmarch

Marrinswalk—one of the March Kingdoms

Maze—in the Funderling Depths

Midlan's Mount—rock in Brenn's Bay upon which Southmarch is built

Moonstone Hall—in the Funderling Depths

Mount Gowkha—burial place of old Xixian desert kings

Mount Xandos—mythical giant mountain that stood where Xand now lies

Northmarch Road—the old road between Southmarch and the north

Observatory House—Chaven's residence

Old Quarry Way—road off the Copper Ring

Orms—city in Helobine country

Oscastle—a city in Marrinswalk

Pellos– a river in Silverside

Qul-na-Qar—ancient home of the Qar or Twilight People

Raven's Gate—entrance to Southmarch Castle's inner keep

Royal Highway—aka King Karal's Road

Salt Pool—underground sea-pool in Funderling Town

Settland—small, mountainous country southwest of the March Kingdoms; ally of Southmarch

Shadowline, the—line of demarcation between lands of Qar and human lands

Sheeps Hill Road—along Sheeps Hill at the base of the New Walls in Southmarch

Shivering Plain—site of a great Qar battle

Siege of Always-Winter—a mythical castle

Silk Door—a place beneath Funderling Town

Silky Wood—a forest behind the Shadowline

Silvertrail—river on the Shivering Plain

Skimmer's Lagoon—body of water inside Southmarch walls, connected to Brenn's Bay

Southmarch—seat of the March Kings, sometimes called "Shadowmarch"

Staple Street—a street in Southmarch Castle's outer keep

Stonebeneath—Funderling settlement under Hierosol

Summerfield Court—ducal seat of Gailon and the Tolly family

Syan—once-dominant empire, still a powerful kingdom in center of Eion

Templeyard—neighborhood in the southwest part of the Southmarch inner keep

Tessis—capitol city of Syan

The Whale Horse—a riverside tavern in Tessis

Three Gods—a triangular plaza in Southmarch; a populous district around that plaza

Tolos—a kingdom, now absorbed by Syan

Torvio—an island nation between Eion and Xand

Tribute Hall—hall outside Briony's bedroom passage (added rewrite)

Tuan—native country of Shaso and Dawet

Tufa's Bag—cul-de-sac off Old Quarry Way

Ugenion—city in northern Syan
Underbridge—Funderling (Kallikan) city in Tessis
Wedge Road—Chert and Opal's street
Well of Finneth—a holy site in Brenland
Westcliff—old Funderling city in Settland
Whitewood—a forest on the border between Silverside and Marrinswalk
Xand—the southern continent
Xis—largest kingdom of Xand; its master is the autarch (adjective, "Xixian")
Yist—once a fairy city in Xand

THINGS (and ANIMALS)

A Country Priest's Tale—a play
Aelian's Fluxative—a poison
Annals of the War in Heaven—a lost and forbidden book
Antipolemarch—a high-ranking Xixian general
Astion—a Funderling symbol of authority
Badger's Boots—a tavern in Southmarch
Basiphae—a name for the organism inside Vo
Blueroot—favorite Funderling tea-herb
Book of Regret—Qar sacred text
Book of the Trigon—a late-era adaptation of original texts about all three gods
Broadhall Palace—seat of King Enander of Syan
Chamber-shells—nautilus shells, symbol to Erivor priesthood
Copper Ring—a road around the perimeter of the Funderling Town roads
Crackbolt—Perin's (Sky man's) hammer
Day of First Delving—a Funderling religious holiday
Days of Cooling—legendary time in Funderling history and myth
Ever-Wounded Maid—a famous story
Feast of the Rising—Xixian festival at the end of the rainy season
Feast of Onir Zakkas—Trigonate holiday when people wear asphodel crowns
Great Death—plague that killed large part of Eion's population
Guild Market—yearly gathering of Funderlings
Hartstangle—type of shadowland tree
Henbane Crown—autarch's ceremonial headgear
Hierosoline—the language of Hierosol, found in many religious services and scientific books, etc.
Horns of Zmeos—a constellation, also called the Old Serpent
Ice Lily—a flower
Iktis—a fitch, a kind of small, burrowing animal in the weasel family

Lastday—end of the tennight

Laws of Shakh Xis—rules to govern second and third Xixian empire

Limestone Gate—a gate that used to be an entrance from the mainland to Funderling Town and its Mysteries

Lonely Ones—another name for Skrikers

Mantis—a priest, usually of the Trigon

Ninth Year War—a famous, watershed war in Xis

Onir Plessos—a temple in Summerfield

Optimarch—a military rank, approx. major

Pass-evil—hand sign made to avert bad luck

Pentecount—a troop, numbering fifty

Perin's Eye—design on the throne room floor in Tessis

Procession of Penance—a holy festival

Quiller's Mint—a tavern in Southmarch

Red Serpent Root—a poison

Shining Man—center of the Funderling Mysteries

Shivering Plain—a famous Qar battleground

Silkins—Shadowland creatures

Skrikers—guardians of Sleep

Starfish—small silver coin

Sturgeon—a silver coin, twice as big as a starfish

The Mattock—Metamorphic Brother's abbot's symbol of power

Staff, the—another name for Mount Xandos

Tigersbane—poison made from the sap of the Ice Lily

Trigon—the religious power of Eion, a triumvirate of priesthoods (Perin, Erivor, Kernios)

War of Three Favors—a dynastic war in days of Syannese empire

Whitefire—the sword of Yasammez, also a name for Zmeos

Wildsong Night—a holiday evening, also known as Winter's Eve

Wimmuai—Dreamless word for human slaves

Xawadis—Xixian word for oasis or waterhole

Yanedan—a mountainous island in the southern sea

Zakkas' Wort—a medicinal herb